GODS' CONCUBINE

BOOK TWO OF THE TROY GAME

Sara Douglass

A TOM DOHERTY ASSOCIATES BOOK

NEW YORK

GODS' CONCUBINE: BOOK TWO OF THE TROY GAME

Copyright © 2004 by Sara Douglass Enterprises Pty Ltd.

Map by Ellisa Mitchell

A Tor Book
Published by Tom Doherty Associates, LLC
175 Fifth Avenue
New York, NY 10010

www.tor.com

Tor® is a registered trademark of Tom Doherty Associates, LLC.

Library of Congress Cataloging-in-Publication Data

Douglass, Sara
   Gods' concubine / Sara Douglass.—1st ed.
      p. cm.—(Book two of the Troy game)
   "A Tom Doherty Associates book."
   ISBN 0-765-30541-0
      1. Brutus the Trojan (Legendary character)—Fiction. 2. Great Britain—History—To 449—Fiction. 3. Troy (Extinct city)—Fiction. 4. Labyrinths—Fiction. I. Title.

PR9619.3.D672G63 2004
823'.914—dc22   2003061225

First Edition: February 2004

Printed in the United States of America

0 9 8 7 6 5 4 3 2 1

For all those who over the years have enjoyed WolfStar's lamppost subterfuge—my apologies. I tried, I really, really tried, but when all is said and done, there is no place in Anglo-Saxon England for subversive lampposts. . . .

Saxon London and Environs in 1065

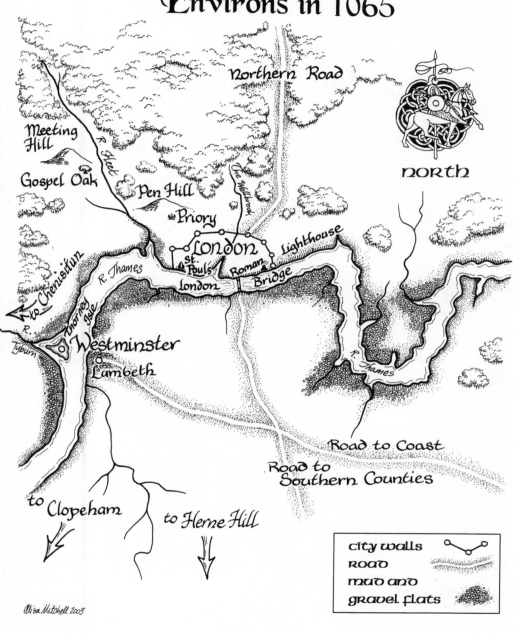

NORTH

Northern Road

Meeting Hill

Gospel Oak

R. Fleet

Pen Hill

The Walbrook

Priory

London

St. Pauls

Roman

Lighthouse

London Bridge

to Chenisitun

R. Thames

Thorney Isle

R. Tyburn

Westminster

Lambeth

R. Thames

Road to Coast

Road to Southern Counties

to Clopeham

to Herne Hill

city walls	
road	
mud and gravel flats	

Alisa Mitchell 2003

PART ONE

ENGLAND AND NORMANDY, 1050

THE GATHERING

Standing on the banks of the Thames on his arrival into Britain,
Brutus said:
> *"I will here, our kind to enjoy,*
> *A city for the love of Troy,*
> *For Troy was so noble a city,*
> *Troia Nova the name shall be . . ."*
> *Then came a king, Lud was his name,*
> *And made a gate in [the wall of] the same,*
> *Caer Lud the name became . . .*
> *When Saxons came that name was strange,*
> *Their own speech they did prefer,*
> *They called the city Luden or London*
> *And the name soon became*
> *London in the Saxon tongue.*
> > *Robert Mannyng of Brunne,* Chronicle, *1303,*
> > *Translated by Sara Douglass*

Chapter One

HE TIMBER HALL WAS HUGE, FULLY EIGHTY FEET end to end and twenty broad. Doors leading to the outside pierced both of the long walls midway down their length, allowing people exit to the latrines, or to the kitchens for more food, while trapdoors in the sixty-foot high-beamed roof allowed the smoke egress when weather permitted: otherwise the fumes from the four heating pits in the floor drifted about the hall until they escaped whenever someone opened an outer door. Many of the hall's upright timbers were painted red and gold in interweaving Celtic designs; the heights were hung with almost one hundred shields.

Tonight, both painted designs and shields were barely visible. The hall was full of smoke, heat, and raucous, good-humored noise. Men and women, warriors and monks, earls, thegns, wives, and maidens sat at the trestle tables, which ran the length of the hall, while thralls, children, and dogs scampered about, either serving wine, cider, or ale, or nosing out the scraps of meat that had fallen to the rush-covered floor. The wedding feast had been in progress some three hours. Now most of the boiled and roasted meats had been consumed, the cheeses were all gone, the sweet-spiced omelettes were little more than congealed yolky fragments on platters, and the scores of loaves of crusty bread had been reduced to the odd crumb that further marred the food and alcohol-stained table linens, and fed the mice, in the rushes, darting among the booted feet of the revelers.

At the head of the hall stood a dais. Before the dais, a juggler sat on a three-legged stool, so drunk, his occasional attempts to tumble his woolen balls and his sharp-edged knives achieved little else save to further bloody his fingers.

A group of musicians with bagpipes and flutes—still sober, although they desperately wished otherwise—stood just to one side of the dais, their music lost within the shouting and singing of the revelers, the thumping of tables by those demanding their wine cups be refilled without delay, and the shrieks and barks of children and dogs writhing hither and thither under the tables and between the legs of the feasters.

In contrast to the wild enthusiasm of the hundreds of guests within the body of the hall, most of the fifteen or so people who sat at the table on the dais were noticeably restrained.

At the center of the table sat a man of some forty or forty-one years, although his long, almost white-blond hair, his scraggly graying beard, his thin, ascetic face and the almost perpetually down-turned corners of his tight mouth made him appear much older. He wore a long, richly textured red and blue heavy linen tunic, embroidered about its neck, sleeves and hem with silken threads and semiprecious stones and girdled with gold and silver. His right hand, idly toying with his golden and jeweled wine cup, was broad and strong, the hand of a swordsman, although his begemmed fingers were soft and pale: it had been many years since that hand had held anything but a pen or a wine cup.

His eyes were of the palest blue, flinty enough to make any miscreant appearing before him blurt out a confession without thought, cold enough to make any woman think twice before attempting to use the arts of Eve upon him. Currently his eyes flitted about the hall, marking every crude remark, every groping hand, every mouth stained red with wine.

And with every movement of his eyes, every sin noted, his mouth crimped just that little bit more until it appeared that he had eaten something so foul his body would insist on spewing it forth at any moment.

On his head rested a golden crown, as thickly encrusted with jewels as his fingers.

He was Edward, king of England, and he was sitting in the hall of the man he regarded as his greatest enemy: Godwine, the earl of Wessex.

Godwine sat on Edward's left hand, booming with cheer and laughter where Edward sat quiet and still. The earl was a large man, thickly muscled after almost forty-five years spent on the battlefield, *his* begemmed hands when they lifted his wine cup to his mouth, sinewy and tanned, his eyes as watchful as Edward's, but without the judgment.

The reason for Godwine's cheer and Edward's bilious silence, as for the entire tumultuous celebration, sat on Edward's right, her eyes downcast to her hands folded demurely in her lap, her food sitting largely untouched on the platter before her.

She was Eadyth, commonly called Caela, Godwine's cherished thirteen-year-old daughter, and now Edward's wife and queen of England.

The marriage had been a compromise, hateful to Edward, triumphant for Godwine. If Edward married the earl's daughter, then Godwine would continue to support his throne. If not . . . well, then Godwine would ensure that Edward would spend the last half of his life in exile as he'd spent the first half (staying as far away from his murderous stepfather, King Cnut, as possible). If Edward wanted to keep the throne, then he needed Godwine's support, and Godwine's support came only at the price of wedding his daughter.

She was a pretty girl, her attractiveness resting more in her extraordinary stillness than in any extravagant feature. Her glossy brown hair, currently tightly braided and hidden under her silken ivory veil (which itself was held in place by a golden circlet of some weight, which may have partly explained why Caela kept her face downward facing for so much of the feast), was one of her best features, as were also her sooty-lashed, deep blue eyes and her flawlessly smooth white skin. Otherwise her features were regular, her teeth small and evenly spaced, her hands dainty, their every movement considered. Caela was dressed almost as richly as her new husband: a heavily embroidered blue surcoat, or outer tunic, over a long, crisp, snowy linen under tunic embroidered with silver threads about its hem and the cuffs of its slim-fitted sleeves. Unlike her husband and her father, however, Caela wore little in the way of jeweled adornment, save for the gold circlet of rank on her brow and a sparkling emerald ring on the heart finger of her left hand.

Edward had shoved it there not four hours earlier during the nuptial mass held in her father's chapel. Now that nuptial ring's large square-cut stone hid a painful bruise on Caela's finger.

Caela's eyes rarely moved from the hands in her lap—someone who did not know her well might have thought she sat admiring that great cold emerald—and she spoke only monosyllabic replies to any who addressed her.

That was rare enough. Edward had not said a word to her, and the only other person who addressed Caela (apart from the occasional shouted enthusiasm from her gloating father) was the man who sat on her right side.

This man, unhappy looking where Edward was sullen and Godwine buoyant, was considerably younger than either of the other two men. In his early twenties, Harold Godwineson was the earl's eldest surviving son and thus heir to all that Godwine controlled (lands, estates, offices, and riches, as well as the English throne, which meant that Edward loathed Harold as much as he did Godwine).

Like his father, Harold was a warrior, blooded and proved in a score of savage, death-ridden battles, but, unlike Godwine, a man who also had the sensitive soul of a bard. That bard's sensibility showed in Harold's face and his dark eyes, in the manner of his movements and his engaging ability to give any who spoke to him his full and undivided attention. His hair was dark blond, already stranded with gray, which he kept warrior-short, as he did the faint stubble of his darker beard. He was a serious man who rarely laughed, but who, when he smiled, could lighten the heart of whomever that smile graced.

Harold was not so richly accoutred as his father and his new brother-in-law, although well-dressed and jewelled enough as befitted his status of one of the most powerful men in England. Like Edward, Harold toyed with his wine cup, rarely bringing it to his lips.

Unlike Edward, Harold spent a great deal of time watching his sister, occasionally reaching out to touch her with a reassuring hand, or to lean close and whisper something that sometimes, almost, made the girl's mouth twitch upward. Harold had adored Caela from birth, had watched over her, had spent an inordinate amount of time with her, and had argued fiercely with their father when he proposed the match with Edward.

Some people had rumored that it was not so much the match that Harold raged about, but that the girl was to be wedded and bedded at all. In recent years, as Caela approached her womanhood, Harold's attachment to his sister had attracted much sniggering comment. There was more than one person in the hall this night who, under the influence of unwatered wine or rich cider and who thought themselves far enough distant from the dais to dare the whisper, had proposed that Godwine's flamboyant happiness this eve was due more to his relief that he'd managed to get his daughter as a virgin to Edward's bed than at the marriage itself, as advantageous as that might be.

If one were to guess, one might think that Harold's wife, sitting on his other side, had been party to (if not the instigator of) many of these whispers. Swanne (also an Eadyth, but known far and wide as Swanne for her beautiful long white neck and elegant head carriage) sat almost as still as Caela, but with her head held high on her lovely neck, her almond-shaped black eyes watching both her husband and his sister with much private amusement.

Swanne was a stunningly beautiful woman. Of an age with Harold, or perhaps a year or two older, she had black hair that, when unveiled and unbound, snapped and twisted down her back in wild abandon. Her skin was as pale as Caela's, but drawn over a face more finely wrought, and framing lips far plumper and redder than her much younger sister-in-law's.

And her eyes . . . a man could sink and drown in those eyes. They were as black as a witch-night, great pools of mystery that entrapped men and savaged their souls.

When combined with her tall, lithe body . . . ah, most men in this hall envied Harold even as they whispered about him (the envy, of course, fueling many of the whispers). Even now, sitting leaning back in her great chair so that her swollen five-month belly strained at the fabric of her white surcoat, most men lusted after Swanne as they had lusted after little else in their lives. She was a woman bred to trigger every man's wildest sexual fantasy, and she was the reason why over a score of men had already dragged female thralls outside to be pushed against a wall and savagely assaulted in a vain attempt to assuage their lust for the lady Swanne.

On this occasion Swanne did not watch her husband or his sister, her black eyes trailed languidly over the hall, her mouth lifted in a knowing smile as she saw men staring at her, lowering frantic hands below the table to grab at the lust straining at their trousers. Swanne was a woman who enjoyed every moment of her dominance, yet loathed those who succumbed to her spell.

Among the other members of the wedding party on the dais sat Harold's younger brother, Tostig, a bright-eyed, lively faced youth, and sundry other noblemen, earls or thegns closely allied with Godwine. But King Edward had a few supporters, two Norman noblemen who had remained at Edward's side since he had returned from his twenty-year exile in Normandy at the young duke's court, and the rising young Norman cleric, Aldred. Aldred had also come to England with the returning Edward's retinue, and now he enjoyed a powerful position within the king's court. Indeed, he had performed the nuptial mass, although most had not failed to note than Aldred spent more time watching Swanne than either his benefactor or the tender bride. Aldred was a thickset man who, having cleaned his own platter, was now leaning over the table to lift uneaten portions of food from the platters of other diners. A trail of spiced wine had thickened his unshaven chin, and stained the front of his clerical robe.

Aldred was not known for the austerity of his tastes.

He snatched a congealing piece of roast goose from the platter of a Saxon thegn, stuffing the morsel inside his mouth.

All the time his eyes—strange, cool gray eyes—never left Swanne's form.

EVENTUALLY CAME THAT MOMENT WHEN GODWINE decided that the wedding was not enough, and that the bedding must now be accomplished.

At his signal (shout, rather), Swanne rose from her husband Harold's side and, together with several other ladies, took Caela and led her toward the stairs at the rear of the hall, which led to the bedchambers above.

The largest and best of the bedchambers had been prepared for the king and his new bride, and once Swanne had Caela inside, she and the other ladies began to strip the girl of her finery.

There were no words spoken, and Swanne's eyes, when they occasionally met Caela's, were harsh and cold.

When Caela at last stood naked, Swanne stood back a pace and regarded the girl's pubescent flesh. Caela's hips were still narrow, her buttocks scrawny, and her pubic hair thin and sparse. Her waist remained that of a girl's: straight and without any of that sweet narrowing that might lead a man's hands toward those delights both above and below it. Her breasts had barely plumped out from their childish flatness.

Swanne ran her eyes down Caela's body, then looked the girl in the eye.

Caela had lifted her hands to her breasts, and was now trembling slightly.

"You have not much to tempt a husband's embraces," Swanne said. She moved slightly, sensuously, her breasts and hips and belly straining against her robes, and then smiled coldly. "I cannot imagine how any husband could want to part your legs, my dear."

At that Caela blinked, flushing in humiliation.

Swanne sighed extravagantly, and the other ladies present smiled, preferring to ally with Swanne rather than this girl who, even now, wedded to the king, promised less prospect of benefaction than did the powerful lady Swanne.

"But we must do what we can," said Swanne and clapped her hands, making Caela start. "The wool, I think, and the posset I prepared earlier."

One of the ladies handed to Swanne a small pouch of linen and a length of red wool, and Swanne stepped close to Caela once more.

"Now," Swanne said, both eyes and voice cold with contempt, "do not flinch. This will get you an heir better than anything . . . save that wild thrusting of a man's thickened member."

She put a hand on her own belly as she spoke, rolling her eyes prettily, and the ladies burst into shrieks of laughter, their hands to their cheeks.

Caela flushed an even darker red.

Swanne bent gracefully to her knees before Caela and first tied the length of wool about the small linen pouch, then tied the pouch to Caela's inner thigh. "This contains the seeds of henbane and coriander, my dear. So long as it doesn't confuse Edward's member too greatly, it will surely drive him to those exertions needed to put a child in that . . ." she paused, her eyes running over Caela's flat abdomen, "*child's* belly of yours."

Again the ladies standing about giggled, but then came the sound of footsteps approaching up the stairs, and the rumble of men's voices and laughter.

"In the bed, I suppose," said Swanne. "He's bound to remember *why* she's there once he climbs in."

With that, the women bustled Caela to the bed, drew back the coverlets over the rich, snowy whiteness of the bridal linens, and bade Caela to slide in.

"We hope to see the red and cream flowers of love spread all over that linen in the morning, my love," said Swanne, pulling the coverlets back to cover Caela's nakedness just as the group of men accompanying Edward entered the chamber.

As Swanne and her ladies had done, so now these men, numbering among them Godwine and his sons Harold and Tostig, attended to Edward, divesting him of his jewels and apparel, and stripping him as naked as Caela.

Then Godwine drew back the coverlets on Edward's side of the bed, and the king, his genitals pitifully white and shriveled in the coldness of the room, clambered into the bed and sat stiffly alongside Caela.

Once he was in bed, one of the men handed him a goblet filled with spiced wine and the raw, sliced genitals of a hare.

"Drink," said Godwine, "and my daughter will soon breed you a fine son."

Edward looked at the goblet, very slowly and reluctantly raised it to his mouth, made a show of sipping it, then placed the goblet on a chest at the side of the bed.

Harold looked at Caela, caught her eyes, and tried to smile for her.

Across the room Swanne laughed, rich and throaty. She pulled her shoulders back, aware that the eyes of most were on her, and splayed her hands over the rich roundness of her belly. "I wish you well, my lord," she said to Edward. "I hope your screams of pleasure, as those of your bride, keep us awake throughout the long hours of this wedding night."

Tostig giggled, and Swanne shot her young brother-in-law an amused glance even as Harold hissed at him to be silent.

As Tostig subsided, Aldred stepped forward, staggering a little drunkenly on his feet, and raised his hand for a mumbled blessing. Then Godwine said something coarse, everyone laughed (save Harold, who watched Caela with eyes filled with sorrow), and then Swanne began to direct people out of the room.

"Our king's member can never rise with this many witnesses," she murmured, to more good-humored laughter.

Swanne was the final person to leave. She stood in the doorway to the chamber, her hand on the latch, and regarded the two stiff people in the bed with a gleam in her wondrous dark eyes.

"Queen at last, Caela," she said. "You must be so pleased."

And then she was gone.

THEY SAT, STIFF, SILENT, COLD, STARING AT THE closed door.

Finally Caela, summoning every piece of courage she could, took her husband's chilled hand and placed it on her breast.

He snatched it away.

"I find you most displeasing," he said, then slid down the bed, rolled over so that his back faced Caela, and stayed like that the entire night.

IN THE MORNING, WHEN SWANNE AND THE REST OF the (largely still drunken) attendants pulled back the covers from the naked pair, there was a moment's silence as the eyes took in the unsullied bleached linens.

Swanne's eyes slowly traveled to Caela's white face, and then she smiled in slow, malicious triumph before she turned her back and left the chamber.

cþapter twO

ROUEN, NORMANDY

ON THE SAME NIGHT THAT CAELA, QUEEN OF EN-
gland, lay sleepless beside her new husband, Edward so also the
duke of Normandy, William, lay sleepless beside his new wife.

But where Edward and Caela's wedding night remained coldly chaste,
William and Matilda's night had been filled with much loving and laughter.
Theirs had been a marriage that *they* had made, and for which they'd had to
combat the combined disapproval of most of the princes of Europe as well the
Holy Father in Rome to be able to achieve.

William lay on his side, his head resting on a hand, his black eyes gentle
as he regarded the sleeping Matilda. *Gods, he'd had to fight so hard for her!*
They'd first met just over three years ago at the court of Matilda's father,
Baldwin, the count of Flanders. Matilda had been fourteen, small and dark
and vivacious, and half the princes and dukes of Europe had sought her hand
(and the considerable dowry and alliances that would come with it). William
had gone to Baldwin's court, not to woo Matilda, but to woo her father, from
whom William hoped to gain much needed financial and military aid in his
constant struggle to repel rival claimants to his dukedom. William had been
struggling to retain Normandy ever since he'd assumed the dukedom at the
age of seven. Not only was his age against him, but also the fact that William
was the bastard-get of the duke, his father, on a tannery wench. In the thirteen years since his ascension and his first sight of Matilda of Flanders,
William had spent the greater part of each year on the battlefield. No one
had expected a bastard son, let alone one of such tender years, to hold out
thirteen years, but during his first vulnerable years, William had enjoyed the
support of a number of powerful allies, notable among them the king of
France. By the time William was fifteen he both led his armies and devised
his strategies himself—almost as if he had been a great leader of men and
armies before.

As if, some rumored, he somehow managed to draw on the experience of a past life as a victorious king instead of a few meager years as the son of a tannery wench.

Thirteen years he'd struggled, and then William had met Matilda. On that fateful day, William's only thought, as he strode toward the count's dais, had been of Baldwin and what the count could do for him, but then his eyes had fallen on the tiny form of Baldwin's daughter standing by her father's throne. William had muttered a cursory greeting to Baldwin, and had then turned to Matilda, took her hand, smiled down into her eyes, and said, "You were made for me."

At that remark there were several audible gasps and one hastily swallowed giggle from among the members of Baldwin's court. Their shocked humor was not simply at William's audacity. At fourteen, Matilda was a mere four feet tall and would grow only another inch throughout the rest of her life.

William was six and a half feet—an amazing height in an age when most men were grateful to achieve five and a half—and with broad shoulders and heavy, tight muscles. Combined with his dark, exotic looks (some questioned the tannery wench maternity, and opined that the previous duke had got his son on some lost Greek princess) and bold demeanor and bearing, William cut an imposing figure.

He certainly looked too large to wed the dainty Matilda without causing her serious bodily damage.

But Matilda had not cared about William's bastardy, nor worried about his large-than-life physicality. She wanted him the instant his mouth grazed her hand and he spoke those words: *You were made for me.*

Europe objected. Frustrated and disappointed princely suitors petitioned the pope, who refused to permit the couple to wed on the grounds such a marriage would violate the Church's laws on consanguinity. William and Matilda shared a distant ancestor, Rollo the Viking, who had founded Normandy, and (as he sat a-counting out the enormous bribes he'd accepted from a number of frustrated suitors) the pope muttered darkly about the evils of allowing such "close" blood-kin to wed. Their union, the pope declared, would offend God to such an extent that doubtless He would smite Christendom with numerous plagues, floods, and boils in the nastiest of places. Matilda stormed, William argued, and, gratefully, eventually the protests waned, the bribes dried up, the pope lost interest, the ban was rescinded (by a lowly clerk within Rome who was sick of the quantity of the duke's protests he'd had to field over the years), and Matilda and William finally wed.

William smiled softly as he lay watching his bride sleep. He lifted a hand and pushed a strand of her dark hair back from her forehead. It was tangled, and damp with sweat, and William's smile grew broader as he remembered the enthusiasm with which both had (*finally!*) consummated their union. Whatever whispers may have rumored, the physical contrast in their heights and builds had made not a single difference to the ease and joy with which they dispensed with Matilda's virginity.

He stroked Matilda's forehead again, his touch less gentle this time, and she sighed, shifted a little in their bed, and opened her eyes.

"I adore you," she whispered.

He leaned down and kissed her, but did not speak.

"And you?" she said very softly, once his mouth lifted from hers.

William hesitated, remembering that other time (*so long ago*) when he had made (*forced*) another marriage. This time, he determined, he would not start with deception and lies.

"You are my wife, my duchess, and I will honor you before any other woman, but. . . ."

His nerve failed him at that moment, and so Matilda did what she had to do in order to found their marriage in such strength that it would never fail.

"But I will not be the great love of your life." she said, propping herself up on one elbow.

"That does not worry you?" he said.

"You and I," she said, tracing one of her tiny hands through the black curls that scattered across his chest, "will make one of the greatest marriages Christendom has ever known. What more could I ask?"

"That is not what I expected to hear," he said, laughing softly in wonderment. "That is not what I had learned to expect from wives." He reached up a hand and cradled her face within its great expanse.

"You have honored and respected me by telling me," Matilda said. "I can accept this." She paused. "You will not dishonor me with her?"

"Never!" William said.

"Romantic love can so often destroy a marriage," said Matilda, "when what is needed is unity of purpose, and unified strength. I will be the best of wives to you, and you shall be the best of husbands to me, and we will marry our ambitions and strengths, and we will never, never regret the choice that we have made."

"I wish I had found you earlier," William said, and Matilda could not have known that with that statement he referred to a time two thousand years past when a former marriage had resulted in such a ruination of dreams and ambitions that a nation had foundered into chaos and disaster. As Brutus, he had failed with Cornelia; William was determined to make a better marriage with this woman.

They made love once again, and then Matilda slipped back to sleep. Once he was sure that she was lost deep in her dreams, William rose from their bed and walked to stand naked before the dying embers of the fire in the hearth of their bedchamber.

The conversation with Matilda had unsettled him. First, the maturity of Matilda's response had astounded William, even though he well knew that she was a princess such as Cornelia had never been, and made him appreciate even more the woman he'd taken to wife. Second, the nature of the conversation had recalled to him Cornelia, and Genvissa, and so much of his previous life.

When he had lived as Brutus, two thousand years previously, in a world wracked by war and catastrophe, he had been a supremely ambitious man. Brutus had allowed nothing to stand in his way. At fifteen, Brutus murdered his father Silvius and took from his dead father's limbs the six golden kingship bands of Troy. In his early thirties, Brutus snatched at the chance to lead the lost Trojan people to a new land and rebuild Troy itself, using the ancient power of the Troy Game which he, as a Kingman, controlled.

In this new land, Llangarlia, now known as England, Brutus had met Genvissa, the Mistress of the Labyrinth, and his partner in the intricate dances of the Troy Game. He and Genvissa had almost succeeded, in their ambition, to build the Game on the banks of the Llan, or Thames, when disaster struck in the form of Brutus' unwilling and unloved wife, Cornelia. Wracked by jealousy, Cornelia had become the pawn of Asterion, the ancient Minotaur and archenemy of the Game, and had murdered Genvissa just as she and Brutus were about to complete the Game.

Even more uncomfortable now that he was thinking of Cornelia, William glanced over his shoulder at Matilda. Gods, there was nothing to compare them! Cornelia wept and sulked and plotted murder. Matilda used reason and wit, and she accepted where Cornelia would have argued. Cornelia had fought with everything she had against Brutus' love for Genvissa. Matilda had shrugged and accepted it as of little consequence to their marriage.

William closed his eyes, feeling the heat of the embers on his face, and finally allowed thoughts of Genvissa to fill his mind. Ah, she had been so beautiful, so powerful! She'd been his Mistress of the Labyrinth, his partner in the Troy Game.

And then she had been cruelly struck down by Cornelia before Brutus or Genvissa could complete the Game.

Had he truly loved Genvissa? William stood, contemplating the issue. After this night with Matilda, and most particularly after their conversation, William wondered if what he'd felt for Genvissa had been an astounding excitement generated by their mutual meeting of ambition and power rather than love. Oh, there had been lust aplenty, but there had been no tenderness, and little sweetness. Instead, William believed, he and Genvissa had been swept away by the realization that united they could achieve immortality through their construction and then manipulation of the Troy Game. They could make both themselves and the Game they controlled immortal.

William smiled wryly. That realization and that ambition had been far, far headier than love.

But both their ambitions foundered into disaster, as Asterion manipulated Cornelia into murdering Genvissa and putting a halt to the Game that would have trapped the Minotaur back into its dark heart.

Disaster, and death. A death that had lasted two thousand years. Why such a delay? William would have thought that his and Genvissa's ambition, as well as the Troy Game's need to be completed, would have brought them back centuries before this. Instead they'd languished in death, frustrated at every attempt at rebirth, kept back from life by a power that they'd both taken a long time to accept: Asterion.

Over two thousand years ago, the Minotaur Asterion had spent his life trapped in the Great Founding Labyrinth on the island of Crete, but he had been released when Ariadne, the then-Mistress of the Labyrinth, and fore-mother of Genvissa, had destroyed the Game within the Aegean world. Now Asterion was the Game's archenemy. He would do anything to ensure its complete destruction, for the Troy Game was the only thing in this world that could control him. Knowing this, after Genvissa's death, Brutus had secreted the ancient kingship bands of Troy about London: Asterion could not destroy the Game if he did not have the bands which had helped create it.

William believed that it had been Asterion who had kept Brutus and Genvissa locked within death for so long, and Asterion who had finally removed the barriers to their rebirth. Both Brutus and Genvissa had con-stantly fought for rebirth, and had as constantly been rebuffed by Asterion's bleak power. He'd been stronger than either had ever expected, and William had thanked whatever ancient gods who still existed, in this strange world into which he'd been reborn, that as Brutus he had secreted the kingship bands of Troy within such powerful magic.

Why had Asterion kept William-reborn and Genvissa-reborn at bay for so long? Had Asterion wanted to find the bands and destroy the Game without risking their rebirth? Well, Asterion had *not* found the bands— William could still sense them, safe in their secret hiding places buried under the city now called London—and so he'd caused Brutus and Genvissa to be reborn, hoping, perhaps, that he could use one or the other to locate the bands.

Asterion had also caused Brutus to be reborn far from London, and (William had no doubt) caused him to exist within such uncertainty, as rival claimant after rival claimant attacked William's right to hold Normandy, that

William had had no chance to think of England at all. Asterion was keeping William at bay for reasons of his own choosing.

William crouched down before the hearth, stretching out his hands to what little warmth the embers emitted. *Oh, but England would be his, it would. England, and London, and the bands and the Troy Game. All of it.*

And Genvissa.

Genvissa had been reborn. William knew it, but he didn't know who, or where, she was. Genvissa-reborn undoubtedly faced the same obstacle. That was their great dilemma. They needed each other desperately so they could reunite and complete the Game, but they did not know who the other was. But wherever or whoever, William knew one thing: Genvissa-reborn would not rest until she had achieved a place within London where the Troy Game was physically located. It was the lodestone for both of them, and unless Asterion had also somehow managed to keep Genvissa-reborn away from the city, William knew she would be there, somewhere.

But who was she? *Who?*

William pondered the fact that as this night was his own wedding night, so also it was Edward of England's wedding night. He knew Edward well, the Saxon king having spent a number of his youthful years at William's court while he was exiled from England by the murderous intentions of his step-father Cnut, and he wondered at this new bride of the man's. Caela, daughter of Godwine, earl of Wessex. William knew the marriage had been forced on Edward by Godwine, but Caela had caught his attention. He was aware that Genvissa, if not actually reborn within the region of London (the Veiled Hills, they'd once called it), would do everything in her power to return to London *and* to a position of power. What better position as queen?

Genvissa would loathe the necessity of becoming a wife, as she would loathe the inherent subjection to a man that marriage meant in this Christian world. It went against her very nature as Mistress of the Labyrinth, an office of such feminine power and mystery that its incumbents refused to subject themselves to any man. Well might a Mistress form a partnership of power and lust and ambition with a Kingman, but never would she subject herself to him.

But William also knew that Genvissa-reborn would do whatever she had to do in order to achieve her ambitions. In this world women had little power. No longer did Mothers rule over households and over their people; the idea of an Assembly of women setting the course of a society was unthinkable now, when men ruled and subjected women to their every whim. Unpalatable as it might be to her, Genvissa *would* subject herself to marriage, if it meant gain.

Marriage to Edward would give her the most gain of all. Queen of England. The highest power a woman could hope for if she held the kind of ambitions that William knew Genvissa secreted.

The moment William heard of Edward's betrothal to Godwine's daughter Caela, William had been almost certain *she* was Genvissa-reborn. True, Caela was by all reports very young, and as timid as a mouse, but maybe that was merely Genvissa's way of disguising her true nature.

William idly wondered what was happening in Edward's bed this night. Had he enjoyed his bedding with the Mistress of the Labyrinth as much as William had enjoyed his with Matilda?

William's face sobered, and he flexed his fingers back and forth before the fading heat, slowly stretching out some of the tension in his body. He needed desperately to contact Genvissa-reborn. He wondered if Caela had any idea who *he* was. Did she suspect William was more than just a struggling duke of Normandy, or did she merely think of him as some bastard upstart who brazened his way about the courts of counts and princes, and of little consequence to her own life and ambitions.

William stared into the fire, then grinned as a means of contacting Genvissa-reborn occurred to him. He would *announce* himself in no uncertain manner. She would know him by his actions, and by his message, and then she would make herself known to him.

"Soon, my love, soon," he whispered.

"William?"

His mind still caught in thoughts of Genvissa-reborn, William jerked to his feet, turning about.

Matilda was sitting up in bed, the coverlets sliding down to her waist and exposing her small breasts. "What are you doing?"

After a moment's hesitation, William walked to the bed, studying Matilda before he slid beneath the coverlets. "Wondering if I dared wake you again," he said. "But, look, now I find you have answered my dreams."

And with that he seized her shoulders, and pushed her back on the bed.

"Matilda," he said, "Matilda, Matilda, Matilda," using the sound of her name in his mouth to suffocate his thoughts of Genvissa.

CᏏAᏢᏆᎬR ᏆᏏRᎬᎬ

S WANNE MOVED THROUGH KING EDWARD'S crowded Great Hall at Westminster, smiling at those she favored, ignoring those she did not. Rather than hold his court in the city of London, Edward, like many of England's previous kings, preferred to keep his court in the community of Westminster on Thorney Isle, which lay at the junction of the Tyburn and the Thames, a mile or so to the southwest of London. Westminster was independent of London, and of its noisy and troublesome crowds, and its equally troublesome civil authority. Better, Westminster was the site of a long-established community of monks (the name Westminster literally meant the minster, or church, west of London), and the pious Edward found them a happier company than the secular profanity of the Londoners. Indeed, Edward was so well disposed toward Westminster's monks that he had summoned court this very day to announce that he would sponsor the rebuilding of the Westminster Abbey Cathedral into the grandest in all of Europe.

The monks were ecstatic, sundry other clerics present were grudging (why Westminster when Edward could have rebuilt *their* church or abbey?). Edward's earls and thegns were resigned and, frankly, Swanne cared not a whit one way or the other whether Edward rebuilt the damned cathedral or not. She was happy to be back on Thorney Isle, happy to be back within the heart of the sacred Veiled Hills of England, happy to be here, now, sliding sinuously through the press of bodies, watching men's eyes light up with desire at the sight of her and women's eyes slide away in disapproval.

Happy to be *alive* and breathing after so long locked in death.

She saw Tostig's eyes on her, saw the darkness in them, and she widened her smile and closed the short distance to his side. "Brother," she said, "you do look well this morn."

His eyes darkened even further. "I am your husband's brother, lady. Not yours."

"As my husband's, so also mine." She leaned close, allowing her breast and rounded belly to brush against him, and kissed him softly on the mouth in a courtly greeting.

As she drew back, Swanne heard his swift intake of breath and decided to deepen the tease. "How *else* should I think of you but as my brother?"

Now Tostig flushed, and Swanne laughed and laid the palm of her hand gently against his cheek, pleased at his patent desire. At fifteen, Tostig still had not learned to conceal his thoughts and needs, nor to discern, or even to realize, that the carefully chosen expressions of others so often concealed contradictory thoughts.

Tostig began to speak, struggling over some meaningless words, and Swanne studied him indulgently. He was not, nor would ever be, as handsome as Harold, but he had a certain charm about him, a darkness of both visage and spirit that Swanne found immensely appealing.

He could be so useful.

"Tostig," she said, and slipped one arm through his. "I am finding this crush quite discomforting. Will you escort me through the hall to my husband's side?" She leaned against him. "I feel quite faint amid this airlessness."

"Of course, my lady!" Tostig said, relieved to have been given something to do, yet flustered all the more by Swanne's attention and the press of her flesh against his. He suddenly found himself wishing that he'd laid eyes on her before Harold, and that he had been the one to demand her hand and her virginity.

Flushing all the deeper with the direction of his thoughts, Tostig began to roughly shove his way through the crowd, Swanne keeping close to his side.

"Aside! Aside for the lady Swanne!" he cried, paying no attention to the irritated glances of thegns and their wives. No one said anything, not to a son of the powerful earl of Wessex, but there were then a few muttered words spoken as soon as Tostig and Swanne had passed on their way.

Within moments, Tostig had led Swanne into the clearer space before Edward's dais. The Great Hall, only recently completed, formed the focus of Edward's entire palace complex at Westminster. It was massive, far vaster than the one Tostig's father had built in Wessex. It was twice as large again, its walls great stone blocks for the first twenty feet, then rising another eighty in thick timber planks. Above the ceiling of the hall, and reached by a great curving staircase behind the dais, were a warren of timber-walled chambers that Edward used for his private apartments, as well as those of his closest retainers.

The focus of the hall was the dais at the southern end. Here Edward currently sat, conversing with Harold who stood just to one side and slightly behind the king's throne, and with Eadwine, the newly appointed abbot of Westminster. Caela, the king's wife, sat ignored on her smaller throne set to her husband's right. Her head was down, her attention on the needlework in her lap, an isolated and lonely figure amid the hubbub of the Great Hall.

Tostig halted as soon as they'd moved into clearer space, and now he stared toward the queen. "Will there be a child soon?" he asked quietly of Swanne.

She laughed, the sound musical and deep, and for an instant Tostig felt her body press the harder against his. "Nay," she said. "There will never be a child of *that* union."

"How can you be so sure?"

Swanne put her lips against Tostig's ear, and felt him shudder. "He will not lay with her," she said. "He believes fornication to be such a great evil that he will not participate in it." She paused. "Especially with a daughter of Godwine. He will have no Godwine heir to the throne. My dear," she said, allowing a little breathlessness to creep into her voice, "can *you* imagine such restraint?"

"With you in his bed, no man, not even Edward, would be capable of it."

"You flatter me with smooth words," she said, but let Tostig see by the warmth in her eyes how well she had received his words.

"But . . ." Tostig struggled to keep his voice even, "but if he has no child of his body, then surely then there *will* be a Godwine heir."

"My husband," she said, laughing. "For surely, for who else? To think, Tostig, you stand here now with the future queen of England pressing herself against you like a foolish young girl. How do you feel?"

Emboldened by her words and touch, Tostig said, "That you will be queen of England there can be no doubt, but who the lucky Godwine brother is that sits beside you as your lord can still be open to question."

That I will be queen of England is undoubted, Swanne thought, laughing with Tostig, encouraging his foolish words, *but that you will ever sit beside me, or Harold, can never be. I have a greater lord awaiting me in the shadows, a mightier lover, a Kingman, and the day he appears, so shall all the Godwine boys be crushed into the dust.*

At that moment Harold looked up from his discussion with Edward, and saw his wife standing too familiarly close to Tostig. He frowned, and spoke swiftly to one of his thegns who stood behind him.

The next moment the thegn had stepped from the dais and was approaching Tostig and Swanne.

"My lady and lord," he said, bowing slightly, "the lord Harold begs leave to interrupt your mirth and requests that his wife join him on the dais. We have received word that a deputation from the duke of Normandy has arrived, and the king wishes to receive him."

"*I* am not invited?" said Tostig.

"You are not my lord's wife," said the thegn.

"I am a Godwineson!" Tostig said, seething.

The thegn was a man of enough years and experience not to be intimidated by the brashness of youth. "All the more reason why our king would not want you standing beside him," he said. "Harold stands there as representative of his father, who cannot attend. Edward tolerates him, but *only* him. My lady, if you will accompany me."

And with that, the thegn led Swanne away, leaving Tostig standing redfaced and humiliated.

HAROLD TOOK SWANNE'S HAND AS SHE MOUNTED the dais, and helped her to a chair. "Was Tostig annoying you?" he asked, smiling gently at his wife. By God, even now he could hardly believe he'd won such a treasure!

"He is a youth," Swanne said, her expression now demure as she sat. "All youths are abrasive, and annoying."

"I will speak to him," Harold said.

"Oh, no!" Swanne said. "It would embarrass him, and only create bad blood. Let it rest, I pray you."

Harold began to say something else, but just then Edward leaned over and hushed them both, waving Harold to his own chair to the king's left.

"I dislike people whispering behind my back!" Edward said, and Harold bowed his head in apology as he sat. Once Edward had returned his attention to the Hall, Harold leaned back, looking behind Edward's throne to where Caela's own throne sat aligned with Harold's chair. He tried to catch her eye, but she was so determinedly focused on her embroidery that she did not, or chose not to, notice his gaze.

Sighing, Harold turned his eyes back to the front. He'd had so little chance to speak with Caela in the past two months, and no chance at all to ask of her in privacy why she wore such a face of misery to the world.

Damn their father for giving such a wondrous girl to such a monstrous husband!

In truth, Harold would vastly have preferred to have spent the morning out hunting, but he'd had to stand in for his father who was not well. Despite the strained and often hostile relations between the earl of Wessex and Edward, Godwine was the leading member of Edward's witan, or council of noblemen advisers, and thus sat, by right, on the dais beside Edward. If God-wine could not attend, then it was best his eldest son and heir do so in his place. Not only would Harold represent Godwine during court proceedings, but his presence would also further cement the Wessex claim to the throne, should Edward's piety prevent him from getting an heir on Caela.

Godwine was determined that one day either he, or his son Harold, or the far less likely prospect of his grandson by Caela, would take the throne of England.

Once the dais was still, Edward waved to the court chamberlain to admit the duke of Normandy's entourage. As the great double doors at the other end of the Hall slowly swung open, and the press of bodies within the Hall parted to allow the entourage passage, Edward allowed himself to relax a little more in his throne. His friendship with Duke William was not only deep, but of long standing. Many years earlier, Edward had been forced into a lengthy exile by his stepfather, King Cnut. Edward had spent the majority of that exile in the duke of Normandy's court where he had come to deeply respect the young William. Not merely respect, but trust. In his own kingdom Edward had to continually fight to maintain his independence from the cursed Godwine clan. Godwine and his clan had sunk their claws of influence and power deep into most of the noble Anglo-Saxon clans, and one of the very few ways that Edward could maintain his authority was to surround himself with Normans, whether in secular or clerical branches of England's administrations.

Edward had two great weapons to use against the Godwine clan: the first was his refusal to get an heir on Caela; the second, his deep ties with the Nor-man court that carried with it the possibility that Edward would name the duke of Normandy as his heir.

As far as Edward was concerned, William was not only a friend and an ally, he was one of the few weapons Edward had against Godwine and his sons.

Edward liked William very much.

The Norman entourage entered the Great Hall with a flourish of horns, drums, the sound of booted and spurred feet ringing out across the flag-stones, and the sweep of heavy cloaks flowing back from broad shoulders. Edward grinned as he recognized several among the entourage that he knew personally.

There were some twenty or twenty-two Normans marching in military for-mation behind William's envoy, Guy Martel. Directly behind Martel came Walter Fitz Osbern and Roger Montgomery, two of William's closest friends. Their presence was a mark of immense respect by William: *See, I hold you in such love, I send my greatest friends to honor you.*

Guy Martel led his entourage to within three paces of the dais, then halted, bending to one knee in a gesture of great gracefulness.

Behind him, each member of the entourage likewise dropped to a knee, bowing his head.

"My greatest lord," Martel said, his voice ringing through the Hall, "I greet you well on behalf of my lord, William of Normandy, and convey to you his heartiest congratulations on the occasion of your marriage."

Edward grunted.

On her chair, Swanne shifted slightly, bored with proceedings. She tried to catch Tostig's eye for some amusement—he was standing to one side of the Hall—but failed. She sighed, and rubbed her belly, wishing she were anywhere but here at this moment. Her mind began to drift, as it so often did, to thoughts of Brutus-reborn, and where he might be, and if he were thinking of her.

"My lord wishes to present you with a token of his love and respect," Martel continued, "and hopes that you are as blessed in your marriage as he is in his."

With that, Martel reached under his cloak, and withdrew a small unadorned wooden box. "My lord, if I may approach . . ."

Mildly curious—and yet disappointed that William's gift was not more proudly packaged—Edward gestured Martel forward, taking the box from him.

"What is this?" he said, opening the lid and staring incredulously at what lay within.

It was nothing but a ball of string. Impressively golden string, but a ball of string nonetheless.

This is what William thought to offer a king as a gift?

Caught by the offense underlying Edward's words, Swanne looked over, wondering what the duke of Normandy had done to so insult Edward.

"What is this?" Edward repeated, and withdrew the ball of string from the box, holding it up and staring at it.

Swanne went cold, and her heart began to pound. She was so shocked that she could not for the moment form a coherent thought.

"A ball of string?" Edward said, the anger in his voice now perfectly apparent.

"If I may," said Martel, taking the string from Edward. "This is a treasure of great mystery." He continued, "May I be permitted to show to you its secret?"

Edward nodded, slowly, reluctantly. *A treasure of great mystery?*

Trembling so badly she could hardly move, Swanne edged forward on her seat. *Oh, please, gods, let this be what I want it to be! Please, gods, please!*

Martel began to unwind the string, which was indeed made of golden thread. His entourage had now formed a long line behind him, and Martel slowly walked down the line, spinning out the string so a portion of it lay in the hands of each member of the line. Once the string had been entirely played out—there were perhaps fifteen or twenty feet of string between each man—Martel walked back toward Edward's dais, holding the end of the string.

Again he bowed. "Pray let me show you," he said, "the road to salvation."

And with that, still keeping a firm hold of the end of the string, he stepped back, and nodded at his men.

They began to move, and within only a moment or two, it became obvious that they moved in a well-choreographed and practiced dance of great beauty. They moved this way and that, in circles and arcs, until each watcher held his or her breath, sure the string was about to become horribly and irredeemably tangled. But it never did, and the men continued in their dance, their faces somber, their movements careful and supple.

Of all the watchers, only Swanne knew what she was truly watching, and only she knew what that ball of string represented: Ariadne's Thread. The secret to the labyrinth.

And gift to Edward be damned. This was a message for her, and her alone!

"Brutus," she whispered, now at the very edge of her seat, her eyes staring wildly at the Normans as they continued in their graceful dance, unwinding the twisted walls of the labyrinth.

Brutus . . . none other than William of Normandy!

"Thank all the gods in creation," she said, again in a whisper, and her eyes filled with tears and her heart pounded with such great emotion that Swanne was not entirely sure that she would not faint with the strength of it at any moment.

With a final flourish the dancers halted, paused, and then in a concluding, single movement, each laid his portion of the string on the ground, and then moved away from it, their task completed.

Soon the flagstone area before Edward's throne was empty, save for the golden thread, now laid out in a perfect representation of the pathways of a unicursal labyrinth.

Edward had risen to his feet, and his eyes moved slowly between the golden labyrinth laid out on the floor and Guy Martel.

"The road to salvation?" he said in a puzzled tone.

"My lord duke well knows of your piety," Martel said, "and of your great disappointment that you have been unable to tread those paths within Jerusalem where once Christ's feet trod. Behold the labyrinth. Its entrance lies before you, and when you enter it, you do so as a man born of woman, and thus weighted down with grievous sin. But as you traverse the paths of the labyrinth, thinking only of Christ and his goodness, you will find when you enter the heart of the labyrinth that Christ and his redemption await you. When you exit the labyrinth, retracing your steps through its twisting paths, you do so in a state of grace, and you will truly be stepping on the pathway toward your own redemption. This labyrinth, great lord and king of England, represents the pilgrim's journey to Jerusalem. He goes there weighted down with sin, but having prayed within that land where Christ once lived, he returns to his own land in a state of grace. He retraces his steps into redemption. This, my great lord of England, is Normandy's gift to you."

No, thought Swanne, the tears running freely down her cheeks, *this is Brutus-reborn's gift to me.*

Edward was clapping his hands, his cheeks pink with joy, and he began to converse animatedly with Martel. But Harold was staring at Swanne, and leaned over to her, concerned. "My dear, what ails you?"

Clearly overcome with emotion, her eyes locked onto the golden labyrinth, Swanne had to struggle to speak. When she did, her voice was only a hoarse whisper.

"The child," she said, and rested a trembling hand on her belly. "The child has caused me some upset. I will retire to our chamber, I think, and rest."

Harold leaned closer, worry now clearly etched on his face. "Should I send for the midwives?"

"No! No, I need only to rest. The heat and the crowd in this Hall have made me feel faint. I will be well enough. Please, Harold, let me be."

And with that she rose and, a little unsteadily at first, made her way from the Hall.

Harold might have followed her, but as Swanne passed behind Caela's chair, he saw that his sister was staring at the labyrinth with almost as much emotion as Swanne had been. Harold sent a final glance Swanne's way—she was walking much more steadily now, and his worry for her eased—then he rose himself and went to Caela's side.

"Sister, what ails you?"

She tore her eyes from the labyrinth, and looked at Harold. "How do we know," she said, "that Christ is in the heart of the labyrinth, instead of some dark monster? Promise me, Harold, that you will never enter that pathway."

He attempted a smile for her. "Should you not be warning your husband?"

"I care not who he meets within the heart of the labyrinth, brother. Christ, or a monster."

And with that she, too, was gone, rising to exit with her ladies.

LATER, AS MARTEL WAS SHOWING EDWARD THE INTRI-
cacies of laying out the string into the form of the labyrinth, a man leaned

against the wall of the Great Hall and watched with a cynical half smile on his face as the king of England tried to learn the pathways of the labyrinth.

He was a man of some influence within Edward's court, and that influence was growing stronger day by day. He was a man liked and trusted by many, disliked by some others, overlooked by many more, and used by none. He was a man far greater than his outward appearance and station within society would suggest.

He was Asterion, the great Minotaur, lover of Ariadne, and victim of Theseus. Many thousands of years ago, Asterion had been trapped within the heart of the Great Founding Labyrinth of Crete. There Theseus had come to him and, aided by Ariadne, Asterion's half sister, had slain him. But then Theseus had abandoned Ariadne and, in revenge, she colluded with Asterion's shade, promising him rebirth into the world of the living if he passed over to her the Darkcraft, the dark power of evil that the Game had been created to imprison. Asterion had agreed, handing over to Ariadne the ancient Dark-craft for her promise that she would destroy the Game completely.

But Ariadne had lied, and one of her daughter-heirs, Genvissa, had sought to resurrect the Game with her lover Kingman, Brutus. That attempt had ended in disaster and death—two of the things Asterion was best at manipulating—but the attempt had given Asterion cause for thought.

What if, instead of completely destroying the Game, he sought to control it?

Asterion stood within the Great Hall of Westminster, clothed in the guise he wore every day to confuse and deflect, watching Edward in his labyrinth, his thoughts all on that great prize: the Troy Game. To control the Game, Asterion needed the six kingship bands of Troy, which were instrumental not only in the Game's creation, but in its controlling.

The bands were a pitiful prize, considering that Asterion had the power to raise and destroy empires, but these bands continued to elude him as they had from that moment when Asterion, in his rebirth as Amorian the Poiteran, had invaded and razed Brutus' Troia Nova. He had not been able to find the bands then. He had continued to fail in their retrieval for two thousand years. Brutus had hid them well, embuing their secret places with such protective magic that they remained hidden from Asterion.

And, by all the gods and imps in creation, how Asterion had tried to uncover their location! He had thrown *everything* he had at the city in order to discover their locations. He knew they were somewhere within London's walls, just as he knew that the Game Genvissa and Brutus had begun was alive and well.

Asterion knew it, because every time he destroyed the city, whether in sheer fury or in order to try again to unearth the bands, the city regrew. Under Asterion's direction, the Celts, the Romans, the Scotti, the Picts, the

various tribes of the Anglo-Saxons, and finally the Vikings had invaded the
land and razed or otherwise destroyed London in its entirety or by sections.
In those lifetimes, when invasion had not threatened, Asterion sent mysterious fires that swept through buildings, reducing swathes of the city to smoking cinders, or agonizing plagues, which left the city's streets full of rotting
corpses.

Every time the city was struck down, it somehow recovered. Perhaps not
overnight, but it *did* recover. Other cities would have succumbed and vanished
beneath the waving grasses of wild meadows. But not London. It refused to
stay dead.

This told Asterion several things. One, that the bands *were* still here, for
otherwise the Troy Game would not be able to function. Two, that the Game
begun so long ago remained alive and well and grew more vital with each disaster, as it absorbed the evil that attacked it. Finally, the city's continued
regeneration told Asterion where the Game was—where lay its heart.

When Asterion, as Amorian, had razed Brutus' Troia Nova, he had not
been able to determine the location of the actual Troy Game itself, where lay
the labyrinth. For decades the area surrounding the Llan River and the Veiled
Hills had remained desolate. Then, very gradually, a modest village grew in
the small valley between Og's and Mag's hills. The villagers traded with com-
munities further upriver, and the village grew and became a small, prosperous
town.

Flushed with their success, which they attributed to the benefice of the
gods, the town's citizens built a temple of standing stones atop Og's Hill. The
town grew space—and was then torn apart by Asterion's fury in the guise of
the invading Celts. The area surrounding the ancient Veiled Hills remained
desolate for almost a century.

Then the Celtic Britons built there a larger town this time, in the same
spot that Brutus had erected Troia Nova, their streets following the contours
of his streets. The town prospered, and the Celtic Druids erected a circle atop
Og's Hill, which they now called Lud Hill after one of their gods. This community Asterion murdered with disease—a horrific plague that wiped out
much of the population of southern Britain in the third century before Christ.

Then came the Romans, who built a magnificent city reflecting their own
pride and achievements. It, like the Celtic township, also followed the contours of Brutus' Troia Nova, and atop Og's Hill—now Lud Hill—the Romans
built a great temple to Diana.

Diana, the Roman Goddess of the Hunt, who had been known during the
time of the Greeks as Artemis.

Asterion, who walked through Roman London as one of Rome's overabundant generals, looked at that temple, and *knew*.

The labyrinth was there. It had to be. It attracted to it the veneration and temples of every people who lived within the city.

And yet the Game and the labyrinth it hid would not allow Asterion to uncover it. No matter how many times he caused the temples and churches atop Lud Hill to be razed, Asterion could never discover the labyrinth.

No matter how deep he caused his minions to dig.

Now a Christian cathedral graced the top of the hill. St. Paul's was the third construction on this hill to bear that name after Asterion had caused the first to be consumed with fire and the second to be razed by the Danes.

To his eyes, still yearning for the grace and color and beauty of the temples and halls of the ancient Aegean world, St. Paul's was a homely, stooped thing. To the English Saxons, Asterion supposed, it was a wondrous construction, given that most of the other buildings in London were wattle and daub, wood, or ungracious and poorly laid stone. Shaped as a long hall, a rounded apse to one end and a squat, ugly tower straddling the nave's mid-section, the cathedral sat in a cleared space running east-west along the top of Lud Hill. The Londoners certainly adored it enough, and not merely for reasons of worship—most days the nave was almost as filled with market stalls as was Cheapside.

Suddenly Asterion's eyes refocused on Edward in the Great Hall. The fool had worked his way through the labyrinth to its heart, and then back out again. Now he was calling for cups of wine to be handed about so he could raise a toast to William of Normandy.

A servant handed Asterion a cup, and Asterion put a smile on his face, nodding cheerfully to Edward when the king looked at him, and toasted William of Normandy with wine while in his heart he cursed him.

Asterion was wary of William. Very wary. As Brutus, William's magic had been powerful enough to outwit Asterion in his hunt for the kingship bands. Brutus' power was the principal reason Asterion had for two thousand years kept those blocks in place that prevented William and Genvissa's rebirth (and thus preventing everyone else's rebirth who had been caught up in this battle).

But Asterion had not been able to discover the bands, and thus, a few decades ago, frustrated beyond measure, he had removed the blocks. One by one, women across western Europe had fallen pregnant and given birth to babies who, as they grew, drew on the remembered experiences and ambitions of a past life to shape their decision in this life.

Asterion had taken the added caution of ensuring that, first, William was reborn far from London (a nice touch, Asterion thought, remembering how Genvissa's mother, Herron, had caused Asterion to be reborn far from Llangarlia so many lifetimes ago), and, secondly, William was kept busy and

distracted with problems within his own duchy. Asterion did not want to meet
William until he, Asterion, was well and ready.

And Asterion did not want to meet William, or to have to cope with the
problem of William, until he had the bands and . . . *her*.

His eyes slid from Edward to the door through which Swanne had
vanished.

"Enjoy what happiness you can find, Swanne," Asterion said. "It won't last
long."

CbAPGER FOUR

ARRIAGE TO HAROLD HAD BROUGHT SWANNE
many benefits—her current proximity to London and the Troy
Game being prominent among them—but at this very moment
Swanne was grateful only for the fact that their seniority within Edward's
court meant they had a private bedchamber.

She had brushed aside Harold's concerns, she had brushed aside the concerns of her attending woman Hawise, and now Swanne stood wonderfully
alone, her back against the closed door of the bedchamber.

"Brutus," she whispered, the tears now flowing again down her cheeks.
Then, more loudly, more emphatically, *"William!"*

William of Normandy! Oh, what a fine jest that was, to place Brutus-reborn
within the land where the savage Poiterans had lived so long ago. Yet how
right it seemed: Brutus once again born as the military adventurer, the strug-
gler, the achiever . . . the *foreigner*. With her new knowledge, the future
became instantly clear to Swanne: once again Brutus would invade, once
again he would seize control of the land.

Once again he would reign as king over England and London and over her
heart. And this time, they would succeed immortality.

"William," she whispered yet one more time, rolling the word about her
mouth, loving the feel of it, joyous in her new discovery.

*He had sent that ball of string as a message to her! He yearned for her as much
as she for him!*

It seemed such a simple thing, discovering what name Brutus went by in
this life, but its lack had meant that Swanne had not, to this point, been able
to discover or contact Brutus-reborn. She needed to know who he was to
be able to contact him, and likewise he had to know her name. Much of her
life to this point had been spent in that search: *Where are you Brutus? Where?*

Always that search had been frustrated over and over again by circumstance.

Swanne had been born in a county a long, long way from London to a
nobleman of little consequence. For years, ever since she had been some ten

or eleven years old and had come to a full awareness—and remembrance—
Swanne had been desperate to leave her father's home and get to London.
Somehow. Anyhow.

To get back *home*.

To find Brutus and to finish what had been so terribly interrupted.

But Swanne had been reborn into a life and a world in which women had
very little power, and even less say over the destiny of their lives. Her father
had laughed at her pleadings to be allowed to live in London, and he said that
she needed a husband to tame her waywardness.

The thought of a *husband* made Swanne even more desperate—no Mistress
of the Labyrinth submitted to a *husband*—but as she grew older, and rejected
the hand of every suitor her father tossed her way, she grew ever more desperate. She'd hoped Brutus-reborn would one day ride into her father's estate and
claim her, but he didn't, and Swanne realized he probably wouldn't.

As she did not know him, so he did not know her.

The only way out of her father's house, and the only way to London
(where, pray to all gods, Brutus might be waiting for her!), was via that hateful institution of marriage. Maybe she *would* need to submit to a husband, if
only to use him for her own ends.

Then one day Harold Godwineson had ridden, laughing and strong, into
her father's courtyard, and the instant Swanne had seen his face, felt his eyes
upon her, she had *known*.

She had known who Harold was reborn, and she knew she could use him.
He would be her bridge to Brutus-reborn and to London and the Game. Coel.
Swanne wasn't sure why he had been reborn, what had pulled him back, but
the thought of using Coel-reborn to get to London, and eventually to Brutus,
was of some amusement to Swanne.

The blessing in all of this was that Harold himself had no memory of
his past life. If he'd had, Swanne would have had no chance at him at all. She
had no idea as to why this was so—perhaps it was merely an indication of
Harold's complete meaningless in what was to come—but she was very, very
grateful.

And so Swanne had smiled, and shaken out her jet-black hair, and tilted
her lovely head on her graceful neck, and had won Harold before he'd even
dismounted from his horse. She went to his bed that night, and in return he
had taken her from her father's house the next morning.

They were wed, but under Danelaw rather than Christian. That had been
Swanne's demand, and Harold, desperately in love with her, had agreed without
complaint. A Danelaw marriage gave Swanne more independence, and far more
control over her extensive lands, which had been her dowry, than a Christian

marriage would have done. Under the hated Christian law, everything—her estates, her chattels, even her very soul—would have become Harold's. Under Danelaw it remained Swanne's

And thus to London. To be certain, they spent some time each year in Wessex, dreaded cold, rainy place that it was, but most of the year, Godwine made sure his eldest son and heir kept him company within Edward's court.

Swanne had been certain that Brutus-reborn would linger somewhere within Westminster . . . but it was not so, and in the eighteen months or so of her marriage, Swanne had had to fight away despair.

Where was Brutus? What was his name in this reborn life?

But now she knew, and all she wanted to do was go to him, and, in this want and need, Swanne succumbed to a fit of hatred so great that she actually sank to the floor, beating at her belly with her fists.

All she wanted to do was go to her lover, to go to William, and here she was, almost seven months swollen with another man's child.

Harold! She spat the name, all her gratefulness for his usefulness vanishing in her anguish. She wanted to go to William. *She wanted to so badly, she could taste the need in her mouth, feel it in her body, and here she was, great with another man's child!*

Coel's child.

Swanne went cold with apprehension. Oh gods . . . Coel's child. *How could she explain that to William?*

She hit her belly hard with the closed fist of her right hand, beating at it until she bruised her skin beneath its linens and silks. Coel-Harold's child.

And a son.

She conceived the baby only after many months of marriage, when it had become apparent to her that Brutus-reborn was nowhere within Edward's court, and likely nowhere within England. She'd conceived a son, going against her every instinct and need as Mistress of the Labyrinth, because a son would bind Harold the tighter to her, and further ensure her a place within the Westminster court.

"*Curse you, Harold, for getting this child in me!*" she said, low and vicious, and she barely avoided using her power as Mistress of the Labyrinth to visit him with a death-dealing curse then and there.

No, no, she must be careful. She must be prudent. She was very well aware that Asterion lurked somewhere, and, after the mistakes of the past life, Swanne was not going to make another ill-considered move until she knew precisely where Asterion was and what power he commanded. As Genvissa, she had thought he was weak and essentially powerless. What a fool she had been. Asterion had played with them all, had *toyed* with them, and had used Cornelia to stop the Game in its tracks.

Swanne had tried to scry out Asterion's identity—she had managed it easily enough when she had been Genvissa and had realized the fact of Asterion's rebirth within the Poiteran people—but now, in this life, Asterion appeared to have grown so greatly in power and in cunning that she could not know where, or who, he was.

Even if she didn't know who he was, Swanne knew precisely what Asterion wanted. To destroy the Game once and for all, and to destroy Swanne and William with it.

No, you bastard, she thought, her eyes still closed, her lovely face set in uncommonly harsh lines. *No. And this time you can be sure we won't allow you to use Caela as your dagger's hand.*

Ah, Caela! Swanne's eyes opened, and they were hard with hatred. *Caela!* Swanne couldn't believe it when she first met Harold's sister. She would have murdered the bitch then and there, had it not been for the fact that she still needed Harold's goodwill (and body and bed and children) to assure her a place by his side at court.

Then, as if her very existence were not bad enough, Caela had become *queen!* Still Swanne did nothing. The murder of Caela would expose her to far too much risk. Not only would it alienate her from Harold (and how she despised being tied by need to the man) but it would overexpose her to Asterion. For all Swanne knew, Asterion was hoping that Swanne *would* murder Caela.

So she stilled her hand, and contented herself with whispering viciousness into the poor girl's ear whenever she had the chance.

The blessing in all of this was the fact that Harold and Caela had been reborn as siblings. Swanne wasn't sure who was responsible for that piece of mischief—whether fate or Asterion—but it had provided her with a never-ending source of amusement. Poor, lost, insipid Caela, for whatever reason, not remembering a thing of her previous life, and horrified at her constant yearning for a man who was her brother. And the equally un-remembering Harold yearning for her.

All that suppressed lust.

Swanne could understand why Harold might not remember his previous life (he was hardly important in the scheme of things, was he?), but she was surprised that Caela did not remember (if also gratifying, as it gave Swanne so many opportunities to torment the woman). Caela still carried the ancient mother goddess Mag within her womb *(was there nothing that could eject that damn goddess from Cornelia-Caela's womb?)*, but even Mag seemed faded, lost, forgetful.

Useless.

Swanne shrugged to herself. Well, neither of them were of much account now.

Swanne slowly rose to her feet, drying her tears and straightening her robe, her thoughts now back to William. There was a large mirror of burnished bronze in the corner of the chamber, and Swanne walked over to it, regarding herself within its depths.

Would he like her? Would he desire her? Pregnancy aside, Swanne was taller and slimmer in this life than she had been as Genvissa. Elegant, where once she had been earthy. Swanne pulled the veil from her head and tossed it contemptuously to the far corner of the chamber: all Anglo-Saxon ladies wore lawn or silk veils over their head in public, and Swanne loathed this single badge of womanly subjection more than any other. Who could imagine it? Veiling a woman's beauty! Pulling the pins from her hair with almost the same amount of vigor as she'd pulled away the veil, Swanne tipped her head to one side, letting her heavy hair fall over her shoulder, admiring the way her long neck glowed like ivory in the candlelight. As a child, Swanne had been named for her long, exquisite neck, combined with her manner of holding her head. Even as a baby, apparently, her beauty had been remarkable. Now, as a mature woman, she could stop men open-mouthed in their tracks.

"Thank the gods this child has swollen only my belly and not my feet, or even my face," Swanne muttered. She continued to study herself critically, unfastening her heavy outer surcoat and allowing it to fall away from her shoulders and arms to the floor so that she stood only in her under gown of pale linen.

She remembered how Tostig had lusted after her in the Great Hall earlier.

She remembered how other men had followed her with their eyes.

She remembered how Harold still used her body, night after night, in their bed.

She remembered how she and Brutus used to make love when, as Genvissa, she had been heavily pregnant with their daughter. Her belly hadn't deterred him then . . . why would it now?

She smiled. So her belly was all crowded out with child—that made her no less desirable.

"I won't tell him about Coel," she murmured. "Why? What does it matter?"

Her hands stilled, and her eyes stared at her reflection. "William," she whispered. *Ah, gods, he was so close!* "William!"

Then again, her voice riddled with desire: *"William!"*

Finally, her mind so consumed with need and want and desire that all thought of Asterion and of prudence disappeared, Swanne opened her arms, cried out one more time, *"William!"* and vanished.

CDAPTER FIVE

ROUEN, NORMANDY

ILLIAM STOOD IN THE TACK ROOM OF THE
stable complex in his castle at Rouen, going over the saddles he used for hunting and for war with his Master of the
Horse, Alain Roussel. They did this several times a year, checking war and
hunting gear for faults, fractures, or worn spots that needed repair. Better to
spend a few hours here and there in the relative warmth of the stables, peering
at metal and leather then to have it give way suddenly amid the heat of battle.

They had just decided that one of William's most prized saddles needed
one of its seams restitched when William suddenly raised his head and peered
into the middle distance, his eyes unfocused, his face drawn.

"My lord?" Roussel asked softly, wondering if his duke had heard the
sounds of a distant battle that his own aging ears had yet to discern.

"Leave me," William whispered.

"My lord—"

"*Leave me!*" Then, in a more moderate tone that was nonetheless tense,
"Ensure that no one disturbs me."

"Yes, my lord." Roussel bowed his head, turned on his heel, and left. Whatever he thought at the abrupt and strange command did not show on his face.

The instant Roussel had departed, William began to pace back and forth
within the relatively narrow confines of the tack room.

Genvissa! She had seen, or heard about, his gift to Edward, and recognized
it for what it was.

She was on her way.

William felt nerves flutter in his belly. *Gods, he wanted to see her, to hold
her!* Yet, at the same time, William worried, his eyes roving from this dark
corner to that, wondering if somehow this would expose Genvissa-reborn or
himself. If somehow this demonstration of power on her part would awake
Asterion into madness . . .

And then she was there, directly before him, breathless, laughing, tears running down her cheeks, her arms held out, and William forgot everything else and snatched her into his arms, holding her tight, laughing and crying with her. He was kissing her, she was pressing her body into his, her hands grabbing at his arms, his shoulders, running through the short black curls on his head.

"You've lost your great mane," she said, somehow managing to get the words out between kisses.

"It did not suit a Norman man-of-war," he said. Then, summoning all his control, he put his hands on her shoulders and pushed her back a little so he could see her face, and study it.

"You're beautiful," he said, and the wonder and admiration in his voice made her laugh and cry all over again. "More beautiful than ever. Sweet Lord Christ, Genvissa, thank *all* the gods that we've found each other!"

"I was desperate. I didn't know who you were, where . . . and then your damned envoy arrived this morning, and presented Edward with that wonderful ball of string, and I knew, I *knew*, I could hear you screaming for me . . . I came . . ."

They embraced and kissed again, and then again William pushed her back, gently. "I had thought Edward a pious man," he said, grinning at her, "but I see he has wasted no time getting an heir on you."

Swanne's expression stilled. "What?"

William laid a hand on her swollen belly. "You've been married only, what? Two months? And yet this is a six or seven month belly you carry."

She frowned all the more.

William opened his mouth, hesitated, then said, "You are Caela, are you not?"

Her reaction stunned William. She tore out of his arms, stepped back, and looked so angry that William almost thought she might hit him.

"I am not *that* fool!" she said. "I am Swanne, lady of Wessex. Caela! *Caela?* Why her? Why did you think I was her?"

"Swanne—what a lovely name—Swanne, I am sorry. Like you, I worried for years where you were, and who. Then I heard Edward was taking a wife, and I wondered if this was you. It seemed to fit . . . I knew you would do everything in your power to consolidate yourself within London and the Veiled Hills, and what better way than as queen?" He smiled, trying to restore her good humor, and ran a thumb down her cheek. "*I* was the fool, my love. I should have known. Caela is but a girl, is she not? And you . . ." His voice deepened. "You are a wondrous woman, all grown into what I need."

Swanne was not appeased. "Caela is Cornelia-reborn."

William stilled, his hand partway down Swanne's cheek. "*Cornelia?* By the gods, what is she doing here? What mischief does she plan?"

Swanne's mouth curled. "She couldn't plan the curdling of a milk pudding, my dear. Fate has this time been kind to us. Cornelia has been reborn as the timid, helpless daughter of Godwine, so sexless and so undesirable, that *she* at least will never be swelling with child. William, hate her all you might, for that at least she deserves, but do not fear her. She has been reborn into such weakness that she does not even remember her past life!"

William frowned. "She doesn't remember?"

"No." Now Swanne moved back into him again, running her hands over his body, and her mouth, slowly and teasingly, over his neck and jaw.

He drew in a deep breath, and she smiled, and nipped at him with her teeth. "She is of no account," she whispered. "None."

Again he breathed deeply, then ran a hand over her belly. "So who gave you this then, if not Edward? You said you were a lady of Wessex . . . you have married into Godwine's family?"

"Aye. His eldest son, Harold."

There was something in her voice, a tightness, and William took her face between his fingers and tilted her face up to his. "Harold? A powerful catch."

"He has been my path into London, and into the center of power." Her face twisted a little. "To think, that circumstance should force me to stoop to marriage. Me, a Mistress of the Labyrinth."

"And who *is* Harold, Swanne?"

She twisted her face out of his fingers and kissed his neck again. "No one. Only a man."

"He is no one reborn?"

She laughed throatily. "Of course not." Her teeth nipped into his skin, and he felt tiny pinpricks of pain as her sharp teeth drew blood, and he forgot Harold in the rising tide of his desire.

"You should have chosen a better place to come to me, my love. This dusty tack room isn't quite—"

"It will do," she said, and loosened the laces holding together the neck of her under robe so that he could run his hand over her breasts. "For all the gods' sakes, William . . ."

The agony of wanting in her voice undid him. He hauled the skirts of her gown up, running his hands over her thighs and bare buttocks. Then he lifted her up, resting her buttocks on a shelf and, as she wrapped her legs about his hips, fumbled desperately with his own clothing that he might bury himself within her.

As he did so, as he moaned and dug his fingers into her buttocks, pulling her hard against him, there came the faint memory of Matilda's words two months earlier: *You will not dishonor me with her?*

Never! He had cried.

Never.

He thrust deeply into Swanne again, and then again, and she cried out and tightened her legs about him.

Never.

And then William became aware of that damned belly of Swanne's digging into his, and he wondered if she had cried out like this under Harold of Wessex, and whether or not she had ever promised Harold what William had promised Matilda.

Never.

"I can't," he said, groaning, and pulled out of Swanne abruptly so that she almost tumbled to the floor.

She flushed, and he knew her well enough to know it was anger.

"Not yet," he said, readjusting his own clothing.

"What?" she hissed. "You don't want to dishonor your *wife?*"

William's face reddened—she had picked up his thoughts. "She is important to me," he said.

"And I *not?*" Swanne said, dangerously quiet.

"Listen to me, Swanne." William stepped close to her and took her chin between fingers less gently than they had been earlier. "Neither of us can afford to relax our guard. Each of us has a part to play so that, eventually, we can both play our parts *together*. Yes, Matilda is important to me. She brings at her back military might and alliances that I can ill afford to ignore if I am to seize the throne of England. For the love of Christ and His army of damned Christian saints, Swanne, have you not heard of my dilemma? I spend eleven months of the year, year in, year out, fighting rival claimants to Normandy, men and armies sent by *Asterion*—I have no doubt—to keep me occupied and away from England. I need Matilda and her dowry of military support and alliances, if ever I am to consolidate my hold on Normandy and then turn to England. Matilda . . . dammit, Swanne, Matilda is my way to you and to the Troy Game!"

She had quietened and relaxed a little as he spoke, and now she reluctantly gave a small nod. "You think Asterion sends these armies to annoy you?"

"Aye. Again and again they come back. That's Asterion's hand, none other." He paused. "Is he in England? Do you know him?"

She shook her head. "I cannot tell who he is, but the 'where' . . . well, I am certain he is in England. I can *feel* his presence sometimes, generally when Edward is holding court, but that sense is only faint, and there are so many people about . . ."

"We must be wary, Swanne."

"Yes. I know."

He kissed her. "It won't be long. Surely . . . not now."

She gave a half smile. "No. It won't be long." Then . . . "Where are your Kingship bands, William? You feel naked without them."

He grimaced. "After . . . after you died—"

"After my *murder* at that bitch's hands!"

"Aye. After Cornelia murdered you, I burned you atop a great pyre on Og's Hill. Then, mindful of your warning—*Save the Game! Hide it, for Asterion is surely on his way!*—I took the bands from my limbs and secreted them about London. They lie there still, even though I think Asterion hunted through two thousand years for them so he could use them to destroy the Game."

She shivered, and moved in close against him. "I do not know what amazes me more, William. That for two thousand years Asterion sought those bands— and kept us apart—or that you have such power that you could frustrate him for that long. William, can you still feel the bands? You know they are safe?"

He nodded. "They are safe. I would know the instant anyone touched them."

"And the Game?" she said. "Do you feel it, even as far from it as you are?"

He nodded. "It is strong still. Unweakened by the time it has been left by itself."

There was a small silence.

"It is different, William."

He hesitated before answering. *Yes, the Game* was *different.*

"Could the Game have changed in the two thousand years it was left alone?" Swanne said.

"Perhaps," William said, but his voice was slow and unreassuring. "We had not closed it, it was still alive, and still in that phase of its existence where it was actively growing. Who knows what . . ."

He stopped then, but his unspoken words were clear. *Who knows what it could have grown into.*

"Oh, gods, William," Swanne said. "How long before you can come?"

He gave a small shrug. "With the resources Matilda brings at her back? With her father and her entire clan as allies? A year, maybe two at the most. Swanne, listen to me—we cannot risk this again."

"Meeting like this? Are you afraid that next time your Matilda might discover us?"

He tensed, and she knew the truth of her words.

"I cannot afford to alienate her, Swanne. But, no, I fear more for what Asterion might do. You can be sure that he's somewhere, watching us. Manipulating us." He paused. "Is there anyone at Edward's court that you can trust to carry messages between us?"

She thought, frowning, then her brow cleared. "Yes. Do you know the cleric Aldred? He is a Norman, so . . ."

"Yes, indeed. I know him well." William paused, thought, then gave a decisive nod. "He is an excellent choice. Either he, or some of his subordinates, travel to and from Normandy throughout the year."

"And he favors you. I have heard him talk well of you to Edward."

William smiled. "Aldred then. But be careful, for—"

He stopped suddenly, his head up. "Gods, Matilda is but fifty paces away! She is looking for me! Go, Swanne, *Go!*"

"William . . ."

"Go!" He kissed her once, hard. "Go! It won't be long. I swear. It won't be long . . . *go!*"

And then she was gone, and William staggered, caught his balance, and looked up to see Matilda staring at him from the doorway.

CHAPTER SIX

SHE WAS ONLY SEVENTEEN, THE CROWN OF HER head scarcely reached his chest, and she had none of the mystical power of the woman who had just left him, but Matilda's simple, still presence and her clear, questioning gaze made William's heart thud with nerves.

"There has been someone with you," she said, and walked into the room, her eyes now sliding this way and that about the tack room.

Suddenly her eyes were back on him, very still. "Someone unsettling enough that your breath rasps in your throat and your cheeks flush. What is this, William? That look I only thought to see in the more intimate moments of our marriage."

"You surprised me."

"I think I should have surprised you a moment or two earlier than I did. Yes?"

William thought of what Matilda *might* have seen had she been that bit earlier. Swanne, legs about his hips, moaning in abandon? Gods . . .

"You vowed," Matilda's voice was harsher now, and William could hear the grate of pain and judgment underlying it, "that you would never dishonor me with her. Not two months since."

Gods, what had she seen? Or was Matilda more perceptive than he had credited?

William thought of all the lies he could tell, *would* have told had this been Cornelia instead of Matilda, and he thought that when he began to speak, one of those glib lies would slip smoothly out. But he found himself remembering their marriage night, and what benefits the truth had brought him then, and so when he spoke, it was truth rather than falsehoods. "She was here, that woman of whom I spoke, and she begged me to take her. Oh God, Matilda, I wanted to. Thus my breath. Thus my flushed cheeks."

"And you did not?" Matilda had not moved, and her eyes were very steady on his.

"I began," he said. "I was roused, and for a moment I did not think. Then I remembered you, and I stepped back from her."

"You remembered what I bring at my back, more like."

"I remembered *you*, Matilda. If it had been your dowry at the forefront of my mind then I could have lied to you just now."

"Who is she, William?"

"She is the lady Swanne, Harold of Wessex's wife."

"I have heard of her, and of her legendary beauty. How came she here, William?"

Oh gods, how to explain this to her?

"She was raised among the ancient ways," he said, "and when a baby suckled at the breasts of faeries. She . . . she commands powers that many would condemn."

Matilda stared at her husband for many long minutes, digesting this piece of information. "A witch?" she said finally, her voice a mere whisper.

William opened, then closed his mouth. He gave a single nod.

"By Christ himself, William, what interest has she in you?"

"Even witches can find me attractive, Matilda."

Matilda laughed, and William was profoundly relieved to hear genuine amusement in it.

"As also daughters of Flanders," she said. "Very well. I believe you. I think you spoke truth to me just now. That was well done, William. Not many husbands would have done it. Now tell me more. Was that," she waved a hand at his groin, "the only reason she used her witchcraft to reach you?"

"No. Matilda . . . I have spoken long and often to you of my plans for my . . . for *our* future. But there is one burning ambition of which I have not yet spoken to you."

She raised an eyebrow.

"I long for the throne of England. I *yearn* for it."

She gave a disbelieving laugh. "Fighting for Normandy isn't enough for you?"

"When Normandy is secure, then I am turning my eyes to England, Matilda. You are already duchess of Normandy—"

"Those bits of it you command," she said sotto voce.

"How much more would you like to be queen of England?"

She thought about it. "Very much, I think. I have heard it is a fine land, and rich, and its people pliable. But I have also heard that there are many people who lust for England. The Anglo-Saxon earls for one, notable among them the Godwine family, and what of the Danes and Norwegians? They have ever longed for England."

He grinned, mischievously. "I thought the challenge would appeal to you."

"Oh, aye, challenge *does* appeal to me. Why else marry you?"

They both laughed, their eyes locking, and William relaxed even more. He moved close to her, and bent down to kiss her, but she moved away.

"Not when your mouth still stinks of this Swanne. Later, perhaps, when you have washed away her taste with wine."

William was not perturbed by Matilda's refusal, for there was no hatred or viciousness in her voice. Indeed, her tone had been matter-of-fact, as if all she had complained about was that his mouth still stank of the leeks he'd eaten for his noon meal.

"I will secure Normandy," he said. "And then I will go for England. I *will* be king of England, Matilda. And you my queen."

"Not this Swanne?"

He shook his head, his eyes unwavering. "No. You. Swanne is . . . Swanne is my eyes and ears within Edward's court. My ambition for England is also her ambition."

"And yet she does not want to be your queen in return for all this disloyalty to her country and husband?"

"What she might *want*," William said quietly, "is not what she might necessarily get." Stunningly, he realized that was no lie.

She regarded him very steadily for some time before finally speaking. "Do you not want to know the reason I came seeking you? What made me dare the stables and all its dirt?"

He smiled. "What, my love?"

Now she drew close to him and, taking his hand, put it on her stomach. "The midwives have just confirmed to me what I have suspected now for a week or more. I am with child, William."

He looked at her, then drew her in close, holding her in silence for a long time. Eventually Matilda drew back, her face softer than it had been at any time before in this conversation.

"Do you think you could still bear to make love to me when I am swollen with this child, William?"

He smiled, but for a moment the memory of Swanne's pregnant body pressed against his consumed him. "I will find it no difficulty at all," he said.

"Then let us quit this tired and dusty stable, and seek our bedchamber and some wine to wash the taste of Swanne from your mouth. I do not think that tightness of breath nor that flush in your cheeks should be wasted."

HE SLEPT ONCE THEY'D MADE LOVE, BUT MATILDA lay awake under the heaviness of his body, thinking over all that had happened this day.

Matilda had known the instant she'd stepped into that tack room what had been happening, although she'd not been able to understand the how of it, for there was no exit from that chamber save the doorway she herself stood in.

But there William had stood before her, as aroused as ever she'd seen him, and behind her had stood the Master of the Horse, Alain Roussel, who had begged her not to enter.

So Matilda had done the only thing she could. She had closed the door on Roussel and had done what she had to in order to not only save her marriage from disintegrating into sham, but to fashion it into something even stronger than it had been.

William had been engaged in making love with another woman (and a witch, no less!) that he'd already admitted (on their wedding night, no less!) was the first love of his life. Matilda could have whined and sulked, or she could have cried and stormed and threatened, but she did none of these things, realizing that would have lost her William's respect. Instead she had remained calm and reasonable, allowing William to judge himself by his own words rather than by hers. She realized also that a marriage could be made on stronger ties than love and that, in the end, these ties would defeat whatever love or lust William felt for this lady Swanne.

Whatever William had said to her, Matilda was not entirely sure that it was *love* that bound these two. Something else bound them . . . their equal ambition for the throne of England, perhaps? Matilda believed William when he said that she, Matilda, would be his queen . . . but Matilda did not think that Swanne would let go her ambition easily. Whatever William might believe, Swanne fully intended to sit beside William as his lover and as his queen.

You might be a witch, lady Swanne, Matilda thought, *but you have not yet matched your wits against a daughter of Flanders, have you?*

William sighed, then half waking, shifted his body a little, running a hand over Matilda's breast and cupping it gently in his hand before falling back into a deeper sleep.

And you are not the one lying under his body, and with his child in her belly. Beautiful and powerful you might be, Swanne, but you are deluded if you think that love and lust will mean more to William than loyalty and friendship and the bonds of a strong marriage.

Matilda resolved to never tax William with Swanne again. If she did so, then it would be Matilda herself who would fracture their marriage.

No, she would not tax William about Swanne, but she would do her utmost to make sure that *she* had *her* ears and eyes at Edward's court. Two agents were better than one when it came to a throne . . . and a marriage.

CHAPTER SEVEN

I N THE SIX MONTHS FOLLOWING EDWARD'S MAR-
riage to Caela, the court at Westminster grew apace. Edward had
announced plans to build a great cathedral abbey church on Thorney Isle, as well as extend and refurbish his own palace. Builders and laborers
thronged the site.

To cater to the growing workforce, as also the growing complexity of
Edward's court, so also the numbers of servants and their families grew.
Westminster almost tripled its population, and a small town grew up about
the palace and abbey complex.

Many new arrivals thronged the community of Westminster, but among
them there were three who had deeper purposes than merely finding employ-
ment.

Some three months after Edward's marriage, a young widowed and destitute peasant woman had come to the palace, asking for work as a laundress,
or perhaps a dairy maid . . . whatever work there was, she begged. Damson,
she called herself, after a variety of exotic plum.

A damson, thought Edward's chamberlain, studying her silently, was
the last thing she looked like. The woman was already tired and worn, despite her relative youth, with stooped shoulders, waxen cheeks marred by
broken veins, and pale blue eyes that looked about to fade away to nothing.
Nevertheless, she claimed to be a skilled laundress, and with a queen in
residence, and all the ladies she attracted about her, and all the linens they
wore, or sewed, or commissioned . . . well, another laundress was always
needed.

"Very well, then," said the chamberlain severely, "but you'll work under my
direct orders for the time being, until I can be sure you're trustworthy."

Damson's eyes brightened at the prospect of a home, and the chamberlain
softened. He patted her on her cheek and sent her away to join the women
already carrying heavy wicker baskets of laundry down to the river.

Within a week he had forgotten about her.

Edward was a particularly pious king, and among the builders and laborers

and sundry laundresses that flocked to Westminster, also arrived a correspon-
ding number of clerics. Among these came many hoping that Edward would
sponsor their religious order, as well as that of the Westminster abbey monks.
Many of these he did indeed aid, some he turned away.

One he almost turned away was a woman of a particularly annoying frank-
ness and air of independence. She presented herself at Edward's court in
order to petition him to fund the establishment of a female religious priory.

"In honor of St. Margaret the Martyr," the woman said to the king as she
knelt before his throne.

Edward watched her silently, not only wondering precisely *who* St. Margaret
the Martyr was (possibly one of those forgettable Roman noblewomen who had
somehow managed to achieve martyrdom and subsequent sainthood on the
strength of their donations to the emerging church) but how he could rid
himself and his court of this unsettling woman as quickly as possible. She was
of some forty years, rotund and with a cheerful round face . . . but the strength
and determination underlaying that cheerfulness did truly unsettle Edward.
Women should know their place, and he was not sure that this one did at all.

"I am afraid—" he began, when, to his amazement, his wife broke in, leaning forward in her own throne and speaking to her husband.

"My husband, may I perhaps take this care from your already over-burdened
shoulders?"

Edward stared at Caela, his mouth open. This was the first time he could
ever remember her speaking openly in court, let alone interrupting him.

"My father has endowed me well," Caela continued, her cheeks flushed as
if she realized her transgression, "and I would like this opportunity to repay
Christ and His saints for their goodness to me. Perhaps I could use a small
portion of my own reserves to endow this holy woman's priory?"

At this, her courage failed her—by this time over half the court were staring open-mouthed at Caela—but Edward smiled, suddenly pleased with her.
If she was this pious, then perhaps she could eventually retire to the order she
founded and he could be rid of her.

His smile broadened. "Of course, my dear. As you will."

Caela blushed even further, perhaps astounded at her own temerity, but
she turned to the woman still kneeling before Edward (but with her round
and generous face now turned to Caela) and asked of her, her name.

"You may call me Mother Ecub," said the woman, and then looked at
Caela as if she expected some reaction.

But Caela only smiled in politeness, and begged Mother Ecub to visit her
within her own private chamber on the morrow.

Mother Ecub bowed, rose to her feet, and left.

And as she left, so she locked eyes momentarily with Swanne, Harold of

Wessex's wife, newly risen from childbed. Both understood each other immediately; each sent ill-will coursing the other's way before each turned aside,
and pretended indifference.

Thus was the Priory of St. Margaret the Martyr founded, with Mother Ecub
as its prioress. The small priory was built at the foot of Pen Hill just to the
north of London, and within a year it had attracted some twelve or thirteen
women who secreted themselves within its walls. The nuns contented themselves with good works to travelers, lepers, and the destitute, and soon earned
themselves such a good name among the Londoners that they called the priory
Mother Mag's as a measure of their affection.

It pleased Mother Ecub no end.

The third arrival into Edward's court, in this first year of his marriage, caused
great comment where the other two had caused scarcely a ripple. King Edward
had recently suffered pain caused by increased swelling and heat in the joints of
his hands, elbows and knees. Many physicians attended him, but there was only
one who consistently relieved Edward's discomfort, and he was the youngest of
all those who presented the king with their herbals and unguents.

His name was Saeweald, and was but some eighteen or nineteen years of
age. Born to the north of London, he had only recently completed his appren-
ticeship. Despite his youth, Saeweald combined an assurance, knowledge,
and skill that most of his older fellows envied, and the youth quickly became
a fixture at Edward's side.

Saeweald attracted much attention, but not only because of his youth and
his talent. He was very dark, bespeaking more of the ancient British blood
than the Saxon in his veins, but this was not what made him stand out physically at court. Saeweald's right hip and leg had been brutally mangled during
his birth, and the newly appointed royal physician walked only with the
greatest difficulty, dragging his deformed leg behind him, and, on his worst
days, requiring crutches to stand upright. In a strange manner this endeared
him to many. Saeweald's rasping breath of discomfort, the drag of his leg, the
tap of his crutches and the constant jingling of the small copper boxes of
herbs, which hung at his belt, announced his imminent arrival more effi-
ciently than any clarion of horn; no one could ever accuse the physician of
spying, for there was no means by which he could creep unheard upon any
conversation.

Yet Saeweald himself did keep secrets, and it was Tostig, younger brother
to Harold of Wessex, who discovered one of these a few months after
Saeweald's appointment as royal physician. Tostig and Saeweald had become
friends soon after the physician's arrival at court. To many onlookers this
outwardly seemed a strange friendship, for Tostig was a youth dedicated to
the military arts, to heroic action, and to the bravado of the warrior, while

Saeweald was far more introspective and given to the pursuit of thought and mystery rather than a warrior's heroisms.

This was, after all, all that his leg would allow him.

Tostig and Saeweald did find some common ground, however, perhaps their mutual youth, as well as their mutual indulgence in some of the fleshly delights the court and community of Westminster offered them (such fleshly delights kept well away from Edward's attention). Thus it was one afternoon, when Tostig was trying to find Saeweald so they might plan which of the accommodating ladies they might prevail upon this night, that he found him soaking away the aches of his leg in a great tub of heated water redolent with herbs.

Edward had given Saeweald three chambers (an unheard of private space for this crowded community) in one of the palace outbuildings. Saeweald used the space to live and sleep, as well as store and dispense his herbs. The first chamber was given over to the herbs and a dispensary, the second, Saeweald used as his sleeping and living quarters, and the third . . . well, the third Tostig had never entered. But this day, as he walked silently through the first and then second chamber seeking his friend, Tostig heard the sound of splashing coming from this third chamber, and so, without any announcement (assuming his friend was merely enjoying a soak) Tostig walked straight in.

Saeweald jumped in surprise—which was unfortunate, because it was that action that instantly gave Tostig full view of something he'd not ever suspected of his friend. True, previously he'd never seen Saeweald utterly naked, but Tostig had always assumed that was because Saeweald was sensitive about his deformed hip and leg.

Now he saw there was another reason—a far darker one.

"What is this?" he said quietly, coming to stand at the side of the tub.

Saeweald had sunk under the water, but now, seeing the expression on Tostig's face, he allowed himself to sit upright, allowing Tostig full view of his chest.

Tostig looked at Saeweald's chest, then at his face, then back to the man's chest. He stepped closer and, very slowly, lowered his hand onto Saeweald's wet skin.

Saeweald's skin jumped a little as Tostig's hand touched him, and the man tensed, but then he relaxed as he saw the expression on Tostig's face.

Awe. Reverence.

Tostig breathed in very deeply and, as Saeweald remained still, moved his fingers over Saeweald's chest and shoulders, their-tips tracing the dark blue tattooed outline of a full magnificent spread of stag antlers.

"I should have known," Tostig whispered.

Saeweald said nothing, his still, dark eyes unmoving from Tostig's face.

"You follow the ancient ways," said Tostig, still very quiet. "By the gods, Saeweald, no wonder you are so skilled with the healing herbs!"

He lifted his hand from Saeweald's chest and looked the man full in the face. "This mark is enough, my friend, to have you executed at the order of our most Christian of kings."

Still Saeweald said nothing, still he watched Tostig carefully.

Tostig breathed in deeply again, deeply affected by what he had discovered. "Moreover, this tattoo marks you as just not a follower of the ancient ways, but as . . . as . . ."

"Are you too afraid to say it, Tostig? Then I will, for already you know enough to have me killed. I am Saeweald, but I am also of that direct bloodline that traces back to the ancient priests of this land. I am the heir to that bloodline, and to the power of the ancient Stag God of the forests."

Tostig paled, and took a step back, his round eyes fixed on Saeweald's face, but Saeweald continued on remorselessly.

"One day that god will rise from his grave, Tostig, and on that day *I* will speak with his voice."

"You are his Druid," Tostig whispered.

"Aye. I am his Druid," Saeweald said, using a word and concept Tostig would understand.

Tostig blinked, and with heartfelt relief Saeweald saw tears slide down the youth's cheeks.

"Then I am your man, and you have more friends here at court than you can possibly realize."

Saeweald grimaced. "There is more at this court than *you* can possibly realize, my friend."

Tostig held out his hand, and Saeweald took it, using his friend's strength to pull himself out of the tub. Tostig stood watching Saeweald as the man dried himself. "Have you met my brother Harold, yet?"

Saeweald shook his head. "He has been south in his estates for some weeks. No doubt I will make his acquaintance soon enough."

"He needs to see this, too, Saeweald." Tostig reached out once more and touched gently the mark on Saeweald's chest. "I think he is going to be as a good a friend to you as I am."

A MONTH AFTER THIS INCIDENT, A MONTH DURING which Edward became increasingly reliant on his young, brilliant physician, the king asked Saeweald to attend his wife.

Saeweald stood before Edward who had retired from his Great Hall to hold his evening court within his private chambers situated above the Hall.

Here gathered relatively few people: some of the king's closest attendants, three or four of the queen's attending ladies, a few servants, invariably the abbot of Westminster, and perhaps one or two other guests. The atmosphere was much more informal than that of the court held within the Great Hall, but Saeweald nonetheless kept his head partly bowed and his face cleansed of anything but deferential respect.

Despite his demeanor, Saeweald was intensely aware of everyone in the chamber. On his way through the door, he had caught the eye of the lady Swanne, here this evening without her husband.

They had known each other instantly, and Saeweald was somewhat surprised that the silent bolt of hatred that shot between them had not sent the entire court into chaos.

But now Saeweald had all but forgotten Swanne. He was intently aware of Caela, who sat in a carved wooden throne a pace or two to Edward's right, and who was almost as rigid as the frame of her chair.

"My wife," Edward began, flickering to Caela, "is unwell. Consistently unwell. She suffers from a great disquiet of her womb, which causes me some anxiety."

Saeweald understood very well by this that Edward was not anxious for Caela's sake, but anxious and irritated that she displayed such womanly weakness. No doubt, Saeweald thought, Edward would believe in the physical manifestation of Eve's sinful presence within all women and, as such, undeserving of any sympathy. He looked at Caela from under the lowered lids of his eyes.

She was, if possible, even more rigid, and pink with humiliation.

"Sire," said Saeweald in the strong, quiet voice he always used with the king, "I have many medications that will ease the problem. Be assured that I can ease your anxiety." For an instant Saeweald's mind was consumed with that terrible night so long ago when Caela had been Cornelia, and he Loth, and Cornelia had lain on the floor of her house, her womb and the child it had carried lying torn and bloody between her legs.

"Good. Perhaps you can attend her now?"

Saeweald bowed his head, more to hide his jubilation than in any real respect for Edward. *Finally, he was going to have a chance to speak with Caela!*

Caela rose stiffly from her chair, her eyes staring ahead so that she did not have to see either her husband or Saeweald, and she walked from the chamber, two of her ladies in close attendance.

With a final bow to the king, Saeweald followed.

WITHIN THE REGAL BEDCHAMBER, SAEWEALD'S "examination" consisted of merely holding Caela's hand in his, feeling the fluttering of her nervous pulse, and asking her a few quiet questions. The queen's two ladies stood a respectful distance away, and, although they kept their eyes on the proceedings, Saeweald was able to converse with Caela in relative privacy.

"Madam," Saeweald began, "I am sorry to hear of your affliction."

She said nothing, merely turning her face very slightly aside.

"It might not be so unexpected, however?"

She turned back to study him. "What do you mean, physician?"

Saeweald did not know what to expect at the distance within her voice. Surely she knew who he was?

"Your previous troubles . . ." Saeweald murmured, hoping that Caela would realize he spoke of her life as Cornelia, and Genvissa's terrible attack on her.

She did not reply, and Saeweald could sense an immense withdrawal within her.

"Cornelia," he whispered. "Do you not know me? I am Loth, reborn."

She snatched her hand from his. "Are your wits addled, physician?"

Her words were angry, but Saeweald could hear a desperate fear beneath them.

Gods, he thought, *what is going on?*

"Madam," he said, "I am sorry." His thoughts raced, wondering what he should do or say next. *Why wouldn't she recognize him?* "I took a concoction for the ache in my leg earlier this evening, and I fear that somehow it has muddled my thoughts."

He felt her relax and, very gently, he took her hand back in his. *She was so frail . . .* For a few minutes Saeweald asked her questions about her monthly fluxes, how they had changed in recent times, and how they discomforted her.

Despite the intimacy of their discussion, Caela relaxed further at the detached tone of his voice.

"You are not with child?" Saeweald asked eventually.

"No."

"There is no possibility . . .?"

"No."

Saeweald licked his lips, phrasing his next questions as delicately as he could. "Madam, has the king ever—"

To his relief, she answered before he had time to form all the words. "No. He will not lie with me."

Saeweald could not help the sudden twitch of his lips. "And does that bother madam over much?"

He more than half expected Caela to snatch her hand from his, but to his astonishment her lips curled in a very slight smile as well. "You are the first person not to offer me sympathy over the issue, physician."

He grinned, delighted, for in that single instant he saw some of Cornelia's old spirit light Caela's face. *She was there, but buried deep.* Caela had also responded to him as an intimate friend—something they were not yet in this life—for that question should have seen any person, favored royal physician or not, immediately ejected from the queen's presence.

"There are many men more deserving of you, madam," he said, and then, not wanting to push Caela any further, began to speak of some of the medications he would mix for her.

When Saeweald eventually sat back, setting Caela's hand loose, he risked one more incursion into their shared past. "Do not think your womb is useless," he said. "It harbors a greater power than I think you can currently know."

Or remember.

She frowned at him.

"Mag," he said, hoping that this single word, the name of the goddess who had inhabited Caela in her previous life, would summon some response from the queen.

Mag, are you there?

But Caela's frown only deepened, and, with a brief, respectful few words, Saeweald rose and left her.

THREE DAYS LATER, SAEWEALD WAS IN THE FRONT room of his chambers, which served as a dispensary, when the outer door opened and a woman came in.

Saeweald stared at her, then stepped forward, taking the woman's hands in his and kissing both her cheeks in welcome before enveloping her in a huge embrace.

"Mother Ecub!"

"Aye," she said, hugging him as tightly as he did her. "Mother Ecub indeed—and *still* Mother Ecub."

"I know," Saeweald said, standing back and grinning at her. "I have heard of you. I have never heard of a more undevout Christian prioress!"

"The priory serves me well enough," said Ecub, "and I have gathered to my side many sisters who, while mouthing their Christian prayers, instead turn for inspiration and hope to the circle of stones standing atop Pen Hill. Whatever Edward and his flock of clerics want to believe, the ancient ways still throb deep within the hearts and souls of the people. But, oh, Saeweald, look at you! How can Fate treat you so badly?"

He touched his hip and grimaced. "I have learned to live with this, Mother Ecub. You need spare no pity for me." Then he smiled. "Just the sight of you, and the knowledge you are back, has eased so much of my pain."

Ecub knew he was not referring only to his physical aches.

"Who else?" she said, softly.

"Genvissa, but then you must know that."

Now it was Ecub who made the face. "Yes. The gracious and beautiful lady Swanne. She and I have exchanged bitter looks, and a few even more bitter words, but my duties within the priory—and to the stones atop Pen Hill— allows me to avoid much of her poison. You?"

"We have spoken only once when she crowed with delight at this." Again Saeweald tapped his hip. "As with you, I avoid her."

"Harold?" Ecub said very softly, watching Saeweald's face.

"Oh, Ecub! How did that witch trap him?"

"He does not remember, does he?"

Saeweald shook his head. "In the past few weeks I have come to know him well. We have re-formed our old friendship and bonds, although Harold is not consciously aware of it." He sighed. "Ecub . . . it is a mercy for him, I believe, that he does not remember. I think it best that way. But that Cornelia and Coel were reborn as brother and sister! To yearn for each other, and yet to believe that to touch would be the ultimate vice! What evil mischief is this? Fate, or Asterion?"

"Who can tell, Saeweald. But you are sure that Harold *is* Coel-reborn?"

"Yes. *Yes.* Like so many people, he adheres to the old ways while he mouths Christian pieties. He is my old and beloved friend, Ecub. Ah! How I hate to see him tied to that witch!"

Ecub grinned. "But he is her husband, and thus she his chattel by the Christian law of this land. Is that not deliciously amusing? Have you not thought how Swanne must chafe under that? And she must bear him sons . . . oh, I laughed when I heard she had birthed a male child. How that must have riled the oh-so-powerful Mistress of the Labyrinth."

"Where is Brutus, do you think?"

"You know where and who he is, as well as I. You have seen that 'gift' he sent to Edward, and have seen Edward crawling through that evil labyrinth on his hands and knees, thinking he is crawling toward Jerusalem and salvation instead of toward monstrous terror."

"Aye. I know who he is, and knowing that, I can foresee the sorrow that is to come. It will be Coel against Brutus, Harold against William, the moment that Edward dies. Edward means to get no heir on Caela. Thus, when he dies, England will disintegrate under those who will claim the throne."

"Coel against Brutus," Ecub repeated softly, "Harold against William. And Swanne, rising in all her malevolent witchcraft to ensure that it shall be William to succeed. Gods, Saeweald, how long do we have?

"How long do we have for *what,* Ecub?"

She was silent, dropping her face to study her work-worn hands.

"Caela," Saeweald said for both of them, finally bringing up the name they had both been avoiding. "I can understand why Harold does not remember his previous life as Coel—that is nothing short of a kindness to him. But Caela? *Gods*, Ecub! She carries Mag within her womb. She is our only hope against Swanne and William and the ever-cursed Troy Game! *And she does not remember!*"

"You have spoken to her, then."

Saeweald nodded tersely.

"As have I," Ecub said. "We have engaged in several conversations over the past months. Sometimes I push a little—mention a name, a deed—but she does not respond, save to stiffen, as if the name I mention causes her great fear. And yet Cornelia *is* there. Caela founded my priory when she had no need to, and I hear her womb bleeds, as if Mag weeps within her."

Again Saeweald nodded.

"Then there is nothing we can do," said Ecub, "but to wait and trust in both Mag and Caela."

"And wait for Edward to die," said Saeweald.

"And wait for the storm to gather," said Ecub. "Saeweald, sometimes I sit on Pen Hill and cast my eyes down to London, to the cathedral of St. Paul's that now sits atop Genvissa and Brutus' foul piece of Aegean magic, and I shudder in horror. It still lives there, Saeweald. I can *feel* it, festering under the city and the feet of the people who inhabit it, poisoning this land."

"Ecub," Saeweald said. "We can do nothing until Caela—"

At that moment they both jumped as the outer door opened, jerking their heads about as if this were the storm approaching now, or perhaps even the Game itself stepping out to consume them.

But it was only the laundress, Damson, come to collect Saeweald's linens, and both Saeweald and Ecub relaxed into silence as the unassuming peasant woman did her task, then left.

PART TWO

As in days of old, the labyrinth in lofty Crete is said to have possessed a way, emmeshed 'mid baffling walls and the tangled mystery of a thousand paths, that there, a trickery that none could grasp, and whence was no return . . . just so the sons of Troy entangle their paths at a gallop, and interweave flight and combat in sport . . . this mode of exercise and these contests first did Ascanius* revive, when he girdled Alba Longa with walls, and taught our Latin forefathers to celebrate after the fashion in which he himself when a boy, and with him the Trojan youth, had celebrated them . . . even now the game is called Troy, and the boys are called the Trojan Band.

                                             Virgil, The Aeneid, *Book V*

---

*Father of Silvius and grandfather of Brutus.

*J*ACK SKELTON WOKE JUST BEFORE DAWN. HE LAY IN *the cold gray light, staring at the just-discernible shape of his uniform hanging on the back of the door. Violet Bentley had put him in the tiny spare bedroom on the first floor of her and Frank's cramped terrace house in Highbury. It was a child's bedroom, really, kitted out with what was probably either Frank's or Violet's own childhood single bed that was far too short for Skelton's tall frame, and with a garishly bright hooked rug on the floor, plywood closet, a ladder-backed wooden chair, and floral cotton curtains that were, if the roll of heavy black twill behind the chair was any indication, soon to be replaced with blackout curtains.*

Skelton thought he'd never been in a more depressing room, not in any of his lives. Its melancholy lay not in the cheap hand-me-down furniture, nor in its austerity, but in the sad attempt to make it homely. If Violet had just managed to resist the rug then the room may have managed some dignity.

If only.

But then, was not life full of "if onlys"?

If only he'd recognized earlier Genvissa's true nature.

If only he'd realized earlier the treasure he'd had in Cornelia.

If only he'd reached St. Paul's sooner . . . before the rafters had collapsed . . . before the fire had consumed his entire world.

Jack lay still, barely breathing, dragging his mind away from that terrible moment when the rafters had given way. He thought about his walk through London last night, remembered Genvissa—Stella Wentworth now—and her stunning beauty, and the way she had turned away from him when he had asked after Cornelia. Had she not known where Cornelia was, or did she not want to tell him? He remembered Loth, Walter Herne now, who had tormented him with questions and who had promised him nothing.

And Asterion, haunting his footsteps as he had haunted them for three thousand years. Always one step ahead.

"Cornelia?" Skelton whispered into the sorry gray dawn light.

Then, after a long moment: "Eaving?"

There was no reply, and Skelton had not truly expected one.

CHAPTER ONE

ENGLAND, 1065

AUTUMN

OTHER ECUB, PRIORESS OF THE SMALL BUT well-endowed Priory of St. Margaret the Martyr, which lay just off the northern road from London, sat worshipping in the weak mid-morning sun.

She did not sit in the chapel of her priory, which had been well constructed of the best local stone and decorated with beautiful carvings and statues, as well as rare and costly stained glass windows.

Neither did Mother Ecub sit before the altar in her solitary cell, nor in the refectory where hung a cross on the wall, nor even in the herb and vegetable gardens of the priory, which were close enough to the wall of the chapel to access in a crisis.

Mother Ecub did not worship within the walls of the priory, nor even within shouting distance of them.

Rather, Mother Ecub sat worshiping atop the small hill, which rose two hundred paces west of the priory.

Pen Hill, as it was known both in ancient times and in present.

The ring of stones that had graced the hill two thousand years ago still stood, although they were now far more weather-beaten than once they had been, and there were gaps where the Romans had hauled away the better stones to use as milestones on their roads. Two of these milestones now stood guarding the London-side approach to the bridge over the Thames. Londoners called them Gog and Magog, and carved crude faces into them, claiming the stones housed the spirits of the ancient ones who had built the city.

Their faith made Mother Ecub, and the seventeen personally picked female members of her order, smile and manage to keep the faith. If people remembered the ancient gods of this land, the stag-god Og and the mother-goddess Mag, even in this corrupted form, then that was all well and good.

Then all was not lost.

Mother Ecub had come to the top of Pen Hill not only to worship the land, which she could see spread about her (and where better for her to do that?), but to gather her thoughts for this evening's audience with Queen Caela.

She shuddered at the thought, distracting herself with the view. To the south, some three or four miles distant, lay London behind its ancient Roman walls (which stood on the even more ancient foundations of the walls that Brutus had built). The city enclosed many acres of grounds, only about a third of it built upon. Most of it, in fact, was given over to the cultivation of orchards, vegetables, and corpses—London had an inordinate number of Christian churches, all of which closely guarded their right to bury the dead members of their flocks within spitting distance of the church walls. The fluids from the rotting corpses invariably found their way into the wells and streams that watered the city, prompting outbreaks of disease in the summer and autumn of most years, but nothing could make the Church give up its right to bury its dead within London's walls.

For that matter, nothing could make the Christian faithful give up their right to be buried as close to their church as possible. After all, come Judgment Day, when all the dead would rise once more, one didn't want to totter too far to get to the church altar and, hopefully, eternal salvation, on barely held-together bits of crumbled bone and rotted flesh.

Ecub's mouth twisted in derision at the thought, and she made a convoluted gesture with her left hand, which, to the initiated, would have instantly recalled the movements of Mag's Nuptial Dance, which Ecub had once watched Blangan and Cornelia perform within Mag's Dance itself.

She squinted a little in the winter sun, focusing on the stone cathedral that sat atop Lud Hill—once Og's Hill. Here, where Brutus had constructed his labyrinth, now stood a great Christian cathedral: St. Paul's. Ecub wondered if the monks and priests and sundry clerics who shuffled about the cathedral's nave in absorbed self-importance had any idea what lay so far beneath their feet.

How *alive* it was.

Ecub's face, as wrinkled as it was with lines of laughter and care, went completely expressionless as a momentary hopelessness overcame her.

It had been fifteen years now since she'd first come to London to establish her priory. Fifteen years of waiting for Caela to remember her duty to Mag, or for Mag herself to make some sign that she was ready to begin the campaign that would witness the final destruction of the Troy Game and the devastation of Swanne and William's hopes. Fifteen years of waiting for that time when the ancient gods Mag and Og could once again take their place within the land and restore its harmony and goodness.

Fifteen years.

Fifteen years she and Saeweald had waited, the last three shared with a noblewoman called Judith, who was Erith-reborn. The widow Judith had come to Westminster and had taken a place as one of Caela's attending women. Unsurprisingly, over those three years, Caela had come to like and trust Judith greatly, and now, of Ecub and Saeweald, but it was Judith who enjoyed the closest and most trusting relationship with the queen.

Ecub and Saeweald had hoped that Judith's appearance had been what Caela or Mag had been waiting for . . . but nothing. Caela persisted in her unremembering; Mag still lingered useless and ineffectual within the queen's womb.

Why this delay? Ecub did not know. Was it the Game itself? Asterion? Mere fate? Mag? No one was sure, but what Ecub knew for certain was that if Caela or Mag did not do something soon then all hope would be lost.

Edward was now an old man. He would not last many more years. When he died, Ecub knew that Duke William would swarm across the seas and reclaim the Darkwitch (his former lover) and the city and the Game . . . taking the throne of England almost as an afterthought.

Even worse was the possibility that Edward's death would sting Asterion into some terrible action. Ecub knew of Asterion from Loth, as well as from the knowledge she had gained during the long death between her last life and this one. Asterion might want the same end as she and Saeweald, the destruction of the Game, but what he would replace it with—the frightful reign of the unrestrained malevolence of the Minotaur—was even a more frightful future than a Troy Game triumphant.

"I trust in Mag," Ecub muttered, "I trust in Mag," repeating the mantra over and over until she restored some peace in her heart.

Caela's continuing forgetfulness no doubt kept the Darkwitch Swanne giggling in delight, but it left Ecub, Saeweald, and Judith in despair. They could do little but stay close to Caela and support her, and wait for her to come to her senses and do whatever it was that Mag required of her. Still, there was hope, as Saeweald constantly reminded Ecub and Judith. Caela had endowed Ecub's priory, and continued to support it, when Edward had refused (and Caela had done this for no other religious order). Caela had also taken Erith-reborn, Judith, under her wing as the most senior of her attending ladies without any prompting from either Saeweald or Ecub. She kept Saeweald and Ecub close to her, although she did not have to. She was patently *drawn* to her allies from her former life . . . but she just would not recall them from this former life.

"Mag directs her thoughts and action," Saeweald often told Ecub, and with this Ecub had to be content. Although in her darkest moment, she wondered if Mag had forgotten as well.

Ecub sighed and thought about rising. She was almost sixty years old, far too old to be spending an entire morning sitting cross-legged in this damp grass, even if such close proximity to one of the sacred sites of Llangarlia brought her peace of mind and spirit. Damp grass aside, Ecub needed to return to the priory to brush out her robes, and set out on the slow ride south to Westminster. This evening she was required at court, to present to the queen an account of the priory's activities this past quarter. Ecub grinned broadly as she contemplated what she could tell Caela, and what Caela herself probably wanted to hear.

What Caela would want to hear were accounts of how many hours a day the sisters of St. Margaret the Martyr spent on their knees in prayer to the Virgin herself, or how many days a week they spent attending the needs of the sick and ill, or how best they had distributed the alms Caela provided among the small community of lepers that lived five miles further to the north.

What Ecub *could* tell her, if she had had the nerve, was how many nights the sisters spent dancing naked among the ancient stones of Pen Hill, or how they whispered to the milestones of Gog and Magog on their numerous visits to London, and of their efforts in keeping alive the ancient ways and beliefs among the people in and about London.

Or perhaps Ecub could tell the queen of how she and the sisters of St. Margaret the Martyr spent their nights praying to Mag within Caela's womb to give them a sign, and to show them she still lived and cared, and that there was hope for this land amid all the horror that had visited it.

"And perhaps not," muttered Ecub, wincing at the ache in her joints as, finally, she rose slowly to her feet. She spent a moment testing her legs to make sure they could bear her weight, and straightened her somewhat grass-stained and dampened robe, before taking the first step toward the slope that led back to St. Margaret the Martyr's priory.

One step only, and then Ecub froze, her heart thudding in her chest.

Something was . . . wrong.

The hairs on the back of her neck rose, and the breath in her throat caught and held.

Something was . . . different.

Very carefully, trying to keep her fright under control, Ecub slowly turned about, looking around the top of the hill.

Nothing. A blue sky, interspersed with heavy dark clouds that foretold rain for the afternoon.

Thick, wet green grass that moved sluggishly in the slight breeze.

Stones, twenty-five or -six of them, encircling the entire hilltop . . .

Ecub's heart felt as though it had stopped entirely.

The stones.

There was something about the stones.

"Oh, sweet Mother Mag," Ecub whispered and, unaware of the discomfort, dropped to her knees and clasped her hands before her.

The stones were humming.

Ecub's mind could hardly comprehend it.

The stones were *humming*! Moreover, their harsh outlines were softening, as though the stones were dissolving into warmth and movement.

As though they were living.

In her previous life, Ecub had heard of tales that were ancient, even in that time. Tales of how the stone circles had come to be, and why they were so important to the worship of Mag herself.

Could it possibly be that they were true?

"You are singing!" Ecub exclaimed, her mind still struggling to comprehend what was happening about her.

Indeed, the stones were now singing—a sad, haunting, lilting melody.

Moreover, the stones were now swaying back and forth in a liquid, delicious movement, as if they wanted to dance.

Then, before Ecub's astounded eyes, they let go the shape of stones and took on their true forms.

Although each had individual aspects, all shared similar characteristics. They were tall with rather long, sinewy arms, their hands broad and long-fingered. Above their thin mobile mouths and hooked noses, each had dark brown hair, shot through with flecks of iron gray; their eyes were of the same color, also flecked with gray, and despite their bleakness, managed to convey a surprising sense of humor, perhaps even mischievousness.

They were very watchful, these eyes, and Ecub realized that all the creatures' eyes moved at the same time; if one looked slightly to the left, all eyes looked slightly to the left. It was very unsettling, and gave Ecub the impression that they shared a silent communication.

All wore the same clothes: undistinguished and well-worn leather jerkins and trousers.

All had bare feet, their toes curling into the grass.

All sang, the sound humming through their thin-lipped mouths, and the song was very sad, and very bleak, and very beautiful. It reminded Ecub of the whispering, sorrowing sound that the wind made when it hummed through the stones of Mag's Dance.

She felt conflicting emotions surge through her. Joy, that she should have been privileged to see this. Fear, that the stones' metamorphosis portended doom. Reverence, before the oldest and most sacred creatures this land had ever known.

Terror, that she should not prove worthy of . . .

The Sidlesaghes. The most ancient inhabitants of this land, so ancient, they were the land, who rested within the stones.

By Mag herself, Ecub thought, *I had thought them only legend!*

She momentarily closed her eyes, blinking away her tears.

Very slowly, inch-by-inch, hand-in-hand, the Sidlesaghes closed their circle about Ecub.

When, finally, not a handspan separated Ecub from the circle of Sidlesaghes, the tallest and most watchful of them leaned forward, touched Ecub on top of her head, and began to speak.

SOME SIX MILES TO THE SOUTHWEST STOOD ANOTHER of the sacred hills of the ancient and forgotten realm of Llangarlia. While Pen Hill still retained a similar aspect to that of two thousand years previously, Tot Hill, now Tothill, had changed enormously. In Brutus and Genvissa's time it had housed only a simple rectangular building, the Meeting House, and a platform of stone at its peak. Now Tothill boasted a thriving community consisting of Westminster itself as well as King Edward's vast palace complex—not merely the Great Hall, but the kitchens, dormitories, barracks, chapels, storerooms, infirmaries, scriptoriums, as well as offices for a score of officials, a dairy, meat-houses, bake-houses, and all the other buildings, orchards, herberies, vegetable gardens, and necessities required for a lively and growing community. Westminster had now become the site of government within the kingdom of England, a rival city a mile or so to the southwest of London.

Fifteen years ago, Edward had begun the reconstruction of the abbey. Now the almost-finished abbey reared into the sky, one of the greatest constructions in western Europe, and a monument not so much to God, but to Edward's piety.

Here in Westminster, just to the north of the palace in an open space on Tothill that overlooked the gray-green sweep of the Thames to the east and the smudge of London on the great northeast bend of the river, stood the man who would control not only Westminster, but London, and all of England, and all of everything else besides.

Asterion. He stood, staring northeast toward London, very still, very watchful.

He could feel the Troy Game moving. A shudder, part apprehension and part excitement, swept through Asterion's body.

The Troy Game was moving, and it was time for Asterion to put into motion the plan that he had spent this entire lifetime constructing.

He turned slightly so that Edward's palace came into view. There she waited. The one who would deliver to him everything. The bands. The Game. William. *Power.*

"It is time," Asterion muttered. "Time to begin *my* game."

A death, a seduction, followed by another death. A plan of beauteous simplicity. That's all it would take, and the kingship bands and the Troy Game would be his.

CHAPTER TWO

CAELA SPEAKS

I WONDER HOW MANY WOMEN KNOW WHAT IT IS like to endure the hatred of one's husband for fifteen long years? Many, I suppose, for while marriage might be a consecrated thing in the sight of God, His saints and the Holy Church, it was often a burden to us lesser mortals, the daughters of Eve who had to bear the torturous punishment for her Great Sin in our marriage and childbeds.

Not that I had to bear anything but the sharpness of Edward's tongue in our marriage bed and, for total lack of the warmth of his body, I never had to endure the agonies of childbed.

Fifteen years a wife, and still a virgin. It was a shameful thing, and not one I had to bear alone, for Edward made sure that the entire court knew that he'd never laid a finger on me. I remembered our marriage night so long ago when, a nervous and excited thirteen-year-old, I had allowed my sister-in-law to settle me into my marital bed with my new husband.

I had been so fearful, and yet still excited. Not only had I become a wife, soon to learn the secrets of my marital bed (or so I had naïvely thought then) and chatelaine over the realm of my own household; I was also queen of England. My father, the great Earl Godwine of Wessex, had successfully negotiated for me marriage with Edward. I hadn't know then that Edward hated and feared my father, and took me as wife only because he knew that if he refused, my father would see him tipped off the throne.

Without my father's support, Edward would have lost his crown years ago.

Edward hated me, for I was the constant visible reminder of his humiliating dependence on Godwine and, later, his equally humiliating dependence on my eldest brother Harold who assumed the earldom of Wessex when our father died. Yet on that night, as I lay trembling and naked beneath the uncomfortably stiff linens of my new husband's bed, I had no idea that my husband already hated me as much as ever he would. I thought only of my induction into womanhood, and of the joy and pride I would feel as I bore Edward an heir.

When Edward, sullen and joyless, joined me in bed that first night, he turned to me, gazed at me with the greatest contempt, and said: "I find you most displeasing."

Then he humped over, and went to sleep, and I was left trembling and silently weeping, wondering what I had done wrong.

I eventually slept that night, and when I did I dreamed. I dreamed of another man, his face lost in shadows, who regarded me with contempt, and who spat at me words of hatred.

He also had called me "wife."

I had gone to sleep weeping, and I woke weeping, and it seemed that the first five or six years of my marriage were spent weeping.

Everyone at court knew that Edward would not lay with me. Edward put it about variously that I was a whore (on one occasion he even sent me into exile for a year over that particular lie); then, when I protested my virginity and had it proven by a midwifely examination, he said that I refused his attempts to make a true wife of me. Latterly, Edward liked to claim that I was Satan's temptation put into his path to tease him away from salvation.

Edward the Confessor, his people had taken to calling my husband, in tribute to his piety.

Gods' Concubine, they called me, for it appeared that in Edward's pious disinterest he had passed over the sexual proprietorship of his wife to God Himself (not that God seemed interested, either). Some smirked at this appellation, and pitied me, but most seemed to feel that Edward's saintliness had somehow rubbed off on me (how, I have no idea, for most certainly our flesh had never rubbed enough for the transfer).

Gods' Concubine. I hated that label. Ho doubt some wit would soon make the connection and start calling me the Virgin Mary's apprentice.

Latterly, Edward's attempts to humiliate me had taken a more disturbing turn. My father Godwine had died some years previously, and now my eldest brother Harold held sway, not only as earl of Wessex, but as the power behind my husband's throne. Edward could not command enough men and arms to keep his throne safe from the ambitions of the Danes and Norwegians. For that he needed the immense power of the Wessex lands and the men within its army, and the king's dependence on the assets of Wessex gave whoever held the earldom a powerful hold over Edward. Edward resented this dependence, and he hated Harold as much as he had hated our father, and almost as much as he hated me.

Harold and I were close, and Edward saw that closeness, and made of it a terrible thing. He hinted to me in our cold bed in the dark hours of night—he would not dare say it aloud where Harold might hear the words—that he knew Harold and I were unnatural lovers. He watched the way that Harold's laughing eyes followed me about a chamber and said that Harold lusted for me.

This tactic terrified me. I feared for Harold far more than for myself. I wished great things for Harold—the throne, for one, once my frightful husband had departed for his place at God's right hand, but above all, joy and contentment and achievement.

Edward could destroy this with a single, hateful remark. I could imagine it now. Edward finally deciding that he no longer needed Harold's support for this throne and remarking at court, as if in passing, "Ah, yes, the earl of Wessex. His sister's lover, don't you know?"

Maybe that would not be enough to destroy Harold. Maybe my brother was powerful enough to overcome even that slur.

Maybe.

And maybe Edward's threat had so much power over me because, in my heart of hearts, I wished that it *were* true. Because, in my dreams at night, I often imagined myself in Harold's bed.

I closed my eyes tight, hating myself. I could hear Edward's voice murmuring as he spoke to some of his pet priests, and I felt more loathsome than the darkest worm.

Mother Mary, I was *repulsive!* To lust after my own brother! When I was a child, I adored Harold. As I grew, that adoration grew into something . . . else. Something that should not grow between a brother and a sister. Harold knew it, for sometimes I caught him watching me strangely, darkly, as if *I* represented a threat to him.

It was rare now that Harold allowed himself to be in a chamber alone with me. We should have been close, Harold and I, but instead we found ourselves avoiding each other, sliding our eyes away from the other, our words stumbling to an awkward close whenever we found ourselves addressing each other.

Edward had noticed it, and I am sure most others did also. I *know* that Harold's achingly desirable wife, Swanne, saw it and recognized the awkwardness for what it was.

I know it for a fact, for one day soon after my loveless marriage had begun, Swanne leaned her elegant, beautiful head close to me, and with her soft, red lips whispered in my ear, "Shall I tell you, my dear, of how fine a lover your brother is? How he makes me squeal and twist under him? Would you like to hear that, my poor virgin girl? Would you? Would you like *it*, my dear? I'm sure Harold has enough for you as well."

And then she'd leaned back, and laughed, and made a comment so crude that even now I could not bear to form the words in my head.

"Wife?"

I jumped, then blushed, for I was sure that somehow Edward could read my thoughts. He sat in a chair some distance from me, although not, unfortunately, so far distant that it prohibited conversation. About us in the Lesser Hall (that smaller hall we used when not holding great court), our small evening court had fallen silent, watching, and wondering what humiliation Edward had in store for his wife tonight.

A tongue-lashing, perhaps?

An order to spend the night on her knees confessing her sins to Eadwine, the abbot of Westminster?

A tirade on the sins of the flesh, at the least . . .

"My dear . . ."

Only Edward could make an insult of those two words.

"Are you not going to greet the Lady Prioress? She has been standing before you for the past few minutes while you have wandered in your thoughts. You have duties as queen, Caela. I would that you occasionally remembered them."

Humiliated, and not the least because I knew I deserved the reprimand, I looked before me.

There, sure enough, her own cheeks stained pink in embarrassment, stood Mother Ecub as she had probably been standing waiting for my regard for the past half an hour.

"Mother," I said, stammering in my discomfiture, "I beg you forgive me." I held out my hand, and Mother Ecub shuffled forward—*Lord Christ, when had she grown so old and arthritic?*—and took it briefly, laying her mouth against the great emerald ring I wore on my heart finger.

Edward had given me that as a wedding ring. Christ alone knew *he* had never kissed it.

"My apologies to you, good prioress," I said, as Ecub stepped back and slowly straightened. "I have kept you standing far longer than I should. Judith . . ." I turned my head slightly, and beckoned to the favorite and most senior of my ladies. "Fetch a chair for Mother Ecub, I beg you."

As Judith hurried to do my will, the court slowly relaxed, and muted conversation started to again fill the background. Our evenings were usually spent in this smaller hall rather than the great audience hall, and only the closest and most valued among the court attended us after supper. About Edward clustered several members of the witan, all looking grave, perhaps with the latest news from France, or Normandy, or with tidings of another crop failure. They were true men, and hardy, but they never seemed cheerful.

Just behind that group stood Saeweald, physician to both Edward and myself. He saw me looking at him, and lowered one eyelid in a slow, reassuring wink.

I looked away, both grateful for the gesture and annoyed at his presumption. I liked Saeweald, I truly did (how could a man stay so cheerful when his right leg and hip were so twisted as to make every one of his steps a painful, tottering journey?), but that liking had taken years to mature. Saeweald had been attending court since the first year of my marriage, but my liking for him had taken some time to establish itself. During the first six months at court, he had greatly unsettled me.

When first we met, Saeweald had called me by another name—what was it again? Corvessa? Contaleia? Analia?—and had seemed irritated with me when I would not respond to it. I had tried to be patient—after all, the pain in his leg must surely addle his mind somewhat from time to time—but all the same his insistence had greatly unsettled me. Over a period of some weeks and months, Saeweald tried to talk to me of a time long ago, and I had bade him to be silent, for I had no mind to hear of the witchery that must have made him scry out such memories of so long ago. He begged me to remember a woman, Mag, he called her, to whom I apparently owed a debt . . . or some such . . .

I would have none of his wanderings, and commanded him to silence with the greatest sharpness. I had said to him that even though he be the greatest physician within Christendom, I would have none of him at court if he carried on so.

I wept.

Eventually Saeweald, weeping himself, had lowered himself to his knees before me (and what agony that must have been for him!) and had said that he would talk of these matters no more. I had nodded, once, stiffly, and motioned him to rise, and Saeweald had done so, and had kissed my hand, and had kept his word and held his tongue.

That had been many years ago now, and even if Saeweald had held his tongue, I still often came upon him watching me as though he expected me to . . . to do *what*, I do not know, but that very expectation in his gaze unsettled me.

I had grown close to him, nonetheless. He was witty, and comforting, and largely nonjudgmental, and, through several murmured remarks over the years, I knew that Saeweald honored me far above my husband. That was largely a novel sentiment (only Judith and Mother Ecub seemed to feel thus), and one that predisposed me toward much good feeling for the man.

And, last, I liked Saeweald because as my physician he was the only person who had the requisite skill with herbs and potions to ease my monthly fluxes, which had become an increasing trouble over the past few years. One might have thought that my womb, finding itself not needed, would have settled into a quietude of resignation, but, no, apparently it resented its empty state so greatly that it wept increasingly copiously and painfully each month.

Ecub had settled herself before me by this stage, and I smiled at her, and paid her my full attention.

"My good prioress," I said. "What have you to report?"

Ecub began a monotony of her priory's good works, and even though I kept my eyes on her and a half-smile on my face, my mind drifted off again. I could hear Aldred, the archbishop of York and a frequent visitor to both London and Westminster, arguing with Abbot Eadwine over some trifling matter of theology, and behind their male, arrogant voices I could hear the soft whisperings and giggles of the five or six of my ladies who sat at their needlework just behind me. Judith, my sweet, dear friend, was standing directly behind my chair, her hand resting on its back just behind my right shoulder, and from its warmth I gathered all the love and support I could. It was not that Ecub bored me, never that, for I took the greatest interest in her priory and the well-being of its inhabitants, but in the past few hours my mind had seemed to drift off to strange, unknown regions of its own accord, as if it had business elsewhere, and resented bitterly my every effort to concentrate it on the task at hand.

"Madam?"

There, my mind had betrayed me once again!

"Ah, Ecub," I said, blushing yet once again (one would think me still thirteen years old, and not the twenty-eight-year-old woman I was). "You must forgive me this evening. I cannot think what has come over me. I . . . I . . . ."

Oddly, for she never usually was so bold, Ecub leaned forward to close the space between us and held my hand briefly.

"You will feel better soon, madam," she said. "I have it on good authority."

"Ecub?"

But the prioress was already rising. "I will stay the night within the women's dormitory, if it pleases you. The way back to St. Margaret the Martyr is long and cold for an old woman like myself, and I would rather attempt it on the morrow than tonight."

"Of course," I said, rising also (a movement that made Edward half-start up, as if he suspected I was going to dash for the palace portal as if I were a hind escaping the huntsmen; my bevy of twittering ladies started likewise, their needlework shuffling to the floor with the suddenness of their movement).

"Perhaps, if it please you madam," Ecub continued, looking at me with those intense brown eyes of hers, "I might stay a day or two beyond this night? I have need to consult with Master Saeweald, and perhaps also to gossip with the lady Judith about mutual memories."

"Of course," I said again, feeling stupider by the moment. *What "mutual memories*"? I wondered momentarily if Saeweald had a potion against stupidity secreted somewhere, then managing to summon the few wits that remained to me, smiled graciously at Ecub, murmured my apologies to my husband, stating that my head ached and I must needs to bed, then made my exit accompanied by Judith and the other of my ladies.

Perhaps sleep would untwist my wits.

SLEEP BROUGHT ME NO PEACE. INSTEAD, I SWEAR that as soon as I had closed my eyes I slipped into a dream.

I dreamed I walked through the center of a stone hall so vast there appeared to be no end to it. It stretched east to west—I felt, if not saw, the presence of the rising sun toward the very top of the hall—and above me a golden dome soared into the heavens. Beneath my feet lay a beautifully patterned marbled floor; to my sides soared stone arches protecting shadowy, mysterious spaces. Even though great thick walls rose beyond those arches, I could still somehow see through them to the countryside beyond where a majestic silver river wound its way through gentle verdant hills and fertile pastures. It was an ancient and deeply mysterious land, and it was *my* land, England, although an England such as I could not remember ever seeing.

I turned my eyes back to the hall. Although this was a strange, vast place, I felt no fear, only a sense of homecoming. I also had the sense that I had spent many nights dreaming of this hall, although I never remembered the dream in the mornings.

Suddenly I realized I was not alone. A small, fey, dark woman walked toward me.

My eyes filled with tears, although I did not know why.

"Peace, lovely lady," the woman said as she reached me. She half started forward as if she meant to embrace me, but then thought better of it and merely reached up a hand to touch briefly a cheek.

"Are you ready?" she said.

"Ready for what?"

"The battle begins," she replied. "You must be ready, Cornelia, my dear."

I frowned, for *this* was the name Saeweald had called me so many years ago. Was this woman as deluded as he?

"Remember," the woman said, "to meet us in the water cathedral beyond death."

"What are you talking about?" I said, taking a step back. The woman was mad! A witch, no doubt!

She laughed, as if I had made a jest. "Then follow Long Tom, my darling girl. Listen to him. He will show you—"

"You! Will I never be rid of you?"

A man's voice thundered about us, and the small, dark woman gave a sad half smile, then vanished with only a word or two reverberating in my mind. *Remember, Cornelia, my dear . . . remember . . . remember . . .*

"What do you here?"

I forgot the woman, and looked at the man striding toward me.

I gasped, for although I swear I did not recognize him, nonetheless I felt I knew him intimately. Tall and well-built, the man had cropped, almost blue-black hair, a strong, handsome, and clean-shaven face and compelling dark eyes that seemed to have noted my every flaw, for, as he neared, an expression of distaste seemed to come over his face. He was dressed in the finery of a Norman nobleman: a vivid blue and stunningly embroidered knee-length tunic over breeches and boots, and a sword at his hip.

For some reason my eyes kept blurring, and I saw him with short black curls one moment, then with long curls that streamed and snapped in the breeze.

"Cornelia? Is this you?" He looked at me puzzled, as if I was some half remembered companion to him.

"I am not Cornelia!" I cried. "I am Caela. *Caela!*"

He had stopped before me now, his black eyes unreadable. "You will always be Cornelia," he said. "Always ready to betray me to Asterion—"

I do not know why, but at the mention of that name a feeling of such fear came over me that I thought I would collapse.

He took another step toward me, very close now, and he grasped my chin in his hand. "You are much more beautiful now than you were as Cornelia." He paused, his black eyes running over my face as if he wanted to consume it. "Far more beautiful . . . but still as desirable."

His mouth twisted, cold, and malicious. "But if the reports I hear are true, then Edward has more sense than I would have credited him, and has not touched you. *I* should have known better than to lay with you, bitch daughter of Hades."

At the contempt in his voice I cried out, and tried to wrench my chin from his hand. But he was too strong, and I remained caught in his hateful grip.

"You want me to kiss you? Well, I will not kiss you, Cornelia, or Caela, as now you are, my queen of England. I have a wife; I do not need *your* womb. I have a lover who awaits me; I do not need *your* kisses." He paused, and something changed in his face, and his fingers became gentle and caressing, as did his voice. "But oh . . . oh, how lovely you are."

His face bent closer, and his breath fanned over my cheek. I shuddered, and he felt it. Then his mouth grazed the skin beneath my ear, then grabbed and held it, and I cried out, and would have sagged had he not let go my chin and caught my shoulders.

Something occurred to me, almost a memory, save I know I had never met this man before, and I said: "Do you hate me still?"

He had raised his head away from me, and I saw his lips form the word "Yes," but then his own face became puzzled. "I never hated you," he said. "Not really."

"But you just called me," *God help me, I wanted him to hold me close again, and do again with his mouth what he had just done,* "bitch daughter of Hades."

He laughed, low and soft, and pulled me close enough that he *did* lay his mouth against my cheek again. "I am sorry for that. That was habit. Who knows if you deserve that epithet now?"

"They call me God's Concubine," I said, relaxing even more with this strange Norman. "*That* I hate."

"You should have children," he said, standing back from me. "You were a good mother."

Now it was I who laughed. "I? A good mother? And when, pray, did I have a chance for that?"

"Tell me," he said. "How is Swanne?"

"Swanne?"

"It is so long since I have seen her. Fifteen years. I miss her. I want her. Will you tell her that? Will you tell her how much I want her?"

He was walking away now, his booted strides ringing out through the stone hall.

"Tell Swanne I want her," he said, throwing the words back over his shoulder, "and that I cannot wait for that happy day when we can be together."

Then he was gone, and I stood there in that cold stone hall, and wept, for that I felt so alone, and so empty.

Far away, in Normandy, William woke with a hoarse cry, sitting bolt upright in his bed.

At his side, Matilda roused, muttered sleepily, then sat herself, laying a loving hand on his arm.

"William, what ails you?"

He smiled, although it was an effort. "A bad dream only, my love. Let it not concern you."

Then he took her chin in gentle fingers, and lowered his mouth to hers, and kissed away the memory of that cursed stone hall and the woman who haunted it.

* * *

THE NEXT AFTERNOON SWANNE JOINED MY CIRCLE
of women as we sat and gossiped over our needlework. I sighed, for I
had good enough reason to dislike my brother's wife, but her presence
reminded me abruptly of the strange dream that had gripped me the previous
night.

"My lady Swanne," I said, putting my needle down, "I dreamed most
unusually last night."

She tipped her head slightly, the movement one of supreme indifference.

"I dreamed of a most handsome man, a Norman, with close-cropped black
curls."

Several of the younger women tittered, and I managed to fight down the
urge to blush. No doubt they thought I sought my pleasure in dream where I
could not find it in my marriage bed. Suddenly I wished I had not brought up
the topic, and would have dismissed it with a laugh had not Swanne leaned
forward, her pale face now almost bloodless, her own dark eyes intense.

"Yes?" she said.

I made a deprecatory gesture. "Oh, I am sure it was nothing, save that this
dream-man asked to be remembered to you."

"Yes?" The word sounded as if Swanne had forced it through lips of stone.

I almost smiled as I remembered his message. "He told me to say, 'I want
her and I cannot wait for that happy day when we can be together.' He said it
had been fifteen years since you had been together, and that he missed you.
Why, sister, who can this be that is not your husband?"

Swanne sat upright, rigid with emotion. Her eyes glistened, and she
seemed unaware that everyone in our circle now stared at her.

"Who is this man?" I asked again, softly.

"A lord such as shall never love *you*," she said, then rose and made her
exit.

CHAPTER THREE

AEWEALD SAT WITH ECUB BY THE DYING FIRE IN the pit in the center of the Lesser Hall where Edward held his evening court. Edward and Caela had long retired, and the only people left in the chamber, save for them, were two servants, sweeping away the detritus of the night's activities.

They were silent. Uncomfortably so, on Saeweald's part, for he wanted to grip Ecub by the shoulders and shake out of her whatever it was that she had to say to him, and far more comfortably so on Ecub's part, for she still basked in the glow of what the Sidlesaghes had said to her.

They awaited Judith, who had to complete her evening attendance on the queen before she could join them.

They sat, silent, eyes set to the floor, until even the servants had gone for the night.

The moment the door had closed behind the last of them, Saeweald turned to Ecub and opened his mouth.

"Wait," she said, forestalling whatever it was he'd been about to say.

He mumbled something inaudible, then turned back to resume his silent vigil.

Eventually Judith joined them, looking both weary and worried, a reflection of Saeweald's own expression. She drew a stool up to Ecub and Saeweald, glanced at the physician, then looked at Ecub.

"What has happened?" she said.

Ecub took a very long, deep breath, then beamed, her entire face almost splitting in two with the width of her smile. "Today I sat amid the stones atop Pen Hill," she said.

"Yes?" said Saeweald.

"They spoke to me."

There was a long moment of complete silence, during which time Saeweald and Judith stared at Ecub, their minds trying to make sense of what she'd just said.

"They 'spoke' to you?" Saeweald finally said, enunciating very carefully.

"Aye, they did. Saeweald, what do you know of the ancient tales of the Stone Dances?"

"Only that they were raised by hands unknown, long ago, before even the Llangarlians came to step on this land."

"Aye, that is what you would have heard. But I think that Judith may have heard something else. Judith?"

Judith looked at Saeweald, but he was still staring at Ecub. She looked back to the prioress, who was studying her with a maddening calm, and licked her lips, trying to remember.

"They were raised in monument to Mag, to the Mother and the land," she said. "They are more Mag-monument than Og, although by association—"

"Yes, yes," said Ecub. "But tell me what you know of their raising."

Judith made a disparaging gesture, unsettled by Ecub's questioning. "Oh, Ecub, they were only tales that children told each other."

"Often the greatest mysteries are hidden within children's tales," Ecub said. "What safer place for them? Where every adult will discount them?"

Again Judith looked at Saeweald, and this time he met her eyes.

"Judith," he said. "*What* tales?"

Judith shrugged her shoulders, not ready to believe that the tales she'd heard as a child in her previous life were fact rather than sheer childish imagination. "I heard . . . it was told . . ."

"Judith," Ecub said, "just spit the words out!"

"The Stone Dances, or, rather, the stones themselves, are in actuality the surviving memory of the ancient creatures who walked this land long before mankind set foot here."

"Very good," said Ecub. "And their names?"

"Sidlesaghes," said Judith. "The Sad Songsters." Then, surprisingly, her mouth quirked in amusement. "Long Toms, we used to call them, for the height of the stones. Children's tales, though. Surely."

"Yet all this," Ecub said, soft but clear, "is true, my dears. Come now, Judith, tell me more of your 'children's tales.' Why do the Sidlesaghes stand as stones and not trail their melancholy amid the meadows?"

Judith's mouth fell open, and she stared wide-eyed and unbelieving at Ecub, as her mind suddenly made the leap to what Ecub was trying to get her to say.

"They . . ." Judith's voice hoarsened, and she had to clear her throat before she could continue. "They only wake and sing when it is time to midwife Mag's birth."

Ecub nodded, smiling. "Aye." She looked apologetically at Saeweald, who was looking goggle-eyed between the two women. "This is a mystery only discussed among girl-children, my dear. You would probably not have heard it as Loth. Midwifery and birth are the realms of women only."

"Wait," said Saeweald, shaking his head as if he were trying to shake his thoughts into some kind of order. "I don't understand. Are you saying that, when you were atop Pen Hill, these 'Sidlesaghes' appeared to you?"

"Aye."

"And you agree with what Judith just said, that they only 'wake and sing' when it is time to midwife Mag's birth?"

"Aye."

"But Mag already *is!* How can she be born again?"

"Because tomorrow, Asterion is going to murder her, my loves. And then Mag is going to need to be reborn."

Saeweald and Judith just stared at Ecub, aghast, then they both began to babble at once.

Ecub let them speak for a few minutes, then she held up her hand for silence, and repeated to them what the Sidlesaghes had told her.

Finally, Saeweald said, "But why can't Caela *remember?*"

"For her own protection, Saeweald. For her own protection. She will remember soon enough. Be patient."

But Judith frowned, and looked at Ecub. "But . . . but where will Mag be reborn? In who?"

Ecub smiled beatifically, then shrugged. "With that knowledge they did not grace me."

CHAPTER FOUR

OSTIG SAT WITH HIS BROTHER HAROLD BEFORE one of the fire pits in Harold's own great hall that Harold had built two years previously just to the south of Edward's palace complex in Westminster. While not rivaling Edward's construction, Harold's hall did nonetheless represent a significant challenge to Edward's authority, and did nothing to allay the king's resentment of the earl.

The past fifteen years had treated Harold and Tostig kindly. Both had grown: Harold into a greater maturity—the only physical changes wrought by the passing years were the sprinkling of gray through his dark blond hair and some more creases of care about his eyes—and Tostig into full manhood. Eight years previously Godwine had settled the earldom of Northumbria upon Tostig, and it was this earldom and the responsibilities that went with it that now directed the conversation between the two brothers.

Tostig was a dark, handsome man. The insecurities of youth, which had once so amused Swanne, had been set aside for a sometimes overbearing assurance of manner that could border on the arrogant. Now, as he and Harold sat before the glowing embers of the fire, alone, save for the soft presence of servants clearing away the tables in the hall behind them, Tostig leaned forward, his face set, his eyes snapping, and stabbed a finger at Harold.

"Their insolence is unbelievable!" Tostig said.

Harold, slouched back in his chair as if half asleep, sent Tostig an unreadable look from under lowered lids, but said nothing.

"They demand that I step down from the earldom!"

Harold closed his eyes briefly, resisting the urge to lean across to Tostig and shake some sense into the man. Tostig had ruled Northumbria well for years, but over the past eighteen months had begun to meddle in local politics with disastrous consequences. The situation had been exacerbated by Tostig's assassination of two popular noblemen several months previously. Now Northumbria was threatening to rise up in revolt.

"Tostig," Harold said, "stifling opposition by murdering the voices who speak it has never been the best course of action."

"I have had to withdraw forces from the border regions closer to home," Tostig went on, ignoring Harold, "with the result that now the Scots threaten to invade. Harold, you must aid me."

Harold leaned forward and emptied the dregs of his wine cup into the fire pit.

The embers hissed momentarily, then fell quiet.

"No," he said.

"No?"

"That earldom is yours to keep or to lose as you will, Tostig. If you currently find yourself mired in mutinous resentment, then may I suggest you have only yourself to blame."

"You have an *army* at your disposal," Tostig hissed. "Give it to me!"

Harold sat up straight in his chair, his hands resting on the armrests, the only sign of his anger, the gentle thrumming of his fingers against the wood. "No."

Tostig stared at his brother, then abruptly spat into the fire. "You think only of yourself."

"I think only of England."

Tostig sneered.

"Edward is old," Harold continued in an even voice. "His days are numbered. He has no heir and, in his own sweet recalcitrant manner, refuses to name one. If he takes this truculence to the grave with him, England will disintegrate into crisis. I will need the army *here* when that happens, Tostig, not trapped in the north, trying to settle your domestic disputes."

"You mean you want to grab the throne yourself. *I* can go to hell for all you care."

Harold took a moment to respond. "My primary responsibility is to the realm, Tostig. Not to you."

Tostig rose, his face twisted with anger. "Desert your family, brother, and you may find yourself without either throne or realm!"

With that, Tostig turned on his heel and stalked off.

Harold sighed, refilled his wine cup, and spent the next hour staring into the fire as he slowly sipped the wine.

Finally he rose, and went to his bedchamber for the night.

CHAPTER FIVE

HAWISE CHECKED TO MAKE SURE THAT HER LADY'S gown was safely folded and set into the chest, then turned back to her mistress. Swanne sat before a burnished mirror, brushing out her thick mass of curly ebony hair with long, slow strokes, and Hawise hesitated before walking over and taking her leave for the night.

Sweet Mother Mary, but she was beautiful!

In the mirror, Swanne's eyes slid Hawise's way, and the woman dropped her own eyes and fidgeted with her skirt, embarrassed at being caught staring.

"I am done with you for the night," Swanne said.

Hawise nodded, colored a little—she had served Swanne for twenty-five years, but the woman still retained the ability to make her uncomfortable—dropped a small curtsy and walked from the private bedchamber that sat above Harold's hall.

As the heavy drapery that served as a door fell closed behind Hawise, Swanne smiled at herself in the mirror. "Oh, aye, my dear," she murmured, "I am beautiful indeed."

Then her smile faded a little. What use was such beauty when William lingered within Normandy? Fifteen years ago they had believed that only a year or two separated them from each other and from their dream of completing the Game. But William's problems in Normandy had continued, he could not turn for England, and Swanne had been forced to wait far longer than she'd anticipated. She might have tried to see William again, to touch him, but both he and she had felt Asterion's malevolent, cruel, and close presence, and they had not dared. Together, they would have presented the Minotaur with too tempting a target.

Fifteen years since she had seen him. Fifteen years of frustration and of being tied to *Harold*. Swanne had never loved Harold, but now she resented him as she never had previously. Fifteen years of Harold when she could have had William.

And it had been that bitch whom he had visited in dream! It still rankled her that William had graced Caela's dreams, and not hers. William was so concerned about Asterion that he kept his mind and powers closely shut-tered; Swanne had tried to touch him through dream previously and had not been able to get past the barriers he'd put in place.

But he'd visited Caela in dream. It mattered not that William had appar-ently done nothing but speak of Swanne.

He had visited *Caela* in dream and *not Swanne*!

"You foolish virgin bitch," Swanne muttered, "even now you can't resist trying your petty, childish charms on him, can you?"

There was a movement at the door.

Harold.

Swanne smiled easily at him—at least those fifteen years had made her the mistress of deception—and turned back to her reflection in the mirror as Harold undressed and slid beneath the bedcovers.

Finally, tiring of her pose, Swanne shook her head so that her ebony hair rippled luxuriously down her back, and put down the brush. She stood, slowly and elegantly, aware of every movement that she made, and smoothed down over her body (still slim and fine after the six children she'd borne to remain in Harold's graces, thank the gods!) the thin lawn nightrobe whose delicate weave scarcely hid any detail of the body over which it was draped.

She placed a hand over her stomach, flattening the lawn against her body, and again admired herself in the mirror.

"Do you think yourself with child again?"

For an instant, Swanne's eyes hardened to a flat bleakness, but then she turned to the man who had spoken, and in that movement she masked her hatred with a well-practiced coquetry.

"Are six children not enough for you, my love? Do you want me to swell again so that your manhood can be proven before all at court yet one more time?"

He was laying on his back on the bed, the covers pulled down to his stom-ach, exposing his well-muscled chest, hands behind his head, studying her with unreadable eyes. "Are you with child?"

"No." Swanne sauntered over to the bed, allowing herself to admire the man's physique and handsome face even if she loathed who and what he was.

Swanne parted her lips, allowing him to see the wetness of her tongue between her white teeth. Slowly she tugged the robe over her shoulders so that it fell to the floor, then climbed onto the bed, pulling the bed covers further down over his body, then lifting one leg over him so that she straddled his body as she settled her weight atop his warmth.

His eyes darkened almost to blackness, and she could see the muscles tense in his upper arms. *You are a very lucky man, Harold,* she thought, *to have me in your bed at night.*

Her lips parted even more, and she moved her hips very slowly atop his.

He moved his hands, and grasped her hips, pulling her the tighter against him.

She drew in a deep breath, and watched his eyes drift to her breasts. *I should have taken you as a lover when you were Coel. You were wasted on Cornelia.*

"Harold," she said, and leaned down so that he could take one of her nipples between his teeth. Hate him she might, but for the moment Swanne saw no reason to deny herself his body and the skills he employed as a lover.

LATER, WHEN SHE COULD HEAR HIM BREATHING IN the deep steadiness of sleep, she moved away from the warmth of his body, rose from the bed, and used the washbowl that Hawise had left to wipe away the traces of his semen from her thighs. Tomorrow she would take the bag of herbs she had secreted at the bottom of her clothes chest, and brew a cupful of the tea that would ensure she'd not conceive. Six children were enough, indeed, and the last thing Swanne wanted was to be big-bellied with child when . . .

When *he* would soon be here, please to the gods!

Swanne dried herself, then wrapped about her nakedness the robe she had discarded earlier, shivering a little in the cold night air. She sat on a stool by the brazier, warming herself, and looked back to check that Harold was indeed fast asleep.

He was breathing deep, and Swanne relaxed. She turned back to the brazier, placed her hands on her knees, closed her eyes, and sent her senses scrying out into the night. There was only one benefit that Harold brought her, and that was to give her the excuse to live so close to the Game.

Ah, there . . . there it was . . .

Swanne relaxed even further, wrapping her senses about the Game, feeling its strength. Gods, it was powerful! She and Brutus had built it so well. Whenever Swanne was despondent, or frustrated, or felt that she could cope no longer with Harold, or with the pointlessness of her life in this damnable Christian court, Swanne found a quiet place so that she could communicate with the Game. Touch its power, feel its promise, believe in the future that she and William would build together once they'd completed the Game and trapped Asterion within its dark heart.

So powerful, and yet . . . different. Swanne recalled again, as she so often did, that conversation she'd had with William in that single brief encounter fifteen years earlier.

Could the Game have changed in the two thousand years it was left alone? she'd asked.

Perhaps, he'd answered too slowly, his own concern obvious. *We had not closed it, it was still alive, and still in that phase of its existence where it was actively growing. Who knows what . . .*

He'd stopped then, but even now the unspoken words rang in Swanne's mind. *Who knows what it could have grown into.*

Swanne reached out with her power and touched the Game. Always before, it had responded to her.

Tonight, although she could feel its presence and vitality, it did not.

A coldness swept through Swanne, and for one panicky moment she almost succumbed to her terror and projected herself into William's presence. But she didn't; it was too dangerous. As well as the Game, Swanne could feel Asterion more strongly than ever before. He was stalking the grounds and spaces of the Westminster, waiting and watching.

And so Swanne drew in a deep breath, steadied herself. Then she rose and, ensuring Harold still lay asleep, she went to her needlework basket and withdrew from its depths a small scrap of parchment upon which she scribbled a few lines of writing with a piece of sharpened charcoal.

IN THE HOUR AFTER SHE AND HAROLD HAD BROKEN their fast, and Harold had departed to meet with some of his thegns, Swanne took the parchment, now folded and sealed, and handed it to her woman Hawise.

"Take this," she said, "and hand it to the good archbishop of York."

Hawise, who knew far better than to ask what the message contained, merely nodded and slipped the parchment into the pocket of her robe.

DEEP UNDER LONDON AND THE HILLS AND RIVERS that surrounded it, the Troy Game dreamed as it had dreamed for aeons.

It dreamed of a time when its Mistress and Kingman would return and complete it, when it would be whole, and strong, and clean. It dreamed of a time when the kingship bands would be restored to the limbs of the Kingman, and when he and his Mistress would dance out the Game into immortality.

The Game also dreamed of things that its creators, Brutus and Genvissa, could never have realized. It dreamed of the stone circles that still dotted the land, and it dreamed of those ancient days when the stones danced under the stars.

In its dreaming, the Game began to whisper, the stones responded, and the dream turned into reality.

CHAPTER SIX

"AEWEALD?"

Saeweald jerked from sleep, the dark-haired woman beside him murmuring sleepily.

"It is I, Tostig."

Saeweald relaxed a little, but not a great deal. He and Tostig had once been great friends, but as Tostig had grown first into manhood, and then into his distant earldom, their friendship had ebbed away.

Saeweald slowly swung his legs out of bed, wincing as his right hip caught within the blankets and twisted uncomfortably.

The woman beside him also started to rise, but he laid a hand on her shoulder. "No, keep my space warm for me, Judith. I will not be long."

Tostig had disappeared into one of the outer chambers, and now he returned with a small oil lamp. He grinned at the sight of the woman. "I know you," he said. "You are one of the queen's ladies."

Judith inclined her head. "Indeed," she said, "and a better mistress I could not hope to serve."

"Does she know you spend your nights here?"

"I cannot imagine that the queen would object," Saeweald said tersely, pulling on his robe and belting it about his waist. "Tostig, what do you here?'

Tostig shifted his eyes from Judith to the physician. "I need your advice," he said. "And your . . . Sight."

Again his eyes slid back to Judith.

"She knows who and what I am," Saeweald said. "You need have no concern for her."

He led Tostig back into the next chamber. "What can be so urgent that you need to wake me from my bed?"

"Edward," Tostig said, then grinned charmingly, which instantly put Saeweald on guard. "I need to know how long he shall live."

"You and most of England," said Saeweald. "Why? Why so urgent?"

"I . . . I am concerned for my brother. I need to know what I can do that shall most aid him to the throne."

Saeweald studied the earl of Northumbria through narrowed eyes. "That is not what you want to know."

Tostig abandoned his charm. He grabbed at Saeweald's arm. "I want to know *my* future," he said. "I want to know where *I* stand."

"Why?"

"Does not every man want to know what lies before him?"

Saeweald gave a hollow laugh. "Some say that a wise man would give all his worldly goods not to know, Tostig."

"*I want to know.* Why won't you tell me . . . do you want gold? Is that it? Does the physician Druid need gold to share his Sight?"

"If you think yourself brave enough, Tostig, then I can share my Sight with you. Give your gold to the beggars who haunt the wastelands beyond the gates of London. They need it more than I."

Saeweald reached for the oil lamp that Tostig still held. The lamp consisted of a small, shallow pottery dish in which swilled oil rendered from animal fats. A wick extended partway out, resting on the rim of the dish, spluttering and flickering.

Saeweald rested the shallow dish in the palm of his left hand, passing his right palm over it several times.

"Well?" Tostig demanded.

Saeweald's eyes lifted from the lamp, and in the thin glimmer of light, they appeared very dark, as if they had turned to obsidian rather than their usual green.

Wait, he mouthed before bending his face back down to the lamp.

Tostig stared at Saeweald, then lowered his own eyes.

And gasped, taking an involuntarily step backward.

That tiny lamp seemed to have grown until it appeared half an arm's length in diameter, although it still balanced easily in Saeweald's hand. The oil was now black and odorless, lapping at the rim of the dish as if caught in some great magical tide.

The wick sputtered, and the smoke that rose from it thickened and then sank, twisting into the oil itself until the dish of the lamp contained a writhing mass of smoke and black liquid.

What do you wish to know?

"How long does Edward have to live?" said Tostig, unaware that Saeweald had not spoken with his own voice.

The oil and smoke boiled, then cleared and in its depths Tostig saw Edward lying wan and skeletal on his bed, a dark, loathsome miasma clouding above his nostrils and mouth.

"What does it mean?" he asked.

The clouds gather. He does not have long. What else do you want to know?

"Harold," Tostig said in a tight voice. "Tell me of Harold."

Again the oil and smoke boiled then cleared, and Tostig bent close.

He saw Harold climbing a hill. He was dressed in battle gear, although he did not carry a sword, and he appeared weary and disheartened. He reached the top of the hill, and suddenly a shaft of light slid down from the heavens, wrapping Harold in gold, and Tostig saw that Harold wore a crown on his head and that the weariness had lifted from his face.

Then Harold turned about, and Tostig drew in a sharp breath, for Harold's face was both beautiful and wrathful and consumed with power all at once. As Tostig stared, Harold very slowly raised his hands, palms upward, and light shone forth from them, as if they carried living, breathing gold within them.

"By the gods!" Saeweald muttered, and he suddenly dropped the dish, spattering oil over both men's robes and legs.

"I need to see more!" cried Tostig, but Saeweald shook his head. "You have seen enough," he said. "Edward has not long, and Harold will be a king such as England has never seen. What more can you want to know? What more can you desire for your blood-kin?"

Tostig stared through the gloom toward Saeweald, but he could not make out the man's face. Then, wordlessly, he turned on his heel and left.

Saeweald stood very still for a long time; the remnants of the oil dripping down his robe.

Eventually he turned, went back to the bedchamber, disrobed, and crawled back in beside Judith.

"I think I know why Coel is back," he said.

ChAPTER SEVEN

*W*ILLIAM STOOD ON THE HILL, THE WESTERLY
wind ruffling the short dark curls of his head, the sun making him narrow his almost-black eyes. Behind him a group
of his men-at-arms chattered quietly where they stood by the horses, and his
close friend Walter Fitz Osbern sat in the grass, watching him carefully.

To his side stood Matilda. She was heavily pregnant, only weeks away
from giving birth, and she and William were engaged in what had become
one of the rituals of their marriage. In each of her pregnancies, a few weeks
before she gave birth, Matilda asked William to bring her to the coast where
she could stand and feel the sea wind in her hair and ruffling through her
clothes. It was this, and its memory, which enabled her to endure the weeks of
confinement just before and after the birth of a child. Matilda hated the sense
of detainment, almost of capture, that surrounded the rituals of childbirth;
this single day of freedom, of feeling the wind in her hair and her husband
standing beside her, gave Matilda enough strength to endure it. Despite her
diminutive stature, Matilda gave birth easily, although she found it desperately painful: this child would be their seventh.

Matilda also liked to stand here, her belly swelling toward the sea, because
it gave her a sense of superiority over this witch that William still dreamed of.
Well might Swanne be the first love of William's life, but it was not she who
bore his children, and it was not she who stood here now, William's companion and mate.

She looked at William, and saw that he had his eyes fixed on the wild tossing gray seas, and that faint smudge in the far distance, that line of white
cliffs.

England.

"How you lust for that land," she murmured, and William flickered his
eyes her way.

"Aye. And it will be mine soon enough."

She nodded. In the past two years, William had finally managed to bring
Normandy under his control. Rival claimants had been quashed, dissent had

evaporated, and William enjoyed power such as he'd never had previously. Normandy was his, and would stand behind him, whatever he ventured. Matilda only hoped that when William *did* venture, she wouldn't be so heavy with child again that she could not accompany him.

Their marriage was strong, stronger than Matilda had ever envisaged in their early months together. They had both agreed that truth was the only possible foundation on which they could build their partnership, and the truth had served them well.

Of course, there were always a few small secrets and, on William's part, the occasional infidelity, but neither small secrets nor infidelities rocked the essential core of their marriage: Matilda and William were good for each other. Together, they managed far more than either of them could have managed individually.

"When?" said Matilda, although she well knew the answer.

"When Edward dies," he said. William was strong enough to venture an invasion now, but he also wanted to coat his claim with legitimacy, and he could not do that if he tried to wrest a throne from the incumbent king.

Once Edward was dead, however, then the path would be open for him.

William shifted slightly, as if uncomfortable, and he frowned as he gazed across the gray waters of the channel that separated Normandy and England.

"What is it?" said Matilda.

"There is something about to happen . . . matters are moving," he said. He lifted his closed fist and beat it softly against his chest, underscoring his words. "I feel it in *here*."

Matilda felt a thrill of superstitious awe run up and down her spine. Fifteen years had been far long enough for her to realize that there were depths to her husband that she had not yet plumbed.

If the witch Swanne loved him, then why was that so? Was it because some power in William called to Swanne?

"It is not Edward," she said, and William looked at her.

"How so? What do *you* know?"

Matilda managed to suppress the small smile that threatened to break through. One of the "small" secrets she had kept from William was that Matilda had her own agent in place within Edward's court.

"I think you will find," Matilda said, "that Edward's queen shall be at the heart of it."

"Caela? Why?"

Now Matilda allowed that secretive smile to break through. "A woman's intuition, my dear. Nothing else."

Caela intrigued Matilda. Initially, Matilda had set her agent to watching Swanne, but that watchfulness had, over the years, grown to include the queen as well. At first this had been because Swanne so clearly and evidently hated Caela, and that made Matilda wonder if Swanne feared the queen as well, and further wondered why this might be so. But then, as the years passed, Matilda came to understand, via her agent, that there was a small but dedicated coterie that surrounded the queen, and that Caela herself sometimes exuded an air of strangeness that Matilda's agent found difficult to express.

"Caela is nothing," William said, and the harsh tone of his voice made Matilda look sharply at him.

I wonder, she thought.

AS WILLIAM LIFTED MATILDA BACK TO HER HORSE, his mind drifted to the dream he'd had some nights previously. Cornelia, or Caela, as she was now called, in her stone hall. That dream had been so real. The stone had felt hard beneath his feet, Caela's flesh so warm beneath his fingers.

The plea in her eyes as vivid as if he'd stood there in reality.

William had dreamed of her previously—would this woman never cease to torment him?—but never had the dream seemed so real.

Nor Caela so close. She was older than she had been as Cornelia, and lovelier. Her hair was darker, her skin paler, but her eyes still had that strange depth of blue that they had two thousand years previously.

She had still held her face up to his, and yearned for him to kiss her.

And he *had* wanted to kiss her, whatever he might have said to her. He'd wanted to kiss her more than he'd ever wanted anything else in his life. More than the Game? Aye, at that moment, when Caela's face had been so close, William thought he might have squandered even the Game itself in order to feel her mouth yield under his, to taste her sweetness . . .

Yet he'd stopped himself, just in time.

Was she the trap Asterion had laid?

Again?

William turned from Matilda—watching him curiously—and stared back across the wild tossing seas.

Soon. It was starting today—he could *feel* it surging through his blood— and within a year all would be won or lost.

Chapter Eight

The Great Hall, Westminster

AROLD GODWINESON, EARL OF WESSEX, slouched in his great chair in its habitual place to the right of King Edward's dais. His dark eyes were hooded, his right hand rubbed through the short dark hairs of his moustache and beard, his left arm lay draped, apparently relaxed, over the carved armrest of the great chair, his legs stretched out before him, one foot idly tapping out a rhythm only Harold could hear.

He looked almost half asleep, but in reality Harold was coiled, tense and waiting. Harold had spent his life either at court or on the battlefield, and over the years he'd developed a sense of danger so acute he could almost smell its approach.

His nose had been full of the stink of danger ever since last night.

Ever since Swanne had dropped her robe and straddled him with her naked, tight body.

Ever since he'd lain awake all night, observing her sitting before the brazier through his heavy-lidded eyes.

Ever since he'd seen her scratch out that secret communication and hide it within the folds of her clothes.

Now he watched and waited, more certain of this than anything else he'd known in this life. There was danger afoot, and Swanne was somehow connected with it. Harold knew he should worry about Tostig as well, but for the moment the sense of danger that seemed to surround Swanne was so acute that he pushed all thought of his brother to the side.

His eyes moved slowly over the crowd gathered for King Edward's harvest court in the vast Great Hall of Westminster palace, seeking Swanne out. Ah, there she was, chatting with several members of the witan.

Harold's expression remained studiously neutral as he watched his wife. This morning she looked lovelier than ever, her ivory gown clinging to the swell of her breasts and hips, pinching in about the narrowness of her waist, both swell and slenderness emphasized every time she moved.

He no longer loved her, nor even respected her. Oh, once he had adored her, patterned his life about her every movement and want. But that lovelorn man had been left behind years ago, murdered through years of cohabitation with the lady he'd taken as his common-law wife. Now that the delusion of love had been stripped from his eyes, Harold could see that there was a coldness about Swanne that even she, most expert of deceivers, could not entirely hide. There was a sense of *waiting* about her that made him think of the deadliness of a coiled snake about to strike.

Harold had absolutely no doubt that, were it to suit her purposes, Swanne would not hesitate to murder him.

A great wave of blackness washed over him, and Harold had to close his eyes momentarily, trying to recover his equilibrium. All his life he'd been plagued with terrible dreams, of a love and a land lost; of Swanne standing over his murdered body, laughing; of a man with raging, snapping black hair reaching out over his corpse to a woman whose face was that of . . . that of . . .

Harold opened his eyes, staring at Swanne, forcing his mind away from his dreams. In his youth, they'd been the province of the night only, nightmares he could laugh away in the sanity of wakefulness. But over the past few months, they'd been taking over his waking hours as well.

And whenever he looked at his sister, his mind was filled with such carnal thoughts that Harold was sure the devil himself must have ensnared him.

Last night, when Swanne had lowered herself to him, he'd closed his eyes and imagined that it was not Swanne atop him, but . . .

No! He must stop this. God, what was happening to him? Was this some sickness of the mind? Some devilish possession? Desperate for distraction, Harold looked slowly about the Great Hall, seeking whatever it was (apart from his thoughts of his sister) that was causing chills to run up and down his spine, and nerves to flutter in his belly.

The Hall was filled with Normans . . . who would imagine that this was a Saxon kingdom, and at its head a Saxon king? No wonder his nerves were afire when his king preferred the Normans to his own countrymen.

This Hall was far vaster than the one his father had built in Wessex. Above the ceiling of the Hall, and reached by a great curving staircase behind the dais, was a warren of timber-walled chambers that Edward used for his private apartments, as well as those of his closest retainers.

Currently, Edward sat on his carved wooden throne on his dais, his snowy hair and beard flowing over his shoulders and chest, robed in the Norman manner as if he were a woman rather than a warrior, a crucifix in his hand, an expression of wisdom and dignity affixed on his aged face. Harold's eyes narrowed. Edward cultivated the demeanor of the scholarly yet shrewd king, but Harold doubted that any honest appraisal of the man would value him at anything more than the mediocre. Edward had begun his reign twenty-five years previously in a burst of bright hope, and it looked as if he'd end it in an agony of indecision.

Edward's advisers—sycophants all—were gathered about him, nodding and smiling and agreeing and sympathizing as the occasion demanded. A Norman nobleman, no doubt from Duke William's court, was smiling and laughing and presenting the duke's compliments. Several churchmen, never slow to flatter such a powerful benefactor, bowed their heads in assumed wisdom and piety. Within the cluster, Harold recognized Bishop Wulfstan of Worcester and the much traveled Norman sympathizer Aldred, archbishop of York (now much fatter than he'd been when he'd officiated at Edward's wedding so many years previously). There also was Eadwine, the abbot of Westminster Abbey, nodding and smiling whenever Edward so much as looked his way.

Fools, all.

Saeweald stood slightly behind and to one side of the adoring cluster, his copper vials of herbs and potions dangling from his belt and catching the light. He leaned on a crutch that Harold knew he only used on days of supreme discomfort. The physician's face was masked in blandness, but Harold knew him well enough to recognize the irony that lay behind his expression. Saeweald hated the Normans as much as Harold did.

Saeweald caught Harold's appraisal and, very slowly, lowered one eyelid in a wink.

Despite his continuing sense of imminent danger, Harold's mouth twitched beneath his hand. It was Tostig who had first introduced him to the physician many years ago, but despite the current tension between Harold and his brother, his friendship with Saeweald remained strong. It was not simple liking that bound the two men (although sometimes Harold wondered at the rapidity with which they had established such a deep friendship, almost as if they'd been renewing it, not forming it) but also their common preference to the ancient pagan ways of the country. They shared a mutual loving and reverence for the land itself, for the turf and the stones and the meanderings of the streams and rivulets. A love and reverence that meant far more to them than the petty mouthings of Christian priests. Sometimes, in the depths of winter, Saeweald would take Harold to the top of one of the hills that surrounded London, and there he would shuck off his robe and, naked save for the tattoo that marked him as a priest of the ancient paths, would take Harold on journeys of such mystery and power that left the earl shaking for hours afterward.

Always, after these mysteries, Saeweald would half smile at Harold and say, *One day . . . one day . . .*

Harold never knew what he meant, and never dared ask.

Saeweald also took Harold to some far less private, although still very exclusive, celebrations. On the winter solstices, the equinoxes, the festivals of Beltane, of Maytide and of the Green Man, Saeweald took Harold to the very top of Pen Hill to meet with (Harold had laughed in disbelief the first night he'd attended such a celebration) Mother Ecub and her very unvirginal nuns, as well as a host of men and women he'd recognized from the councils and markets of London. There he'd partaken in the dances and meanderings, the fires and the spirit-soarings, the choruses and (Harold shivered with remembered longing) the strange matings within the circles of stone about the hills of London.

Harold's mouth curled behind his hand: if only Edward knew what went on in his realm while he knelt before his altar . . .

A snippet of conversation from around the king reached Harold's ears. Abbot Eadwine had begun a long and loud boast about the beauty of the almost-completed abbey.

Edward was hanging on every word, almost drooling in his excitement, and Harold's lips thinned in disgust. Eadwine was Edward's special creature. Many years previously, the king had selected Eadwine, from among the gaggle of black-robed monks who lived within the abbey precincts, to be the new abbot *and* had then glorified both abbey and abbot by financing one of the most spectacular building programs ever seen in England—or Europe—come to that. Westminster Abbey had gone from being a damp, dark, sullen stone church, with too many draughts for any but the most desperately pious to enjoy, to an imposing church and abbey that now rose atop Tothill. The new abbey, due to be completed within the next few months, was one of the most beautiful and impressive churches within all of Christendom.

Edward meant it as a fitting burial chamber and memorial to his reign. Harold thought the entire matter beyond contempt. Other men, other kings, would have preferred that their deeds and victories remain as their memorials.

Not Edward. Childless, victory-less, and increasingly meaningless in his essential impotence and powerlessness, even within his own kingdom, Edward had chosen to erect a monument of stone to his glory.

Harold had no doubt that the Church would eventually canonize the king for it. Spectacular donations were ever the easy road to sainthood.

Saeweald was still watching Harold, and seemed to understand some of the earl's thoughts, for his own mouth curled in amusement.

Harold finally looked away from Saeweald. Soon the damned physician would have him smiling openly, and in this court that would never do.

His gaze drifted, as it so often did, to Caela. She looked particularly beautiful—and particularly sad within that beauty—on this morning. She was robed in soft blue silk over a crisp white under tunic, a mantle of snowy linen about her shoulders and draped demurely over her dark hair. The colors suited her, and Harold found himself thinking on how beautiful she would look, were she within her and Edward's private chambers, where she could remove her veil, and let that blue silk shimmer against the darkness of her hair . . .

Caela turned slightly on her seat, handing some needlework to a woman behind her, and as she did so the material of her robe twisted and tightened about her waist and breasts.

Harold stilled, his very breathing stopped.

Caela spoke softly to the woman, and then laughed at some small jest the woman made to her, and Harold let his breath out, horrified to hear its raggedness.

Damn it! Look elsewhere, lecher!

Desperate, Harold dragged his gaze away from his sister and toward the back of the Great Hall where thronged the thegns and stewards, and even several ceorls, who came each day to court in the hope of gaining a moment of the king's time for their supplications.

Harold saw several that he knew, and nodded a terse greeting to them. And there was Tostig, just entered.

Tostig saw Harold looking, even across this distance, and pointedly looked away.

Harold sighed. Perhaps he should send one of his thegns down to his brother and bid him sit with Harold. Then they could talk, perhaps, and jest away the tensions that had arisen between them the previous night.

But, just as he was about to summon a thegn and send him to Tostig, Harold stilled in puzzlement.

To the very rear of the Hall, where opened the doors to the outer chambers, stood a tall, pale figure.

Harold blinked, for the figure seemed very slightly out of focus . . . as if it stood behind a veil of water. Whatever—whoever—it was, the figure was very tall, and dressed in plain, poorly sewn garments.

A beggar, come to elicit pennies?

For an instant, just an instant, the veil lifted, and Harold found himself staring at intense gray-flecked brown eyes. The eyes transfixed him, they were so clear, even from this distance, that he did not think to expand his view to the larger face.

Then the veil was back again, and the figure muted.

Suddenly his sense of imminent danger exploded, and Harold straightened and slid to the edge of his chair, a hand to the knife at his belt.

Even as Harold was rising, the strange, discomforting figure gave a discernible moan, raised a long, thin, almost diaphanous arm, and pointed toward Caela.

Before Harold could say or do anything further, Caela half rose from her seat, her face a mask of terror and pain, and cried out with a half-strangled moan.

Asterion marched through the stone hall that represented Caela's womb, his booted footsteps ringing most satisfactorily.

It was time, finally, to make the opening move in this most exquisite, if deadly, of dances.

Asterion laughed aloud—and to think only he knew the tune!

Then he sobered, and slowed his pace as he walked through the hall, his head swinging this way and that as he tried to spy out where she'd put herself.

She wouldn't have hidden herself too well, that he knew. After all, Mag was the one who wanted herself murdered.

Wasn't that all a part of her Grand Plan?

Asterion almost laughed again, remembering how, in their previous life, Mag and Hera had plotted to outwit Asterion. Hera, the dying Greek goddess, had called to the Llangarlian goddess Mag, telling her that they could use Cornelia to trick Asterion into an alliance with Mag.

Then Mag, using Cornelia, could turn against Asterion.

Neither Hera nor Mag realized that Asterion knew of their entire, inept plan.

Gods thought to outwit him, Mistresses of the Labyrinth thought to deceive him, and Asterion was a step ahead of all of them. They would dance to his tune, not he to theirs.

"Come on, Mag," Asterion whispered. "Show thyself. It is, after all, your execution day, and you wouldn't want to be tardy for such an important appointment, would you?"

There was a slight movement to one side, within one of the shadowy recesses of the arched side aisles.

Nothing. A trickery only. Something designed to make him feel as though what he did now was real. Worthwhile, even.

"Oh come on, you silly bitch," Asterion muttered. "I haven't got all day."

Ah! There she was! About time . . .

Asterion's gait increased in pace and, as it did so, so his entire form became huge and black, a great amorphous mass of murderous intent.

Mag had appeared at the far end of the stone hall. She looked tiny and wizened from her long period of inactivity, and darted terrified from the shadow of one great column to the next. She wailed, the sound thin and frightened, and she clasped her hands about her shoulders as if that single, futile gesture might save her.

Oh, for goodness sake, thought Asterion, that act wouldn't fool a toddling child.

"Did you think that you had outwitted me?" he snarled (one had to play out the absurdity, after all).

"No!" Mag cried. "No! Let me be, Asterion. I can help you! I can—"

Something dark and horrible, a bear's claw although magnified ten times over, roared through the air, and Mag threw herself to one side.

The claw buried itself in one of the great columns of the stone hall, and blood gushed forth from the stone.

Asterion began to giggle.

"I beg you!" screamed Mag. "I beg—"

The claw flashed through the air once more, save that this time it became as the head of a great cat halfway through its swing, and its fangs snapped, barely missing the goddess, who rolled desperately across the floor.

"Bitch!" seethed Asterion, and he leaped high into the air. His form turned into a murderous cloud, its entire bulk shrouding Mag completely. From a cloud it changed into a bubbling mass of plague, sorrow, and death, and it poured itself over Mag, it flowed over her, and in that one movement, that one moment, Asterion did what Genvissa had always wanted to do.

He destroyed the goddess. He annihilated her.

Just as she wanted.

Blood flowed.

Asterion laughed.

So many things happened all at once within the Great Hall that all Harold could do was leap from his chair, and then just stand, helpless and appalled.

Caela staggered from her chair, her face suddenly so pale that all the life appeared to have drained from her, her eyes wide, her mouth in a surprised "O," her hands clutching to her belly. Blood—*a flood of it!*—stained first about her lower belly and then thickened down her lower skirts until her feet slipped in it and she fell to the timber flooring.

Edward, his own face stunned, stumbled from his throne to stand, staring at his wife as she writhed in agony on the floor.

Caela's ladies, standing together in one amorphous mass, hands to mouths, eyes wide in shock. *What queen ever acted this way?*

Swanne turned from the three men she'd been seducing with her grace and wit and loveliness and regarded Caela's sudden, unexplained agony with something akin to speculation.

Judith was the first to make any attempt to aid Caela, bending down to her and gathering the stricken woman in her arms. The next instant, Saeweald had joined her, almost falling to the floor as he tossed aside his crutch.

Harold also went forward, his eyes glancing back to where the strange, pale figure had stood—it was gone, now—and bent down beside Saeweald and Judith. Appalled at his sister's distress, Harold lifted his head to say something to Edward, who was standing close by with an expression of revulsion on his face, when he was forestalled by Aldred, the archbishop of York.

"See," the archbishop said, his voice roiling with contempt, "your queen miscarries of a child. I had not known, majesty, that you had put one in her. You should have been more forthcoming in boasting of your achievement."

Edward gasped, his rosy cheeks turning almost as wan as Caela's now bloodless ones. "The whore!" he said. "I have remained celibate of her body! I have put no child within her!"

And he turned, his face now triumphant, and stared at Harold.

"For mercy's sake!" Harold shouted, murderously furious at Edward and frightened for Caela all in one. "Your wife bleeds to death before you, and all you can think of is to accuse her of *whoredom?*"

He spun his face about in Caela's ladies who, too terrified both by Caela's sudden, horrifying hemorrhage and by Edward's accusation, stood incapable of movement. "Aid her!" Harold cried. "*Aid* her, for sweet mercy!"

He rose, as if he meant to force the ladies down to help Judith and Saeweald, but then the physician himself spoke.

"Send for the midwives," Saeweald said. "*Now!*"

Then, stunningly, he grabbed at Harold's wrist, pulled him close, and whispered, "Be at peace, Harold. This is not as bad as it might appear."

MUCH LATER, WHEN THE COURT WAS STILL ABUZZ with shock and speculation, the head midwife, a woman called Gerberga, came before Edward.

"Well?" said the king. "What can you tell me of my wife's shame?"

To one side, Harold made as if he would stand forth and speak, but Edward waved him to silence with a curt gesture.

"Well?" said the king. "Speak!"

Gerberga's eyes flitted to Harold, then settled on the king. She raised her head, and spoke clearly. "Your wife the queen carries no shame, Your Majesty. She remains a virgin still, as intact as when she was birthed. To this I swear, as will any other of the five midwives who have examined her."

"But she miscarried!" Edward said, his hands tightened about the armrests of his throne.

Gerberga shook her head slowly from side to side. "She did not miscarry, my king. Some women, if left virgin too long, grow congested and cramped within their wombs. What happened today was the sudden release of such congestion. A monthly flux, although far worse than what most women endure."

"Caela will recover?" Harold said.

"Aye," said Gerberga, "although she shall need rest and good food and sweet words of comfort."

"Then she shall have it," said Harold.

Edward snorted, and relaxed back in the throne. "The *court* shall be the sweeter place without her," he observed, and, by his side, Archbishop Aldred laughed.

TOSTIG HAD OBSERVED THE ENTIRE DRAMA FROM HIS place far back in the Hall. He had not moved to aid Caela, nor even to make inquiries after her health, contenting himself instead with watching the words and actions of those on the dais with a cynical half smile on his lips.

As he turned to leave, a man standing just behind him made a small bow of respect, stepping back to allow Tostig to pass.

But, just as the earl made to step forward, the man said, "You must be concerned for your sister, my lord. How fortunate that all seems better than first it appeared."

Tostig snorted. "That farce? It concerned me not. England is in a sorry state indeed if the actions of its king and his deputies revolve about the weakness of a woman's womb."

"Edward . . ." the man half shrugged dismissively. "He is an old man, and weak because of it. But Harold . . ."

"Harold is as weak and foolish," Tostig snapped, "for his wits are so addled he cares not for any within this kingdom save our sister. Now stand aside, man, for I would pass."

As the earl pushed by, the man looked across the Hall to where a companion stood. They exchanged a glance, and then each turned aside with a small smile of satisfaction on their faces.

Tostig would bear watching.

CHAPTER NINE

ISGUISED IN THE BODY HE INHABITED FROM
time to time, Asterion walked through Edward's Great Hall,
mounted the stairs at its far end, and moved through the upper
floor toward the chamber where lay Caela.

As he passed, people stood to one side and bowed in respect.

Many of them asked for his blessing, and Asterion was pleased to pause,
and make above their heads the sign of the cross, and to murmur a few words
of prayer to comfort them.

So amusing. So quaint. The world was full of fools.

When he reached Caela's chamber, the midwives allowed him entry
instantly, standing aside as he approached her bed. Further back, the physician Saeweald sat in a chair, looking tired and wrung out, as if it were he who
had suffered the flux rather than the queen.

Saeweald rose awkwardly, made a small bow of respect, then sank down
again at Asterion's good-natured gesture.

"My beloved lady," Asterion said, his voice an extravagance of sympathy,
turning now to the queen in her bed, "the entire court expresses its concern
for your malaise. The well-wishes are many and rich."

Caela lay very still and very white under the coverlets. "I doubt that very
much, my lord."

"We were all shocked," Asterion said, accepting the stool that one of the
midwives brought to him, and pulling it close enough to the bed that he could
take Caela's still, cold hand. "Some of us perhaps uttered hasty words." He
made a small moue of regret.

Caela gave a small, humorless smile, and remained silent.

Asterion sent out his power, searching, as the queen's hand lay in his. He
knew what he would find, but it always paid to be careful, and he had to go
through the motions. To do what was expected of him. People were watching,
and who knew their powers of perception?

As he had expected, there was nothing. Mag was gone from Caela's womb
as surely as if . . . she had never been there.

Asterion smirked, then turned it quickly into an expression of concern as he patted Caela's hand.

"Poor child," he said. "You have suffered so terribly."

And shall suffer even more.

Then he rose, mumbling something conciliatory, winked at Saeweald, and walked away, well pleased with himself.

The trap was set, but he must not rest upon his achievements thus far. The Game was moving, and he must needs move with it.

Once he reached the stairs that led down to the Great Hall, Asterion began whistling a cheerful little ditty that he'd heard used by the fishermen at the wharves.

AELA LAY, DEEPLY ASLEEP. HER HUSBAND, THE king, had taken himself off to another chamber for the night, claiming he did not wish to disturb his wife in her recovery.

He fooled no one. Edward had forever been repulsed by the normal workings of a woman's body and had always insisted Caela move to a different bed during the nights of her monthly flux. His decision on this occasion to quit the marital chamber instead of requiring Caela to do so was a singular event, and perhaps a further expression of regret for his thoughtless accusations at court earlier in the day. Edward had visited his wife, along with a dozen other notables who had dropped in one by one, had patted her hand awkwardly, muttered some even more awkward words, and had then left with patent relief.

Now, as night closed in, Saeweald, Judith, and Ecub sat about the brazier on the far side of the chamber from Caela's heavily curtained bed. The midwives had gone, Caela's bevy of lesser-attending ladies had gone, and now only the physician, the prioress, and the senior of the queen's ladies remained.

For a long time they sat without speaking, perhaps being careful, perhaps just bone-weary themselves.

Finally, with a sigh, Saeweald spoke. "It has happened as the Sidlesaghes said it would."

"Aye," said Ecub.

"Asterion showed his hand," Saeweald said.

"In a manner," said Ecub. "He acted, yes, but who saw his hand, then? You? Or you, Judith?"

"All of us," said Judith, repressing a shiver. "We were at court this morning . . . and we all know he would have been among those to come to this chamber this afternoon or evening. To make sure Mag was gone."

"Oh, aye, indeed," Ecub said very softly. "But which one was he?"

All three knew from their previous lives, from their conversations with Cornelia in that time between when she'd "died" during the dreadful birth of her daughter, a time when Mag had spoken to her, and the time that Cornelia had murdered Genvissa, that Mag had made an alliance with Asterion. Mag had warned Cornelia then—and Cornelia had subsequently mentioned this to Loth—that in the next life Asterion would renege on the alliance. For him, Mag was nothing but a complication and a nuisance. Something which must needs be removed on his path to destroying the Game.

Until very recently, neither Ecub, Saeweald, nor Judith had any idea what Mag had planned. They'd thought that the presence of Mag within Caela's womb was the real Mag, but from the Sidlesaghes, Ecub had discovered that this Mag was only a sham, an illusion, set within Cornelia's stone hall, her womb, to deceive Asterion. To trick him into thinking he had disposed of Mag.

They'd known from the instant Caela had collapsed in court what was happening. At least the Sidlesaghes' warning had meant they were not as terrified or distraught as they would have been, had they thought Asterion was truly murdering Mag, but even so, Caela's distress had sickened and frightened them.

As had the procession of people into Caela's bedchamber throughout the day. Ostensibly all these visitors were there to assure themselves of the queen's well-being, that she had not bled, nor would not bleed, to death, but the three friends knew that among these visitors almost certainly would have been the disguised Asterion, come to check that Mag had indeed been killed.

"It could have been any one of them—and as much one of the women as one of the men," said Saeweald.

Ecub harrumphed. "And not a single one of them stank of bull."

Again, silence as they sat, watching the curtains pulled about Caela's bed, listening to her quiet breathing.

"Where is Mag?" said Judith. "Where *has* she been hiding all this time? How will she be reborn?"

Both Saeweald and Ecub shrugged.

"*She* should know," Saeweald said, nodding at the bed. "Mag would have told her."

"Cornelia never told you?" Ecub said.

Saeweald shook his head.

"Caela *should* know, but Caela is unchanged!" Judith said, despair making her voice higher than it normally was. "She has not opened her eyes and said, 'I remember.' She has simply opened her eyes and been as she has always been in this life—unknowing, unwitting, unremembering."

"The Sidlesaghes told me," Ecub said, "that all will come to pass as it should. So we shall wait, my friends. We shall wait and we shall trust."

Saeweald was about to respond, but just then there came a knock at the door, and all three seated about the fire jumped.

Glancing warily at Saeweald and Ecub, Judith rose and went to the door. She opened it, peeked through the gap, then visibly relaxed and opened the door to the visitor.

It was Harold, looking almost as wan and exhausted as Caela did in her sleep.

He walked quietly to the bed, held aside one of the drapes momentarily as he looked down on his sleeping sister, then came over to the fire where Judith had rejoined Ecub and Saeweald.

Ecub began to rise, her eyes on a stool standing in a corner, but Harold motioned her to remain seated, and fetched the stool himself.

"My sister the queen?" he said softly as he sat down with them.

"She will be well enough," Saeweald said. "Her monthly flux was bloodier than normal, but that is all that it was. With rest and good food, Caela shall be well enough."

Gods, how he hated to lie to this man, but it were better Harold not know of the love and loss of his previous life. To know would be only to torment.

"To so accuse her!" Harold said, low and angry, and it took the others a moment to realize that he referred to Edward's hateful accusation at court. "My sister should have babies and love and laughter, but all she has is . . . is *this!*" He waved a hand about the chamber, but taking in with that gesture the entire palace and her life as Edward's wife.

To that there was nothing to say, so the others merely nodded.

Harold's shoulders slumped and his face suddenly looked old and gray. "I wanted to come sooner, but Edward detained me, first with this nonsense and then that, and then sent me to interrogate some fool who had imagined he'd seen a pair of dragons mating in the skies over London during the afternoon. Now," he glanced at the bed, "it is too late, and Caela sleeps. Well, I shall not wake her, and will leave my visit until the morrow. Mother Ecub, Judith, if she wakes during the night, will you tell her that I came, and that I cared?"

Ecub nodded, and Harold gave a small half smile. "Tell me," he said, "has Tostig been here to ask after Caela?"

Saeweald shook his head, and Harold sighed. "Ah well, I expect he was detained as was I."

He rose, made his farewells, and was gone.

When he had gone, Ecub sighed. "Such a waste," she said, and even though she did not elucidate on that statement, the other two knew precisely what she meant.

"And now," Ecub continued, smiling at Saeweald and Judith, "I will sit with the queen through the night, and you two can have some precious time together."

Judith started to protest, but Saeweald took her hand, squeezed it so that she subsided, and smiled in his turn at Ecub. "I thank you, Mother Ecub," he said. "You will send for us if . . .?"

"If there is any trouble, which there shall not be," the prioress said. Then she winked. "Enjoy your rest."

SAEWEALD'S APARTMENTS WITHIN THE WESTMINSTER complex were spacious and well-appointed, a sign of the regard in which Edward held him. Situated in a long, half-timbered, half-stone building situated fifty paces from the palace and (for Saeweald) a comfortable one hundred paces from the abbey complex, his building housed the domestic apartments of various court officials, the occasional visiting nobleman and his family, and a few highly placed servants. Saeweald's quarters, three well-sized and airy chambers, were at the very end of the building, and he had his own entrance-way so that he could make his way to the beds of the sick at all times of the night and day without disturbing the other residents of the building.

Of course, this also meant that Saeweald had far more privacy than others when it came to the comings and goings from his chambers.

Now, several hours after they had left Caela's chambers, he and Judith lounged naked before the hearth on coverlets they'd pulled from the bed. They had made love, but the greatest intimacy came now, when Judith gently, lovingly, massaged soothing oils into Saeweald's twisted leg and hip. This was an intimacy that he allowed no one else, the touching of his deformity, and that he allowed Judith to was a measure of the love and trust he held for her.

They'd been lovers ever since she'd come to court to serve Caela. The instant they first met in this life, and *knew*, there had been such a sense of relief and of companionship renewed, that their first bedding had been accomplished with unseemly haste.

In a stable, which had been the first place they'd been able to find that had some relative privacy.

Save for the resident horse, of course, who had been quite agitated and who had snorted his disquiet for the fifteen turgid minutes it had taken the pair to sort themselves out.

Since that day, Saeweald and Judith found every spare hour they could to spend together. The love-making was evidence not so much of lust, but of the deepest friendship and respect *and* of shared purpose. To serve Caela and Mag, and to serve the land, in whatever means that were possible.

They were extremely discreet. Ecub knew, of course, and Judith thought that Caela, and perhaps even Harold, suspected, but (apart from the horse, who still watched them warily whenever he saw one or the other cross the stable yard and tended to utter panic when he saw both of them together) no one else knew. In King Edward's court, stiff with morality and piety, that was just as well.

In a world where Asterion strode, unknowable and unrestrainable, their secret was doubly important, for even this simple knowledge may have given the Minotaur a piece of priceless information he could use at his destructive leisure.

Judith ran her hands down Saeweald's leg, leaning her weight into his crippled flesh, massaging away tensions and cramps and aches. Saeweald's hip had been so brutally twisted during his birth (and who had commanded *that* midwife's hands? Judith had often wondered. Fate? Brutus' deadly hand from two thousand years' previous? Asterion? Genvissa's lingering malicious humor?) that the ball of his hip joint jutted out beneath his right buttock, making even sitting uncomfortable for the man. As a consequence, Saeweald either stood, or balanced precariously on the very edge of stools and seats; when he rode, as he needed to if he was to get about at all, he had to sit twisted on the saddle so that his left buttock bore most of his weight. Even then, riding was often agony.

At least he could walk. Praise Mag that at least he could walk.

"What do you think will happen?" Judith said.

Saeweald, who was lying on his left side, his head propped up on a hand, watched the movement of Judith's body in the firelight appreciatively. "Hmmm?" he said.

Judith looked at him, then grinned. "You would have me to be your slave forever, would you not, physician? Bending over your body, rubbing away your aches . . ."

"Are you offering?"

Her expression sobered. "Would it help?"

In response he only held out his free hand, and she gripped it silently. They locked eyes, and for a moment nothing at all needed to be spoken.

"Mag," Judith finally said. "Where is she, do you think?"

Saeweald sighed. "Caela would know . . . but how to make her remember. Ah! She cannot be pushed, yet . . ."

" 'Be patient,' Ecub said."

Saeweald muttered something that Judith was rather glad she did not catch. She grinned again, and was about to say something when, stunningly, horrifyingly, the door to the chamber swung open and a man stepped through.

"STAY," HE SAID TO THE STARTLED COUPLE, RAISING A hand, palm up, a gesture that was both conciliatory and reassuring.

Judith looked at Saeweald, who stared unbelievingly at the man, then she unhurriedly reached for her linen under tunic and pulled it over her shoulders.

"Your name, good man?" she said.

The stranger's mouth lifted in a small, admiring smile at her composure. He was a strikingly good-looking man of middle age. His long black curly hair was pulled back into a leather thong behind his neck, a few strands escaping to trail over his broad shoulders. His chest was broad and well muscled, his limbs long and strong. He wore nothing but a snowy white waistcloth threaded over a wide leather belt and leather-strapped sandals.

His face was stern and handsome, and not at all marred by the leather patch he wore over his left eye. His right eye was dark, gleaming with humor and power.

It was not the stranger who answered Judith, but Saeweald.

"Silvius," he breathed, leaning forward so that Judith, now standing, could lend him her hand and aid him up.

At the mention of that name, Judith's eyes flew sharply to the man. *Silvius? Brutus' father? The man Brutus had murdered at fifteen in order to seize his heritage?*

"Aye," the man said, "Silvius, indeed. It has been a long time, Loth, since we met within the dark heart of the labyrinth." His eyes slid down Saeweald's body, marking the deformities. "My God, boy, does Brutus' hand still mark you?"

"As much as it marks you," Saeweald said, his tone still cautious, but nodding toward the patch over Silvius' empty left eye socket. Judith passed Saeweald his robe and he, too, clothed himself. "Silvius, what . . ."

"What do I here?" Silvius' face suddenly seemed weary, and he raised his eyebrows at a chair that stood to one side of the hearth.

Saeweald nodded, and Silvius sat down with an audible sigh. "I am as trapped as you, Saeweald, and," he looked at Judith, "as I suppose you are, my dear. I take it from your intimacy with Loth here—"

"Saeweald," Judith put in quietly.

"Your intimacy with Saeweald here, that you, too, are reborn from that time previous when we all suffered at the hands of Brutus and that woman," he spat the word out, "he tried to make the Game with?"

"Aye," she said. "My name was Erith then, and now I am Judith."

Silvius nodded, his expression still weary. "Asterion is back."

"We know," said Saeweald. "Silvius. *What do you here? And how?*"

"Brutus trapped me at the heart of his Game with my murder," Silvius said. "I am as trapped as any of you."

"But you seem flesh, not shade," Saeweald said.

Silvius grunted. "You'd be astounded at what has happened in the past two thousand years, my boy. I sat there within the heart of the labyrinth, and somehow I took power from the Game. I am as much a player in the battle that is to come as either of you two are."

"But you cannot move from the Game," Saeweald said. "You were trapped within its heart."

Silvius looked up at him, his one good eye seething with knowledge and power. "Who says I have moved from the Game?" he said quietly.

Saeweald and Judith said nothing.

"The Game was left unfinished," Silvius continued. "It continued to attract evil . . . and it grew."

"Grew?" said Saeweald. He shared an appalled glance with Judith.

"Oh, aye. Grew. Grew in power and knowledge *and* in magnitude, my boy. You think that the Game, the labyrinth, occupies only the top of Og's Hill— Lud Hill, as now you call it—where my son first built it?"

The other two were silent, staring at Silvius.

Silvius' mouth twisted. "Nay," he said, very softly now, and he threw his hand about, as if encompassing not only Saeweald's chamber, but all the Westminster complex. "The Game occupies the *entire* area of the Veiled Hills now, my boy. It has burrowed deep, indeed."

Then Silvius leaned forward, resting his forearms on his thighs, and looked at them intently. "I have had enough of this disaster my son helped construct. I feel partly responsible, and so I am here to help you." He paused. "To help Caela."

Saeweald narrowed his eyes suspiciously. "Caela?"

"Oh, for the gods' sakes, boy! You think me a fool? I know Caela is Cornelia-reborn, and I know how important she is to you, and to your Mag and Og besides. And I know she does not remember, and this she needs to do. Yes?"

Silence.

"And Caela is the only one who is likely to know where Mag truly is, yes?" More silence.

"Yes, and yes again," Silvius answered for them. "Caela needs to remember very badly, for if she does not then all of our causes are lost. Saeweald, perhaps all that Cornelia needs is something from her past life to jolt her into awareness."

"What?" said Saeweald, finally, grudgingly deciding to trust Silvius just a little bit. "What possibly remains from her previous life, save want and need and hope?"

Silvius grinned, holding Saeweald's eye. "A bracelet," he said.

Saeweald frowned, but it was Judith who spoke. "Saeweald, you may have never seen it, but Cornelia had a bracelet, a beautiful thing of gold and rubies that she brought with her from her life as a princess of Mesopotama. She rarely wore it here in Llangarlia, but I know she looked upon it occasionally, remembering her life as a girl."

"Aye," said Silvius. "*That* bracelet. What would happen, do you think, if we slipped it on her wrist again?"

Saeweald was still frowning. "And you know where it is?"

Silvius nodded. "But to retrieve it safely I need you and whatever ancient magic of this land you still command. Saeweald, will you aid me?"

"No," Judith said, but it was already too late, for she could see the light in Saeweald's eyes.

CHAPTER ELEVEN

ERY LATE THAT NIGHT, WHEN THE MOON HAD sunk and the streets of London were lost in silent stillness, two men on horseback approached London Bridge from Southwark.

"They will not allow us to pass," Saeweald muttered, squirming uncomfortably in the saddle. His mare, Maggie, was well used to her rider's habitual wriggling, and strode on unperturbed.

"Is that so?" said Silvius, his teeth flashing white in the darkness, and Saeweald saw him make a gesture with his left hand.

"A sign of the Game," Silvius said. "Look."

Ahead was a guardhouse that protected the entrance to the bridge. Normally four or five men stood night watch here, but as they approached, Saeweald saw through the open doorway into the dimly lit interior that all slouched dozing about a brazier.

"They shall not wake," said Silvius. "And likewise with the guards who stand watch at the other end of the bridge. The way shall be open for us."

"You can manipulate the power of the Game?" Saeweald said, and Silvius glanced at him, hearing the distrust in his voice.

"I was a Kingman, too, remember? Yes, I can use parts of the Game's power. But, believe me, Saeweald, I want what you do—to stop my son at any cost from completing the Game with his Darkwitch. I do *not* want him finding those bands and completing his horror."

Silvius visibly shuddered, and Saeweald relaxed slightly. "You look so much like him," Saeweald said. "I am sorry if I remain on guard."

"I tried to help you before, didn't I?"

"Yes. Yes, you did," Saeweald said, remembering how Silvius had tried to aid Loth when he'd challenged Brutus to battle within the heart of the labyrinth. "I am sorry, Silvius."

Silvius nodded, accepting Saeweald's apology, and led the way on to the bridge, which was largely built over with houses and shops, leaving only a narrow, barely lit tunnel for foot and horse passengers to walk. The horses' hooves echoed loudly in the enclosed space, and Saeweald glanced back at the guardhouse.

There was no movement.

"They remain unaware," said Silvius.

From the bridge they turned right along Thames street (Saeweald looking curiously at the stones of Gog and Magog sitting inscrutable at the London-side entrance to the bridge), pushing their horses into a trot and then a canter.

"We have little time," said Silvius. "It shall be dawn in a few hours."

"Where do we go?" Saeweald said, having to raise his voice above the clattering of hooves.

Silvius nodded ahead. There, rising out of the gloom, was the White Mount that occupied the eastern-most corner of London. At its top rose a dilapidated stone and timber structure: a lighthouse, constructed by the Romans almost a thousand years earlier. As they neared it, Silvius pulled his horse back to a walk, waited for Saeweald to do the same, and began to talk.

"Aha," said Saeweald, knowing now where it was that Silvius led him.

"The Romans built this," Silvius said. "You know that?"

Saeweald nodded.

"The Romans were a people from the same world as the Trojans, although from a later time, when the mysteries of the Game had been forgotten. They were drawn to this land and to this place by the siren song of the Game, although they did not recognize it. On this mound, one of your sacred hills, they built a great lighthouse, a beacon tower."

"But the tower is of no importance."

"No. You are right."

"It is what lies beneath it."

"Aye."

"The well," Saeweald said. The Romans had built their lighthouse atop the White Mount, which, in Saeweald's previous lifetime, covered a sacred well. Brutus had caused the opening to the well to be covered over when he built his palace atop the mound, but Saeweald supposed the well was still there, guarding its mysteries.

But what was the bracelet doing down the well?

"Cornelia was buried there," Silvius said softly. "Did you not know? Ah, of course not, for you were dead many years before she. When Brutus died, and then Cornelia took her own life, their sons carried them to the well, and buried them within it."

"And the bracelet was buried with her," said Saeweald.

"Indeed."

The horses climbed the grassy slopes of the mount toward the derelict tower, Saeweald clinging to Maggie's saddle and studying the tower as she climbed. The Romans had built the tower of white ragstone, well-buttressed and founded. It had once soared over thirty paces into the air, but during the past nine hundred years the top courses of stonework had tumbled down to lie in untidy heaps about the foundations, and the highest rooms were open to the night air. The Romans had used this tower to watch the river approaches to the city, and to set atop its heights a great beacon to warn both London and surrounding areas of any danger that approached. Now it was used for little more than a place for boys to hide from their mothers, and for those who still followed the old ways to light fires during the solstices.

At the tower's base, Silvius and Saeweald dismounted from their horses, leaving their reins untied so they could nibble the grass about the top of the hill. Once inside, Silvius led Saeweald to the tower's lowest rooms. The approaches to the basements were half obscured with tumbled beams and stones, and Saeweald reluctantly had to allow Silvius to aid him over the obstructions.

Eventually they stood in the very lowest level of the tower where stood an uneven floor of great stone slabs.

Here Silvius dropped his cloak to one side.

"Cornelia's and Brutus' corpses are beneath these slabs?" Saeweald asked.

"Aye."

"And you want *me* to lift these slabs?"

"No. Your power I shall need later." With one hand Silvius made another gesture over the stone flagging. "That was but a slight alteration to that magic that would have raised the flower gate," he said. "Never forget that once I, too, was—"

"A Kingman. Yes, Silvius. I remember."

Then Saeweald gasped, for just as he spoke, several of the flagstones wavered and then vanished, revealing a great chasm.

Silvius stepped close, his feet careful about the edge of the chasm, and peered down.

"Gods," he murmured. "I had not expected this to be so beautiful."

Saeweald looked away from Silvius and back to the well, drawing himself carefully closer. The way opened into a rough circular shape that spiraled downward in great twists of rough rock. Far, far beneath rippled an emerald pool of water, and Saeweald knew that the depths of this pool were unknowable, even to such as himself. As he watched, the waters surged, their waves lapping higher and higher up the wild walls of the well, as if trying to reach him. A dull roar reached his ears.

Shaken by the power of the raging waters, Saeweald studied the rock walls of the well. They did not consist of the well-finished masonry of human hands, but instead twisted and spiraled down in wild, sharp ledges. This was a savage and untamed cleft, and a place of great magic and power.

Saeweald's face sagged in astonishment. "I can't believe the well still retains this much power! Gods, Silvius, did Brutus and Cornelia's sons see *this* when they buried their parents?"

"No," said Silvius. "They saw only ordinariness, and a convenient place to rest their parents."

"How in all that's good and merciful," Saeweald said, "did Brutus and Cornelia's sons manage their way down?"

"The well made it easy for them," shouted Silvius. "All they and the mourners saw were smooth, even courses of stones for the walls, a dribble of a puddle far below, and a easy flight of steps that wound its way about the side of the well. To them this place was nothing more than a source of water for Brutus' palace, and not a very reliable one at that."

"I have never seen the well so vibrant," Seaweald said.

"You know it as a vital part of this land," said Silvius. "But did you know that there are others about the world?"

Saeweald finally dragged his eyes from the well to Silvius. "No."

"There was one like this in my world also—we called it God's Well. It was the heart of the city of Atlantis, which was itself the heart of Thera. When the Darkwitch Ariadne destroyed Thera, she also destroyed its God Well."

"Thank the gods that Genvissa didn't manage to destroy *this* one," said Saeweald.

"And to why I need you here," said Silvius. "The well is open now, and who knows who can feel it, besides you and me? Saeweald—"

"I cannot go down," Saeweald said, looking again at the rough walls. It was not the magic which deterred him, but the simple fact that his twisted body would not allow him to even attempt the climb down. "You need me to stay here, and guard the entrance to the well with whatever power I can summon, while you retrieve the bracelet. In case . . ."

"Aye," said Silvius. "I will be as fast as I might, but still. . . ." He stepped close to Saeweald, and put a hand on the man's shoulder. "One day, my friend, you *will* be whole again, and then you also may go down."

"Be careful," said Saeweald.

Silvius nodded, then dropped to the edge of the well, carefully lowering himself down to the first of the twisting edges. Above him, Saeweald stripped off his robe and, naked, the light from the well playing over the antler tattoo over his chest and shoulders, began to hum a strange melody.

Within moments the entrance to the well had clouded over, and then vanished, as if all that Saeweald stared at was a rough, uneven flooring of gravel.

Silvius glanced above to make sure that Saeweald had concealed the entrance, grinned, then concentrated on the climb. The way down was difficult, but not impossible, and Silvius' pace quickened once he became more confident in finding his hand and footholds.

After some time had passed, Silvius spied what he was looking for: an opening into the rock wall, partway around the well from where he clung to a ledge. The roaring from the waters—still far below—had now increased greatly in volume, and the rocks had grown ever more slippery with condensation, and Silvius was more than glad he had found the entrance to the burial chamber. Even more careful, now that his destination was in sight, Silvius concentrated on climbing about the rock walls to the opening.

In a few short minutes he breathed a sigh of relief and leaped lightly down to the floor of the passageway. He made a gesture with his hand, and immediately the passageway was filled with a soft, golden light.

Unlike the rock walls of the well, the passageway had smooth walls and an even, dustless rock floor, and Silvius wasted no time in striding down its length.

It was only some thirty or thirty-five paces long, leading directly into a rounded chamber that looked as if it had been water-carved from the living rock.

In the center of the chamber were two waist-high rock plinths, some three feet wide and seven long, and on each of these plinths rested cloth-wrapped figures.

The corpses of Brutus and Cornelia.

Silvius halted the instant he stepped inside the chamber, staring at the plinths.

A sardonic smile creased his face as he walked to the plinth that bore the larger and taller of the cloth-wrapped corpses. He lifted his hands and rested them gently, almost hesitantly, on the wrappings that covered the corpse's head. "So much power that you have wasted, Brutus."

Silvius drew in a deep breath, then raised both his head and his hands from the corpse of his son.

"Cornelia," he said, as he stared at the corpse that lay on the other plinth.

"Poor Cornelia," he said very slowly. "Poor, dead Cornelia. Used and abused by all about you." He walked over. "Cornelia," Silvius said again, "is it time to wake?"

He grinned to himself. "Why, I do believe so!" Then he reached down with both hands to the cloths that wove about her breasts and, sliding his fingers between them, tore them apart. "Cornelia!"

Something fell from amid the bandages, then toppled from the plinth and clattered to the floor where it lay glinting.

Silvius drew in a deep breath, then leaned down and picked it up.

"Gods," he whispered, "the Greeks always knew how to make a fine piece of jewelry."

In his palm nestled an exquisitely worked gold and ruby bracelet.

Then, suddenly, Silvius' head jerked upward.

SAEWEALD FELT IT BEFORE HE ACTUALLY HEARD OR saw anything.

A coldness seeping out from the cracks of the lighthouse basement's stone walls that rose about him. The night was cold, yes, but this was different.

Malevolent.

Seeing.

Saeweald glanced at the well, made sure the conjuration hiding the well's opening remained in place, then he twisted about, trying to see in every direction at once, tottering and almost falling as he tried to find a place to hide. Cursed his power that enabled him to hide (however insubstantially) other objects, but not himself!

You poor fool. What brought you back to this calamity?

Saeweald felt the voice, rather than heard it. He turned about, trying to locate it.

There was a movement in the air. Something large, shifting. Behind him? No! To his left!

Do you look for me?

Saeweald cried out, terrified. The Minotaur had materialized directly in front of him, no more than two paces away. He was massive, taller than any man Saeweald had ever seen, tightly muscled, overpowering in his presence.

His ebony bull's head, almost majestic, swayed slowly from side to side, and bright, savage eyes pinned Saeweald where he stood.

Tell me—what do you here?

Saeweald found himself compelled to speak. It was though a ghostly hand had seized his throat, squeezing the words from him. "I am tied to the land! I am *for* the land!"

That's pathetic. I am for power, did you know that?

The word was crushed from Saeweald's chest. "Yes."

And what is this then, that you try so miserably to hide? Suddenly the gravel dissolved, and the God Well lay exposed. The Minotaur's gaze jerked back to Saeweald, and the man cried out as invisible claws ripped agonizingly into his body.

"It is . . . ah! It is a God Well!" Saeweald's body began to shake, jerking up and down as the Minotaur's power began to crush him.

Asterion began to laugh, a great belly-shaking amusement that filled the basement with his merriment. *A God Well! How sweet! Shall I destroy it?*

Saeweald had begun to cry. He was no longer capable of speech.

Shall I destroy you, friend?

Then, just as Saeweald was sure he was about to be torn to shreds, the Minotaur's eyes widened, and the creature snarled. *Who is here with you? Who?*

Saeweald somewhere found breath enough to speak a single word. "Silvius."

A Kingman? The Minotaur was still staring at the God Well. The next moment he'd taken a step back, then another, and then he was fading from view. *A Kingman?*

And then he was gone, and Saeweald collapsed unknowingly to the ground.

HE WOKE TO FIND SILVIUS CROUCHED OVER HIM.

"What happened?" Silvius said.

"Asterion . . ."

"Asterion was *here*?"

Saeweald nodded. His body was throbbing horribly, but it felt as if the Minotaur had not quite torn him to shreds after all. It had just felt like it at the time. "Aid me to rise. Please."

Silvius lent him his hand. *"What happened?"*

Saeweald briefly told him as he managed to regain his balance, a hand on Silvius' shoulder for support. "The instant he heard your name, he vanished. 'A Kingman?' he said, as if it were the last thing he wanted to hear, and then he was gone."

Silvius frowned. "I had not thought I had the power to overly perturb him," he said.

"You are the one who keeps reminding me that you were once a Kingman. Maybe Asterion has not forgotten it, even if occasionally I do." He managed a small smile. "Perhaps I will trust you, after all, Silvius. Having about me a man who can terrify even Asterion is bound to come in handy."

Silvius patted Saeweald's hand where it still rested on his shoulder. "I need to see you safe back to your chambers." He managed his own grin, but it was a weak thing. "I think you have need of Judith's ministering hands."

"Did you find it?"

Silvius nodded, and held out a hand. In its palm rested the bracelet.

"Pray to Mag that it works," muttered Saeweald.

CHAPTER TWELVE

CAELA SPEAKS

HEN I WOKE THE NEXT MORNING, I LAY FOR A very long time, cold and stiff, my belly a terrible, painful weight, and waited for my usual sense of futility to sweep over me.

This futility was my own constant burden. I had carried it about ever since that first night with Edward (*I find you most displeasing*) and I had born it as a woman, as a wife, as a queen. Poor Caela, they whispered.

Poor Caela. How I *hated* it!

The drapes were partly pulled back from the bed—and, oh, the sweetness of having this bed to myself for an entire night—and I could see that someone sat by the hearth, her chin on her chest.

Slim build, delicate face, dark sweep of hair escaping from the veil askew over her brow.

Judith. I smiled drowsily, happy in this moment. Alone in my bed, watched over by Judith.

"You're awake."

Startled, my eyes jerked to the person who now stood by my side: he must have been sitting toward the head of the bed where the drapes had obscured him.

"Saeweald." Sweet Lord Christ, he looked worse than I felt. There were great dark circles under his eyes, his skin was blotched, and there were deep lines of pain about his mouth. "Saeweald," I said again, holding out my hand. "Have you not slept?"

He took my hand and kissed it. "You seem rested, madam."

"I am well enough, Saeweald." And, surprisingly, I *was* well enough. Although my belly ached, the great wave of futility and melancholy that had so often been my intimate companion had, apparently, decided to stay away for this day. "But you? Saeweald . . . have you been battling demons all night?"

He laughed. "Indeed, madam. Keeping them from your bed."

Judith appeared at his shoulder, her tiny hands lifting to straighten her veil and push away the dark wing of hair that had fallen loose.

Saeweald had sobered, and now he looked at me with an unreadable expression. "Did you dream well, madam?"

Ah, sweet lord, why did he so constantly inquire after my dreams? "I slept dreamlessly, physician. I am sorry to disappoint you."

Judith and Saeweald shared a glance, and for some reason that made me angry.

"I am sorry to disappoint you," I said again, my tone decidedly waspish now. "If I had known you were so concerned at my dreaming I would have had a nightmare to delight you."

"I did not mean to offend you, madam," Saeweald said.

I sighed, turning aside my face. How I hated these strange, uncomfortable conversations with Saeweald. He always seemed to be waiting for me to say something for which I could not form the words. At times he appeared to be teetering forward on his uncertain legs, as if I were supposed to remember something of great import and then hand it to him to enchant him.

Although I could not see it, I *felt* Judith and Saeweald glance at each other once more.

"Bring me water," I said, looking back to Judith, "and cloths. I am not so sick that I want to break my fast stinking of my night sweat. Saeweald, I feel greatly improved this morning. You may take some of your own rest, and, should you need to again inquire after my health, then you may do so this afternoon."

And with that, and yet one *more* of those cursed glances between the two, Saeweald bowed and retired.

LATER, WHEN I HAD EATEN A SMALL BOWL OF BROTH and a piece of new-baked bread, washed, and assured both myself and Judith (who would doubtless report the fact to Saeweald) that I had not bled afresh during the night, and when the linens of my bed had been changed and the coverlets shaken, I lay back upon my pillows and prepared to receive what visitors there were. I would have risen, save that apparently Saeweald had threatened both Judith and everyone of my other attending ladies with dire warnings of my undoubted demise should I rise from my bed too soon, and so I was condemned to yet another day's rest within my bedchamber.

To be honest, I was not so very unhappy with that thought. A day abed meant a day of peace: Edward would avoid me, the majority of the court

would find other scandals and intrigues to amuse themselves, and perhaps . . .
perhaps Harold might come to talk awhile with me.

He had not come yesterday, at least not while I was awake.

I remembered that there had been a constant stream of people come to
view me, to poke and prod me, physically, emotionally and spiritually, to
ensure I was still breathing and to depart with further gossip for the court.
None of them had been Harold; none of them had been particularly welcome.
Edward had come, and said words that I think he meant to be conciliatory
(but how could I forget him standing over me, as I lay in humiliation on the
floor of his court, screaming at me that I was a whore? *How could I ever set
that memory aside?*), and had then, gratefully, departed, all thin-lipped and
pinch-nosed. Several churchmen had come, and leaned forward with wet lips
and gleaming eyes to hear what sins of the flesh I had to confess (of which I,
boring creature that I am, had none at all, save a weakness of the womb,
which was neither my fault nor theirs). A woman or two, wives of senior
members of the court, had come, and twittered all about me.

Judith saw them off with thankful alacrity.

Today, perhaps, Harold would come to see me. I closed my eyes, the soft
movements of my ladies about the chamber a soothing lullaby and, thinking
of Harold, drifted into a light doze.

I DREAMED OF THAT STRANGE STONE HALL AGAIN,
and in this dream it felt such a familiar place to me that I knew I had dreamed
of it previously; and often at that.

I smiled in my dream, for now, at least, I might have something to tell
Saeweald.

I walked through the hall, noting as I went that there were great patches
of dried blood staining the columns and the floor. Oddly, this did not disturb
me, nor did I seem to find it strange.

There was a step behind me and I turned. Harold! And yet not Harold, for
this man wore no beard, and he was dressed in strange clothes, and his face
had a different aspect—and yet still I knew it was Harold.

"Harold!" I said, and, glad beyond knowing, I held out my hands.

Joy lit his face, and he strode toward me. "Cornelia," he said. "How strange
you appear to me."

I laughed, thinking this some jest of Harold's. "My name is not Cornelia."

"Is that so?" he said, and then he had taken my hands, and pulled me in
toward him, and I had no thought at all of stopping him. He leaned down
until our mouths almost touched—and at this moment I abruptly recalled
another dream I'd had recently . . . a night ago, two nights ago? . . . when

another man had lowered his face to me, and chosen not to lay his mouth to mine.

He had called me Hades' daughter, and I knew I'd heard those words before— shouted at me, as if in accusation. And I had known that man intimately, too. But where? Where? In dream? Or in some unknown day or week or month of my life that I'd somehow managed to forget? Who was he, this man of whom I dreamed?

I tensed, my mind in turmoil, but Harold only smiled gently, and lowered his mouth to mine.

I should not allow this, I thought. *He is my brother.*

And yet, even thinking so, I opened my mouth under his, and felt the sweet bitter taste of his tongue, and then the pressure of his hand against my back as he pressed me against him.

And then, to one side, a sweet laugh.

Harold and I pulled apart. Standing not three or four paces from us was the most compelling creature I had ever seen. He was very tall, and wore only a crudely fashioned leather jerkin and trousers. His face was both bleak and joyful all at once, his eyes great mysteries that saw far more than just the objects within their sight. He laughed, raising his hands at the end of long, thin, strong arms, and I saw that his square teeth were rimmed with light, as if he would always be incapable of speaking anything but the truth.

Harold's arm tightened about me, but I could feel that he was not frightened of this apparition, nor angry at its imposition into our intimacy.

"Are you one of the ancient ones?" Harold asked of the strange creature.

"I am Long Tom," the creature said, and I frowned, trying to remember something that tugged at my mind. *Hadn't a wise woman said something to me about a Long Tom only recently? What was it? What . . .?*

The creature began to say something else, but then it turned slightly, and cried out at what it saw.

Then Harold was wrenched from my arms, and I saw the man who had called me Hades' daughter, and now he had a sword in his angry hand, and as Harold fell over backward, his throat white and vulnerable, the sword came slashing down . . .

I THINK I SCREAMED. I KNOW I JERKED AWAKE WITH such violence I almost fell from my bed.

That I did not was due to the fact that someone—a man—was holding my shoulders.

I twisted away, sure that it was that brutal man of my nightmare come to murder me, but whoever it was tightened his hands, keeping me safe, and a much beloved voice cried out.

"Caela! Caela! Wake, I beg you, for this is nothing but a dream."

My eyes cleared, and Harold's face came into focus before me.

"Caela," he said again, his voice now a groan, and I took a deep breath, and stilled, and then fell forward into his arms.

There was a moment, a long moment, when Harold's hand cupped the back of my head, tipping it back, and his face lowered to mine, his mouth so close to mine I could feel its warmth, and then he gave a harsh laugh and laid me back against the pillows.

Sweet Christ, he had almost kissed me! The memory of my dream still lingered, and I knew that if he had, I would have responded. What were we, Harold and I, that this sin consumed us?

"By all the spirits of the night, Caela, of what were you dreaming?"

I could not lie, not after what had just—almost—happened. "I dreamed of you, that you were with me—"

He winced.

"—and that—"

"Caela, do not say it!"

I stopped, and drew in a deep breath. "I dreamed I saw a Norman drag you away from me, and raise his sword. Then I woke."

"Caela . . ."

"I wish to God," I said very quietly, holding his eyes, "that I had not been born your sister."

There was a silence, neither of us looking away from the other. The silence grew intense, and I wondered if we were both teetering at the edge of a cliff, and if I would truly mind very much if we fell over.

He sighed, and the sound was ragged.

"Harold . . ."

"Caela, we can't—"

I sat forward, the memory of his sweet dream kiss still very much with me, and laid my mouth very softly against his.

I didn't know how to progress. I had never been kissed in passion before, and I was not sure . . .

Harold's mouth moved against mine. Very slowly, very gently, and I felt his breath mingle with mine. I opened my mouth, pressing it more firmly against his.

I felt him hesitate, then respond, and then he was pushing me back again. "Caela, we can't. Someone could well walk in."

Not "We can't, for it is a shameful thing." But only, "Someone could well walk in."

I smiled. At that moment I was so intensely happy that I did not care that we had, for a moment, slipped over the edge of that precipice. "I love you, Harold," I said.

He slid a hand over my mouth, but I could see the emotion in his eyes, part joy, part longing, part fear of what we had done. It was not the kiss that was so frightening to him, I think, but the fact that we'd opened a door that might prove impossible to close again.

"Not now," he whispered, and his hand fell away from my mouth.

"Harold," I said, trying to lighten the mood somewhat. "You are here, at last. I looked for you yesterday. I wanted to thank you for what you said in court. For a moment I thought no one would dare a word in my defense."

"Your husband does not deserve you," he said, and in my mind I heard what he meant to say: *I would be the better husband for you.* "I did come last night, but late, and you were already asleep. I did not want to wake you."

"So he came to me, instead," said another voice, and I felt my own face stiffen even as I saw Harold's lose all expression as Swanne's face appeared over his shoulder.

Oh, Lord Christ, that the "someone" who should walk in would be her.

She looked serene and beautiful and powerful—very sure of herself as I never truly was—and as she moved up to Harold she put a hand on his shoulder and looked down on me.

"You quite enlivened your husband's court yesterday, my dear," Swanne said. "Are you quite well now?"

Harold's eyes had dropped away from both of us, his head turned slightly down and away. I felt a great sorrow then, for I understood that where once Harold had loved Swanne, now he found her irritating, and an embarrassment.

"Aye, sister," I replied. "It was but my monthly flux, more burdensome than usual."

"Is that truly so?" she said. A very slight frown creased her forehead, then she lifted her hand from Harold's shoulder and placed it on the coverlets of the bed, over my belly.

"Swanne . . ." Harold began, but I shook my head—she could surely do no harm—and he subsided.

"Is that truly so?" Swanne repeated, and her frown increased. Something shadowy and unknowable darkened her eyes and the pressure of her hand increased slightly, although not uncomfortably so.

"My lady?" I said, glancing at Harold who was watching Swanne's face.

"Your womb is empty," Swanne said, and her voice was slightly puzzled. She leaned back, raising her hand away from me, and looked at me, the frown still marking her lovely face.

"Do you believe, too, that I have a lover, and lost his child?" I said, bitterly. "I am a virgin still, Swanne."

My eyes briefly, meaningfully, locked with Harold's.

She nodded, and made a small smile with her mouth, but I could see that her mind was consumed with something other than our conversation.

"So," she said softly. "He has made his first move. I wonder why this was so important to him . . ." Her voice drifted off.

By now both Harold and myself were staring at her. "Swanne?" Harold said. "Of whom do you speak?"

She blinked, and her face set into hard, cold lines. "Of no one who concerns you, my dear."

And with that she turned and left us.

CHAPTER THIRTEEN

SWANNE WALKED FROM THE QUEEN'S APART-
ments, her gait smooth and elegant, her shoulders back, her
beautiful face held high. She walked until she reached the head
of the staircase where windows overlooked the Thames, and there she
stopped, folded her hands before her, and stared out the window.

She had felt nothing in Caela's womb. Nothing, and yet, for all the time
she's known Caela in this life, the woman's womb had always held a faint
trace of Mag.

Swanne sighed, ignoring the stares of servants and officials who hurried
by, and once more a small frown wrinkled the otherwise smooth skin of her
forehead. Swanne had been reborn into this life with her powers as Mistress
of the Labyrinth intact, but with her two other sources of power strangely
muted. In her former life as Genvissa, Swanne had been the powerful
MagaLlan, or high priestess to the goddess Mag, commanding great powers
of magic that she drew from the goddess herself. In this life her powers as
MagaLlan were virtually nonexistent. This had not surprised Swanne. Mag
was all but dead, clinging to life only in the dim recesses of Caela's womb
(and, as a virgin, Caela would have provided the goddess of fertility and
motherhood with no power at all) and the ancient power of the land that
Swanne had known as Genvissa was hidden under a heavy cloak of time and
forgetfulness. There was no source of power for a MagaLlan, and Swanne
spent no time weeping over what she had lost.

What did frighten Swanne was that the dark power of the heart of the
labyrinth, which she'd inherited from her foremothers, and which Ariadne
had won from Asterion, was all but gone as well. Why? Was that Asterion's
malicious hand? Or because her mother in this life had been but an ordinary
woman, and Swanne had needed the direct blood link from a mother who
wielded the darkcraft in order to wield it herself? She didn't know, and that
frustrated and frightened her.

Her power as Mistress of the Labyrinth should be all that she needed, but
Swanne had wanted the darkcraft as well. Badly.

If she had it now, perhaps she'd have more of an idea of what was happening about her. She would certainly have more hope of influencing and directing it.

Whatever power she did or did not command, Swanne had managed enough of it to be able to recognize the faint trace of Mag within Caela's womb.

Today, even that faint trace was gone.

Its absence could have been attributable to a number of causes: Mag had simply faded away completely, Swanne had perhaps lost touch with enough of her own remaining power to lose contact with Mag, something, or someone else had destroyed Mag within Caela's womb.

Swanne knew it was the latter. Caela had been attacked yesterday, and whatever faint trace of Mag remained had been deliberately murdered.

And there was only one person who had the power to accomplish that *and* had possible reason to want to accomplish Mag's death.

Asterion.

Swanne stared out at the gray waters of the Thames. It was a cold, blustery day with sheets of rain driving in from the northeast at periodic intervals. Winter was not far away.

"Why?" Swanne whispered. "Why?"

Why would Asterion want that final, helpless remnant of Mag dead? Swanne well knew of the previous life's alliance between Mag and Asterion, using Cornelia to destroy Genvissa and stop the completion of the Game. Swanne could also understand why Asterion might want to tidy up loose ends; if nothing else, the Minotaur was a methodical creature, and he most certainly needed neither Mag's nor Caela's, all but useless, hand.

So why not kill Caela and dispose of both of them at the same time? Why leave Caela alive?

Why go to all the trouble of removing Mag in such a spectacular fashion when he could just as easily have murdered Caela and left no loose ends at all?

What are you up to, Asterion? Swanne thought. To be honest, Swanne had no idea why even *she* was alive. Asterion wanted to destroy the Game. If that was all he wanted, then that was easily enough accomplished.

Kill her. Kill the Mistress of the Labyrinth. If there was no Mistress of the Labyrinth, there was no Game. As simple as that.

Or kill William, Brutus-reborn. If there was no Kingman, then there was no Game.

What was happening that she couldn't understand? Swanne's frown deepened, and she chewed her lower lip as her thoughts tumbled over and over. The Game had changed, she could feel that herself. Even incomplete, was it a danger to Asterion? Did he fear to be trapped by it, even though she and Brutus-reborn hadn't managed the final Dance? Was the only way Aster-ion could destroy the Game completely was to use either her or William?

"The bands," she muttered, keeping her face turned full to the window so that none of the passersby could see her mumbling to herself. "It must be Brutus' kingship bands. Asterion needs those, either to destroy them, or to use them to destroy the Game. Dammit, Brutus, *where did you hide them? Where?*"

Suddenly irritated beyond measure by her inaction, Swanne abruptly turned away from the window and walked, as fast as possible without attract-ing undue attention, down the stairs, through the Great Hall and back to the quarters she shared with Harold.

She could put to good use the free time Harold had given her by his spending the morning mooning over his sister's sickbed.

HAROLD LISTENED TO THE SOUND OF HIS WIFE'S footsteps fading away. *Gods, had she seen what was going on?* Another moment or two and Harold had been sure he would have thrown all caution to the wind and taken his sister there and then.

What a fine sight that would have been for Swanne, had she been a few moments later. Her husband squirming frantically atop his own sister's body. It would have cost him everything.

It would have cost Caela more.

For the first time in his life, Harold cursed the high birth of himself and his sister. If they had been lowly peasants, they could have simply moved to a far distant village, and lived as man and wife.

But the earl of Wessex could not just abscond with the queen . . .

"Harold? What did Swanne mean? 'He has made his first move.'" Caela was looking at him with a puzzled face.

Harold pulled his thoughts back into order. *Where had his self-control gone?* "Do not ask me to interpret what she means, Caela, for I cannot!"

"Sometimes she makes me feel as though she carries about with her such a great secret that could destroy all our lives," Caela said. "Sometimes when she looks at me . . . ah!" She gave a small smile. "I do not know what to make of your wife, Harold."

"Nor I, indeed," he said, then paused. "She envies you, I think. She thinks she would do better wearing the crown herself."

Caela studied him silently for a moment. "And will she wear it, Harold?"

Harold took Caela's hand between both of his, using the excuse to drop his eyes away from her scrutiny. *By all the gods, what did she mean with that ques-tion?* He rubbed at the back of her hand with his thumbs, gently, caressingly, deciding to take Caela's question at face value, and using the time it bought him to think over all the issues it raised.

Ah, the throne. Edward was an old man, likely to die within the next few years, and still he had to name a successor. In theory, the members of the witan elected a new king, but in practice whoever was named by the former king had a powerful claim.

Edward was driving his witan, and well most of the Anglo-Saxon nobles in England, into despair over the issue. It was stunningly important that he name a successor, if only because there were so many men who wished to claim the throne: not merely Harold, who had the strongest claim, but the Danes, the Norwegians, the Normans, the French . . . half of Europe, come to that, entertained ambitions to add the English throne to what they already held. If Edward continued to prevaricate then he risked tumbling England into chaos on his death.

Caela watched Harold's face, knowing what he was thinking. "You are the only one who can take the throne, Harold. Even Edward must know that."

Harold snorted softly. "And has Edward actually *spoken* to you of this?"

"Does Edward speak to me of the succession?" Caela laughed softly, bitterly. "Nay, of course he does not. He has 'spoken' only with his body, keeping it from me, that I may not breed him a Godwineson as his heir."

For an instant Harold entertained the vision of Edward making love to Caela, and his heart almost went cold in horror. "Then he is a fool. Better, surely, that a child of his own body take the throne than risk the slaughter of half of England as rival princes fight it out."

There was a lengthy silence, neither looking at the other, which was finally broken by Caela.

"I have not seen Tostig," she said, "yet I know he lingers about Westminster. Have you . . ." her voice drifted off at the expression on Harold's face.

"We have fought," he said, "and now Tostig wastes his time in sulks. I wish that he put aside his disagreement with me long enough to wish you well."

"Over what have you disagreed?"

"Tostig wants me to send my army north to subdue Northumbria to his wishes. I refused . . . I cannot afford to waste men and arms in the north when I may need them here."

"Tostig has not done well this past year," Caela said. "If only . . ."

"Yes," Harold said. "If only, indeed."

She squeezed his hand. "All will be well, Harold. Surely. You are brothers, and disagreements will be set aside soon enough."

"Brothers can be enemies as well as any other men, Caela. I pray only that we can resolve our differences before Edward dies."

"And what," Caela said, determined to change the subject yet again, "have you heard of William?"

Harold sighed, and sat back, letting Caela's hand drop to the coverlet. Tostig was a trifling threat when compared to William of Normandy. Not only was William a seasoned warrior with a seasoned army behind him (he'd spent over twenty-five years battling half of Europe to keep Normandy, and he could just as easily turn that army on England), but he also had a claim to the throne. Edward's mother, Emma, was a Norman woman, and close kin to William; close enough that William might make a claim through her blood. It wasn't much of a claim, but it was there, *and* it was strengthened by the fact that during his many years in exile (necessitated by the Danish Cnut's seizure of the throne on the death of Edward's father) Edward had formed strong bonds with William and had spent many years an honored guest in the Norman court. Some men rumored that in his gratitude Edward had promised England to William on Edward's death—and if Edward would not lay with Caela, then this was the reason: he did not want to breed an heir that would break his vow to William.

Personally, Harold did not believe it. No man, surely, could hand over a throne in gratitude for some bread and wine and a bed for a few years.

Could he? Harold shook his head very slightly. Edward was fool enough for anything, and who knew what he might have promised William one drunken night when Edward might have thought he'd never regain the English throne from Cnut?

"Edward has never said anything?" he said to Caela.

Caela shook her head. "I know only that they exchange letters."

Harold grunted. "William is preparing the ground to claim that Edward has always wanted him as heir."

"Edward is preparing that ground," Caela said, "with the Normans he keeps at court."

Harold said nothing. God knows Edward had brought enough of Normandy back with him when he'd finally managed to regain the throne on Cnut's death, and the bonds between Edward and William had been strengthened with further treaties over the years.

Had any of those treaties encompassed a promise that William could have the throne after Edward's death? No one knew, least of all Harold, and that lack of knowledge kept him awake many hours into too many nights.

Harold wanted the throne. Moreover, he felt that he deserved it. He alone had kept Edward safe from internal disputes and the ambitions of the Saxon earls. He alone had the moral and military strength behind him to not only take the throne, but to hold it once Edward died.

He was the only choice, the only *Saxon* choice, unless England decided it wanted a foreigner.

Or, if a foreigner decided he wanted England.

Now, as Edward declined into old age, and as it became obvious that he would never consent to get an heir on Caela, the issue of who was to succeed him was becoming ever more critical.

"If I take the throne," Harold said, reverting to Caela's original question, "Swanne will not be my queen."

Caela arched an eyebrow, but there was a strange relief in her eyes.

"Once, perhaps, I would have fought to the death to have her crowned at my side."

He paused, and Caela did not speak.

"Once," Harold finally continued. "Not now. She and I have grown apart in these past few years. Strangers, almost."

"Then that must explain the birth of your sixth child and third son last year."

Harold took a moment to respond to that. "She has ceased to please me, even in bed," he finally said. "We rarely touch . . . and even when we do, I find myself thinking of . . ."

He stopped suddenly, unable to say that *you.*

A silence where both avoided each others' eyes, then Harold resumed. "Swanne cannot be my queen, even should I wish it. We were wed under Danelaw, not Christian, and the Church does not recognize our union. England is too Christian a realm now to try and flout their laws. If I am to be crowned, then I cannot afford to alienate a church which must anoint my right to that throne."

"You will put her aside?" Caela looked incredulous, as if she could not believe for a moment that Swanne would be content to be "put aside."

"If I am to be accepted by the Church . . . if my claim to the throne is to be *backed* by the Church, then, yes, I must put her aside."

"She knows this?"

"We have not spoken of it but, yes, I think she knows of it." He made a harsh sound in his throat. "It would certainly explain her growing distance and coldness this past year and more."

Caela thought for a moment, then said, "And who will you take for a wife? For your queen?"

The instant she spoke, the awkwardness again rose between them.

"That was a foolish thing for me to ask," she said, "considering how stupidly I behaved earlier."

"There could never be a better queen for this country than you," Harold said.

"I shall find you a queen," Caela said, her voice forced. "A good woman, and worthy of you."

Harold reached out a hand and touched her mouth briefly with his finger-tips.

"I will honor whomever you choose," he said softly, "but never so much as I honor you." He hesitated. "If I thought for an instant that I could take the throne *and* flout Church law," he said very softly, holding her eyes, "then I would ensure my grip on the throne by marrying my predecessor's widow."

And with that, and before Caela could find breath enough to reply, he rose from the bed and left.

CHAPTER FOURTEEN

ACH YEAR LONDON HELD A CELEBRATION TO MARK the (hopefully) successful conclusion of the harvest. It was held in conjunction with the more important autumn hiring and poultry fairs, with the city guilds, the merchants, and the folk of at least a dozen of the outlying villages. This festival was held on a Saturday (the preceding three days being taken up with the market fairs), and was one of the few occasions in the year when the city came to an almost complete standstill for the celebrations. In the morning the guilds held a great parade through the streets of London, and in the afternoons virtually the entire city repaired for games, competitions, and general revelry to the great fields of Smithfield northwest of the city, just beyond the ancient walls.

Edward and Caela, as most of the court, usually attended the afternoon's festivities at Smithfield. It was a good chance for the king to display himself (and his wealth and power and might) to the general public, and to make generous offerings of prizes to those who won the games. All in all, the day was generally one of lighthearted fun and competition and, so long as the weather held clear and the crowd didn't become too raucous with the overabundant supply of ale and beer, Caela generally enjoyed herself immensely.

This year promised even greater enjoyment.

The night before the festival, Edward had succumbed to a black headache. He'd retired to his bed, and demanded that he be left alone, save for two monks who were to sit in a corner and recite psalms. Saeweald had given him a broth and applied a poultice that had eased the king's aching head somewhat, but when Saturday dawned, and Edward's head still throbbed uncomfortably and his belly threatened to spew forth with every movement, the king decided to forgo the fun of Smithfield for the continued stillness and peace of his bedchamber.

The queen should still attend, Harold escorting her—this was, indeed, a true indication of just how deeply Edward's aching head had disturbed his state of mind. To make matters even better for Caela (and for Harold), Swanne decided to remain behind as well, vaguely stating some indisposition, which she felt would only be exacerbated by the noise and frivolity of Smithfield.

Thus it was that, two hours past noon, Caela found herself seated with Harold in a great temporary wooden stand on the north side of Smithfield. In truth, she also should perhaps have remained behind, her collapse in court only being but ten days previous . . . but she declared that nothing could keep her from attending, and the sheer joy she felt escaping the confines of Westminster showed in her bright eyes, her constantly smiling mouth, and in every movement.

She was dressed splendidly in a deep ruby silken surcoat embroidered all over with golden English dragons, a matching golden veil, and a jeweled crown. Beside her, Harold had dressed somewhat similarly, if in bright sky blue rather than ruby. His surcoat was also embroidered with English dragons, although his beasts snarled and struck out with their talons while Caela's merely scampered playfully. Harold wore a golden circlet on his brow, gold-encrusted embroidery weighting down the tight-fitting lower sleeves of his linen undertunic, heavy jeweled rings on his fingers and, to remind everyone of his exploits and renown as a warrior, a great sword hanging at his hip. He looked the king as Edward never had: vital, healthy, handsome, powerful, and the crowd gathered in Smithfield roared in acclaim when he and Caela took their places.

They stood to receive the cheers, waving and smiling, and the breeze caught at Caela's veil and blew it back from her face.

"They adore you," Harold said, softly.

"They adore *you*," she responded, turning to laugh at him.

The crowd continued to roar, and as the sound pounded over them in wave after wave, Harold took Caela's hand and held her eyes. "I meant what I said to you, that day I came to you in your bedchamber," he said, his voice only loud enough that she could hear him. "There could be no better queen for me than you. No woman I could want more."

The laughter died from her face. "Harold . . ."

"I know," he said. "I know. But I needed to say that. Just once." His face lightened away from its seriousness. "And what better place than here, and now, when perhaps we can pretend?"

"Harold, it can't be."

"Of course not," he said, and leaned forward and kissed her cheek, where perhaps his lips lingered a moment longer than they should and where, as he finally moved his face away, too slowly, she felt the soft momentary graze of his tongue.

"Unfortunately," he finished, and then the sound was fading away, and they sat, and Caela used the excuse of settling her skirts to hide her pinked cheeks from her brother.

Behind and to one side of them, Judith and Saeweald exchanged a worried glance.

THE AFTERNOON WAS FILLED WITH GOOD-NATURED sport and competitions. Men wrestled, ran, leaped and shot arrows into distant targets. To each winner, Caela graciously gave a prize: a carved box here, a fine linen shirt there, a copper ring to someone else. Each time she rose, and the successful sweating combatant knelt down before her, the crowd cheered, and called good-natured jests, and when Caela had done with handing the victor his gift, then she smiled, and waved and patently reveled in the good cheer of the day.

The final event was something the city guilds and fathers had spent weeks planning. It was a new contest, one designed not only to demonstrate the grace and athletic abilities of its participants, but also to delight and astound the crowd.

A man, clothed only in trousers, strode into the center of the arena, beating a drum that hung from a cord about his neck. He was a fine man, tall and well-muscled, and had been the winner of two of the earlier events. He walked to a spot some ten paces before the stand in which Caela, Harold, and their attendants sat and, still beating the drum, cried: "Behold!"

At his word two lines of horsemen entered the arena from opposite gates. They rode bareback, the horses controled only with bridles through which had been threaded late autumn greenery, while the riders themselves wore only trousers, leaving their shoulders and chests bare. Each man carried a long wooden lance, tipped with iron. Each line was headed by a rider dressed slightly more elaborately than those he led. At the head of one line rode a man wearing a chain mail tunic and Saxon helmet. He carried a bow, fitted with an arrow.

At the head of the other line rode a man wearing nothing but a snowy white waist cloth, sandals on otherwise muscular brown bare legs, and a great bronze helmet, of a design and shape that was not only unfamiliar but markedly exotic. A plait of very black, oiled hair protruded from beneath the helmet, and hung halfway down the man's back. About his biceps and upper forearms twined lengths of scarlet ribbon, as about his legs, just below his knees. This man carried a sword.

Caela frowned, leaning forward slightly. "What event is this?" she asked softly, but to her side Harold only shrugged, and no one else had a response.

The man beating the drum waited until all the riders were in the arena, the lines pulled to a halt on opposite sides of the great square, then he abruptly gave a flurry of much louder and more insistent beats, then his hands fell still.

"Behold," he cried. "The Troy Game!"

The crowd roared, intrigued at the display thus far and at the novelty of the event. Judith and Saeweald went rigid with shock. Harold grinned, anticipating some military game that might well prove entertaining, while Caela's frown merely deepened.

"The Troy Game," she whispered to herself, and shivered.

"Behold!" cried the man with the drum once more. "Listen well to the rules of the Game! Two lines, two ambitions, two corps of riders skilled beyond compare. Two kings! One the king of the Greeks," he indicated the man wearing the chain mail and the Saxon helmet, "and one the monarch of that ancient, wondrous realm—Troy!" and he indicated the beribboned warrior wearing the bronze helmet and the simple linen waist cloth.

The crowd roared again. History pageants and games of all sorts were always popular.

The king of the Greeks kicked his horse forward a few paces, as did the king of Troy. They raised their arms above their heads, flexing their biceps, then shook their fists, each at the other.

"What can we do?" whispered Judith, her face drained of all color.

"Nothing, but watch and see," said Saeweald. He was watching the king of Troy, and his eyes narrowed.

"We propose a dance!" cried the drummer. "He who is quickest and most agile, he who is most skilled shall win. He who falls first . . . *loses!*"

Again the crowd roared in anticipation.

As the drummer ran to safety, the two lines of horsemen began to move. First at a walk, then a trot, then at a carefully controled canter the lines of horsemen moved into an intricate and dangerous dance, the two lines first interweaving as they each crossed the arena on opposite diagonals, then in a dozen different points as the lines performed circles and serpentines.

As the horses cantered, their paces carefully measured, the riders swung their lances in great arcs from side to side: at all the intersecting points where the opposing lines crossed there was only ever a half a breath between the flashing down of one lance and the passage of another rider. A single misstep, a minor miscalculation, and the wicked blade, which tipped the end of one lance, might cut another rider in half.

The drummer had climbed atop the fence, which kept the crowd safe from the riders, and was now speaking again, calling out over the riders with a clear, carrying voice. He was minus his drum now, the thud of the horses' hooves and the wicked swishing of the swinging lances the only accompaniment he needed.

"See!" he cried. "The Trojan king re-creates the walls of Troy—seven walls, seven circuits to defeat the Greeks! Will the Greek king defeat him? Will he penetrate the labyrinth of Troy's defense?"

Harold was leaning forward now, his eyes gleaming. "By God!" he said. "See their skill!"

Caela was staring at the performance before her, her face expressionless, her hands carefully folded and very still in her lap.

The two leaders, the "kings," controlled the tempo of the dangerous dance. It was they who sped up, or slowed down the rhythm of their followers, and each had to keep a wary eye on the other. If one slowed down too soon, or too late, or if one did not take speedy note of what the other commanded, then his line of warriors would be broken by the lances of his foe. The two lines of riders were now interweaving at an impossible pace, the tips of their lances gleaming in the sun, sweat dripping from shoulders, horses snorting as they fought both for balance and for breath.

The crowd had begun to scream for their favorites. "Greece! Greece!" or "Troy! Troy!" and, among the acclaim, it was most apparent that the screams for Troy were the loudest.

Then, as it appeared that the speed of the dance could not possibly grow faster, or the swinging of the lances more dangerous, there came a surprised grunt from one quadrant of the arena as a horse, turned too tight, lost its balance and collapsed, throwing its rider under the flashing hooves of those who came behind.

Instantly there was mayhem. Horses and riders collided everywhere, the rhythm of the dance was entirely lost, and the crowd began to shriek in appreciation as the blood spattered through the air.

Then, stunningly, from out of the melee, came one line of riders still in perfect formation, their lances still flashing back and forth in a controlled manner, their riders untouched, save for their sweat.

It was the line led by the Trojan king.

They cantered in a line across the back of the arena, their foes lying mostly unhorsed and bleeding in the center of the arena, then all turned in one beautifully coordinated movement so that they faced into the arena, looking toward the royal stand at the far end.

The Trojan king raised his sword, then pointed it toward the stand. The line exploded forward as the horses, still perfectly in line, galloped toward the royal stand.

As they met the confusion in the center of the arena, each horse leapt in perfect alignment with its neighbors so that for an instant, the entire line was suspended high in the air, then every horse thudded back to earth, their vanquished foes safely behind them, and galloped to the end of the arena beneath the royal stand, where their leader brought them to a stunning, perfectly controlled halt.

Harold leapt to his feet, shouting, punching his fist into the air, applauding the victor.

Caela sat, still motionless, expressionless, staring at the Trojan king, now sitting on his horse directly before her.

The man's chest heaved as he fought to get air into his lungs, his face was mostly hidden by his helmet—but still nothing could hide his great toothy smile.

"My lady," he cried, brandishing his sword. "I hand you Troy!"

CHAPTER FIFTEEN

CAELA SPEAKS

STARED, GAPE-MOUTHED. I HAVE NO IDEA WHAT had come over me. I felt disembodied, dislocated, disorientated. "Climb up!" cried Harold beside me, and I swear I leapt almost a foot, he surprised me so. "Climb up and accept your prize!"

At least he'd broken the trance that had claimed me. I managed to look at Harold: he was bright-eyed and flushed, flashing a brilliant smile.

"By God, Caela," Harold said to me as the Trojan king was clattering up the wooden steps that led to the small platform before our seats, "never before have I seen such skill! Such horsemanship!"

And then the man was with us, his heat and his sweat and the powerful presence of his body commanding my attention. He stood before us, and bowed deeply.

"You honor us, sir," said Harold. "May we know your face? Your name?"

That great toothy grin flashed again in the darkness behind the helmet, and the man lifted both his hands to his helmet (his sword already taken by one of Harold's men-at-arms) and raised it from his head.

I must confess, my heart was racing. *Who was it?*

"A stranger to our shores, by your countenance," Harold said. "Who are you, and your allegiance?"

For the moment the man did not reply. He was staring at me, and I at him. The instant he'd taken the helmet from his head I felt overwhelmed by a strange disappointment. His face was familiar—

Almost the face of the man who had come to me in dream, and who had almost but not quite kissed me.

—and yet not. Not the face some part of me seemed to have been expecting.

Oh, but he was handsome! He had dark skin and very black hair. Very long, very curly. Regular, strong features . . . and that smile, it was stunning. The only discordant note in his entire aspect was the leather patch over his left eye, yet even that lent him a rakish air that moderated his otherwise over-powering presence.

"I am Silvius," said the man, replying to Harold but not taking his eyes from me. "And I am truly king of Troy. My allegiance? Why, that belongs to your lady here, to the queen, my heart."

And he lifted his hand, took mine, and kissed it before any could move to stop him.

Harold laughed, but the laughter held a trace of tenseness in it now, and, glancing at him, I saw that his smile had died.

"Well, then," he said, "welcome, king of Troy. I admit myself envious of your military skills."

Now this man Silvius did look at Harold. "Oh, I have had many years in which to hone them, my lord. Very many indeed."

"Your prize, good man," I said, collecting myself. I turned, ready to take the gift of a finely woven and embroidered mantle from Judith, who stood behind me (and, by heaven, *she* was staring at this strange king of Troy as if she were trapped by his masculinity as well!), but before I could lay hold to it, Silvius spoke again.

"Nay, my lady. Lay that aside, I beg you. It is *I* who shall gift the prize, *I* who shall award the honor."

"A *most* strange man," said Harold, watching Silvius warily.

I noticed that several men-at-arms had moved quietly closer.

Silvius reached into his helmet, then withdrew from it the most beautifully worked bracelet that I think I have ever seen. *(And yet some part of me insisted that I had seen it previously.)* It was of twisted gold, and set with a score of cut rubies.

"In my world," said Silvius, his voice now very soft, "it belonged to a princess and a great queen. It deserves no better home now than on your arm, gracious lady."

He reached forward, then stopped as both Harold and the men-at-arms laid hands to their swords. The mood was now very tense among us, and I wondered at that, at what had changed between us that Harold should now be so wary.

"Madam," Judith said very softly behind me, and in that word she some-how managed to convey both reassurance and the message that I should, indeed, accept the gift.

"Ah," I said, smiling a little too brightly at Harold, "put away your sword, brother. Shall this bracelet bite? Shall it sting? Nay, of course not."

Then, to Silvius. "This is most gracious of you, and I shall not be so churlish as to refuse." I held out my left hand, stretching it slightly so that the sleeve drew back from my wrist.

Silvius reached it forth and, just before he snapped it closed about my wrist, he said, "It is very ancient, my lady, and contains many memories."

It clicked shut, its metal cold about the heat of my skin, and I blinked, and looked at Silvius.

And saw before me, not Silvius, but a man very much like him but with, if possible, an even more powerful presence, and whose face made my stomach clench.

It was the man from my dream, save with long hair and dressed as Silvius was now dressed.

And with great golden bands about his limbs where Silvius wore scarlet wool.

Then the man who was not Silvius spoke, and he said: "I am Brutus, and I am god-favored. It is not wise to deny me." He smiled, holding my eyes, and it was one of the coldest expressions I have ever seen. "I control Mesopotama. I control this palace. I control you. Be wise. Do not deny me."

"Brutus?" I whispered.

And then I fainted.

I HAVE ONLY JUDITH AND HAROLD'S RELATION TO SAY what happened next. Harold and Judith both grabbed at me, and the men-at-arms lunged forth, sure that the strange man Silvius had somehow murdered me.

In the confusion, apparently he slipped away. Harold sent men after him, but he was never discovered. When Harold questioned the guildsmen who had taken part in the strange event, they shrugged and said that he was a foreign merchant who had seemed perfect for the role as king of Troy, but when asked to remember his name and country, they blinked, and each recounted a different name and origin.

The man Silvius was never found.

I woke after only a few moments, seemingly well, and Harold calmed down once he saw me smiling and apologizing for the fuss. I lifted my arm, and studied the bracelet. It *was* beautiful, and the stones glittered in the late afternoon sunshine, and so I decided that it would do me no harm to wear it an hour or two longer.

So, as the crowds dispersed, Harold and I and our retinue made our way back to Westminster. There I repaired to bed, claiming a headache myself, and taking a smaller chamber next to Edward's to sleep in so that I should not disturb him.

I left the bracelet on as I slept. I do not know why, but perhaps it was that which caused me again to dream strangely.

* * *

I walked through the great stone hall in which I'd found myself previously.

And there, as if waiting for me, was this man called Silvius.

He stepped forward and, as if the most natural thing in the world, kissed me hard on the mouth.

I wondered if this were my frustrated virginity causing me to dream of all these men who kissed me.

"You and I," he said, "shall be greater friends than you can possibly realize."

Then he was gone, and I slipped out of the stone hall and back into dreamlessness.

In the morning, as she aided me to dress, Judith said, "Madam . . . are you well?"

I frowned, because I felt there was much more to her question than her bold words. "Of course I am, Judith. Now, watch what you do with that sleeve, it is all twisted."

Much later, at court (Edward having risen, his ache dissipated), I saw Judith lean close to Saeweald. He asked a question, glancing at me, and she shook her head, as if imparting news of the greatest sorrow.

I do not know the import of that question, but Judith's answer made Saeweald frown, and sigh, then turn away, and I had to fight down an unwarranted irritation at their behavior.

CHAPTER SIXTEEN

AROLD HAD KEPT LATE HOURS WITH SEVERAL OF his thegns, returning to his bedchamber when Swanne was already asleep, so it was that she only heard of what had happened at Smithfield the next morning.

Harold, imparting the news as if it were of not much interest to her, was stunned by her reaction.

In all his years of intimacy with Swanne, he'd never seen her so shocked that she could barely speak.

"They played *what*?" she said, her voice barely above a whisper.

Harold watched her carefully, trying to discern the reason behind her shock. "The Troy Game. It was one of the most skillful displays of horsemanship I have ever seen."

"Describe it," she said.

"Two lines of riders, each executing a series of twists and turns that intersected and interwove." He paused, thinking. "Labyrinthianlike, truly."

Swanne paled, but Harold kept on speaking. "The Trojan king, who led one of the lines, and was the ultimate victor, re-created the walls of Troy with his dance—seven walls, seven circuits. It was up to the Greek king, who led the opposing line, to defeat him." He gave a small shrug. "But Troy won out. Its circuits held against the Greeks, who were left trampled in disarray in the dust. Swanne? Why does this intrigue you so greatly?"

She gave a light laugh, but Harold could see the effort it cost her. "It is not something I could ever imagine the common guildsmen re-creating, my love. The legend of Troy? Why, who among the commoners of London's back alleyways have ever heard of it?"

"Many, my lady," said Hawise, who had just entered the chamber to see to the bed linens.

Swanne, who had literally jumped when Hawise spoke, now regarded her with a frown. "Many? Explain yourself, Hawise."

The woman licked her lips, wondering if she had spoken out of turn.

"Hawise?" said Harold, curious himself.

"The story of Troy is retold many a night about kitchen hearths, my lady," Hawise said. "How the Trojans escaped the destruction of their wondrous city, and fled here to ancient Britain, led by a man named Brutus. Why," Hawise smiled, finally relaxing as she realized she had the undivided attention of both Swanne and Harold, "is it not true that London itself was founded by Brutus?"

There was a silence, during which Swanne continued to stare at Hawise and Harold looked at Swanne.

Then Swanne smiled, an expression that seemed to Harold to be one of the few genuine smiles he had ever seen her give, and touched Hawise gently on the cheek.

"So it is said," Swanne said softly. "And so it may be. And do the Londoners say anything else about the Troy Game?"

"Oh," said Hawise, "it is but a foolish game, my lady. Children have played it in the streets for years, dancing a pretty pattern across the flagstones outside St. Paul's, claiming that whoever steps on the lines first shall be eaten alive by a monster from hell."

"And that is what the horse game of yesterday was based on, Hawise?" Harold said.

"Aye, my lord. One of the guildsmen was watching his daughters dancing out their childish game across the flagstones when he thought that perhaps their play could be modified and made into a far more spectacular sport."

"Well," said Harold wryly, turning away to pick up his over-mantle, "it surely was that."

WHEN, MUCH LATER, SHE MANAGED TO FIND SOME quiet time to herself in the palace orchard, closely wrapped in a heavy woolen cloak, Swanne finally allowed herself to take a deep breath and think on what she had heard.

The Londoners were playing the Troy Game?

Whether children or skilled horsemen mattered not . . . *they were playing the Troy Game?*

Oh, it was not the Game that she and William would control, but it was clearly a derivative of it. It would not command the magic and power of the Game she and William would play, but it was surely a memory of it.

How had they known? How had this come to be?

There were many possibilities, the least unsettling of which was that the Trojans of Troia Nova had passed the Dance of the Torches (that they had witnessed her and Brutus dancing) down to their children. The story of the Troy Game may well have survived the generations between that day Brutus alighted on the shores of Llangarlia and now, even if the city and surrounding country had been ravaged so many times, and so mercilessly. It took only one person to remember the tales, and to speak them, for a memory to become a permanent myth.

And yet what Harold had described, and then what Hawise had said about the children's games, was too accurate to be "myth." The horsed game had been devised by an expert, someone who had known the Game intimately.

Or . . . Swanne took another deep breath . . . or the entire event had somehow been arranged by the Game itself.

Was the Game seeping up through the very foundations of London? Was it making London, and its inhabitants, its very own?

For years, ever since she had come to London, Swanne had felt that the Game had changed, become more aware.

But *this* aware? Gods, that was terrifying. What if it refused to allow her and William control over it?

Swanne gave a small, disbelieving laugh. What if the Game decided it would rather have some dirt-smudged child from London's backstreets to dance it to a conclusion?

"My lady?"

Swanne jumped again, some stray disassociated part of her mind thinking that she truly needed to ask Saeweald for some herbal potion to calm her nerves.

It was Aldred, the archbishop of York.

"My lady," he said, grunting with effort as he sat on the bench beside her. "I do hope I am not disturbing you. It is just that I saw you sitting alone in the orchard while I was taking my afternoon stroll, and I thought to pass a few words."

Taking my afternoon stroll, indeed! thought Swanne. *I have never before seen you walk farther than from one banqueting table to the next.*

"I was thinking," she said, "about that spectacular horsed game the Londoners put on yesterday in Smithfield. Harold seemed quite taken with the skills evidenced."

"Ah, yes," Aldred said, tweaking at a corner of his robe where it had become uncomfortably stuck under his bulk. "I have heard tell of that extravagance myself."

"You were not there?"

"Alas, no, my lady. I thought it better to stay close to our beloved king, should he need me."

Thought it better to stay close so that you could insinuate yourself even further into his graces, she thought.

"Aldred," Swanne said slowly. "I may have another letter for you to pass on within the day. You will be able to arrange . . . ?"

"I shall be able to expedite its delivery, my lady, with all speed."

She inclined her head. "I do thank you, my good archbishop."

He beamed, and patted her knee, which made Swanne wince.

ANOTHER MEETING TOOK PLACE IN THE ORCHARD that afternoon, but an hour or two after Swanne and Aldred had abandoned the trees.

Tostig was walking through the orchard on his way from his own quarters to Edward's palace when he heard the sound of a footfall behind him.

Stopping, and both turning about and drawing his dagger in one fluid movement, Tostig saw that two men approached, one of whom he recognized as that man who had talked to him as he'd left the Great Hall after Caela's sudden illness.

"My lord," both the men said, and bowed as one.

Tostig's hand had not left his dagger.

"What is it you wish?" he said.

"To talk only, my lord," said the first of the men. Both of them were fair, but this man's hair and beard were fair to the point of whiteness, and even in the weak afternoon sun it shone brilliantly.

"I am Halldorr Olafson," said the man, "and this is my companion Örn Bollason. Because we want you to trust us, and believe in us, we give you our true names, and not those we go under while at Edward's court."

Tostig narrowed his eyes. His hand had not strayed from the haft of his dagger. "You are Hardrada's men," he said. He'd heard that the Norwegian king had agents within Edward's court . . . but what were they doing approaching him?

"We mean you no harm," said Bollason. "Indeed, we speak with Hardrada's voice. Our words are his, and spoken with his authority."

"And they are . . . ?" said Tostig.

"Hardrada wants England," said Olafson. "He would like you to aid him."

Tostig snorted, and half turned to walk away.

"In return," said Bollason, "he will give you all of the north. Not just Northumbria, but *all* of the north."

Tostig stopped, although he did not look at the two men.

"Hardrada is a fair man," said Olafson. "He does not need it all. He has asked us to treaty with you. If you pave the way for Hardrada's successful ascension to the English throne after Edward's death . . ."

"Then I get the north?" said Tostig, turning back to stare searchingly at each of the two men who faced him. "And the means by which to hold it?"

"And the means by which to hold it."

"Talk on," said Tostig, and his hand fell away from his dagger.

While they talked, all three men noticed the round-shouldered woman walking through the orchard ten or fifteen paces to their left carrying a wicker basket of late-fallen winter apples. They saw her, but they paid her no attention.

She was but a serving woman, scrounging the orchard for something to see her and her family through the long winter months.

They did not know that, instead of carrying the apples to where Damson kept her pitifully few belongings, she instead went straight to the river where, after a few moments waiting, a waterman poled his flat skiff to where she waited. Damson handed the basket to the waterman, then bent close for a hurried conversation.

The waterman nodded and then, as Damson walked away, continued on his journey down the Thames.

LATE THAT NIGHT, WHEN MOST OF LONDON AND Westminster slumbered, one of the standing stones atop Pen Hill shimmered, then changed into its ancient form. It was the senior among the Sidlesaghes, a creature who had once been a great poet, songster, lover, and humorist.

His name he had long forgotten, but he had grown used to the childish whims of the men and women who had peopled this island after he and his kind had taken to their stonelike watchfulness, and so this Sidlesaghe called himself Long Tom. As he walked, his every movement soft and fluid, Long Tom hummed to himself snatches of melody, the fingers of one hand occasionally snapping in time to the beat of his music.

The Sidlesaghe skirted London about its western wall, taking the road to Westminster. The Thames was on his left, and as he walked, the river rose up in strange, luminous, rolling waves as he passed, as if it were greeting him.

"Soon!" the Sidlesaghe whispered, and the river subsided.

Soon.

"Soon," the Sidlesaghe said again, and shivered in excitement.

Far beneath his feet, something rumbled and hissed, as if a great dragon was passing through a long-forgotten mine.

"One day," said the Sidlesaghe, "but not yet, not yet."

The beast beneath his feet fell still, and groaned.

Long Tom's pace picked up as he neared Westminster. There was someone he had to see, to touch, to make words with. A woman of darkness and long memory.

A woman who could bring him what he needed.

* * *

JUDITH HAD SPENT THE GREATER PART OF THE NIGHT
with Saeweald. Now, as dawn approached, she made her way swiftly and
silently from Saeweald's chambers back toward the palace. Locked in
thought—and her warm memories of the night past—Judith almost passed
out from fright when a long arm grabbed at her from the darkness.

Before she could shriek—and she'd drawn a huge breath to do just that—
a large, hard hand had enveloped half of her face.

"Peace, little lady," said the Sidlesaghe, drawing close. "It is only I."

The moment Judith saw the long, hook-nosed face with those strange,
watchful, melancholy eyes, Judith recognized it immediately for a Sidlesaghe.
She relaxed, not much, but enough, and the Sidlesaghe managed a small
smile and let her go.

"How may I aid you?" Judith said, not sure *what* she should say to the
Sidlesaghe, but deciding that question was as good as any.

"It is time for Caela," said the Sidlesaghe. "Time for her to remember."

"But the bracelet did no good."

"The bracelet?" The Sidlesaghe's face crinkled up into a hundred lines of
question.

"The ancient bracelet of Mesopotama, that which Silvius gave her yesterday."

"Silvius?"

"*Yes!* Silvius!"

"Silvius was out of the heart of the labyrinth?"

"Yes." Judith repressed a sigh. "At Smithfield yesterday."

Long Tom was looking increasingly puzzled.

"The Troy Game?" Judith said, hoping that would be enough to prod him
into remembering.

"Oh," the Sidlesaghe said, sighing hugely, then smiling. "Yes. That's why I
am here. Caela needs to take her place within the Game."

Now it was Judith who was confused. "I am sorry. I do not know how I
might aid you."

The Sidlesaghe leaned forward and enveloped both of her hands in his
large ones. "You already do more than enough," he said. "But seeing as you
offer . . . bring Caela to the banks of the Thames tomorrow night. By Tothill."

"At night? She will not come! How can I—"

He squeezed her hands. "That is for you to determine, my dear. Tomorrow
night, on the banks of the Thames. We have some midwiving to do."

Then he was gone, and Judith was left to stare into the night, feeling both
bewildered and blessed.

CHAPTER SEVENTEEN

M ADAM?" JUDITH LOOKED CAREFULLY AT HER
mistress. The evening was closing in, and she couldn't help a
quick, impatient look at the as-yet unshuttered windows in
the queen's chamber. Caela sat by the fire, some needlework in her hands, her
lovely face relaxed almost to the point of dreaminess. Twelve days after her
hemorrhage she looked rested and well, buoyed by good food, rest, and twice
daily visits both from Harold and from Saeweald who kept their voices and
words light, and made her laugh with every third remark. The outing to
Smithfield had also lifted Caela's spirits immensely, even though the outcome
was not quite what Judith and Saeweald had hoped.

"Madam?" Judith said again, trying to gain the attention of Caela who had
drifted away somewhere unknowable over her embroidery. Tonight Judith
somehow had to inveigle Caela down to the banks of the Thames.

Caela gave a slight start, then looked to Judith and smiled. "If you have
finished your duties," she said, "perhaps you would like to sit and aid me with
this embroidery. It is for the high altar in Westminster's new abbey, and I should
like it to be finished for the abbey's consecration."

"Madam . . . I had wondered . . ."

Caela gave up all pretense at her needlework, allowing it to slip to her lap
as she raised her face to Judith and laughed. "Am I keeping you from some
great pleasure, Judith?"

Judith blushed, more from her current state of tension than embarrassment.

Caela's smile died and she set her embroidery to one side. "What is it,
Judith?"

Judith abandoned caution and plunged straight into the lie. "Madam, your
brother Harold spoke to me earlier."

Caela raised an eyebrow, no more than mildly curious.

"He asked that I bring you to the banks of the Thames just below Tothill
tonight, when all is still and silent in the palace."

Caela's face retained its pleasant expression, but Judith could see the
incomprehension growing in her eyes.

"Your husband has decided to spend the night in prayer on his knees before the altar in the abbey, madam." Judith had told Saeweald and Ecub (visiting this day from her priory) about the visit from the Sidlesaghe. Edward's decision to spend all night in prayer was Saeweald's doing, although Judith had no idea how he'd managed it. Did he inform the king that if he prayed all night before the altar, his amulet against the arthritis would double its potency? Or was this just a sign of Edward's increasing piety? "He will not notice you gone."

"Judith—"

"Madam, Harold was most insistent."

Caela's brow creased, and she looked cross. "Judith, before heaven, what is Harold doing? Sneaking about like a mischievous child? A surreptitious midnight picnic by water's edge? *What is going on?*"

"Madam, *please*. I beg you, Harold needs you."

"Then why not beg me himself? Why ask through you?"

"It is about Swanne," Judith said, desperate now. "Swanne . . . Swanne is . . ."

"Ah . . . ," said Caela, and her posture relaxed very slightly. "Swanne is causing trouble." She furrowed her brow, thinking. "It must be that Swanne and . . . and Tostig, perhaps . . ."

"The palace has ears, madam." Judith had no idea quite what she meant by that, but it seemed to confirm something in Caela's mind.

"Yes." She nodded. "What chamber *is* safe in this palace, eh? I swear that Edward has paid ears against every door." Then Caela smiled, and it was the kind of smile that Judith had never seen her give: girlish, mischievous, uninhibited. Judith's breath caught in her throat. *Sweet gods, if ever she smiled that way upon a man. . . .*

Then Caela's smile faded. "But how can I leave the palace? I can have no excuse, and the fact of my leaving will surely reach Edward's ears long before dawn."

Judith allowed her shoulders to relax: she had not been aware how tense she had been. *Pray that Caela forgive her when she realizes the deception.* "I shall fetch you my third-best robe, and we shall drape a serving woman's hood and cloak about you, and none shall be the wiser."

THEY WAITED UNTIL WELL-PAST MIDNIGHT, THEN, heavily cloaked and veiled, made their way to one of the postern gates in the wall about Westminster (the guard long gone, persuaded away from his post by the gold of Saeweald's purse). From here Judith led Caela south along the river path toward a spot some hundred paces south of the palace complex where the southern branch of the Tyburn River joined with the Thames.

Perhaps some ten or fifteen paces ahead of them, waiting on a broad expanse of gravel laid bare by low tide, waited three cloaked figures.

"Who can be with Harold?" said Caela.

"Saeweald," said Judith. "See how he drags that leg?"

Caela nodded. One of the figures had moved slightly at their approach, and he did indeed drag his right leg in the manner of Saeweald.

"Saeweald!" Judith called softly as she and Caela approached. "Is that you?"

"Aye." Saeweald threw back the hood of his cloak. "Madam, you are well? We thank you for agreeing to come."

Caela peered at the smaller of the remaining figures, and it turned about, revealing Ecub.

"Mother Ecub," said Caela, "what do you here?"

Ecub bowed her head, a gesture of deep respect, and smiled, but she did not respond with words.

Caela stared at her, then looked to the final figure. Strange, for out here in the night Harold looked much taller than—

The other figure turned about, and as it did so, the cloak about its form faded as if it had never been, and Caela saw that it was—stunningly—the same creature that she had seen in her dream.

Long Tom.

"It is a Sidlesaghe, my dear," said Ecub, but Caela was staring at the creature in horror, taking a step backward.

"Caela," Saeweald said softly, hobbling forward a little. "Please, it is all right. You will be safe."

Caela shrunk back from him, her eyes riveted on the Sidlesaghe, standing with a strange, dark, watchful expression about two or three paces from her. His eyes, as dark as they were, seemed to reflect the small amount of moonlight, and they glittered at Caela eerily.

"What . . . is . . . this?" Caela said very slowly, enunciating every word very carefully. She shot Saeweald a look, and it was full of anger.

"Madam," Judith said, placing a hand on Caela's elbow.

"Don't touch me!" Caela hissed. Her eyes swung between Saeweald, Ecub, and Judith. *"What have you done?"*

Whatever they may have said was forestalled by the Sidlesaghe, who suddenly almost doubled over in a sweeping, elegant gesture of reverence.

"My lady," he said, "forgive the means by which these three delivered you to me."

Caela stared at the Sidlesaghe, her posture as tense as that of a startled deer. "What are you?" she said harshly.

The Sidlesaghe smiled, his teeth gleaming in the trickle of moonlight. "I am your welcomer," he said. "Do you not remember the last time I greeted you?"

For a moment Caela did not respond. Then she shook her head slowly.

"I am here once more," said the Sidlesaghe, "as is all my kind." He lifted one of his long-fingered hands and gestured.

Caela's eyes darted around her, and she gasped. Where a moment before had been empty graveled shoreline, now stood rank upon rank of creatures similar to the one that stood before her.

"We are all here," the Sidlesaghe, "to welcome you anew."

"Caela," said Saeweald, his tone pleading. "Please trust—"

"No," she said, and took another step backward. Then she glanced over her shoulder, as if ensuring her way were still open.

"It is time," said the Sidlesaghe, and, with a movement as quick and as fluid as that of the fox, darted forward and seized Caela.

She gave a half shriek, grabbing at the Sidlesaghe as if she meant to push it away, but the creature cradled her against his body, holding her almost as if she were a baby. Caela struggled, but caught in the Sidlesaghe's firm, loving grip, she could do nothing.

For an instant the Sidlesaghe stood, Caela in his arms close against his body, smiling at her as if she were his own much beloved child.

Then, stunningly, he lifted her high above his head and, as all the Sidlesaghes let out a long moan, tossed her into the river.

Caela hit the water with a frightful splash and almost instantly sank beneath its surface.

The final sight that Judith had of Caela was of her terrified white face, and then her extended arms and hands as, slowly, inevitably, she sank into the rolling gray waters.

chapter eighteen

CAELA SPEAKS

H, GODS, THE TOUCH OF THAT WATER!
Something ruptured within my head—the pain was excruciating, overwhelming, and within the space of a single breath that agony had become my entire existence.

I was terrified, but what of I cannot say. Not of the water, nor even of death (an activity I was undoubtedly engaged in, for the water flowed down my throat as I gasped and gulped, and some tiny part of me understood that it was filling my lungs), but of the fact that I was in the grip of something so powerful, so unknowable, that even death could not save me from it.

Death could not be an escape from it.

My head was on fire, the pain now beyond the excruciating, and I gave up even trying to stay afloat. I sank down through the waters—strangely deep for the shallows of the river—descending into an icy bleakness.

And still my head rang with agony.

I screamed, and river water surged down my throat.

Now my lungs felt as if they, too, were going to explode with the weight of the river within them and I gave myself over entirely to the water and the pain, and hoped only that they would have done with me as fast as they possibly could.

My last single coherent thought was that if Edward could see me now he would only nod his head knowingly, and turn his head to say to one of his ever-present sycophants: *I always knew the Devil was in her.*

The instant she gave up the struggle, tiny hands reached out for her, pulling her deeper and deeper, not so much into the river, although that was what encased them, but deeper into a realm that was unknowable to any who watched from above.

The water sprites waited until her body was cold and still, drifting lifeless in the current, and then they stripped her of all her clothing, leaving only the ruby and gold bracelet she wore about her wrist.

I blinked, and woke, and found myself lying curled into a tight ball on a cold stone floor, utterly naked and dripping wet. For the longest time I did not move. I just lay there, my arms hugging my knees to my chest (not quite naked, for I could feel a band of jewelry about my wrist that cut into the soft flesh just below one of my knees), blinking, not thinking, just *being*.

Then, very softly, the sound of a name being called. Was it my name? I did not think so, but then, lying there, I was not even sure of *what* my name was.

Then the faint sound of thrumming hooves, coming ever closer, and I raised myself on one elbow just as, at the very reaches of my vision, a white stag burst into the stone hall in which I lay.

He was huge, vital, brimming with power and sexuality and meaning, and he lifted his head and cried out, *trumpeted* out, tidings of such joy that I cried out myself, and raised myself to my knees.

The stag ran closer, closer, and I could feel his heat and feel his breath on me, and then I saw . . .

I saw . . .

I saw about his delicate, tightly muscled limbs the golden bands of Troy, two on each of his forelimbs and a pair about his hind limbs.

And I remembered . . . and I knew where we were going and where we had been.

I gave one incoherent cry, and then, as the beast came to a halt before me, and lowered his noble head, and I felt his lips gently move within my river-dampened hair, I said: "Og, Og, can we truly manage this?"

He said, "We must . . ." And then he groaned, and I both felt and saw his body crumble about me, crumble away to nothingness until there was nothing but six golden bands, rolling about on the stone floor . . .

I woke, and I was no longer who once I had been, although I was what I had always been.

I LAY NAKED AT TIDE'S EDGE, MY LOWER BODY STILL rocked by the gentle waves of the river.

The Sidlesaghe was leaning down over me, his dark face smiling with such love I thought I could not bear it.

"*Resurgam*, pretty lady," he said, and his voice was full of simple, unrestrained joy.

PART THREE

It is an opinion generally received, that the tournament originated from a childish pastime practised by youths called Ludus Troia (the Troy Game), said to have been so named because it was derived from the Trojans . . .

In the middle ages, when the tournaments were in their splendour, the Troy Game was still continued, and distinguished by a different denomination; it was then called in Latin, behordicum, *and in French,* bohourt or behourt, *and was a kind of lance game, in which the young nobility exercised themselves, to acquire address in handling of their arms, and to prove their strength.*

Joseph Strutt, Sports & Pastimes of the People of England,
Late 18th century

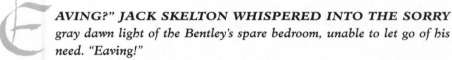

AVING?" JACK SKELTON WHISPERED INTO THE SORRY *gray dawn light of the Bentley's spare bedroom, unable to let go of his* *need. "Eaving!"*

For a moment nothing, then a creaking noise somewhere deep within the house.

Skelton leaped out of bed, his heart racing, and then realized, horribly, that Violet Bentley had made the noise. She was moving from her and Frank's bedroom, down the stairs, and to the small kitchen on the ground floor where she was doubt- less about to prepare Skelton one of those horribly fatty English fried breakfasts.

Skelton subsided back to the bed, almost hating Violet for causing him to hope so terribly, and so momentarily.

Eventually he made the effort to sit up and swing his legs over the edge of the bed. He paused there, then dropped his head into his hands, trying to find the energy to rise and wash and then dress for his first day in his new posting.

And then it came. From outside the window this time, not inside where Violet was making an increasing amount of clatter over the breakfast.

The sound of a child's voice. A breathless, joyful catch of laughter. A spoken word, murmured.

Daddy.

"Gods!" Skelton said, his voice a harsh, shocked whisper.

She was dead! Dead! He'd recovered her charred bones from the ruins of St. Paul's himself, wept over them, refused to allow anyone else to touch them.

Her bones, as those of her mother's.

She was dead. Dead!

Daddy.

Skelton felt the hope rise like bile in his throat. He scrambled to the window, almost falling in his haste, and stared out.

On the street below, looking up at the window, was a little girl of some seven or eight years. She had very black curly hair, an image of Skelton's own, and a pale face with deep blue eyes ringed with sooty lashes.

Daddy, *she mouthed.*

And then she held out her hands.

In each palm rested one of the golden kingship bands of Troy.

The two lost bands of Troy, for which both Skelton and Asterion had searched for centuries.

ChAPTER ONE

ROUEN, NORMANDY

*M*ATILDA, DUCHESS OF NORMANDY, SHIFTED slightly in her chair, easing her still-tender muscles, and looked to where her husband sat on his dais at the head of the bright, commodious hall. William had returned from his morning hunt not an hour before, and now sprawled in his great chair, his face still flushed with excitement, one hand gesturing effusively as he relived the chase with his two closest companions, Walter Fitz Osbern and Roger Montgomery.

She smiled, happy that he was, for the moment, content.

Then she sighed, and shifted yet again to ease her aching muscles. She'd given birth a few weeks previously—another daughter—and had only just rejoined William's public court. She would also, Matilda thought, as she watched William's eye slipping to wander over the form of one of her more youthful waiting women, shortly have to rejoin him in their marital bed. William's natural lusts made him wander sometimes, and Matilda knew full well that on occasion he bedded a village woman and had sired three or four bastards about his many estates, but the knowledge did not perturb her overmuch.

She was the woman he respected and honored before all others, *she* was the one to whom he confided his most secret thoughts and greatest ambitions, and *she* was the one to whom he turned for advice and counsel.

Matilda felt a tiny kernel of fear. She was the woman he trusted and honored and respected above all others, but what would happen once he won England? England—and thus Swanne—had been so distant for so long that Matilda had all but forgotten her fears regarding Swanne. But now . . . now that Edward's health was declining . . . suddenly neither England nor Swanne were far away at all.

* * *

WILLIAM GRINNED AT THE EXPRESSION ON HIS WIFE'S
face, knowing full well she'd seen him ogling the luscious form of Adeliza.

Adeliza would be sent home to her family estates and Matilda would be
back in his bed before a new day dawned.

That thought contented William. The tedium of birthing always annoyed
him; he appreciated the fine healthy children Matilda gave him, but he was
irritated that it should remove Matilda from his bed in the weeks immediately
preceding and then following the birth. He missed those hours holding her,
and talking through his problems with her, in that one place where they had
utter privacy and need not guard their words.

Matilda was worth to him more than all the gold in Christendom. William
did not think he could have borne the uncertainty and fear of the past years if
it had not been for her.

He valued her beyond measure . . . and yet he had not found within himself the courage to talk to her of that one thing which consumed so much of
his life.

The Troy Game.

How could he ever explain that to her?

So William couched his thoughts of the Game within talk of his ambition
for the English throne, and that ambition Matilda understood very well. All
men lusted for more estates and power, and what was more normal than
William, having finally secured his own duchy, to lust for a throne to which he
had some small right, in any case?

A sound distracted William from his thoughts, and he looked to the
doorway.

The guards had admitted a short and very slight priest, still with his
stained traveling cloak flapping wetly about his shoulders, and now that priest
was striding toward where William sat.

William tensed, sitting a little higher in his chair, and his companions
Walter and Roger shared knowing glances.

"My good lord," said the priest, sweeping in a low bow before the duke's
chair, "I greet you well, and am glad to have arrived in your sweet abode after
the mud and strain of the road."

"Greetings, Yves," William said. "I welcome you indeed." He waved to his
chamberlain, who sent a man forward with a stool for the priest. "You were
not troubled by brigands on your way?"

"Nay," said Yves, handing his cloak to the chamberlain and seating himself
with patent relief, "just the rain and the sleet. Winter has set in early."

"I welcome you also, Yves," said Matilda, wandering over to stand by
William's side. She perched one hand on his shoulder. "It is too long since we
have seen you."

There was something in her tone that made William glance at her face, but she wore a bland, unreadable expression that gave no clue as to her thoughts. He looked back to Walter and Roger, sitting forward on their seats with expressions of perfectly readable curiosity on their faces, and he turned those expressions into ones of disappointment by asking them to leave himself and his wife alone for a while with the new arrival.

"We have matters of some delicacy to discuss," William said, and Walter and Roger, who were certain as to what those matters might be, reluctantly rose, bowed to both their duke and duchess, and joined the greater part of the court seated at some distance from the dais.

Matilda took one of the chairs vacated by the departing men. She folded her hands in her lap and waited, leaving it to her husband to conduct the conversation.

"Well?" said William softly.

"I have a communication for you," said Yves and, glancing about in a manner that must have incited the suspicions of the entire court, handed to William a carefully cloth-wrapped small bundle.

"From my husband's agent at Edward's court?" said Matilda.

Yves inclined his head, and Matilda and William shared a meaningful glance. William would not open this now, not here.

"And how goes Edward's court?" said William.

"The king ages apace," said Yves. "His mind lingers less on worldly matters than on the salvation that awaits him. Most days he spends with the monks and priests of Westminster Abbey, or walking within its rising walls. He thinks to build for himself a place of great glory, so that the world might not forget him when death takes him."

William grunted, turning the small cloth-wrapped bundle over and over in his hands, as if impatient to read its contents.

"There is no sign of an heir?" he said.

Yves gave a short laugh. "Queen Caela is not so blessed as my lady here," he said, inclining his head to Matilda, who accepted the compliment with a small, polite smile. "Edward refuses to corrupt his piety, or his possible salvation and deification, with any sins of the flesh. There will be no heir of his body."

He hesitated, and William looked at him sharply.

"What do you *not* say?" he said.

"Only that Queen Caela was struck with a most untimely bloody flux of her womb at court two weeks before I left," said Yves. "Some said that she had miscarried of a bastard child, but the midwives who examined her said she was a virgin still. Edward," again Yves gave his short, strange bark of laughter, "has his reputation as intact as his wife's virginity."

Matilda had been watching her husband as Yves spoke, and she frowned, puzzled, at what she saw in his face. Regret? Unhappiness? *Uncertainty?* She could not read it, nor understand it completely. Again she resolved to discover all she could about this enigmatic queen.

"Harold?" William asked, and Matilda relaxed, for now there was nothing in William's face at all but ambition and cunning.

"His strength grows, my lord," said Yves. "He knows, as does everyone, that Edward has his eyes more on the next world than he does on this one."

"And so how does Harold conduct himself, knowing the throne shall be vacant in so little a time?" said Matilda.

"He sits, and watches, and gathers his forces. The witan is all but sure to elect him to the throne on Edward's death—"

"But William has the greater claim," said Matilda, unable to suppress an outburst of loyalty. "Edward all but promised it to him when my husband sheltered him in his court during the man's exile, and through Emma, Edward's mother, William and Edward are close cousins. There is no one closer in blood than William."

Yves shrugged. "The witan will not want a foreigner marching in and forcing the Saxon earls to his will."

"They may have to accept it!" snapped Matilda.

William smiled at her, then looked back to Yves. "I thank you for your care in bringing this," he tapped the bundle, "to me. Will you accept my hospitality for the next few days as I decide whether or not to respond?"

Yves rose, knowing a dismissal when he heard one. He bowed, first to William, then to Matilda, and left the hall.

The instant he had turned his back, both William and Matilda looked at the bundle he held.

"I will open it later," William said, and slipped it inside his tunic.

"We will open it together," Matilda said firmly, and William sighed, and nodded.

CHAPTER TWO

CAELA SPEAKS

OW CAN I EXPLAIN HOW I FELT AT THAT MOMENT? When I opened my eyes and saw the Sidlesaghe look down at me, and smile, and say "*Resurgam*, pretty lady!" with such joy and welcome?

I felt relief. That was the first, overwhelming emotion. Sheer, thankful relief. We'd managed it—Hera, Mag, and I. The first and most critical part of our journey was done.

And who was *I*? Why Caela, of course, as I had been Cornelia, but far more than that.

Far more.

How can I put into words what that felt like? It is as if . . . it is as if you had wandered naked all your life, and then someone approached and placed a mantle about your shoulders. This mantle protected and nurtured, and because of the warmth and comfort it gave, it made you much more than you had been when naked. Moreover, the threads of the mantle magically wound themselves into your flesh so that it became an integral and living part of you.

The mantle had not truly changed who you were, it had just made you *more*.

I lay at tide's edge that still, cold night, and I felt the land beneath my back and the waters about my legs. It was not just that I felt their solidity or wetness, I felt *them*. The essence of them—how they felt, how they turned, their wants and needs and loves as well. I could feel the land closing in upon itself for its winter death-sleep; I could feel the seeds of spring and the bones of the dead sleeping within its flesh; I could feel the roots of the trees stretching down, down, down; and I could feel the chatter of the moles and the bark of foxes and the sweetness of the worms who inhabited its flesh.

My flesh.

In the waters I could hear the laughter of distant lands, and feel the siren song of the moon, for love of whom the tides and inlets danced. I could feel my heart in its depths, and feel the love of the water-sprites who, with the ancient ones, the Sidlesaghes, had overseen my birth.

I was aware that the water-sprites still hovered close to the surface of the water, and that the Sidlesaghes lined the banks of the river in their thousands, and that Ecub and Saeweald and Judith stood close by, staring down upon my naked flesh in varying degrees of stupefaction and awe, but, for the moment, I concentrated only on myself.

I closed my eyes, and did what Judith, Saeweald, and Ecub had been wanting me to do for so long.

I remembered.

I remembered that terrible night when Genvissa had torn my daughter from my body, and I had died. I remembered how Mag had come to me then (even as Loth was sobbing over my cooling flesh), and how she had talked to me, and shown me the way ahead.

I remembered how dismayed I had been, not only dismayed at the thought of how *far* we had to go, the intricacies involved (where so much could go wrong) and the dangers inherent in that journey, but of how unworthy I was of the responsibility. But Mag had loved me, and held me, and promised me that all would be well. That all I had to do was to believe and to trust, and to summon the courage to dare.

I lay there at tide's edge, my eyes closed, my heart full of contentment, and felt the land and waters move about me. When, as Cornelia, I had stabbed myself in the neck, thus causing my own death, Mag within my womb had died with me. When I had been reborn as Caela, so had Mag—or her potential, rather than her precisely—been reborn also, but not within my womb.

Within me. As much a part of my flesh as that imagined mantle.

There was no difference between us now. I was not only Caela, Cornelia-reborn, but also everything that Mag had been.

Mag-reborn. That strange mantle, seamlessly wound through my flesh, that made me more than I had been previously. Not different, just *more*.

I knew that about me stood those who needed a word, and who needed reassurance, but first I wanted to do one more thing . . . I allowed my memory to roam free. Oh, but it encompassed so much! I could remember when this land was still young, when it was still bound by a thin land bridge to the great continent to the east, and when great bear and elk and wolves scampered across that bridge to fill this bounteous land.

I remembered when Mag had walked across that land bridge, and was welcomed to this land by the Sidlesaghes who now stood about me, welcomers once more.

I remembered the joy of turning about one day, and seeing standing there the great white stag, and knowing that he would be my one mate throughout eternity.

And I remembered that bleak day when the Darkwitch Ariadne came to this land, and Mag welcomed her, not realizing her malignancy and her contempt.

Finally, I remembered the arrival of the Trojans, carrying with them Mag nurtured within the womb of their leader's wife, Cornelia. Mag, arriving once more to this land, bringing with her . . . *me*.

Filled with joy, I looked deeper.

And found an empty space. A well of nothingness. An incompleteness.

Had something failed? Had my transformation not been complete?

Startled, and not a little scared at that discovery, I opened my eyes. I would think on it later when I had peace and solitude. This was only the beginning, after all. I could not expect everything all at once.

The Sidlesaghe reached down his hand and I took it, and rose, glimpsing as I did so at the gold and ruby bracelet that glinted about my wrist. I half smiled at that, seeing in it everything that Cornelia had suffered but yet would become, then I looked to my three faithful companions who had been reborn into this life with me, and, in turn, I took their faces in my hands and kissed them softly on their mouths.

"You are Mag?" stammered Saeweald.

I hesitated. I was not *Mag* precisely, but did not know how best to express myself. So, foolishly perhaps, I let him think what he wanted, for it was easier. "Aye," I said, and felt a faint flutter of discomfort deep within my belly.

"But . . . I had no idea . . . I would not have . . ."

"Wait," I said. "This is not the place nor the time to discuss it." I turned back to the Sidlesaghe, and I kissed him also on the mouth. "Long Tom," I said, for that was truly his name, "thank you for greeting me. I am sorry I was so nervous and that I attempted to obstruct you."

Long Tom smiled, and, as I had in my dream, I saw a faint suggestion of light spill from his mouth. "We are happy to see you as well, lady. Do not worry for what you may have said. We are happy only to see you."

My smile slipped. "I need to speak with you."

"Aye, and we with you. But not now. I will come to you again. We will walk the paths."

"Aye," I said, "that we will."

Then I turned back to Saeweald and the two women, and I grimaced, and I said, "May I borrow a cloak or some other covering from you? This night is chill, and there is a long walk back to the palace."

And so, huddled beneath Saeweald's cloak, with the Sidlesaghes fading into the night, and the physician, the prioress and my attending lady beside me, I went back to the palace via the graveled flats of the Thames until we reached the wharves of Westminster, thence up the paths and steps to the palace itself where doors opened and sentries stood unnoticing. We went to the very door of my bedchamber and there, I smiled again, and kissed them all once more, and said, "We shall have a chance to speak tomorrow. Be still until that moment."

Then I opened the door, and walked inside and, shucking away the cloak, crawled into my empty, cold bed (Edward was, most apparently, still on his knees before his altar, and the bowerthegn who usually slept by the door must also be with him).

I lay down naked, and I closed my eyes, and I put my hands on my breasts, and I dreamed—not of the young boy Melanthus whom I had thought to love in my previous life as Cornelia, nor even of Brutus-now-William, but I dreamed of my beloved white stag with the bloodred antlers, pounding through the forest toward me.

One day, I thought. *One day, beloved.*

And then I began to weep.

Silently, deep into the night.

chapter three

*M*ATILDA WATCHED THROUGH HOODED EYES AS William, as naked as the day he had been born, stood before the fire in their bedchamber, reading the letter that Yves had delivered earlier.

They had retired some hours ago, made love (which Matilda hoped had driven all thought of Adeliza from William's mind for the time being), talked, and then William had waited until he thought Matilda asleep.

Now he stood before the fire, his head bent over the letter, frowning.

HE COULDN'T ALLOW MATILDA TO SEE THIS! WILLIAM thanked all the gods that existed that he'd delayed opening the communication until Matilda had been asleep. Previously, Swanne always had been circumspect in her communications, but now she had abandoned caution. Swanne wanted him to tell her where the kingship bands were. She wanted to move them before Asterion could get to them. She needed to do it before William arrived, or else it would be too late. She wrote of the strange events of the day the Troy Game was enacted in Smithfield, and of the children who played at the Game on the flagstones outside of St. Paul's. They needed to act fast, before everything disintegrated out of their control. Her unwritten fear, but one William discerned easily, was that Swanne was just as worried about the Troy Game's intentions as she was about Asterion's.

William understood Swanne's fear about Asterion. It was evident that matters were careening toward a head: Edward was sliding toward death, the new abbey was almost complete . . . and now the Londoners were dancing the Troy Game? Children playing it across paving stones?

To be honest, William was not surprised at the manifestation of the Game above the stones. It had existed for two thousand years, it was no shock to find that the people who lived their daily lives above it should also find their feet moving unwittingly in its steps. Swanne's belief that the Game was trying to take matters into its own hands, however, was an overreaction. William could not conceive for a moment that the Game would ever try to divorce itself from its Mistress and its Kingman.

But the bands. On that subject William was prepared to share Swanne's concern. The golden bands of Troy were vital. If Asterion had them, then all hope that William and Swanne could work the final Dance of the Flowers and complete the Game—thus trapping Asterion within its heart forever—were gone.

If *William* could retrieve them, however . . .

William's body tensed, his eyes staring unfocused into the fire. *If he had the bands, if he wore them, and if he and Swanne had the time and space to raise the Flower Gate . . .*

Then all would be won, and he and Swanne would live forever within the stones of London.

Strange, that he should feel no joy at this thought. "I must be getting old," William muttered. Once, every bone in his body would have been screaming with joy at the thought of controlling the Game completely.

Again William collected his thoughts and concentrated on what Swanne asked him: *Tell me where lie the bands of Troy, and I shall take them, and keep them safe for you. What do you want otherwise? That Asterion should snatch them before you can collect yourself enough to arrive?*

The tone of that last sentence irritated William immensely. What did she think, that he had idled his life away in his court of Normandy? Drinking fine wines and laughing at the antics of court jesters? By the gods, did she not know that he'd had to battle rivals and enemies for the past thirty years? That he'd spent each and every day of those thirty years ensuring his survival? That there had not been a single chance—not a *one!*—to turn his armies for England and for London so that he could, at last, take his rightful place on its throne?

William well realized that his troubles had been caused by Asterion's meddling. He knew that Asterion had his own dark, malevolent reasons for ensuring William kept his distance from London for all these years.

And William knew, with every instinct in his body, that the fact that all these internal problems within Normandy had miraculously receded over the past couple of years meant that Asterion was preparing the way for the confrontation they all knew was coming.

"What news?" said Matilda from their bed, surprising William so much he visibly jumped.

"Little," he said as lightly as he could, and tossed the paper into the fire.

It crackled, flaring in sudden flame and burning to ash within moments.

"You did not want me to read it?" Matilda said.

"No."

"Why?"

"Swanne was incautious." William looked Matilda directly in the eye. "She spoke of things I did not want you to see."

"What things?" Matilda hissed, finally allowing her jealousy free reign. She rose from the bed, snatching at a robe to cover herself as she did so, hating the fact that her body was still swollen from the child she had so recently borne, and hating Swanne even more bitterly for the fact that all the news Matilda received of her spoke of a beautiful and elegant woman, despite the six children she'd birthed.

"She did not speak of love," William said, walking over to Matilda and kissing her gently on the forehead. "But there are matters so terrible that you will be safer not knowing of them. I speak nothing but truth, Matilda, when I say that what Swanne wrote has irritated me. I did not throw that letter into the flames because I am a shame-faced adulterer, but because I was angry with she who wrote it."

"I should not have taxed you over the matter," Matilda said, more angry with herself now that she'd allowed her jealousy to speak tartly.

"You had every right," William said very softly, his lips resting in her hair. "You are my wife, and I honor you before all others."

"But Swanne is the great love of your life," Matilda said, keeping her voice light.

"When I spoke those words to you, fifteen years ago," he said, "then I thought I spoke truth. Now I am not so sure."

"What do you mean?" Matilda leaned back so she could see his face.

Again William paused, trying to find the best words with which to respond. "You have taught me a great deal during our marriage," he said eventually. "You have taught me strength, and tolerance, and you have given me maturity. What I thought, and felt, fifteen years ago, are no longer so clear to me."

Again Matilda arched an eyebrow. "Are you saying that *I* have suddenly become the great love of your life?"

William laughed, knowing from all their years together that she jested with him. "What I am saying, my dear, is that 'great love' no longer appeals to me as once it did."

She held his eyes, her jesting manner vanished. "When you win England—"

When, not *if.* William loved her for that.

"—a marriage to Swanne would consolidate your hold on the throne, especially if, as we expect, the witan elects Harold as king to succeed Edward.

When you have dealt with Harold, what better move for you than to marry his widow?"

"I will never renounce you!" William said. "Never! *You* will be queen of England at my side. Believe it!"

Matilda, studying the fervor in his eyes, believed it, and was content.

CHAPTER FOUR

*J*UDITH THOUGHT THE CHANGE IN CAELA SO stunningly obvious that the entire realm would have taken one gigantic breath and screamed its incredulity, but she supposed, on second thought, that maybe most people who came into contact with the queen on that following day thought her "eccentricity" merely a result of the turbulent state of her womb.

She woke Caela as she usually did, just after dawn, with a murmured word and the offering of a warm, damp flannel with which to wipe the sleep from her eyes.

Caela took the cloth, smiling, and wiped her face. Then she stretched cat-like under the covers, then pushed them back and rose in one fluid, beautiful movement, apparently unconcerned at her nakedness.

Edward's bowerthegn, or bed chamberlain, aiding his king to dress, stilled and stared.

Normally, Caela stayed modestly covered in bed until both her husband and his servants had left the chamber.

Now she walked slowly over to one of the closed windows, threw back the shutters, and stood gloriously outlined—and gloriously naked—in the dawning light.

"Wife! What do you? Clothe yourself instantly!"

Judith froze, wondering if Caela would strike him down.

Instead Caela only inclined her head toward Edward's direction, as if she found his presence mildly surprising. "My nakedness disturbs you?" she asked.

And turned about.

Judith bit her lip, suppressing a deadly desire to giggle. Both Edward and the bowerthegn were staring goggle-eyed at the queen.

Caela smiled, sweet and innocent, and drew in a deep breath.

The bowerthegn's mouth dropped open, and, frankly, Judith was not surprised. Caela looked magnificent, her pale skin subtly shaded by the rosy light of dawn, her mussed hair gleaming in an aura about her face and shoulders.

Her body, which Judith knew so intimately from their long association, appeared somehow different, and it took Judith a moment to realize that where once Caela's body, although slim, had been soft from her life of inactivity at court, was now taut and finely muscled, as if she spent her time, not at rest at her needlework, but running through the forests, or slipping wraith-like through the waters.

"A robe perhaps, Judith," Caela murmured, turning slightly so that the slack-jawed men could see her body in profile.

Judith hurried to comply, not daring to look at Caela's face.

"That was most unseemly, wife," said Edward.

"I am sorry my nakedness offends," said Caela, allowing Judith to slip a soft woolen robe over her head and shoulders.

Even then, the soft robe clinging to every curve and hugging every narrowness, Caela managed to give the impression of nakedness as she moved slowly about the chamber, lifting this, inspecting that, and Edward finished his dressing in red-cheeked affront before he hurried from the room.

The bowerthegn, hastening after him, shot Caela one final wide-eyed glance, which made Caela grin.

"How sad," she remarked to Judith, dropping the robe from her body so that she might wash, "that Edward should be so afraid of a woman's body, and that the bowerthegn should be so shy in admiring it."

Fortunately for Judith's peace of mind, Caela managed to perform her usual duties about court demurely and quietly, although with an air of slight distraction. Several people looked at her oddly, frowning, as if trying to place what was unusual about Caela (among them Swanne, who stopped dead when first she saw Caela enter court, then wrinkled her brow as she patently tried to discern exactly what was different about the queen on this morning).

When Harold came to her, and wished her a good morning, Caela visibly glowed, and Harold responded in kind. He, too, looked puzzled by her, but also pleased, and he stayed longer than he normally would when he had business elsewhere, laughing and chatting over inconsequential matters as other members of the court circled close by.

I wonder if some part of him knows, wondered Judith, hovering nearby and wondering if Caela was being a trifle indiscreet with her openness and patent happiness in the presence of her brother. There was a subdued sexuality to every one of her movements that had never been there before, and Judith prayed that no other observer noted it and spread further dark and malignant gossip about the queen and her brother.

Edward, certainly, kept a close eye on his wife, closer than usual.

However, when Caela bid her brother a good morning, and turned her attention instead to chatting with one of her more recently arrived attending ladies, a young widow called Alditha, then Edward relaxed and allowed himself to be distracted by the priests and bishops who hovered about him.

In the late morning, Caela beckoned Judith closer. "I have decided to take an interest in my lady Alditha," she said, gracing the said lady with a lovely smile. "I wonder if you could see to it that her sleeping arrangements are changed. Currently poor Alditha shares with five other of my ladies, as well as one of the under-cooks, and she sleeps badly. Perhaps . . ." Caela paused as if thinking, one finger tapping gently against her lower lip. "Perhaps Alditha can take over that chamber in the annex that runs between our palace and Harold's hall? You know the one, surely. The bishop of Kent occupied it before he so sorrowfully succumbed to his ailments."

Judith blinked, trying to mask her confusion. She glanced at Alditha, a pretty woman with a heart-shaped face and generous hazel eyes, who looked as confused with the attention she was receiving as Judith felt. And the chamber of the (sorrowfully now deceased) bishop of Kent? Why, not only was that a sumptuous chamber, it was also a very private chamber in a palace complex where privacy was a highly valued thing indeed. She wondered what Caela was about . . . why establish Alditha in such a fine, and finely private, chamber?

And one so close to Harold's own private apartments?

"Of course, madam," she said, inclining her head.

"And when you have done that, and settled Alditha comfortably," Caela continued, "I wonder if you might bring the physician Saeweald to attend me? And the prioress Ecub? Mother Ecub has been complaining so greatly recently about her aching knees that I think it time I grant her a consultation with Edward's own physician. Don't you think?"

"Yes, madam." Judith locked eyes with Caela, understanding.

"Perhaps in my solar," said Caela. "I think I may withdraw for a little while."

"Yes, madam."

"I AM SORRY THAT FOR SO LONG I HAD NO MEMORY, and that you were sorrowed and troubled because of it," Caela said, once Saeweald, Ecub, and Judith had gathered in her solar. They were not entirely alone, for below the windows sat three of the queen's ladies, their heads bent over their needlework, but Caela and her three companions were far enough distant in their chairs about the hearth that they could talk in reasonable privacy. To have insisted that the ladies take their needlework elsewhere was to have invited gossip and unwelcome curiosity.

"But you remember now . . . madam?" Saeweald said. He hesitated at the end of the question before adding the "madam." His concern was obvious. How should he address this woman, his friend, queen and, now, reborn goddess?

Caela nodded. "Most things, yes, although there are still some vaguenesses." She shifted a little in her chair, her eyes glancing over at the group of ladies under the window. "My friends, I am still Caela to you in private, and madam in public. I am nothing else."

"You are Mag," Ecub said.

Caela hesitated a fraction before replying. "I have her within me, her power and knowledge and memory, but I am still Caela, Cornelia-reborn. I am simply *more* than she had once been."

Ecub gave a small smile, her creased face kind and loving. "And perhaps not. When you first came to this land we knew you were somehow different. You were always, and will always be, beloved."

At that Caela lowered her face, drawing in a deep breath as she blinked back tears. "I say again," she said, as she raised her face and looked in turn at each of the three, "that I have been well served in you and that you have my unending gratitude for staying by me, even when you thought I had no memory, and when you had every reason to suspect me of uselessness in the struggle that is to come."

"To destroy the Game," Saeweald said.

Caela looked at him, her gaze clear and direct. She opened her mouth as if to speak, then closed it again, having reconsidered. "Let me tell you, briefly, how things came to pass. In the world where Cornelia came from, the Aegean world, there was a great goddess named Hera. She had once been all-powerful, magnificent, but had been cruelly crippled by Ariadne's darkcraft. Before she died, she approached Mag—also suffering from the Darkwitches' malevolence—and suggested a plan. A means by which the Darkwitches could be outwitted, and Mag's land saved."

"But not Hera's world?" Judith said.

"No. That was too badly corrupted. It was dying. There was nothing Hera or Mag could do about that. But Hera could aid Mag and Mag's land, and she did so by passing on her knowledge and cunning."

"How to destroy the Game," Saeweald said, and again Caela glanced at him, this time with her brow very slightly furrowed.

"Mag needed a place to hide," Caela continued, "and Hera showed her Cornelia. But Cornelia . . . but *I* . . . was not simply a place to hide. In rebirth—and Hera and Mag knew that what needed to be done would take more than one lifetime—Mag would be reborn within my flesh, giving her power and potential new vitality."

Judith frowned. "But Mag was within your womb . . ."

"No," Caela said. "That was merely a phantom. A decoy, if you will. Hera and Mag had known about Asterion, and had known of his malevolence and danger. Mag pretended an alliance with the Minotaur, but knew that eventually he would turn against her. She had no illusions about that. Thus the phantom within my womb that he could murder, and my lack of memory. Asterion had to be convinced that he had disposed of Mag, and subsequently that I was no threat. He did just that, murdering the phantom Mag, and convincing himself that poor Caela was of no consequence. Now I am safe, we are safe, for Asterion thinks us all of little consequence or danger to him in the Game ahead."

"And the Sidlesaghes?" asked Ecub.

"The Sidlesaghes have always been intimately connected with a goddess's rebirth. They also knew something of Mag's plan. When they felt Asterion readying himself, they walked. When Asterion murdered Mag, and convinced himself that I was no threat, then it would be time to rebirth the goddess."

"And thus they approached me," said Ecub, "and then Judith."

"Yes," said Caela.

"Tell us, great Mother," said Saeweald, his face alive with eagerness, "how will you destroy the Game? How shall you return this land to its purity?"

There was a moment's silence, a stillness, during which Caela visibly steeled herself.

"I have no intention of destroying the Game," she said eventually, watching Saeweald carefully.

"What?" Saeweald said, tensing as if to rise.

"Be still!" Caela hissed, and Saeweald subsided at the command in her voice.

Again Caela glanced at the ladies under the window, but they had not moved, nor glanced up from their needlework.

"The Troy Game will *save* this land," Caela continued, her voice low and compelling. "It will be completed, but not by Swanne and William. *Not* by Genvissa- and Brutus-reborn."

Her three companions stared at her, their bewilderment patent.

"*I* will complete the Game," Caela said. "With Og-reborn."

There was a long hush as Saeweald, Ecub, and Judith stared at Caela, then exchanged glances between themselves.

"Og-reborn?" Saeweald said, very slowly, and a flush mottled his cheeks. *Og-reborn!* He could not help a thrill of excitement.

"How can this be so?" Ecub said eventually. "My lady, we . . . we do not understand. The Game completed? By you, and Og-reborn?"

"The Troy Game is not the evil thing that you believe," Caela said. "You only saw it so because its creators, Genvissa and Brutus, worked it with corruption rather than with good intention and meaning. Used correctly, the Game *is* a powerful and beneficial thing, and it can be used to protect this land as nothing else can. But to use the Game to its full potential, to use it to aid this land, then we need to wrest control of it away from Swanne and William."

"Gods," Ecub muttered. "No wonder you needed to divert Asterion's attention away from you. It is enough that you have set yourself against Swanne and William; you do not need to contend with Asterion as well."

"Since the time Genvissa and Brutus left the Game unfinished," Caela said, "the Game has all but merged with the land. The land and the Troy Game have, if you like, negotiated an alliance. Hera told Mag that this would be so. That if the Darkwitch and Brutus were stopped before they completed the Game, and the Game and the land upon which it sat were left to their own devices, then they would come to an understanding, if you will."

"Og-reborn?" said Saeweald, who had paid little attention to anything else Caela had said. *"Where? When?"* He paused. "In *whom?"*

Caela smiled, and leaned forward so she could put a warm hand on Saeweald's arm. "Not yet," she said. "He will not be reborn until it is safe for him to be so."

In whom? Saeweald thought, and would have repeated the question save that Ecub spoke first.

"When will it be safe for Og to be reborn?" she said.

"When Asterion is negated, and when . . ." Caela faltered, then resumed, "and when Swanne can pass on to me the arts and secrets of the Mistress of the Labyrinth."

Judith's mouth fell open, her expression mirroring that of Saeweald's and Ecub's. "*Swanne* hand to *you* the powers of the Mistress of the Labyrinth?"

"I will need them in order to complete the Game, as so also will Og-reborn require the powers of the Kingman. Land and Game merged, completely. Mag and Og, Mistress and Kingman of the Labyrinth."

"That is not my query," said Judith, still aghast, "but this: *how in creation's name will you get Swanne to hand to you her powers as Mistress of the Labyrinth?"*

"There is a way, I *know* this," Caela beat a clenched hand softly against her breast. "But for the moment this way remains unknown to me. Eventually I will find it—or it will find me."

Saeweald gave a short, harsh bark of laughter, making the ladies under the window look at him in surprise.

He waited until their attention had returned to their needlework. "I wish I had your certainty, Caela. Swanne will never do it, just as William will never hand to Og his powers as Kingman! Both are too devoted to their ambitions, and to their shared vision of immortality. They will *never* do it!"

"You misjudge both of them," Caela said quietly. "I think they will. Eventually. When circumstances are right."

There was quiet for a while, each lost in their own thoughts. Judith and Ecub were trying to come to terms with the idea that they should actually use the Game, rather than destroy it; Saeweald's mind remained consumed with the idea of Og-reborn. *Who? Who? Who?*

The thoughts of all three stumbled at the idea that Caela, Mag-reborn, actually thought she could make Swanne hand over her powers as Mistress of the Labyrinth, and that William would do likewise with his powers as King-man.

Eventually Caela, having watched the doubts flood the faces of the other three, shrugged her shoulders as if in a silent apology. "There is still much to be decided. I will need to speak with the Sidlesaghes. They have been watching these past two thousand years. They will show me the direction I should take."

Ecub, somewhat reluctantly, gave a single nod. "May I ask, great lady, whom Asterion masquerades as? He is among us, we can all feel that, but who is he?"

Caela colored slightly. "I do not know."

"You do not *know*?" Saeweald said, incredulously.

Caela shot him another hard glance, but Saeweald met it unhesitatingly.

"He hides himself well," she said curtly. "Too well. I cannot know him. But he must have come to see me in the hours after Mag's death. Who visited me then? My mind was sleepy and muddled, and I can remember only a procession of vague faces."

"Half the cursed court visited you," Saeweald muttered. "How is it you cannot tell Asterion's guise? By all the stars in heaven, Caela, you do not know how to persuade Swanne to hand over her powers, you do not know who Asterion is . . . what else do you 'not know'?"

"There are still vaguenesses, and still things I need to learn," Caela said. "I am not omniscient, neither was Mag, nor even Og. But, if you worry about Asterion, then pray put that to one side. For the moment Asterion is concentrating on Swanne and William. I am no longer of any concern to him." She drew in a deep breath. "Now, I have some questions of you. Harold . . ." her voice broke a little. "For all the gods' sakes, why does he not remember? Why have none of you told him?"

"As to why he cannot remember," Saeweald said, "I do not understand this, but I suspect it is because it is kinder to him that it be so. And that is the reason none of us have taken him aside, and explained to him the tragedy of his previous life. What would you have had us say, my lady? That his sister in this life is the great love of his life? That if he indulges in that love, he not only threatens her well-being, but throws away all he could attain in this life? By all the gods, Caela! Harold is the man who can lead England to a victory against William, but England will not follow him if he is accused of fornication with his own sister!"

"But he is married to *Swanne!*" Caela said.

"And that marriage took place before any of us knew him," said Ecub. "That fact changes little."

Caela's face twisted in revulsion. "But *Swanne* . . . she arranged his murder in his last life."

"And what can you do about it?" said Saeweald. "If you walk up to him now, and reveal all that can be revealed, then you risk destroying his life."

Caela did not answer.

Saeweald again leaned forward. "Is *Harold* Og-reborn?"

Caela shook her head.

"Then what purpose is there in revealing his past to him?" said Saeweald. "What purpose, save to batter his emotions, and show him what he cannot have in this life?"

Caela nodded with obvious reluctance.

"Silvius," she said, lifting her wrist a little so she could see the bracelet he'd given her. "What in heaven's name does he do here?"

"He is part of the Game," Saeweald said. "Brutus made him so."

"He says he is here to help," Judith put in. "He thought that the bracelet might make you remember. None of us then knew quite what you truly were, or what was needed to make you remember . . ."

There was a slight reproach in her last remark, and Caela's cheeks again colored a little at it. "Well," she said, "I suppose I will speak to him eventually."

She was about to say more, but at that moment the door to the solar opened, and Edward's chamberlain entered with a request that Caela rejoin her husband to greet an ambassador from Venice.

With a smile, and a gracious inclination of her head, Caela rose.

LATER THAT NIGHT, WHEN JUDITH STOOD BEHIND Caela in her bedchamber, combing out her long hair, Caela half turned, and spoke quietly.

"Judith . . ." Caela hesitated. "William . . . I have not met him in this life . . . have I? He and Edward were very close when Edward was younger— gods, Edward spent a decade or more at William's court when he was exiled by Cnut—but I do not think William has come to our English court. Has he? Ah, I have searched my memory and cannot remember, and I do not know if that is because I have not in truth met him, or because if I have met him then I dismissed him, not knowing who he was . . ."

Her voice broke a little on that last, and Judith frowned.

"Caela, remember how this William treated you in your former life. He was *vile* to you! He—"

"I *loved* him. And now I need to know. Judith, tell me . . . *have* we met?"

"You have not met."

Caela sighed. "And his wife, Matilda? I have paid little attention to what I've ever heard of her. What do you know?"

"Caela, you can be doing yourself little good by—"

"I want to know. Please."

"She is a strong woman, quick to temper, sure of herself and her place in life. I . . . I have heard that she and William have made a good pairing."

"And children?" Caela said.

"Many, sons as well as daughters."

Caela winced.

"They have been blessed," Judith finished.

Caela turned aside her head.

"Caela . . ." Judith said softly.

"My hair is untangled enough, Judith. You may leave me now."

Judith went to Saeweald, needing to talk through all she had heard that day.

"I still find it difficult," she said, as she lay naked in Saeweald's arms on his bed, bundles of drying herbs hanging from the low beam above them, "that the reborn Mag and Og will complete the Game instead of destroying it. For so long we have hated and loathed the Troy Game, wanted it gone. Now . . . now we must reconcile ourselves to the idea that it will be with us always. Part of us."

Seaweald did not immediately reply, and, curious at his silence, Judith raised herself on an elbow so she could see his face. "Saeweald?"

"While you spent the evening with Caela, I went to sit on the edge of the river. I prayed, and thought, and sought answers."

"And did you find any?"

His hand stroked gently over Judith's shoulder, and down her upper arm, making her shiver and smile. "Aye. Caela—*Mag*—is right. Imagine the power and strength of this land if it is wedded to the Game."

"But the Game is so . . . foreign."

"Now? After so many years? I don't believe so, not anymore. You may as well say that Caela is 'foreign' and unacceptable, yet Mag chose her for her rebirth. The Sidlesaghes, most ancient of creatures, have accepted both Caela and the Game. *Imagine* the power of all these things combined—the ancients, the gods, and the Troy Game."

Judith frowned a little at Saeweald's emphasis on power. "And if Caela is

Mag-reborn, and will become the Mistress of the Labyrinth, then who is to become Og-reborn?"

Saeweald was silent, but he smiled very slightly as he stared upward toward the ceiling where strings of drying herbs swung gently in the warm air that radiated out from the brazier.

"By Mag herself," Judith said softly, "you think it will be you!"

Saeweald focused on her face. "And who else, eh? I cannot think myself worthy of the honor . . . but who *else*? Not Harold, for Caela said so, and surely he is the only other one among us who Og's spirit could inhabit."

"Saeweald . . ."

He grinned, and lifted his head enough to kiss the tip of her nose. "Ah, I know. You think of the intimacy that must exist between the Mistress and the Kingman, but that is a mere part of the ritual, a step in the dance, and you should not take it personally. Besides, when did you assume such a cloak of Christian morality? We have both had different lovers, in both our lives."

"That was not what I meant."

"Then what?"

She hesitated, then gave a half smile and lay her head back on his chest so that he could no longer see her face. "Nothing," she said. "I think it is all just too much to absorb at once. Mag and Og, reborn, and dancing the Game. Imagine."

He laughed, and they chatted some more about inconsequential things, and then they made love, and Saeweald spoke no more of his ambition to become Og reincarnate.

But all Judith could think of, as she lay with Saeweald through that night, was that moment in their previous life when Loth had challenged Brutus within the labyrinth. Brutus had seized Loth, and had lifted his sword to take the man's head off, but then Og himself, by some supernatural effort, had careened from the forest and dislodged Brutus' sword arm so that, instead of decapitating Loth, Brutus had merely crippled him.

Had that been happenchance (Brutus' sword must go somewhere, and better in Loth's spine than through his neck), or design? Had that sword stroke been as much Og's judgement on Loth as Brutus' displaced anger?

Was Loth's crippling, in this life as well as then, Og's judgment? If so, then Saeweald would never become Og-reborn.

Whatever he himself believed.

And if not Saeweald, then who?

CHAPTER FIVE

WANNE HAD NOTICED SOMETHING DIFFERENT about Caela during the past few days, and it disturbed her greatly. There was something altered in the way that Caela moved, in the way that she sat—very, very still—and in the way Caela looked about her when she observed her husband's court.

There was certainly something very different in the manner Caela looked at Swanne—with sadness and regret, almost—and that difference was driving Swanne almost to distraction.

There was already enough to worry about. She did not need to fret about what Caela was doing as well.

Consequently, when an opportunity presented itself one afternoon when the court had adjourned for the day (Edward had retired to murmur and mutter in a chapel), Swanne took it in both hands. She asked for admittance into Caela's private chamber, received it, and then asked that she and the queen be allowed to speak in some privacy for a time.

As Caela's serving women and attending ladies retreated, Swanne took a seat close to where Caela sat at her ever-present needlework.

"You wonder what is changed about me," Caela said simply, put her needlework down, and lifted her deep blue eyes to Swanne's face. "It is merely this: I have remembered."

Momentarily shocked, Swanne's expression froze. "Remembered what?" she said, stupidly.

"That I am," Caela said in a very even voice, "merely a body to be penetrated and a pair of legs to be parted . . . if I remember rightly how you taunted me so long ago."

Swanne stared, saying nothing, still trying to absorb the shock.

"Why Harold?" said Caela. "Why *him*? What pleasure did you take, then, in seducing Coel-reborn to your bed?"

"Do *you* want him now?" said Swanne, finally finding her voice. "I find that I have tired of him, somewhat."

"William must be close then. Do you send him reports of Harold? Beg him to invade and take you?"

Swanne's face flushed. "He will ever be distant to *you!*"

"Did you not know," Caela said, her demeanor remaining very calm, "that once you were dead he took me back as his wife? Back to his bed? I bore him two more children." Caela lowered her face, resuming her needlework as if this conversation were of no importance to her.

Now Swanne's face drained of all color. "*Never!* I cannot believe that lie."

Caela shrugged slightly, disinterestedly.

"He loathed you," Swanne continued. "He found you vile!" She drew in a deep breath, then resumed in a more even tone. "How is it that you have suddenly remembered all that you were, and all that you did? Did Asterion draw close, and plant an enchanted kiss upon your lips to wake you?"

Caela's needle threaded in and out, in and out. "Asterion has not—"

"Has he roused you from your slumber so that you might once again work his will? Hark!" Swanne put her hands to her face in mock fright. "Is that a *dagger* I see at your girdle?"

Despite herself, Caela's eyes jerked upward, and her cheeks reddened. She immediately looked away, hating the smile of triumph on Swanne's face.

"Where is he, Caela? Where is Asterion?"

"I do not know."

"Ah! Do not expect me to believe that! You are his handmaiden! His *dagger-hand!*"

"No! I will not again—"

"Have you taken him to your bed yet, Caela? If I caused the midwives to examine you again, would they now not find you the same virgin you were a few weeks past?"

"I am a virgin still, Swanne. Unlike yourself, I do not need to use my bed to make my way in life."

"Ah, poor little virgin, can you not even find one man eager to take it from you? And now even Mag has deserted you. Poor worthless bitch goddess. Dead. Was *that* what woke you, Caela? The corpse of your one true friend slithering dead in the hot blood running down your thighs?"

Ignoring the look of distaste on Caela's face, Swanne leaned forward, jerked the needlework out of the way, then took Caela's hands in her own. To any of Caela's ladies watching from across the chamber it seemed only that the lady Swanne was comforting their queen.

"My only regret is that Asterion did not murder you as well. You are as useless as ever you were, Caela. Take my advice and cast yourself into the cold waters of the Thames. Who wants you? No one. You are a pathetic queen—even your husband cannot bear to take you. When William comes, and come he will, Caela, then *I* shall be his queen, and you shall be locked away in a nunnery in the cold, gray reaches of the north where even the scurrying rats will be hard put to remember your name."

She let go Caela's hands and sat back.

"You were ever the failure at being the wife. An, no! I lie! There is one small thing at which you ever excelled as the wife, Caela, and that is in attracting husbands who despise you, and who can hardly bear to touch you."

Finished, Swanne raised an eyebrow, as if daring Caela to even attempt a response.

"How strange," said Caela very softly, her eyes unwavering on Swanne's face, "that you should say that my husbands despise me, Swanne, when you have misnamed both my husbands."

Swanne's face assumed an expression of affected curiosity.

"I am married to this *land*, Swanne, and it is not *me* that this land despises."

Swanne's expression froze, and she did not move as Caela rose and walked away, brushing aside Swanne's skirts as she did so.

By all the gods, Caela, Swanne thought, keeping her face expressionless under the regard of the other ladies in the chamber, *I will make you suffer once William is here, and the Game, and England are ours.*

CHAPTER SIX

CAELA SPEAKS

J LAY AT NIGHT BESIDE MY STILL, COLD HUSBAND—
one part of me thinking that, ironically, nothing had changed—and
tested my memory and powers.

It all felt so comfortable and so overwhelmingly *right*, but still . . . still . . .

There was still something missing, as I had felt it on the banks of the
Thames. Something not quite as it should be. An emptiness. In that first
euphoric day after the Sidlesaghe had thrown me into the river, and I had
remembered and, in remembering, I had thought that if I had actually felt anything wrong, then that was merely because of the newness of my awareness.

Now, in the days following that awakening, and, more particularly, during
the long nights following, I had more than adequate time to investigate.

That exploration unnerved me. I found a fullness of memory and experience, a growing sense of power and knowledge, but at the very heart of all
this . . . a cold emptiness. Not so much that there was something "missing,"
but that I could not determine what it was.

Only that I was slightly "emptier" than I should be.

I consoled myself with the thought that the Sidlesaghes still had to come
to me. I knew that they had visions to show me, and words to share, and I
thought that what was "missing" (whatever it was) could be supplied by them.
They would be the ones to show me how Swanne could be persuaded to part
with her powers. They were the ones to show me the means whereby Asterion
could be subdued.

They would be the ones to show me how William . . . no, I would not dare
to think about that now. There was too much else to be accomplished before
then.

On the fourth night after that of my awakening, I lay beside Edward
thinking deep into the early hours of the morning. Finally I fell into a fitful
sleep.

I dreamed.

I walked the stone hall again, *my* stone hall, my special place. I studied it, seeing that perhaps one day it could be a place of great joy.

Perhaps. If all went well.

I recalled that, not so long ago, when I had been Caela-unremembering, William had come to me in this hall and so, when I heard the soft footfall behind me, I turned, a glad smile on my face, thinking that it would be him again.

It was Silvius, and some of the gladness went out of my smile.

Oh, but he was so much like Brutus! He was as tall, and as dark, but not so heavily muscled, and his face, almost a mirror of Brutus' own (save for that patch over his empty eye), was gentler and far more weary than I had ever remembered my husband's. That gentleness and weariness made my gut wrench, and endeared him to me as nothing else could have done.

Silvius was dressed as he would have been in his Trojan prime: beautifully tooled-leather waistband, soft ivory waistcloth, laced boots that came partway up his calves, and a variety of gold and bronze jewelry about his fingers and dangling from his ears. His long, curly black hair was tied with a thong in the nape of his neck.

About Silvius' limbs, around his biceps, forearms, and just below his knees, circled broad bands of paler flesh, as if someone had only recently taken from him the bands that had once graced his body.

I saw that my fading smile had hurt him, and so I held out my hands in greeting, and rearranged the smile upon my face.

"Silvius," I said. "What do you here?"

He took my hands, one of his fingers reaching out to touch the bracelet on my wrist, and smiled in answer to my own. "Come to see this lovely, magical woman," he said. "Why, oh why, did Brutus never appreciate you? Not know what a treasure he held in his arms?"

His hands tightened about mine as he spoke, and their warmth and dry softness made the breath catch in my throat. *Oh, he was so much like Brutus!*

"What do you here?" I asked again, hearing the quaver in my voice and hoping Silvius would not know the reason for it. "What have you been doing, wandering the streets above, and conversing with Saeweald and Judith?"

"I am a part of the Game," he said. "Brutus left me to wander its twists eternally. That is what I do here. I am part of the Game." With his hands, he drew me in close to him, so that I could feel the heat from his flesh, and feel the waft of his breath across my face.

"Gods," he whispered. "I am so glad to see you as you truly should be."

And then he leaned forward and kissed me, gently, warmly, lingeringly, on my mouth.

I was stunned at my reaction. Silvius had just dared far too much, but . . .

oh, I had always longed to have Brutus kiss me, and had hated it that this was the one intimacy he denied me.

And so, when Silvius leaned forward and presumed so greatly as to place his mouth on mine, I sighed, mingling my breath with his, and opened my mouth under his.

He was surprised, I think, for he drew back, half-laughing. "Lady," he said, "do not mistake me for my son."

I let his hands go, and smiled apologetically. "I am sorry for that. For a moment . . ."

"I am not my son."

"I know."

To distract him, and myself, I lifted a hand to the patch over his eye. For a moment, I hesitated, and then I lifted the patch, and winced at the shadows that I saw writhing within the empty socket.

For two thousand years the Troy Game had been attracting evil into its heart, and for two thousand years Silvius had waited within that same heart, where Brutus' corruption had placed him. The shadows I saw within Silvius' empty socket was the physical manifestation of evil at the heart of the Game.

"You carry this about with you?" I whispered.

He nodded. "I must."

I turned away, unable to bear it. "I wish I could undo that which Brutus has done to you."

"Perhaps one day you will."

Distracted, both by his presence, and by the thought of what Silvius had been forced to bear these two thousand years, I lifted my left arm and allowed the bracelet to sparkle between us. "I thank you for this. It was a fine gift."

"It did not make you remember."

"A little." I allowed myself to look at him again. "It prepared the way, I think."

He laughed softly. "You are very kind." He stepped close to me again, and touched my hair. "When you killed Genvissa, Brutus kept you imprisoned in a dank, airless hovel for three years. And then for another twenty-four he took you back to his bed and tormented you. Oh gods, how is it that I had bred such a son!"

Abruptly he turned away. "Do you know," he said, half looking over his shoulder, "that when my wife was pregnant with Brutus, a seer told me that I should cause the child to be aborted, for it would be the death of both me and her."

He laughed shortly. "She was wrong. He was far more than just the death of me. He imprisoned me in torment, as he did you. He—"

"Stop," I said. "Please."

"You still love him," he said, wonderingly. "How can that be so?" Now he swiveled back to me again. "How can that be so when he caused you so much suffering?"

"But *you* still love him."

His eye went very dark, and his face stilled. "Oh, aye, I still love him. He is my son. My flesh." Silvius hesitated, and when he spoke again his voice was soft, pleading. "Caela, will you come see me sometime, and allow me to come to you? I have been so lonely . . ."

"Of course." I would be glad of it, I thought, to speak with Brutus' father. *And it would serve both Brutus and myself in good stead, when it came time for Brutus-reborn to make his peace with his father, and with himself.*

Thus I reasoned, although, in truth, when I looked at Silvius, all I really saw was Brutus' face. It was a selfish foolishness on my part, but I had been a woman helplessly in love, and despite whom I had become, a part of that love still lingered.

"Tell me," Silvius said, "Now that you are in touch with your true nature, and know of where you must go—"

The doubt at his knowledge of that must have shown on my face, for he laughed.

"Of course I know what you plan, and where you want to go. I have sat in the heart of the Game, remember? Do you think that I do not *know?* You want to complete the Game yourself, with your lover, and make of it a shining thing, rather than the corrupt monster of Genvissa and Brutus' construction."

I let most of my doubts go at that point, and laughed slightly. "Is there anything you do *not* know?"

He made a show of thinking, and I grinned even more. Silvius had a sense of fun about him that his son had never demonstrated. I felt doubly attracted to him, and now it was not merely because of his resemblance to Brutus.

"Aye," Silvius said eventually. "Do you know," he touched the pale flesh about his biceps, "that even though I was once a Kingman, and had kinship with the bands of Troy, that I cannot feel where Brutus has put them. Can you feel them?"

I frowned, then shook my head. "No. He will find them, eventually. Surely."

"Aye. He will. Meantime, there is but you and me."

He smiled, and it made him look so handsome, and so appealing, that I felt my heart race a little, and I knew that he realized it.

"Caela," Silvius said, then he stepped close to me, and leaned forward once more, and laid his mouth on mine, and the last thing I remember as

I rose toward wakefulness was the taste and strength of his tongue in my mouth, and I swear that taste stayed with me all through the day, and at times that memory made me tremble and wonder if Silvius was everything that Brutus had not been.

CbApGER seveN

WILLIAM? WILLIAM?" MATILDA SHOOK HER
husband's shoulder, concerned at his tossing and muttering,
Sweet Christ, of what was he dreaming? *"William!"*

He jerked away, suddenly sitting upright so abruptly he almost knocked
Matilda out of the way.

"Ah," he said, blinking. "I am sorry, my love. A nightmare engulfed me,
and for a moment I thought I was lost to it."

"A nightmare?" She slid an arm about his waist, pulling him gently against
her, and kissed his shoulder. "Tell me of it, for then it will lose all power over
you."

He licked his lips, and for a moment Matilda thought he would not respond, but just as she was about to broach the silence he began to speak in a
harsh tone.

"I dreamed I was in the labyrinth, trying to save . . . I don't know whom,
but someone who was so important to me that I would have died if I could
have given this person freedom."

"The labyrinth?" Matilda said softly, kissing his shoulder once again.

"She was trapped—"

Matilda held her breath at that "she."

"—and I could not find her. The blackness swarmed all about, and I thought
it would overwhelm me . . . *had* overwhelmed her . . . ah, Matilda, this is
making no sense, and I am sorry for it. It makes no sense to me, either."

"But why dream of a labyrinth?"

He gave a half shrug. "It no doubt has meaning that the local village wise-
woman can decode for me."

"Perhaps it represents England, and your fear that England shall be a
trap."

"Perhaps," he said eventually.

"William," Matilda said, unnerved by her husband's dream, "there is something I should say to you."

She saw a flash of his white teeth as he grinned. "What, wife? You feel the need to confess a passion for the stableman? For the houndsman? You need to tell me that none of my children were fathered by me, but by a variety of rough-speaking peasants?"

She did not grin as he had expected her to. "Matilda?"

"William, perhaps England *will* be a trap."

"What do you know?"

"Hardrada lusts for England. You know this."

He nodded. "The king of Norway has long cast envious eyes south. What of it?"

"It is possible that he conspires with Tostig, Harold's brother."

"Against Harold?"

"Who else?"

"How do you know this?" William asked eventually.

"Womanly gossip, my love."

He regarded her silently for some time, then nodded. If she would not tell him, he would respect that for the moment.

For the moment.

CHAPTER EIGHT

SWANNE GLANCED OVER HER SHOULDER, SAW that Harold was ensconced in some doubtless dry conversation with Earl Ralph, Edward's nephew; Wulfstan, the bishop of Worcester; and his younger brother, Tostig. Swanne knew there had been some bad blood between Harold and Tostig recently, but they seemed to have resolved whatever differences they had in the past few days, and now were back to their old, easy friendship. There was an empty chair set next to Harold's: Swanne's chair, but she had no intention of filling it this evening. Just behind the group of men, sitting attentive on a bench, were Harold and Swanne's eldest sons, Beorn and Alan. Saeweald was sitting with the boys as well, and managed to catch Swanne's eye during her brief glance.

She arched an eyebrow at him, then deliberately turned her back, walking slowly and gracefully down the hall toward a gathering of southern thegns listening to the sweet voice of a Welsh bard. Swanne smiled as the group rose to greet her, then accepted a seat from one of the thegns.

This would be a far pleasanter means of spending the evening than having to pretend a smile at Harold. Truly, now that events moved apace, and William was surely so close, she would not have to submit to him for much longer.

The king had retired early, well before Vespers, whining about a headache and a congestion of his belly. Freed from the necessity of attending the king during evening court, Harold and his retinue had retired thankfully to the earl's own hall and chambers at the southern end of the palace complex. Caela, Swanne assumed as she settled down and allowed the thegns and bard to fawn over her, was trapped with her husband, wiping either his brow or his arse, whichever needed the most attention at the moment.

Her grin broadening, Swanne relaxed and tried to concentrate on the song the bard was now singing for her. In truth, she'd not had many settled moments these past few days. Something had happened . . . something had *shifted*.

Oh, yes, part of it was Caela suddenly recalling all that had been—for no apparent reason—but that was not all.

Was it something about the land? The very soil and the forests and the waters? It made Swanne uncomfortable. Once she would have known. Once she had been the MagaLlan, and *nothing* occurred within and to the land without her being fully apprised of it. But Swanne's powers as MagaLlan had passed with her previous life, and her darkcraft lay untouchable, and something was moving beneath her feet that she was not privy to.

Asterion, no doubt.

Damn you, William, Swanne thought, keeping the smile light on her mouth and the desperation from her eyes, *Reach out to me! Let me know that you, at least, are well!*

William still hadn't replied to her request that he tell her where the golden bands of Troy were. *Damn him* for delaying the information! They were all in danger of dancing to Asterion's call . . . and Swanne had no doubt at all that Asterion would be trying to locate those bands *before* William arrived in England to claim his throne and his heritage.

Hadn't that been what Asterion had been doing these two thousand years, while delaying their rebirth?

She had to find those bands now! Before Asterion.

Swanne could not entirely prevent the shiver of apprehension that shot from the base of her spine to her neck. If Asterion found those bands, then he would effectively prevent William and her from dancing the final Dance of the Flowers and completing the Game. It was all Asterion had to do. He need not even face William.

He only had to find and hide, or destroy, those bands.

From the corner of her eye, Swanne saw the great door at the end of the Hall open, and glanced over.

More churchmen! Was the entire land swarming with them? The archbishop of York, Aldred, and Eadwine, abbot of Westminster Abbey, had entered, smiling and nodding, *and*—damn them!—were making their way toward Swanne and her group of musicians and admirers.

Swanne's smile slipped, but she had it back in place by the time Aldred and Eadwine sat themselves down a few places from her, bobbing their heads pleasantly to all about. Eadwine began a muted conversation with the thegn beside him, while Aldred waved the bard to continue as he sat back, and, closing his eyes, folded his hands over his huge belly. His expression relaxed into one of total enjoyment, and Swanne had to admit that perhaps the archbishop did find the soulful music of the Welsh bard a more enjoyable entertainment than the constant wail of sinners and beggars, and the incoherent mumble of monkish prayers that must surely fill most of his days.

The great door opened again, admitting yet another party, but this time

Swanne ignored it, as she finally relaxed under the spell of the bard's beautiful voice.

It would be another group of clerics, or sycophants perhaps, come to scry out the lay of the land in the court of, possibly, the king to follow Edward.

If only they knew, Swanne thought, closing her eyes herself and allowing her body to sway slightly to the rhythm of the bard's music. *If only they knew.*

William, her lips formed slowly, and, briefly, the tip of her tongue glistened between her teeth.

Asterion saw her from his place within the hall, and read her thoughts, and kept his face bland and pleasant, and his thoughts to himself.

When Swanne reopened her eyes, it was to notice that the entire world seemed to have changed.

No longer was she the sole object of attention within her circle of clerics, thegns, and musicians.

Instead, all of their eyes—indeed, every eye within the hall!—was watching as Caela and several of her attending ladies walked slowly and assuredly up the hall toward Harold and his company.

It must have been *Caela* and her party who had entered the hall after Aldred. But why wasn't Caela with her husband? *What was she doing here?* Swanne had never known Caela to do something like this.

It was far too bold for the contemptuous wretch.

And the way she walked. She was so confident, so majestic.

So sure of herself.

Every eye in the hall was riveted on Caela, and not merely because of her surprising entrance.

Because of the way she walked. That wasn't like Caela at all. Not even a Caela who had suddenly recalled her previous life.

Swanne felt her heart thudding within her chest. There was something about the way Caela moved, something in the way she held herself. Something Swanne should have recognized, and yet remained curiously just out of recognition's reach. *Damn her!*

She swiveled about on her seat, and stared toward Caela who was, by now, within ten paces of Harold.

And the empty chair beside him.

Nausea and cold disbelief gripped Swanne in equal amounts. Caela was about to take *Swanne's* place at Harold's side!

Apart from making an inelegant and highly embarrassing dash to get to the chair before Caela, there was absolutely nothing Swanne could do about it.

Caela was about to take Swanne's place at the top of the hall. *Caela!*

That Caela, both as queen of England and as Harold's sister and equal, had every right to take that chair, did not enter Swanne's mind. That she herself had disdained to sit with Harold did not for a moment occur to Swanne. All she could think of was that Caela was going to take *her* place at the head of the hall.

Then, just as Caela reached the group of now-standing men, she turned about in a move so elegant and lissome that Swanne had trouble believing that it *was* Caela standing there at all. She faced Swanne, and extended one long, white, graceful hand and arm behind her to the chair by Harold's side.

"If I may, sister?" she said, smiling with great sweetness at Swanne. "This is your seat, after all."

Swanne was so furious that her entire body tensed, and she almost growled. Caela had her trapped. Swanne simply could *not* refuse her permission without appearing scandalously ungracious.

Every eye in the hall was on her.

A moment passed.

Something changed within Caela's smile, something so subtle that Swanne was sure no one but her would have noted it. Swanne realized that Caela was deliberately provoking her. For the sheer enjoyment of it.

"As my queen wishes," Swanne said. Then, as Caela bowed her head in acceptance, and started to turn back to Harold, Swanne added, "And, if you wish, you can also take my place in your brother's bed. We all know how much you have both lusted for it."

Absolute silence filled the hall. No one could believe Swanne had said that. Rumor and innuendo was one thing, outright accusation another.

As one, eyes turned from Swanne to Caela.

Among them, Asterion was absolutely incredulous. If he didn't mind his way, Swanne would dig her own grave before he could manage it for her! Gods! The Intemperance of the woman!

He narrowed his eyes, intrigued as to how Caela would react.

Caela tilted her head slightly, her still face composed, and regarded Swanne thoughtfully. "Even if your own tastes have been bred within the dung heap, sister, you should think twice before ascribing them to others. If you find my purity unbearable, then think not to besmirch it with your own foulness."

Swanne froze in humiliation and fury, unable for the moment to respond.

Caela's eyes shifted slightly, looking to Archbishop Aldred, sitting a few places from Swanne, and looking as shocked as everyone else. "Perhaps, my Lord Archbishop," she said, "you might take my lady Swanne aside for some instruction in manners. Such careless accusations, bred within privy pits and spoken with spitefulness, are the wont only of barnyard sows accustomed to rolling in muck. They are not becoming to those who believe themselves great ladies of the realm."

With that, Caela turned her back to Swanne, smiled at Harold (who had been glaring at Swanne with silent promises of later retribution), took his hand and allowed herself to be escorted to the chair beside his.

Behind her, thegns slowly began to drift away from Swanne's group, thinning it to such an extent that within minutes there remained only Swanne, the highly embarrassed archbishop, the equally embarrassed, but also angry, abbot, and a Welsh bard, who looked as if he did not know whether to continue singing or not.

"I am most sorry for that," Harold murmured as Caela sat down. He was studying her as many others were, surprised that the queen had managed to best Swanne in the verbal exchange. "You spoke well, sister. Swanne has ever had a vicious tongue, and that little jest of hers was unbecoming in the extreme."

It was what Harold had to say, even if, in his heart, he was writhing in shame. *What had Swanne seen when she'd walked in on him and Caela that single time they'd let their passions rule their heads?*

Caela shrugged, looking utterly unperturbed. "Swanne is . . . Swanne. It is no matter to me, brother. Now, Judith shall stay with me, and my other ladies may interest themselves as they may in the hall."

She waved away her attending ladies, save for Judith, who sat on a stool Saeweald had placed beside Caela's chair, and nodded greetings to her brother Tostig and the other men who were now resuming their seats about Harold. Tostig was regarding her as thoughtfully as most others were: that exchange was not what he would have suspected from the girl he had known so many years.

"What great conference have I interrupted, Harold, Tostig?" Caela said. "Such grave faces you all wear!"

Harold glanced at Judith, and Caela reached down a hand to the woman, keeping her eyes steady on Harold's face. "I trust Judith with my life," she said. "You may, also."

Harold looked again to Judith, then to Saeweald, who gave a very slight nod.

"Very well," he said, then he sighed, and rubbed a hand over his suddenly haggard face. "Not good news, Caela. I have heard that Harold Hardrada has agents within this court. I fear their intent."

Tostig rolled his eyes. "Our brother has turned to womanly fancies, sister."

"The intelligence is good!" Harold snapped.

"Of what do you fear, Harold?" Caela said.

"Hardrada wants England, he has made no secret of this. I worry that he will try to smooth his way to the throne with some silent, treacherous action."

"Do you fear for yourself, Harold?" Tostig asked softly. "Why, the last I heard, you had surrounded yourself with an army to keep unwanted daggers at bay."

Harold gave Tostig a dark look, but did not respond to his taunt.

"Can you discover who they are?" Caela said.

Harold nodded. "Within a day or two. My men know where one of the agents, a man named Ölafson, hides. I will have him taken, and questioned."

Caela grimaced. She knew precisely what Harold meant by "questioned."

To one side, Tostig's face had suddenly gone very still.

"Ah!" Harold continued, "If only I had the knowledge of the angels on my side, and knew when Edward will finally gasp his last. Then I could plan the better to meet any challengers. But," he shrugged, smiling wryly now, "who can know such things."

Caela started to speak, then stopped, indecision written across her face. She exchanged a glance with Saeweald, then dropped her gaze to her lap.

"What do you know, sister?" Harold asked very quietly. "You share his chamber intimately. Is there something you can share?"

She lifted her eyes to his. "Edward will not live more than a few days past the New Year celebrations."

There was an utter silence as everyone stared at her.

"How can you know this?" asked Wulfstan, his eyes narrowed suspiciously. "Such knowledge is witchery, surely."

Caela regarded the bishop very calmly. "I know this," she said, "because, as Harold has said, I am my husband's wife, and I know his every breath and manner. And I know this because my husband's physician," again she glanced at Saeweald, "tells me that Edward has not long to live. And . . . and I have dreamed it. An angel has indeed come to me and told me as much."

People nodded, accepting her explanation. But again, as before, Tostig's face was very still, his eyes watchful.

"And my fate?" asked Harold. "What is *my* fate, then, if you speak to angels in your dreams?"

Caela leaned forward and took both of Harold's hands in hers. Her expression was one of great sadness and joy combined. "You will become a hero such as this land has never seen before," she said. "You will live in glory."

To his side, Tostig and Saeweald exchanged glances, then as quickly looked away from each other again.

Harold stared at her, then his mouth quirked. "That may be read as either a glorious death, or a glorious reign, sister. No! Do not explain yourself, for I regret the asking of the question in the first place. But do tell me, since you seem to know so much, who is it I should fear the most? Who stands as the greatest obstacle between me and the throne of England?"

She tipped her head, and regarded him. "Your enemies shall flock like crows, Harold. I am not the warrior to tell you which one shall be the most cunning."

Harold gave a hard bark of laughter. "You do not *want* to tell me!"

Something hardened in Caela's eyes. "Beware of William, brother, for at his back shall ride the greatest enemy this land shall ever know."

"Now you speak in riddles, Caela. Should I fear his wife, Matilda? But, oh yes, William . . ." he drifted into silence, one hand rubbing at his short, stubbled beard.

"Has there been any more spoken," said Wulfstan, "of that contract Edward and William are rumored to have made between them fourteen years ago?"

Harold chewed his lip. Twelve years ago Edward had moved briefly—but with great effect—against the Godwine clan. The entire family, even Caela, had been exiled for almost a year, and only the great cunning of Earl Godwine himself had seen their eventual restoration to power. They had regained their place, but ever since that time it had been rumored that, while free of the Godwine family's influence, Edward had made a pact with William, promising him the throne of England on Edward's death.

"There is always a great deal rumored about William," Harold said quietly, his eyes unfocused, "and very little spoken that is known fact. What does William plan? How shall he justify his ambitions before God and the other thrones of Europe? I don't know . . . I don't know . . ."

And there lies the rub, thought Harold. *No one knows what William is or is not planning. And without that knowledge, anything I plan is certain to be torn asunder the instant I act on it. What are you planning, William? Will you content yourself with Normandy, or do you want this green isle, as well?*

CHAPTER NINE

"HE *HUMILIATED* ME, AND YOU SAID NOTHING!" Swanne said, as she watched her husband disrobe.

Harold remained silent, unlacing his tunic, sliding it over his head and tossing it across a chest.

Swanne stalked closer, her hands balled into fists, her face white with fury, her black eyes snapping. "You have a duty to me. I am your *wife*. I—"

Harold suddenly turned about from laying his shirt atop his tunic and grabbed her chin in his hand. "You have a vile tongue, Swanne, and, I am learning, a mind to go with it! Be silent, I beg you, before I lose what little regard I have left for you!"

She twisted out of his grip. "You've always lusted after her."

He went white, but said or did nothing.

"You dream about it, don't you? I've heard you, mumbling at night, planning your incestuous assault on your sister's body—"

He slapped her, then grabbed her wrist as she tried to strike him and twisted it so violently she cried out. "Caela was right," he said, "when she said you had been bred within a dunghill, Swanne. You are the get of a worm and the night; there is no sweetness within you at all, merely vileness."

Again Harold turned from her, twisting off his boots and then his trousers and tossing them toward the chest.

Swanne nursed her wrist, watching him with, finally, all of her loathing and contempt writhing across her face. "And there is nothing for you *but* the dunghill, Harold. You cast your eyes toward the throne, but you should know that—"

She stopped suddenly, both her eyes and those of Harold's flying to the door that had suddenly opened.

Tostig stood there, his face equal amounts incredulity and humor as he regarded his naked brother and Swanne standing before him.

"My, my," he said softly, closing the door and walking slowly into the room. His eyes were very wary.

"Is this the future king and queen of England I see before me? Nay, I think not. This behavior cannot surely be that of—"

"What do you want, Tostig?" Harold said roughly.

Tostig had been watching Swanne who, correctly reading the look on his face, took three or four steps back, spreading her hands out at her sides. Now, he turned back to his brother.

"Only this, Harold," he said softly, "that Hardrada sends his greetings, and bids you a well-earned death."

And, lightening quick, he drew his dagger from the belt at his waist and plunged it toward Harold's heart.

Harold had nothing with which to defend himself save his hands. He grabbed Tostig's wrist just as the dagger reached his chest, and managed to stop the blade before it had penetrated more than a finger's thickness into his body. With all the strength he had, he wrenched the dagger backward, but he could do nothing about Tostig's weight that, leaning down with the force of his plunge forward, pushed Harold back onto the bed.

"For God's sake, Swanne!" Harold shouted. "Send for aid! *Now!*"

Swanne watched, her face still slack in shock at the suddenness of the attack. Then, as Harold screamed at her again, she smiled, very slightly, and stood back, folding her arms across her breasts.

"No," she said, and then laughed softly as the two men writhed their deadly dance across the bed.

CAELA WAS ASLEEP, WHEN SUDDENLY HER INNOCU-
ous dream slid into horror.

His face was torn from her hands by a great black shadow that loomed over them, and she saw a glint of metal that swept in a vicious arc across Coel's throat. His body, still deep within hers, convulsed, and she screamed, and blood spurted over her in a hot, sticky flood.

Brutus took a firmer grip on Coel's hair, then he tore him from her, tearing him painfully out from her, and all she could do was cry, "No! No! Oh, gods, Brutus, no! Not Coel!"

And then she heard Swanne laugh . . .

Caela jerked upright in bed, shrieking so loudly that both Edward, Judith, and the bowerthegn woke shouting as well.

"Assassins!" Caela screamed, stumbling in her haste to leap from the bed and grabbing her robe as soon as her feet hit the floor. "Assassins! Harold's chambers. Oh, God, assassins! *Help him!*"

"No!" hissed Edward, but by then both Judith and the bowerthegn had rushed from the chamber and were rousing the guards.

"It will be too late," Caela whispered, standing as if stunned, or still caught by dream. "He is too far from us."

HAROLD AND TOSTIG TWISTED ACROSS THE BED, rolling this way and that, each man grunting with effort, neither man able to gain the upper hand from an opponent as strong and as battle-hardened as the other.

"For the gods' sakes, Tostig," Swanne muttered, her look now anxious. "Do not mismanage this as you have so many other matters!"

At that moment Harold cried out, and Swanne saw a thick smear of blood mar the surface of the creamy bed linens.

"Good," she said. "Very good."

THE PALACE WAS AWAKE AND IN FULL CRY, GUARDS grabbing weapons and rushing through halls and chambers toward exits and, eventually, Harold's hall to the south of Edward's palace.

Caela ran with them, her robe flapping and barely knotted about her waist, terrified, hearing Swanne laugh, hearing also Harold's cry of pain and fear.

They would never get there in time!

Summoning all the power she could through her panic, she sent a shaft of alarm directly to the men she knew stood guard within Harold's own hall.

Your lord fights away an assassin! Aid him, aid him, now!

Then, to her immense relief, Caela felt within her an echoing answer of panic as the guards within Harold's hall rushed toward his bedchamber.

TOSTIG SUDDENLY CRIED OUT, ROLLING AWAY FROM Harold, a deep cut across his belly. Harold lurched upright, his own chest and belly covered in blood and, ignoring the dagger, struck Tostig an immense blow to his jaw.

The blow sent Tostig tumbling to the floor. Harold lurched forward, meaning to throw himself after his brother, but one of his legs tangled in a sheet, and he fell, hitting the floor with a heavy thud and cry of pain.

Tostig rolled to his knees, gripping the dagger, and exchanging a quick glance with Swanne who was stepping forth, her hands held out in entreaty— *finish him! For the gods' sakes, finish him!*—but just then Tostig heard the distant footfalls of the guards rushing up the stairs and, with a bitter curse, he sheathed the dagger in his belt, stumbled to his feet, and disappeared out the door.

WHEN CAELA ARRIVED WITH JUDITH, THE BOWERTHEGN, and what seemed like an entire company of guards from Edward's palace, it was to find Harold sitting on his bed, one of his guards by his side holding a thick wad of bedding to Harold's chest and belly to staunch the bleeding, and Swanne standing by the window, staring out, her face closed, her arms folded.

"Harold!" Caela said and ran to him, pushing away the guard's hand so that she could examine her brother's wound. "Harold? Are you well? Oh, gods, I dreamed of treachery—" *I dreamed that Genvissa had set Brutus to your death all over again* "—and came as fast as I could."

"It was Tostig," Harold said, wincing as Caela's probing fingers bit a little too deeply.

Caela went very still. "Tostig?" she whispered. "Oh gods . . . Tostig . . ."

"Tostig was ever the fool," Swanne said in a toneless voice. She still kept her back to them as she stood by the window.

Harold looked his wife's way, and the black hate in his eyes was enough to make Caela recoil.

"Swanne?" she whispered. *"Again?"*

Swanne turned about. "Me? Nay, Caela. I was surprised as any by Tostig's attack."

"She stood back," Harold said. "She laughed, refusing to aid me."

"I was afraid for my own life!" Swanne cried, her face now a mask of fright. "I thought he would take his blade to me the instant he had done with you!"

Harold was about to say more, but just then Saeweald pushed his way past the guards standing about, and the movement was enough to make the bowerthegn spring into action.

"What are you standing about for!" he cried, his face purpling. "Seek out the assassin! *Now!*"

Within three heartbeats, the chamber had almost emptied again as the bowerthegn hurried the guards out the door, leaving for the moment only Harold, Swanne, Judith, and Caela.

"Let me see," said Saeweald as he sat on Harold's other side. He pushed away Caela's hands, pulled back the wad of bedding that was being used to staunch the bleeding and, with fingers considerably less gentle than Caela's had been, pulled back the flap of skin on the cut that ran across Harold's belly, and then probed the puncture wound in his chest.

Harold cursed, pulling away, but Saeweald would not leave him be until he'd finished his examination.

He grunted finally, allowing Caela to wipe away the blood, and sat back. "You're lucky," Saeweald said. "The chest wound did not go deep enough to reach either your heart or your lungs. It will be sore enough for a few days, but it will leave you with hardly a scar. The belly wound I will need to stitch, but only because of its length, it is even less deep than that wound in your chest."

Swanne laughed, harsh and bitter, making everyone jerk their heads toward her. "Well now," she said, "what a scene this is. Is it only someone with my sense of humor who could possibly enjoy it? Ah, I see no need to pretend, not with who we have here in this chamber."

She sauntered forward. "Lucky, lucky Caela," she said, very low, her eyes vicious, "isn't this just what you always wanted? Sitting on a bed next to your naked lover—only this time he has survived the assassin's knife. Tell me, should we leave you in peace so you and your lover can consummate your love . . . I'm sure those wounds won't stop him."

Caela's face hardened as she opened her mouth to speak, but Harold forestalled her. He pushed aside Saeweald's hands, strode over to his wife, and grabbed her arm with a tight hand.

"Get you gone from here, you snake-tongued bitch," he said and, despite her protests, pushed her through the door and slammed it shut after her. Then Harold turned about, his face more determined now than angry, walked over to where Caela sat, leaned down, and kissed her hard on the mouth.

"I am no longer ashamed of what I feel for you," he said, standing upright again. "On the night that my brother tried to murder me, and my wife begged him to succeed, I have no reluctance in admitting before all present," his eyes swept over Saeweald and Judith, "that I love you more than any other woman, more than life itself."

Caela rose slowly, her eyes riveted on Harold's. "Harold . . ." She sighed, closed her eyes briefly, then leaned forward and kissed him very softly on the mouth. "We cannot. We each have different paths to travel. If we were to act on this love, it would destroy this realm. What we feel for each other would be used against us, and this land and its people would be the ones to suffer. We cannot, and I, for one, am most sorry for it."

She turned away, and, her head bowed, left the chamber.

ChAPTER TEN

CAELA SPEAKS

AROLD CAME TO SEE ME THE DAY AFTER TOSTIG'S vile treachery. It was in the late afternoon, and many among the court, my husband included, had gone to vespers services within the abbey church. Edward had only shrugged when told of the drama within Harold's bedchamber the previous night, and commented: "I'd thought Tostig was a better marksman than that."

I was seated before the fire in the Lesser Hall that Edward and I used for our smaller courts when Harold arrived. He nodded away Judith and the two other ladies who were seated with me as I rose to greet him.

Under normal circumstances I would have kissed him on the mouth—that was normal greeting between close relatives—but "normal circumstance" between us had been shattered the previous night. I took his hands between mine, and pressed them, then let them go and silently cursed the awkwardness between us.

"Harold . . . are you well? Your wounds?"

"They sting a little," he said, and I could see that in the stiffness of his movement as he lowered himself into the chair, "but they shall be no more trouble. Saeweald has done well."

"And Tostig has done badly," I said. "Oh, Harold, I cannot believe that our brother—"

"Leave Tostig for the moment," he said. "Caela, what happened last night, what I said—"

"What you said was truth, and best spoken," I said. "Do I feel this pull between us? Yes, of course I do. But we *cannot* act on it, Harold. We cannot. We are each more than just a man and a woman unhappily yearning each for the other. What each of us does affects an entire realm and its people. We cannot."

I cannot kill you again through my ill-considered passions, Coel. Please understand that. Please.

His mouth twisted wryly. "You state your case as clearly as you did last night. I am sorry that I have so discomforted you."

"You comfort me through all my life, Harold," I said as softly and lovingly as I could.

He looked away, overcome, I think, with emotion, and for long moments we were silent.

Finally, unable to bear it any longer, I said, "Tostig?"

He sighed. "Last night's debacle was my own fault. You remember that when we sat in court in the evening, I mentioned that I'd heard that Hardrada had agents within Westminster, and I had the means to shortly discover them, and their purpose?"

I nodded.

His mouth twisted wryly. "Even then I suspected Tostig. I had thought to goad him into action . . . but I had no idea how deadly that action might be."

I closed my eyes momentarily, unable to bear the thought that Tostig might have succeeded. "Have you found him?"

"No. He slipped away."

Aided, no doubt, by Swanne's witchcraft, I thought. *How she must have enjoyed last night.*

He reached a hand out and took one of mine. I tensed, but then relaxed. A hand was not much. "You aided me," he said. "I am not sure how, but I know it was you. My men said they were roused by the sound of your voice screaming in their heads, screaming that an assassin was upon me."

I said nothing, but my eyes filled with tears. All I could think of was how Brutus had torn him from me, and ripped out his throat. To have that happen again . . .

"Ah," he said, very softly, "you do not deny it. Then I do owe you my life."

"You are very beloved to me, Harold," I whispered.

He smiled, and it contained no demands, nor hurt. Nothing but love.

"Swanne?" I said, wanting to distract both him and myself.

"Ah, Swanne. After Saeweald attended me last night I returned with him to his own chamber, mostly to avoid my damnable wife, as to avoid the stink of murder in my bedchamber, but also partly as a precaution should Tostig have decided to try again. I have not seen her this morning, nor shall I seek her out."

"Be wary of her."

"You do not need to warn me of *that!* God, Caela, she stood there and laughed as Tostig tried to murder me."

"She can do far worse, Harold. Please . . ."

"I *will* be wary of her, my love. Now, to the reason I came to you this morning, apart from my desire to lay my eyes on your beautiful face yet again, and to thank you for saving my life. Caela, I need your aid further to what you have already done for me."

"You have it."

"You may not be so willing to offer it when you hear what I need from you."

"You will always have my aid, Harold. Whatever you plan."

"I have put it about that in four days' time I intend to return to my home estates in Wessex. My stewards have some problems that I need to attend. Besides, I need the peace to recover from Tostig's brutal attack."

I inclined my head. Nothing thus far seemed very difficult.

He held my eyes steady. "But Wessex is not my true destination, sister."

I raised an eyebrow.

"I go to see William of Normandy."

"Harold!"

"Shush! Keep your voice down! No one must know of this, Caela! I need you to help maintain the ruse that I am in Wessex."

"Why? *Why?*" My heart was pounding in my breast, and my emotions were so tangled that I could not sort them out. *Oh, gods, William was his murderer in his previous life . . . why go to see him now?* "Why, Harold?"

"I need to know William's intentions. I need to know his ambitions. Caela, the crows are gathering for Edward's death. I need to know who my rivals for the throne shall be. After last night, I can now be certain that Tostig will be against me, and will probably ally with Hardrada—only the gods know what Hardrada has promised Tostig in return. But William is an unknown. He could be either my rival or my ally. What does *he* plan?"

Ah, mercies, I knew exactly what he planned, but how could I tell Harold this without shaking him to the very core of his being with the tale of his previous life? Harold needed strength and equanimity to survive what faced him. Saeweald and Ecub were surely right when they argued that he did not need to be distracted or perhaps even tipped into uncertainty by what had happened to Coel. I believed that Harold had a better chance against William without the burdens of both their previous lives.

"I need him to know, if he does not know it already," Harold said, "that England shall stand united behind me. Perhaps if he knows that, then he will ally with me, continue the partnership he had with Edward. He may not be such a willing rival if he knows how England will stand behind me."

Ha! I thought, but again felt that it would be better that Harold discovered now where William's ambitions lay than delude himself with the hope he might be an ally. "The witan will elect you king?" I said.

"Aye. They have given me their word."

"And you hope that, in informing William of this, he might retract his ambitions? Reconsider his likelihood of success? Consider instead an alliance before a challenge?"

"He already has Normandy safe in hand. Why lust for England as well when it might well kill him?"

Oh, what could I say? That William-once-Brutus would have no compunction in slaughtering the entire witan, in razing the entire land, if he thought it would clear his way to London, to Swanne, and to his Trojan kingship bands?

And yet what harm could Harold's trip do?

Particularly if I armed Harold as best I could for his venture.

Besides, this he *did* need to know.

"Harold," I said, laying a hand on his knee. "I have some deeply privy information for you that has only just come to my ears."

Had just come to my own understanding, more like, but there was no means by which I could explain this to Harold.

"Yes?" he said.

"It will be useful for you at William's court," I continued. "A weapon."

"Yes?"

"William has an agent, a spy, within Edward's court."

He gave a harsh bark of laughter. "I am not startled to hear of it. There are agents everywhere, I think."

"It is Swanne."

Nothing I could have said would have shocked Harold more. Well, perhaps one or two revelations may have shocked him more, but this one certainly had no small effect.

He stared, white-faced. *"Swanne?"*

I nodded.

"Why? *Why?*"

What could I say but the truth? "She lusts for him, and she lusts to sit as queen beside him."

Harold cursed. "Then no wonder she stood by and laughed as Tostig tried to murder me. Ah, I have misjudged both her and Tostig. I knew she disliked me, but to betray me to William? I had not thought she would go that far."

What could I say? That Swanne wanted William, not for the title as queen, but because he was her Kingman, and with him she could achieve a greater immortality than she ever could as wife to Harold?

Harold was a hindrance to the Mistress of the Labyrinth. William was a much-loved necessity.

"There can be no doubt that I *will* set her aside after her behavior last night, as well knowing her betrayal of me to William," Harold added, his face now rigid with anger. "By Christ himself, Caela, does Swanne not know that William is already wed, and securely so by all accounts?"

A wife has never stood in her path before, I thought, *and she will not allow one to do so now.*

"Be careful," I said, meaning so much with those two simple words.

"Aye," Harold said, smiling in what I suppose he hoped would be a reassuring manner. He rose. "You will put it about that I am in Wessex, and perhaps send communications to me there, so that all may think I truly am within my estates?"

"Aye, of course. Harold . . ." I took his hand as he was about to step away. "Will you do something for me?"

"Anything."

"Will you talk to Matilda, William's wife, and discover what kind of woman she is? I have heard so many rumors of her, and I would like to hear a report from eyes I can trust."

I was curious. Feverishly so. Matilda might make all the difference if she was indeed as strong as rumor had it. William had been married to her for some fifteen years. They had many children together.

"Harold," I continued, "will you tell me if . . . if she is someone William respects?"

I could see he was agog with curiosity as to my motives, but he merely nodded. "Of course."

And will you tell me of William? I wanted to ask, but did not.

Oh, merciful heavens, how I wanted to be there when Coel-who-was and Brutus-who-was met again for the first time in two thousand years.

I hoped that William had learned enough that he would not instantly slide a sword through Harold's throat.

CHAPTER ELEVEN

WHEN HAROLD HAD BEEN GONE THREE DAYS, ostensibly to visit his estates in Wessex, and the court quietened in its traditional lull between harvest celebrations and Christmastide festivities, Caela lay asleep beside her husband the king in the quiet, dark night.

The night was very still and, now that autumn had taken firm grip on the land, very cold, readying itself for a heavy frost at dawn. Nothing moved, not so much as a night owl, not even a breath of air.

King Edward's and Queen Caela's bedchamber lay as still and cold as the rest of Edward's kingdom, as heavy and unyielding as the wall Edward had built between himself and the woman who lay at his side. It was a large chamber, its floorboards covered in part with thick rugs, its timber-planked walls hung with woolen tapestries and drapes. A great bed occupied the central portion of the chamber, its embroidered drapes pulled partway about the great mattress where lay the king and queen, their motionless forms huddled far apart.

The king's bowerthegn occupied a trestle bed closer to the door. Beside the bed, lying unscabbarded on the floorboards, lay a sword so that the bowerthegn could set his hand to it the instant danger threatened.

Unusually, the bowerthegn appeared to have forgotten to shutter the windows before he retired and now faint moonlight, occasionally shadowed by thin clouds that scudded across the night sky, spilled through the chamber.

The sleepers did not move, save in the gentle breath of sleep.

The moonlight intensified, almost as if the moon had suddenly waxed to its full girth within the space of a breath.

A stray cloud scudded briefly across its face and, when it moved on, the strange, intense moonlight flooded the chamber once more.

The chamber was not as it had been before the cloud had so briefly obscured the moon.

Now, in that expanse of bare floorboards between the great bed and that of the bowerthegn by the door, there appeared a trapdoor. As yet it was little more than a faint outlining of lines within the boards but, as the moonlight grew ever stronger and the breathing of the sleepers ever heavier, the lines thickened and deepened until the trapdoor became a new reality within the chamber.

Everyone slept on.

The trapdoor quivered, then rose, achingly slowly, utterly silently.

An arm lifted with the door, its hand gripping the bolt that raised the door. It was a very long arm, browned, and roped with muscle. There was a moment of stillness, as if whatever awaited beneath the trapdoor hesitated, to ensure all was well, then, satisfied that all was as it should be, a Sidlesaghe rose entirely from the trapdoor, laying it open silently against the floor.

Again the Sidlesaghe hesitated, looking first at the bowerthegn, then at the sleeping king whose lips rattled wetly as a small snore escaped his throat. Finally, content that all was at it should be, the Sidlesaghe walked to Caela's side of the bed, folded his hands before him, and waited.

A moment later Caela's eyes opened. She saw the Sidlesaghe, and then, without comment, turned back the bedclothes as he held out a hand for her.

Once she had risen, the Sidlesaghe handed her a cloak that had mysteriously appeared in one of his hands, then he nodded at the trapdoor.

She stared at it, clearly puzzled, for directly beneath this bedchamber lay the dais of the Great Hall. She looked at the Sidlesaghe, raising her eyebrows.

He merely nodded once more at the blackness revealed in the mouth of the trapdoor.

Caela gave a slight shrug, then walked to the trapdoor and descended through it into the unknown. The Sidlesaghe stepped down after her, and in the next moment the trapdoor had closed, and there was nothing in the chamber save for the smooth floor and the heavy shadows of the beds, coffers and the two sleepers. There was no Great Hall beneath the trapdoor, nor even the foundations of the Hall, nor even the worm-infested earth that lay beneath. Instead, the Sidlesaghe led Caela into the softly shadowed, barely discernible track of a vast forest. About her reared massive trees—trees such as the land had last seen many millennia ago—tangled with vines and sweetly scented flowers.

Was this the forest and the land of her youth? Of *Mag*'s youth?

Caela tipped back her head and visibly stretched, almost catlike, and drew in a deep breath. "This is so wondrous!" she said.

"Aye," said the Sidlesaghe, coming to stand beside her. "Do you recognize it?"

She frowned, only slightly, just enough to crinkle the skin between her brows. "This is the land, as once it was. Yes?"

He shook his head. "Not entirely correct. The land is not as once it was."

She shivered, and pulled the cloak a little more tightly about her shoulders, as if she had suddenly felt more acutely the fact of her nakedness beneath it. "Ah," she said. "We are in the Game."

"Aye. This is where Brutus and Silvius played the Game. This is where Brutus murdered his father."

"Why are we here?"

"To learn," said the Sidlesaghe. "To remember."

She turned from her regard of the forest and studied the Sidlesaghe. "Long Tom," she said, "when you threw me into the waters, and I came to understand myself as I truly am, I saw many things. I saw my lover, Og, running through the forest," her eyes flickered about the great trees dwarfing them both, "wearing the golden bands that once graced the Kingmen of Troy." Her voice dropped almost to a whisper. "That once graced my husband's limbs."

"What did you learn from that vision, Caela? What did it tell you?"

"It told me where the Game is going, Long Tom. It told me where the land is going, and where I must, too, tread."

"Aye."

"How?" she said. "How did the Game and this land become as one? Can you show me?"

In answer the Sidlesaghe inclined his head, nodding to the path that had opened up through the trees before them. "Will you walk with me?"

She nodded and, taking his hand, they walked through the forest track.

As they want, the Sidlesaghe continued to speak. "The Game has grown, as you know. When you were Cornelia, and you witnessed Brutus and Genvissa dance the Dance of the Torches, what was the Troy Game then?"

"A labyrinth, atop Og's Hill. A thing made of stone and gravel."

"Aye. And then when you had murdered Genvissa, and halted the Game before its completion, what became of the Game and its stone and gravel labyrinth?"

Caela licked her lips, remembering. "Brutus buried it," she said. "He caused it to sink into the hill, and atop it he built a temple." She laughed, short and hard. "Which he dedicated to Artemis."

"And his kingship bands? What did he do with those?"

Caela stopped, and faced the Sidlesaghe. "I don't know. I can't even *feel* them. They merely vanished. When Brutus pulled me from my three-year confinement—and that was the first time I had set eyes on him since that day I'd murdered Genvissa—he was not wearing them and, to be frank, I was so much in fear of my life at that point, so much in fear of *him*, that I did not ask what had become of them. Not ever.

"Silvius asked me about those bands a few nights ago," she said, her mouth quirking in either memory or humor. "*Everyone* wants to know about them."

"They are vital," said the Sidlesaghe. "We dream of them as well. But first,

I will show you what happened to this land and to the Game in the two thousand years that have passed, and then we will need to talk about the bands."

"You know where they are, don't you?" she said, searching his face with her eyes.

The Sidlesaghe smiled. "Of course! Did Brutus not bury them within this *land*? They have been itching at us for centuries."

She laughed, delighted at the humor that lurked behind the Sidlesaghe's otherwise bleak face, and allowed him to lead her farther down the track.

"The Troy Game that Brutus made has grown," the Sidlesaghe said once more. "Now that you understand who you are, and are beginning to understand the extent of yourself, perhaps you can tell me exactly where we are within the Game."

Caela chewed her lower lip, her eyes on the ground, thinking, *feeling* the ground beneath her feet.

"We are within the Game, yes," she said eventually, her eyes still on the ground, "but we are walking within that part of the Game that twists under the northern shore of the River Thames. We were walking north, but are now moving more eastward." She paused. "We are walking toward the heart of the labyrinth. Toward St. Paul's within London, atop what was once Og's Hill. Gods, Long Tom, how far does the Game extend?"

"As far south as Westminster, and a little under the river on the opposite bank to Westminster where once stood Llanbank, and where now stands the village of Lambeth. Eastward the Game now encompasses all that stands within the walls of London. To the northwest the Game stretches toward . . ."

"Toward the Llandin," Caela said. "What the people now call the Meeting Hill."

"Aye, and north—"

"North to Pen Hill. The Game has grown to encompass all of the Veiled Hills. Blessed Lady," the Sidlesaghe stopped, and as he faced Caela he dropped the hand he held and put both of his on her shoulders, "the Game wants to grow even further. It needs to, if it is to overcome what lays ahead. You need to help it do that."

She drew in a deep breath, nodding. "I still need to know—"

"How it grew? Yes, be patient now. We are almost there."

They resumed walking again, and soon the sense of a close forest fell back. Light—not sunlight and yet not quite moonlight either—filled the spaces between the trees, and the borders to either side of the path broadened.

Caela visibly tensed, as if she knew what they walked toward.

Then suddenly they were there.

An emerald green glade, encircled by trees. In the center of the glade lay a roughly circular pond, its waters still.

On the far side of the pond, perhaps some six or seven paces from the water's edge, and halfway between the edge of the forest and the pond, lay the form of a white stag with blood-red antlers.

His heart, half torn from his body, lay on the creamy pelt of his chest.

Caela groaned, and made as if to step forward about the pond, but the Sidlesaghe seized her arm.

"No! Touch him and you kill him!"

She twisted about, partly trying to tear herself free from his grasp, partly in an agony of emotion. "Why? Why can not I go to him? Why?"

"Because you are not yet strong enough to heal him, or to help him in any manner. All you will do is push him toward the final precipice. One day you will be able to aid him, and midwive him through his rebirth, but you are not strong enough to do it now!"

Caela sobbed, her knees slowly bending until she sank to the ground, and the Sidlesaghe let her go.

"Can I not just touch him?" Caela said through her tears. "Just lay a hand to his face, and kiss him?"

"No," the Sidlesaghe said, then laid his own hand on the crown of her head. "He knows you are here. It is enough for him for the moment. It is enough that he knows *you* are reborn, and are growing stronger."

Caela lowered her face into her hands and cried disconsolately, rocking back and forth. The Sidlesaghe, his own gray-brown eyes filled with tears, kept his hand on her head, letting her cry out her sorrow.

"I want to touch him," Caela said once more, but the Sidlesaghe did not respond. He knew she said it, not to him, but to the Stag God himself, and he knew that she said it as a comfort, both to Og and to herself.

Eventually Caela composed herself, wiped the tears from her eyes and cheeks with the backs of her hands, and rose again. "Thank you," she said simply, and the Sidlesaghe nodded.

"We need to go to the pool," he said.

Again they walked forward until they stood at the edge of the pool. Before Caela looked down to the waters, she glanced upward, then gasped, truly shocked.

Instead of a sky, or the arching and intertwining branches of the trees, a great golden dome soared above them.

"We are in the stone hall!" Caela cried.

"We are deep under it," the Sidlesaghe said. "Deep under St. Paul's." He paused. "Deep in the heart of the labyrinth." He looked across the pond again, toward Og, and now Caela saw that Og lay not alone, but that a man sat with him, cradling the wretched stag's head in his lap.

Silvius.

"And there lies the evil the labyrinth attracts," the Sidlesaghe said, his voice hard, merciless, nodding at Silvius.

"I know," Caela whispered. "Poor Silvius."

Silvius looked up as if he had heard her, and he stretched out a hand. His face held both a frightful yearning, as well a terrified aspect, and it unsettled Caela, for Silvius had seemed so confident, so calm, on the two occasions she had met with him. He opened his mouth, and it moved, but no words came out, and his eyes filled with tears, and before Caela's appalled gaze Silvius began to cry.

Caela started forward, but again the Sidlesaghe held her back. "Ignore him," he said. "He is not why we are here now."

She gave Silvius a half-sad, half-reassuring smile, hoping he knew why she could not approach him at the moment. He held her gaze, than lowered his face, looking away from her and back to the stag.

Caela watched him for a further long moment, wishing she could speak with Silvius, and comfort him of whatever had troubled him. Eventually she sighed, and looked again at the water. "The waters will show me what happened to the Game?"

"Aye," said the Sidlesaghe. "Of all people, you should know how to read them."

In answer she walked forward a step or two until the water touched her bare toes.

For long minutes Caela did nothing but stare at the water.

Then, she sighed, only very slightly, but the entire surface of the pond rippled as if disturbed by a heavy wind, and when it settled again, the waters showed Caela what she wanted to know.

Brutus, standing and screaming with grief and rage in the center of the labyrinth atop Og's Hill under a sky laden with roiling black clouds.

Genvissa's body at his feet, her cold pregnant belly mounding toward the sky.

Time, passing.

Brutus, again standing atop Og's Hill, again under the laden black sky, but now Genvissa's corpse lay atop a great burning pyre.

Time, passing.

Brutus, burying Genvissa's ashes at the entrance to the labyrinth.

Then Brutus doing . . . doing *something,* but his actions were cloaked with the grayness of enchantment, and Caela could not discern his actions.

"He is hiding the Trojan kingship bands," she murmured, and behind her the Sidlesaghe nodded.

Time, passing. *Much* time passing. Many years.

Now a great temple stood atop Og's Hill, hiding the labyrinth beneath its stone flooring, but somehow the waters of the pond showed Caela what was happening *beneath* the temple floor.

The labyrinth, sinking.

Deeper and deeper, writhing through the dirt and rock and gravel of the hill like a worm.

And the hill, embracing it.

Time passing.

Above, atop the hill, swarms of blue-clay-daubed naked warriors led by a man of such beauty and such evilness, that he appeared to suck all of the world's life into him.

Below, the labyrinth sinking deeper, deeper, embraced by the land.

The naked warrior—*Asterion!*—raging as Brutus had once raged, but for differing reasons.

Time, passing.

The labyrinth now lay buried far into the land. As yet it had not grown appreciably in physical size but, as Caela watched, she saw that small earthen creatures wandered its twists and paths—worms and moles and beetles, and foxes and badgers, too, who had burrowed deep to see what it was that hummed so beautifully within their midst.

Time, passing.

Tree roots, extending (*reaching*) out from the northern and western forests, touched the extremities of the labyrinth.

Drew back, then, carefully, touched again.

And the tree roots, as the moles and badgers and foxes and worms sighed, found that touch good, and merged with the labyrinth.

It was a process that Caela understood happened over many hundreds of years, perhaps over a millennium, and she understood that it happened principally because Og rested within the heart of the labyrinth, and his presence drew in the creatures and the forest. But once met, the labyrinth—the Troy Game—and the land and its creatures found each other well met, and discovered that they could live together with ease, and that, above all, they could be *good* for each other.

And this, Caela understood, was what Mag-who-once-had-been and who now lived as Caela's flesh had known so long ago, and what she had foreseen.

The Sidlesaghe moved close enough behind Caela that their bodies touched briefly, and Caela shuddered.

"See," he whispered, extending a hand to the waters. "See how the Game has spread its tentacles, grown its labyrinth under the area of the Veiled Hills. It tunnels and it worms, and it waits."

"For . . ."

"For you, of course, and for its Kingman."

Caela's eyes flickered to where Og lay motionless, then she looked back to the images within the pond.

"Look," she said, and now it was she who pointed.

A dark stain was spreading over the pond from its eastern extremity. A cloud of malignancy.

"Asterion," the Sidlesaghe said.

"He lurks within the court," said Caela. "But he is too powerful, too cunning for me to perceive him. Long Tom, why is that so? I *should* be able to perceive him, to know him."

The Sidlesaghe frowned, and his mouth dropped open in a low moan. "Oh," he said, and the sound was more a low moan than a spoken word. "You cannot see him? You cannot see him?"

"No. Long Tom—"

"Oh! You cannot know him?"

"Do *you* know who he is?" Caela said sharply.

The Sidlesaghe's mouth thinned, and he shook his head.

"Are you sure?" Caela asked.

The Sidlesaghe nodded. "He is dangerous," he said. "Highly so."

"Yes. I know."

"He wants to destroy the Game."

"I know."

"We must keep it safe."

"Yes, I know, but, Long Tom—"

"Asterion is very, very dangerous, dear girl."

"I know this, Long Tom!" Now Caela was getting frustrated.

"We want you to move the bands. Keep us safe. Keep the land safe. Both the Game and the land want you to do this. It will aid both, but principally it will aid the Game to grow in strength as well as in magnitude."

Caela's mouth dropped open. "*That* is what the Game needs me to do to help it?" Then, "*Can* I move them?"

The Sidlesaghe regarded her, and for a moment Caela felt as if she were being judged. "Yes," he said finally, "this is how you can help the Game, and, yes, you will be able to move them. The Game wants you to move the kingship bands of Troy. If Asterion cannot find the bands, then not only shall the Game remain safe for the time being, but you shall have time to—"

"To discover the means to persuade Swanne to hand to me her powers," Caela said, "and to establish those circumstances in which Og can be reborn. Yes, I can understand why the Game wants the bands moved."

The Sidlesaghe gave a nod, his eyes still watchful.

"And it will not be difficult." Caela had not said that as a question, but the instant the words had left her mouth the Sidlesaghe's eyes narrowed, and his very being stilled.

"Will it?" Caela said.

The Sidlesaghe hesitated. "Not inherently."

"Not *'inherently'*?"

The Sidlesaghe sighed. "The instant you touch the bands, Caela, Asterion will know. And William and Swanne will know. And the instant they know the bands have been found, and *are being moved,* they will panic . . . and then they will hit out."

CHAPTER TWELVE

ROUEN, NORMANDY

ILLIAM'S BODY MOVED EASILY WITH THAT OF his horse, a great bay stallion he'd bred and trained himself. His face was relaxed and his eyes dreamy as he let his mind wander in the late autumn sunshine. He wore no armor, merely a heavy tunic against the cool wind and a cloak thrown back over his shoulders and left to drape as it would across the stallion's rump. A sword hung at his left hip, a bow and quiver of arrows were slung across his back.

About him rode his companions, nobles and retainers. No one spoke, easy in their companionship and the delight of the day. All were in more or less the same state as the duke: easy, dreamy, relaxed, waiting.

Some fifty paces ahead of the band of riders spread a semicircle of twelve or thirteen men on foot. In counterpoint to the men on horseback, they were taut and watchful, their eyes constantly sliding about the sparse forest about them.

In their hands they held either crossbows or short hand bows; quivers of arrows jounced across their backs. At their heels stalked huge, well-trained, tense, silent pale hounds.

It was a good morning for the hunt. The sun was two hours risen, and the dawn mist cleared from the ground. The quarry—deer and boar, and perhaps even a wolf—would be moving from the open grass and meadowlands back into the comparative safety of the forest.

This was the part of the hunt that William enjoyed the most. Oh, the heat and excitement of both chase and kill were fine enough, and the back-slapping, jesting camaraderie that came after, but nothing surpassed this gentle dreamtime as they stalked the prey.

Did the stag and the boar know what came? wondered William. Did some primeval part of them, some *forestal* part of them, understand that today men would come stalking, and that only strength and courage and daring might save them from the arrows that pierced the air? Were they even now standing still, quivering, heads raised, ears and nostrils twitching, striving to catch that first noise, that initial scent, which would give them leave to leap into flight?

He drew in a deep breath—part suppressed excitement, part sublime happiness—and exchanged a glance and a smile with Walter Fitz Osbern who rode several paces away to his right. How many hunts had they participated in together? How many times had Walter stood to one side, sounding the horn, as William bent down with his short, broad knife to finish off the stag at his feet?

William relaxed further, his every movement part of those of the horse beneath him. A small smile played over his face as he remembered the previous night's loving with Matilda. Gods, but he and Matilda were well-matched! He hadn't thought to find one like her. William had known from an early age who he was, and what lay both behind him and before him. *Who* lay behind and before him. When William was a young man he'd hungered for Genvissa—for Swanne—and he'd remembered Cornelia with bitterness and anger. He'd known he would take a wife, but he'd thought she would simply be a bedmate, a mother to the heirs he needed, a chatelaine for his estates and castles and manors, and someone to be easily and quietly set aside when William had achieved what and whom he needed.

But Matilda! Ah! He had not thought she would make such a difference to him and to his life. Strong, loyal, passionate, a match and counterpoint to his every mood and want.

If he'd had her in his earlier life . . . William grinned to himself. If it had been Matilda instead of Cornelia who had plotted his ruin in Mesopotama, then William had no doubt that he would have been murdered and cast into the bay beside the city. Matilda would have succeeded with flair and triumph (and more than a few scorching words), where Cornelia had only failed miserably.

William remembered what he'd said to Matilda that night a few weeks past: *You have taught me a great deal during our marriage . . . strength, and tolerance, and maturity. What I thought, and felt, fifteen years ago, are no longer so clear to me.*

He'd thought about those words a great deal since. William had initially spoken them as a comfort to Matilda, but even as they slid smoothly from his lips, William had realized their truth—and the greater truth that lay beneath them. Matilda had been god-sent, he was sure of it. He *had* learned from her strength and tolerance and maturity, and it was not simply that what he had felt fifteen years ago was not now so clear to him.

What he had felt *two thousand years* ago was now not so clear to him. The great peaks of love and hate he'd felt then had been smoothed out by his marriage to Matilda. Bitterness and hatred and love all had been . . . modified.

Gentled. He did not yearn for Swanne with the passion he once had, and when he thought on Caela, then his thoughts were strangely tolerant, given his once all-consuming hatred of her when she had been Cornelia. Above all, Matilda had taught him what it was to be a good husband, and William was aware that he had once been a very bad husband, indeed.

He shifted a little on his horse, newly uncomfortable. How might his life have been different two thousand years earlier if he had been a tolerant husband, rather than a hateful one? How might his life have been altered if he had studied Cornelia with the understanding Matilda had given him, rather than with Brutus' indifferent callousness?

Suddenly one of the hounds bayed, and the huntsmen shouted, and William jerked out of his reverie.

"There!" cried Walter, and William followed his friend's pointing finger and, indeed, there it ran—a huge red stag, bounding through the dappled shadows of the forest.

William swept the bow from his back and fitted an arrow, digging his heels into the flanks of his stallion and guiding him only with voice and knees.

The horse surged forward, his hooves pounding through the grassland, then crashing through the first line of shrubs in the forest.

The stag careened before William, leaping first this way, now that, his head raised, his eyes panicked, his nostrils flaring.

Behind William crashed the horses of his companions, but they raced a full six or seven paces behind him, and it was William who had the first, clear shot.

The stag bounded behind a dense thicket, and William let his arrow fly.

It struck, he *heard* it, as he heard the cry of the stag and the sound of its heavy body plunging to the forest floor.

"I have him!" William cried as he seized the reins of his stallion and pulled the beast to a plunging, snorting halt. He lifted his right leg over the horse's wither, jumping to the ground, and ran behind the thicket, his knife drawn.

The stag lay convulsing in a carpet of fallen leaves and dried summer grasses, the arrow through his left eye.

William's stride slowed, and he drifted to a halt, staring at the stag.

Except it was no longer a stag lying there at all, but his father, Silvius, his hands to the arrow, his voice screaming to his son for aid.

Sick to his stomach, William took a step forward, then stopped, the knife suddenly loose in his sweat-dampened hand.

Silvius was no longer screaming. Instead he stared at his son, his hands still about the arrow, blood and gore dripping down his cheek. *You shall not have her!* he whispered within William's mind. *Never have her! You had your chance. She's mine, now.*

"No!" William said, very low. His gaze transfixed on his father.

Never have her . . .

Something *flowed* forth from Silvius, and William took an intuitive step back. It was evil. Malignant evil, seeping from every pore of his father's body.

You shall never have her . . . she's lost to you, now . . .

"No!" William said again.

And took another step back.

"My lord?" Walter Fitz Osbern walked up beside William, his eyes drifting between William and the downed stag, now screaming with a harsh, guttural cry. "My lord? Should I . . .?"

There were more steps behind William: other fellow hunters, and the huntsmen. They were quiet, watching William, one or two of them wincing at the terrible sound made by the stricken stag.

Walter's eyes settled on William's face. The duke was staring fixedly at the stag, his skin pale and clammy, as if he saw before him a devil, or some imp from hell. "My lord?" he said yet one more time, hoping that William would break free of whatever spell had claimed him.

Still no response, and Walter exchanged a worried look with one of the other nobles.

"Damn you!" William suddenly whispered, and Walter jumped, thinking his duke spoke to him.

But William was still staring fixedly at the stag, and now he stepped forward, almost stumbling. The stag cried out yet more harshly, his hooves flailing dangerously, and Walter was sure the duke would be struck, but somehow William managed to avoid the stag's hooves and legs. He stepped around behind the stag, sheathed his knife, grasped one of the stag's magnificent antlers to steady the beast's head, then took the arrow with his other hand and, frightfully, sickeningly, thrust the arrow deep into the stag's brain.

The creature gave one more frightful spasm, and then lay still, save for one hind leg, which continued to quiver slightly.

"Butcher it," said William harshly, standing back. "Butcher it *now!*"

He turned away, but then staggered, and Walter stepped close and took one of his arms to steady him.

"My lord?"

"Will he never leave me be?" whispered William, bending over as if he were going to vomit. He gagged, then again a little more violently, before managing to regain control of his stomach. "Will he never leave me be?"

One of the huntsmen came forward, taking William's other arm, but then William straightened, wiped his mouth, and managed a smile.

"I am well enough," he said, seemingly himself again, and the two men relaxed—as did all the others standing about watching with worried countenances.

"Likely the meat you took for breakfast was rotten," Walter said, and William accepted the excuse.

"Aye, likely it was. My apologies if I have concerned you, but I am well enough now. Where is my horse? Ah, thank you, Ranuld."

He took the stallion's reins from the huntsman who had brought him forward, and swung into the saddle.

But just as he settled on the horse's back, gathering up the reins, there came a distant shout, then the sound of approaching hooves.

"What is wrong?" said William, swinging his stallion about so he could see.

There was a rider hurtling across the meadowlands toward the patch of forest where William had downed the stag. He wore the duke's livery, and William recognized him as one of the squires from his garrison within the castle of Rouen.

"It's Oderic," mumbled Walter.

"And with dire news," said Ranuld, the huntsman who had also come to William's aid. "See the lather on his horse."

"My lord duke!" Oderic called as he pulled his exhausted horse to a stumbling halt. "My lord duke!"

"What?" snarled William, kicking his stallion forth and grabbing Oderic by the shoulder of his tunic before almost hauling Oderic from his mount. "What news, man?"

"Earl Harold of England," Oderic managed to gasp. "Earl Harold . . ."

"Yes? Yes" William gave Oderic an impatient shake.

"Earl Harold . . ." Oderic could barely speak, caught between the extremity of his news, his desperate battle for breath, and his duke's furious grasp on his shoulder.

"*Yes?*" William thought he would strangle the news from the man if he did not spit out the words within an instant.

"Earl Harold awaits in your castle, my lord duke."

"What?" William was so surprised he let Oderic go, and the squire almost fell off his horse as a surprised, concerned buzz of comment rose among William's retainers and huntsmen.

Earl Harold awaited in Duke William's castle?

"*My* castle?" said William stupidly, unable to comprehend what Oderic said. "Here? In Rouen?"

"Aye, my lord. A patrol discovered him last night, he had embarked from a fishing vessel on the coast two nights previous."

"What does he *do* here?" William mumbled to himself, then waved away the question. "Never mind. Walter. We ride. *Now!*"

PART FOUR

Pay me my fare, or by Gog and Magog, you shall feel the smart
of my whipcord!

Coachman to passengers at Barthlomew Fair,
London, late 1700s, cited in William Hone,
Ancient Mysteries Described, *1823*

ADDY!

Dear gods, his daughter! He'd thought her dead, a victim first of Genvissa's malevolence, and then of Asterion's.

And yet there she was, standing in the street outside Frank's house, holding the two lost kingship bands of Troy, and calling to him.

Skelton pulled on his uniform trousers, fumbling with the buttons on his fly, then hauled on a shirt, opened the door, and took the stairs three at a time before he'd done up a single button.

Violet stepped out of the kitchen, butter knife in hand. "Major?"

Skelton ignored her, opened the front door and ran into the street.

The little girl was gone.

He stood there, barefooted, his shirt flapping in the cold wind, staring up and down the street.

Gone.

"Major?" Violet was at the front door now, her pretty face crinkled up with doubt, her voice cautious. "Is there anything the matter?"

"Old chap?" said Frank, now standing directly behind Violet, a hand on her shoulder, staring at Skelton. He had raced out of his bedroom when he'd heard Skelton's mad dash for the front door.

Skelton ignored them. He turned this way, then that, his movements abrupt, frantic, his face distraught.

Frank's hand tightened momentarily on Violet's shoulder, then he walked over to Skelton. "Old chap . . . what's up?"

"She was here," Skelton muttered, the skin of his face gray. "She was."

Frank glanced back at Violet. "Who?"

"My daughter."

Now Frank openly stared. "I say, I didn't know you had . . . in England?"

"A long time ago," Skelton whispered.

The door to one of the neighbors' houses opened, and two women came out. They were both in their late thirties, their short waved hair freshly combed, and with matching dark blue candlewick dressing gowns tied about their trim figures. Both looked somewhat amused at the sight of Major Skelton standing half-naked and crazed in the street.

Frank looked embarrassed. "I'm sorry, Mrs. Flanders. A bit of a disturbance, I'm afraid."

Mrs. Flanders pursed her lips, but her eyes sparkled with humor. "And just as I have my sister staying, Mr. Bentley. Mrs. Ecub is quite overwrought by such a sight, I'm sure."

At that Skelton turned about and stared at the two women. "My God," *he said.* "Matilda? Ecub?"

They both grinned at him.

"We're all gathered," *said Matilda, whom Frank had addressed as Mrs. Flanders.* "Every one of us."

Skelton took a step forward. "Where is my daughter?" *he said.*

"Perhaps Stella has her," *said Mrs. Ecub.*

"I do apologize," *said Frank,* "But Mrs. Flanders, how can you possibly know Major Skelton?"

"We've had many dealings over many years," *said Matilda Flanders. Then her face softened from humor into pity, and she stepped forward, took Skelton's hands, and kissed him softly on the mouth.* "Welcome back, my love," *she said so softly that only he could hear.* "Welcome back."

ChAPTER ONE

CAELA SPEAKS

*I*SAT WITH MY LADIES—HOW I HATED THIS SITTING
about, spending my days in nothing but courtly gossips and embroi-
deries!—and understood that Harold had arrived in Rouen. I shivered, unable to keep at bay that memory of William tearing Coel's lifeless
body from mine.

Coel's blood had been so very warm, as he had himself been so very warm,
and so very loving.

I could feel—very faintly, but the knowledge was there—William's confusion, anger, and uncertainty as he heard of Harold's arrival. Everything, in
fact, he had felt that night Genvissa had sent him to murder me.

Keep him safe, I prayed silently. *Keep him safe.*

I closed my eyes, and in the strength of my prayer I think my body
wavered somewhat, for instantly, concerned voices were raised about me, and
tentative hands touched my arm.

"Madam? Madam? Are you well?"

I opened my eyes, and caught Judith's gaze. She nodded, understanding.

"No," I murmured, allowing my voice to waver just so very slightly. "I am
not well. I should rest awhile before our noonday meal. Judith . . .?"

She took my arm, and I nodded a dismissal at the other women who clustered about me. Slowly we retreated from the private solar, where I spent
most of the day when I was not in court, to the bedchamber, where I spent all
my cold, loveless nights.

Once the door closed behind us, I straightened and Judith dropped my arm.

"Madam?" she said.

I smiled wryly. I wished she would call me Caela in private, but now that I
was doubly "royal" in Judith's eyes, I doubted there would be little chance of
that now.

"I am glad that we have this time alone," she said. "There is something I need to speak of to you."

"Yes?"

"Saeweald . . . over the past days I have spoken to Saeweald on many occasions on this matter . . ."

Her voice had drifted off, her cheeks mottling, and her eyes avoiding mine.

"Judith?" I said. "What is wrong?"

"It is something of which you spoke to us—that you and Og-reborn will complete the Game as Mistress and Kingman of the Labyrinth."

"You find this difficult to accept."

"It is difficult enough," she said, "but this is not what eats at me."

"And that is?"

She hesitated, mouth hanging partly open, eyes averted. "It is that Saeweald believes he shall be Og-reborn."

There, it was out, and Judith finally allowed herself to look at me from under her lashes.

"Oh," I said on a long breath, and now it was I who averted my eyes.

"Ah," said Judith.

By the gods, we were playing some silly childish prattling game! "Oh" here and "Ah" there!

"Is Saeweald . . .? Will he . . .?" Judith said.

Then, gods help me, I lied, for if I told her who Og-reborn *was* fated to be, then I would have lost her, as well Saeweald and Ecub, in one foul-tasting word.

"I cannot know," I said, holding her gaze. "It shall be who the Troy Game and the land demands. Maybe Saeweald, maybe not . . . but I dislike it that he already has voiced his ambitions to the office." I put some distaste into that final phrase, some goddess-like offense, and it diverted Judith magnificently.

"I should not have presumed—"

"*He* should not have presumed!"

Judith dropped her gaze again, her cheeks mottling an even deeper shade of humiliation. I placed a hand on her arm. "I am sorry to snap, Judith. I had not thought that Saeweald would have jumped so easily to that possibility. But it is nothing to do with you, and I am glad you have told me. Here," I kissed her face. "I am not cross with you."

"I will tell him—"

"No. Do not mention it. I shall speak to him when appropriate." *And yet when was appropriate? "I am sorry, Saeweald, but you have no place in what is to come?" Oh, I could not lose him so quickly. I had need of him yet. As did . . . as did he who would become Og.*

"And now," I continued, all business, "I asked you here because I have need of your aid."

"Anything," Judith said, trying to atone.

I felt abashed, and took her hand and led her to a covered chest, which stood beneath the chamber's only window. We sat down, and I kept hold of her hand, although I think I was trying to reassure myself more than her.

"Judith, there are tasks I will need to do, places I shall need to go. I will need to spend much time away from the palace. Both at night, and during the day."

She nodded, the eagerness to please in her eyes intensifying.

"This will be difficult for me. I am the queen, I cannot just wander about the streets as I need—"

"But at night . . ."

I shrugged slightly. "Nights contain more freedom for me, surely, but even they are dangerous. What if Edward or his bowerthegn should wake, and I not be there? More importantly, there are days when I will have the need to leave the palace. I need more freedom, far more than my existence as 'queen' allows."

I also needed more security if I was to move the bands, or even to communicate with the Sidlesaghes as I needed. I constantly worried that some action or ill-considered word might draw either Swanne's or Asterion's suspicion; had I already said or done something that may have alerted them? This concern ate at me. I needed to move about both more freely *and* unobserved. How to do this as the constantly watched queen, whose every movement was noted?

I had struggled with this problem over the past few days, and could see only one solution. I hated to do it, for it would put another in the danger that I sought to escape, but if I was careful, then maybe she would not suffer.

Maybe.

"Judith, I need a glamour."

Her eyes grew huge, and she drew in a deep breath and held it for a long moment as she watched me unblinkingly. "A glamour?" she said finally. "Do you want to use me to—"

I shook my head. "Not you, for I will need you awake and aware of what goes on about me." I grinned briefly. "If I can drag you away from Saeweald's bed long enough . . ."

She blushed, and I thought that if she kept this up I would need to ask Saeweald for some whitening alloy to dab on Judith's cheeks.

"No, I will need someone else with which to create the glamour."

"Ah. You would like me to find her for you?"

"Aye. Judith, I hate to do this—to use an unwitting woman as my dupe. I

fear for her, and what might happen to her if she . . . is discovered. But without her I shall be too constrained for my purposes. Judith, do you know of
anyone who lives in Westminster, who has no children or husband who . . .
who . . ." *Who would be left bereft if my mistake killed her.*

Judith dropped her gaze to where our hands lay entwined, thinking. Eventually she raised her face, then nodded.

"There is a woman who I think would serve you well. Her name is Damson,
and she is the widow of a stone-cutter and now partly earns her way as a laundress. She is, oh, some forty-five or fifty years of age, and has the freedom of
both Westminster and London as she wanders looking for small pieces of
work. Everyone knows her. Damson is a simple woman, but true and good-
hearted. If you ask her I am certain that—"

"I cannot 'ask,' Judith. She must not have any understanding of what I do,
or else the glamour shall not work sufficiently—it will not be *deep* enough.
Can you bring her to me, and say only that I have need of her services? Would
she accept that?"

"Aye."

"When could you bring her to me?"

"I saw Damson about the palace courtyard this morning, probably looking
for work in the laundries, or even the dairy. If I find her quickly, then I could
have her before you within the hour."

"Go, then, and find me this Damson."

CHAPTER TWO

A BRIGHT DAY IT MIGHT BE, BUT INSIDE ROUEN'S castle the sunshine had yet to penetrate. The air was chilled and the breath frosted from the mouths of those not fortunate enough to have secured a close position by the fire that burned within Duke William's Great Hall.

Matilda and Earl Harold were two of the fortunate few. They sat in intricately carved oak chairs only two paces distant from where the fire cracked and leapt in the stone hearth, cups of the duke's best wine in their hands, making conversation until the duke himself could be summoned from the hunt. Rather than Norman French or Anglo-Saxon, they spoke in the more general French dialect that most European nobles (as merchants and craftsmen) learned as children.

Their ability to converse in a mutually comfortable language was not the only reason both found the conversation relatively effortless. Matilda was fascinated with the earl and he, quite obviously, with her. This might be their first meeting, but each had heard so much of the other over the years that they felt each other already well acquainted.

"My husband shall doubtless be surprised to find you here," said Matilda, gracing the earl with a smile over the rim of her wine cup. She was deeply intrigued by his face, for although it wore the hard lines of a warrior and man used to great command, it also had an aura of sensitivity, even mysticism, that one found generally only in the faces of poets, or religious recluses.

Or, indeed, in lovers.

Apart from that sense of mysticism, Harold was a highly attractive man, with his dark eyes framed by his graying blond hair and darker beard. Matilda liked the fact that, unlike so many Saxons, Harold kept that beard very short and neat, and did not hide beneath a shrubby, flea-ridden haystack.

"There was a time," said Harold, intrigued in his own way by this tiny, stern-faced woman before him, "when dukes and earls and princes spent their time only in the pursuit of the bloody sport of war, and it was with war that they solved every one of their dilemmas. I like to think that I and your husband are more civilized men, and that words and vows might be used to accomplish more than the agony and futility of war. I come to court an ally, not to incense an enemy."

"You *are* a poet!" Matilda murmured into her wine cup before taking a sip of the heavily spiced wine within.

Harold gave a small, sad smile. "I am a man, and a father, and a leader of many men and fathers. I value life before needless death. Thus I sit here with you this fair morn, waiting for your lord to return from the hunt."

"And for my part," said Matilda, "I am more than pleased to have this chance to sit and pass words with you. Tell me, how goes Edward?"

"Heavily, and with bad grace," said Harold. "He thinks only of the next life, and of his salvation. He is less the king, and more the repentant, mewling constantly for a chance to redeem himself before whichever altar he can find."

"And thus you are here," said Matilda. "I understand. So, if Edward declines, then may I ask after your own family? Your wife, and children? Your sister, and brother?"

Harold studied her, wondering what she knew. "My wife . . ." He shrugged as his voice drifted off in uncertainty as to what to say, and was then surprised at the glint of understanding in Matilda's face.

"She does not suit you, then."

He did not answer, and Matilda smiled into her wine as she sipped it. "Your children are well?"

This time she was rewarded with a natural and very warm smile, and her regard for the man grew. He loved his children.

"Aye," Harold said. "They are my delight."

"The queen?" Matilda said. "I have heard she has been unwell."

"She is better now."

Harold's manner had become extremely guarded, and Matilda wondered further if some of the more salacious rumors she'd heard about Harold's relationship with his sister might, in fact, have a kernel of truth to them.

"And Tostig . . ." she said.

"Madam," Harold snapped, "your manner is more direct than any of the Holy Father's inquisitors!"

Matilda laughed. "I have heard rumors of Tostig's penchant to treachery. Moreover, I suspect that Hardrada is tempting Tostig away from his loyalty to his family."

"Then I could do with access to your intelligence, madam, for I think it better than mine."

Matilda began to say something, but then there came a clatter of hooves in the courtyard beyond the narrow windows, and the shouts of men.

"My husband," she said, watching Harold carefully, and noting the manner in which his face closed over and he set his wine cup aside with great care. He took a deep breath, and Matilda saw that he was nervous.

Strangely, this gave her no sense of satisfaction, nor of advantage, but only saddened her somewhat. *This man,* she thought, *has no business seeking out the throne. He is too good, and too valuable, to be wasted on kingship.*

The doors at the end of the Great Hall flung open, and William strode into the Hall.

Harold and Matilda rose.

"My lord duke," said Matilda as William strode up to them.

William ignored her. He was sweaty from his hard ride back to the castle, his hair—even as short as it was—was disheveled, and his black eyes were as hard as flint.

They did not waver from Harold's face.

"My lord duke," Matilda said again, unperturbed by William's disregard. "My lord Harold, Earl of Wessex and favored of King Edward, has graced our castle with his presence. He has come with words, not swords, and speaks of peace and alliances where others might speak of hard deeds and war."

There, she thought, glancing at Harold. *I have done my best for you.* Strangely, Matilda's sympathies tended more to Harold in this encounter than to William, even though she lusted for the spoils of England almost as much as her husband.

William suddenly appeared to notice that Matilda had spoken, and he gave a brief nod in her direction. His eyes did not move from Harold's face.

"I greet you well, Harold," William said, recovering some of his usual calm demeanor, and he stepped forward and offered Harold his hand. "Welcome to Rouen, and to my duchy of Normandy."

Harold took William's between both of his, and the instant he did so, William's world turned upside down.

As Harold's flesh touched his, William knew who he was reborn. Coel. Coel!

A thousand emotions surged through William: jealousy and fright at their head. He remembered that terrible night he'd burst into his house in Llanbank to find Coel atop Cornelia's body, sweating in the labors of love. He remembered that appalling moment that he'd caught his hand into Coel's hair, and hauled back his head so that for an instant they'd stared deep into each other's souls, before Brutus had sliced his sword across Coel's throat.

Cornelia's cry of terror and loss, Coel's eyes still locked into his as he died.

Coel? Coel had reappeared in this guise on the same day that Silvius had once again writhed on the forest floor before him? What, in the gods' names was going on? What frightful magic had them in its hold?

And why had Swanne not told him this? Gods, Swanne had taken Coel to her bed, bred him children, and she had not told William of it?

William recalled what Swanne had said that day so long ago when they'd met. He'd asked her then if Harold was anyone reborn, and she had said no. He was a mere man. *Gods! She had* lied *to him! Why? Why?*

"William?"

William realized he was not only still gripping Harold's hand, but he was staring maniacally at the man. In the same moment William also realized that Harold had no memory of his life as Coel. He had come only as Harold, Earl of Wessex and pretender to the English throne, not as Cornelia's lover come for revenge . . . or whatever else it might be that he sought.

But this was no coincidence. Surely. And what was Coel doing back? What?

"William?" Matilda said again.

"Forgive me," William managed, dropping Harold's hand. He even managed to find the strength and fortitude of spirit to give Harold a small smile. "Your arrival has truly surprised me, my lord of Wessex."

"Aye, I see that it has." Harold, his hand now free, had taken a step back, and was watching William speculatively.

"Wine, husband?" Matilda murmured. She stood holding out a freshly poured cup to her husband, and very apparently taken aback by her husband's reaction.

A servant hurried forward with another chair, and William waved them all down, his equanimity now apparently fully restored.

"It has been a most surprising morning," William said. "First, I brought down a great stag, who reproached me with his dying."

Matilda gasped in superstitious dread, but Harold only watched William with narrowed eyes.

"And now," William continued, "I find before me England's greatest lord, save for Edward. A most strange and unexpected visitor, given the circumstances. What mysteries swirl about us today, I wonder?"

The question was half rhetorical, half real. *A most strange and unexpected visitor, given the circumstances. There, answer me that, Harold-Coel, if you dare.*

"No mysteries but those of mortal men," said Harold. He had set his wine cup to one side, and now leaned forward in his chair. "You must know why I am here, William."

To reproach me for your death? "To beg me to take England's throne once Edward is dead?'

Matilda repressed a wince at the bluntness of both men. So much for the soft beauty of poets.

Harold held William's stare a long moment before answering. "I come for

England," he said softly, "I come *as* England." William's face assumed a strange expression at that, but Harold ignored it. "We are both great lords here, William. To be blunt, I come wondering if you shall be my ally, as you have been Edward's, or my rival. Which one, William?"

William sat back in his chair, his dark eyes hooded. "I am ally to Edward for only one reason, my friend."

Harold's mouth quirked at that "my friend." "Not ally, then."

William gave a small smile, but his eyes were humorless.

"Edward is heirless," Harold said, "and the unfortunateness about all this is that we both have a claim to the throne. You through your great-aunt Emma, Edward's Norman mother, I through my place and standing as England's pre-eminent lord, defacto ruler throughout Edward's long, pious slide into irrelevancy and death."

Ah, thought William. *You and I again, Coel, standing on each side of the chasm. You for the old, dark ways of the land, I for the new bright ways of the foreigner. I won last time, Coel. What does that say about this encounter?*

"I not only claim through the distant blood of Emma," William said, "but also through Edward's promise."

Harold raised a patently disbelieving eyebrow.

"I sheltered Edward for many years during his time of exile," William said. "During those years when Cnut held England captive. For my aid, when no one else would help him, Edward promised to me the throne of England, should he die without heir to his body." He paused. "I believe that he has no heir, unless Queen Caela quickens with a child I do not know about—and that possibly Edward does not know about?"

Something in William's voice and face became aggressively confrontational with that last sentence, and Harold frowned over it.

"There is no heir, either walking or breeding," he said. "Caela remains chaste and untouched. Gods' Concubine, they call her, for the fact that the saintly Edward has so consistently refused to have dealings with her."

William gave a strange half smile. "So, then, Edward's promise to me stands."

"England has only your word for that," said Harold, "*I* have only your word for it, and neither England nor I will ever accept it."

"Truly?" said William, his tone now far more aggressive.

"England has had enough of foreigners imposing their word and law over us!" Harold said, his eyes snapping with anger. "England will not accept you. I have the witan's promise that come that day when Edward fails, then they will elect me to the throne. England wants Saxon rule, William. Not Norman."

"England is *already* half Norman! God, Harold, half your clergy are Norman imports, while Norman interests hold high office and control much land. Norman—"

"Those interests and offices shall not continue long past the day I am crowned," Harold said, very quiet now. "The clergy shall be replaced with Saxon men, loyal to England. Norman influence in England ceases with Edward's death. Completely. That is the message I bring you."

"You are afraid of me," William said, his own voice now very quiet. "*That*, essentially, is the message you bring me."

"England will stand against you, William. We are not boys, playing with wooden swords. We are seasoned *men*, and we will fight for our land. Come at your own peril but, for your own sake, and that of this lady your wife, and for the sake of all Englishmen, I ask you to rest content with Normandy, for what more could a man want?"

Immortality, thought William, staring at Harold. *Power beyond knowing. The Troy Game, in my hands.*

"England will stand against me?" William said. "Really? How strange, for the reports I have so recently received suggest very much the opposite."

Harold glanced at Matilda. "You mean my brother Tostig." He put down his cup of wine, then rolled up the short tunic he wore and undid his shirt.

His chest and upper belly were marred by red scarcely healed scars.

"*This* is Tostig," said Harold softly. "He thought to murder me." He did up his shirt and pulled his tunic down. "He came to me as I and my wife were preparing for bed, and he thought to earn a reward from Hardrada for his actions."

"But you bested him, or you would not be here to show me the scars."

"Aye," said Harold. "But only through the aid of my sister, who sent aid. My wife," he spoke the word contemptuously, "merely stood back and laughed as Tostig tried to murder me."

William went very still, and Matilda sent him an unreadable look.

"That was not the action of an honorable woman, let alone a wife," she said to Harold.

"It was the action of a woman who lives by deceit," Harold said. "She is not a woman to be trusted."

William dropped his eyes to his wine, swirling it about his wine cup.

"I say that," Harold said softly, not taking his eyes from William, "because I think you need to know very particularly, my lord of Normandy."

William looked up, his gaze unreadable.

"I know Swanne is your eyes and ears at court, William. Does she send you her love besides?"

Harold suddenly shifted his gaze to Matilda. "Did you know, my lady duchess, that my wife Swanne thinks to plot against me for William, and against you as well? She hopes to take your place at William's side, should he ever win for himself the throne of England. She has said that William has promised her this."

Harold looked back to William, sitting open-mouthed in shock, staring at Harold. "How long has she been whoring for you, William? And how *can* you plan to set aside this wondrous wife of yours to take Swanne Snake-Tongue as your queen, if you ever gain England?"

cḃapꞇer ꞇḣree

CAELA SPEAKS

I WAS LYING ON THE BED WHEN JUDITH BROUGHT Damson to the bedchamber, and as they entered I had to smile at what my other ladies must have thought of this simple woman who I admitted to my presence when they were left in the solar.

Damson was a woman well marked by her years and her travail. She was fair of hair, and ruddy of complexion, with stooped shoulders wearied by life, and hands roughened and gnarled by labor. Her eyes were pale water-blue, currently filled with anxiety.

"My lady queen!" she cried the instant she saw me, dropping to her knees despite Judith's hand on her arm. "I have meant no harm through my actions!"

I was rising from the bed as she said this, and my own eyes filled with tears at the thought that the only reason Damson could conceive for her presence before me was to be accused of some transgression.

"Of course not, Damson," I said in as gentle a manner as I could. "I have asked you before me only to serve me, not to reproach you."

Damson's face crumpled in relief, and my sorrow for her increased.

"My lady Judith has told me of your difficulties," I said, "and I thought only to help."

And may all the gods forgive me for *that* particular lie.

Damson had her hands clasped before her face, which was lowered almost to her breast: the poor woman could not even look upon me.

What trials had this land been through that women acted in such a manner?

I shared a glance with Judith, then bent to Damson, grasped her hands between mine, and raised her to her feet.

Damson finally managed to lift her face, and she visibly gulped, then blinked some of her tears free from her eyes.

"I have many fine linens, and rare embroideries," I said, "and I hear tell that you are the finest and most trustworthy of laundresses. Will you take charge of my linens, Damson, and watch over them for me, and attend to them as needed?"

All those years I had spent as unknowing Caela, my head bent over my sewing, watching the needle ply in and out, in and out, in and out. *Years,* I had spent curled about my damned needlework.

Frankly, I did not care if Damson took the entire corpus of my embroideries and hurled them into the mud of the river's low tide. I did not think I could bear a single hour more bent over my needles and wools.

"My lady . . ." Damson said.

"You agree?" I said, and hated myself, for I was asking Damson to agree to much more than the care of my ever-cursed linens.

"Oh. Aye, madam. I would do *anything* for you! Anything!"

The hope and happiness in her eyes almost made me waver, but I steeled myself.

"Damson," I whispered and, summoning both courage and power, I leaned forward and kissed her full on the mouth, sliding my tongue gently between her parted lips.

THE FIRST THING I BECAME AWARE OF AS I GAZED OUT of Damson's eyes and into my own bemused face was the scratchiness of her rough and ill-fitting clothes. Then I became aware of the different weight and feel of her body, of the way it moved. And then I became aware of its aches and pains, its sadnesses and strains, and I almost wept for the poverty of this woman's life.

"What is happening?" said my voice, issuing out of my face.

Poor Damson.

"It is nothing but a dream," I said very softly, and reached forward and cradled Caela's confused face in my hands. "Nothing but a dream. Sleep now, and when you wake you will remember nothing of this."

"Sleep . . . yes, I would like to sleep . . ." she said.

I led Caela-inhabited-by-Damson to the bed, and lay her down, pulling a coverlet over her.

Within an instant, she was asleep.

Caela, so it would appear to everyone who saw, asleep on her bed.

And so it was, but only Caela's body, not her soul or her spirit. They now lived in Damson's body, able to use Damson's body to move relatively unhindered wherever they wanted to go.

"Madam?" said Judith, and reached out a hand to my (*Damson's*) face.

"Aye," I said. "It is me." I shivered, embarrassed that I so loathed this body. I was grateful that Damson's thoughts and memories had traveled with her into my body; I did not think I could cope with whatever weight of worry she carried about with her through her dreary days and nights.

"Madam, what if I need you to return while you are gone? What can I do to summon you?"

I nodded at the figure asleep on my bed. "Shake my—*her* shoulder, and call my name forcefully. I should return at that."

"In body?"

I hesitated. "No. In soul and spirit only. So do this only if highly troubled, Judith. Otherwise you risk having Damson wake within herself in circumstances which may drive her witless."

"I understand." She paused. "What will you do now?"

"Now?" I grinned. "Why now I shall gather some linens, and I shall walk from this chamber with my head and shoulders bowed, and then I shall spend the rest of the day wandering free."

My smile widened at the thought, and then it faded. "Judith, stay here with . . ." I looked to where Damson-in-Caela lay on the bed. "Stay with *her,* and let no one touch her. Tell everyone that I am unwell, and want only to rest. I shall not be long. Not this first time."

Poor Caela. I had the feeling that she was going to be spending a great many days lying unwell on her bed over the coming months.

With another reassuring smile for Judith, I gathered up some linens, and left the chamber.

CHAPTER FOUR

WELL?"

Matilda's anger was evident in the rigidity of her stance, her flinty eyes, and the tight, clipped tone of her voice. She and William had retired to their bedchamber, Harold and his companions seen to their own chamber and offered food and the means to refresh themselves.

"He is bolder than I had thought him." William turned his back to his wife, and walked to the window, fiddling with the catch on one of the shutters.

"I was not talking of Harold. I am talking of the fact that you have apparently promised this Swanne a place at your side as queen."

"I have never promised that!"

Matilda's only answer consisted of her archly raised eyebrows.

"*Never!*"

"You swore that you would not betray me," she said, walking to and fro in her agitation. "You swore that I would be queen. *Not* Swanne! Did you lie? Do you truly mean *me* to be queen of England at your side? You have been lying to one of us. So, which one? Me, or Swanne?"

He caught at her wrist as she swished past him, and forced her to a halt. "*You!*" he said, his voice low and vibrating with emotion. "*You!* I meant that vow . . . dammit, Matilda, Swanne will never be my queen. *You* will. *You!*"

"Does *she* understand that?" Matilda asked quietly, then gave a soft, harsh laugh as William averted his eyes.

"You promise me one thing, husband, and you allow her to believe another. Where do any of us stand in your affections, eh?"

"*You* will be my queen, Matilda."

"You cannot trust her, William, if only because too many people know she is your agent. For sweet Christ's sakes, husband, did you not hear what Harold said? That she stood by and *laughed* as Tostig tried to murder her husband?"

William closed his eyes, trying to repress the memory of Coel lying dead at his feet, and Genvissa standing before them, laughing . . .

"And you trust that kind of witch?"

"I . . ." *She lied to me about Harold. He is Coel. Coel! And she lied to me about it . . .*

"She does not harbor a soul that can be trusted, husband," Matilda said very low. "And Harold knows she is your agent! If he knows, then who else?"

"For all we know, only Harold—"

"Harold is one too many people, my love," she countered.

"Aye. I know." William's shoulders suddenly slumped, and he walked to a chair and sat down heavily.

"Harold is far more knowledgeable than any of us thought. Had you ever considered that he knew of his wife's efforts on your behalf?"

"No. I had not thought he might know."

"And how does that affect our plans, William?"

"I would imagine it shall affect them very little."

"Don't play me for a fool!" Matilda snapped. *"Harold knows his wife has been your spy at Edward's court!* Have you not thought through the implications?"

William was silent, his face impassive. Matilda did not know if he was holding back, if he was so furious to learn that Harold knew of Swanne's treachery that he could not yet speak of it, or if this knowledge had so thrown him that he did not know what to say, or how now to act.

"How long do you think Harold has known, William?"

Silence.

"How long do you think Harold has been feeding misinformation to his wife and then to us?"

William's face, if anything, grew even more impassive.

Matilda all but hissed. "You are so certain of this woman?'

William hesitated, opened his mouth, and then closed it.

"Are you more certain of her than you are of me?"

"No." He finally met her eyes. "I have never been more certain of anyone in my life than I am of you."

She softened slightly. "My love, how can you trust a woman who stands by and *laughs* as her husband is murdered? That is not mere disloyalty, that is witchcraft so bleak and so deadly that *none* can ever trust it! Not even you, my love, no matter how much she protests that she loves you."

Swanne lied to me about Harold, William thought, unable to let the thought go. *She lied to me about Harold. Why? What purpose could that have served, save to intentionally deceive me?*

"William, what I see in Harold is nothing but honor. What I understand about Swanne is that she is a Darkwitch who will destroy anything and anyone who stands in her path."

Cornelia's face suddenly flashed before William's eyes, and he blinked.

"I cannot believe that you are certain you are immune."

"Enough," William said wearily. "God, does Harold have any understanding of how bitterly he has struck into the very heart of my household?"

"It is Swanne who has struck into the very heart of our household, husband. Not Harold." Then Matilda sighed. "Ah, I shall not continue haranguing you about her. Harold is the guest within our household, and it is with Harold that we should concern ourselves."

Matilda walked over to a table, which held a ewer of wine and some cups. "Harold is far stronger than we thought," she said, pouring out two cups of wine, handing one to her husband.

"Aye." He took a long draught of the wine.

"Edward was terrified of the father . . . how now should you feel of the son?"

"I am not 'terrified' of him!"

"I think you should be very wary of him, William. He cannot be discounted."

Again William sighed. "I know that." *He is Coel-reborn. He is back for a reason.*

"William . . ." Matilda came to his chair, and sank to her knees beside him. She placed her hands on his thigh, and looked earnestly into his face. "William, England is not going to lay down and offer itself to you on a golden plate the moment Edward dies. What Harold says is truth—the Saxon earls are not going to want a foreigner to rule over them. They *will* unite behind him."

William was silent, the fingers of one hand scratching through his clipped beard, his eyes unfocused as he thought.

"You spent thirty years uniting Normandy behind you," Matilda continued, her eyes steady on her husband's face. "Can you afford to wait another thirty to gain full control of England? Can any of us afford to wait that long? Is England worth it, truly?"

"Yes!" William said quietly. He looked down at Matilda's face, still looking into his so earnestly, and smiled. "The mere fact that Harold is here tells me something."

"Yes?"

"He is uncertain. No man sure of his support would come all this way to tell me to abandon my own ambitions. Tostig's attack—as Swanne's treachery—has unnerved him."

"Perhaps he truly thought he might persuade you to an alliance against Hardrada and Tostig. Harold does not want his countrymen and women's blood wasted in futile war."

"Harold fears simultaneous invasions on Edward's death. He is here to try and deflect at least one of them."

Matilda shrugged. "Simultaneous invasions could work against you and me, *and* Hardrada, as well as against Harold."

"Aye . . ." William's voice trailed off as he drifted back into thought.

"Caela," Matilda suddenly said, very firmly. "Caela is important."

"What?" William jerked up in his chair. *"Caela?"* Then he narrowed his eyes at his wife. "What has your own spy told you?"

Matilda chose her words carefully—not in any attempt to deceive her husband, but only because she, and her agent at Edward's court, relied so greatly on their shared intuition about the queen.

"She is," Matilda finally said, "so very quiet, some would say timid, and yet so strong. People are drawn to her. I have heard it said by some military strategists that the most important and influential person in any realm, or battle, or diplomatic negotiation, is not the person who speaks the loudest, or who bullies or acts in the most aggressive manner, but that person who sits silent and watchful and then, at the critical moment, utters a single quiet word, a word which alters the course of nations and history. Caela strikes me as such a person. There is a storm gathering, husband, and she sits quiet and unmoving, and so very, very strong, in the very heart of it."

"She sounds like a person not to be trusted."

"I think that, besides Harold, Caela is the person *most* to be trusted in the tempest ahead of us. Not Swanne, William. Never Swanne."

William sighed, and for a moment Matilda feared she had gone too far.

"Then what do you counsel me to do about Harold?" he said, and she relaxed.

"I think you should befriend him, husband, for he shall be a friend such as you have never had before."

THAT NIGHT, AS WILLIAM SLEPT, HIS DREAMS DREW him back again to that terrible night when he'd rushed from Genvissa's bed to find Coel atop Cornelia.

He recalled how he'd been overwhelmed by an anger and—oh gods, and by a *jealousy!*—so profound, he had drawn his sword and acted without thought.

Without humanity.

He saw again the blood that had streamed from Coel's body, the tragedy in Cornelia's face.

Genvissa, laughing.

In his dream, Matilda stood there also, and she was studying him with such a mixture of pity and disgust on her face that he could not bear it, and turned away.

ChAPTER FIVE

CAELA SPEAKS

*J*SPENT MANY DAYS WANDERING IN DAMSON'S body, and I spent most of this time within London itself. Here I found many signs, subtle and otherwise, of the influence of the Troy Game on the Londoners. Children, playing a hopping game on flagstones, weaving a path through a maze of cracks and flagstone edgings to what they called "home"—safety. "Step on a crack," they sang, "and the monster will snatch." Women also, embroidering or weaving simplified patterns of the labyrinth into their clothes: I found the pathways of Brutus' labyrinth decorating many a collar and cuff, or twirling about the hem of a robe. In the center of the marketplace that ran off Cheapside was inscribed a stylized labyrinth: here traders and housewives alike could pause in the business of market day and play a game with sticks and balls through the labyrinth. They called the game "Threading Ariadne's Needle," which I might have found amusing under any other circumstances.

And, of course, the Troy Game that Silvius had led on Smithfield. As tempting as it might be to believe he had directed the entire enterprise, apparently he had not. It was the men of London who were responsible for the games that day. They had thought up the game, patterning it on the legends of the fall of Troy. Silvius had only come late to these preparations, suggesting himself as the leader of one of the lines, and then proving his suitability on the practice field a week beforehand.

As the Troy Game had merged with the land, so it had also merged with the city. Whatever was built on this site would always become a living extension of the Troy Game. As the Londoners went about their daily tasks, so also they stepped out in the intricate patterns of the Game in a hundred different ways. Even the pattern of the streets . . . so many parts of the city now reflected the purpose of the Game.

I wondered if Brutus had ever realized how powerful his Game would become.

During these wanders I invariably found myself drawn to St. Paul's Cathedral. At first I supposed this was because the cathedral sat directly over the site where Brutus had originally built the labyrinth. The Game, and its labyrinth, had grown, I knew that, but still here lay its heart.

Then, as I sat within the nave, ignoring all the people who prayed and chattered and wept about me, I came to another realization, one that stunned me. *St. Paul's was the stone hall of my dream.*

Not precisely. It was not as grand as the stone hall of my dream, but there was something about it, some sense, some voice that called silently to me, that told me this was, indeed, the stone hall of my vision.

But my vision showed it as it would one day be: not in this lifetime, but in one to come.

And what *that* told me was that all would not be accomplished within this lifetime. The hall had to grow, and once that was done, then I and the Game could accomplish our mutual goal.

I can't say precisely how my understanding that all would not be accomplished within this lifetime made me feel. Sad, certainly. Frightened, a little.

Frustrated, beyond measure.

Yet, unsurprised. Mag and Hera had known, I think, that it would take a very long time. That there were so many twists to be taken that several lives might be needed. But, oh, to have to come back again and again . . .

Beyond all this, as I sat in the gloomy, frigid interior of the cathedral, staring at the altar and yet seeing none of it, I felt a deep fear.

I should have known this, surely? Not only that St. Paul's was the stone hall of my vision, but that the playing out of the Game to its conclusion would take so long? Mag and Hera had known it . . . but was I not Mag-reborn? Did I not hold Mag and all that she was within my flesh? Was I not everything that she had been, yet *more*?

So why had I not known this? Why had it taken me this long to realize, rather than instinctively *know*?

The sense deepened that there was an emptiness, some "unrightness" about my power, my bond with the land. I was far more than I had been as Cornelia, but I was not yet all that I should be.

What was missing? What had I yet to learn?

Was this some omission on my part? Had Mag been wrong in trusting me to be all that was needed?

I wanted to talk to one of the Sidlesaghes—oh, how I wished I had discussed this with Long Tom when we walked the forest paths of the Game—but no matter how much I wandered, and wanted, I saw none of them. They seemed to have their own sense of time, and of how events should be placed and paced out within that time, but I knew none of it. Long Tom had told me I needed to move the bands, but had then left me alone all this time—a week, longer, without a word.

And so I had wandered, about Westminster, about London, and invariably to St. Paul's where I sat, and worried.

One market day, when the lowing of cattle and the bleating of sheep and goats from the markets of Cheapside disturbed even the relative calm of St. Paul's, I sat huddled on a bench in one of the aisles. Many of the traders and their customers had come inside the nave of the cathedral to do their business—I supposed it was raining outside, and the cathedral more conducive to trade than the rain-washed street—and the aisle was one of the few spots within the cathedral where remained any peace. I had decided to return to Westminster, the walk would take me an hour, and poor Damson needed her body back for her evening chores, and so I had shuffled forward on the bench in preparation to rising, when a cloaked figure dropped down beside me, making me cringe back on the bench. What was this? A robber? A lecher? Worse, a monk come to pry out my sins?

"Don't leave," said Silvius.

I stared at him, not sure if he knew *who* it was within this poor woman's body.

"My lord," I began, but Silvius laughed, and waved a hand in the air.

"Oh, no need for such formalities, Caela. But this body . . ." His eyes traveled over Damson's squat outlines with patent disapproval. "You could not find better?"

"How did you know it was me?"

His teeth flashed inside the hood. "I know all about glamours, Caela. I am no fool."

"I did not ever mistake you for one," I said quietly. My eyes had got used to the darkness beneath the enveloping hood, and now I could see his face clearly. He was grinning, obviously enjoying my discomfiture.

"Glamours were used in the ancient Aegean world, as well as here," he said. "Mag was not the only one to know of them."

"Ah. I did not know."

"I have watched you these past days," he said, all teasing dropped from his voice. "You keep coming back here. Why?"

"It is the stone hall of my vision."

He nodded. "I had wondered when you would see that."

"Is there anything you do not know?"

Again he laughed. "Very little, although I suspect that what I don't know is what you need desperately to know, and perhaps why you sit here with Damson's rough-worked face all wrinkled with worry."

I wondered how to reply to that, then finally decided that it would not hurt to talk to Silvius. I felt safe about him, cared for and comforted, and I knew he was someone in whom I could confide.

"There are several things all at worry within me," I said.

"And they are?"

"Well . . . the lesser is that Judith has told me that Saeweald expects himself to become Og-reborn."

Silvius grinned. "The pretentious fool," he said. "Has he no idea?"

I shook my head. "Should I tell him?"

"Oh, nay. I think not! Imagine the consequences. Ah, Caela, do not worry. He will come to terms with his disappointment, I am sure. He will do what is best for the land."

"I hope so," I said, lowly.

"He *will*."

I chewed at my lip, then nodded.

"Very well. What else eats at you?"

"There is something missing within me," I said. "Some part of who I should be is . . . not there."

He frowned. "What do you mean?"

I lifted one hand, then let it drop uselessly. "An emptiness, Silvius. An unrightness. I can explain it no more than that."

"You are not all you should be?"

"Yes. That is it, perfectly."

He was silent, and I looked at him. He was smiling gently, his face so like, and yet unlike, Brutus' in its gentleness that I felt like weeping.

I was suddenly very sorry that I was here in Damson's body and not my true one.

His smile widened a little. "I could tell you what is so amiss, but you might not want to know."

"What is it?"

Now he was grinning enough that I could see his teeth, and the wetness of his tongue behind them. I smiled, responding to the mischievousness in his face, and to the warmth and life dancing about in his remaining eye.

"Let me see," he said. "How can I put this without having you shriek down the cathedral?"

"Tell me!" I said. Then I laughed, for suddenly it seemed as if Silvius had taken all my cares into his capable hands, rolled them up into an insignificant ball, and tossed them carelessly aside.

"Well now." He struck a pose, as if considering deeply, and without thinking I reached out and touched him.

"Tell me."

He took my hand, curling it within his own.

His flesh was very warm. Very dry. Very sensuous.

My heart began to thud strangely within my breast, and I knew he could feel the pulse leap within my wrist.

"Let me see," he said again, but now all the laughter had gone from his voice, and his gaze as it held mine was direct and strong. Confrontational, but still reassuring.

"You are Mag-reborn within Caela. Yes?"

My hesitation was only slight. "Yes."

"And you are queen of England, wife to the oh-so-pious Edward. Yes?"

"Yes."

"As Mag you are the land, fertility personified, you are *Mother* Mag. You are the *bounty* of the land."

I had a glimmer where he was going. "Oh."

"Oh, indeed. But as Caela, queen of England, wife of Edward the Confessor, you are," his lips twitched, "God's Concubine. A virgin. Imagine," he said, "how this undermines everything you are as Mag-reborn."

"Oh." I let out a long breath—I had not realized I'd been holding it.

"No wonder you feel a lack," he said, and he laughed, breathily, and his hand tightened about mine.

"But what can I—"

He roared with laughter, and I looked about, sure the entire cathedral would be staring at us.

But in the hustle and bustle, no one was paying us any attention and so I looked back to Silvius.

"You are a poor wretch indeed," he said, "if you do not know how to fix the situation."

I could see nothing but his black eye, feel nothing but the pressure of his hand, the warmth of his body, the skittering of *his* pulse. I could read the solution in his eye, feel it in his touch.

"I am not my son," he said, very softly. "Never mistake me for Brutus."

I knew what he saying. *Do not take me only because I remind you of Brutus.*

I swallowed, and pulled my hand away.

He let it go easily. "It would be best," he said, "that, if you do decide to relinquish your state as God's Concubine, that you do not do it in Damson's body."

"Yes," I said, adding, without thinking, "she is no virgin, in any case."

"Is that so?" He laughed again, and I colored.

I forced my mind back to what he had said. *As Caela I was a virgin, and that contradicted everything I should be as Mag, as Mother of this land, as its fertility.*

"The winter solstice approaches," Silvius said. "It would be the best night."

The best night in which to lose my virginity.

"In which to wed yourself entirely to the land." His gaze had not once wandered from my face. "To fill that lack."

He was right. *Everything* he said was right. Virginity was anathema to Mag and to all she represented, and the night of the winter solstice, the night when the land needed every particle of aid and fertility it could summon to see it through the long, frigid winter, was the perfect occasion to . . .

"To wed myself entirely to the land," I whispered.

"And to the Game," he said, as low as I, "should you choose aright."

Ah, I knew what he suggested, and I knew then what I would do.

"Do not come to me as Damson," he said, and his voice was thick with desire. "Not as Damson."

"No," I whispered. "Not as Damson."

CHAPTER SIX

WANNE WAS FEELING EDGIER BY THE DAY. There was something happening, yet she could not scry out the "what" of that happening. Caela had changed, had become far more confident within herself, and Swanne did not like that. The Game was setting children to hopping over lines in the flagstones outside St. Paul's (and their fathers to battling out the Troy Game in labyrinthine horse games). Harold had vanished, ostensibly to his estates in Wessex, but Swanne had sent him a message there several days ago and he had yet to reply.

Was it that Harold was ignoring her . . . or was it that he was not in Wessex at all? Was this punishment for her failure to aid him during Tostig's attack? For her laughter? Damn! Swanne supposed she should have managed some pretense at caring . . . but then, Harold was no threat, surely. Was he?

As Harold irritated and worried Swanne, so also did William. Rather, his refusal to answer her pleas for the location of the kingship bands of Troy irritated her. Gods, he must know that Asterion hunted them down! He could not afford to let them lie vulnerable!

To cap all of this was Edward's decision to request Swanne to accompany himself, the queen, and a small group of courtiers and clerics to view the almost-completed abbey of Westminster. Swanne could not understand why he'd invited her. Edward and she barely spoke, and Swanne only attended the king's court when Harold was in attendance. On the occasions when they did speak, their mutual dislike was obvious. Edward disliked the Danelaw wife of Harold, not only for the sensual beauty that Swanne never bothered to drape with modesty, but because Swanne and Harold's union was not recognized by the Holy Church and was therefore, in Edward's eyes, a horribly sinful affair. He even had referred to her and Harold's children as bastards on more than one occasion.

In Swanne's view, Edward was a contemptuous and cowardly old man, hiding behind his religion and his sharp, sarcastic tongue.

Edward's one great love was the almost-completed abbey. It had been fifteen years in the building (the fact that Edward had been married to

Caela for fifteen years as well, and that his Grand Plan for the abbey was conceived at the same time he wed her was the occasion of much ribald comment: Edward found in stones and mortar what he could not find in his wife) and had absorbed one-tenth of the entire wealth of the realm. Edward meant the building to be a marvel of its kind, the most wondrous abbey in Europe and, Swanne supposed, most Christians would think he had mostly succeeded.

The abbey was enormous, by far the largest single structure in England. It occupied the western portion of Thorney Isle, its central tower crowned with a cupola of wood, rising some several hundred feet into the air, its cruciform layout (still a novelty in Europe) stretching over five hundred feet east to west. The abbey was constructed of great blocks of gray stone, unusual in a country where most churches—indeed, most buildings—were constructed of wood or wattle and daub, had a magnificent lead roof, a graceful rounded apse at its eastern end, and dazzlingly beautiful stained glass filling its windows. In the two towers at the western end of the abbey hung five great bells that were to be rung for the first time this day. From the southern wall extended the foundations and partly constructed walls of the cloisters, infirmary, rectory, and the infirmary gardens: that would be completed within the next few years.

Edward, accompanied by Eadwine, abbot of Westminster, a bevy of other clerics including Aldred, Wulfstan of Worcester, and the bishop of London, his queen, Caela, two or three of her ladies, a handful of earls and a score of lesser thegns, guards, hangers-on, and three ragged children who tacked themselves on to the very end of the party, set out for the short walk on foot from his palace to the abbey at midmorning. Swanne, who had decided that attending might give her a better opportunity for observing Caela than that provided her within the confines of court, walked a few paces behind the queen and her ladies. It was a fine day, if crisp and cold, and most people had wrapped themselves in fur-lined cloaks and heavy woolen robes, with sturdy leather boots on their feet. A fresh southerly breeze blew, tugging at the veils of the women and making everyone's eyes water.

Swanne kept her eyes on the ground, her skirts lifted delicately away from the ever-present mud. *Gods,* she thought, *could not Edward have seen to the laying of a few flagstones to make the way a little easier?*

As they approached the eastern apse, the bells of the western towers suddenly burst into tongue.

Swanne flinched, as did most people. Although everyone had known the bells were to sound out for the first time this morning to welcome the great king into the new abbey, the actuality of their tremendous peal was a shock to both ears and nerves.

If Swanne flinched, then Edward stopped dead in his tracks (forcing everyone to stumble to a halt behind him) and crowed with delight, clapping his hands and raising his face heavenward.

"Glory be to God on high!" he shouted, and the shout was dutifully taken up by the clerics clustered in a small adoring flock behind him.

Glory be to God on high!

Swanne mumbled something that she hoped would be taken for a similar response, feeling such a rush of loathing for the entire Christian church and its damned crucified sons, saints, and sundry martyrs that for an instant she had a surge of sentimental longing for Mag. At least that silly bitch hadn't wrapped herself and her followers about with ridiculous conditions, sins, and unachievable objectives in order to keep them unthinking and under control.

At least Mag hadn't demanded the building of cold, dark, and useless stone tombs in which to herd her mindless minions.

Swanne looked ahead, and realized with a jolt that Caela had turned and was looking at her with a small smile on her face—almost as if she knew exactly what Swanne was thinking. The fine linen veil Caela wore about her forehead and over her hair had fluttered loose in the wind, as had a few wisps of her dark hair. The wind had also brought a glow to her cheeks and a sparkle to her eye, and for a moment, a single moment, Swanne was struck at how lovely the woman looked.

How certain. How happy.

Then Swanne hardened both her heart and her face, and Caela turned away as Edward resumed his triumphant march into his abbey and his immortality.

AS SWANNE HAD EXPECTED, THE INTERNAL SPACE OF the abbey could have been a block of ice, for all its warmth. The abbey's nave was also full of dust, dirt, and a few remaining scaffolds for workmen to put the final touches to the sculptures about Edward's soaring walls.

At least the screech of the bells was muted in here.

Edward was almost capering in his joy, pointing out this and that for his equally joyous sycophants.

Swanne turned away, trying to seek out Caela in the shafts of weak sunlight that filtered through the stained glass windows.

"Is this not a sight to gladden one's heart?" came a voice behind her, and Swanne managed, just, to put a pleasant smile on her face as she turned about.

It was Aldred, the archbishop of York, beaming at her as if she would truly think this abbey the most wondrous site in creation.

"Indeed," she said, inclining her head politely.

Aldred looked about, checking that no one was within hearing distance. "And won't William enjoy it, don't you think? So . . . *Norman.*"

Swanne drew in a sharp breath of dismay, her eyes glancing about, praying to whatever gods were listening this morning that no one had heard Aldred's remark. *The fat fool!*

"You need not be so indiscreet!" she hissed.

His face hardened. "Indiscreet, madam, is passing written intelligence from your chamber to his!"

"To which you have ever been a willing party," she retorted.

Aldred had been her means to contact William for the past eight or nine years. He was a Norman who had come to England when Edward returned from exile some twenty years previously. As part of his admiration of all things Norman (and his desire to irritate the Saxon Godwineson clan at every opportunity), Edward had elevated Aldred from mere monk to bishop to, eventually, archbishop. The cleric's girth increasing in direct proportion to the importance of each elevation. In between clerical promotions, Edward also used Aldred as his ambassador to Rome, Cologne, and Jerusalem, and as many smaller and less important realms.

Swanne found him repulsive, but he was necessary to her cause. Aldred was a man of great influence, who knew many people and was a Norman sympathizer. Over the years he had told her (in foul-breathed whispers . . . his liking of sweet pastries had rotted away most of his teeth) that he would like nothing else than to see William ensconced on England's throne, and would work with her to ensure this end.

Swanne wasn't sure if she could truly trust the man . . . but he had not failed her over all the years she'd been communicating with William, and Swanne was sure that if a treachery was to have been forthcoming, then it would have engulfed her by now.

Now Aldred had his hands clasped across his not-inconsiderable girth, his eyes narrowed as he studied her. "I have heard that Harold has set Caela to procuring him a more suitable wife, my dear. One who can comfortably sit next to him on a Christian throne. One who is not . . ." he drew out his pause with infinite delicacy ". . . tainted."

Swanne ignored the jibe; Aldred, after all, was a cruel man underneath his jovial flab and enjoyed a taunt almost as much as he enjoyed a pastry. "Are you certain?"

Aldred raised an eyebrow. "Of course, my dear. Now you are more, ahem, married to William's cause than ever, eh? A pity about Matilda, though. I hear also—"

Swanne gritted her teeth.

"—that William has promised Matilda that she shall be crowned next to him. What place for you in all this, then? Neither man seems to want to publicly associate himself with you. And yet, one or the other shall surely be England's king."

"William will never—" she began, leaning close to the archbishop, when his eyes widened, and one plump hand whipped out and seized her forearm.

Swanne snapped her mouth closed.

"My good lord archbishop," Caela said, inclining her head politely to both Aldred and Swanne as she walked close, "do you find this abbey pleasing?"

"Most pleasing, gracious queen," Aldred said. "It is a true monument to Edward."

Caela glanced about the frigid, empty stone interior. "Oh, aye, it is that," she said, not a hint of sarcasm in her voice. "And you, my lady sister, what think you?"

Swanne tried to smile politely, then abandoned the effort, realizing she was failing miserably. "I find it empty," she said, tired with all the pretense and the lies. "And cold."

Caela nodded slightly at her, consideringly. "Not many people would have spoken such truth, sister. That was well done of you."

Swanne momentarily closed her eyes, fighting back the impulse to slap the patronizing bitch across her glowing cheeks.

At that moment, one of Swanne's sons, Alan, who had accompanied the party, came over and greeted his mother and the archbishop. He exchanged one or two words with them, then made a small bow to Caela.

"Madam," he said, "forgive me for not speaking to you first, but your beauty this morning, in this cold gray hall, struck me dumb, and I could not find the words with which to adequately greet you."

His eyes sparkled as he spoke, and Caela burst into delighted laughter.

"Ah, I was standing in the good archbishop's shadow, my dear," she said, "and it was only now that you saw me. You thought to cloak oversight with flattery." She paused, her grin widening. "You shall make a true courtier, indeed."

Well, well, thought Swanne. *You grace my son with your laughter and insult the archbishop all in one. From where did you discover this courage?* She glanced at Aldred, saw his face tighten with humiliation, and she had to dampen a moment's grudging admiration for Caela.

Her boy had turned to Aldred, engaging him in a conversation about the estates of his archbishopric, and Caela moved a little closer to Swanne, taking her arm and moving her away a pace or two.

"I am glad to have you to myself a moment," she said, "and Alan's delightful interruption has made me curious about something. Let me phrase this as delicately as I might, considering always that there are other ears about."

Swanne stiffened. She held Caela's gaze with easy arrogance, but the queen did not let her eyes drop.

"Swanne," Caela said, "I remember that you, a very long time ago when I was but a naïve girl, said that you only ever wanted daughters. Yet here you are, a mother of three fine sons to Harold. How can this be? Has my recently returned memory somehow . . . misremembered?"

Swanne knew what Caela was truly asking. *How does a Mistress of the Labyrinth bear sons when she only truly wants daughters?*

"I am glad for the sons," Swanne said, sure she could actually hear her teeth grate, "for otherwise Harold would have set me aside."

"Ah," said Caela, and the expression on her face said: *The truth of the matter.*

And then Swanne knew, as surely as she drew breath, that Caela was hiding something from her. Something *deep*.

She remembered how long ago, long, long ago, when she had been Genvissa and Caela had been Cornelia, how she had continually felt something strange about Cornelia. Something *hidden*.

Now she felt it again. The woman was hiding something, something *sly*.

What? What? Not Mag, for Mag was dead.

What else?

Again Swanne felt a shiver of fear slide through her. *What else?*

Alan had departed, and Swanne became aware that Aldred was looking most peculiarly between the two woman.

Swanne laughed, daintily and prettily, and patted his hand.

"You must forgive us, Father, for our chatter about babies. I am sure you are bored by it."

"Indeed not, madam. You would be surprised at how much matters of the womb amuse me."

Then he changed the subject, talking first about the abbey, and how splendid it must be for Eadwine to be able to conduct services within its grandeur ("My cathedral of York is, I am afraid, a sad affair, indeed"), then about Harold ("Has anyone seen the great earl recently? I confess to have missed his wit about the king's court this past week"), then about the River Thames itself ("So gray and lifeless, don't you think? I cannot but agree with those Holy Fathers who preach that such wide expanses of water are but examples of sinful wasteland, unfit for consideration"), before, eventually, bringing the subject back to the matter of children.

"My dear, gracious queen—"

Swanne looked at Caela, and saw that her face was strained and paler than it had been. Either Aldred himself was beginning to try her (a distinct possibility, as far as Swanne was concerned) or some of what Aldred had bean talking about had somehow upset her, and Swanne found herself intrigued by that possibility.

"—I have always sorrowed that your womb has borne no fruit," Aldred continued, his face all wrapped up in palpably false sorrow and concern. "It must be a great tragedy for you that—"

"I am afraid, my good archbishop, that I can see my husband looking about for me. I should rejoin him."

Swanne's eyes had not left Caela's face. So, she *was* upset over something.

"—you have proved so barren," he finished. "Should I pray for you?"

From the corner of her eye, Swanne saw something quite horrible slither across his face. She half turned so she could see him more clearly, when Caela gave an audible, and patently horrified, gasp.

Swanne looked back to her, then saw that Caela was staring at the altar, some distance away.

Curious to see what it was that had so distracted Caela, Swanne looked also . . .

. . . and froze, so terrified she could barely continue to breathe.

The altar was not yet fully completed, and there was still some scaffolding behind it. This scaffolding was perhaps some fifteen or twenty feet high, and hanging from its central supports, in a frightful parody of the Christian crucifixion, stretched Asterion.

He was completely naked, his muscular body gleaming with sweat, his black bull's head twisting slowly from side to side as if he moaned in agony.

Swanne was vaguely aware that Aldred was still babbling on about babies and wombs and barrenness, but she could not truly distinguish a word he said. All she could see was Asterion, crucified before her, blood trickling down his arms, his chest, his belly.

Then, horrifyingly, Asterion's head stopped rolling from side to side, and his eyes opened, and they stared directly at Swanne.

Do you know, the Minotaur whispered in her mind, *of what Ariadne promised me? Do you know, of how much she enjoyed me?*

Swanne realized, frightfully, that the Minotaur was fully erect.

Do you have any idea of how much good I could do you?

And then he was gone, and Swanne was left staring open-mouthed at the altar, trembling so badly that she thought she would tumble to the flagging floor at any moment.

"Swanne!" she heard Caela say, and felt the woman grasp at her arm. "Swanne!"

And then, in her mind, *It was trickery, Swanne. Ignore it! He thinks only to taunt you!*

Swanne, so slowly she could feel the tendons behind her eyes popping with the movement, dragged her eyes away from the altar and to Caela. The woman was staring at her, looking almost as horrified as Swanne felt.

"Swanne," Caela whispered, close enough now that she could put an arm about Swanne's waist. "Ignore him, I beg you."

"Ignore me?" Aldred said indignantly, staring bemusedly between the two women. "Have I said something to upset such noble ladies?"

CDAPGER SEVEN

XHAUSTED BY HIS DAY SPENT INSPECTING THE
abbey, Edward fell into a dreamless sleep as soon as he closed his
eyes. The bowerthegn likewise, prompted less by exhaustion than a
little too much ale taken at supper. Judith, who often slept in the trestle bed
at the foot of the king and queen's great bed, was not there. Caela had told
her she could spend the night with Saeweald, if she wished. That she, Caela,
had no need for her.

In truth, Caela did not want Judith—who had not realized Asterion's
appearance—awake and near, fretting over Caela's patent and unexplained
worry. And so Caela lay awake and alone, staring at the canopy over the bed,
replaying the events of the day over and over in her mind.

Her hands lay over the bedcovers, twisting and warping the material until,
eventually, broken threads began to work themselves loose from the weave.

The night deepened.

Well past midnight, when even the owls were silent, Caela's hands paused,
and she raised herself up on one elbow.

A trapdoor had materialized within the floor.

"Praise the lady moon!" Caela whispered and, rising from the bed, she
threw a gown hastily over her nakedness, slipped her feet into some shoes,
and snatched at her cloak that hung from the back of the doorway.

The trapdoor opened, and an arm and hand emerged, beckoning Caela.

She stepped through the trapdoor as the arm disappeared, unhesitant.

SHE WALKED WITH THE SIDLESAGHE THROUGH A
tunnel that seemed not of this world, or of any that Caela could remember.
Above them and to either side, curved walls made of red clay bricks of a
uniformity of shape and color and of size that Caela had never seen
previously.

Even stranger, the floor of the tunnel consisted of a thick layer of gravel
upon which her feet continually slipped and slithered. Stranger yet, through

this gravel ran two ribbons of shiny metal as wide and as high as the palm of her hand.

Every so often Caela noted that the ribbons of metal quivered violently, shaking to and fro, and when they did this, then a moment later, there invariably came a rush of air so violent that it almost blew Caela off her uncertain feet.

"We walk through a part of the Game that is yet to be," said the Sidlesaghe. "Sometimes this happens."

Caela nodded, curious but not unbearably so. Asterion, his naked form, his malevolent words, rich with unknown meaning, kept repeating themselves over and over in her head.

Eventually they came to an opening within the wall on their right. It was the height and just over the width of a man, and the Sidlesaghe turned and entered the aperture.

Caela followed, swallowing down her apprehension.

The footing was firmer here, gravel no longer, but what felt like brick.

Whatever relief the footing afforded was consumed almost immediately by the fear caused by the dark. Caela put her hands to either side of her, using the enclosing brick walls to orientate herself and to give her some comfort within the blackness. She could not see anything before her, but could hear the Sidlesaghe's footsteps ahead of her.

Occasionally she bumped into his back, and, whenever she did that, Caela lifted one of her hands from the brick walls and rested it momentarily on the Sidlesaghe's shoulder, seeking reassurance in his nearness and warmth.

They walked for what seemed like hours, but which, Caela realized, was probably for only a fraction of that time, until a faint light emerged before them.

A doorway into the night.

Caela gave a great sigh of relief as she followed the Sidlesaghe into the cold night, taking a moment to recover from her claustrophobia before she looked about her.

They stood within London before the northern approach to the bridge. Immediately before Caela was the bridge itself; the two stones of Magog and Gog standing to either side of its entrance-way.

The Sidlesaghe put a hand in the small of Caela's back, and she walked forward.

As she did so, the stones wavered in the gloom, and metamorphosed into Sidlesaghes, slightly shorter than Long Tom, who had brought her through the tunnel, but otherwise virtually indistinguishable.

"We saw Asterion," said the one who had been the stone Magog.

Caela nodded, her hands pulling the cloak closer about her shoulders.

"He spoke," said the one who was Gog.

"It was vile," said Long Tom.

"What did he mean?" said Caela, looking between the three Sidlesaghes. "What did Ariadne promise Asterion?"

"Who can tell?" said the Gog. "Perhaps it was a falsehood, sent to disturb you, and Swanne also. Perhaps it was a truth."

"If it is a truth," said Caela, "then it will be a dangerous one."

"We agree," said all three Sidlesaghes simultaneously.

"We have little time," added Long Tom.

"The bands," Caela said.

"You must move the first one tomorrow night," said Magog. "Long Tom shall aid you."

Caela shivered, and Long Tom placed a surprisingly warm hand on her shoulder.

cbapter eight

Rouen

HEY HAD LEFT THE CASTLE AT ROUEN BEFORE dawn, heavily cloaked against the frost, their horses' hooves dull thuds on the straw-strewn cobbles of the castle courtyard, and then the frost-hardened mire of the streets that led to the city gate. They were a small party: William of Normandy; Harold of Wessex; Walter Fitz Osbern; Ranuld the huntsman, on horseback himself for this dangerous adventure; Thorkell, a thegn from Sussex, and Hugh, a thegn from Kent, both of them close companions of Harold's who had accompanied him on his journey to Normandy; and, finally, two men-at-arms from William's own personal guard at Rouen. All eight men were heavily armed with swords and knives and the men-at-arms also carried with them wickedly-sharp, long pikes, two apiece, which they could share with any other of the hunters as need be.

The gatekeepers were awake and alert, having been forewarned of this expedition the previous night. They bowed as William rode up on his black stallion, then set in motion the grinding and clanking which signaled the rising of the portcullis. William and Harold and their companions sat waiting silently, their eyes set ahead, their expressions drawn, their thoughts on what lay before them, while their horses stamped and flicked their tails with impatience, lowering their heads and testing the strength of bit and rein and the hand of the man who held them.

The portcullis rattled into its place in the heights of the gate, and the riders kicked their horses forward.

"Which way?" William said over his shoulder to Ranuld, riding several paces behind.

Ranuld nodded toward the line of trees that stretched along a creek some two miles distant. "There, my lord. The report I had last night said they had nested along that creek bed."

"Take the lead," William said, and Ranuld kicked his horse forward, guiding the party toward the distant trees.

For the first few minutes of the ride, they kept to the road, and William pulled his horse back until he rode side by side with Harold. He'd given the Saxon earl one of his best stallions, better even than the one William himself rode, and William noted that Harold controlled the spirited bay easily and gently. The horse was unmanageable for most riders, and William had given it to Harold as a test.

Strangely, as he'd watched Harold gather the stallion's reins and mount, William had found himself hoping that Harold *would* be able to control the beast. He didn't want to see Harold tossed into the mire of the stable yard, or suffer the humiliation of having the horse bolt from under him while half the garrison watched from dormitory doorways or leaned over the parapets.

And why not? Brutus would have relished the chance to arrange Coel's humiliation.

Wouldn't he?

The horse had given one initial plunge as he felt Harold's weight settle on his back, but then Harold had taken control, soothing the stallion with a calm but firm voice, reining him in with a determined yet gentle hand, and stroking the horse's muscled neck when he'd finally settled.

Then Harold had turned amused eyes to William, knowing full well that he'd just been set a test.

William had given the earl a single nod—*that was well done*—and then mounted himself, leading the party out.

They'd not spoken since. But now, riding through the hoar-frosted countryside beyond Rouen's walls, William felt the need to talk.

Honestly.

Harold had been with William now for some time, and all this time had, after their initial conversation, been spent in hedging and wary verbal circling, interspersed with long and significant periods of eye contact over the rims of wine cups. Neither wanted to concede anything to the other, but both wanted to scry out the other's strengths and weaknesses as much as possible.

They were, after all, likely to meet on the battlefield, and this time spent together was as much a part of that distant battle as would be the eventual clash of sword on sword.

Through all of this, William had not forgotten Matilda's injunction to be Harold's friend. His wary circling had as much been sounding out Harold's character as it had his strengths and weaknesses.

And William had discovered that he did, indeed, like Harold. The earl was as honest and true a man as ever William had met, in either of his lives, and William had come to regret bitterly the actions of his previous life.

William checked to ensure that Ranuld, as the riders following them, were not within easy earshot, and said, "Tell me of Swanne." He made no attempt at dissimulation, for that would have been an insult to Harold's own integrity. "Did you ever love her, and she you?" *Is that why she lied to me about you, because then she loved you?*

Harold shot William a wry look. "What is this, William? She has not told you everything that has passed between us?"

No. "She has only mentioned that she is your wife, but nothing more."

Harold raised his eyebrows, although his gaze had returned to the road before them. "I am her husband, I am the man who should rightfully succeed Edward, and I am thus the one she betrays the most, both as husband and as future king. How strange that she has not mentioned me, apart from naming me as her husband."

He turned his head, looking at William once more. "If Matilda betrayed you with, for instance, the duke of Gascony, and plotted to hand him your duchy, would you not expect her to hand him some reason for this betrayal? Would you not expect the duke to ask, 'Why, madam, do you betray your husband and your homeland in this manner?' I find it passing strange, William, that Swanne does not 'mention me.' You never thought to ask?"

"I asked her once, many years ago. She said you were but a man. Nothing more."

Harold laughed bitterly. "Just a man. Nothing more. When I first married her I loved her more dearly than I had thought possible. She bewitched me. You have surely heard of her loveliness, if not seen for yourself."

William nodded, his eyes now on the road before them.

"God, William. I could not believe I had won such a trophy to my bed. In the early years together, she provided me with bed sport such as I'd never enjoyed before."

William winced.

"And then . . ." Harold hesitated.

"And then . . .?"

"And then, as years passed, I realized that Swanne's loveliness was only a brittle thing. A sham, meant to bewilder and entrap. Swanne uses her beauty and love only as a weapon." He paused. "I do not think Swanne knows what love is. Not truly. William, how is it you have fallen under her spell? What did she use to entrap you?"

Power. Ambition. The promise of immortality. "I am not 'trapped,'" William said.

Harold grunted.

"I hear tell you lust for your sister," William said, stung into attack. To his amazement, Harold only laughed.

"You would have done far better to recruit Caela to your cause, William. Caela could have been born the lowliest of peasant women, and still she would have been a queen." He looked directly at William, forcing the duke to meet his gaze. "*She* has true power, William, not Swanne, and that is beauty of spirit, not darkness of soul."

"Caela is well served in you, Harold. She has always been so."

"And I in her," Harold said quietly, and for a time they rode in silence, each wrapped in their own thoughts.

"Harold," William said eventually, "you cannot fight me. When Edward dies, I have the closest blood link to the English throne. I will have the stronger claim. Don't oppose me." *Please.*

Harold grinned, easy and comfortable, and William felt his stomach turn over. Gods! Was this *guilt?* A conscience?

"A tenuous blood link," said Harold, "through your great-aunt, and well you know that the English throne is not handed automatically from father to son . . . or from king to—what are you?—great nephew through marriage. The witan approves and elects each new king. If there is a strong son with a good claim, then it will lean to him . . . but they will not elect you, William. Never."

They lapsed into silence again. Ranuld had led them from the road, and now their horses were cantering through stubbled meadowlands, the hay long since cut and carted for winter fodder. The pace had quickened, and everyone's hearts beat a little faster.

The tree line of the creek bed loomed.

"I *will* invade," William said. "Believe it."

Harold shrugged. "Then you will meet the might of the Saxon army. You will meet *England*."

"For sweet Christ's sake, Harold, I have a battle-hardened force second to none! I have spent thirty years fighting for this duchy, and I will loose all that experience on you!"

Unwittingly, Harold echoed Matilda's words. "And you are prepared to waste another thirty trying to seize England, William? For I assure you, thirty years of Norman spilled blood is what it is going to take."

Furious now—although at quite what, William was not sure—he kicked his horse forward with a terse, "As you will."

They descended into the all-but-dry creek bed, their horses slipping and sliding down the steep slope before splashing into the bare inch of water that wound its sludgy way around the larger of the stones of the bed.

At the head of the party, Ranuld reined his horse to a halt and held up his hand. "Prepare yourselves," he said once the seven other men had pulled up behind him. "They are not far."

He extended the hand he'd held up until it was pointing straight ahead. "There," he said, his tone quieter now. "See? In those bushes lining that slope?"

The other men peered, some swallowing in nervous anticipation, others tightening their mouths in grim attempts at fortitude.

All reached for weapons, and Thorkell and Hugh, Harold's men, took a pike each from the men-at-arms.

All eight looked between each other, then forward again, to the distant bushes.

At this time of morning, when the sun had barely risen, the shadows were so long and strong about the shrubs that it was difficult to distinguish detail.

Then a shadow moved, deepened lightly, and a single ray of sunlight, penetrating the deep creek bed, revealed the roundness of flesh.

A shoulder, perhaps, or even a haunch.

The shadow moved, shuffling about, and then, for an instant, the watchers saw a head with thick curved tusks and small, bright, mean eyes.

William very slowly withdrew his sword from its leather scabbard and, even with that slight sound, the creature hiding in the bushes squealed in anger, and the world erupted into a seething mass of leaves and branches and hot flesh and terrible grinding tusks.

The riders scattered, the horses—even as well trained as they were—terrified by the suddenness of the attack.

A boar, half the size of a horse, its hairy hide mottled tan and black and pink, had *roared* from the shrubs and charged down the creek bed toward the group of riders. It moved with the agility, grace, and power of a master swordsman, and it used its vicious, deadly tusks with as much effect, breaking a leg on no less than three horses on its first charge.

The horses went down in a flurry of snorting fear and flailing legs, tossing their riders onto the sharp stones of the creek walls and bed.

A man-at-arms was one of those who was tossed. Horribly, he had fallen directly in the path of the boar, which had made a nimble turn, and was making a returning charge at the now disarrayed hunting party.

The man screamed, rolling away. He got to his knees, his hands reaching for the roots of a tree higher up the bank, his feet scrabbling for purchase, then the boar slammed into his back, driving its tusks deep into his ribs.

The man-at-arms screeched, so terrified—or so paralyzed by pain and shock—that he did not even think to reach for his sword or knife.

The boar twisted its head and, aided by the immense muscles in its neck and shoulders, bodily lifted the man off the ground and tossed him some feet away.

The man, still screeching, landed with a sickening thud, his head smashing into a large rock.

He convulsed, then lay still.

The rest of the party had either gotten their horses back under control or, in the case of the two riderless men who had regained their feet relatively uninjured, had grabbed pikes. Now the remaining seven men closed in on the boar, which had now turned its ire on one of the luckless horses, disembowel-ing it with two vicious sweeps of its tusks.

Harold was the closest and, guiding his horse in with the pressure of his knees and calves, he hefted his sword. As the boar swung to meet him, he plunged it with all his strength into the boar's back.

The blade of the sword missed the boar's spinal cord by a mere inch, bury-ing itself into the thick muscle that bounded the creature's ribs.

Harold leaned back, meaning to pull the sword free so he could strike again.

The boar screamed in rage, rather than pain or despair. Before Harold could twist the sword free, the boar twisted himself, throwing the weight of his body against the legs of Harold's horse.

The stallion slipped to its haunches and Harold, still gripping the haft of the sword, was pulled out of the saddle both by the motion of the horse and by the continual maddened twisting of the boar.

He fell, grunting in surprise as he hit the stones of the creek bed, and slipped in the shallow water as he tried to right himself.

The boar, Harold's sword still sticking from its back, had turned and was now watching Harold with his vicious, intelligent eyes.

Even though there were other men and horses milling about, and even though Harold could hear the frantic shouting of Ranuld and William, and of his two companions Thorkell and Hugh, it felt to him as if there were only two creatures in this world on this morn: himself, and the maddened, murderous boar.

Very slowly, Harold managed to rise to his knees, his eyes never leaving those of the boar, and slowly drew free the long-bladed knife from his belt.

To one side, William kneed his horse forward, grabbing a pike from one of the other men, and hefting it in his hand.

The boar had its back to him, and would be an easy target.

"No," whispered Walter Fitz Osbern. Then, a little more strongly, "No!"

He grabbed at the reins of William's horse, pulling it to a sudden halt and almost unseating William.

"Let the boar and Harold settle this," Walter said, meeting William's stunned and furious gaze. "Let God decide who has the right to take England's throne, here and now."

"You fool!" William yelled, and, leaning forward, struck Walter a great blow across the face that almost unseated the man from his horse.

Frantic, not even wondering why he should be so frightened, nor so determined, William turned his horse back toward where the boar faced Harold in
the bed of the creek.

To his side, Thorkell and Hugh were already moving forward.

They were all too late.

The boar had charged.

Harold was still on his knees, weaving backward and forward unsteadily
from either the force of the initial impact in the fall from his horse or in panic
at the boar's murderous rush, and had barely time to raise his knife.

"*Harold!*" William yelled, discarding the pike and jumping down from his
horse. He dashed forward, his sword drawn.

The boar was roaring again, a horrible, terrible noise of squealing and grunting and screaming, all in one, and as it came to within two paces of Harold,
it tucked its head down against its chest, presenting its tusks and broad
forehead.

In that instant, that instant when the boar could not see, Harold fell back,
his legs before him, the back of his head slamming into the trickle of cold
water.

The boar was upon him, terrible pounding feet, hot, foul breath, a grunting and screeching that sounded as if it emanated from hell.

Harold cried out involuntarily as the boar's front feet slammed into his
belly and chest and then, as the boar surged forward, as the boar's great pen-
dulous abdomen brushed over Harold's chest, Harold brought up the knife
with all the strength he had left, plunging it into the boar's soft underbelly and
allowing the forward motion of the creature to tear itself open.

Blood and bowels erupted over Harold, smothering him, and in the next
moment the entire weight of the boar crashed into his neck and head, then,
mercifully, rolled off to one side.

"Harold! Harold!"

William was upon him, sure that the blood and entrails that coated Harold
must be the man's own.

"Harold!" William fell to his knees, straddling Harold's body, and pushing
aside the worst of the gore.

Beneath it, Harold slowly opened his eyes.

"Harold?"

Harold raised a hand, waving it weakly from side to side. He was gasping
for air, and William realized that the boar's death plunge must have winded
him severely.

If not worse.

"Harold?"

"I have . . . have . . . but lost . . . my breath . . . ," Harold eventually managed. "And . . . and my chest and belly throb from where the boar stood on Tostig's treacherous scars. But I think it is nothing more than bruises."

William breathed a sigh of unpretended relief. "Thank Christ, our Lord," he said.

"I thought the boar had me," Harold said.

"I have never seen such bravery," William said, and all who now crowded about heard the admiration and respect in his voice.

William rose.

"I had thought you might have hoped the boar would have taken me," said Harold, slowly raising himself into a sitting position. He grimaced as he saw the blood and entrails and pig shit that coated him, and in that grimace missed the cold look that William shot Walter Fitz Osbern.

"You are my guest, and my equal. I had not wanted you dead," William said.

Harold looked up at him. "And you didn't think that my death here and now would be only to your advantage?"

William stared at Harold for a long moment before answering. "I did not want your death now," he finally said, quietly but with great feeling, "as I do not want it for the future. England would always be the sorrier place for your lack, Harold. I would be the sorrier man for your death."

And he held out his hand.

"You are a most strange adversary," Harold said, gripping William's hand and using it to pull himself upright.

"I am not your enemy," William said. "I will not be one to laugh over your corpse, Harold."

Now upright, Harold changed his grasp so that now both men gripped each other by the forearm rather than by the hand. Strangely, he seemed to know what William was thinking. "Do not trust Swanne," Harold said softly, only for William's ears. "Never trust her."

In answer, William merely stared, then gave a very small nod. In this they understood each other.

Then he let Harold's arm go, turned, and dealt Walter Fitz Osbern such a heavy blow to his chin that the man staggered and fell to his knees.

"Never dishonor me again," William said, then stalked off for his horse.

ChAPTER NINE

CAELA SPEAKS

MOVING THE BANDS HAD SO MANY INHERENT dangers, yet the first and most difficult task (or so I believed at the time) was simply ensuring I was not missed. Moving the band was something Long Tom had told me I could not do as Damson, so somehow I had to ensure that no one would make note of the queen's absence for what might be virtually the entire night.

In the end, this first obstacle was reasonably and easily accomplished. I gave a moan during our supper, placed a hand on my belly, and looked apologetically at Edward, who had paused with a spoon of broth half raised to his open mouth.

I managed to color. "My flux," I murmured, lowering my eyes modestly.

And so I removed myself to the solar, where I usually slept during these phases of the moon. Edward kept his bowerthegn, and I dismissed all my ladies, save for Judith.

There, at the darkest hour of the night, Long Tom came to me.

WE DESCENDED THROUGH ANOTHER OF HIS STRANGE, eerie trapdoors (I resolved that I should ask him how he managed it, this descent into the twists of the labyrinth), and into that even stranger tunnel he had led me only the previous night. Again the metal rails that lined the gravel bed trembled and vibrated from time to time, and again I was overwhelmed as, from time to time, a great rush of air filled the tunnel and rushed past us.

A part of the Game that is yet to be.

"We will have to be very careful tonight," the Sidlesaghe said, and I nodded, lost in thought of what was to come.

"This will be the one time you are going to be able to do this in relative safety," he continued.

"I know," I said. "Once Asterion and William and Swanne realize that one band has been moved, then they will be alert for a further . . ." I stopped, not knowing how to express myself.

"Intrusion," said the Sidlesaghe, and again I nodded. He took my hand, and squeezed it. "So we will make the most of this night, eh?"

I tried to smile for him, but in truth I was nervous. Not so much by the thought of Asterion's—or any other's—wrath and reaction, but at touching the bands themselves. I remembered how they had always been so much a part of Brutus, so much a *wholeness* with him, that I could barely imagine the thought of the bands away from him.

And yet they were apart from him, were they not? And were they not also to be given to another, in time? I remembered the vision of the Stag God Og, alive and vibrating with power, running through the forest, the bands about his legs. *My* lover, and thus I must be the one to take these bands, and give them to him.

At this moment, walking down this otherworldly tunnel with the Sidlesaghe, it all seemed impossible.

"Faith," said Long Tom, giving my hand another squeeze. "What seems hopeless when you look across a vast distance, to what must be ultimately accomplished, seems possible when you only look at the task a step at a time. Tonight you will move one of the bands and make the Game and this land just that little bit safer. In a little while, perhaps a week, perhaps a month, you will move another band, and we will cope together with whatever danger threatens us on that occasion."

"You say *I* must move the bands. Are you not able to touch them?"

"No," he said. "Only the Kingman or the Mistress of the Labyrinth can truly touch them, and not suffer."

"Then how can I? I am not yet—"

"But you *will* one day be." The Sidlesaghe paused, both in speech and in walking, and I stopped as well and watched him as he tried to find words for what he wanted to express. "The Game sometimes shows portions of itself which are yet to be," he said, "and sometimes it can accept things that are not yet, but which will be."

"Because it wants me to be the Mistress of—"

"No. Because you *will* one day be the Mistress of the Labyrinth."

My mouth twisted. "The Game *hopes*?"

"The Game *knows*. It has already created the future, and in some manner, already lives it."

I was suddenly, inexplicably, angry. "Then why do I fight, or strive, if all this *will* be. Why do I *worry*, if all this is set into stone as surely as . . . as . . ." I waved my hand about the strange tunnel.

Just then there was an eerie whining in the tunnel, and one of those almost incomprehensible rushes of air. The gravel rattled under our feet, and the metal strips vibrated and sang, and both the Sidlesaghe and I had to take a deep breath and steady ourselves until the phenomenon had passed.

"Because," the Sidlesaghe said, very gently once the wind had passed, and our world had calmed, "the Game needs you to strive."

I stood there, gazing into the creature's gentle face, and felt like weeping. At that moment I did not feel like Mag, or the queen of England—I just felt . . . I just felt like poor, lost Cornelia, caught in a struggle that she neither wished for nor instigated.

The Sidlesaghe reached out his large hand and laid it softly, warmly against my cheek. "There are many futures," he said, "all existing side by side. We all need to strive to ensure we reach the *right* future."

I nodded wordlessly, hating the tears in my eyes. That I could live with. The possibility of many futures, not just one certain one.

"And in all of them," he said, "you will be the Mistress of the Labyrinth. Thus you can touch the bands."

I nodded again, feeling a little better.

"And in some of them," the Sidlesaghe continued, "you will also be Asterion's whore, his creature, his vassal. We must avoid that future."

My mouth dropped open in my horror. "You can see—"

"I know only of the possibilities," he said. "No more."

I shuddered, and we walked forward. We held our silence for some time, then I spoke again, wanting to hear the Sidlesaghe's amicable voice again.

"I sometimes feel an emptiness within me," I said. "An incompleteness. Is this because I am a virgin, and this is anathema to what I should be as Mag?"

Long Tom nodded. "This is very true. I am glad you thought of it."

It was Silvius who had thought of it, but I thought it best to let the Sidlesaghe believe I had come to this understanding on my own. "I need to unite myself to the land. Mate with it."

"Aye," the Sidlesaghe said, looking sideways at me, his mouth curling in a smile. "Choose well," he said, and winked.

I laughed, partly at his mischievousness, but mostly because he had allayed those few niggling reservations I'd had about what Silvius had suggested.

"Oh," I said, "I shall." Who better than Silvius, who was so closely associated with the Troy Game?

We lapsed into silence once more, and eventually the Sidlesaghe led me into a side tunnel, as narrow as that which once had brought me to the approach to London Bridge.

This time we did not emerge before the bridge, but just before the great west gate of London. In former times, when I had been Cornelia, the sad, abused wife of Brutus, this gate had been called Og's Gate. Now the people called it Ludgate, after Lud Hill.

The gates—thick, wooden constructions—hung between two ten-pace-high stone towers. The towers had narrow slit windows so that archers could shoot at any approaching enemy—I half expected an arrow to fly toward us at any moment—and parapets at their tops where further archers and spearmen could let fly their missiles.

Beyond the gates stretched the ancient stone and brick walls of London: part Roman construction, part British, part Saxon and, for what I understood of them and of what had founded them, of part magical construction as well.

I looked back to the towers to either side of the barred gates. I knew that normally guards watched atop these towers at night. I peered closely, and saw motionless shadows just behind some of the stone ramparts.

I looked at the Sidlesaghe.

"Shall they see us?" he said softly, returning my querying look with one of his own.

It was a test, but of understanding rather than of power.

"No," I said. "We do not exist within their perception. We are here, but not within their own expectations of reality. We are *beyond* what they expect, or can even imagine, and so they will not see us."

"And if it were Asterion, or Swanne, or William watching on those towers?"

"Then we would be discovered."

"Aye. Come."

We walked forward and when we reached the gates, they swung open as if by invisible hands, closing silently behind us once we had walked through. The Sidlesaghe led me through the empty street leading to St. Paul's atop Lud Hill, and as he did so, I thought about what I had said.

The guards could not see us because we existed beyond their expectations of reality; beyond what they could even imagine.

If that was so, then what could I see if I truly opened my eyes?

The instant that thought had passed through my mind, and I had opened myself to possibilities *beyond* what I expected, the empty street suddenly filled with life. A great, shadowy crowd thronged the street. These people were not alive, not in *this* present, but they were the memories of people who had been and the possibilities of people who would be.

I stopped, gazing open-mouthed at people dressed in the strangest of apparel, the great draperies of Roman senators, or the tightly clothed passengers, who sat in horseless vehicles that seemed to move of their own volition, placing burning fags in their mouths, as if in enjoyment!

"*Don't!*" the Sidlesaghe said.

I jerked my eyes to his face.

"We have not the time for this now," he said.

And I heard his unspoken thought, *Besides, if you see the myriad possibilities inherent in the many futures that await you, then you may not have the heart to continue.*

I blinked, suppressing . . . not the vision as such, but the understanding of the possibility of it.

Slowly, the shadowy, unnatural throng faded from view.

"You have the power to see too much," the Sidlesaghe said, more gently now, "and you will overwhelm yourself. Now, come with me, and we will walk softly for a time."

In a short while we stood at the base of the steps leading to the western—and main—doors of St. Paul's. I raised my foot to begin the climb, but the Sidlesaghe's grip on my hand tightened, and I stopped.

"We do not enter?" I said.

"No."

"Where do we go?" I said.

"Tonight we will move the closest band. Brutus hid them both within the city, and about its boundaries."

I turned slightly so I could look down the street we had traveled to reach St. Paul's. "Ludgate?"

"Aye," he said. "An obvious choice, and one Asterion himself thought of."

"Why couldn't he find it, then? There cannot be many places to hide a golden-limb band for one who is prepared to raze everything to the foundations and beyond."

"Because the band must be approached in a certain manner." He faced me completely, taking both my hands in his. "Caela, what do you understand of Asterion? Of his nature?"

I thought, remembering all I had been told, and what I had gleaned during my long wait in death. "He is the Minotaur, the creature in the heart of the labyrinth whom Theseus slew."

"Aye. And . . .?"

"Asterion controls great power, dark power, the power of the heart of the labyrinth, which is . . . which is . . ." I did not know quite how to phrase it, and the Sidlesaghe, seeing that I understood and lacked only the ability to explain in words, finished the sentence for me.

"Asterion controls the power of the heart of the labyrinth, *his dark power is kept in check by the labyrinth, by the Game, itself.*"

"Yes, thus Asterion wants the Game destroyed so that he and his dark power can ravage free across the world."

"Brutus hid the golden kingship bands by using the power of the Game, which—"

"Which Asterion does not yet know how to use or control, thus he cannot find them!"

The Sidlesaghe laughed in delight. "Yes!"

Now it was my turn to smile. "But you know the Game, and you are of the land. Both land and Game know where the bands lie. *You* know how to approach them." I paused. "But only I can touch them."

"So I will show you the path, and walk it with you, but when it comes to the band itself, you are the only one who can touch it. *You* are the only one who will be a part of their future."

I thought of my lover, running wild and free and strong through the forest, the bands glinting about his limbs. "Apart from . . . him."

"Aye." Again he squeezed my hands. "Caela, I must say something. When we reach the band, there will be a shock waiting there for you."

I did not like the sound of this. "A shock?"

"Brutus," he said.

CHAPTER TEN

HE SWALLOWED, AND THE SIDLESAGHE COULD see the fear, and want, and the desperate love in her face.

"I do not know if I dare see him again," she said, and began to weep.

The Sidlesaghe groaned, and gathered her to him, rocking her back and forth until her weeping had abated somewhat. Caela might face dragons and imps from hell, and the Sidlesaghe knew she would face them with courage and resolve, but confront her with the man she had loved so desperately and Caela's resolve and courage vanished in an instant.

"You must," he eventually said. "It will not be as difficult as you think."

"How so?" she said, leaning back and dashing away her tears with her hand.

"He will not know you are there, but only, *only* if you do not allow your eyes to meet with his. I will be with you, and I must abide by the same command myself. Neither of us can allow our eyes to meet with his. If we keep our eyes cast down, then he will overlook us, just as the guards in the towers overlooked us."

She nodded, some of her composure regained. "And if he sees us?"

"Then we, and this land, are undone. The band will vanish, turn to dust. Asterion shall have won."

Caela closed her eyes, drew in a deep breath, held it, then let it out. "Long Tom . . . where are we going to move the band to?"

The Sidlesaghe laughed, and stroked one of her cheeks with a thumb. "We will move this one in honor of your brother, Harold."

She frowned, puzzled.

"To the west of Westminster," the Sidlesaghe said, "is a small manor and village where once Earl Harold held court in the hall of a trusted friend."

Her frown deepened, then suddenly cleared. "Cynesige, who controls the estates and village of Chenesitun. He has ever been a true friend to not only Harold, but to our entire family."

"Aye. Chenesitun is the place to where the Game wants this first band moved."

"Why there?"

"Because the earl's court will become a focal point in the Game that is yet to be played," the Sidlesaghe said, then grinned wryly at the confusion on Caela's face. "Or where it *is* playing, in some corner of the Game's existence. This is what the Game requires, and so this is what we shall do. It will make the land a little stronger. Once the band has been moved, you will *feel* the renewed strength within yourself and within this land."

"Long Tom," Caela said, frowning a little, "how is it that you—and your kind—and the Game 'talk'? How *do* you know these things?"

The Sidlesaghe laughed, joyous, and Caela realized that he must spend much of his existence laughing. "We sing to each other, my love. Under the starlight. We *hum*."

"Oh," she said, not quite able to imagine this.

The Sidlesaghe grinned. "Now, are you ready?"

She nodded, but the Sidlesaghe saw that her knuckles had whitened where her hands clutched at the cloak.

"We will survive this night, at least," he said, "if you remember what I said about not meeting Brutus' eyes."

Again Caela nodded, and so the Sidlesaghe took one of her hands, and he led her about St. Paul's, first sun-wise, then counter-sun-wise. He walked deliberately but briskly, keeping Caela close by his side so that they walked almost as one.

Once they had completed the counter-sun-wise circuit of the boundary of St. Paul's, the Sidlesaghe led her north along a narrow street, then after a few minutes executed a sharp turn to the east, crossing through a vegetable garden.

"What . . ." Caela began to ask, then apparently realized herself. "We are traversing the labyrinth," she said.

"Aye. Not quite the same labyrinth that Brutus caused to be built atop Og's Hill, but one very similar if a little more convoluted. He hid each band within its own labyrinth—or, rather, guarded it by its own labyrinthine enchantment—so that only one skilled in the ways of the labyrinth could find them again." He paused. "Or one whom the labyrinth allowed to enter."

"The Game will not allow Asterion to traverse the labyrinthine ways to the bands."

"No. There are six labyrinthine enchantments for each of the six golden bands of Troy, and Asterion does not know them. *He* cannot traverse them."

"Without either Brutus—William—or you, or another of your kind."

"Or you," the Sidlesaghe said, noting, but not this time laughing at, the sudden frown on Caela's face. "And he shall not have me, nor as many of the bands as we can hide from William. Come, enough chatter. The night fades, and we have much work to do before morning."

They continued to walk through London, their pace picking up further speed, the greater distance they traveled through the labyrinthine enchantment. The Sidlesaghe led Caela through twists and turns, great circles and tight curves, traversing the greater part of the city west of the bridge.

Eventually the Sidlesaghe brought Caela to a stop before Ludgate.

Save that now the twin towers and the walls and the very gates themselves had vanished.

Instead there rose before them a small circle of standing stones, like, yet unlike, the Stone Dances that Caela had seen in her travels as Cornelia. They were as tall as the uprights in the Stone Dances, but more graceful, being composed of tapered fluted columns, which were topped with stone scrollwork. There were twelve of these columns, and they encircled a clear space that was lit with a soft golden radiance.

"These stones," Caela murmured, transfixed by the sight. "Are they . . .?"

"Aye. They are of our number as well. When Brutus first constructed this enchantment, they were of his world, bloodless, lifeless creatures. But as the years passed, we inhabited them, one by one."

"So now the Sidlesaghes stand guard over the bands."

"And you, now." The Sidlesaghe's hold on Caela's hand tightened momentarily, then he led her forward.

As they approached the columned circle, he paused, and whispered against Caela's ear, "Remember, do not meet his eyes."

She nodded, her eyes on the radiance beyond the columns.

They walked forward slowly.

As they reached the columns, and paused between two of them, the Sidlesaghe felt Caela tense. "Remember!" he whispered, and she managed a tight nod.

Brutus stood in the center of the circle.

He was naked, save for the six golden bands of Troy he wore about his limbs. His tightly curled black hair flowed down his back, lifting a little in some unfelt breeze.

He was walking very slowly and very deliberately about the center of the circle, his head down, his eyes fixed on the ground intently, as if he studied it for flaws.

Then suddenly he stopped, and raised his head, and looked directly toward where the Sidlesaghe and Caela stood.

The Sidlesaghe looked at Caela's face, then tugged urgently at her hand.

Caela had been looking straight at Brutus, as he'd stopped and raised his eyes to them, a look of utter want on her face, and she only managed to jerk her eyes downward in the barest instant before her gaze would have met that of Brutus'.

The Sidlesaghe kept his eyes fixed on Caela's face. "Remember!" he hissed at her.

Brutus walked slowly toward them.

The Sidlesaghe felt Caela tremble.

Brutus halted a pace away and the Sidlesaghe could sense his puzzlement, even if he could not directly look at Brutus' face.

"Genvissa?" Brutus said. "Is that you? Genvissa?"

Caela moaned, then bit her lip, and the Sidlesaghe understood the effort it took her not to look at Brutus.

"Genvissa?" Brutus said one more time. He stood still, looking forward intently, and the Sidlesaghe knew that Brutus felt *something*.

"Oh gods," Brutus said, his voice breaking, "where are you, Genvissa?"

The Sidlesaghe thought Caela would break at that moment. Her breath was coming in short jerks, her entire body was shaking, her head was trembling uncontrollably.

Any moment she was going to lift her eyes to Brutus, and call his name.

"In one of your futures," the Sidlesaghe said, very softly, "it will not be *her* name he calls, and then you will be able to lift your head and meet his eyes. Remember that."

The compassion in his voice steadied Caela. She closed her eyes, gained some control of herself, then squeezed the Sidlesaghe's hand very slightly.

I will not look.

"Genvissa?" Brutus said one more time, but his tone was less sure now, less urgent, and after a moment he turned and walked back to the center of the circle.

He stood—fortunately now with his back to the Sidlesaghe and Caela, which meant they could watch him directly—and looked down for a long time, then he sighed and seemed to come to a decision within himself. He lifted his left hand and, slowly, with great precision, slid the golden band that encircled his right forearm down over his wrist.

He hesitated as it reached his hand, and, the muscles of his back visibly clenching, he slid the band over his hand, squatted, and placed the band on the ground before him. He lifted his right hand, and made a complex movement over the band as it lay on the ground.

"He is creating the labyrinthine enchantment that we just traversed," the Sidlesaghe whispered into Caela's ear, and she gave a small nod.

Brutus finished, standing upright.

And then, in the space of a breath, he vanished, and both Caela and the Sidlesaghe let out their breaths in long, relieved sighs.

"Take it," the Sidlesaghe said, nodding to the band where it lay on the ground. "Take it. You will be safe."

Caela paused, then walked into the circle. She stood before the band, then leaned down and, without any hesitation, picked it up.

PART FIVE

Don't jump on the cracks, or the monster will snatch!
Traditional children's hopscotch song

LONDON, MARCH 1939

*M*ATILDA FLANDERS TURNED TO FRANK BENTLEY, *who was still looking at her open-mouthed. "Frank," she said, "I wasn't a staid widow all my life. I was a young girl once." She* glanced at Jack Skelton, then looked back to Frank and winked. *"And kicked up my heels a bit, if you know what I mean."*

Bentley blushed.

"With Major Skelton?" Violet Bentley said.

"I wasn't always so old and haggard," Skelton said dryly. "Matilda, Ecub, I need to speak with you. Please."

"Major—" said Frank.

"Just for fifteen minutes," said Skelton, turning to Bentley. "I won't hold you up. Go inside now, and have that breakfast Violet has cooked."

Bentley stifled his curiosity, nodded, then put his arm about Violet's shoulder and led her back into their house.

The instant the door closed behind them, Skelton turned back to the two women.

"Where is my daughter?"

Matilda and Ecub glanced at each other.

"Probably with Stella," said Matilda. Then, hastily, as Skelton's face registered his dismay, added, "Stella will—"

"My daughter is with the greatest of Darkwitches that ever lived?" Skelton said, his voice rising. "With Asterion's whore?"

Ecub stepped forward, grabbed his arm, and pulled him toward Matilda's front door. "Don't be a fool, Jack. 'Asterion's whore' can take care of her as well as anyone."

"But—"

"For gods' sakes, Jack!" Ecub hissed. "Don't you know that in her last life Cornelia asked Stella to look after the child should . . ."

Her voice trailed away.

"Should Asterion take Cornelia," Skelton said woodenly. "So Asterion does have Cornelia."

"Come inside," said Matilda, taking his hand, "and have a cup of tea."

CHAPTER ONE

*M*ATILDA WAS ALWAYS A LIGHT SLEEPER, drifting in and out of awareness as a night progressed. She would wake to hear William's heavy breathing beside her, and she would smile, and touch him, knowing all was well with her world, and drift back into a deeper unconsciousness for a time. William lapsed into deep sleep the instant he lay down, sleeping soundly the entire night through, but Matilda did not for an instant begrudge him his deep sleep. Those secret, brief moments when she would wake, and touch him, were precious to her.

She woke this night as she so often did, still half-dreaming, and reached out to touch William's arm.

The instant her fingertips touched his skin, he burst from the bed, shouting, *screaming*, incoherent with . . . *what?* Matilda did not know. She cried out herself, stunned, unable for the moment to make any sense of a world that had so suddenly erupted into the unexplainable.

Were they under attack?

Were there assassins in the bedchamber?

William was raging about the chamber, crying out insensibly, beating at walls, at his head, smashing a ewer and several wine cups halfway across the chamber.

The door burst open, and men-at-arms and valets and chamberlains, groggy themselves with either sleep or shock or both, staggered into the room to instantly reel out of the way as William continued his maddened rampage.

"William!" Matilda shouted, snatching at a robe to clothe herself as she stumbled from the bed. *"William!"*

"The band!" he screamed. "The band!"

Matilda burst into terrified sobs, certain that her husband had been struck with a brain fever so appalling he would shortly drop dead. She sank to her knees, unable to cope, her hands laced over her bowed head, while above her William continued to shout, to rage, and to *roar.*

"The band! Who has laid hand to the band?"

* * *

LIKE WILLIAM, SWANNE ALSO KNEW ONE OF THE
bands had been touched, *handled* by someone *other* than she or William.

Who? Who? Who?

Unlike William, Swanne did not roar and rage. Instead she curled up in
her bed, sweating in terror, the coverlets pulled up about her chin, staring
frantic-eyed about the darkness of her chamber.

If it were William who had laid a hand to the Kingman band, she would
have known it.

But this was not William's doing. This was the work of someone else.

Who?

No! No! Not . . . Asterion?

Swanne whimpered, feeling all her habitual arrogance and surety bleed
away into the unknown night. It was no accident, surely, that so soon after
Asterion had taunted her (*Do you know of what Ariadne promised me? Do you
know of how much she enjoyed me?*) a band was moved.

Swanne fought back panic.

She had never felt so alone, so powerless, in her entire life.

ASTERION HAD BEEN AWAKE, TORTURING WITH CRUEL
words and spiteful fingers a small naked boy he had tied face down, spread-
eagled across his bed.

He stopped suddenly, frozen half-bent over the sobbing boy, then he
slowly raised his head, his eyes narrowed, his lips drawing back over his teeth
in a silent snarl.

"Who?" he hissed. "Who? Who has found a band?"

William? Had William slunk unnoticed into the country?

Asterion felt a moment of intense fear. *He had not expected William to be
this bold!*

And yet, why not, eh? What if William was not willing to dance to Asterion's
tune? What if he had decided to circumvent everything Asterion had so carefully planned?

*What if William had donned the garb of a merchant, or common seaman, and
jumped off ship at a London dock, seeking out the bands before Asterion was
ready to intercept him?*

"No!" Asterion said. "It cannot be William. *Think,* man."

He looked down to the boy who continued to cry, save that now his wails
grew louder as he twisted his face about and saw the expression on the face of
the man standing over him.

The man reached down and touched the boy, *tweaked* him, and the boy shrieked.

"Not William," said Asterion softly. "Not William at all."

Who then?

Her. It had to be. Damn her to all hells. It had to be her.

"But how has she found them? What magic has she employed?"

Was she stronger than he thought?

That thought disturbed Asterion, and he sighed, and considered the boy. It would have been fun to play with him a little longer, but . . .

He took hold of a large wooden crucifix that hung on the wall next to the bed and dealt the boy a shattering blow to the back of his head, then one to the back of his ribs, and then yet again to the boy's neck.

When he had done, the boy lay still, barely alive, blood seeping from his battered body.

In any other circumstances, the sight would have stimulated Asterion into the heights of sexual passion. Tonight, however, he merely tossed the crucifix down onto the boy's body with a grunt, and reached for his robe.

When he had garbed himself, and wiped away those splatters of the boy's blood that had marked his face, he left the chamber.

"Throw him in the river," he said to the shadowy man waiting patiently outside, and the man nodded, and slipped inside the door.

By the time the servant emerged, the boy's shattered body wrapped in a blanket, Asterion had long vanished into the night.

"HAROLD!" WILLIAM SUDDENLY DECLARED, AND Matilda carefully raised her head.

There had been the suggestion of sanity in that single utterance.

"Harold," William said again, his voice firmer now. "Harold."

To Matilda, it seemed as if William uttered that name as a mantra, as the lifeline that would pull him back into reality.

She very carefully rose to her feet. About the chamber stood various men-at-arms and servants, all staring, none knowing what to do or say.

"Harold," William said one more time, then, as naked as that moment he'd erupted from the bed, shouldered his way through the watching men, and half ran through the halls and chambers of the castle toward Harold's chamber.

Grabbing a cloak, Matilda hurried after him.

CҺAPꞆꞆꞂ ꞆWꞀO

AROLD SHARED A CHAMBER WITH THORKELL
and Hugh off a cloistered walk some distance away in the castle
complex.

That distance gave William time to think.

At first he'd raced from the bedchamber he shared with Matilda, as though
every moment it took to reach Harold would somehow mean another moment
in which *whoever it was* had to steal the arm band away completely. William
could *feel* which band it was—the lower right forearm band, which he'd
secreted at the western gate of Troia Nova—and could feel its movement *away*.

He couldn't have explained that sense of "away" to anyone else, let alone
himself. The arm band, *his kingship band, his power, his future,* was being
stolen away from him.

Away.

And yet how could this be? That band, *all the bands*, were protected by a
labyrinthine enchantment that meant only another Kingman or William's
partner in the Game, Swanne, could touch it, let alone find it.

And it could not be Swanne, for he had not told her where the bands
were.

Yet she had asked for their location. Could she have scried out the bands'
resting places, and decided to move them anyway?

It was the only explanation that William could think of, unless . . . unless
Asterion had somehow managed to find a band.

Could he move it?

William didn't know. Possibly. Asterion was a creature of the labyrinth
and of the Game; he was the brother of Ariadne, the most powerful Mistress
of the Labyrinth there had ever been; and he had increased in power and
knowledge through all the lives he had passed through since Ariadne had set
him free from both death and the Game.

Could it be Asterion?

"Oh God," William groaned, and stumbled to a halt just as he reached the
door of Harold's chamber.

He was vaguely aware that he'd been followed in his mad dash through the castle by a bevy of servants, men-at-arms, and Matilda, all of whom doubtless thought he was about to murder Harold in a state of dream-induced madness.

And what was he going to do now that he *was* here? Break down the door, haul Harold from his bed and demand the name of whoever it was who had the arm band?

Harold would not know. He was not even aware of what part he played in this cursed Game.

Was he?

What if Harold *was* aware, and had thus far deluded William into thinking he had no idea who he had been?

What if Harold and Swanne were in league, against William?

No! No, that could not be.

William suddenly realized he was standing inanely by the closed door to Harold's chamber, so close his forehead was actually resting on the wood, and the sentry who stood further down the cloistered walk was staring at him as if he were moon-crazed.

William sighed, straightened, and looking to where Matilda stood several paces away with his cloak, smiled ruefully and held out his hand.

"Are you well, husband?" she asked, as she stepped up to him. From what William could see of her expression in this barely lit place, her eyes were narrowed and suspicious.

"I have had ill news given to me in dream," he said. "I need to speak with Harold."

"Be careful," she said, and William knew she was not saying *Be careful of Harold*, but, *Do not harm Harold.*

William nodded, threw the cloak about his shoulders, and dismissed the crowd of watchful, concerned men who stood at some distance. "Go now," he said to them. "I am sorry that I have disturbed your night."

"William?" said Matilda.

"I will talk awhile with Harold," he said, and bent down to kiss her. "Do not fret. I shall not slaughter him. But perhaps he can calm my mind. Wait for me in our chamber."

When she had gone, the servants and men-at-arms trailing behind her, William turned once more to Harold's door, and thumped softly on it with his fist.

It opened almost immediately.

Harold stood behind the door, fully dressed, his chamber glowing with the light of several lamps.

Thorkell and Hugh stood only a pace behind Harold, their expressions wary, hands on the knives in their belts.

"You're awake?" said William, and again doubts assailed him. Why? *Had he made that much commotion in his mad race from his own bedchamber to Harold's?*

"There is trouble," Harold said, and William's eyes narrowed.

"Oh, aye, there *is* trouble. But how do you know of it?"

In answer, Harold looked to Thorkell and Hugh, then to William, then back to his two companions.

"I would speak awhile with William," he said, and, understanding the message, Thorkell and Hugh left the chamber, pushing past William with set, careful expressions on their faces.

"You will find warmth and light and companionship in the kitchens," William said to them. "I have no doubt that most of the castle is awake and restless this night."

The instant Harold closed the door behind him, William spoke again. "There is great trouble in London," he said, searching Harold's face for knowledge of what had—*was*—happening.

"You dreamed it?" Harold said. He walked to a stool by a glowing brazier, and sat down heavily.

"Aye, I dreamed of it. But it was a dream of reality, not of fancy." William stayed by the door, watching Harold closely.

The Saxon earl looked haggard, as if he, too, had dreamed horribly. William saw him rub gently at his belly, and wince slightly as he shifted on the stool, and thought that the wild boar's bruises must be paining him.

"Caela is in danger," Harold said, and William's jaw almost sagged in surprise.

"Caela? You dreamed of Caela?"

"Aye. She and I have ever been close—"

William's mouth twisted.

"—closer than most brothers and sisters. Sometimes, when she has been frightened or unwell I have known it, even though she be at a great distance. Tonight . . . tonight I dreamed that a great beast, something *monstrous*, pursued her through a land of broken stone and tumbled walls. Ah!" Harold lifted his hand from his belly and rubbed at his eyes. "I cannot understand it. What I *do* understand is that there is trouble afoot, great trouble, and that somehow it involves Caela."

When has there ever been trouble about that has not involved her? William thought, but there was no hatred in that thought. He took a stool opposite Harold, pulling the cloak comfortably about his body, and leaning forward close to the brazier. "Something is wrong tonight," he said. "I also had a dream."

"Of Caela?"

William looked at Harold sharply, but saw nothing in the man's face other than genuine concern and puzzlement. "No," he said. "Just of . . . of trouble. Harold . . ."

"Aye?"

"Harold, are you in league with Swanne against me?"

Harold stared at William, then grinned, genuinely and freely. "Nay, William. Put that from your mind. I do not plot with Swanne against you. I may plot with the rest of England against you, but I do not plot with Swanne."

William stared at Harold, then laughed softly, deprecatingly. How twisted his life had become to be so relieved that Harold only plotted with all of England against him, but not with a single woman! And Harold *was* telling the truth. William could see it. Coel had never lied, could never lie, could not even begin to contemplate the art of dissimulation, and Coel's spirit shone so true and bright from Harold's eyes that William believed utterly that he was telling the truth.

Whatever else Harold might be doing, he wasn't doing it in league with Swanne.

"Will you share some wine?" said Harold, standing and walking to a chest, atop which stood several jugs and cups. "I think Thorkell and Hugh may have left us a drop."

"Aye," said William. "Thank you."

But as he drank, and as he exchanged friendly words with Harold, William's mind drifted back to London, where he could feel the arm band moving farther and farther from that place where he'd left it.

Caela? No, surely not. Surely?

And if so, how?

William suddenly remembered that moment when he and Genvissa had been dancing the final dance, which would have completed the Game, building the gate of flowers to the entrance of the labyrinth. He remembered that single horrifying moment when he had seen Cornelia stepping forth, running forth, drawing from her robe Asterion's wicked blade.

Caela?

Caela and Asterion?

God! Was Caela now so completely Asterion's creature that she could manipulate the Game's mysteries?

William realized that Harold had stopped, as if he'd said something that required William's comment.

"What?" he said stupidly.

"I asked," said Harold, "if you would swear your support to my succession to the English throne. Your lips were forming the word, 'Yes,' I think."

William shot him an amused look. "That was not what you asked."

"Well . . . no. But I thought you so lost in your own thoughts that I might catch you unawares and gain your support for my accession without a single blow being struck."

"I do not want to kill you, Harold."

"No," Harold said softly. "I don't believe you do. If you and I had met under different circumstances, I think we would have been true friends."

William nodded, accepting the truth of it. "Harold . . ." he said.

"Aye?"

"Will you tell me of Caela?"

"How strange," said Harold, "for when I return to my homeland, I have every expectation that Caela will ask me to tell her of you."

CHAPTER THREE

CAELA SPEAKS

HE SIDLESAGHE HAD TOLD ME THIS MOVING OF the first Kingman band would be a true test of my abilities and understanding, but I found it far easier than he had intimated. I picked up the band, and held it in my cupped hands, studying it.

How it reminded me of Brutus. How many times had this band and its fellows rubbed against me, pressed against me, as Brutus lay with me? Earlier in our marriage I had loathed it, for those bands and their pressing against me represented his victory over me. Later, when I had come more to my senses, I had loved the feel of them against my skin as I had loved the feel of Brutus against me.

Then, later still, when I had murdered Genvissa, and Brutus had taken me back to wife in order to hate and punish me, I had missed those bands. Brutus had hidden them, and their lack represented all that had been buried and hidden between us: love, respect, warmth, want.

I breathed in deeply, *feeling* the band as it rested in my hands. It was not cold, as one might expect metal—even golden metal—to be, but was warm, as if it still retained the warmth and vitality of Brutus' body. Of course, now I understood differently. These bands had power and life of their own, and this warmth reflected that life as also the life and power of the Game.

The band was beautiful. Strangely, given that I had spent so much time with Brutus in the two years or so before I destroyed everything before us in the interest of land and Game, I had never truly examined them before this moment. Almost three fingers wide, the band was incredibly finely wrought in metal that was itself so refined it visibly glowed. About its surface, craftsmen had worked the symbol of the Trojan kings: the stylized crown spinning over the labyrinth.

I rubbed a thumb over the decoration, and as I did so, I swear that Brutus' scent rose from the gold.

"Caela."

The Sidlesaghe's voice brought me to my senses, and I looked up.

"This you must do by yourself," he said from where he still stood just out-side the circle of columns.

I frowned. "You will not come with me?"

"No. You must be the one to move it. This travail only you can accomplish. Use your skills, Caela. Take it to Chenesitun."

I looked back to the band.

"You have not long, Caela. You must be back in Edward's bed by dawn."

I was irritated with the Sidlesaghe now, for all I truly wanted was to stand and inhale the feel and scent of Brutus from this band . . . but he was right, and so I looked away from the Sidlesaghe toward the southeastern quadrant of the circle.

I concentrated, my eyes narrowing.

I became the land, and I saw.

There, a trail, winding through a rocky landscape. Not the landscape that was reality, for that was sweet meadowland and marsh where the grasses bordered the river, but some *other* landscape. I did not immediately recognize it, but it felt safe to me, and right, and so I stepped forth.

The instant I left the circle, the columns faded, but the golden radiance that had lit that circle now strengthened to such a degree that I felt I was walking through the noonday sunlight. A path stretched before me. Composed of dirt and scattered gravel, it wound its way between great piles of tumbled rock.

Paving, I saw as I took my first steps along that path, the golden band still held in my cupped hands.

I was walking through the ruins of a once great and mighty city.

Tears filled my eyes. I knew this place, even though I had never been there. I knew it because I had heard stories of it from so many people: Brutus, Hicetaon, Corineus, even Aethylla. It was Troy. Troy destroyed.

I was seeing this because this is what the band remembered. It had *been* here, it had barely escaped the destruction itself, and it still sorrowed and wept for the great, beautiful city of its birth and initial purpose.

I realized also that I was seeing this for another and more vital reason. I had become the land in order to find my way to Chenesitun, but what the land became—in conjunction with the band—was Troy. My land—my *self*—and the Game had merged to such an extent that this land *was* Troy. Or, at least, it had absorbed the vitality and memories of that long-ruined place, until Troy's past had become part of its own past.

Or was it that I saw only one of many possible futures for this land that the Game played out, over and over?

I continued walking. Great drifts of tumbled masonry extended to either side of me. In some places the stones still leaked smoke from fires that raged within, in other, sadder places, bloodied bodies lay sprawled across the stones.

I wept, so sickened was I by the destruction and the carnage.

All this a part of Ariadne's Catastrophe. All this a part of her pact with her hateful brother, the Minotaur Asterion.

And what was in that pact that Asterion thought to use it to taunt Swanne? What part did I not understand?

Thought of Asterion made me hurry my feet. They would know now that the band was being moved: William, Swanne, and Asterion. Still in Normandy, William would do nothing but rage and fret. Swanne? Swanne would rage as well, and she might also fly into the night, seeking that person who had dared touch the band.

Or would she? In Swanne's mind the only conceivable person who might touch the band apart from William was Asterion, and I did not think Swanne ready for a confrontation with him.

No, I thought it unlikely that at this initial time Swanne would make a physical move.

That left Asterion, and I admit that thought of him did worry me. I didn't know Asterion, I couldn't scry him out, I didn't know the extent of his power, and I couldn't be sure that he might not be lurking behind the next pile of rubble I walked about.

So I hurried my feet. I was walking amid enchantment, so that I knew the way to Chenesitun would take me only a fraction of the time it would if I walked the land in reality, but still I hurried. I began to fret about what I would find when I reached Chenesitun—where could I hide the band? Did *I* have the skills to secret it from Asterion, as well as William and Swanne?

About me the destruction and horror grew even greater. The piles of masonry grew higher, the smoke and fires thicker, the stench of the corpses more sickening. Blood now trickled in small rivulets across the path, and every third or fourth step I had to make a small leap to avoid soiling either my feet or robe.

My hands tightened about the band, for I was fearful it might dislodge. Somehow I knew that if I let it fall, if it rolled away between the tumbled stones, then it would be lost forever.

My breathing grew quicker, deeper, harsher, and I prayed silently that I would soon reach my destination.

I dared a glance ahead, and what I saw dismayed me. The smoking ruins of Troy seemingly stretched on forever.

It would take me all night, surely!

I began to panic and, in that panic, one of my feet slipped on some loose gravel. I almost lost my footing, and I cried out as my hands grabbed frantically at the band.

I stopped walking, taking a moment to try and calm myself. Gods, this was but the first band, and surely was going to be the easiest to move! I could not let a vision of the past upset me!

Or was this a vision of the future? Not of old Troy destroyed, but of this Troy—London—destroyed?

Panic again threatened to overwhelm me, but then I pushed it down with every ounce of strength that I had, and I pushed ahead, one foot after the other, one foot after the other, and so I endured.

Within minutes, so it seemed, I walked in the space of three footsteps from the devastation of Troy into the strangest, most frightening chamber I had ever encountered.

In all of my existences.

Somehow I knew that this was Chenesitun, but not the Chenesitun I had once seen. Here were no scattering of wattle and daub dwellings, here no low-roofed timber house of the thegn called Cynesige. Here no barns or the soft lowing of cattle.

Instead, I stood within a chamber so vast I could barely comprehend it. It reminded me somewhat of my vision of the stone hall that I'd had as Cornelia, but only in its dimensions. Here was no peace, but the madly scurrying bodies of people dressed in alien clothes. Here was no joy, but the irritation of bustling people—I could feel from them a cacophony of words and emotions: *late, late, late, hurry, hurry, hurry, delay, delay, delay, what is the time? Where is the platform? Where is my ticket? Have you a timetable?*

And then, more ominously: *Hurry! Flee! Down! Down! The sirens have sounded!*

A woman, dressed in a close-cut coat and skirt of a weave and material I could barely imagine, stepped up to me and stared me in the face. Her own face was garishly painted, her shoulder-length hair was elaborately curled and stiffened by some unseen agent. She held a small boy, dressed in close-cut clothes similar to hers, save that he wore trousers rather than a skirt, and a striped cap pulled low over his eyes.

"Do you know the way?" she asked me, her eyes wild with fear, I thought, and perhaps even some desperation. "Which platform do I need?"

"I . . ." What could I say? Everything about me was so strange, so foreign, more terrifying even than Troy's destruction.

"You cannot just *stand* here!" the woman said. "Save yourself!" Then, thankfully, she turned her back and scurried off, pulling the boy behind her.

He sent me a single pleading look over his shoulder, and then they vanished into the hurrying crowd.

"My dear," said a voice, and it was so soft and familiar I grabbed on to it. "My dear . . ."

I turned to my left, and saw some ten or fifteen paces away a collection of tables and chairs. At one of the tables sat a man who, even though he was sitting, was of noticeable height. He was also very thin, and he had a calf-length brown coat belted tightly about him, and a curiously-shaped soft hat pulled low over his long, thin, pale face.

Even so curiously disguised, I could recognize who it was.

A Sidlesaghe. Not Long Tom, but one of his kind.

His soft voice reached me again. "Old thing. Is that my cup of tea? I will have it, if you please."

I looked down at my hands, and noticed several things all at once. I was no longer dressed in my robe and cloak, but a tightly belted dress of starched white material that seemed like linen and yet was not. My legs were encased in fine, woolenlike stockings, and on my feet were brown leather shoes of sturdy construction.

I no longer held the golden band of Troy, but a small round platter on which stood a cup. Both were made of a fine white pottery. The cup held a steaming, milky-brown substance.

"My cup of tea, old thing, if you don't mind."

Again the Sidlesaghe's voice cut into my thoughts, and I walked over to him.

His eyes locked into mine.

"On the table, there's a dear."

I hesitated, then placed the cup before him.

The instant I set it down he reached out a hand and grabbed my wrist.

"The band is safe for the moment, but you must be careful, darling. *He's* coming up the stairs."

I knew immediately who he meant, if not quite *what* he meant.

Asterion.

"Flee," the Sidlesaghe said.

ChAPTER FOUR

THE GAME STRETCHED, AND GREW. NOT IN power so much as in potential.

One band had been moved and the Game's boundaries had been physically expanded.

Five more to go.

ASTERION HAD ASSUMED HIS NATURAL APPEARANCE the instant it was safe for him to do so unobserved.

Power was so much easier to manipulate when he walked in his man-bull form.

London was quiet and dark—save for that glow in the northern section where a building appeared to be afire. Asterion knew well what that was—a distraction, something to keep the watch occupied while the *real* crime of the night took place.

Asterion was close to glow-in-the-dark furious. *She*—she!—*was moving a band!*

Not only was she shifting the band, but she accomplished it under a cloak of such enchantment that he had difficulty sensing any information about it at all.

To know that a band was so close, so tantalizingly *exposed,* and yet still so out of reach . . .

And how? *How?* The unknowingness of that only fed Asterion's rage.

Asterion roamed the streets of London, seeking something, *anything,* that could provide him with a clue.

Nothing.

How could he have so misjudged her?

His pace became ever more frantic, his fury edging ever closer to the out-of-control, but still . . . nothing.

Quiet, dark streets.

Here! Ah! Nothing but a dog, a cur of a beast that was hiding behind the wheel of a cart.

Asterion slaughtered it.

He moved on, dashing in short bursts along the streets, pausing to sniff the air, to peer closely into shadows, then lay a hand to a wall and *feel*, feel for anything, anything at all . . .

And, just before dawn, he *did* feel it. Just a suggestion, nothing more.

A memory that tugged insistently in his mind . . . Troy. Troy.

Troy!

Asterion had been there for the final destruction of Troy, as he had participated in the majority of the destructions Ariadne had worked with her Catastrophe. He had walked through the ruins, through the raging fires, through the piles of bodies—adding to fire and ruin and death whenever he had the chance. During that wonderful day, Asterion had known of the escape of Aeneas, the Kingman who had then worn the kingship bands of Troy.

Then, of course, Asterion had not known what a role these bands would play in a later life, but even so, Asterion had tried to snatch Aeneas. It had been for fun, for joy, for amusement, for the pleasure of the hunt. Aeneas was the son of Aphrodite, he was wearing the golden bands that allowed him to play the Game, and Asterion had thought it would be more than entertaining to tear the man apart limb from limb. One more Kingman dead, one more set of bands destroyed, one more nail in the coffin of the Game.

But Asterion had never caught Aeneas. He'd tracked him through the ruins and through the rivulets of blood. He had heard and seen and smelled him, but Asterion had never managed to catch Aeneas. Aphrodite had aided him, of course—how else could he have escaped?—but even so, Asterion had felt the trickery of the man and his damnable bands . . .

And he was feeling something similar here this night in London.

Asterion was close to the western wall of London when these memories flooded back to haunt him, and he stopped, and paused.

He sniffed the air, his magnificent bull's head held high.

He sniffed again . . . and then he hunched over, arms held out, as if he were ready to attack.

And then . . . he vanished.

HE RUSHED THROUGH THE BLOODIED, TUMBLED remains of Troy, their smell and sight as vivid as that day he'd participated in the city's destruction.

She was somehow using this landscape to do it!

And why not? Asterion could understand that. The bands were of Troy, they had breathed the same air, and *she* was using that ancient escape to effect this one.

Grinning from ear to ear, Asterion jogged through the ruins. He followed the same path of the band, he could *smell* it, and any moment, any moment . . .

Any moment he would be upon her . . . and the band would be his.

Asterion could have howled in joy, but he didn't; not when he was hunting. He ran lightly, effortlessly, down the path, his feet splashing through puddles of water and blood, his eyes fixed ahead.

His right foot splashed down into a puddle of water, and before it could lift again, a thin, white hand reached out of the water and grasped Asterion's ankle tightly.

The Minotaur tumbled over, hitting the ground with a great crack. Within the instant, he had half risen, his own hands reaching for the hand that had his ankle.

Before they could reach it, the strange hand had vanished amid a tinkle of feminine laughter.

Asterion scrambled to his feet. A trap left by Aphrodite, he had no doubt. Even dead, that goddess was proving more than trying. But that was of no concern to Asterion now. What he *needed* to do was catch the bandshifter who trod the path just a twist or two ahead in the ruins.

But he was too late. Just as he rounded a corner, sure to find there the woman he sought, the landscape of Troy fell away, and Asterion found himself standing in the midst of a trackway that wound between several low farm buildings.

There was no one there.

CHAPTER FIVE

HE INSTANT CAELA MATERIALIZED ON THE trackway before him, the Sidlesaghe Long Tom reached out and grabbed her.

She gave a cry of terror. "Asterion!"

"I know," the Sidlesaghe said. "He will be here at any moment. The band . . . it is safe?"

She nodded. "Yes, but—"

"There is no time for 'buts' now. Quick, quick, if the band is safe, if it is *here*, then we can escape."

He dragged Caela toward one of the farm buildings, pushing aside the unlatched, rough door with a shoulder and all but threw Caela inside.

Inside there were no cattle, or sheep, or pigs, nor even piles of new-mown hay. Instead there stretched one of the Game's strange tunnels.

"Newly built," said the Sidlesaghe, the relief evident in his voice as he hurried Caela forward. "The instant you laid that band in its new resting place."

"Asterion?"

"He cannot follow us down here. The labyrinth, the *Game*, is still protected by those enchantments Brutus wove over it. More protected, now that one of the bands is moved and the Game has expanded. Now, hurry, hurry, hurry. Dawn is close, and Edward's eyes will shortly open. Hurry, hurry, hurry."

ASTERION STOOD IN THE CENTER OF THE TRACKWAY, *feeling* the escape of the damnable bandshifter, but not able to do anything about it.

Then he caught at his thoughts, and he flushed hot at the realization that he *didn't* have to do anything about it, did he?

She could move the bands all she liked, but so long as he managed that one small task that lay ahead, then that was of no matter. That one, single, pleasurable task, then she could move them to the very sun and it wouldn't matter, would it?

"My dear," he murmured. "You think you know which way the attack will come. But you have no idea, do you?"

The Sidlesaghe led Caela to that place in the Game's magical tunnel that lay beneath her solar.

"Asterion smelt you," he said. "When you walked the path to Chenesitun, what path did the game construct for you?"

"The ruins of Troy," Caela said, glancing above her. She could *feel* Judith pacing back and forth, back and forth.

The Sidlesaghe sighed softly. "Then no wonder he discovered it! Doubtless Asterion aided in Troy's ruin as he must have aided in the ruin of so many wondrous cities. Caela, we must be careful. We must wait awhile before you try to move another band. He knows the path you will take . . . we cannot risk him *waiting* for you the next time, or any other time. Now, go. Go! The world wakes!"

She leaned forward, laid a quick kiss on his mouth, then vanished.

SWANNE HUDDLED IN HER LONELY BED, CONSUMED with the knowledge of what had happened this night. It must be Asterion who had moved the band. Who else? Who else?

And if it was he, then all was lost, surely.

"William," she whispered. "William . . ."

WILLIAM SAT BEFORE THE NEWLY STOKED FIRE IN HIS slowly lighting bedchamber. He stared at the flames, but his thoughts were elsewhere.

A band had been moved, and yet the Game had not been harmed. Indeed, its strength had increased. William could feel that even from this distance. The Game had *grown*.

It was not Asterion who had moved the band. If it had been, William would have felt the diminution, or the alteration, in the Game's power that Asterion's touch would have caused. But nothing like that had occurred. In fact, William could feel a faint echo of Asterion's anger.

Asterion had been caught as much unaware as William.

So who then had moved the arm band?

Caela? Caela in league with Asterion? William fretted it over. Caela had betrayed him with Asterion once before to pull the Game to a wrenching halt.

William knew he could not afford to ignore the possibility that she may have betrayed him (*and the Game*) once more.

But if it was Caela who had moved the band, Caela in concert or alliance with Asterion, then would not William have felt that? Felt Asterion's presence within the endeavor? If Caela had moved the band using Asterion's power and/or knowledge, then William would have known it.

Yet the only presence of Asterion's he *had* felt was that of anger and frustration. So not Caela under Asterion's direction?

Caela by herself? No, no, it could not be. Caela had no power, and certainly no knowledge of where the bands lay. She simply could not have moved it. She was just a woman, a woman of no power or enchantment . . . and, besides, the band would not have allowed her to touch it, let alone find it.

It *must* have been Swanne. Swanne was the only other person alive who could have touched the band and successfully moved it. She was the Mistress of the Labyrinth, and cofounder of this Game. She *could* have managed it.

But Swanne didn't know where the band was. Could she have discovered it? William wasn't sure. If she had found the band, then she had more power than William had thought.

It had to be Swanne. It *had* to be. There was no one else. And if it was her, then she was risking everything. If Asterion caught her, or if he found one of those bands . . . *gods, the thought was not bearable!*

William shifted in his chair, uncomfortable and restless. *If only he could invade now! If only he could take those bands now!*

But invasion was not an option. Not during the winter, when storms were likely to wreck any invasion fleet within a half day's sail from port. Certainly not while Edward was still alive. To take England, William needed the support (and private armies) of several score noblemen and counts from Gascony to Flanders to Burgundy and all the duchies and kingdoms in between. If they thought he had a legal claim to the English throne, and a viable chance of winning it, then they'd not hesitate to join him for a share of the spoils. If they thought that his claim was *not* legal (as it would be if he tried to wrest England from Edward rather than Harold), then they'd hesitate. Half the European princes, dukes, and kings would denounce the invasion. The pope, like as not, would place William and Normandy under interdict. William's support base would melt away, and Edward's army (which would be led by Harold, dammit, rather than the dying king!) would likely defeat William's much reduced invading force.

William's only chance, and it was a good one, was to invade only after Edward had died, when he could viably claim the throne.

Not before.

Not before, even if an unknown "someone" was moving the kingship bands.

It must be Swanne! It must!

William sat and stared into the flames.

On the bed, Matilda sat and stared at William.

For hours, until well after the sun had risen, neither moved, nor said a word.

Then, as Matilda dressed and made for the door, William raised his head. "Matilda?"

She turned, and looked at him.

"Can you ask your agent, whosoever he or she may be, to watch both Swanne and Caela?"

"That is most certainly possible."

William considered, wording his request carefully. "Then can you ask if . . . if either ever manages to escape the court unnoticed, or keeps strange company? Or if they . . ." *Oh gods, how to phrase this?* "If they have within their possession any finely wrought golden bands with a spinning crown over a labyrinth worked into them."

Matilda's eyes widened very slightly, but she understood that her husband was in no mood for explanations. "I can do that for you."

"For us," William said softly. "For *us*."

CHAPTER SIX

WILLIAM GRUNTED, THEN SIGHED. HE STILL sat before the fire in his bedchamber, but now Matilda was gone, and in her place—in a chair opposite William rather than sitting on the bed—was Harold.

Between Harold and William sat a chessboard on a low table.

The men had been shifting pieces back and forth for almost an hour, and that time spent at the one game did not reflect their skill, nor their determination to keep the other at bay, but instead was an indication of both men's almost total lack of interest in the game. Both had squandered chances to trap the other, both had exposed their own men to the ravages of the other's, both still had most of their pieces on the board.

"I am returning to England," Harold eventually said. It was the first time either of them had spoken since they'd sat down.

William grunted again. He did not raise his eyes from the chessboard.

"You will not hold me?" Harold said.

William shot him a glance, but just as quickly returned his gaze to the board. "It would do me no favor," he said. "I would alienate half of Europe, let alone most of England." He paused, his long fingers hovering over his king. "Besides, Edward would as likely as not disinherit me for the act."

"Edward would likely as not spend an entire week capering about Westminster in joy if he thought there was the faintest possibility you might put a sword through my throat."

William's hand froze over the chess piece, then he slowly sat back from the board and looked Harold full in the face.

"Why did you come, Harold?" Oh, William *knew* why Harold had come. It was the unacknowledged Coel within him, driving him forward to meet face to face with his doom. It is what Coel would have done, it is what drove Harold over to Normandy. Still, William wanted to know what Harold believed had driven him here.

"We will meet one day on the battlefield," Harold said. "I wanted to know you beforehand." He relaxed a little in his chair, his attention now as removed from the chessboard as was William's. "And, of course, I had hoped to gain your total support for my own succession to England's throne."

Both men grinned, and then both men's grins faded as quickly.

"I needed to *know* you, William," Harold said again. "But I did not expect to like you. I did not expect to respect you."

There was silence. William's eyes dropped to his lap where he was slowly rubbing the thumb of one hand between the forefinger and thumb of the other. He fiddled some minutes, thinking. Aye, he liked Harold, too. He *liked* him. In other circumstances, William knew he could probably have counted on Harold to be his most loyal and trustworthy companion.

Harold . . . *Coel*. Who would have thought it? But then, when had Brutus ever taken the time to understand Coel, or even to know him beyond a passing acquaintance?

William suddenly understood that he needed to have reached this revelation, this state of liking and of friendship, with Harold-who-was-once-Coel. It was something William needed to do, just as Harold needed to like and respect him.

Why? What part of what larger game was this?

Finally, William raised his gaze back to Harold. "I wish . . ." he began, then could not continue.

"Aye," said Harold. He blinked, as if he had tears in his eyes, then leaned forward and held out a hand to William.

William took it without hesitation. "I do not want to kill you," he said.

"Aye, and I do not want to have to kill you."

They gripped hands, their eyes locking, then both let go and sat back, half-embarrassed smiles playing over their faces.

"If I win," William said, only half-jokingly, "and you do not survive, may I say that you pledged to me that I might take the throne?"

Harold considered. Such a statement would inevitably blacken Harold's name. He had pledged to William that he might take the throne on Edward's death, and then Harold had backed down on his word, and sought through force to deny William his rights.

Yet the revelation of such a vow would unite England as nothing else had done. It would prevent the country from tearing itself apart trying to resist William's rule. If William won on the battlefield, and then said that God had judged in William's favor because Harold had reneged on his word, the English would accept it. They might not like it, but they would accept it.

What did he want more? His honor, or England's well-being?

He nodded. "Aye. You may say that." He paused, a slow smile spreading over his mouth. "If you also agree that should I win, and you die, then I can spread it about that you were the motherless son of one of Hell's imps."

William burst out laughing. "A deal!" He held out his hand as Harold had just held out his.

But Harold hesitated. "And that if you do so win against me, and I die on the battlefield, then you shall respect the life and property of my sons and daughters, and that of my sister, Caela. You shall honor my children, and my sister, and do them no harm."

William's face grew serious. "A deal, Harold."

Harold nodded, and took William's hand.

"I wish you well," said William softly.

"And I you," said Harold.

And with those words, each man felt an immense weight lifted off his shoulders, while, under London, the Stag God Og stirred, and his heart (still lying so cruelly torn from his breast) beat a fraction more strongly.

CHAPTER SEVEN

CAELA SPEAKS

*A*DAY OR TWO AFTER I HAD MOVED THE BAND, I arranged it so that Ecub, Judith, and Saeweald sat with me in some privacy within my solar. Again, other ladies were in attendance, along with one or two of Edward's thegns (paying attention to one or two of my ladies rather than me), but they were grouped at some distance, and I felt that if I kept my voice low enough then we should have seclusion enough.

I told them of the moving of the band, and of how Asterion tried to snatch me and it. They shuddered, as did I in the retelling, and begged me be careful in the future.

Then, because they needed and deserved to know, I told them of how I had felt empty, un-right, of how I had felt some loss of connection to the land. How I was not all that I should be.

"But how can this be?" Saeweald began, rather officious and put out, as if I had conceived of this problem only to irritate him, and I held up a hand to quiet him.

"I have talked of this to both Silvius and the Sidlesaghes—"

"And not us?" Saeweald said quietly.

"She talks of it now!" snapped Ecub, and silently I blessed her for her intervention. "Think yourself not so important that you be her first counsel on every occasion."

Saeweald's mouth thinned as he compressed his lips, but he said no more. Judith caught my eye, but I looked away and resumed my speaking.

"I have talked of this both to Silvius and the Sidlesaghes," I said, "and the answer is alarmingly simple." I gave a soft, depreciatory laugh. "Here I am, the enchanted representation of fertility and birth and growth, the health of the land, and I am—" I lowered my voice "—a virgin! To unite completely with the land, to be at one with whom I should be, I need to consummate my self with the land. Unite completely with the land."

"Lose your virginity," Ecub said, ever practical.

Gods help me, I blushed. "Yes."

"With whom?" said Saeweald, and I felt both his and Judith's eyes steady on me.

"Silvius," I said.

"*Silvius?*" Saeweald said.

"Shush!" I said. "Is there better without Og-reborn to comfort me?" I kept my eyes steady on Saeweald as I said this, and he dropped his eyes away from mine.

"He does not truly represent the land," said Ecub. "Surely . . ."

"He represents the Game," I said. "And the Game and the land *are* united. Allied. Besides," I softened my voice, "it need only be a man, and I may choose as I will."

"He looks like Brutus," Saeweald said, his voice hard. "That is why you chose him."

"And if it *is* why, then that is *no* concern of yours!"

For a moment no one spoke. Finally, Saeweald broke the silence.

"I put myself forward," he said. "It would be appropriate."

Oh, gods, damn his ambition!

"I have chosen as *I* think appropriate. I am not looking for applications, Saeweald."

His face hardened, and he looked away.

ChAPTER EIGHT

ON THE MORNING OF THE FESTIVAL OF ST. THOMAS, Edward accepted an invitation from Spearhafoc, the bishop of London, to celebrate mass within St. Paul's cathedral. Although Edward generally preferred to worship within Westminster, whether at the abbey or the chapel within his palace, he did make a point of worshipping within St. Paul's on four or five occasions a year. If the weather was kind, then the king proceeded to St. Paul's via the road that led from Westminster to the Strand and thence through Ludgate to the cathedral; if, as on this day, the weather was inclement, then Edward and the immediate members of his court rode the royal barge to St. Paul's wharf and then traveled on horseback, under a canopy, up the hill to the cathedral.

Whichever way the king traveled, the crowds always lined his processional route, often three-or-four-people deep, cheering and applauding. Sometimes supplicants tried to reach forth, but these poor folk were always kept at bay by the king's men-at-arms.

Caela, of course, came with the rest of the court. Although her previous visits to St. Paul's had held little significance, she now, with her restored memory and new knowledge of who and what she was, looked very greatly forward to the outing. Not to the service, which Caela had every intention of ignoring, but merely the visit to St. Paul's itself.

Today, as always for a king's visit, the cathedral was packed. Caela and Edward, together with several members of the witan, two earls, several thegns, and a variety of wives, took their places on chairs set out for them to one side of the altar. A large and beautifully carved wooden rood screen shielded them from the eyes of the majority of the congregation; today, unusually, flowers had been woven through the spaces in the screen, filling the royal seating area with the heady scent of late autumn roses.

Caela took her seat by her husband, resting her feet gratefully on the covered heated stone that had been placed before it. The cathedral's interior was frigid, and Judith stepped forward and ensured that Caela's fur-lined cloak sat

closely about the queen's shoulders before she took her own place further
back in the rows of seats.

The service began.

Halfway through, when a visiting cleric was engaged in a lengthy dialogue
about the sins of Adam and Eve, Caela noticed a movement to her left, and
glanced over.

She froze, her eyes wide, disbelieving.

Silvius, in all his Trojan finery, was walking toward her through the ranks
of clerics, courtiers, and sundry monks who filled the aisles to the side of the
altar.

Having stared at Silvius, Caela's eyes then flew to the people grouped
about her, doubtlessly expecting most of them to be staring gape-mouthed at
this apparition who walked so arrogantly among them.

But no one was paying any attention.

Caela looked back to Silvius, who was now grinning at her confusion.

"Peace, lady," he said as he walked to her chair, leaned down, and planted
a light kiss on her still-startled face. "They are unaware of me, and, as for you,
why, all they see is their queen with her head bowed in prayerful contemplation."

Again Caela glanced about her. It was as Silvius said. No one paid them
any attention, and even the movements of the cleric intoning before the altar
were strangely slowed and muted, as if in dream.

"You have done this?" she said.

"Aye. Another piece of Aegean trickery. Did Brutus never do this? Never
play this particular hoax on his comrades?"

"If so, then I was unaware of it."

Silvius laughed, softly, and dragged an empty chair close to Caela's. "The
trick, my dear, *is* to leave people unaware of it." His face sobered. "I needed
to see you, Caela."

Still rattled by Silvius' piece of magicking, Caela only raised slightly her
eyebrows.

Silvius put his hand on the back of her chair; he was very close. "That was
well done," he said, looking her in the eye. "Moving the band."

She let out a long breath. "Ah. You realized it?"

He gave a small smile. "How could I not? I am, after all, a part of the
Game." He paused, his black eye roving slowly over the planes of Caela's face.
"I did not realize you were that powerful."

She gave a small shrug. "I had help." Then she gave a small laugh at the
puzzlement on Silvius' face. "Long Tom, of course! I am surprised he has not
told you every detail himself."

Silvius managed a grin, although it looked a little forced. "Of course. Long Tom. A true friend, eh?"

"Better than you know . . . or maybe you do. I am sure that you and he have spent many a long conversation together. You remember, surely, when he brought me to see you and Og within the heart of the labyrinth?"

Silvius hesitated a long moment before answering. "I did not speak to you then . . ."

"No. You need not apologize for it. But, ah, what Long Tom showed me!"

"He is powerful . . ."

"Oh, aye, he and all his companions."

Silvius half lifted his hand that rested on the back of the chair, hesitated with it elevated slightly, then finished the movement, sliding Caela's veil back a little from the crown of her head.

"Be careful," Caela said, stiffening slightly. "I do not want your spell snapped, and all to see me with my veil and hair disarranged." Her mouth quirked. "My husband would surely claim that I had been visited by the devil."

Silvius' hand slid down to her cheek, his fingers very gently stroking at her smooth skin. "I am sorry for that. Caela . . . have you given any more thought to what I said the last time we met?"

"Here," she said. "In this cathedral."

He smiled. "Aye."

She gave a small nod. "Yes, I have. What you suggested is right, and needed."

Silvius' smile broadened.

"Long Tom also agrees," Caela continued, and Silvius' smile slipped.

"Oh," she said, "should I not have spoken of it to him?"

His grin reappeared. "If he agrees, then I am rightly pleased that you *did* mention it! When, Caela? When?"

"The winter solstice, you said."

He nodded. "Can you manage an escape from . . . ?" He nodded to Edward.

"Yes. Silvius . . ."

"No more words," he said, and, leaning into the gap between them, placed his mouth on hers, gently, not demanding.

She hesitated, but only an instant, then she leaned forward into him, giving him her mouth. They kissed, passionately, then Silvius managed to pull back, laughing softly, breathlessly.

"I must stop, for I cannot keep this sorcery intact much longer, Caela. Oh gods, I am sorry." He rose, shifting his chair back to its original position as Caela rearranged her veil.

"The solstice," he said. "Meet me in your stone hall. Now, be still, and bend your head back to prayer."

She did, and in the next instant Silvius was gone, and all awakened about her.

Caela paid no attention to the rest of the service, imagining only what it might be like to have Silvius take her virginity.

Eventually, without consciously realizing the transition, Caela's thoughts turned entirely to Brutus, and she remembered that night she had offered herself to him under the stars on the way to the Veiled Hills, and the passion with which they'd made love . . . almost as if there had been love between them.

Meanwhile, at Thorney Isle, a barge containing the earl of Wessex drew softly to Westminster's wharf.

CHAPTER NINE

AROLD STRODE INTO THE BEDCHAMBER HE shared with his wife, tore the covers from Swanne's body and, before she could move or speak, grabbed her hair and hauled her from their bed.

Swanne finally found her voice as she half-tumbled naked to the floor. "What . . . ? Harold! No! *No!*"

Now he had her by her arm and dragged Swanne to her feet. With his free hand he dealt her a stinging blow to her cheek, and then another, and then yet one more, before she had time to collect herself.

"That first was for the damage done to me with your treachery," he snarled. "The second was for the damage you have done to England! And the third, you black-hearted witch, was for standing by and laughing as my brother sought to murder me! Did you report *that* to William? *Answer me!*"

Swanne was stunned, not only by the suddenness and savagery of Harold's attack, but by his knowledge.

How dare he lay a hand to her!

How did he know?

"I haven't . . . I don't . . . ," she stumbled, unable for the moment to string a coherent sentence together.

"William told me how much you delight in passing him your little tidbits of communication," Harold said, and pushed Swanne back so that she sprawled across the bed. "Did he tell you also how he shares them with Matilda?"

"No! *William?*"

Shared with Matilda? No!

Swanne edged back in the bed, trying to put as much distance between her and Harold as possible.

"I have been to Normandy, Swanne. Did not William think to tell you?"

"What were you doing there?" Swanne had reached the far edge of the bed, and now carefully rose to her feet. She put one hand to her reddened cheek, but made no attempt to otherwise cover her nakedness.

"Discussing your whoring ways with William."

"No," she said, looking at him with all the contempt she could muster. "William would not have told you."

Harold's face twisted: Swanne did not even attempt to deny it. "We have reached an agreement, William and I," he said, "and you form no part of it."

"Liar!" she spat.

"I renounce our marriage, Swanne. You—"

"No!"

"What? You fear to lose me? *You?* Who laughed as Tostig knifed me?"

She stared at Harold, her breasts rising and falling with the rapidity of her breathing. "I was sure that Tostig would kill you. I was terrified. Terrified! I wanted to live. I thought laughter would save me. . . . I'm sorry. I know I should have leapt to your aid . . . but I was so frightened. I was not thinking. . . ." She let her voice drift into a whimper with her last sentence, and contorted her features into something approximating fear.

Harold's face twisted with loathing. "It doomed you, witch. Begone from my life. You have your estates and manors that your father and uncles bequeathed you. You shall lack for nothing."

"You *cannot* do this!"

"Every noble, every court in this country shall support me!" he snarled, striding about the bed and grabbing Swanne's hand away from her cheek. "No man stands for a wife who betrays him in this manner! I shall have a wife, but she shall be a true wife, Swanne. Not what you have given me!"

"The Church will not let you put me—"

"The Church did not ratify our marriage, they do not recognize it. We were Danelaw-wed, Swanne. That was your insistence, not mine. Well, now you reap the harvest of your insistence, your all-consuming desire for independence. By God, Swanne, had you thought that once William was in a position to fight for the throne that you could renounce *me?*"

Swanne tried to wrench her arm away from Harold's grasp, but he would not let it go.

"I am pregnant with your child," she said, her panic tipping her into the lie. *William had shared their communications with Matilda?* "You cannot set me to one side."

"Truly?" Harold raised his eyebrows, his eyes running slowly up and down her figure. "Your slenderness belies *that* lie, my dear."

"You lay with me before . . . before you left for your sly voyage to William. Why can't I be with child?"

"Because I know you too well. Because you would not want to be thick with my child when you think you might have William instead! Be gone from my life, Swanne. I have had enough of you."

"You cannot put me aside!"

"Ah, you do not fear losing me, do you? You fear losing your place within this court, because without me as your husband you shall be forced to retire to one of your country estates. And what can you betray to William there? The state of the apple harvest? How many ewes have lambed this spring? You'll be as useless to him as you are now to me."

Swanne finally managed to free her arm. *"I will be queen of this land beside William!"*

"I have seen how William regards his wife, Matilda. I suspect you shall be queen of nothing but the peasant rabble who shall work your fields."

She spat at him, but Harold could see the fear in her eyes, and he smiled coldly.

"Clothe yourself, Swanne. I have already left instructions with the servants that you shall be removing to the country by this afternoon."

And with that, Harold turned and left the chamber.

Swanne stared after him for long moments, her eyes wild, her expression a mixture of fear and shock and disbelief. She could not afford to be banished to the countryside!

Gods . . . *gods!* How had Harold known? William could not have betrayed her to Harold.

He could not.

Could he?

CHAPTER TEN

HAROLD WENT STRAIGHT FROM HIS BEDCHAMBER
to that of Caela's, hoping she had returned from St. Paul's by now.
      He burst into her chamber almost as abruptly as he had into
his own to find Judith and two other ladies removing Caela's outer clothing.

"Harold!" Caela spun about to face him, waving a dismissal in her ladies at
the same time.

"Caela, thank God you have returned from your worship." Harold walked
across to her as the women left the chamber and, placing his hands on her
shoulders, bent to kiss her briefly and dispassionately on the mouth. "You are
well?"

"Aye, I am. But, Harold . . . ah, thank God to see you well!"

Harold managed a smile and, checking to see that all of Caela's attending
ladies had left the room, said, "William did not murder me, sister. He is not a
man of Tostig's treachery."

She let out a long breath of sheer relief, and placed the palm of her hand
against his cheek. "What . . . ah, Harold, *what happened?*"

He took her by the hand and led her back to the bed so they could both sit
down. As he talked, relating to her all that he'd seen and heard and talked of
with William, he kept her hand tight in his own.

"He is a good man," Harold finished. "I cannot find it in my heart to hate
him." He let out a short, dry laugh. "Even to distrust him. And what a thing
that is to say about a man who makes no attempt to hide his own ambition for
the English throne!"

"You liked him," Caela said, her eyes searching Harold's face.

"Aye, that I did. In a strange manner, we have become friends, even though
our ambitions make us sworn enemies. He is an honorable man, Caela."

She smiled, and Harold thought he'd never seen her look lovelier. "How
he has changed," she said. "I am glad. I am so glad."

Harold frowned. "'How he has changed'? But you have never met him."

Caela looked away, her face closing over. "I have only heard rumors,
brother."

And William spoke of Caela in a manner that made me wonder if ever he had met her, Harold thought. He lifted his hand, and gently turned Caela's face back to meet his.

"Is Swanne the *only* one who has been secretly communicating with William?" he said. "William was as interested in you as you have been in him. Why all this interest, Caela?"

"I have had no communication with William," she said, her gaze unflinching, and he believed her.

"And I am interested in William for the same reason you are, Harold. He seeks the English throne."

"You do not need to fear him, Caela. Not personally. He has sworn to me that if . . . if fate favors him in this wrestle for England, then he will do you no harm, nor harm to any of my children."

"He said that?" Caela smiled, although it was tinged with sadness. "I had thought he might be vindictive . . . hard. It is what I had . . . heard of him."

"Vicious rumor only. William is an honorable man," he said again.

"Ah, Harold, I hope his promises never have to be kept."

There was a silence, and Caela became uncomfortable under Harold's regard. "Harold, tell me, what manner of man *is* William? Come now, hold nothing back. Tell me of William and Matilda."

He laughed softly. "William is a tall man, and strong in build. And *handsome,* with black, dancing eyes and a magnetism about him that surely draws women to him like bees to the honey pot. Mayhap you will think he will be a prettier face to have about this court than mine."

"Never."

"Aye, well . . . I think he looks at no one but Matilda. I do not think even Swanne can draw him away from her."

"Do you think that William knows Swanne for what she is, and thus leans toward Matilda?"

"William respects and trusts and treasures his wife. I think he knows that is not something he could achieve with Swanne."

Again Caela breathed out as if in deep relief, and Harold looked carefully at her. "Caela, will you promise me something?"

"Anything."

"If by wicked fate, William defeats me to take the throne, will you support him?"

"How can you ask that of me?"

"If I am defeated I do not want to think that England will tear itself apart trying to resist William. You will be the dowager queen; people will listen to you—"

"Listen to *me?* Gods' Concubine? The always-dismissed wife of Edward? Harold, I do not think that—"

"You are far more than that, Caela. Do you think I cannot see? That I do not watch the way you move, and what you say, and watch how other people respond to you? In the past weeks . . . I don't know . . . in the past weeks you have somehow come into your true self. People have always listened to you, and respected you, whatever Edward has said and done. Now, I think there might be something even more than 'respect' behind their regard." He sighed, dropped his eyes, and stroked her hand where it rested in his.

"Caela, please. Do this for me if you do nothing else. If William takes the throne over my dead body, then support him. The witan will take what you say and consider it. They will not dismiss you. The people will not dismiss you, nor what you say. Caela, please, I ask you this for the sake of the land—"

Something flitted across her face, an expression Harold could not read, and her hands jumped slightly where they clasped his.

"—*for England,* and everything that it is, will you do this for me? Will you support William if . . . if it comes to pass?"

"Oh, Harold . . ." her voice broke. "Do not speak of your death!"

"Promise me this!"

She blinked away her tears, then nodded. "For the land, I promise, Harold."

"Thank you." He leaned forward and kissed her again, but this time did not immediately draw away. Their mouths locked, and Harold's free hand slipped behind Caela's head and pressed her the more firmly into him.

She moaned, softly, and probably with desire rather than distress, but it was enough to make Harold draw back.

"Oh God," he breathed. "Caela, I am sorry."

"No! *Never* say that! Be sorry for the fact we cannot be together, but not for the fact that you love me."

He kissed her again, softly, and then shifted his mouth to her ear. "Cruel fate," he whispered.

"Crueler than you realize," she said.

For a long moment they sat there, their faces close, feeling the play of the other's breath over their faces, then Harold sighed, and sat back.

"I have heard news of Tostig this morning," he said softly.

"I do not know if I want to hear of it."

"He has gone to Hardrada."

She was silent.

"He will not defeat me. I promise you this. But William . . . well, William I respect. That's why I asked you to pledge as you did."

"What of Swanne?" Caela said. "Have you seen her since you returned?"

"Ah, *Swanne!* I think William distrusts her as much as I do, Caela."

"Really?"

"And, yes, I have finally done with her. I visited our chamber before coming here. I severed the ties between us. She is gone, and you, my dear," he hesitated an instant, "must find me a new wife, someone suitable to be a queen."

She looked away, composed herself, then nodded. "I have found a woman," she said, her face and voice very quiet. "Do you wish to hear of her?"

"Does she bear your name?"

"Harold . . ."

"I am sorry. Yes, tell me of this woman."

"Do you remember Alditha, Harold? She is the sister of—"

"The earls Edwin and Morcar, aye, I know of her. But she is married to that Welsh lord. Ah! I can never remember his name!"

"He died some months previous, Harold. And now the pretty lady Alditha, with all her lands and estates and ancestry and alliances, sleeps unattended in the chamber, which once was the bishop of Kent's. So close to yours."

Harold's eyes had grown very dark. "I wish it were you lying unattended and alone in the chamber of the bishop of Kent," he said. "I wish it were you lying alone and widowed at night."

"I cannot," she whispered, her face stricken. "If you truly want this throne, Harold, then I *cannot!*"

"What say you, sister? That should I renounce my ambition for the throne, then you will be mine?"

"We cannot, Harold." She shifted on the bed, putting space between herself and him. "Alditha is a good woman. I am sure you will manage."

"I would rather a woman I could love." He saw the stricken expression on her face. "Ah, I am sorry, Caela. This does neither of us any good. Aye. Alditha will do well enough for me, and that you have chosen her, well, that will bless the match. If you wish me to go to Alditha and warm her nights, then that I can 'manage.'"

Her face closed over, and he sighed. "What happened three nights ago, Caela? Both William and I had evil dreams, and mine was all about you. I thought you in great danger, and thus I hurried from William's court back home."

"What happened? Why, nothing, brother!" She smiled, but it was false, and Harold knew that she kept something from him. "And William dreamed of me as well? What did he say? What did he do?"

William again! thought Harold. *Why does she speak so much about William?*

"He did not say he dreamed of you, Caela. He said he dreamed of great trouble."

"Ah. He was angry?"

"Caela? You said that nothing had happened. Is that the truth?"

"I am in no danger, Harold. Believe it."

Harold didn't. She was hiding something from him, just as surely as

William had hid something from him that night he'd burst into Harold's chamber.

What was the interest these two had in each other? Harold felt a wave of jealousy wash over him.

"Caela—"

"Trust me," she whispered, her great blue eyes staring steadily into his. "Trust me. Please."

This time he allowed himself to believe her. "Yes," he said. "I do."

LATER, WHEN CAELA HAD SETTLED TO HER EVER-present needlework (claiming that a headache kept her from the bustle of Edward's court), Swanne came to the chamber, and requested an audience with the queen.

Surprised, Caela allowed the request, then further granted Swanne some privacy by asking Judith and the other ladies to retire some distance away.

"Harold has doubtless spoken to you," Swanne said, her voice hard.

Caela inclined her head. She did not look up from her needlework.

Swanne's lips compressed into a hard, vicious line. "Grant me duty within your ladies. I cannot lose my place at court."

Caela finally lifted her eyes. "My attending ladies are my only haven of peace, sister. You want that I should shatter that with your presence?" She sighed, shaking her head slightly. "I cannot offer you a place within my own tiny court. It would go against Harold's wishes."

"Harold! Have you slept with him yet, little virgin girl? Are you the reason he has turned so viciously against me?"

"How dare you ask me that!" Spots of color reddened Caela's cheeks. "How dare you, when—" she glanced at her ladies on the other side of the chamber, ensuring they were not within hearing range "—when in our previous life it was *you* who arranged his death! If he turns 'viciously against' you, Swanne, do you think that my doing, or that of Fate, weaving out what must be?"

"There is nowhere for me to go."

"You have your own lands and estates, Swanne."

"I cannot leave court!"

"Why *not*? What mischief do you plan? And if you want a court to shine within, then why not choose William's?"

"Oh, I will. You will never have a place at *his* side!"

"I do not wish it," Caela said, calm again. "But neither do I think you will ever have that queenly throne on his right hand, Swanne. From all reports, that is Matilda's so firmly that you could wish the moon from the sky more easily than wish for that seat. But have no fear, William has no doubt planned a backroom for you. If you wish, I can inform him of what remote county you linger in, and he can send a horse for you."

Swanne rose, her face stiff with anger. "Is this your little victory over me, then? Then enjoy it, for one day—and soon—it shall be you cast into the cold, and crying out for succor."

WHEN SHE HAD GONE, CAELA LEANED HER HEAD against the high back of her chair, and closed her eyes. *I should not have done that. I should have offered a hand, and my friendship, not harsh words and the door. Oh, merciful heavens, how could I have allowed my own petty need for revenge dictate my actions?*

CHAPTER ELEVEN

LDRED, ARCHBISHOP OF YORK, WAS SITTING AT his noonday meal in his palace just within the walls of London when one of his manservants hurried over to him.

"My lord," he said, bowing respectfully. "The lady Swanne begs audience."

Aldred paused with a knife, a tempting piece of juicy meat speared on its blade, halfway to his mouth. He blinked, his mouth hanging open, a dribble of saliva glistening at one corner, and stared at the servant.

"The lady Swanne?" he said.

"Aye, my lord. She begs audience. Urgently. My lord, she is in a state of some distress."

Aldred blinked again, then slowly, and obviously very reluctantly, put the knife and its tempting morsel back on the plate.

"Well, I suppose I'd better see her," he said. Then, hopefully, "She might not wait until I have finished eating?"

The servant glanced at the table with its array of over fourteen different dishes. "I think not, my lord. She *does* appear to be in some need."

Aldred sighed, and rearranged his fleshy features into a scowl. "Oh, very well then. Send her in."

The servant hurried out, and as he went, one of the corners of Aldred's mouth upturned briefly, as if in a smile.

SWANNE ENTERED IN A SWISH OF SKIRTS AND CLOAK. Her eyes were bright, her cheeks flushed (which fortunately hid the slight bruise that was deepening on one of them) and her abundant black hair artfully arranged atop her head.

She wore no veil, and Aldred noted that her gown was most unseemly for this hour of the day. It was one a noble lady might more properly wear to a private banquet, for its neck was square cut and low, unlike the high necklines of public gowns.

"My lord!" she said, and dropped in a deep curtsy.

Aldred blinked yet once more, finding it difficult to lift his eyes away from the sight of her breasts straining at that low neckline.

"Ahem," he managed as Swanne rose to her feet. "What can be the matter, my dear lady?"

"Harold has abandoned me," she said. "He has renounced our marriage."

Aldred spluttered, then succumbed to a fit of coughing so violent he had to cover his mouth with a napkin lest he spray pieces of half-chewed food over the table.

"How is this possible?" he finally asked. "Why? Why?"

"He wants a good wife under Christian law," Swanne said, sitting down at a bench at the side of the table. "He wants the throne, my good lord archbishop, as you have doubtless known, and he thinks it more likely the church, witan, and England will accept him with a Christian-law wife, rather than a Danelaw one."

"But this is . . . is . . . so . . ."

"After all I have done for him!" Swanne's eyes filled with tears, and her breasts heaved with the strength of her emotion. "What can I do? What? I have been abandoned . . . *abandoned!*"

"My dear woman," Aldred said, laying aside his napkin. "You need not pretend such distress to me. Harold has discovered your communications with William, yes? His reaction can hardly be of great surprise to you."

"Did *you* tell him?"

"No. I did not."

"Well, that may be as may be. My lord archbishop, I need your aid as never before. Your vast palace has many spaces and chambers. May I not inhabit one of them?"

Aldred's mouth dropped open yet again. "My lady! What would people think!"

Swanne shrugged. "They can think what they like, my lord. Besides, it will do you no harm. Many of the higher clerics keep mistresses, even wives, without any repercussion."

"You are offering yourself to me as . . . as . . ."

"No!" Swanne fought briefly with herself, managing to keep the disgust from her face. "No, not at all my lord. I was only arguing that even should people think the blackest, it would not harm your reputation. Indeed, it may even add to it." She attempted a coquettish smile, but it faded almost as soon as it had lit her face. "I only want a chamber, my lord."

"But . . . why? You have estates in your own right. I would have thought that—"

"No! No, I must stay in Westminster, or London."

"Why?"

"For my children's sakes, my lord. I need to be assured that Harold will not forsake them as he has forsaken me. I fear that should I vanish to the countryside, he will disinherit them as he has me." Swanne felt like screaming: *I have to stay in London!*

Aldred sighed. "I asked you not to pretend with me, my lady. You have no thought for your children. You never mention them, never think of them. They have only ever been but a means to keep Harold tied to you, and thus you to Westminster and Edward's court. You think Edward has not long to live, you think William is coming, you want to be here to greet him. Thus you beg me for a chamber, and care not what rumor suggests happens within that chamber."

He made a face, as if disinterested. "You don't think that might ruin whatever you hope for with William?"

"William and I have an alliance that goes back much further than you can guess at, my lord. He will not think any the worse of me for begging shelter from you."

Aldred shrugged. "Very well, then, my lady. You may 'shelter' within my palace." *And when I demand my price for this generosity, my dear Swanne, you will wish you had never thought to throw yourself to my mercy.*

CHAPTER TWELVE

WANNE WAITED A FULL DAY FOR A TIME WHEN
she had an hour or two undisturbed in the chamber that
Aldred had given her, before she succumbed to her sense of panic.

Who had moved the band?

How?

*Had William told Harold about her? Had he really shared her messages with
Matilda? No, surely not. That was just Harold's lies. Surely. And if William
had . . . then why? Why? Why?*

She needed answers, she needed reassurance, and she needed both so
badly that she knew she could not wait for the slow passage of written communication, between her and William.

Besides, she no longer trusted Aldred completely. The man had been too
sure of himself recently. What did he plan behind her back?

No, she needed to see William. To meet him again, face to face, as much
to satisfy her emotional needs and as much to answer her questions.

Since her first meeting with William, Swanne had always been supremely
careful with the use of her power. She had never known where Asterion was,
or if he would be able to scry out her use of power, and, most importantly,
what he might do if he felt her use such power.

But the past day or so had witnessed the loss of most of Swanne's assurance.

*She needed William again, if only for a moment or two, just to see him, to
reach out and touch him. To hear him reassure her that Harold had only lied.*

And so she did what she had not yet dared to do for the past fifteen
years.

She used her power as Mistress of the Labyrinth to visit William.

ONCE HAROLD HAD DEPARTED, WILLIAM HAD TAKEN
his horse, a few companions, and ridden for the coast to a small estate he had
near Fécamp. There he spent two days staring northwest from the tower of
the small castle that dominated the estate.

Then, on this morning, he had ridden from the castle, curtly telling his companions to give him time and space alone for a few hours, and galloped for the coast some three miles distant.

He pulled his horse to a halt on a small hill that overlooked the sea. Above his head wheeled scores of seabirds, filling the air with their harsh voices; about him there was nothing but the rolling turf of untilled meadows; before him there was nothing but the wild gray sea, whipped into a frenzy by a bitter northerly wind.

The distant view was hazy, the nearer view distorted by the spray sent skyward by the crashing waves, but William could *feel* England just beyond his eyesight. There it lay, so close, so close . . .

Something within him *tugged*. Almost as if an invisible hand had laid hold of his gut and pulled.

He groaned, bending forward a little in the saddle, and his horse shifted uneasily underneath him.

Again, the strange, painful tug, and this time William realized what it was.

"No!" he cried. *Damn, it was Swanne!* "No! Stop!"

But it was too late. Some twenty paces away, where the hill started to dip toward the rocky beach, the haze consolidated into, first, a misty pillar, and then into a discernible female form.

"Swanne! *No!*" William cried again, almost beside himself with a crazed mixture of fear and anger. *She dared not do this! She dared not! Not now, when it was so dangerous!* He swung down from his horse and ran toward the figure just as it consolidated into its final form.

Swanne, running to meet him.

She looked older than before, but just as beautiful: the black, curling hair, snapping free in the wind; the sensuous figure; the round white arms held out to him; the face, more beautiful than he could ever have imagined.

The red mouth silently framing his name. *William! William!*

"Swanne!" he grunted in that instant before she hurled herself into his arms. She pulled his head down and kissed him, but within a moment he pushed her back, his hands on her shoulders, staring at her.

"Gods, Swanne! What do you here?"

"William!" she cried, and buried her face against his chest, her arms tight about him. "William."

Again he pushed her back, harder this time. "What do you here? What is wrong?"

"You know what! Someone has moved a—"

"It was not you?" William's hands tightened about Swanne's shoulders.

"No! *No!* I thought that perhaps you . . . somehow . . . ."

"No." William looked away from her and looked over the wild sea.

"Who? No one could touch those bands but you and me. William . . . William, was it Asterion?"

"No. I felt that Asterion was as surprised as me. As *you*, now, I find. Gods, Swanne, I was sure that you had moved the band." *Had prayed that it was you who had moved the band.*

Swanne's hands had lessened their grip about William a little, and now she moved them to his chest, and she leaned in closer, and pressed her hands against him. She could feel the heat of his body radiating out through the layers of his tunic and undershirt, and Swanne closed her eyes momentarily, and breathed in deeply. "Then who?" she said.

"Caela," William said in a voice almost a whisper. He was still staring out to sea.

"No."

"No?" William remembered what Matilda and Harold had said about her. "Are you sure? She has surprised us before."

"She has no power, William. Not like us." Again her hands pressed against him. "Asterion destroyed Mag within her. She has nothing left."

"What?" Swanne had finally said something that pulled William's eyes from the sea back to her. "What in Hades' name do you mean?"

"Mag," Swanne said, "within Caela's womb. As she lived within Cornelia's womb. Did you not . . ."

Swanne suddenly stopped. *Had Brutus ever known of this?* She had not mentioned it to him, not in those few brief months between when she had discovered it herself and when Cornelia, the bitch, had murdered her. And then Cornelia would never, surely, have mentioned it.

Besides, Cornelia would have had no chance to tell him, for Brutus would have killed her the instant that Cornelia had stepped back from Genvissa's dead body.

Wouldn't he? Caela was speaking only lies when she'd said she'd lived with Brutus for decades after Genvissa's death, and borne him more children.

Wasn't she?

"How long *did* Cornelia live after she killed me?" Swanne asked. "An hour? A day, at most?"

"As long as I did, at least," said William, vaguely, not thinking through why Swanne might have been asking this. "And that was, what? Some thirty years or so."

"*What?* You did not kill her?"

William dropped his hands and took a step backward, breaking the contact between Swanne and himself. "No. Eventually I took her back as my wife, but I—"

"You kept her as your wife for some thirty years after she had killed me?" There

was a terrible pain in her chest, and Swanne could hardly breathe for its fire.

Betrayal, she realized dimly. That's what that pain was. Betrayal.

"I did it to punish her, Swanne. I never spoke to her again."

Swanne gave a bitter laugh. "But you lay with her." A pause. "Yes?"

He did not answer, and that was all the answer Swanne needed.

Above them the circling seabirds cried our in their harsh tones, as if barking in laughter at Swanne's anguish.

She lifted a hand, as if to strike William, but he seized it before she could act.

"And you told Harold of our correspondence," she said, her voice flinty, trying but not succeeding to wrench her wrist from William's grasp. "And, I discover, shared it with *Matilda!* How could you betray me like that? Ah!" She gave a hard laugh. "How stupid of me. If you could lay with Cornelia after she'd murdered me, then what would such a small betrayal as telling Harold of our communications and sharing it with your *wife* cost you? Eh? I swear before all gods, William, that I believe you collect wives only so you can betray me with them!"

William remained silent a long moment, staring at her with a face as tight and as angry as hers. "How can *you* speak of betrayal, my love, when you have been sleeping side by side with Coel all these years?"

There was a flash of panic in Swanne's eyes, then she collected herself and pouted. "It was of no importance."

"It was of no importance," William repeated, then laughed hollowly. "No importance . . . ha!"

Swanne's face hardened. "You took your Matilda, did you not? I took Harold. There is no difference."

"Matilda has no part in this deadly game we play! But *Coel!* That was something you held back deliberately. And I *asked* you about him!" William's voice hardened to granite. "And you lied to me. You lied. Deliberately."

"I was afraid. I did not want you jealous."

William's jaw tightened, and he looked away from her.

"Is that why you told him about you and me?" she said, watching William's expression carefully. "You were upset when you realized Harold was Coel, and that I'd kept that information from you? Is that why—"

"I did not tell Harold," William said. "He knew before he came to my court."

"He knew?" Swanne frowned, then her brow cleared. "Ah, well then, it must have been Aldred, no doubt hedging his bets against a Harold victory rather than a William victory."

"You were speaking of Mag," William said, finally looking back at Swanne. "Living within Cornelia's womb, you said?"

Swanne's mouth twisted, but she managed to bring her emotions under control. "Mag hid herself within Cornelia's womb. If Cornelia allied with Asterion, then that alliance was as much an alliance between Mag and Asterion as between Cornelia and Asterion."

Now William's face was wearing a strange, unreadable expression. "Cornelia carried Mag within her womb? Truly?"

Whatever that expression was, Swanne did not like it. "Aye. Both the bitches conspired against you. *And* me. But we need not worry now. Whatever assurances and promises Asterion made to Mag, whatever reward he offered for her aid, he meant none of it. He destroyed Mag, murdered her completely, a few months ago."

"And Caela?"

"*What of Caela?* Why speak of her when—"

"Because I need to know if she has the power to move that band!" William shouted. "*I need to know who it was!*"

Swanne's face set sulkily. "Caela has no power. Believe me, William, she does not have the ability to find and move any of those kingship bands. She barely has the capability to *dress* in the morning. It must have been someone else. Who?"

"Very well, then," William said finally, although his mind still rankled over what Matilda and Harold had said about Caela; they had not described a woman who didn't even have the power to "dress in the morning," "if not Caela, then . . ." He paused, thinking. *Who?*

Swanne gave a small shrug. "I cannot tell. The puzzle has kept me awake at nights."

"Silvius," he said. "Perhaps it is Silvius."

"Your father? How?"

William remembered how he'd met Silvius in the heart of the labyrinth; how he'd killed him again as he had that day so long ago when he, the fifteen-year-old Brutus, had killed Silvius. And he remembered what Silvius had said to Brutus as he'd faced Silvius yet one more time that day Loth had challenged Brutus: *I am your conscience, I am this land, and I am the Game.*

"I am the Game," William whispered. Then he refocused his eyes on Swanne. "Silvius lives within the Game," he said. "And Silvius once wore those bands. He *knows* those band, and they him. He could have moved them."

He must have! Who else?

"Why?" said Swanne.

"To foil me," William said, a sad smile hovering about his face. "To murder my ambitions."

Swanne cursed, foully enough to make William stare at her in barely disguised distaste.

"What can we do to stop him?" she said.

"At the moment, not much." *If only it were Silvius.* William wanted to believe that very much; it made everything so simple. Still, he was glad Matilda had her agent within Westminster. Just in case . . . someone . . . was lying to him.

"If Silvius moved them then I can find them," William said, trying to settle the matter in his own mind. "We are of the same blood, the same training. If he moved them, then I can find them."

William forced himself to smile slightly. "It is not as desperate as I'd thought. It will not be long before I can come," he said. "Do not worry."

Above them one of the seabirds, now circling much lower, gave another harsh cry as if of laughter.

Swanne smiled, and lifted her face to William's. "Kiss me," she said.

He did so, but not as deeply as Swanne would have liked. She drew him close, meaning to kiss him again, but William pushed her back. "Go now," he said. "Go. And don't ever dare this again. It is too dangerous. It won't be long until I can be with you in truth. It won't be."

"You said that fifteen years ago."

"Fifteen years ago I was a fool." *Two thousand years ago I was a fool, too.* "It won't be long now, we can both feel it."

"William . . ."

"Go!" he said, and gave her shoulders a push. "Go."

When she finally disappeared, William was not so very surprised to feel a profound sense of relief sweep through him.

Deep within the Game, Og's heart beat infinitesimally stronger.

ASTERION SLOWLY RECOMPOSED HIS AWARENESS FROM the seabird—after all, he was the master of glamours—back to his own body sprawled in a great chair before the fire in his hall.

The silly witch, thinking he would not have known she would do something like that.

In truth, Asterion had been expecting it ever since Swanne had forced herself on Aldred, the obese buffoon, and had been mildly surprised she'd waited as long as she had.

He thrust thoughts of Swanne aside, and concentrated on the matter at hand. Silvius? They had decided Silvius was moving the bands.

Asterion grinned, staring into the flames. Silvius. . . .

DAMSON WAS DOWN AT THE RIVER'S EDGE, CAREFULLY folding wet linens and placing them within her basket, when the waterman poled his craft close to her.

"Damson!" he called softly, and she set her washing aside, lifted her skirts, and walked over to him.

"A new challenge," he said. "Our mistress requires you to watch the queen as well as the Wessex witch. What company do they keep? Do they slip into the night unattended?"

Damson rolled her eyes. "A fine request indeed, and to come at such a time! The lady Swanne had been bundled out of Westminster and has found solace within the archbishop of York's house within London's walls. What does our mistress expect me to do, scurry back and forth, back and forth, and expect no one to notice?"

The waterman leaned on his pole and regarded Damson speculatively. "In the past weeks I have seen you scurrying often between Westminster and London. What is one or two more scurries among those you already accomplish?"

"I have not left Westminster in months!"

The waterman chuckled. "So you have a lover then, and seek to deny it. I hope you do not confess our mistress' secrets to him."

Damson glared at him. "I have *not* left Westminster!"

He shrugged. "As you will. But, listen, there is more. Pray watch carefully, if you can, among either the queen's or lady Swanne's possessions for a golden band or two, with a spinning crown over a labyrinth set into them."

"She wishes me to steal it?"

The waterman shook his head. "Just to observe its presence."

"I can do that."

"Give my best to your lover," the waterman said, standing up straight and hefting the pole. "He must be good if you seek to deny him so mightily."

Damson scowled, marched back to her basket, then stalked off, leaving the sound of the waterman's laughter ringing over the river.

CHAPTER THIRTEEN

*I*T WAS THE NIGHT OF THE WINTER SOLSTICE; THE death of the year. That night, which marked the nadir of the sun's journey through the heavens, the shortest day, the longest night; that moment when the sun either would triumph against the darkness and rise the next morning toward an eventual spring, or it would fail, and plunge the world and all creation into never-ending gloom and death.

It was the night when the land held its breath. If the sun failed, then the land failed, and spring would never grace its body again. If the sun failed, then the land would wither and die, and all who lived on her would wither also.

It was the night when the land strived for the dawn, for the light, for its resurgent fertility.

It was the night Caela could act, where she could *do* for the land.

"MY LORD?"

Edward, who had been contemplating something unfathomable in the middle distance of the Great Hall in the palace of Westminster, turned to study his wife. They sat on the dais, digesting their evening meal, listening to some minstrels play.

The Hall was all but deserted, and this emptiness had put Edward in a foul mood.

Tonight was the winter solstice, and he knew that great festivities were planned for the fields and hills beyond the northern walls of London. Fire dances and games were to be enacted by all and sundry. The fire festivities were aeons old, meant to encourage the sun's rise the following morning and to frighten away all evil spirits who hoped for the sun's death and for never-ending gloom. Most of London's population, as well as that of the surrounding villages and hamlets, were gathering at Pen Hill, awaiting the first strike of the flint, and the first spark that would signal the festivities.

And half the court had gone as well, if the emptiness of this Hall was any indication.

Edward had spent the past week expressly forbidding the pagan ceremonies.

That not only the general population, but also so many of the court had completely ignored him, had sent him spinning into so ferocious a temper that Judith, who was sitting a few paces away, wondered at Caela's courage in even speaking to him.

"Yes?" Edward snapped.

"My lord, I beg your sanction to take my leave of you this night. I would—"

"*You* also would take your part in these devilish practices? *You* also want to dance with the heathens? How *dare* you, wife! Christ's birthday is but days away, *and you want to revel in heathenish practices expressly forbidden by our Lord?*" His vehemence was so great that Edward peppered Caela's face with fine globules of spit.

Judith winced, hating the king and all he stood for. She looked to Caela, knowing her mistress wanted above all else to scream *Yes!* Instead, Judith watched with growing admiration as Caela kept her face humble and submissive.

"Never!" Caela said. "I grieve for their souls in their ignorance. Nay, I wanted to ask your leave not to join in these heathenish and most vile practices, but to spend the night in humility before the altar of St. Paul's, that I might pray for the souls of all who succumb to sin this night."

Edward was momentarily lost for words. Caela wanted to spend the night in prayer? He was consumed by a sudden rush of warmth for his wife. Perhaps, in her maturity, she was learning a greater grace and humility than he had ever thought her capable.

But . . .

"St. Paul's?" he said. "Would you not be better served by our own abbey church of Westminster? There I could join you."

Judith kept her face impassive, but her stomach clenched.

"I have ever felt closer to God in St. Paul's, my lord. And it is in the heart of London itself." *It is the heart of London.* "There I feel my prayers might have the greater effect on the souls of those Londoners who might otherwise lose themselves tonight. I beg you, grant me my wish. I feel that much prayer shall be needed tonight to counter the effects of these dire, devilish dances."

Judith had to bite her lip at that last phrase, and she could see the corner of Caela's mouth twitch as well. *Control yourself!* Judith thought, and in that instant Caela did, and her face became as a great pool of sadness and piety.

"Caela!" Edward said, and reached out both his hands to take one of Caela's. "I wish that your brother had your sense of Christian duty, for I note full well that he is also absent from the hall this night. Very well, I grant your wish, and I shall send with you an escort of armed men that you may be kept safe throughout your night of prayer."

Caela bowed her head and, as Edward's attention drifted elsewhere, winked at Judith.

TWO HOURS LATER CAELA, ACCOMPANIED BY JUDITH, Saeweald, an escort numbering some thirty-five armed men (looking unhappy that duty called this night when they would much rather be dancing on the hills), and seven monks from Westminster Abbey, entered the cathedral of St. Paul's via the great western doors.

There were few people about. A priest or two, several Londoners—among those very few who had not wanted to partake in the revelries—and an aged workman, huddled in one corner with a tattered cloak wrapped about him.

It was very cold, and the party's breath frosted about their faces.

"Madam?" murmured Saeweald. He had been very quiet on the journey to St. Paul's.

"I will pray before the altar," Caela said, and led the way through the nave toward the great gilded altar. There burned several fat candles, and dishes of incense, and, in the floor immediately before the altar, offerings of gold, oils, and coins, left by pilgrims grateful to St. Paul for whatever healing he had bestowed upon them.

Caela walked directly to the altar, bent and kissed the crucifix, which sat upon it, then turned once more to Judith and Saeweald, who stood close by her.

"I will lay prostrate before the altar," Caela murmured. "For the entire night."

"Madam," said Judith, glancing at Saeweald.

"What I do," said Caela quietly, "I do for this land, *not* for any Christian monstrosity. I need to merge entirely with the land so that it and I are seamless, and tonight . . . tonight, this is what I shall accomplish."

"Caela," Saeweald said slowly, "are you sure that you go to the right man?" *Should it not be me? As Og-reborn?*

Caela studied Saeweald, then smiled, and kissed him on the forehead. Briefly. Gently. No more than a brush of dry lips. "This is right for me, here and now," she said. "Later, perhaps . . . besides, you have other duties tonight."

He nodded. "I understand." Saeweald paused. "Be well," he finished, and at his blessing, grudging as it was, Caela's face relaxed.

"Caela . . ." Judith began, her gaze darting between Caela and Saeweald.

"I *need* to do this," Caela said.

Judith sighed, nodded, then kissed Caela's cheek. "Be well, then." She managed to summon a small smile. "And enjoy, for it is meaningless without enjoyment."

"I shall stay all night," Caela said again. "When I am . . . gone, then there is no need for either you or Saeweald to stay to watch over me. You shall be better employed elsewhere. Perhaps," her eyes danced, "with Ecub, atop Pen Hill?"

Judith looked at Saeweald, both knowing that Caela's suggestion was in fact more like a command.

"Come," said Caela. "Aid me to this floor. And be here to greet me at dawn, when I am sure my bones shall be still and cold from this stone!"

Judith took Caela's elbow, and aided her to the floor where, having bowed several times and crossed herself even more, Caela sank down until she lay prone, her arms extended to the side, her face to the floor.

Saeweald gestured to the escort to stand back at a respectful distance— they removed themselves until they stood in a semicircle about the prostrate form of their queen at a distance of some fifteen paces—and then he folded his hands inside his voluminous sleeves, and bowed his head as if in prayer.

Slightly to his side, and a pace behind him, Judith did the same.

In reality, they had their eyes fixed on Caela.

IN ROUEN, WHERE THE POPULATION WAS ENGAGED IN much the same activities as the Londoners, William begged leave from his wife.

"I have drunk too excessively of the wine this afternoon, my dear. My head throbs horribly. I would retire, I think, and let it settle."

"What?" said Matilda, her eyebrows raised. "You would miss the revels?" Unlike Edward, she and William always normally attended the excitement of the winter solstice fires.

"You go, if you wish," said William, his face apologetic as he leaned forward and kissed her mouth. "But I must to bed, or I think my head will burst. Nay, do not think to stay and nurse me. It is but the wine."

Matilda shook her head. William *had* drunk a little excessively this day. "I should force you to drink only milk, like a child," she said.

William made a face, then smiled, kissed her hand, and left her. He went straight to his bedchamber, where he disrobed and slid beneath the coverlets.

Despite the terrible ache in his head, he was asleep within minutes.

JUDITH AND SAEWEALD SAW THE INSTANT THAT CAELA "left." There was a sudden, strange stillness about her body, and although it still breathed, they knew that Caela was no longer there.

Saeweald glanced about at the armed men and monks standing about. They, too, seemed locked in an eerie stillness.

He reached down and grasped Judith's hand. "Come," he whispered. "The hills call."

THE MAIN SITE OF THE REVELS FOR LONDON WAS ON Pen Hill, a mile or so beyond the northern wall of the city. Here crowds had been gathering since dusk and now, as full night fell, they grew increasingly restless.

Atop the hill itself, standing within the circle of worn stones, which had graced the hilltop since antiquity, an elderly woman, clad in little more than a diaphanous robe, cried out, and held aloft a burning brand.

The light revealed her face, and those close enough could see that this year's mistress of the ceremonies was, as it had been for the past twelve years, Ecub—the strange, enigmatic prioress of St. Margaret the Martyr.

Standing just to Ecub's right was a man and a woman, their eyes riveted on Ecub's face: Judith and Saeweald, the hoods of their cloaks drawn about their faces.

Ecub dipped the brand groundward with an inchoate cry, and fire erupted about the hilltop. A great bone-fire burned, the stench of the bones meant to drive away evil spirits and witches who might be flying overhead, and men and women rolled forward great hay and wickerwork wheels.

The prioress gave a signal, and from brands dipped in the bone-fire, the wheel holders lit the wheels, and, once they were well alight, sent them rolling down the hill on all sides.

It was the moment the crowd had been waiting for. With a great roar, the revels began.

On the hill, Saeweald turned to Judith and gathered her in hungry arms.

"May tonight increase the herd," he said, thinking of Caela.

"May she tie herself and this land in everlasting harmony," she whispered, and lifted her mouth to his.

"Amen," murmured Ecub to one side.

* * *

THE STONE HALL STOOD EMPTY, WAITING AS IT HAD waited for so many thousands of years. Tonight, however, there was an expectancy in the air, almost a vibration.

There was a movement in the deep shadows in one of the side aisles.

Then another. A rustling, as if someone had dropped a cloak or a robe, and dragged it momentarily across the stone flagging.

And then she walked forth. Caela, yet not Caela. Mag, and yet not Mag. A woman, if nothing else, of startling loveliness.

She was completely naked, and utterly beautiful in that nakedness. Her glossy dark hair cascaded down her back and across one shoulder. Her blue eyes were deep and very calm and sure. Her body was slim, strong, lithe.

She walked into the center of the stone hall, and looked about, as if expecting someone.

After a moment, she began to pace impatiently.

William tossed and turned in his sleep as dream gripped him.

He moaned, desperate, for this dream was no stranger.

It had first come to him two thousand years ago, when he had been Brutus and Caela had been his wife, Cornelia. Then, the dream had undermined his marriage. Now, it terrified him.

He stood, as Brutus, in a stone hall so vast that he could barely comprehend the skill required to build it. The roof soared so far above his head he could hardly see it, while to either side, long aisles of perfectly rounded stone columns guarded shadowy, esoteric places.

This was a place of great mystery and power.

There was a movement in the shadows behind one of the ranks of columns, and Cornelia—utterly naked—walked out into the open space of the hall.

Brutus drew in a sharp, audible breath, but she did not acknowledge his presence, and Brutus was aware that even though they stood close, she had no idea he was present.

Cornelia looked different, and it took Brutus a long moment to work out why. She was older, perhaps by ten or fifteen years, far more mature, far, far lovelier.

Brutus realized he was holding his breath and let it out slowly, studying her. Her body was leaner and stronger than he knew it, her hips and breasts more rounded, her flanks and legs smoother and more graceful. Her face had thinned, revealing a fine bone structure, and there were lines of care and laughter about her eyes and mouth that accentuated her loveliness rather than detracted from it.

"Cornelia," Brutus said, and stretched out his hand.

She paid him no attention, wandering back and forth, first this way, then that, her eyes anxious, and Brutus understood that she was waiting for someone.

Completely unaware that hundreds of miles away William was caught in a two-thousand-year-old nightmare, Caela stopped, and stared, and breathed an audible sigh of relief.

"I thought you would not come!" she said.

The approaching man smiled, and held out his hands.

He was utterly naked, save for the patch that covered his left eye.

She ran to him, and took his hands. "Silvius." Her voice was filled with longing. "It is the death of the year. It is time."

There was some uncertainty in his face, even though he was clearly aroused by her naked body and the yearning in her voice.

"I am not Brutus," he said. "I am not—"

"You are everything I want," she said, and drew him in against her. "Really. This is truly a special night, Silvius."

"I pray I do right by you."

He was trembling, and she let go his hands and ran her hands over his body. He was lean, no fat, and with hard muscles and clean limbs, and she found herself wanting him very, very badly. She was Caela-Mag, she was this land, and she could bear her virginity no longer.

Not on this night, of all nights. Not on a night when those who still remembered, and cared, lit fires and danced the ancient fertility rituals, begging the land to hold fast through the winter and to emerge fertile and bountiful in spring. To allow her virgin state to last beyond this night, of all nights, would have been vile.

"Tonight," she repeated, her voice little more than a murmur, "this land and I, merged forever. This land and the *Game,*" she touched his face, "wedded forever."

She ran her hands up his back, and drew him in for a hard kiss.

He pulled his head back, just for a moment, just so he could gaze at her with a strange, triumphant light in his eye. "Wedded forever, you and I, the Game and the land," he said. "Oh, aye. *Aye.*"

Then he gathered her to him fiercely.

William cried out in his sleep, his arms flailing as he tossed and rolled over, tangling the covers about his legs.

"I thought you would not come!" she said, and Brutus almost groaned at the love in her eyes and voice.

"Cornelia!" Brutus said again, taking a step forward, his heart gladder than he could have thought possible.

And then he staggered as a man brushed past him and walked toward Cornelia.

This was the man that Cornelia had smiled at and spoken to, and he was as unaware of Brutus' presence as Cornelia was.

A deep, vile anger consumed Brutus. Who was this that she met?

The man was as naked as Cornelia, and Brutus saw that he was fully roused. Who was he? Corineus? Yes . . . no. Brutus had an unobstructed view of the man's face, yet could not make it out. First he was sure that he wore Corineus' fair features, then they darkened, and became those of a man unknown.

Cornelia said the man's name, her voice rich with love, and it, too, was indiscernible to Brutus' ears.

"Do you know the ways of Llangarlian love?" said the man.

"Of course," said Cornelia, and she walked directly into the man's arms, her arms slipping softly about his body, and offered her mouth to his.

They kissed, passionately, the kiss of a man and a woman well used to each other, and Brutus found his hands were clenched at his side.

"Caela," Silvius said, his voice rich with love. "Do you know the ways of Llangarlian love?"

"Ah, I would learn. Will you teach me?"

"I am not Brutus. I am not my son. Know that."

"I know that."

"Yet you choose me? Freely?"

"Yes. *Yes!* Freely, *yes!* Gods, Silvius, enough words! I have had *enough* of this virginity!"

"As you wish," he whispered, and grabbed at her mouth once more with his, and pulled her against him. She pressed her body against his, moaning, and together they half sank, half fell to the floor.

All his apparent doubts gone, Silvius wasted no time, nor did he seem to have a care for Caela's sensibilities. He put a hand on one of her shoulders, pushing her hard against the stone, and with the other hand he parted her legs and mounted her, thrusting deep inside.

Caela cried out as she felt the warmth of her virgin blood spill across the stone flooring. She struggled a little under Silvius, but he did not tolerate any resistance, and, both his hands now on her shoulders, he thrust again and again.

His face, and the one eye that shone from it, were very hard.

After a short while she subsided, accepting him, and then moaned.

* * *

"No!" William shouted, and lurched upright in the bed, grabbing frantically at the bedclothes. His eyes stared straight ahead, but they did not see his own bedchamber.

They only saw dream.

"No!" Brutus shouted, and would have stepped forward and grabbed at the man now moving over Cornelia with long, powerful strokes, save that he found himself unable to move.

He could witness, but he could not interfere.

The lovers' tempo and passion intensified, and Cornelia moaned and twisted, encouraging her lover in every way she could, and they kissed again, their bodies now so completely entwined, so completely merged, that they seemed but one.

Caela held on to Silvius' shoulders, remembering with every one of his movements, those nights she had lain with his son, remembering how Brutus had felt inside her, remembering how he had made her feel, and she wept, silently and softly, because Silvius made her feel none of these things. Silvius was a powerful lover, almost cruel in his strength, but all he accomplished with his body and his sweat and his effort was to make her long for his son.

Silvius saw her tears, and his mouth caught at hers, demanding, powerful. He lifted his face away from hers for a moment.

"Do not weep," he rasped, "for this is all you asked for."

Then he lowered his mouth again, his teeth biting and grabbing at her neck and breasts, drawing blood here and there.

And then he paused, still buried deep inside her, and raised himself on an elbow, looking down.

His face was flushed and sweaty, his black hair tangled, his breathing harsh and heavy.

"Do you wish I was Brutus?" he said.

"No," she said.

A strange look came over his face. "You lie."

"I'm sorry," she whispered.

"It does not matter," he said, and she felt him move again inside her. "All that matters is that *I* am here, and that you took me freely."

His hips rocked back and forth, smooth and practiced. "Hang on to me," he said, fiercely, and her hands tightened about his shoulders, "and remember that you freely accepted what now I give you."

"I feel nothing," she said. "Silvius, what is wrong? I feel nothing."

"All that matters," he said, then grunted, thrusting more fiercely than he had heretofore, "is that *I* feel, my lady, and that your body lies beneath mine."

Caela closed her eyes, wincing at Silvius' now violent action, and then, as she felt the sudden wetness of his semen within her, cried out, her eyes flying open.

WILLIAM SAT UPRIGHT IN BED, HIS BODY BATHED IN sweat, his breath heaving in and out.

His eyes still stared wildly, his hands clutched among the bed linens.

He had seen, finally, the man's face.

His father, Silvius, lay with Cornelia-Caela and whatever else it was that she had become.

And yet, Silvius notwithstanding, in that terrible moment when William had seen his father's face, and heard him cry out as he shuddered over Caela's body, William could only see the vision, and how it had ended.

The man's form changed, blurring slightly. He was grunting now, almost animalistic, and for the first time Brutus saw that Cornelia had her hands on the man's shoulders as if to push him off.

She cried out, and it was the sound of pain, not passion.

Brutus still could not move, and he watched in horror as the man's form blurred again, and became something horrible and violent.

A man, yes, with a thick, muscled body, but impossibly with the head of a bull.

The creature tipped back its head and roared, and both Cornelia and Brutus screamed at the same moment.

The creature's movements became violent, murderous, and Brutus saw that he was using his body as a weapon.

There was blood now, smearing across Cornelia's belly and flanks, and her head was tipped back, her face screwed up in agony, and her fists beat a useless tattoo across the creature's back and shoulders.

"Cornelia! Cornelia!" Brutus screamed, and for once both Cornelia and the creature heard him, and both turned their faces to him, and the creature roared once more, and Brutus knew who it was.

Asterion. Cornelia had invited evil incarnate to ride her.

"Caela?" William whispered. He rose from the bed, throwing back the sheets angrily when they tangled briefly in his legs, and walked to stand naked before the window.

"Caela?" he whispered again, staring into the blackness and distance. "What have you done?"

SILVIUS PULLED OUT FROM CAELA'S BODY, BUT DID not roll away. Instead he gazed at her, his face hard and watchful.

She lay as if asleep, her face flushed, her breasts rising and falling.

Silvius ran a hand over them, and then down to her belly.

At that, her eyes opened.

"Well?" he said, his expression now soft.

She frowned. And then smiled, but it was half-hearted, and troubled. "Thank you," she said.

"I was not what you wanted," he said, and then laid a hand over her mouth as she tried to speak. "Never mind," he continued, his voice a little hard, a little disappointed. "You were all that *I* wanted."

Then he rose from her, and was gone.

Oh gods, it was not what I had expected. He had constantly told me he was not Brutus, and yet all I could think about when he mounted me was Brutus, and all I wanted was Brutus.

"Do not take me only because I remind you of Brutus," he'd said.

But I think that was why I had lain with him, the only reason, because his face was that of Brutus', only kinder, and his body was also that of Brutus', only sweeter and gentler.

And yet, when Silvius had mounted me, I could barely restrain from shouting Brutus' name, from screaming for him. Gods, it was as if he'd been there, watching. All I had wanted was Brutus. All I had thought about was Brutus. All I had felt was Brutus.

So was that why I felt no different—save, of course, for that throbbing heat and the lingering discomfort between my thighs? Is that why that emptiness still echoed within me, why that sense of 'un-rightness' had, if anything, grown? Was this my fault, my weakness?

I laid my hand on my belly. My womb felt strangely sore, although I knew there would be no child from this encounter. For that I was heartily glad. I hated to think what mischief my womb might breed from lying with one man while all the while dreaming of another.

I let my head roll to one side. "Brutus," I whispered. "How is it you can torment me so?"

And then I wept, for the sheer stupidity of that question, and for all the good this night had done me.

* * *

LATER, WHEN CAELA HAD LONG GONE, ASTERION STOOD IN
the stone hall, staring at the dark stain of her virgin blood on the stone floor.

He stood there for a long while, his face expressionless, then he finally
permitted himself a tight smile, and vanished.

CHAPTER FOURTEEN

J PRAY YOU, LADIES, DO NOT RISE."

The three women who slept in the chamber outside Swanne's bedchamber, still blinking sleep from their eyes, glanced at each other in uncertainty.

"I merely go to the lady Swanne," the archbishop of York said, grinning benignly, his fingers laced over his huge stomach. "As her ladyship and I had agreed. As part of our contract. Surely she mentioned this to you."

The senior among Swanne's ladies, Hawise, slowly shook her head, her eyes fixed on the archbishop.

Aldred grinned. "What? Swanne modestly unforthcoming? I cannot believe this. And she *begged* me!"

"I cannot think that my lady—" began Hawise.

"Well, my lady *did* agree," Aldred snapped, suddenly waspish. "Do you think that I would have risked Edward and, for the sweet Lord's sake, *Harold's* wrath merely out of the goodness of my heart? No, my lady has a payment to make, and tonight she is going to make good her debts."

And with that, he brushed straight past the one among the women who had risen from her bed, and opened the door into Swanne's bedchamber.

SWANNE HAD BEEN FAST ASLEEP WHEN THE SOUND of a raised, querulous male voice, had started to pull her from her dreams into wakefulness. Before she could fully rouse, the door to her bedchamber had opened, and a vast bulk had moved through the opening, then the door had closed again.

Firmly.

Then came the sound of a bolt sliding home.

Alarmed, even though she was not yet fully aware, Swanne half raised herself, clutching the bed covers to her naked breasts.

"Who . . .?"

"Your beloved archbishop, my dear. Come to claim his debt."

"What?" Swanne had been so deeply asleep that she was still not completely awake.

The man—*the vast bulk*—moved close to her bed, and Swanne instinctively slid away until the bare skin of her back touched the stone wall against which her bed was placed.

Aldred—Swanne had recognized him—started to fumble at the neckline of his robe, where ties held it in place.

Swanne's mind suddenly snapped into full alertness. Full awareness.

"Begone from here!" she hissed. "Get *out!*"

"Nonsense, my dear." The robe now slid from his body and, in the faint light from the partly unshuttered window, Swanne saw the immense expanse of dimpled white flesh that stood before her.

The sight of this sickening mass of a man, the very *thought* of him clambering atop her, made Swanne feel nauseous, but that initial reaction was instantly overridden by a wave of immense anger.

"Remove yourself!" she shouted.

Aldred took a single pace forward, the numerous rolls of fat over his chest and down to the mound of his belly undulating like a river at high tide, and placed a hand over Swanne's mouth, forcing her back against the wall.

Swanne's round and furious eyes glared at him over the top of her hand, and she opened her mouth further, meaning to bite him, but just before she could bring her teeth down, something surged through her . . .

A sense of terror.

Her breath stopped. The terror had not come from Aldred, nor from the situation in which she found herself. Nor even from herself, for Swanne was furious, not terrified.

It came from memory.

It came from the memory of a woman silently screaming inside Swanne's skull.

No! No! No!

Then Swanne did feel the first inkling of dread, for she knew who that was. Ariadne.

No, no, no . . .

Aldred had clambered onto the bed now, his hand still held brutally tight over Swanne's mouth, and was kneeling over her, straddling her with his legs.

Something, perhaps the sound of Ariadne's terror, made Swanne look over his shoulder.

The faint illumination from the window cast Aldred's shadow on to the far wall.

This shadow was not that of the fat, loathsome man who straddled her.

It was of a fit man, tightly muscled . . .

. . . and with the head of a bull.

Up to this moment Swanne had been struggling with the huge man who had forced her back against the wall. Now her efforts became utterly frenzied. She struck at him with her fists, beating without pause, and tried to jerk her knees into him.

She tried to bite him, but his hand had pushed her upper lip hard up against her nose, and she could not force her jaw to close.

He laughed softly, joyously.

"You know me for who I am now, Swanne?"

She made a strangled sound under his hand, her body trying to buck under his.

"Come now, Swanne. No need for such histrionics. Ariadne didn't put up a fight like this. You knew, of course, that she and I were lovers as well as siblings?"

Swanne's eyes were wide with terror, but still her efforts to repel him doubled.

"Enough!" barked Aldred, and the hand and arm that held Swanne became as stone. He shifted his hand slightly so that it covered both Swanne's nose and her mouth.

She stiffened underneath him, her breasts heaving in their frantic fight for air.

Suddenly, desperate beyond knowing, sure she was about to die, Swanne sent forth a surge of power, trying to push him away with that power where her muscles had failed.

"No, my dear," Aldred whispered. "We can't have that, can we?" Without any seeming effort he blocked the power, and sent it churning back into Swanne.

She heaved beneath him, unable to bear the twin agonies of lack of oxygen and the painful bite of her power within her own flesh.

A moan gurgled in her throat, and her eyes rolled back into her head. Her struggles lessened, her hands relaxing away from their fists and sliding slowly down the broad expanse of his back.

"Listen to me," Aldred whispered, leaning over her until his eyes stared into her dying ones. "I will not allow you to slip into either unconsciousness, or even into death. None of that escape for *you*. Indeed, not. Instead, you can listen to what I have to say, and watch what I have to show you." He paused. Then, "Can you hear me, Swanne, my dear?"

Swanne's eyelids slowly dropped in acknowledgment.

Aldred could feel her body twisting beneath his, and he grinned, pleased.

She would exist in this agony of half-death until he thought to release her.

Then, of course, she would endure something much more terrible.

"Swanne, beloved . . . I may call you that, yes?"

She made no response, but Aldred carried on regardless.

"You may be suffering under some disillusionment," he said. "You may think that the darkcraft is yours, free and clear—even if it hasn't been of much use to you in this life. You may have believed that Ariadne won it from me completely."

His voice and body both became rigid with threat. "But there was a condition, my sweet. A condition. And now has come the time for you to pay it out."

Swanne, who lay suspended half between life and death, found her mind filled with images so clear, they might have been enacted before her.

Ariadne clasped to Asterion, the Minotaur's hand in her waistband.

"Give me the darkcraft of the heart of the labyrinth," she begged. "You are the only one who has ever learned to manipulate the power in the dark heart of the Labyrinth. Now I want you to teach me that darkcraft. I will combine your darkcraft with my powers as Mistress of the Labyrinth, Asterion, to free you completely."

At this point Ariadne paused, and rested her hands on Asterion's ruined chest. "I will combine our powers together, beloved brother, to tear apart the Game once and for all. Never again will it ensnare you. That will be my recompense to you for my stupidity in betraying you to Theseus and my payment to you for giving me the power to tear apart Theseus and all he stands for."

"She was persuasive, wasn't she?" Aldred whispered. "Who could resist such hair, such eyes, such a mouth . . . and those breasts! She had just betrayed me to her lover, she had arranged my murder, and here she was, cooing all over me, offering herself to me, and asking me to give myself and my power to her completely. Of course I allowed myself to be tempted! After all, Ariadne was offering me the ultimate aphrodisiac: a life where I'd thought to endure only death."

He paused, and he grabbed at one of Swanne's breasts, squeezing it painfully. "Of course, I was no fool for her completely."

He held her eyes steady, looking for deception. "You would destroy the Game? Free me completely so that I may be reborn into life as I will?"

"Yes! This is something that only I can do, you know that . . . but you must also know I need the use of your darkcraft to do it. Teach it to me, I beg you."

"If you lie—"

"I do not!"

"If you do not destroy the Game—"

"I will!"

He gazed at her, unsure, unwilling to believe her. "If I give to you the darkcraft," he said, "and you misuse it in any manner—to trick me or trap me—then I will destroy you."

She started to speak, but he hushed her. "I will, for there is one thing else that I shall demand of you Ariadne, Mistress of the Labyrinth."

"Yes?"

"That in return for teaching you the darkcraft, for opening to you completely the dark heart of the Labyrinth, you shall not only destroy the Game forever, but you will allow me to become your ruler. Your lord. Call it what you want, but know that if you ever attempt to betray me again, if you do not destroy the Game completely, I demand that you shall fall to the ground before me, and become my creature entirely."

"Of course!"

His expression did not change. " 'Of course!'? With not even a breath to consider? How quickly you agree."

"I will not betray you again, Asterion. Teach me the darkcraft and I swear—on the life of my daughter!—that I will use it to destroy the Game utterly. It shall never entrap you again."

Aldred's fingers were still groping at Swanne's breasts, but the pain of his sharp-nailed fingers could do nothing to eclipse the sickening dread that now coursed through Swanne.

Aldred's hand on Swanne's mouth and nose loosened a little, allowing a thin draught of air to trickle between his fingers, and Swanne's chest bucked in its effort to heave precious oxygen into her lungs.

"And what did you do, Swanne-who-was-once-Genvissa?" Aldred whispered. "What did you do? Why, you started the Game again, thinking that I was too far distant to stop you. I don't care to hear of your excuses and your reasons, for I know them all. All I do care to hear is your acknowledgment of Ariadne's oath. She is the one who is going to destroy you, Swanne. Not me."

His hand removed entirely from her mouth, and Swanne gulped air into her lungs. Aldred sat back, sitting on her lower legs, one fat, dimpled knee to either side of her hips, his hands to his own hips, regarding her with amusement.

"Well?" he said.

"What?" Swanne gasped, and then screamed, her body contorting again as Asterion's power surged through her.

"Do you acknowledge Ariadne's oath?"

She was still shrieking, and Aldred lifted a hand and struck her hard across the face.

Blood spattered in an arc across the bed.

"Do you acknowledge Ariadne's oath?"

"Oh gods," Swanne moaned. "How can I . . ."

She screamed again as a counter blow sent her head smashing into the wall.

"It was an oath made on power and on the life of Ariadne's daughter, my dear. One that bound not only Ariadne, but through that daughter, all Ariadne's daughter-heirs. What a foremother, hey? What a legacy!" Aldred laughed, the sound rich and deeply amused. "Now, do you acknowledge Ariadne's oath?"

She tried to deny it. She tried with every fiber of her being, but, even desperate as she was, Swanne could not force the denial from her throat again. Instead, there came a voice from her mouth that was not so much hers, not only Ariadne's, but the voice of all her foremothers, Ariadne and her five daughter-heirs before Genvissa.

"Yes," that voice whispered, a ghastly, echoing utterance that coiled about the room. "Yes, I—*we*—acknowledge the oath."

Aldred's body tensed, and Swanne was dimly aware that it was because he had drawn in a great breath of triumph. "You know what is going to happen now, Swanne, don't you?"

Swanne whimpered. It was all she could articulate in her overwhelming sense of horror.

"You are going to fulfill Ariadne's bargain for her, seeing as she is no longer about to do so herself. And well you *should* pay, Swanne, since it was you who began the Game again! *You* who tried to trap me!"

"No, no! I beg you. Anything but—"

"*Everything*, Swanne. Everything."

"Please . . . no . . ."

Aldred's hands were now fumbling under the great dewlap of his belly, and before Swanne's appalled gaze, he brought forth his erection.

"No!"

"And now, my lovely, we are going to cement Ariadne's bargain by the same means she and I originally cemented it. Are you ready?"

Swanne tried to scream, but she felt Asterion wrap his power about her, and she could do nothing but whimper.

She tried to hit at him, but her arms were leaden.

She tried to roll away from him, but because Asterion still chose to cloak himself within Aldred's massive bulk—the ultimate humiliation—she could do nothing.

Aldred lay down over Swanne, resting his full weight on her, and grunted.

Swanne felt something vile, something cold, probe at her.

She tried to writhe, but could do nothing, nothing, as Aldred shifted his hips, and grunted again.

Something so cold and so painful that it felt like splintered, jagged ice slithered its way inside her.

Aldred's hips bucked, then pushed down deeply.

Agony coursed between her hips and deep into her belly, but even beyond this, Swanne felt something else.

Something cold and painful, a splinter of sharp-edged ice, twisting its way into her soul.

"You're mine now," whispered Aldred, and he forced his mouth over Swanne's, and pushed his tongue inside her.

His hips began to work frantically, and Swanne knew that she would have died under the suffering of his brutal assault—both on her body and her soul—had not Asterion deliberately kept her alive.

Aldred lifted his mouth a little away from hers, his fat face wobbling with his efforts, and slicked with sweat that rolled from his skin's open pores.

"*Everything* you shall lay bare to me!" he said, and Swanne felt her entire being sliced open, her every secret laid bare, her every knowledge made understandable to this horror inside her.

She felt her soul, her very being, kneeling in subjection before him.

And then something terrifying, unendurably agonizing, exploded within her belly, and Swanne mercifully lost consciousness.

WHEN SHE WOKE, HER BODY THROBBING IN TOR-
ment, Aldred was sitting—fully dressed—on the edge of her bed.

"There," he said. "That wasn't so bad, was it?"

Swanne tried to swallow, but her throat felt as if it had been stripped of its flesh, and she gasped in agony partway through the movement.

"Poor dear," Aldred said, and patted her hand where it lay on the bed.

Then his entire demeanor changed, and malevolence shone through the man's fat features. "You are now my creature entirely," he hissed, and his hand tightened clawlike about hers. "You may make no move, and you may make no utterance without my permission and guidance. You shall use your powers as Mistress of the Labyrinth only as I direct. Do you understand me?"

Tears now coursed down Swanne's face, but she managed a tiny nod.

And then a wince, as if even that tiny movement caused her pain.

Aldred's rubbery lips stretched in a grin. "I may not always be close, but there is a part of me always with you, always watching you, always *knowing*. Do you feel it?"

Benumbed, Swanne could do little but blink at him in incomprehension.

"This," said Aldred, and lifted Swanne's hand so that it lay on her belly.

He pressed her hand down.

Swanne's eyes slowly widened in appalled understanding.

"My little incubus," said Aldred, his very voice as sibilant as a snake's. "Always within you, always ready to bite and to whisper and to *be*. You are my creature entirely, Swanne." He laughed. "The Game is half mine."

Then Aldred sobered, and bent his vile face close to Swanne's. "And all you have to do is please me, my dear. To start with, I think you can bring me William.

A pause. "Won't that be nice for you? Eh?"

Within her belly, the incubus bit deep with its tiny, icy fangs, and Swanne's mouth opened in a silent scream.

Her body arched and bucked, and Aldred waited patiently until the agony had subsided enough that Swanne lay relatively still again, even though her moans had not quietened.

"Later," he said, "I might find some errands for you to run. Yes?"

She gave a single, agonized nod.

"You *will* do whatever I want," he said, and Swanne sobbed, hopeless, knowing that indeed, yes, she would do it.

Within her, Asterion's little incubus twisted happily.

Darkcraft come to life and form.

IN THE MORNING, HAWISE EXCLAIMED IN HORROR AT the blood covering her mistress's sheet, and at the haggard pain-filled face of Swanne herself.

But Aldred, arranging the heavy golden crucifix on its chain over his chest, told Hawise that there was little point. "It is but Swanne's monthly flux," he said. "A little more burdensome than usual. No need to send for the physician."

He turned to Swanne, fixing her with a cold, hard eye. "My lady should perhaps take as her inspiration the queen, who so valiantly struggles with her own womanly complaints. The physician is not needed, eh?"

Swanne looked at him, then at Hawise, staring incredulously at her. "The physician is not needed," she said hoarsely.

PART SIX

With Edward's gentle piety was blended a strange hardness towards those to whom he was most bound . . . his alienation from his wife, even in that fantastic age, was thought extremely questionable.

A. P. Stanley, Memorials of Westminster Abbey, 1886

"*HAT DO YOU KNOW OF EAVING?" SKELTON* *said as he stirred the sugar into his tea. He stared unabashedly at Ecub and Matilda, noting the similarities in their finely drawn features. True-born sisters now; twins, he thought, as there was no age difference between them.*

Who had controlled their rebirth? Surely not Asterion. They must be a part of the Troy Game itself now, their souls entwined with the labyrinth.

"Very little," said Matilda. "Jack, you know me, and know what once I was to you. If I knew, I would tell you."

"Is she with Coel?"

"You asked Loth that last night," said Ecub. "Would you blame her if she was?"

"Curse you, Ecub!" Skelton said, pushing aside his cup and saucer. "I love her! Where is she?"

"Coel has ever been the gentler choice for her," Ecub responded.

"Coel is not the man for her," Skelton responded, very quietly, his eyes steady on Ecub's. "Now tell me, you ancient witch, where is Eaving? You are bound to her. You must know where she is!"

Ecub looked at Matilda, then back to Skelton. She smiled. "You are going to have to fight for both Eaving and your daughter. Are you prepared to do that?"

"Yes, dammit. Yes!"

"Are you prepared to do everything in your power to—"

"Yes!"

Ecub raised her eyebrows, and shared a look with Matilda.

"I will destroy the world if that is what it takes," said Skelton. "Please . . ."

Ecub studied him, seeing in his haggard face all she needed to know.

"What if I said to you," she said, "that 'destroying the world' means giving Eaving to Coel, forever and aye?"

Skelton sat back in his chair and studied Mother Ecub through narrowed eyes. "No," he said slowly. "You say that only to taunt me. Giving Eaving to Coel is not required, nor is it even a concept within the understanding of what Eaving is. She cannot be given to Coel. Nor would he accept her."

"But you having her is a concept within understanding?" Matilda asked.

Skelton looked at the woman who, so many years ago, had once been his wife. His only answer was a small, tight smile and the slightest of nods.

Both Ecub and Matilda burst into delighted laughter as if he were a favorite child who had just passed a crucial test. Matilda rose, and, stepping forward, placed her hand on his bare chest.

His skin was very warm, the muscles beneath very tight, and her touch brought back many memories for the both of them.

"Tell me what to do," Skelton said. "tell me what I have to do to win Eaving back from whatever darkness consumes her."

CHAPTER ONE

AELA WAS TRAPPED WITHIN HER MARRIAGE AND
Edward's court throughout the Christmas festivities. For six long
days she smiled and danced and jested and, in the mornings and
evenings, attended chapel or abbey services with Edward.

At night she lay beside Edward who, for once, did not sleep well, but
tossed and turned and muttered throughout the nights, gripped with a slight
fever that presaged a chest cold. If she left for even an instant he would have
missed her.

There was no time to herself. No time to talk with any of the Sidlesaghes,
nor, hardly, with Judith.

No time to kiss Damson on the mouth and effect a glamour so that, at
least, she could move within the laundress's body.

Caela had emerged from her almost catatonic state before the altar of
St. Paul's to find Judith and Saeweald, and the remainder of her escort, waiting for her. There had been no chance to talk then, not with the men-at-arms
and monks so close, and little chance once she returned to the palace, for
Edward was in an unaccountably good mood and insisted on sitting in her
chamber (behind a blanket that Judith hastily erected) while Caela took
her bath and dressed.

From there it was to chapel, and from there to court, and from there it
was a merciless slide into Yuletide and all those days of celebration that it
entailed.

Normally Caela enjoyed the Yuletide festivities. This year she loathed
them.

She finally had a chance to exchange a few hasty words with Judith on
Christmas Eve, the day after she'd returned from St. Paul's. They were sitting
within Caela's solar, and several other of the queen's attending ladies were
present, but bending over a chest full of linens in the far corner, muttering
about some damp sheets which would need to be aired.

"Madam?" Judith whispered. "We have not had a chance to speak. How
went it?"

Caela's eyes filled with tears. "Not well. Oh," she said, glancing at Judith's face, "I lost my virginity well enough, but it did not bring me the closeness to the land I had thought it would. It was just . . ."

Bestial, she thought, and hated herself for the calamity of that bare truth. If it was nothing but the humping and grunting of animals, then that was, surely, her fault.

"It was not a true marriage," Caela finished. "And I do not know why."

"You still feel the emptiness?"

"Yes. I have taken a wrong turning somewhere, and I do not know how, or what I should have done instead." Caela rested a hand lightly on her belly. "Even my womb feels it, for it pains me greatly."

"Caela," Judith began, laying a hand on the woman's shoulder, but then two of the other ladies came over, a sheet draped over their arms, and distress written over their faces.

"Madam!" one of them said. "Your bed linens have been quite soiled."

There was a silence, and Judith closed her eyes briefly, appalled at the timing of the woman's concern.

"I am very well aware of that," said Caela softly, and turned her head aside.

LATER, JUDITH SAID TO SAEWEALD: "IT DID NOT WORK. Caela still feels her lack."

"And why am I not surprised to hear of that?" said Saeweald, his voice weary despite the inherent sarcasm of his words.

She chose wrong, he thought.

Christmas day itself was unseasonably wild. A storm front surged down from the north, laying snow two feet deep on the ground and trapping people inside with its icy blasts.

Thus it was that no one was about to see, at dusk, the figure capering atop the Llandin, now known as the Meeting Hill. It was something of the utmost evilness, now a man, now a bull, now something even worse, shifting and twisting into shape after shape, growing into something dark and humped and monstrous, then shrinking violently into something that existed only as a spark of light dancing among the driving snowflakes.

It was Asterion, celebrating.

Not Jesus Christ's nativity, but the success of his own schemes.

"She's mine!" he sang, again and again, arms wild, legs cavorting. "She's mine!"

And then stillness, only the darkness of his eyes glowing through the storm.

"She has no will now, but mine."

* * *

IT WAS SAEWEALD WHO HELPED, IN THE END. FOUR DAYS after the celebration of Christ's Nativity, and after a long discussion with Judith, Saeweald brought to the king in his evening chamber a particularly strong sleeping draught.

"It is to aid you to sleep, gracious lord," Saeweald said as Edward sat on the edge of his bed in his nightshirt, his chest heaving in and out as he tried to catch his breath.

On the other side of the chamber Caela stood in her own night robe, a light wrap thrown over her shoulders, her hair loose for the night. She looked as tired and drawn as the king; more in need, in fact, of the sleeping draught than Edward.

Saeweald glanced at her, then looked back to the king. "Madam your wife has told me how ill you sleep," he said, his voice soothing and gentle. "Drink of this, I pray you, for you cannot exist much longer without the restorative power of a good sleep."

"Aye," said Edward, sighing heavily. "Aye. You are right."

And he took the draught, and drank heavily of it.

Later, when the king was already fast asleep, snoring mightily, the bower-thegn accepted with a smile the cup of spiced wine Judith brought to him.

Soon he, too, was deep in sleep.

WHEN ALL WAS STILL, AND THE ONLY SOUND THAT OF the snores of the two men, Caela rose. She slipped a cloak about her shoulders, shivering a little in the coldness of the air, slipped her feet into leather shoes, and padded quietly to stand in the center of the chamber.

"Madam?" It was Judith, half rising from the trestle bed at the foot of Caela and Edward's bed.

Caela put her finger to her lips. *I go to the Sidlesaghe, Judith. Be still.*

"Be fast," Judith mouthed. "And be careful."

Caela nodded, then stared at the floorboards.

A trapdoor slowly materialized, and Caela bent down, lifted it and, with a smile for Judith, vanished below.

THE SIDLESAGHE WAS WAITING FOR HER IN THE strange, brick-lined tunnel.

"Oh, Long Tom!" Caela said, and stepped forward so that he could wrap his strong arms about her, and hug her to his chest.

"What is wrong?" the Sidlesaghe said.

Caela sighed. "I am still not as whole as I should be. I still . . . *lack*. Long Tom, what is wrong with me?"

He frowned, puzzled. "You need to unite yourself to the land to attain your full self, sweet one. You know that."

"But I did!"

The Sidlesaghe's expression of puzzlement deepened. "You did?"

"Yes! The night of the winter solstice. I lay with Silvius. You said . . ." Caela stopped as she finally looked at the Sidlesaghe's face.

"Silvius?" he said. "He who sits and waits within the heart of the labyrinth?"

"Yes. Long Tom—"

"You lay with him?"

"Yes!"

The Sidlesaghe shrugged. "No matter. Was he enjoyable?"

Caela gave a tiny laugh. "Well enough, I suppose, although I thought of no one but . . ."

"But of *him*."

"Yes."

"Well, at that I am not surprised."

"But did that not destroy . . . well, whatever was supposed to happen? Long Tom, I feel such a fool. Silvius tried so hard—"

The Sidlesaghe put a hand to his mouth, and actually chuckled.

Caela could not help herself, she laughed as well. "Well, you know what I mean. And, surely, by thinking of no one but Brutus, and imagining him with me instead of Silvius, I destroyed the magic that would have united me completely to the land."

The Sidlesaghe shook his head. "It would have made no difference. You merely chose the wrong partner."

"Oh? And who, pray tell, *is* the right partner?"

The Sidlesaghe grew soulful. "When you see him, lady, you will know."

"So I have lost my virginity to the wrong man?"

"Your virginity is neither here nor there, sweet one. A marriage can be effected with or without it. But why do we talk of this inconsequential? There is greater danger afoot."

Caela frowned. "What?"

"Seven nights ago," the Sidlesaghe said, "something *bad* invaded this land."

"How so?"

The Sidlesaghe was now shifting his weight from foot to foot, clearly agitated.

"There has been a fundamental shift in the land," he said. "*And,* I think, in the Game. Something has happened. Something corrupt. Something *wrong*."

"Asterion?"

He shook his head. "Perhaps. Maybe. We don't know. Something has happened that has altered the foundations of the Game and of this land . . . something has *tilted* it slightly . . . I cannot know how else to describe it."

"Something 'bad'?"

"Oh, aye," the Sidlesaghe whispered. "Very bad." He had been looking down the tunnel, but now he refocused on Caela's face. "You must move another band. Tonight. And the others as soon as we may."

Caela shivered. "Asterion . . ."

"He will be waiting for us, yes. Surely."

"Long Tom . . ."

The Sidlesaghe reached out a hand and took hers, enveloping it within his. "We will watch for you," he said, his voice somehow immensely soothing. "As we have always watched for you."

CHAPTER TWO

HIS TIME THE SIDLESAGHE LED CAELA THROUGH a complex labyrinthine enchantment that eventually brought them to the low arched opening in London's wall, which allowed the Walbrook entry into the city. They stood once more just beyond the ring of columns that encircled Brutus who, once again, was taking a band from his arm—his left forearm this time—and placing it in the center of the columned circle. He made the complex enchantment with his left hand, the band vanished, and then so did Brutus.

As Brutus disappeared, the Sidlesaghe felt Caela relax under his touch.

"One day," he whispered to her, "you can allow him to meet your eyes."

She made a dismissive motion with her head, clearly not wanting to talk about Brutus.

"Sweet one," said the Sidlesaghe, "if Asterion meets you within the ruins of Troy while you are moving the band, he *will* kill you. Caela," the creature's voice roughened, and he had to pause and clear his throat, "don't walk through those ruins. Run. *Run*, for your life depends on it."

She drew in a deep breath. "To Holy Oak," she said. It had been the Holy Oak when she had been Cornelia, and still it graced the tiny bubbling spring at the foot of the Llandin.

Mag's Pond, still there after all these years, and Caela's natural escape route, should she need one.

"I will be there to meet you," the Sidlesaghe said, and his voice had dropped so low that Caela had to strain closer to hear him. "Be safe, sweet lady. Be safe on the journey."

She touched his cheek, then stepped forth into the circle of glowing light, and picked up the band.

ASTERION WAS ROAMING. HE'D KNOWN EVEN BEFORE the sun sank that tonight would be special, that tonight *she* would attempt to move another of the bands.

Asterion grinned. And if she did move a band, it was of no matter. He didn't care if she moved it to the cold heart of the moon, for he would still be able to find it.

Now that he controlled *her*.

But he had to play his part. There was no point in causing suspicion—and thus unexpected behavior—through inactivity. So he needed to make it appear as if he wanted to snatch the band as it was being moved. He needed to appear *angry*.

"Frustrated," he whispered. "Inept!"

And he laughed.

He did not want to attempt the ruins of Troy again. The memory of that snatching hand was still too vivid.

Besides, the ruins bored him. Best to make an appearance where she would emerge . . . which was . . . Asterion lifted his bull nose to the wind and sniffed.

North.

It would be north . . . northwest.

Asterion's smile stretched even further. He knew where she was going.

CAELA ONCE AGAIN TRAVERSED THE TERRIBLE PATH that wound through the ruins of Troy, the band clutched tightly in her hands.

But this time, mindful of the Sidlesaghe's concerns, she ran as fast as she could while still able to avoid tripping over loose rocks or the rigid hand or foot of a corpse that lay partway across the path.

Troy lay bloody about her, the dead lay moldering in their stinking heaps as they had previously, but Caela did not find them so disturbing this time. Instead she concentrated on the band lying in her hands, keeping her every sense strained for indication of pursuit. Every twenty or thirty steps she paused and half turned, her breath still, her body motionless, her face white, listening.

Nothing, save the dying of Troy.

Then she would hurry forward, her face even more strained, perversely, but she did not hear the sound of someone behind her.

Was he ahead? Crouching behind rocks to her side?

The further Caela moved through the destruction of Troy, the quicker became her steps, the tighter her face.

Eventually, safely, she reached the end of her journey.

ASTERION COULD *FEEL* THE PASSAGE OF THE BAND, *feel* its movement closer and closer toward him. It almost felt as if the band were rushing to meet him, and, as he stood before the rock pond under the Holy Oak, Asterion literally held out his hands as he intuited *her* imminent arrival.

There was a sound, a great sound of rushing water and wind and song, and suddenly a figure *burst* from the air before him, directly into his arms.

He laughed in sheer enjoyment, but turned it into a roar, as if of fury, and grappled clumsily with the figure, allowing it to slip partly from his grasp. He grabbed at it again, meaning to pinch a little, but just as he tightened his fingers, it seemed as if the air itself erupted about him.

Asterion's composure evaporated entirely as tall, bleak figures surrounded him. He panicked, not so much because he was afraid, but because these *strangenesses* were so entirely unexpected. The figure, *she,* slipped completely from his grip, but he was not worried about that, only the who and the what of that which attacked him.

Gods, they were singing, and such a mournful sound!

Asterion began to flail about with his arms, trying to see what it was that surrounded him, what gripped him, what was trying to smother him, but all he could make out was enveloping grayness, as if he were enclosed within a thick, viscous fog.

There was the sound of water splashing, and he knew that *she* had escaped. Furious (not with her escape, but with the unknowns that attacked him), Asterion lashed out with virtually the full extent of his darkcraft.

The air exploded, and there came the sound of moaning as the strange creatures fell back.

There came the sound of a single sob, and then Asterion was standing alone by Mag's Pond, the ancient Holy Oak stretching out its bare limbs cold and dark above him.

CAELA HEAVED IN GREAT GULPING BREATHS, HARDLY daring to believe she had escaped the Minotaur. *Oh gods, the feel of his hands upon her, the heat of his body, the stench of his breath!*

She looked about. She still stood close by the Holy Oak, save that now the countryside had vanished, replaced with a terrible aspect that, for one frightening moment, made Caela believe she had fallen back into the ruins of Troy.

She stood in a landscape covered over with bricks and mortar, hard, pale, smooth stone, and a wide roadway of hard blackness along which dreadful beasts roared. People moved shadowlike about her, and Caela realized she was seeing with that same awareness she'd tested inside Ludgate on the night she had moved the first band.

Women, mostly, bustling busily about with baskets over their arms, and clothed in tight gowns that came only to their knees. Most of them wore hats, silly, small round bonnets that clung to stiffened curls. Some of the women had children with them, or pushed babies before them in wheeled conveyances that looked to Caela for all the world like backward running carts.

There were some men hurrying among the crowded street. They were black, like ravens, and one or two of them swung sticks covered in material in their hands.

What to do with the band? Where to leave it?

She looked across the road, and saw there a small redbrick building. It was accessed via a large arch, which Caela could see led to an open paved area beyond the building. People stood about on this paved area, looking anxiously about as if expecting something.

She turned her attention back to the building. Just inside was a small window in one of the walls, barred with metal, and behind this window she could see the tall form of a Sidlesaghe.

He was looking at her, and once he saw that he had her attention, he lifted a hand and motioned to her, slowly, yet managing to convey the utmost sense of urgency.

Again Caela looked about her, her hands now gripping the band even tighter in her anxiety.

To reach the building and the Sidlesaghe, she had to cross this strange roadway.

And there were great beasts that periodically roared along the road, black and blue creatures, twice the size of oxen, and red creatures the length of five oxen, and three times as high.

"Oh, gods," she whispered. "What possibility is *this* the Game has created for me?"

She looked at the Sidlesaghe again—he was still motioning to her to *hurry, hurry*—and then back to the road.

It appeared to be clear.

Taking a huge breath, Caela stepped onto the road, moving as fast as she could without risking tripping over the sodden robes that clung about her legs.

Something roared past her.

She shrieked, almost dropping the band, and stopped motionless in the middle of the road.

She didn't know what to do. Her very will seemed frozen. She could step neither forward nor backward, and Caela was certain that her life would be snatched by one of those great speeding beasts at any moment.

"Here, now, miss," said a soothing male voice, and Caela jerked as a firm hand took her by her right elbow. "Can't have you standing about in the street like this, you know."

She risked a glance to her right—then sighed in relief. A Sidlesaghe stood there, although he was dressed in the most extraordinary jacket and trousers of tightly-fitted and very dark blue worsted cloth and with a blue and silver conical helmet on his head held on by a strap under his chin.

"If you will, miss," said the Sidlesaghe, his gray-brown eyes watchful and reassuring beneath his strange helmet, and Caela allowed him to guide her across the street and into the building and thence to the barred window.

There the Sidlesaghe, who had been so impatiently motioning to her, said, "Where to, miss?"

Caela stared at him.

"Miss?" said the Sidlesaghe who stood behind the counter at the window. Now that she was close, Caela could see that he was dressed in similar fashion to the Sidlesaghe in blue still standing beside her, but his close-fitted jacket and trousers were of a maroon color, and on his head he had a peaked cap with a leather brim.

"I think miss would like to go home to Westminster," said the Sidlesaghe standing beside her.

"Will that be a first-class ticket, miss?" said the Sidlesaghe behind the window.

"Definitely," said the other Sidlesaghe.

Caela stood, her eyes not moving off the Sidlesaghe behind the bars, unable to comprehend any part of this conversation.

The Sidlesaghe behind the window held out his hand, palm upward. "A first-class ticket demands payment in gold, miss, if you don't mind. London Transport regulations."

Caela stared at him.

The Sidlesaghe stared at her.

Caela slid the golden band of Troy through the aperture under the bars.

"Thank you very much, miss," said the Sidlesaghe, handing to her a small rectangle of cardboard and placing the band into a drawer full of coins under the counter at which he stood. Then he nodded to his left. "Train's through there, miss. Should be arriving any minute now."

"Thank you," said Caela, who still felt in a state of shocked unreality. "Is Long Tom about?"

"I think you'll find him waiting on the platform, miss," said the Sidlesaghe who had helped her across the road and, hand still on her elbow, led her toward Platform No. 1 at Gospel Oak Station.

IT WAS TOO MUCH. NOT THAT THE BAND HAD BEEN moved, but that *her* strange, unknown companions had thwarted him. Asterion was anxious, unsettled, and, anxious and unsettled, determined to make circumstances just a little more uncomfortable for . . . well, for everyone, really.

Time to begin the process that would see William dead. To bring the Game under his control. Once and for all.

Asterion moved through the night as a shadow, an unreality, rather than as flesh. He entered the palace at Westminster and slid under the door of Edward's bedchamber.

There was a bowerthegn fast asleep on a bed by the door, and a woman on a pallet at the foot of the king's bed.

There was no sign of Caela, and Asterion was not concerned about the absence of the queen. She was not what he needed this night.

His form shimmered, coalescing into a black cloud of miasma, which hovered above the sleeping Edward's face, then, suddenly, it slid down to cover the man's face, then seeped inside his slightly open mouth.

There was a moment of peace, of stillness, and then Edward suddenly reared forth, his eyes starting.

"The Devil!" he screamed. "The Devil has taken me!"

CHAPTER THREE

*L*ONG TOM WAS INDEED WAITING FOR CAELA ON the "platform," and before she could speak, he took her elbow from the Sidlesaghe in blue, saying, "Hurry, there is mischief about at the palace, and you have been missed."

As when she'd moved the band to Chenesitun, a new tunnel awaited them, and Long Tom hurried her along it.

"I have a ticket," she said, holding out the rectangle of cardboard at the Sidlesaghe.

He tut-tutted. "We have no time for that now!" But he took it anyway.

Soon they were underneath the palace of Westminster, and even here, deep in the magical tunnel of possibility, Caela could sense the commotion above her.

"Go," said Long Tom.

CAELA DID NOT DARE TO REAPPEAR WITHIN HER BED-chamber using her power. It was too late. The entire palace was alive with shouting and consternation.

What to do? What to do?

There was little she could do, only one possibility, and Caela seized it. She reappeared in a still corner of the palace—a storeroom that was partway between the royal quarters and the bachelors' quarters—then slid stealthily into the palace proper, arranging her features into those of the panicked wife (something, in truth, she did not have to pretend too much) and ran back to her and Edward's quarters.

People—clerics, servants, thegns, chamberlains, men-at-arms—had thronged the approaches to the quarters, but they stood back as Caela approached, glancing at her curiously.

Where had she been?

Caela ignored them, restraining her pace to something more digni-fied, although she kept the worried expression set on her face, moving through the chambers until she reached the antechamber just before the bedchamber.

Here thronged yet more people—as well as the echoing sound of Edward's shouts—and, thankfully, Judith, whose face reflected even more trepidation than Caela's.

"Madam!" Judith said, then, in a softer tone, "Where have you been?"

Caela put a hand on her arm, and drew her in close.

"Is Saeweald here yet?"

Judith, her eyes round and frightened, shook her head slightly.

Caela drew in a deep breath, which Judith thought had the feel of sheer relief.

"How is my lord?" Caela asked in a stronger voice. "I had felt a change in his breathing as he slept, a horrid rasping, a deep difficulty, and saw a ghastly pallor cross his face. I rose, dreading what this portended, and without thinking to wake anyone else, fled for Saeweald."

Apart from Edward's echoing shouts, the entire antechamber was silent, everyone staring at Caela, watching.

Judith's tongue flickered over her lips, then she managed to speak. "Aye, madam. It must have been your rising that waked me just before my king shouted."

"You did not think to wake *me*, or any other of the king's servants?" said the bowerthegn, staring at Caela with patent disbelief.

"I panicked," said Caela, keeping her voice calm. "I thought only of the physician."

There was a movement at the door, and the shadow of someone entering. Judith glanced over and then, before anyone else could speak, said, "Ah, Saeweald! How fortunate that my mistress reached you so quickly!"

Caela turned, and managed a wan smile at Saeweald, who regarded both women carefully. "I am sorry for rousing you so precipitously, Saeweald, and I thank you for responding so quickly. My lord is ill, desperately so, and I fear greatly for him."

Saeweald bowed slightly to Caela. "The desperation in your voice, madam, roused me as nothing else could have done. Our king is fortunate indeed that he has such a caring wife at his side."

A great smile, clearly one of relief, spread over Caela's face, and Judith hoped that most of the observers standing about would think it merely relief that Saeweald had arrived.

"I, and my king, are fortunate in having you as a servant," she said. "Come, physician, let us waste no more time."

With that, she straightened her shoulders and led Saeweald, Judith directly behind, into the bedchamber.

* * *

EDWARD'S BED WAS SURROUNDED BY ALMOST AS many people as had been waiting in the antechamber. There were several clerics, of which Wulfstan was the greatest, all muttering prayers or wailing invocations for the speedy aid of almost every saint imaginable. Several women, a midwife among them (Judith supposed she had been one of the few people within the immediate vicinity who had any claim to healing skills, and so had been hauled into the chamber), rocked back and forth on their feet, wailing and wringing their hands. The palace chamberlain held position at the very head of the bed, an island of stillness and silence among the commotion, his steely eyes roving about the chamber as if seeking someone to blame for the current crisis. Armed men stood several paces back from the bed, nervous, alert, unsure what they should do. The bowerthegn, entering before Caela, went to stand at the foot of the bed. He picked up the coverlets over the king's toes, squeezing and twisting the material until it seemed he would rip it at any moment.

The instant people realized that Caela, Judith, and Saeweald at her back, had entered the chamber, the murmuring and crying and caterwauling ceased—even Edward, who was sitting bolt upright in the center of the bed, bedclothes twisted to one side, stark naked, sweat glistening over his entire body—and everyone turned to stare at Caela.

"Wife!" croaked Edward in a horrible, thick raspy voice. "Explain your absence!"

"Thank God and all His saints and angels that you still live!" Caela said, her voice one of apparent joy. "See, I have brought Saeweald to your side."

"Your beloved wife realized the change in your vitality even before you woke," Saeweald said, pushing aside several of the clerics and women to reach the side of the bed, Caela directly at his shoulder. "She came to me before anyone else had thought of my name, weeping that you were ill, nigh unto death. How lucky you are, my lord king, to have such a wife!"

Still close to the door, Judith closed her eyes and sent a heartfelt prayer of thankfulness to all water and forest gods in existence for Saeweald's quick wits.

Edward folded his lips into a thin line, his bright, feverish eyes darting between Saeweald and Caela. "You were not here," he finally said, his gaze settling on his wife. "The Devil came a-visiting and you *were not here*."

"My lord," Caela said, and sat on the bed. "I *was* here, until I heard your breath gasp. Then I rushed for the physician." She glanced at the women present. "Hasten now, and bring me cloths and warm rosewater. I would wash this sweat from my lord's flesh."

The women backed away, and Saeweald took Edward's wrist and felt his pulse.

It was weak, fluttering feebly.

"My lord," Saeweald said quietly. "What has happened?"

"The Devil has entered me!" Edward said, sending one more vicious glare in Caela's direction.

She ignored it, her face set in respectful concern, and she took a hastily wetted cloth from one of the women and began to run it over one of Edward's hands.

Edward looked back to Saeweald, and then to Wulfstan, who had maintained his position at the head of the bed opposite from Saeweald.

Wulfstan moaned theatrically, and with a wavering hand made the sign of the cross over Edward. "Begone, Devil!"

"Devil or not," Saeweald muttered, "your chest is sorely congested." With one hand flat on Edward's chest, he tapped its back with the stiffened middle two fingers of his other.

Edward's chest resounded with a thick, horrible thud at every tap. Then the king gasped, his face purpling, and he began to cough in great hacking barks.

"What have you done?" cried Wulfstan, but Saeweald ignored him.

"Expel it!" he said to Edward, who was now bent almost double with the effort of his hacking. "Bring it forth!"

Saeweald grabbed the cloth from Caela, now sitting quite still as she stared in horror at her husband, and brought it to Edward's mouth just as the king ejected a great clot of blood and pus.

There was a collective gasp of horror from those still gathered about the bed and, apart from Saeweald and Caela, everyone took a step back.

"Pestilence!" muttered the palace chamberlain, and his stance stiffened even more, if that were possible.

"Still your hysteria!" snapped Saeweald. "Your king has a great and evil congestion of his lungs, but this is *not* the pestilence!"

There were concerned glances among the onlookers. Pestilence had not struck in over three generations, but the stories of its horror were still whispered about fires and tables.

"Physician," said Caela, leaning forward to touch Saeweald's arm briefly. "What can you do? Please, tell me that you may save my husband's life!"

The distress in her voice did not appear feigned.

"I shall bleed him this night," said Saeweald, "and prepare a poultice for his chest and belly. Will you stay, madam, and aid me?"

"Gladly," she said, then, as one of the women returned with a bowl of warmed rosewater, she rinsed out the cloth thickened with the blood and pus and began gently to sponge down her husband's body.

Chapter Four

IN SOME DEEP, INNER CORNER OF HER BEING, Swanne realized she was drifting toward wakefulness, and she fought it with every ounce of her strength. Better sleep and unknowingness than facing what had occurred last night (as every night in recent, terrifying memory).

To no avail. She felt herself propelled toward consciousness, and at the same time she felt that ghastly, leaden, icy weight in her belly, and she knew the incubus was forcing her to wake.

Asterion must want her.

"No!" Swanne muttered as her eyes sprang open.

She stared directly upward to the wooden ceiling of her chamber.

It looked so ordinary, so nonthreatening, and Swanne wondered why its innocuous wooden planks did not somehow reflect the agony that gripped her.

She moaned, twisting a little in the bed. Her body throbbed and ached in a score of places, the hurt between her legs and deep within her belly the worst of all. There was a warm dampness on her thighs, and even without looking Swanne knew it was fresh blood.

The incubus? Breakfasting?

"William," she moaned softly and, for the first time since Asterion had trapped her, without her thinking or considering the implications, acting only on deep need and on her even deeper terror, Swanne tried to reach out to him.

The next instant a blood-curdling scream ripped through her throat and she convulsed on the bed. The incubus had sunk its teeth into the inner lining of her womb, and had ripped her flesh clean away.

As horrific as the pain was, worse was the frightful feel of the thing's jaws working back and forth, back and forth, as it chewed its morsel.

"My lady?"

The door had burst open at the sound of Swanne's cry, and Hawise and another of Swanne's attending ladies stood there.

The instant they'd entered they'd halted, transfixed by the sight of Swanne writhing beneath her bloody sheets.

"Madam!" Hawise gasped, and would have moved forward save that at that moment Aldred appeared behind them, grabbed both of the women's elbows, and forced them backward toward the door.

"It is but her monthly flux," he said soothingly. "It is still flowing—can you credit it? A nuisance, indeed." He turned from the women and looked benignly at Swanne. "That *is* the problem, is it not, my dear?"

Swanne looked at Aldred, and then felt the incubus within her open its jaws again. A wave of hopelessness all but overwhelmed her.

"Aye," she whispered, and within her the incubus closed its jaws. "It is but my flux. More burdensome than usual."

"But . . ." said Hawise.

"The flux, Hawise," said Swanne, her voice flat. "Nothing more."

"And now," said Aldred, "if you will leave your ladyship and myself alone for a time. We must talk a little over . . . arrangements."

The women, now outside the door, stood motionless, still staring, as Aldred closed the door on them, and then Swanne heard their footsteps retreat.

"No . . ." she whispered, and wondered if that was going to be the only thing she could ever say again.

For so long as her life lasted . . . for so long as Asterion permitted her to live.

"I am glad to see you awake," Aldred said, wobbling forth. "The night has seen some intriguing happenings." He paused, and grinned maliciously. "Not only the lovemaking that transpired between you and me. Yes?"

She said nothing, but Aldred saw her throat constrict as she swallowed.

"I am awaiting your response, my dear." Aldred's voice had hardened into ice, and Swanne felt her head jerked back so that she was forced to stare at him.

"Yes," she whispered, her mouth dry with terror.

"Another of the bands has been moved. Did you not know of it?"

"My . . . my mind was consumed with other things."

Aldred laughed, the sound harsh. "Indeed you were. Indeed you were." He began to tug at the neckline of his robe, pulling it away from his shoulders.

"No!" Swanne cried out, and instantly the incubus inside her bit hard and viciously, and her cry turned into a choked-off shriek, her back arching off the bed in agony, her eyes almost popping from her head.

"I regret I may have misunderstood your response, my dear," said Aldred, now naked. "I *thought* you may have said no."

The agony had hardly dissipated, but Swanne knew her life depended on being able to placate this monster standing before her. All she had to do was survive, somehow to live, and eventually she would be able to find a way to . . .

The incubus bit again, harder and deeper, and the pain was so terrible that Swanne almost lost consciousness. She opened her mouth, but the agony was such she could not draw breath even to cry out.

Her eyes rolled up into their sockets, and her body jerked, and then convulsed.

Aldred smiled amiably and climbed onto the bed.

A moment passed, and then, even though her body was still stiff with suffering, Swanne managed a faint, "Yes."

"Yes . . . what, my dear?"

"Yes, my lord. I am grateful for your attention."

Aldred smiled, cold and malevolent, and forced Swanne's legs apart with one hand. "This bleeding is truly heavy, my dear. You really should learn to say 'Yes' to me a little quicker. Yes?"

"Yes."

"Good girl," he whispered and, grunting with both effort and pleasure, forced himself once more inside her body.

SHE CONTINUED TO EXIST, SOMEHOW, THROUGH THAT grunting, thrusting nightmare. The incubus roiled within her, joyous to feel its master so close, and it nibbled and poked and thrust itself so that her body, from her breasts to her ankles, seemed composed of nothing other than screaming, tearing flesh.

When Aldred had done and had rolled away from her, Swanne barely managed to conceal her tears of relief.

He rose immediately, garbing his hideous body with his robe, then turned back to Swanne who lay motionless amid the dreadful, bloodied sheets.

"None of this lying about, my dear. I have work for you to accomplish."

A tear rolled from Swanne's left eye down her cheek, and the sight of it irritated Aldred. He leaned down and dealt Swanne a blow across the face, making blood spurt from her nose.

"Get up!" he said. "Rise, and wash and clothe yourself. *Now!*"

Swanne managed to struggle to her feet, but was unable to stifle the moan of pain as she did so.

She jerked, as if expecting Aldred to strike her again, but he merely sat down on the bed and regarded her with calm eyes. "Wash and clothe yourself," he repeated, moving toward the door. "I have some matters to attend to elsewhere, but will return shortly. Be waiting for me, a smile on your face."

Grateful that the monster had departed, Swanne nonetheless did as she was told, although she thought several times during the procedure that she would faint with pain. Her belly throbbed unbelievably, and blood continued to trickle from between her legs.

Nothing she had ever endured had been this bad, not even childbirth, and she wondered how she had any blood left in her after the nightmare of the past week.

As she pulled her gown over her shoulders, and twisted a little so she could manage the fastenings, Swanne closed her eyes and indulged in a heartfelt moment of pure hatred for Ariadne.

How could she have done this? How could she have been so stupid? Why had she not warned her daughter-heirs? Had she been so self-conceited, so stupid, so . . .?

"She was wrapped in her own ambitions," said a voice behind her, and it was Asterion's voice rather than Aldred's.

She felt his hands fall about her waist, and she jerked, frightened almost to insensibility.

Asterion had only come to her as Aldred since he'd first forced himself upon her, not in his true form. Now Swanne's heart raced, her breath growing tight and shallow, as she wondered what this portended.

Asterion's hands grew heavy where they rested about her waist, and he turned her about.

The Minotaur stood there, regarding her from his monstrous bull's head with beautiful liquid black eyes.

Swanne grew rigid, but could not tear her eyes from the bull's powerful face. Its terrible aspect was almost hypnotic, and Swanne understood in a moment of clarity just *why* it was that Ariadne had consented to this single, devastating condition.

She had been seduced by the power—and the hope of power—in that great face.

She would have offered him the world if he had asked for it, just for the power he offered.

Ah! What was she thinking? Ariadne *had* with that single ill-considered consent given her cursed brother the world!

Asterion's hands were still about her waist, and now he slipped one of them downward to rub gently over her belly.

Swanne tensed, expecting further suffering, but unbelievably her pain began to dissipate until it was little more than a dull ache. Her entire body sagged in relief, and for an instant she almost loved the Minotaur for releasing her from the agony.

"Aldred has treated you poorly," Asterion said, "Your belly is battered almost to the point of uselessness."

What are you saying? Swanne thought. *You have treated me "poorly"!*

"Very poorly," Asterion murmured, and Swanne relaxed a little further under the touch of his hands, closing her eyes as even more of the pain abated. Just to feel the cessation of pain, just for a moment, was worth this brief compliance.

"Do not judge me by Aldred's actions," Asterion said.

Swanne could do nothing but nod, just once, jerkily. Her eyes were still closed as she concentrated on living every pain-free moment as desperately as she could.

"My dear, I need you to look upon me" said Asterion.

Swanne reluctantly opened her eyes.

"I wish you to present yourself at Edward's side—"

"I cannot! Harold dismissed me from court . . ." she stopped, terrified by the Minotaur's thumbs which had suddenly dug into her belly.

"Remember what Aldred put in you," he said, very softly, *What I put in you while I used Aldred's body.*

"Yes," she said dully. "I will do it. I will go to Edward's court."

"Good. Poor Edward's health appears to have taken a turn for the worst. He is busily engaged in his dying. I wish you to watch for me, be my eyes and ears."

"But you . . . but Aldred has better reason to be there—"

"And be assured he *will* be there. But you have your ear attuned to the world of women, and can be admitted to their presence." He stopped, his black brow wrinkling as if in perplexity. "Now, I know that you and William—the sweet, sweet boy—believe Silvius is moving those bands. That may be so. But whoever *is* moving them has aid. Someone aids him. Or her. If someone *is* aiding Silvius—or whomever—then I need to know who, or what, they might be."

He smiled, and ran his hands up to Swanne's breasts, caressing them gently. "After all, my sweet, you must have some duty to keep you occupied until you deliver William's life into my hands, mustn't you?"

She moaned.

"You *will* deliver William's life into my hands, will you not?"

Silence.

"Will you not?"

Swanne jerked her head once in assent.

"Good."

Asterion let her go, eventually, and Swanne, her face dull, lifted her cloak from where it lay draped over a chest and moved to the door.

"Swanne, my sweet," Asterion called to her just as she laid a hand to the door catch. Her back stiffened as she heard his voice. "I heard a rumor that

Caela was not at Edward's side when he took ill last night. I do rather hope you can discover for me who she might have been with. This is most important. What strange company does Caela keep these nights when she doesn't lie with Edward? You *will* ask her, won't you? I am most curious to know."

LATER THAT MORNING, ALDRED SAT IN HIS BATH, slowly washing himself, puzzling things over in his mind.

Everything this past week had been so dim . . . and yet so vaguely pleasurable. Somehow he seemed to have acquired the lady Swanne as a mistress, but he could not always remember those nights he spent with her so very well.

Yet that he was spending them with her was undoubted. Everyone was looking at him differently—and Swanne herself, why she practically fell over herself to cater to his every wish. The proud lady he'd known for so long seemed to have decided to admit herself as his utter slave.

Aldred smiled, then sighed happily. He wasn't sure about the "why" of his current circumstances, but he wasn't about to complain.

CHAPTER FIVE

CAELA SPEAKS

EDWARD SAT THROUGH THE DAY AND WHEEZED A little further into his dying with every breath, and enjoyed every moment of it.

Finally, he was vindicated. The Devil and his evil roamed everywhere and now, due to the inattention of careless priests and the apathy of Edward's subjects, the king had been struck down in all his glory.

No matter that Edward was an old man anyway.

No matter that he'd whined of his aches and pains and fevers for as long as I had known him (and well before that if the mutterings of his long-suffering mother were any guide).

No. He rambled and he moaned all through that morning: *See how your lack of attention and love has struck me down. See how your lack of piety has allowed the Devil into the very heart and soul of the realm. If only you* (and he took in the entire realm with that single "you," although his feverish eyes did tend to linger on me as he said it) *had loved me and cared for me and tended me as your duty insisted.*

By noon I could gladly have gone to the window, thrown back the shutters, and screamed for the Devil to come back and finish the thing properly.

Oh, I knew it was Asterion, and I knew why. He was pushing matters forward to suit his own pace. Catch us off-balance. Snatch at the Game before any of us, whether William or Swanne or Silvius or myself, or even Saeweald, could snatch back.

What was Asterion planning? I wondered if Long Tom was pacing through the Game, wondering and worrying. I wondered if Silvius worried, and I had an urge to see him, not only to seek his forgiveness for what I could not give him on the night of the solstice, but to just have him hold me, and tell me all would be well. I know *I* had spent the hours after my return, ignoring Edward's vilenesses, wondering and worrying. I was outwardly the dutiful wife, bending my head in contrition at every barb Edward spat my way, aiding Saeweald as first he bled Edward, then applied hot herbal and honey poultices to his armpits and chest and groin, wiping down Edward's face and arms and legs to wash away his stinking sweat.

About us hurried and muttered various court and church officials, moaning and blessing and praying and, no doubt, wondering how best to position themselves in the upheaval following Edward's undoubted soon-to-be death.

Harold came to attend the debacle as well. He'd hurried from Alditha's bed (Harold had wasted no time in knocking at the door of Alditha's chamber, and I knew also that he had broached the subject of marriage with her ecstatic family; I had no doubt that Harold would be making sure of a legal heir as early as possible. He might not, after all, have much time once Edward had succumbed), glanced worriedly at me, then, with the rest of us, endured Edward's ranting throughout the remaining hours of the night and through the morning. He'd pushed a chest against the far wall—as far from Edward's bed as he could manage—and there he had sat and watched, his face haggard, his eyes deep with worry. Occasionally one of the chamberlains or counts or thegns or courtiers would bend close to him, and mutter, but Harold only ever responded with a nod.

My eyes slid his way more often than need be, I expect, but I had so little chance to see him, or be with him, and the sight of him comforted me greatly.

I would have liked—desperately liked—to be able to sit down next to him, and allow him to wrap me in his arms, and to hold and comfort me, but that was impossible under these circumstances.

Under any circumstances, I expect.

Sweet gods, how close had I come to discovery during the night? Or *had* I been discovered? Asterion would have noticed my absence when he'd visited his little dance of death upon Edward. Would it have seemed strange to him? Or would he have thought only that I slept in a different chamber so that Edward's piety would not be disturbed by my female form?

In which case, Asterion must have wondered why my attending lady, Judith, slept on a pallet at the foot of the bed.

Would Asterion have remembered that brief moment when he'd held me by the magical waters of the pond, and connected that woman with my absence from Edward's bed?

As the night progressed, my worry combined with my fatigue to make me nauseous, and, when one of the servants leaned close to me just after dawn and offered me a cup of warm mead, I felt my stomach heave and sweat break out on my face.

Saeweald noticed as well, and grabbed my arm just before I toppled from the bed.

"Madam," he said, sharing a glance first with Harold and then with Judith, "you must rest. You cannot do more for your husband at present than you have."

"What?" screeched Edward, lurching up from where he'd been reclining against the pillows. "The whore feels ill? What, Caela, a bastard child you're breeding there to some peasant lover? A thick-witted boy you're going to claim is mine? A bellyful of some lustful—"

"You go too far, even for a king," snapped Harold, rising and coming to the bed. "If you think yourself dying, Edward, then concentrate on that dying, and ensure your own salvation rather than searching out imaginary faults in those who seek only to aid you."

He turned his back on Edward, who was spluttering and hacking his way through a coughing fit brought on by his own outburst, and Harold took my arm, leading me back to the chest where we both sat down.

Judith hurried over with a freshly dampened cloth to wipe my face, and I smiled my thanks at her.

There was a clear question in her eyes, and I shook my head slightly. There was no baby, I was certain of that, even though my womb had been cramping badly in the past week or so.

Judith wiped away my sweat, then brought me a mixed cup of milk and egg and honey, and I took it gratefully, thanking her as she turned to return to her stool by the door.

"He *is* dying?" Harold said softly, his lips barely moving.

"Yes."

"Saeweald cannot save him?"

"Do you want him to?"

Harold, who had been staring at Edward, now looked at me. "No," he admitted. "I do not. It has come time for me to take my heritage."

I shivered, a black wave of despair making me feel ill all over again. "Harold . . ."

"I know, my love. I know."

That "my love" almost undid me, and I had to set the half-drunk cup of milk down on the floor.

Harold mistook the reason for my distress, and took my hand, no longer caring, I think, what all the watching eyes thought.

"I am strong. I can face whatever comes at me. England will not accept either Hardrada or William."

Oh, Harold, my love, I thought, *you have no idea at all what it is you will face.* I had the sudden, crazed thought that I hoped Asterion *would* best all who raged against him, for then Harold would not have to die. He could reign as king, never knowing that beneath him reigned a far viler lord in a far more wretched land . . .

The thought vanished even before I had completed it. *England would not accept Asterion either.*

Harold's gaze returned to Edward, now lying back on the pillows and struggling for breath. He spoke again, keeping his voice very low. "Edward will die, and he chose the best time of year to do so."

"What do you mean?"

"It is the dead of winter. Neither Hardrada nor William can invade until late summer at the earliest. I have well over six months before . . ."

He stopped, and I squeezed my eyes closed so that he might not see the pain in them. Oh, I knew very well what that "before" encompassed.

Before William came home to kill Coel all over again.

William would win whatever battle he engaged in with Harold. William would become king. Hardrada, if he was to be a player at all, would be little more than a nuisance.

"Do not fear for me, Caela," Harold said in the gentlest voice I have ever heard from any throat. He was going to say more—I was by this stage beyond any coherent speech—but then his head jerked toward the door, and he cursed, not taking the trouble to lower his voice.

I raised my head.

Swanne had entered the room.

She looked . . . I don't know . . . she looked different in some aspect. She was very pale, but then she'd always had pale skin, but it did seem far more translucent than normal. Her eyes were overbright, but then that might be because she had a winter chill.

There was a strange rigidity in the manner in which she held her body, but that was likely because she'd fully heard Harold's curse, and because she undoubtedly knew she would not be much welcomed within this chamber.

Edward had always disliked her (the man had *some* sense!), and Harold had made his feelings for Swanne known all through the court.

Harold was within one or two weeks, at the most, of being crowned the new king, and there was no one in this chamber likely to try and alienate him by taking Swanne's side in their rift.

The chamber was already crowded, and there was little room for movement, but still somehow people managed to draw back from Swanne as if she carried the pestilence within her person.

"What do you here?" Harold asked. He had let go my hand and risen.

Swanne's eyes moved about the room, as if searching for supporters, but she answered Harold calmly enough. "I am here to pay my respects to the king," she said, "and to offer my aid, in howsoever that may be required."

Without waiting for a reply, Swanne moved to the side of Edward's bed—the opposite side from Harold and myself—and sank to the floor in a graceful curtsy, bowing her head almost fully down to her breast.

"My lord and liege," she said to Edward as she finally raised her face to look at him, and I was shocked to see her eyes glistening with tears, "I am sad to see you in such distress. How may I best help?"

Edward was in no mood for courtly niceties. "You can remove yourself from my presence," he said, "and take that slut with you. I have had enough of her."

He waved a hand feebly in my direction.

Harold tensed, and before he could speak I rose myself and said calmly enough, "I will be glad of the time to rest. Judith, perhaps you might bring some bread and cheese so that the lady Swanne and I may break our fast together? We can sit in peace in the solar, I think."

Away from all these people. That would be a relief, at least, even if Swanne's company was not. I determined to rid myself of her as soon as possible. All I wanted was to sleep . . .

Swanne seemed curiously pleased at this suggestion, and she and I made our silent way to the solar—gratefully empty. There was no fire burning in the brazier because of the fuss Edward's sudden sickness had caused, but there were furs and blankets enough to wrap about us, and Judith could send someone to attend to the fire shortly.

"Swanne," I said as we sat down in opposite chairs and arranged the furs about ourselves. "How do you?"

It was but a politeness, but her eyes gleamed strangely, and her mouth worked as if she wanted to say something but dared not.

"Well enough," she said finally. She was staring at me now with a disturbing brightness, and I shifted, uncomfortable. I did not truly feel like trading barbed comments with Swanne at the moment.

"And you are comfortable at the archbishop's palace?" I said. The news of Swanne's move to Aldred's residence had caused a great stir and even more comment in Edward's court.

She jerked her head in what seemed like assent.

I looked to the door, wondering where Judith was. Even the presence of another person in this chamber would be a welcome relief, even if she did nothing to ease the awkwardness of this conversation.

"You must be missing your children," I said.

"Do you remember those golden bands Brutus wore about his limbs?" she said. Her entire body was rigid, and she stared at me unblinkingly.

I froze, although I truly should not have found this unexpected. Swanne would have known another band was moved last night, and I was the only living soul in England with whom she might discuss the matter (apart from Asterion, of course, but then I could not imagine Swanne interrogating him about the bands' movements!). She might even suspect me, although she would not think me capable of their movement.

Still, Swanne-who-once-was-Genvissa had been blaming me for most of the world's ills for these past two thousand years, so that she would blame me for this—without actually believing that I was responsible for it—was hardly a shock.

"Of course," I said. "Brutus treasured them dearly."

"He hid them. After you had murdered me."

"They vanished from his limbs, that I know, but I did not know what he had done with them." *Not then.*

"Now someone is moving them."

I swallowed. It wasn't so much the topic of conversation, but the strange, unreal directness of it that perturbed me. There was something odd about Swanne. Something . . . *un*-Swanne. It was the only way I could think of describing the strangeness that hung about her.

Perhaps it was just her anger and shock at the movement of the band.

"We think it is Silvius," she said.

We? I thought. "Silvius?" I said.

"Oh, come now, you pathetic little wretch, you know who Silvius is."

I fought the urge to drop my eyes from her direct stare. "Oh . . . Brutus' father. Yes? Swanne, you must understand that in our dealings with each other, Brutus and I spent little time talking."

There, let her make of that what she would.

Swanne flushed, and I knew my barb had hit home.

"There are rumors, foul rumors, I am sure," she said, "that you were strangely absent from Edward's bed when he took ill last night. How may that be explained, do you think?"

It was not unexpected that Swanne would have heard this, and certainly not unexpected that she would comment on it to me . . . but that she would do so in the instant after discussing both the band's movement and Silvius?

I gave her the same explanation I'd given everyone else. I'd woken, realized Edward's distress, and run to fetch Saeweald without thinking to wake anyone else.

I finished, but Swanne said nothing. She just stared at me with that unusual light in her eyes.

"I've taken Aldred to my bed," she said. "Did you know that?"

Perhaps if she had said that she was really Og reincarnated, she may have stunned me more, but, frankly, I doubt it. Not only was that comment so totally unexpected, so totally inappropriate to the conversation immediately preceding it, but the fact that *Swanne had taken Aldred to her bed* was . . . unbelievable.

I cannot imagine any woman willingly taking Aldred into her bed, but Swanne? Never! Not when events were so clearly moving toward a reckoning. Not when William was so close!

Later, of course, I may have recognized that comment for what it was—a heavily-veiled scream for help—but at this moment I only sat there, my mouth agape, and finally managed to splutter, "But what about William?"

"He wasn't handy at the time!" she snapped.

"But—"

"Do you know who is moving the bands?"

Again, the sudden twist in the conversation unnerved me. "No."

"Is it Silvius?"

"I don't know to what you refer, Swanne. I—"

"Are you moving the bands, Caela?"

"Me? *Me?* How can I, Swanne? I do not even know why you are so obsessed with these damned bands! And *Brutus* hid them, not me! Surely you have enough wealth and estates. Why tinker after some long-buried relic?"

"Are you moving the bands, Caela?"

"Why are you asking me this, Swanne?"

"You were not with Edward last night when a band was moved."

Gods, and to think I'd been worrying about what Asterion might have thought! "I have explained where —"

"Who do you keep company with, Caela? What strange creatures aid you those nights you are not with Edward?"

"What do you mean?"

She rose suddenly to her feet, the furs and coverlets tumbling about her feet. *"Who else has come back from that terrible life we endured? Who are your friends?"*

I defended with attack. I was now so truly confused, worried, and disorientated by Swanne's bizarre behavior that I could think of no other way to respond.

I, too, leapt to my feet, and with one fist I beat against my belly. "Do you not remember, Swanne? Asterion tore Mag from my womb! I am no more than an ordinary woman—I *have* no insights! No secrets! What? Do you think that I am still Asterion's pawn? Still dancing to his tune?"

Something in Swanne's face changed. There was a moment when she seemed terrified, and I assumed that her terror was because she might truly have thought I *was* Asterion's creature.

"Look," I snarled, spreading my hands wide. "No knife."

She winced, but I carried straight on.

"I want nothing save to be left in peace, Swanne. I have no ambitions save to escape your malevolence and jealousy and retire to some quiet hall in the country where I might live quietly. I do not want to see your and William's triumph, Swanne."

My face was twisting in bitterness now, and I think it was that more than anything else that convinced her. "I do not want William, Swanne. You can have him. I just want to escape you and him and all that has happened. *I just want to escape!*"

I burst into tears, and as I put my hands to my face and sobbed, Judith entered the room, took one appalled look at me, and hastened over.

"Madam!" she said. "What—"

"My lady Swanne is leaving, Judith. Perhaps you can close the door behind her."

Swanne gave me one more strange, searching look, nodded tersely, then left.

TWO DAYS LATER, AS I SAT EXHAUSTED IN EDWARD'S chamber, Silvius came to see me.

I was astounded at his daring—for he did not bother with one of his Aegean sorceries, but came to me openly—and grateful. In truth, Edward's death chamber (once our marital chamber, but now utterly overtaken with the stink and business of his dying) was thronged with clerics, supplicants, nuns, abbesses, physicians, herbalists, nobles, members of the witan, sundry palace servants crowding in for a glimpse of the fun, and a press of other bodies and ambitions I did not bother to recognize. Jesus Christ himself could have entered that chamber, and it would have elicited no comment.

I was sitting on a linen chest on the far side of the chamber, all but hidden from the view of those closely grouped about the bed by a group of nuns (from Mother Ecub's order, I think, which may have given Silvius the courage, knowing they would do their best to keep him hidden from view), when a close-hooded monk came to me, murmured an apology for intruding, and sat on the chest beside me.

"My lady," he said, and took my hand.

I almost jerked it out of the presumptuous man's grasp before I realized who it was. Silvius' good eye gleamed at me from deep within his hood, and I almost burst into tears.

I almost spoke his name, but he put his finger to his lips and winked.

I contented myself with squeezing his hand. "What do you here?" I asked, lowly.

"Come to see if you need any comfort."

Oh, he was too good to me. "Oh," I said. "Good man—" *Damn this audience for not allowing me to say his name!* "—I am glad you are here. I wish to say . . . that . . ."

I *wanted* to apologize to him for how I had acted that night we lay together, for not being what he deserved, but I did not know how to phrase the words.

"Do not worry, my lady, you were all that I deserved, and more. Tell me . . . have you lost that emptiness?"

I shook my head wordlessly.

"Ah, I am sorry for it. I had hoped . . ."

"I know." Again I squeezed his hand. "So much has changed in so few days."

He glanced at the back of the closely grouped nuns, as if he could see Edward through their substance. "I know. There is a disturbance in the Game."

"Long Tom has felt it also." Silvius' eye jerked back to my face as I continued. "The foundations of both land and Game have tilted slightly."

"And does he know what has caused this?"

"No." Now it was I who looked about the chamber. "Swanne is altered. I wonder if it is she who has . . . has . . ."

"Has?"

"I don't know." I felt close to tears, and Silvius lifted his free hand and touched my forehead, making the gesture look like a blessing. I wished he could keep his fingers on my face, but of necessity he needed to drop them away. I took a deep breath and tried again. "Her manner. Her very being. It is different in some way. Sharper, edgier. More acute."

"Then what has happened, has happened to Swanne," he said.

"But what could it be?"

He shrugged.

"Asterion?" I asked, glancing about, wondering if *he* was here, among us. Undoubtedly.

"If Asterion did anything to Swanne, it would be to kill her. *That* I could imagine. Especially if he was angered that another band had been moved. Who else would he suspect, save for Swanne?" said Silvius.

"He could suspect me. He came to Edward while I and Long Tom moved the second band, and he saw I was not here. Then Swanne came to me, and asked questions . . ."

"Lady," Silvius said very gently, "how could he suspect you? He is certain that Mag has been killed. He cannot know you for who you truly are."

I shrugged again, closer to tears than ever. If only I could sleep, rest, close my mind to everything save the delicious relief of dream.

Silvius' hand tightened about mine. "I can feel him," he said, beating his other hand in a closed fist gently against his breast. "I can feel that motherless bastard in here. He is confident. He is *crowing* with confidence. The Game has shifted, and he has caused it. Swanne has 'shifted' and I cannot think but that he has caused this, as well. Caela . . ."

"Yes?"

"If Asterion murders Swanne or otherwise corrupts her, we are lost. You know that, don't you?"

I closed my eyes, and gripped Silvius' hand tightly.

"I know that," I said.

Chapter Six

6th January 1066

DWARD LAY DYING. HE'D TAKEN ALMOST A WEEK about it, but now, in the heart of the bleak midwinter, it was his time.

He was screaming.

There was no need for him to scream so, save that Edward was approaching his salvation, and he wanted everyone to know that he was going to grab at it with both hands. There was no possible means by which salvation was going to avoid him. No possible means by which God and His saints were going to escape an eternity without the Confessor by their side.

Humility had never been Edward's strongest attribute.

His screams were terrible to hear. As he gurgled with the blood and pus that now almost completely filled his lungs, they rippled about the crowded chamber like a rotten sea.

It appeared that anyone who had even the faintest connection with the king had squeezed themselves into the chamber.

Caela was there, the chief mourner and witness. Her face was pale and expressionless, her every movement measured, as if she kept herself under tight control.

Most of the highest clergy, currently within a days' ride of London, were there: Wulfstan, bishop of Worcester; Eadwine, the abbot of the newly consecrated Westminster Abbey; Stigand, the archbishop of Canterbury; Spearhafoc, the bishop of London; Aldred, the archbishop of York, his eyes weeping, his chins wobbling, his plump hands twisting and twining before his ample stomach; and sundry abbots, and deacons, including many from Normandy.

Many earls and counts and senior thegns were there, including the earls Edwin and Morcar, brothers to Alditha, and who were there less to witness Edward's death than to ensure Harold wed their sister as soon as possible. Among the other men of rank who attended were at least eight members of the witan. Their eyes rested on Harold far more than they rested on Edward.

Swanne was there, standing well back and hardly visible, but with her black eyes darting about and watching the crowd more than they watched Edward.

Saeweald also attended. He stood at the king's side, silently using linens to wipe away the worst of the effluent that projected from the king's shrieking mouth before handing them to Mother Ecub, prioress of St. Margaret the Martyr, who placed them in a basket at the bed's head.

No doubt, once the king was dead, the basket's contents would be souvenired by eager hands, kept against the inevitable day when Edward would be sanctified and the purulent linens would become valuable relics.

Finally, packed at the furthest distance and generally jammed against the walls of the chamber, stood the king's most faithful servants: his bowerthegn, his palace chamberlain, his royal men-at-arms, the laundresses (Damson among them) and stable boys who had served Edward with love and devotion and who wondered if Edward were to find himself a place with God and His saints this night, then what place there might be for them in the new court.

This relatively small group of servants were, truly, the only ones there whose primary concern was to mourn.

Everyone else had their own agendas, the most common of which was to ensure themselves a prominent place in the new court. Doubtlessly, the sound first heard, in that moment after Edward drew his final breath, would be the thud of knees hitting the floor as men pledged their allegiance to the new king, Harold.

Edward's shrieks grew louder, more incoherent. It was difficult to distinguish individual words, but no one had much doubt as to their intent: Edward was letting God know of his imminent arrival, and was telling the world that it would be a poorer place indeed for his absence.

The dying king sat propped upright against a welter of goose-down pillows. He had on a linen nightshirt, open at the neck so that it revealed his thin, laboring ribs, and it billowed about his skeletal arms as he waved them about. Edward's staring eyes were fixed on the golden cross held in the trembling hands of a monk who stood at the foot of the bed. The darkened chamber was lit only by eight or nine fat candles in wall sconces, and what light did manage to find its way through to Edward's bed consisted only of graying, shifting shadows.

As Edward's shrieking shrilled yet higher, and the pustulence he emitted from his mouth became thicker and more foul, several members of the witan, who stood close to the huddled clerics, stepped forward and began urgently to whisper to Stigand, Spearhafoc, and Aldred, the three senior clerics present.

The whispered conversations grew heated. Both the members of the witan and the clerics gesturing and, occasionally, looking worriedly at Edward.

Finally Aldred nodded his head, as if he agreed with what the witan argued, and turned to his two fellow clerics, adding his weight and influence to the reasonings of the witan.

After some moments, Stigand and Spearhafoc nodded as well—by this stage most eyes were watching this discussion rather than the king—and Aldred wobbled to the king's side and, holding a careful sleeve to his mouth, lest the king splatter him with his dying, began to speak to Edward in a low, but compelling voice.

"My dearest liege," he said, "your time is upon you. See! God holds out his hands before you! The saints chorus their jubilation!"

On the other side of the bed Saeweald turned his head as he accepted a clean linen from Mother Ecub, taking the opportunity to roll his eyes very slightly at her.

Ecub's face remained expressionless, but Saeweald thought he could see a slight relaxation of the muscles around her eyes: she was as amused as he.

"Yes! Yes!" Edward shrieked—the first two coherent words he'd uttered in the past hour.

"Salvation awaits!" Aldred continued, his eyes gleaming with a fanatical light. "Heaven and the next world awaits! You shall live at God's side for eternity!"

"Salvation!" screamed Edward, his hands flapping at his bed linens. "Eternity!"

Caela winced, then looked away.

"The Devil shall be bested!" shouted Aldred, now working himself into a true fever.

"Bested!" shrieked Edward.

"Evil shall be overcome!"

"Overcome!"

"God and his angels shall prevail!"

"Prevail!"

"Your subjects shall be saved!"

"Saved!"

"Harold shall reign, a true Christian king!"

"A true Christian king!" Edward echoed. Then, more softly, and far more suspiciously. "*Harold?*"

"Harold shall be your heir!"

Edward said nothing, but glared at Aldred.

Across the room Harold also glared at Aldred, who flushed.

"My best and truest lord," Aldred said, his tone unctuous, "evil thinks to create disharmony and confusion within your realm. There is unsurety about your heir. Name him now! Best evil! Ensure that righteousness prevails! Name Harold—"

"Godwine's cursed son?" Edward said. "You want a Godwineson to sit on the throne of—"

He stopped, and uncertainty appeared to overcome him. He coughed, spitting into the linen that Saeweald provided, then looked with watering, tormented eyes to Eadwine, the abbot of Westminster. "What should I do?" he whispered. "What should I do?"

"You must do what is best," Eadwine said.

"What is best?" said Edward.

"Harold," said Eadwine, and, about the chamber breaths were released in profound relief.

"Harold?" said Edward.

"Harold," said Eadwine.

Edward gave a small nod, then looked back to Aldred. "Perhaps Harold *would* be best," he said.

"Name him," Aldred said very softly.

Edward sighed. "Harold shall succeed me." He did not look at Harold as he said this.

For his part, Harold's face flushed with relief. He had been named. He had the right to the throne. If William or Hardrada or even a bevy of church mice tried to lay claim to it then they would do so illegally, both in the sight of God and in the sight of England.

"Harold . . ." Edward said, and his tone was one of immense sadness, as if he felt he had failed somehow, but was not quite sure of that "how."

Aldred laid a heavy hand on Edward's shoulder. "Be at peace, my lord," he said, and with those words Edward slipped quietly into death.

There was a silence, then cries of "Harold! Harold! Harold!"

Through the tumult, Aldred raised his face and caught Swanne's eye.

William, he whispered into her mind. *William is on his way . . . and you shall hand me his life. Yes?*

A pause during which Swanne's face twisted in silent agony and she grabbed with one hand at her belly.

Yes?

Yes, she whimpered back, and her eyes ran with tears.

CHAPTER SEVEN

AROLD'S ELECTION TO THE THRONE WAS A foregone conclusion, the result not only of Harold's careful and ceaseless canvasing of the members of the witan as Edward lay a-dying over the Christmas season, but Aldred's ability to wrangle a succession order from Edward in those moments before he died. Within an hour after Edward's death, Harold's succession was proclaimed over Westminster and through London; within a day it had spread to most parts of the realm.

Edward's chamber was abandoned virtually within moments of his passing, save for Damson, Caela, and several other ladies who attended to his laying out. The rest of the witnesses, the counts and earls, the chamberlains, chancellors, stewards and thegns, the priests and bishops and abbots and abbesses and all their attendants had moved with Harold to the Great Hall of the Westminster palace, there to plan the coronation.

It would take place in the morning at the very newly consecrated Westminster Abbey, directly after the funeral service to bury Edward.

And directly after he was crowned king, Harold would wed Alditha and crown her queen. All would be settled before noon.

The morrow was going to be a rushed day indeed, but that was, as Harold explained to his crowd of old retainers and friends, heavily augmented with new hangers-on and applicants to power, all to his advantage.

"If I leave my coronation until the usual period of official mourning will have passed, then William, Tostig, Hardrada, and half the aging Vikings still left in Norway, for all I know, will have moved." Harold sat on the throne on the dais, having marched there without hesitation the instant he entered the Great Hall.

One of the senior members of the witan, Regenbald, who had been Edward's chancellor, stepped forward. He was an old man, but still radiated a powerful virility, and was renowned across half of Europe for his insights and sagacity.

"Mourning would only take a month," he said. "No one is going to mount an invasion in a month. Not in the bleakness of midwinter. To rush into a coronation might appear to smack of . . . unseemly haste."

There were murmurs of agreement in the five-man-deep throng about Harold.

"Aldred, my friend," said Harold. "What say you?"

The archbishop visibly preened with pride; Harold's prompting for advice was a direct reward for Aldred's success in securing a succession order from Edward.

"I cannot speak for Hardrada," said Aldred, his eyes skimming quickly over the watching faces before returning to Harold, "but I think I can for William. His spies at this court—"

There were murmurs and dark looks exchanged about the gathering, but Harold kept his own gaze steady on Aldred.

"—will have doubtless already sent word regarding Edward's demise," Aldred continued. "William will have been waiting for this news. Surely, yes, he will swing his plans for an invasion into place, but the *first* thing he will do is seek to claim the throne himself. He has, as we are all too well aware, been claiming for years that Edward promised *him* the throne many years ago when Edward sheltered at the Norman court. William will proclaim loud and long all over Europe, from the Papal court to the Holy Roman Empire to Flanders itself that he is the legal king of England. He will do this because he will hope to make the witan think twice about electing Harold. William will do everything he can to make Harold's succession, should it happen, as illegal as possible."

"We will *never* have a Norman king!" said Regenbald.

"We would never elect *William!*" said Robert Fitzwimarch, who had been a member of the witan even longer than Regenbald.

"A Norman *and* a bastard," muttered yet another witan member, Ansgar.

Harold smiled. "If he surrounded London with enough swords you would elect him willingly enough," he said, then carried straight on through the howls of denials. "Aldred is right. If I give William so much as a day of space he will have petitioned most of the reigning princes, dukes, kings, and prelates of Europe regarding his right to the throne and, knowing William's charm and his reputation, most of them shall have agreed to his right to it. If I waited for the full month of mourning before being crowned, I would have the weight of European opinion against me, and William would have his excuse for an invasion. This way," he paused momentarily, his face suddenly looking old and haggard, "this way, perhaps I have a chance of circumventing him."

There was a silence.

"St. Paul's?" said Aldred brightly. "I should send word to the dean that he should ready the cathedral for your—"

"No," said Harold. "I will be crowned in Westminster."

"But kings have always been crowned in St. Paul's!" said Stigand, the archbishop of Canterbury, and Spearhafoc, the bishop of London, as one. Stigand had always been a stickler for tradition, and Spearhafoc could suddenly see the coronation sliding out of his control into the eager hands of Eadwine, the abbot of Westminster.

"Then I shall start a new tradition!" snapped Harold. "Think, damn you! Edward had stipulated that he be buried in Westminster Abbey, and I dare not go against that lest I be seen to disrespect his wishes and his holy corpse. So the funeral service for Edward, with every court member present, will be held in Westminster Abbey in the morning. I am *not* then going to insist that everyone up and move themselves, through the heart of a frozen winter's day, to St. Paul's for my coronation! Westminster it is."

Harold leaned forward on the throne and looked Stigand in the eye. "Is your matter still before Alexander?"

Stigand looked down. "Yes." For several years now Stigand's appointment as archbishop of Canterbury had been in dispute. The matter had gone to the pope for a final decision, but Alexander II, not known for his speed in dealing with business matters not directly connected with either food or young girls, had not yet proclaimed on the problem.

"Then Aldred shall crown me," Harold said.

"No!" Stigand cried, taking a half step forward. Harold raised his hand.

"I cannot afford to be crowned by an archbishop whose appointment is in doubt!" Harold said. "Damn it, Stigand, if Alexander does not rule in your favor, and you *have* crowned me, then my coronation is null and void. Aldred is the second most senior churchman in England, and there is *no* dispute as to his right to the title. He shall crown me."

Stigand shot Aldred a foul look, but the obese archbishop was staring down at his hands laced across his belly, a small smile on his face.

Harold stood up, beckoning to the brothers Edwin and Morcar. "I need to speak to you about your sister, Alditha. If I am to wed her in the morning, then you and I need to finalize her dower arrangements tonight."

And with that, the rest of the crowd was dismissed.

chapter eight

ALDRED HAD SECURED FOR HIMSELF A SMALL BUT private chamber within the Westminster complex. Between the death of the one king and the coronation of the next, there was little time to scurry to and from his palace in London.

Besides he was enjoying himself far too much to waste time in traveling along the frozen Westminster to London road.

"And so then Harold said, 'Aldred shall crown me'!" Aldred said, and grinned. "I could hardly believe it. I . . . *I*, to crown the king of England! Shall I crown William, too, my dear? Do you think?"

Swanne sat at the very edge of the bed, as far away from Aldred as possible. She felt as though she were locked into a black, cold night from which she could never escape. Her belly ached from the incubus's horrid nibbling, her heart ached for all that had happened and for what Asterion promised would happen, and her entire body throbbed painfully from Aldred's just-completed bout of lovemaking . . . if such a brutal assault could be in any way described as 'lovemaking'.

"Shall I, my dear?" Aldred said, now much softer, and Swanne's head jerked in terrified assent, knowing that the incubus could strike at any moment.

He was going to say more, but just then came a knock at the door, and a mumbled request from one of the abbey monks that the archbishop join the abbot of Westminster and the archbishop of Canterbury within the abbot's private chambers as shortly as possible.

Aldred sighed, patted Swanne on the cheek, and departed.

A few minutes later, surprising Swanne who had relaxed just enough to close her eyes, the door reopened, and Asterion, now in his ancient form of the Minotaur, walked in.

He sat on the bed, close to Swanne, who had shrunk back.

She tensed, her black eyes growing huge and terrified, and Asterion reached out a hand and took one of hers gently.

"I will not harm you," he said, sliding close enough that their bodies touched at hip and shoulder.

If anything, her eyes grew even wider.

"I will not harm you," he repeated, and ran his free hand softly over her shoulder, breast, and belly, where the hand lingered a moment before continuing down to rest on her thigh.

She was very cold, and Asterion jerked his eyes toward the brazier.

Instantly a fire roared into life, making Swanne tremble under Asterion's touch.

"Shush," he said, and pulled her tense body close. "I do not mean to treat you harshly."

She made a small noise, part laughter, part groan.

The expression on Asterion's great bull head changed into something curiously like a smile. "Ariadne loved me, you know," he said. "Perhaps you might, too."

"She wanted you dead," Swanne said.

"Oh yes, she did, and thus this." Asterion's hand again rested on Swanne's belly. "I am not going to make the same error with you as I made with Ariadne. But she *did* love me. A long time ago, when we were but half brother and sister, and mated within the great mystery of the labyrinth." He paused, and again smiled, this time more obviously. "It was hardly as if she were a virgin when Theseus first took her, you know."

For the first time since she'd managed to struggle from under Aldred's body to this spot at the end of the bed, Swanne looked at him. And for the first time in many days there was something other than fear in her eyes. A questioning, perhaps.

"Think about it," said Asterion. "Ariadne was the Mistress of the great founding labyrinth. I was . . . almost her Kingman, if you like." His bestial mouth brushed the top of her head, and Swanne winced. "And you well know what relations exist between a Kingman and the Mistress of the Labyrinth," Asterion said, drawing back a little.

"You were not the Kingman of that labyrinth," said Swanne. "You were the blackness and malevolence she kept trapped within its heart."

He laughed. "Ah, you know your history too well, Swanne, my love. Be that as it might, Ariadne nevertheless visited me in the heart of the labyrinth on many an occasion. We *were* lovers, Swanne, and that is what made her betrayal of me to Theseus the more . . . dreadful."

His voice had hardened into ice on that last word, and Swanne shuddered.

"And yet still I gifted her all that I had," Asterion went on. His hands were running all over Swanne's body now, and, as they moved, they smoothed away all the pain and aches she felt. Without realizing it, Swanne leaned very gradually against him. Finally she relaxed enough to rest her face against his broad chest, and to feel without fear the play of his soft, warm breath over the crown of her head.

Swanne closed her eyes. *Oh gods, it felt so good to have all the pain and fear soothed away.* She felt a sudden rush of gratitude toward Asterion for taking away all the pain Aldred had caused, and she did not even pause to think that thought strange.

"You are so very much like her," Asterion continued, his voice now very soft. "Your hair. Your face. Your form." Again he paused, although his hands still kept moving, slowly, gently, soothingly. "Your ambition."

So greatly had she relaxed that Swanne did not even tense at that last phrase, and Asterion smiled to himself over the top of her head. She had learned to hate and loathe Aldred, and that was good.

Better would be the day when she automatically relaxed whenever he appeared as Asterion.

And best would be that day she allowed herself to love him. That she would, he had no doubt. Once she loved him, then Swanne would grant him any wish, if he promised to keep Aldred at bay; a captive creature was all very well, but Swanne would do twice as well for him, should love drive her actions rather than force. Aldred's brutalization had been harsh, but it had been necessary.

"What do you think I plan?" he asked Swanne, in that moment before she fell asleep.

She jerked a little, not in fear, but merely in half-surprise at the question.

"To destroy the Troy Game," she murmured against his chest. She had lifted one hand, and now it rested against his skin, the tips of her fingers slightly tangled in the black hair that curled over his chest.

He took her shoulders and tipped her back so that she could see his face. "No," he said. "I do not seek to *destroy* it, Swanne. Whatever gave you that idea? Some strange half truth that Ariadne passed down through her generations of daughter-heirs? I do not seek to destroy the Game, Swanne. I seek to control it."

She frowned, and would have spoken, save that Asterion laid the fingers of one hand over her lips.

"And if I want to control the Game, my love," he said, his voice now throbbing with reassurance combined with heady promise, "I will need a Mistress of the Labyrinth."

Her eyes widened, then clouded with confusion. *What was he intimating?*

"I will need a Mistress of the Labyrinth, and I will need a set of kingship bands, of which the Trojan bands are the only set left. Swanne, *you* want to control the Game, and for that you need a Kingman and you need his bands. How are we at odds here?"

"But . . ." she murmured behind his fingers.

"But . . . what?"

"But you want to destroy me."

"Nay," he said, laughing softly, and planting a brief kiss on her forehead. "I adored Ariadne. I can adore you, as well."

Swanne's forehead creased as she tried to order her thoughts . . . but she was so warm, and so grateful to be free of pain and fear. "William," she managed to say finally.

Asterion's face became dismissive. "Ah, William. He is not here, is he? He pouts uselessly in some draughty Norman castle. Of what use is such a Kingman to you?"

His mouth brushed her forehead again, the touch firmer this time, and with his touch he used a barely discernible element of his darkcraft. *Love me, Swanne.*

Swanne suddenly realized she did not find the touch of that great beast's mouth loathsome at all.

His mouth brushed against her forehead yet once more. *Love me, Swanne. Trust in whatever I say.*

"When he arrives in England, my dear, we shall have to negate him."

"Really?" Swanne said, so under Asterion's enchantment now that she was not even mildly curious at her total lack of concern at Asterion's proposal.

"Yes, really. There is room for only one Kingman, after all, and to have William scrambling about would be such a nuisance."

She was silent.

"Do you really think," he said, whispering so that she could barely hear, "that William is stronger than me?"

His hands were moving again, firmer, more insistent. "Do you really think," he said, directly into her ear so that his bull breath slid deep into her soul, "that William is *preferable* to me?"

Love me, Swanne. Do whatever I want.

She moaned, and could not think at all. All she could do was lean into Asterion's hands, against his chest once more, and allow herself to be drawn back to the bed.

She felt no fear, only a vague gratefulness that he was not angry at her, and the words he whispered were not those of terror.

"You have the darkcraft within you," he whispered. "I put it into Ariadne, and she has passed it to you. Can you imagine, Swanne, my darling, what kind of Game we could build, what kind of *power* we could command, if we used the darkcraft to control the Game?"

He rolled on top of her, and Swanne felt herself part her legs with something that felt a little like eagerness. Caught in Asterion's sorcery, her mind had now completely forgotten that Asterion also used Aldred's body from time to time. Instead, they had become two separate personalities to her. Aldred caused her pain and humiliation. Asterion relieved that pain, and offered her soft words . . . and *power.*

"Why William," he repeated, sliding sweetly and gently into her, "when you have me?"

"Not William," she whispered.

"No, my sweet. Not William. When he arrives in England, will you kill him for me?"

Swanne moaned, not simply from pleasure at the feel of Asterion's body within hers, but because she could feel him sliding a small piece of the dark power back into her with every thrust.

Oh, that was so sweet!

"Will you kill him for me?"

"Yes! Anything, anything . . ." She gasped, and moved sinuously under the Minotaur, encouraging him with her body.

"And all you will have to do, my love, is to seduce him back to your bed. That won't be too difficult, will it?"

Swanne couldn't think, let alone reason. "No. Anything. Please, give me more of the darkcraft . . . please."

"When you have killed William, I will give it *all* back to you."

She moaned.

SHE WOULD DO ANYTHING FOR HIM NOW. ANYTHING.

Asterion whistled as he wandered along the river path. He'd had to escape Westminster and the confines of petty men, and so had chosen this somewhat muddy walk for the solitude it gave him. He wanted to shout and to scream his power, but in the interest of maintaining some dignity, restrained himself to the occasional hop and skip as he walked along.

The Troy Game was all but his.

The bands he could get any time.

He had his Mistress of the Labyrinth.

All that stood in his way was William.

Asterion sobered a little. He well understood that William was indeed highly dangerous. As dangerous as Theseus had once been—and Theseus' danger had been fatal.

Asterion needed William negated. Murdered. Assassinated. Whatever. *Dead.*

Then nothing would stand in his way. Nothing.

Asterion's face resumed its cheerful aspect and, as he imagined what awaited William the instant he gave into his lust for Swanne and slid inside her body, he chuckled and then burst into laughter, startling the waterfowl which had been hiding in the rushes.

CHAPTER NINE

CAELA SPEAKS

E DWARD HAD DIED, AND I WAS FINALLY FREE.
At least, that is what it felt like. No longer the queen, merely the relict of a dead king, all interest in me evaporated the instant Edward breathed his last. I could have torn the robes from my body and run shrieking about the palace complex and, at best, I would have been regarded with only mild irritation for creating a noise.

Instead, Alditha became the focus of attention (after Harold himself, naturally). Harold had spread the word of his betrothal to her the day of Edward's death and now she, the future queen, became the darling of the sycophants.

She was not the loathed wife.

She was not the detested bedmate.

Alditha was respected and treated with deference by her future husband, and thus the entire court respected and deferred to her.

I did not mind in the least. Not for the world would I have had any other woman suffer what I did in Edward's court. I visited her as soon as Edward had been respectably laid out, and to her credit Alditha admitted me within an instant, dismissing all the flatterers who crowded about her chair, and kissing me on the cheek before embracing me tightly.

"I will not have you move from your quarters," she said. "There is no need."

"There is every need," I said, "for they stink of death. Mother Ecub, the prioress of St. Margaret the Martyr, has offered me lodging and privacy, and I shall move there without delay. You do not need me cluttering up your court, my dear."

Harold had entered then, and as he bent to kiss Alditha, I was pleased—if smitten with a pang of jealousy—that there was clearly not only friendship between them, but the ease of physical intimacy as well. Harold had not been wasting his nights at all.

He had the grace to color slightly when he met my eyes and saw the understanding there. He put a hand to Alditha's shoulder, and said, gently, "You have done well by me, sister. I am grateful."

"And I," said Alditha. Then she sobered. "I think."

Harold and I both burst into laughter, and the awkwardness dissipated.

"I heard you say you were moving to St. Margaret the Martyr's," said Harold. "Caela, there is no need."

"I do need to quit this palace," I said. "It has nothing but bad memories for me." And traps, and eyes, and ears. The freedom of Ecub's establishment promised to be exhilarating. "You may visit me there whenever you wish, Harold. Kingdom and new wife permitting."

Again we laughed, all three of us, and spent some pleasant minutes in idle conversation. Then Harold had to leave—the kingdom waited, and plans for his coronation—and I also did not linger. Alditha had many matters to occupy her as well, and I did not want my presence ever to become a strain.

As we stood, I leaned forward and pressed my cheek against hers and, presumptuously, laid a hand lightly on her belly. "You will have twin sons by Yuletide this year," I whispered. "Do not fear for them."

Then, with Alditha staring bewildered after me, I took my departure.

ALDRED CROWNED HAROLD IN WESTMINSTER ABBEY the next day, an hour after Edward had been laid to his eternal rest inside his cold stone casket, inside his cold stone abbey.

I hoped it comforted him, all that cold stone imprisoning him within his death.

Alditha was crowned alongside Harold, the abbey alive with music and garlands and pennants and the shouting of the Londoners outside. I stood to one side in the shadow of a side aisle, Judith, Ecub, and Saeweald beside me, watching, both glad and saddened for Harold.

I could almost hear the sound of William sharpening his sword across the narrow straits of the sea.

I closed my eyes, fighting to keep back the tears. *Gods, what this land needed was Harold as its king, not William!*

I felt Judith's hand touch my elbow in concern, and I opened my eyes, and gave her a small smile.

Then I looked back to Harold, just as he was standing to receive the acclaim of the witan and the nobles.

A stray shaft of sunlight hit his head, highlighting the golden crown atop his brow, and I frowned, for it seemed to me that I was seeing something very important at that moment, yet not understanding it.

"Caela," Ecub whispered in my ear, and she nodded to a spot within the crowd hailing Harold.

There stood Long Tom, looking at Harold with eyes shining with reverence.

He must have felt me watching, for the Sidlesaghe shifted his gaze from Harold to me. He frowned, and nodded in Harold's direction, and then raised his hands and applauded as most everyone else in the abbey was doing, his eyes constantly dancing between Harold and myself, and then the tears *did* slip down my cheeks, because I knew Long Tom was trying to tell me something, trying to *show* me something, and I was fool enough not to understand what.

THAT NIGHT, MY FIRST AT ST. MARGARET THE MARTYR'S, I climbed to the summit of Pen Hill, and there waited Long Tom.

I asked him what he had been trying to tell me in the abbey, but he only shook his head, and would not answer the question.

"We are worried," he said, changing the subject when I tried to press. "The land feels ill. You do not feel it?"

I shook my head. In truth, the past week I had slept so little that I doubt I would have felt it even if my right arm had been torn from my body.

Then I was consumed by guilt, because I *should* have felt it. I was the land, and if it was not right, then I *should* have felt it.

"It has an imp within it," he said, and moaned so pitifully that I began to weep. "We cannot see where, but that imp will eat at us and this green land and its forests and waters until all are gone."

"Long Tom, I can see and feel nothing. Why? What is wrong with me?"

And to that he did not respond, either, saying only, "You must move another band tonight, sweet lady. It is all we can do."

I did, moving a band that Brutus had hid in the northeastern part of London's wall to a point far to the south of the river, a place called Herne Hill, where waited for me a similar scene as that had greeted me at the Holy Oak, save that this time I handed the band to a man sitting behind a curious wheel in one of those frightful black beasts, this time stationary by the entrance to a similar redbrick building as had stood at Gospel Oak.

My heart raced the entire time, but there was no sign of Asterion.

Somehow that worried me more than anything.

CHAPTER TEN

YVES HAD BEEN AND GONE, AND NOW WILLIAM
stood before Matilda with the unfolded letter in his hands that the
priest had delivered.

He was staring at it without expression.

"Does it . . .?" Matilda said, wanting to snatch at the letter but unable to
tear her eyes from her husband's face.

"Yes," William said, finally raising his own gaze from the letter to look at
Matilda. "It confirms the rumors we've heard for the past two days. Edward
is dead. And Harold has been elected and crowned and anointed king of
England."

Matilda drew in a sharp breath. "He moved fast. But then we always knew
he would." She nodded at the letter. "And Swanne? How has she positioned
herself?"

William's mouth twisted wryly, and he handed the letter to Matilda to
read. "This is not from Swanne, but rather Aldred."

Matilda took the letter, her eyes scanning the thick inked lines. "The archbishop of York?"

"Aye." They had already heard that Harold had set Swanne to one side,
and neither were surprised at this intelligence. William wondered, however,
just how deeply Swanne had taken that to her heart.

He wondered, very privately, and with an intensity that ate at him during
those long wakeful moments in the heart of the night, if it was her anger and
undoubted humiliation that had caused the "shift" he'd felt in the Game over
the past few weeks.

Something had happened—distinct from the movement of the second *and*
third bands that William supposed could be attributed to Silvius—and it had
happened as he had felt a simultaneous "withdrawing" from Swanne. Apart
from their two brief meetings, they'd never been in close contact, but William
had always been able to sense her, *feel* her.

Now that sense had faded.

What was happening?

Well, at least now he had the excuse he needed to move. William took a deep breath, grateful at least for Edward's dying.

At last . . . at last.

He looked to Matilda's face and saw the excitement there, and for the first time he wondered what would happen to her in this forthcoming battle. *Dear gods, let her not be hurt!*

He reached out and touched her face tenderly, and was rewarded by the slight pressure of her cheek against the palm of his hand.

"You will be king," she said.

He smiled, but it did not reach his eyes. "Aye. After all this time . . ."

"William," she said. "I have had news from my agent as well."

"Yes?"

"Swanne has moved into the archbishop of York's palace."

"What?"

"Harold put her aside. This cannot be surprising news, surely."

"That Harold should set Swanne aside? No. In truth, I expected it. But why would Swanne move into the archbishop's household? In what capacity, has your agent discovered that?"

Matilda watched her husband closely as she picked her next words with some care. "It is rumored that Swanne has become Aldred's lover."

William's mouth fell open.

"My love," Matilda said. "After what Harold has told us of her, you cannot be surprised that—"

"That Swanne has chosen a lover? No, I am not surprised at that. I am sure she did it so that she might retain a place at court. Unless she became a laundress—"

Matilda's eyes widened very slightly, but otherwise her face remained remarkably expressionless.

"—there could be little else Swanne *could* do to keep a place within court. Sweet Christ, Harold would not want her there! But Aldred . . . *Aldred!* Matilda, you have met him and seen him for what he is. An obese flatterer with few qualities. He is useful, yes . . . but as a lover . . ."

"Perhaps he is a *good* lover."

William laughed briefly, incredulously. "There are many other men within court who could have served as well as Aldred. Swanne is a beautiful woman—"

"I wouldn't know," murmured Matilda.

"—and she could have any man she . . ." he stopped abruptly. He stepped to Matilda, and cradled her face in his hands. "Matilda, *you* will be queen beside me. I swear it to you."

"I expect to be, William. And Swanne?"

"I don't know." And he didn't. William didn't like to consider what Swanne would say once she learned Matilda was not to be pensioned off to some nunnery in Flanders. He remembered what she had done to Cornelia, how she had brutalized her, come near to murdering her, taken her child from her . . .

"I will protect you," William said to Matilda.

She frowned. What an odd thing to say. Before she could question him on the matter, William had let her go, walking to a chest beneath the window where lay several sheets of parchment and vellum. He picked them up, shuffling them in his hands and signaling through his action that he wanted the subject changed.

"The documents are all prepared," he said, "and the riders are waiting. They will be dispatched by this evening."

Matilda came to stand by him, leaning in close as she stared at the letters before her.

They were addressed to the leaders of Europe: Alexander II, the pope, leader of all Christendom; Henry IV, the Holy Roman Emperor, controller of the largest territory within Europe; Count Baldwin V of Flanders, Matilda's kinsman, who was not only an important prince in his own right, but was also the guardian to the young French king, Philip I; as well as scores of other lesser nobles and prelates. William was going to invade England, come what may, but he was going to make damned sure that he had the political and armed support of Europe behind him.

"I have also sent out word to my magnates," William said. "I will hold a great council in Lillebonne in a few weeks. When they agree, I will have an undivided Normandy behind me."

"Will they agree?" she said.

"Yes. The rewards will be too good to ignore."

"And the ships?" She almost whispered the question.

"I sent word yesterday, once the rumors grew strong." William had actually known the instant Edward had died, but had been forced to stay his hand until he heard the news by more conventional means. He didn't want whispers of murder by poisoning circulating. "The wharves of Dives River are already ringing with the sound of carpenters' hammers and adzes."

"When?" she said, and she had to say no other word for William to know of what she spoke.

"Late summer," he said. "Harold has until summer to enjoy his kingdom."

His stomach clenched. *Only another few months, a few months!*

CḊAPⳐER ELEVEN

WHILE INTELLECTUALLY, SWANNE SHOULD have known that Aldred and Asterion were one and the same man, one and the same *beast*, Asterion's subtle sorcery worked so well that emotionally they were entirely separate in her conscious mind. Once the coronation was past (and how she had *hated* seeing Harold enthroned, and that pale-faced bitch beside him), Aldred had settled her back into his London palace. Here, at least once a day, he brutalized her both physically and emotionally until she cringed whenever she heard his voice, or caught a whiff of his scent on bed linens or a discarded robe.

Asterion usually came to her once Aldred had departed. He would hold her, and soothe away her hurts, and tell her how beautiful and powerful she was, and whisper how good it would be when they ruled the Game together. Swanne never made the connection that Asterion appeared to her immediately after Aldred brutalized her, so that Swanne would grow so dependent on him, and so grateful to him, that she would do anything he wanted. Aldred unhinged Swanne's mind and made her cruelly vulnerable to Asterion's ensuing sweetness. Aldred was danger and pain; Asterion was relief from that pain.

Swanne was so grateful to Asterion, and now so desperately dependent on him, that it was difficult for her to disagree with anything Asterion said to her, or asked of her. Moreover, she found herself longing for those times when Asterion appeared. In a strange, bizarre fashion, she almost enjoyed the worst of Aldred's beatings and rapes because it meant that Asterion was likely to come to her within an hour or so of Aldred, leaving her writhing in agony.

Swanne was not sure what she wanted most from Asterion: the relief he represented; or the *power* he represented.

Strange that previously she had never thought of Asterion as a possible partner in the Game. She'd only ever considered Brutus, or William as he was now, as her Kingman. But she didn't *have* to use William, did she? Asterion was right. All she needed as Mistress of the Labyrinth was a Kingman.

It didn't matter *which* Kingman.

That realization had hit with almost a physical thud one day after Aldred had left her bruised and bleeding.

All she really needed was a Kingman.

She had selected Brutus because she'd thought he was the only one left. Indeed, there was no *selection* about it at all. It was him, or no one. She'd come to love him because of his power and attraction and vitality and because he was what she needed to fulfill her ambitions.

But there had been another choice apart from Brutus, hadn't there? Why hadn't she ever thought of Asterion? This puzzled Swanne in those long, silent afternoons she spent sewing with her ladies, their heads bent over their embroideries, unspeaking at their mistress's demand.

Why hadn't she ever thought of Asterion *beyond* considering him as a threat?

Asterion did not want to destroy the Game. He wanted to control it—a perfectly understandable ambition, had Swanne thought clearly enough about it before now.

To control the Game, all Asterion needed were the bands. And Swanne, the Mistress of the Labyrinth.

Imagine the Game she and he could build together!

The power . . .

The darkcraft in full flower . . .

Swanne could feel her ancient darkcraft reemerging. Every time Asterion lay with her, it became a little bit stronger. Asterion had put the darkcraft into Ariadne, and now he was putting it into Swanne.

She almost loved him for it.

No . . . she *did* love him for it.

As the weeks passed, Swanne found herself hardly thinking about William at all. All she wanted was to be free again, to be the mistress of a resurgent Game.

And all she needed to do that was to ensure that Asterion found the bands.

All she wanted was power, and Asterion seemed to represent the quicker, surer pathway to that than did William.

CbAPGER GWELVE

AWISE HAD SERVED AS SWANNE'S MAID AND THEN as senior attending woman for over twenty-five years. She'd known Swanne as a child in her father's manor, as the young woman who had seduced Harold to her bed, as the mother who had borne him six children, and, by virtue of Swanne's connection with Harold, as one of the most senior women at Edward's court.

Swanne had never been an easy woman, even when Hawise had first known her. She had been reclusive, demanding, cunning, charming. She had never been friendly, nor confiding. She had always seemed sure . . . of *something*, as if even from childhood she entertained a distant vision that only she could discern.

Even if she was never Hawise's friend, Hawise was as close to a friend as Swanne was ever likely to achieve. Thus, it was as a friend that Hawise asked Edward's physician Saeweald to attend her mistress. (After all, it was not as if Edward needed the constant attendance of the man now, was it?)

Swanne had shocked Hawise (as all the other ladies, and as all they gossiped to when she had not only moved herself to Aldred's palace in London, but accepted the corpulent cleric into her bed. If Hawise had been shocked by that action, then she had been stunned by the manner in which Aldred appeared to treat Swanne. Bruises. Bite marks. Bleeding.

Her mistress's face gaunt and haunted, and her eyes brimming with agony every morning.

Matters had improved vastly in the time since Edward's death. On those nights Aldred spent with Swanne (and that was most of them) there still came the sounds of muffled sobbing from behind the locked door of the bedchamber, and often in the morning there would be rusty streaks of dried blood staining the bed linens, but Swanne seemed to have improved within herself, and her bruises and wounds were far less, even nonexistent for days on end.

And yet . . .

Swanne was changed somehow, and most definitely not for the better. Her loveliness had become brittle. Her eyes, if possible, were darker, more unknowable, and often Hawise found Swanne watching her with a calculation and bleakness she found deeply disturbing. And despite her almost incessant bleeding, Swanne also appeared to be with child again (Hawise spent much time on her knees before whatever altar she could find praying that this child was Harold's final gift, and not Aldred's loathsome welcome), although Swanne denied it with vicious, hard words that one time Hawise had dared to venture the question.

And Swanne was growing thinner, as if the child (or whatever it was, if Swanne had been telling truth) was eating her from within. In Swanne's previous pregnancies she had never grown thin, but had blossomed and bloomed.

In essence, Swanne was growing thinner, harder, and darker—and more sharp-tongued as each day passed.

Hawise feared her mistress had a fatal, malignant growth within her and, though she knew Swanne would not thank her for it, took it upon herself to send for Saeweald. It was all she could do, and that Hawise did that much for a woman who had never given her much beyond harsh words, said a great deal about Hawise's generosity of spirit.

"I DID NOT SEND FOR YOU," SWANNE SAID AS Saeweald stood before her, one hand gently fingering the copper box of herbs at his waist. In his other hand, he grasped firmly a large leather satchel that Swanne presumed contained all the tricks of his trade.

Swanne's mouth curled. All Loth's "tricks of his trade" vanished that night he'd murdered Og along with Blangan in Mag's Dance two thousand years before.

"A friend sent for me," Saeweald said, and Swanne's eyes slid toward Hawise, standing calmly a few paces away.

"No friend to *me*," Swanne said, and Saeweald had to refrain from hitting the woman. Gods, as Genvissa she'd at least managed to maintain a semblance of respect toward the women and mothers in her circle. Even as Swanne, she'd managed a fragile veneer of sisterly communion with the women about her.

But this naked contempt. Swanne must be sure of herself indeed, and that worried Saeweald.

He'd been glad when Hawise approached him, handing to him on a platter the perfect excuse to visit—and examine, by all the luck of the gods!—Swanne. He'd heard from Caela how Swanne had accused her, and then how the Sidlesaghes felt there was something wrong with the Game *and* the land, some dark shift, and that it possibly concerned Swanne.

Well, and that was no surprise. Every "dark shift" always somehow concerned Swanne-Genvissa. If there was one lesson he'd learned in all his lives, then that was it.

"Do not discard friendship when it is offered to you," Saeweald said as he set his leather satchel down by his feet. He expected Swanne to sneer again, but she smiled, almost as if genuinely cheered by some thought that had come into her head, and then laughed, and gestured for one of her women to bring a chair forward for Saeweald.

To Saeweald's surprise, he saw that it was Damson, and he asked after her as he took the chair.

"Damson is well enough," said Swanne before the woman had a chance herself to answer, and waved her a dismissal.

"I'm surprised to see Damson in the archbishop's household," Saeweald said as he sat down.

Swanne raised her brows. "*I'm* surprised you even know her."

"I attended her once for a fever."

"Well, she is of no matter, her health of even less. Damson had asked if she might join my household here, and I saw no harm in it. I suppose she thought it preferable to serving that mealy-mouthed jade Harold took to wife."

They were sitting in the chamber that Aldred had put at Swanne's disposal. Saeweald had never been to the archbishop's London palace previously, and he had to admire the comforts with which the good archbishop surrounded himself.

Swanne being one of them, of course.

Like everyone else, Saeweald had wondered about this liaison, particularly as he knew Swanne better than most. Swanne could have had the pick of any noble male protector within the court—but *Aldred?* It was not like Swanne to select the most physically unattractive man about when, as Saeweald well knew from her previous existence, she preferred someone more delectable.

"You look amused," Swanne said, disdainfully raising one carefully plucked black eyebrow as only she could manage.

"I was imagining you with Aldred," Saeweald said, not inclined to play polite word games with her. "I was wondering *why*."

"It is none of your concern," Swanne snapped.

"Everything you do is my concern," Saeweald said. "You have a terrible penchant for destroying my entire world."

She smiled again, but this time it was so icy and so calculating, it made Saeweald's blood run cold.

He reached out a hand and took Swanne's wrist.

She drew back slightly, then relaxed and allowed Saeweald to feel her pulse.

Unable to bear her black-eyed, shrewd scrutiny, Saeweald looked down at her wrist. Her skin was so pale he could see the blue-veined blood vessels beneath, and he could feel the delicate bones shifting beneath his fingers. Her pulse beat strong and full, however.

Whatever had affected Swanne, whatever had caused this pallor and thinness and strange light in her eyes, it had not lessened her strength or, Saeweald suspected, her ambition and purpose.

"You must have heard from William recently," he murmured, making much fuss about feeling her pulse from several points on her wrist and lower forearm.

Swanne gave a tiny shrug of her shoulders.

"And you must be excited that—perhaps—he will shortly be here. I have no doubt that you cannot wait to see him again."

Swanne gave a small sigh, as if the matter was of supreme disinterest to her.

Saeweald's eyes flew to her face. That disinterested sigh had sounded *genuine*. Swanne? Didn't care if she saw William or not? It could not be!

"You do not spend every moment lusting for him?" Saeweald said.

Again that secretive smile. "I have a better lover," Swanne said.

Saeweald gave up any pretense of feeling Swanne's heartbeat. *"Aldred?"*

Something flashed over Swanne's face, and for an instant Saeweald thought it terror, but then an expression of the most supreme contentment took its place. "No," she said. *"Not* Aldred."

"I had thought the Mistress of the Labyrinth would spend her time lusting only for her Kingman."

Yet again Swanne said nothing, but held Saeweald's eyes with a disdain that told him she was hiding something momentous.

What?

And who? Swanne would not just discard William for an athletic lover, however skilled he might be in her bed. She would not just discard her *Kingman*.

Saeweald felt the germ of hope within him. Perhaps Swanne *had* changed. Perhaps she was prepared to abandon her ambitions as Mistress of the—

"Never think that," Swanne said, her voice a low hiss, and Saeweald screened his mind in sudden fright. "I will be the most powerful Mistress of the Labyrinth that ever was. The Game will be mine."

"But for that you will need William," Saeweald said, pushing the point.

Again that shrug, the slight, disdainful lifting of an eyebrow.

Saeweald sighed, hiding his confusion and concern with rummaging about in his satchel for a moment.

"I need none of your potions," Swanne said, irritated by Saeweald's fidgeting. "I am not ill."

Now it was Saeweald's turn to raise an eyebrow. "You do not look particularly well," he said. "You have lost much weight. There is a fever burning in your eyes. Hawise says that you may be pregnant—"

"Hawise is a fool!"

"Perhaps this lover of yours is potent."

Swanne smiled. "Oh, aye, that he is. But he fills me with . . . ah, this is not your concern, Saeweald. It is far and away not *your* concern."

He fills me with power. Saeweald could almost hear the words she had stopped.

"But enough of me," Swanne said, her tone almost girlish now. "I admit myself surprised, Saeweald, that you have not yourself sunk into a great blackness of spirit now that Mag has finally been disposed of. Caela, poor lost soul, must have been your final hope for some kind of . . . oh, some kind of purpose, I suppose."

Saeweald dropped his eyes, dampening that tiny gloat within him. *Well may you think Mag dead, Swanne . . .*

And then he looked back at Swanne again, meaning to say something trivial, and saw the blaze of understanding in her eyes, and knew that he had not been secretive enough.

"Mag is not dead, is she?"

Swanne rose to her feet, pushing Saeweald away. "Mag is not dead! Of course! The secretive, treacherous bitch. I should have known she would do something like this!"

SHE WAITED UNTIL ASTERION WAS ATOP HER, WITHIN her, driving both her and himself into a panting, moaning lust before she told him, gasping the words as she felt Asterion climax within her.

"Mag is alive."

"What?" He pulled himself back from her, raising himself up on straightened arms, his ebony face glistening with sweat.

There was a little trickle of perspiration running down the center of his moist black nose, and Swanne found herself momentarily fascinated by it. "Mag is not dead."

"Of course not. I knew this."

"You thought you killed her!"

He grinned, the expression horrible on his bull's face. "Oh, but I mean to."

She narrowed her eyes, and he thought she looked so beautifully sly that he had to bend his head down and kiss her mouth.

"What do you know that I don't?" she said, pulling her mouth free.

A great deal, he thought. "Only that we have the means to finally trap her," he said. "Would you like that, my love?"

She breathed in deeply, and Asterion's eyes clouded over with renewed desire as he felt her breasts move beneath his chest.

"Oh, aye," she said.

CHAPTER THIRTEEN

CAELA SPEAKS

J RETIRED, EDWARD'S RELICT, TO ST. MARGARET
the Martyr's, that small priory I had endowed so many years
ago.

The sense of independence was astounding. Ecub gave me several small
chambers that were at the very end of the priory's main group of buildings.
Here I had access to the herb garden, the refectory, the chapel, and the outside as much as I wished. Of all my ladies, Judith was the only one to come
with me (the others gratefully transfering themselves to Alditha's household), and Saeweald took the opportunity to take over the running of the priory's herb garden and infirmary. I have no idea what gossip ran through
London about this arrangement—no doubt that the physician spent most of
his time sampling the wares within the sisters' dormitory rather than tasting
the sweetness of his medicinal draughts—but none of that bothered us
within the calm of St Margaret's. Saeweald spent his nights with Judith, and
I . . .

I spent my nights either blessedly alone (ah! The wonder of not having to
share a chamber, let alone a bed!) or even more blessedly in company atop
Pen Hill. Here I climbed late at night, aye, even in the depths of winter, and
here the Sidlesaghes came to me, and sang, and comforted me. Ecub often
joined me, and also Judith and many of the sisters of Ecub's order. The cold
did not perturb us, for we were warm with power and shared femininity and a
shared *oneness* with the land.

It cheered me to think that not all had been lost, and that a few still
remembered the old ways.

One day, I thought, I would be able to dance here with my lover, with Og, with the white stag with the blood-red antlers and the bands of power about his limbs.

One day.

ONE EVENING SAEWEALD CAME TO VISIT ME, AS HE SO often did.

I was seated with Judith and Ecub, and Saeweald joined us about the small fire I had burning in the hearth.

"I have seen Swanne," he said as he sat.

A bleakness overcame my heart. I had almost forgotten her existence. And at that realization I felt dreadful, for I could not afford to forget Swanne, who somehow I had to persuade to pass over her gifts as Mistress of the Labyrinth.

Saeweald's eyes dropped to the hands in his lap. "But before I relate what news I gleaned there, I must make a confession."

We waited. Saeweald finally raised his eyes.

"I was incautious," he said. "She gleaned from my mind that Mag is not as dead as she had thought."

I felt a nasty jab of fear, but quickly suppressed it. "And what can she do with this knowledge, Saeweald? It is unfortunate, perhaps, but the main thing is that Asterion does not know."

I saw Ecub and Judith exchange a worried glance, but I spoke again quickly, before any of them could voice their thoughts. "But what did you discover, Saeweald?"

"She has taken a lover," he said.

Ecub, Judith, and I shrugged simultaneously. Whether as Genvissa or as Swanne, the woman was always taking lovers.

"A lover who has supplanted William in her heart and in her estimation."

"I cannot believe that!" I said. Then . . . "Has she . . ."

"Decided to abandon the cause of the Game?" Saeweald said. "Forsworn her duties as Mistress of the Labyrinth? Nay, I am afraid not, Caela. She made it very clear to me that she is the Mistress of the Labyrinth, she *will* be the Mistress of the Labyrinth, and the Game is hers to control as she pleases."

I felt a twinge of worry. I kept waiting for some enlightenment as to how it was I might persuade Swanne to hand over her powers as Mistress of the Labyrinth but that knowledge continued to elude me. Still, I must trust, and surely it would become plain to me.

But . . . Swanne had found a lover to supplant William?

"She has taken a lover who has supplanted William?" I said. "How can that *possibly* be?"

"Aldred," Judith said. "Who else."

Saeweald shot her a disbelieving look. "Aldred the great lover who has made Swanne forget William? I can hardly credit it."

I could no longer bear inactivity, so I stood and paced back and forth in the narrow space of the semicircle we made before the fire. "*This* must be the shift the Sidlesaghes felt in the Game and the land," I said. "Swanne's lover."

I halted, and fixed Saeweald with a penetrating glare. "Perhaps Swanne is misleading you about this man, this lover, for her own purposes."

"No." Saeweald said. "I would stake my life on her genuine affection and regard for this man."

"But how can that be!" I made an impatient gesture and resumed my pacing. "William can be the only man for her. She needs a Kingman. She can't just *dismiss* William!"

"Aye," Saeweald said. "I do not like this. My foreboding merely grows the stronger for this news."

"We need to know who this man is," said Ecub. "We need to know more about Swanne. What is happening with her? *How can she have decided to abandon William?*"

I exchanged a glance with Saeweald. "I could visit her and—"

"No!" Ecub and Judith said as one.

"Too dangerous, surely," Judith added. "Especially as she knows that Mag still lives."

"Swanne examined me after Asterion killed the false Mag," I said. "She knows there is no Mag in *me*. She will think merely that Mag has hopped elsewhere." I smiled with what I hoped was persuasion. "Swanne might talk to me, if only to brag. She always did enjoy bragging to me about her lovers."

"Still . . ." said Ecub.

"Damson," Saeweald put in, his voice slow. "Damson is with Swanne."

"What?" I said. "With *Swanne?* What is Damson doing with Swanne?"

Saeweald shrugged. "Swanne said that Damson had asked if she might join Swanne's household at Aldred's palace. I have no idea why, for Damson would just as surely have had a place in Harold and Alditha's household as she had in Edward's."

Damson was my responsibility, I thought. *I should have seen her settled somewhere safer—and obviously she felt unsettled enough to go into service with Swanne, of all people. She was my responsibility.*

"Caela . . ." Saeweald said. "Damson is your means to watch Swanne with far more safety than if you attended the witch in person. Swanne will be unguarded about Damson where she will be cunning and sly about you. Damson is your entry into Swanne's world."

I sat silent, not liking it. I had come to hate "using" sweet, trusting Damson in the manner that I did, and to use her in this way was to place her in terrible danger.

I could see that Ecub and Judith were not happy with Saeweald's suggestion, either, but it was too good an opportunity to lose.

"I can fetch her to you," Saeweald said softly.

I looked down at my hands curled tight in my lap, and lowered my head in agreement.

SAEWEALD ARRANGED MY MEETING WITH DAMSON some six days later. By virtue of her service to Aldred, whose palace lay within the boundaries of London, Damson could not stray from London itself, so, accompanied by Mother Ecub and Judith, I traveled heavily draped and veiled to London to meet Damson there. I occupied a room in a sister house to St. Margaret's—Mother Ecub said I was a noble lady who needed solitude and privacy in order to pray for her dead husband's soul—and there I waited.

In the late afternoon Saeweald bought Damson to me.

He'd not told her whom he brought her to meet, only that he needed some assistance with draining fluid from the lungs of a woman who had the creeping blackness in her chest. When Ecub opened the door to Saeweald's soft tap, and Damson saw who awaited her within, her simple, clear face burst into a radiant smile, and she sank into a deep curtsy before me.

"Madam!" she said. "I have prayed for your happiness every night."

My guilt increased. How could I use this woman as I did? I determined that, whatever happened, Damson should not suffer for it.

"Damson," I said, keeping my voice light. I took her hands in mine and raised her to her feet and, leaning forward, kissed her on the mouth.

Instantly our souls transposed.

As I entered Damson, I felt a brief, lingering trace of her unfeigned joy at seeing me and my guilt again stabbed deep.

I would see this woman safe. I would.

ALDRED HAD HIMSELF A FINE PALACE WITHIN London. It was richer and larger than most others—even the bishop of London himself did not command such magnificence, let alone any of the nobles who maintained residences within the city walls. Aldred had made himself rich indeed on Edward's munificence, I thought, as I made my way through the halls and chambers to where Saeweald had told me Swanne had her private apartments. I took care to maintain Damson's habitual modesty of demeanor, and, keeping my shoulders slumped and my face averted, I entered Swanne's outer chamber without any challenge from the guards.

It was late afternoon and Swanne was enjoying a light repast. Hawise, Swanne's senior attending woman, made a sharp remark to me about my tardiness in returning from my errand, but that was the only comment made.

"Here," Hawise said, handing me some linens. "His lordship has spent the afternoon with my lady. Her bed shall need to be changed."

I took the linens silently and, equally as silently, I slipped into Swanne's chamber.

Swanne was sitting by a brazier to one end of the chamber, picking without much apparent interest at a plate of food set before her. She paid me no attention as I made my way to the bed, and I glanced surreptitiously at her.

She seemed very pale, and had lost weight, but even so, she was still fabulously beautiful. Her hair was bound under a veil, although several strands of it straggled over her neck that was, I was concerned to see, slightly reddened in patches, as if someone had grabbed at it with thick fingers.

Swanne must have felt my eyes on her, for she turned to me and snapped, "Just change the linens and remove yourself, Damson. I have no interest in holding a conversation."

I averted my head, terrified she should have seen *more* than Damson in my eyes, but Swanne said no more, and when I glanced once more at her, as I began to strip the coverlets from the bed, I saw that her attention was back on the plate of food.

I looked to the bed, and barely managed to restrain a gasp of horror.

That Aldred had lain with her recently was apparent—there were stains smeared across half the bed—but what was appalling was that there were *also* great streaks of blood marring the creamy linens. *Her flux?* I thought, then dismissed it, for this blood was not that of a woman's monthly courses, but the rich red of arterial flow.

By all the gods in existence, what was Aldred doing to her? This was the lover she had crowed about to Saeweald?

I could feel Swanne's eyes on me once more, so I hurriedly stripped the bed and remade it with the fresh linens.

"Burn those soiled linens," said Swanne. "They are unredeemable."

"Yes, madam," I muttered, and scurried out, the offending linens stuffed under my arm.

* * *

I WAS NOT INVITED BACK INTO SWANNE'S CHAMBER
that day. No one entered save Hawise, and I heard Swanne snarling at her on
those brief occasions when the door opened or closed.

Late at night, long after the bells for compline had rung, Aldred himself
returned. He rumbled into the outer chamber, wrapped in furs against the
night cold, and exuded charm and bonhomie.

Hawise shot him a black look, and did not meet his eyes. Frankly, I was
not surprised. If Swanne had been *my* lady, and even being Swanne, I think I
would have sunk a knife into the fat archbishop's belly for what he did to her.

Aldred called for wine and meat, then vanished into Swanne's chamber.

In the instant before the door swung shut, I saw Swanne's white face.

It radiated sheer dread.

A kitchen hand appeared in due course with both wine and with meat, and
Hawise took them in.

As she came out I heard the door lock behind her.

An hour or so later, as Hawise, myself, and several of Swanne's other
women had settled on our pallets for the night, I heard the first shriek.

The good archbishop had patently finished his meal and had now com-
menced on the evening's entertainment.

There came another shriek and, despite myself, I raised myself up on an
elbow and looked about the chamber. Surely Hawise or the other women
would do something?

But all I received for my concern was a sharp reprimand from Hawise to
go back to sleep.

The sounds of agony issuing from Swanne's chamber were not, most apparently, my concern.

IT CONTINUED FOR WHAT SEEMED LIKE HOURS—THAT
sobbing anguish from behind the locked door. Eventually I could stand no
more and, despite the danger I knew it would bring to both myself and to
Damson, I decided to do something about it.

The other women, while pretending to be asleep, were actually still very
much awake, so I cast over them a gentle enchantment of peace and rest and
they slipped quietly into slumber. Then I rose from my own pallet and
approached the door.

I put my ear to it, and heard nothing.

Perhaps they were asleep.

I risked all. I placed my eye against a slight crack between two of the planks of the door and, again using just a fraction of power, widened that gap so I could see into the chamber.

For a moment all I could make out were shifting shadows, but then they resolved themselves into shapes. A single lamp had been left glowing by the chair where Swanne had been seated earlier and by its shifting light I could make out the bed.

They were not asleep at all. Aldred's massive form was humping over Swanne's gaunt white body, back and forth, back and forth.

Her hands were to her sides, hanging over the sides of the bed, her hands clenched into fists.

Aldred's tempo increased, and something made me look from his body to the shadow his bulk cast on the wall behind the bed.

It showed not *his* form at all, but that of a monstrous bull-headed man.

I DO NOT KNOW HOW I MANAGED TO TEAR MYSELF from that door, nor how I managed to lay back on my pallet as if nothing had happened. I knew I could not risk Damson by fleeing in sudden panic into the night. I would have to wait until morning, then make some excuse so that I could slip back to where Ecub, Judith, and Saeweald guarded my own sleeping form.

I lay there all night, sleepless, terrified that Asterion would thunder from that chamber and assault me.

No wonder that Swanne appeared ill. No wonder she appeared changed. No wonder Silvius had felt something so wrong.

Aldred was Asterion.

Aldred had Swanne. Asterion had her captive.

I remembered that day so many weeks ago when Swanne had come to my chamber and questioned me about the movement of the bands. How she had said to me, *I've taken Aldred to my bed.*

That had surely been a plea for help, but I had not understood it.

How she had looked terrified when I had said, "Do you think that I am still Asterion's pawn? Still dancing to his tune?"

No, I was not the one now dancing to Asterion's tune.

Swanne was now his pawn, by some hold I could not yet understand.

I should have seen it. *I should have seen it.*

I lay there, sleepless, my eyes closed, and wept.

CĐAPTER FOURTEEN

WANNE WOKE CLOSE TO DAWN, ACHING AND
bleeding, and found Asterion pacing the chamber.

She rose, glad beyond knowing, and held out her arms.

He came to her, gathering her close, and soothed away the hurts and
bruises that Aldred had given her.

"How I loathe that man," she whispered as Asterion carried her back to
the blood-sodden bed and began to make love to her.

"I know," he whispered, moving sweetly over her. "I hate what he does to
you as well."

"I wish you would come to me more often," Swanne said, weeping now.
She was entirely lost. Where once Swanne had known Asterion used Aldred's
body to hurt her, now she had become so dependent on Asterion she had forgotten it entirely. She was totally incapable of realizing that Asterion continued to use Aldred to hurt her so that Swanne would become ever more reliant
on Asterion, ever more willing to do whatever he asked of her, ever more vulnerable to his subtle sorcery.

"I come to you as often as I can," he said, bending down his face to kiss
her.

"I adore you," she said, cradling his monstrous head in her hands, loving
the bestial musk of his breath.

"I know."

"I will do anything for you," she said, moaning now as he thrust into her,
feeling his darkcraft fill her.

"Indeed you will," he said, and then they fell speechless as their moans
and groans consumed them.

Later, as dawn broke and they heard Swanne's women rise and move
about in the outer chamber, Asterion nuzzled Swanne's ear and said, very low,
"Mag was here last night."

"What!" Swanne almost fell out of bed as she struggled upright.

"She was watching you with Aldred, using her power to scry through the
door. You did not feel it?"

Swanne frowned, trying to remember, but all she could recall was the agony of Aldred. "Who is she?" she said.

"One of the women within Aldred's household," Asterion said.

"I'll *kill* the bitch! I'll kill them *all*, just to make sure!"

Asterion laughed, and stroked Swanne's naked back, feeling his palm bump over successive ridges of her spine. She was getting too thin. Way too thin, when Asterion needed her to seduce William into her bed. Perhaps he should pull the imp back a little, suppress his appetite a fraction. Even given Brutus and Genvissa's history, Asterion doubted William would succumb to a walking corpse.

"Shall I lay the trap for you, my dear?" he said.

She turned her face to him, and smiled.

THAT NIGHT, IN THE HOUR BEFORE DAWN, AS MONKS and priests across Europe were filing their cold, huddled groups into chapels and cathedrals to sing Matins, a great fire appeared in the sky.

CHAPTER FIFTEEN

*S*AMSON HAD GONE BACK TO ALDRED'S PALACE, and now Caela sat white-faced and trembling before Ecub, Saeweald, and Judith. Silvius was there also, having knocked quietly on the door a few moments after Caela returned. He was standing by a chair, his face dark with worry as he regarded Caela.

The words tumbled out of her mouth. "Aldred is Asterion! Aldred is Asterion. He has Swanne. He has forced her to his will—I have no idea how. Oh, gods, gods . . . Silvius . . . my friends . . . what are we going to do? *He has Swanne!*"

Silvius sat down on a stool with a thump. He exchanged one shocked look with Saeweald, then clenched his fists where they rested on his thighs. "Asterion has Swanne?" he said. "Asterion has the Mistress of the Labyrinth? No wonder the Game has felt so wrong!"

"The entire world feels wrong," Saeweald said. "The great fire in the sky is sure evidence of it."

There was silence, several among the group shuddering. Everyone had risen this morning to the news—*Look! Look! Look to the sky!* All London—all Christendom, surely—was jittery with nerves. It was a comet, the more learned said, but no one had ever seen anything like this before. The blazing fire covered almost a third of the sky. Who rode it? Some devil rider? A fiend from hell itself? And what if it crashed earthward?

Who had it been sent to destroy?

"Caela," Saeweald said. "Do you know anything of this?"

She shook her head. "The fire in the sky is unfamiliar to me. It has nothing of the land or the waters about it. It is cold, angry, alien. Worse even than Asterion." She gave a tight, humorless smile.

No one returned it.

"There is disaster coming," muttered Ecub. "None can doubt it."

"We can only hope it prophesies disaster for Swanne and Asterion rather than for us," said Silvius.

"What if it means Asterion is going to destroy the Game and all our hopes with it?" Judith said. "Is it coincidence that on the night Caela discovers the truth about Swanne and her new lover that this great fire appears hanging above our heads?"

"Asterion *will* use Swanne to destroy the Game," Ecub said. "None can doubt it."

Silvius grunted. "And *you* should become a prophetess of doom, Mother Ecub. None should doubt that."

She shot him a black look.

Saeweald looked at Caela, now with Judith's arm about her shoulders for comfort, then to Silvius.

"If he has the Mistress of the Labyrinth," he said, "and if he wanted to destroy the Game, then all Asterion would need to do is kill her. Swanne is the only woman alive who can command the powers of the Mistress. If Asterion has her alive, then there is a reason for that, surely."

There was a silence, disturbed only by Caela's deep, tremulous breathing as she brought her emotions under control.

"What do you mean?" Silvius said eventually.

Saeweald shrugged. "For the gods' sakes, Silvius, do you not sit in the heart of the Game? Were you not once a Kingman? What I am *saying* is that if Asterion wanted to destroy the Game, and if he controls Swanne, then all he needs to do is to kill her." He paused. "And if he hasn't, then there is a reason for that, and we should determine what that might be."

"What does Asterion need in order to destroy the Game?" Caela said to Silvius. "Could he accomplish it by Swanne's murder?"

"No," Silvius said. "He would need both Swanne and control over the kingship bands. That means he needs control over both Swanne and William."

"Then that is why he hasn't killed Swanne!" Caela said. "He needs to take William as well; whatever else, Asterion can't leave William free." She looked at Silvius, then as quickly looked away again.

"But you are moving the bands," Saeweald said.

"William can still find them easily enough," Caela said. "He is their King-man. They call to him constantly."

"So Asterion needs William to find the bands," Saeweald said. "And for this he has—somehow—taken Swanne. She is both bait and trap. Ah! We may as well assume William's loss now, for he will fall into Swanne's arms as easily as if he were a babe seeking his mother's milk!" He looked at Caela. "And what do *we* need to control the Game, to wed it to this land forever and trap Asterion in his turn?"

"We need Swanne to pass on her powers as Mistress of the Labyrinth to me, and we need—"

"William to pass over his powers as Kingman to . . . to whoever shall rise as Og," said Saeweald. One of his hands raised momentarily to his chest, as if to touch the tattoo beneath, then dropped back to his lap.

"Yes," said Caela, her voice flat.

"Let us concentrate on Swanne for the moment," said Ecub. "We cannot let her remain within Asterion's grasp."

"Do you suggest we somehow rescue her?" said Saeweald.

"A rescued Swanne would undoubtedly be a very grateful Swanne," Judith said. "Prepared, perhaps, to hand over her powers as Mistress of the Labyrinth?"

Silvius nodded. "My thoughts exactly." He turned to Caela. "Saeweald and Judith are right, Caela. You told us earlier that you should have recognized Swanne's scream for help when you heard it. Well, now you *have* heard it. We *know* that Swanne wants to be rescued from Aldred-Asterion's grasp. One of your's, and this land's, greatest problems has always been in the persuasion of Swanne to hand over to you her powers as Mistress of the Labyrinth. Now, perhaps, Asterion has handed us our bargaining power. If Swanne has the choice of handing the power to Asterion, or handing it to you . . ."

"I don't know," said Caela. "For many months I have sought out the means by which Swanne might be persuaded to hand me her powers as Mistress of the Labyrinth. I was—*am*—sure that when I saw or heard of this means, I would recognize it. This does not feel right."

"Why?" said Saeweald.

Caela made a helpless gesture.

"You can't ignore it," said Silvius. "Swanne must be desperate for release from Asterion. This very well could be the chance you've been waiting for, Caela.

"Silvius is right," said Saeweald. "We offer Swanne freedom in exchange for her freely handing to Caela the powers of Mistress of the Labyrinth. Then, once William realizes Swanne has handed on her powers, he will do so as well."

Ecub's mouth twisted. This all sounded very naïve to her. "I'm sorry to disagree," she said. "But surely Swanne would prefer to see the world destroyed before she 'handed over' any of her powers? And why do you assume that she wants to escape Asterion? Did she not boast to Saeweald of her new lover? Of how she apparently preferred him to William? Does none of this sound a note of danger to any of you?"

"There is *no* way that Swanne could ever want to ally herself with Asterion," Silvius said forcefully. "None whatsoever. *Why?* He wants to destroy the Game, Swanne wants to use it to achieve immortal power. She wants Asterion destroyed. She cannot possibly want to ally with him."

There was a silence, finally broken by Caela. "Yes," she said. "I agree with Silvius. Swanne cannot be allied with him. If she has boasted of her new lover, then they were words Asterion forced her to speak. What I saw in that chamber was not an act of love and consent, but of violence and domination. Asterion is murdering Swanne by slow degrees."

"Aye," said Saeweald. "She *is* ill. This cannot be 'want' on her part."

Ecub sighed and nodded. "Very well."

Caela gave her a smile, then addressed the group. "If we manage to free Swanne, can we hide her from Asterion?"

"Yes," said Silvius. "I think so. We can secret her within the Game itself. There she can teach Caela."

"Possibly," said Caela. "I, for one, still doubt that any rescue, even one of this magnitude, will make Swanne so pathetically grateful she'll just pass over her powers. Ah, no need to look so concerned, Silvius. I agree we should at least try. Who knows? Miracles can happen."

There were nods from Silvius, Judith, and Saeweald, and a mild shrug of agreement from Ecub.

"How do we free her from Asterion?" Caela asked. "Surely, if it was a simple matter of just walking away . . ."

"We need to know just what power he holds over her," said Silvius. "Caela, you will need to speak to her. Let her know that she is not alone. That she *will* be rescued."

Caela nodded.

"As Damson."

"Oh, no! Silvius . . . I do not want to do that! It was enough that I risked her as much as I did when—"

"You *cannot* go as yourself!" Saeweald said. "It is too dangerous—especially since Swanne now knows Mag is not dead. What if she has told Asterion? Caela, if you use Damson, then you will have the chance of escape should . . ."

"Should Asterion discover what I do," said Caela, her tone bitter. "In which case Damson will be killed."

"Better her than you," Silvius said. "You know that."

"I owe Damson more than this!"

"You owe this *land* more than Damson," Silvius retorted. "Never lose sight of that."

There was a long silence, then Caela gave one single, reluctant nod.

IN ANY EVENT, IT WAS ALMOST SEVEN WEEKS BEFORE Caela could do anything about approaching Swanne. On the morning that she told Silvius, Saeweald, and Judith of what she'd discovered in Swanne's bedchamber, Harold ordered Aldred north to his see of York. Rebel sentiments were stirring, and Harold needed Aldred to return to York to work on Harold's behalf.

Swanne went with him. A few days after Swanne and Aldred had left, the great fire in the sky faded and then vanished, and everyone breathed a little easier.

Doom had been averted, it appeared.

In itself, Swanne's journey north need not have delayed Silvius' plan to use Damson to approach Swanne, but Damson herself had unexpectedly traveled to her home village in Cornwall where her mother lay dying. Until Damson and Swanne were within the same town, it would be impossible for Caela to use Damson to approach Swanne.

Meanwhile, and now knowing who Asterion was, and, most important, where he was, the Sidlesaghes and Caela moved a fourth band. This time Caela took a band from its hiding place close to the London Bridge and shifted it five miles to the southwest of London to a small village called Clopeham where Caela handed the band to a Sidlesaghe sitting mournfully on a stool at the junction of two roads.

There was no interference, no trouble, no disturbance. The move was effected quickly and smoothly.

Asterion made no attempt to halt them, and Caela supposed that this time it was because he was so far distant.

CHAPTER SIXTEEN

SWANNE ARCHED HER BACK, STRETCHING OUT her stiff muscles, then bent her elegant neck slowly from side to side. The journey back from York had taken three days of hard riding, and three nights of . . .

Swanne forced her mind away from Aldred. She would not think about those nights.

She wouldn't.

Swanne sat down in a chair, as close to the fire as she could manage without setting her rose-colored gown ablaze, thinking on Asterion. She hadn't seen him for over a week. He'd appeared now and again while she and Aldred had been in the north, but far more infrequently than he'd come to her here in London. Swanne missed him—and resented his absences—horribly.

It was not only that Asterion's gentle touch soothed Aldred's agonies, nor even that when he lay with her he increased her darkcraft a fraction more. It was that Swanne simply missed *him*.

How could she ever have lain with Harold . . . and borne him six children?

How could she have ever thought she loved William, and believed him her true mate in power?

How could she have ignored Asterion for all these years? How could she never have *realized*?

Swanne's mind was now so consumed with Asterion, with the need for his presence and touch, that her conscious mind was no longer aware that Aldred and Asterion were one and the same. That Aldred tormented her merely so that Asterion could soothe her.

Aldred she feared and loathed beyond measure. Asterion she craved as much as life and power itself.

Another band had moved during her absence from London (by Silvius, Swanne supposed). The night it had moved, Asterion made one of his rare visits to Swanne while she was in York. Aldred for once had left her alone—he'd gone to spend a day or so at a monastery just to the west of York where he suspected the abbot was falsifying his estate accounts.

Asterion had come to Swanne, and soothed her and held her and loved her and said that the band's movement did not matter.

"William will be able to find it soon enough," he'd said. "As he will all of them. And when William has the bands . . ."

"We pounce," Swanne had whispered into the beast's mouth as he bent to kiss her.

"William will do anything for you," Asterion said.

"Anything," Swanne murmured.

"And when we have him . . . then he will do everything for *us*. Tell me, my love, do you think the bands will look elegant encircling my limbs?"

Swanne had run her hands over the creature's thickly muscled biceps. "They were meant for you," she'd said, and Asterion had smiled, and had given her more of the darkcraft that night than he had hitherto.

Now, Swanne sat by the fire, shivering despite its heat, and waited.

Mag would come to her today. She could *feel* it—not merely that Mag would come, but that the trap she and Asterion had set was about to spring.

Swanne closed her eyes, blessing Asterion for the renewed sense of dark-craft within her, then composed her face and put upon it the expression of the battered victim—that of equal parts; fear, hope, and submission.

The door opened.

Swanne took a deep breath and opened her eyes . . . then could not help widening them as she saw who it was.

Damson?

Ah! Mag had ever had a penchant for obscure, worthless fools.

"Damson?" Swanne said in her most chilling voice—she could not let the tiresome witch know she'd been expected. "What do you here? The linens have already been changed and I have no further use for you. You may leave."

But Damson did not leave, as Swanne knew she would not.

"Madam," Damson said, carefully closing the door behind her and looking about the chamber to ensure they were alone.

"Damson," Swanne said again, stiffening in her chair as if deeply affronted. *"You may leave!"*

"I cannot, Swanne," the Damson-who-was-not-quite-Damson said, and she came directly to Swanne, hesitated, then pulled up a stool close to Swanne's chair and sat herself down.

"How dare you sit in my presence!" Swanne said, allowing a note of anger to creep into her voice.

"I am not Damson," said the woman. "Not entirely."

And she looked directly into Swanne's eyes.

Swanne did not have to fake the surprise that flared across her face.

"Gods!" she whispered. *"Mag?"* This was not the Mag that Swanne had

known in her earlier life, but one infinitely more dangerous, far more powerful. This was, somehow, a *youthful* Mag, a Mag at the beginning of her promise, a Mag who could grow into a true threat.

How had she managed this? Swanne barely managed to keep herself still in
her chair. She had a wild urge to dash to the window and fling aside the shutters, and scream for Asterion.

No, no. She must be calm. He would be here soon enough.

And yet it wouldn't be soon enough, would it? No time would be soon
enough to rid themselves of this unexpectedly powerful enemy.

"Mag," Swanne said again, her voice more controlled now.

Damson-Mag gave a slight nod. "I am she who walks as the mother goddess of this land," she said. "Not dead, after all, Swanne."

"You always did know how to slip away from danger, didn't you?"

"I draw on a long association with the Darkwitches, Swanne. I have
learned well."

Swanne bared her teeth in equal amounts smile and snarl.

"And now you have come to gloat?" she said.

Damson shook her head. "Swanne, I have come to make you an offer."

Oh! The smugness of it! "An *offer*! And what might that be?"

Damson took a deep breath. "In return for your freedom from Asterion's
malicious grip, in return for your *life*, because Asterion is surely murdering
you by degrees, I need you to teach me the ways and powers of the Mistress
of the Labyrinth."

Swanne stared unblinking at Damson, her lips slightly parted, shocked
into total silence. There was nothing, absolutely *nothing*, that Damson could
have said to stun her more. "You . . . *what?*" she finally managed.

"The Game has changed," Damson said. "Altered."

Swanne said nothing, still staring at Damson as if she had turned into a
frog before her eyes.

Damson took a deep breath, as if coming to a decision within herself. "The
Game has grown in the two thousand years that Asterion kept everyone
within death. It has merged with the land itself, allied with it. Now the Game
and the land have a single purpose."

Swanne still said nothing. Her mind was racing, trying to take in all Damson was saying, and what this was leading to. Mag? Wanted to be the Mistress
of the Labyrinth? *Why?*

In her lap, Swanne's hands twisted over and over.

Again Damson took a deep breath. "The Game wants myself and Og to
complete it as the Mistress and Kingman."

Swanne's mouth dropped open even farther, and her eyes widened impossibly. It was not so much that the Game and the land had apparently decided

between themselves that Mag and Og should complete the Game as Mistress and Kingman, although that was unbelievable enough, but that Og still lived! *Og? Alive?*

"Og . . ." Swanne managed to get out, more a groan than a true word. "Og is . . . *alive?*"

Damson gave a single nod.

Swanne slumped back into her chair, unable for the moment to accept it. "But Loth slew him when he slew his mother, Blangan."

"He almost did, yes. But Mag was in that stone dance as well that night, secreted within Cornelia's womb, and she cast an enchantment upon him that has kept him alive, just, all these years. He rests, waiting."

Swanne noted that Damson-Mag still did not say "I," but "Mag." Why that distance? "Where?" she said.

Damson hesitated, then apparently decided that truth would persuade Swanne more quickly than falsehood. "In the heart of the Game."

"Gods," Swanne whispered. Her mind was still whirling. *Asterion should know this! Soon!*

Damson mistook Swanne's shock for indecision, and she leaned forward and took Swanne's hands in her own.

Swanne did not resist.

"Swanne, please, let me help you. You and I share neither friendship, or even a semblance of respect each for the other."

True enough, thought Swanne.

"But I can help you. I can free you from Asterion. I know he masquerades as Aldred."

Swanne wanted to scream at the stupid bitch that Asterion was not Aldred, but managed to hold her tongue.

"If I aid you to freedom, Swanne, I would that you teach me the ways of the Labyrinth in return."

"Foolish" could not possibly encompass the inanity of this suggestion, Swanne thought, allowing a frown of indecision to crease her forehead, as if she truly considered what Damson offered. *Hand to her my powers as Mistress of the Labyrinth? How could she ever have thought that I would do such a thing?*

"A deal, Swanne," Damson said, now grasping Swanne's hands very tightly and leaning in to her very close. "In return for your freedom from Asterion, you hand to me your powers as Mistress of the Labyrinth."

"I . . ." Swanne said, and then her eyes altered slightly, as if she saw something behind Damson.

In an instant Swanne's hands twisted in Damson's, grasping them in a cruel grip.

Damson pulled back, but could not break free from Swanne's grasp, and in the next moment her own face went as slack in shock as Swanne's had been for most of their conversation.

Two heavy hands had fallen on her shoulders, pinning her to the stool.

"Well, well, Mag," said a chilling male voice. "What a posy of surprises *you* have turned out to be."

Damson struggled on the stool, but she was caught in the twin grips of Swanne and Asterion.

Swanne looked to her lover, an expression of unfeigned love and rapture on her face. "Asterion," she breathed. "Oh, how I have missed you."

Both her expression and words were enough for Damson to let out a shocked cry. "No! Swanne! No! What are you doing?"

Swanne turned her face back to Damson, her expression now twisted with hate and loathing. "Think you that I would ever hand *you* my powers? Think you that I have any intention of completing the Game with *William*? Nay, *this* is my lover, my partner, my mate, and *this* time, my dear darling Mag, you are to be given no chance of flight at all."

She let go Damson's hands and, although Caela-within-Damson tried to wrench herself tree of Asterion's hands, and tried to use every piece of power she had against him, he held both her form and her power in check with infinite ease.

Swanne rose and, with deliberate slowness, reached with one hand into the pocket of her robe.

Very gradually, very deliberately, keeping her own eyes steady on Damson's frantic face, she drew her hand forth.

In it she clasped the twisted horn-handled knife of Asterion.

"Do you recognize it, you witless bitch?" Swanne whispered. "Do you remember how you made Cornelia plunge this into *me*? Well, now you feel what it is like, Mag, to have cold metal end your ambitions and hopes."

And with that she hefted the knife, then plunged it into the soft, tender skin at the juncture of Damson's neck and shoulder.

CHAPTER SEVENTEEN

SAEWEALD, ECUB, AND JUDITH WERE SITTING company with Caela's body as it lay still on the bed.

Within, Damson's soul slept unknowing.

Then, suddenly, all three gasped as a bright red spot appeared at the base of Caela's neck, and then flowered into a crimson pool of blood.

"No!" cried Saeweald, and lunged forward.

"OH GODS," SWANNE MOANED, AS IF IN THE ECSTASY of love-making, "how I have *longed* to sink this knife into Mag! At last! At last!"

Behind Damson, Asterion was almost doubled over with laughter, although he kept his hands firmly on Damson's shoulders.

Swanne viciously twisted the knife until the blade sank completely into Damson's body. "I only wish you were Caela, bitch, then my happiness would be complete."

Damson's hands were grasping at Swanne's, but they were slippery with the blood that now pumped out of her neck, and she could not dislodge Swanne's grip on the knife.

"No," she said in a horrible bubbling whisper. "No, Swanne, please . . ."

But Swanne was not listening. Her eyes were wide and glassy, her mouth open, and her hands twisted again and again as she leaned so hard on the knife that she forced even the twisted-horn handle into Damson's body.

SAEWEALD GRABBED AT CAELA'S SHOULDERS, SHAKING her as violently as he could. "Come back now!" he shouted. "Now! For Og's sake, Caela! *Now!*"

Behind him Judith was screaming something, and Ecub was shouting, but Saeweald took no notice of them. "*Return home now!*" he shouted. "*Now! Now!*"

Caela's soul obeyed, even though it did not want to, even though it was almost fatally mated with that twisting, murderous knife in Damson's body.

It left Damson, and fled shrieking back to its own body, passing Damson's soul halfway.

That soul seemed curiously resigned, even peaceful, even though, as it neared its own body, it knew what awaited it.

Death.

CAELA'S BODY CAME TO LIFE UNDER SAEWEALD'S hands, and she grasped instinctively at her neck where blood was pumping forth, even though, strangely, her skin was apparently unbroken.

"No!" she cried out, then fell insensible as the blood flowed from her.

"Stop the bleeding!" Ecub said, rushing to Caela's side as Saeweald tried to staunch the flow of blood.

"It won't stop until Damson's heart stops beating," Saeweald said in a curiously flat tone. "Pray that happens soon."

There was a single, appalling silence.

"Or Caela will die with her."

SWANNE WAS PANTING AS SHE LEANED WITH ALL HER strength into the knife.

Damson had stopped struggling, and was regarding Swanne with flat, hopeless eyes; beyond her Asterion was hopping from foot to foot, his eyes almost popping out of his head as he watched Swanne. *This was so much better than he'd planned!*

Damson's hands were fluttering at her sides, scattering bright drops of blood over both Swanne and Asterion. Her mouth had fallen silent, even though it still moved.

The blood continued to pump from her neck.

"CURSE HER STURDY HEART!" CRIED SAEWEALD, AS HE tried uselessly to stem the flow of blood from Caela's neck. "Why can't the damned peasant woman *die*?"

Judith took one futile step toward the door, as if she meant to run to Aldred's palace and wrench Damson's head from her body.

If Caela died now then all was lost, for the Mag force within her would finally vanish.

* * *

DAMSON GAVE ONE GREAT SHUDDER, AND SWANNE let go the knife and took a step back, staring wide-eyed at Damson.

Damson gave a soft moan, shuddered again, then fell forward, snapping her head back as her chin caught the edge of the stool, which she'd pushed before her during her struggles.

Her neck snapped, and with it snapped Damson's life, and the connection that bound her to Caela.

"IT HAS STOPPED!" SAEWEALD SAID. "SHE HAS DIED AT last. Thank all gods in existence!"

Judith came back to the bed. "Is *she* still alive?"

There was a long, terrible pause.

"Just," Saeweald eventually said. "And *only* just."

SWANNE LOOKED OVER DAMSON'S BODY TO ASTERION.

Both of them were covered in blood.

"My lover," she breathed, and he stepped forward over the corpse and took her in his arms.

LATER, WHILE SAEWEALD, JUDITH, AND ECUB WERE still grouped about Caela, willing her every breath, Silvius rushed through the door, not even bothering to knock.

"Gods!" he cried. "What has happened?"

THE NEXT MORNING, AS THE WATERMAN WAS POLING his craft from the fish wharves just below the bridge toward Lambeth on the southern bank of the river, he saw a bloated white body half submerged in the water.

It did not immediately perturb him—the Thames was the final resting place for hundreds of unfortunates every year—but as he passed it, the current surged, turning the corpse over.

It was Damson, her head almost severed from her body.

CHAPTER EIGHTEEN

*J*T TOOK SAEWEALD FIVE DAYS AND NIGHTS—DAYS and nights when he hardly slept—before he could be sure that Caela would live. He dribbled broths down her throat, he placed medicated lozenges in her mouth to slowly dissolve, he coated her tongue with honey.

And finally, finally, she began to respond to his treatment.

Ecub and Judith also kept vigil within Caela's chamber, as did Silvius. More than anything else, all four wanted to move Caela back to the relative safety of St. Margaret's. This small religious house within London's walls was too close to Swanne and whatever had happened in that chamber (*and how they wanted Caela to wake, and to talk, so that they would know what had happened!*), but Caela lay so close to death that there could be no thought of moving her.

Not yet.

On the sixth day, so wan, she looked like a three-day dead corpse, Caela opened her eyes.

Saeweald, waving Silvius, Judith, and Ecub back, gently fed her some broth with a spoon, then wiped her face with a clean towel.

"Caela," he said, gently. "You're back with us."

She started to weep. "Damson is dead."

"We know," Saeweald said. "But—"

"I killed her. I killed Damson."

"Enough," said Silvius, who had finally managed to find a place beside Saeweald. "It was not you who killed—"

"I put her in harm's way," said Caela, and then wept so violently that Saeweald again motioned Silvius back with a frown, then held Caela's hand while she cried away her grief and guilt.

When, eventually, her tears had abated somewhat, Silvius said, "What happened?"

"Swanne . . ." Caela said, her voice hoarse. Saeweald fed her some more spoonfuls of broth, and she smiled at him gratefully.

The smile died almost the instant it had appeared.

"Swanne had Asterion's black knife," she said, "and with it she murdered Damson. Swanne has allied with Asterion. *He* is her new lover."

There was a chorus of voices, shocked, stunned, angry, disbelieving.

"Wait," Caela whispered. "There is worse. Swanne and Asterion mean to control the Game between them."

"Asterion does not want to destroy it?" Silvius said.

Caela gave a weak shake of her head, prompting Saeweald to murmur in concern and to glare at Silvius, as if his question had seriously weakened Caela.

"He means to control it," Caela said. She began to cry again. "Become its Kingman in place of William. Silvius . . . I am sorry . . . Silvius . . . I told Swanne—before I knew of her bond with Asterion—what the Game has planned. Oh, Silvius, I am so sorry. I should have—"

"Be still," Silvius said gently. "It could not be helped. They trapped you." He took Caela's hand in his, stroking it gently.

Then, suddenly he stilled, and his face went pale.

"What?" said Saeweald, staring at Silvius.

"The Mag force within Caela has gone," he said, his voice hoarse with disbelief and horror. "The Mag within her has *gone!*"

A terrible, bewildered silence.

"Swanne has succeeded," Silvius went on, his voice now barely audible. "She has killed Mag. She has finally killed Mag."

PART SEVEN

Among the school-boys in my memory there was a pastime called Hop-Scotch, which was played in this manner; a parallelogram about 4 or 5 feet wide, and 10 or 12 feet in length, was made upon the ground and divided laterally into 18 or 20 different compartments called beds . . . the players were each provided with a piece of tile . . . which they cast by hand into the different beds in regular succession, and every time the tile was cast, the player's business was to hop on one leg after it, and drive it out of the boundaries at the end . . . if it passed out at the sides, or rested upon any of the marks, it was necessary to repeat the whole of this operation. The boy who performed the whole of this operation by the fewest casts was known as The Conqueror.

Joseph Strutt, Sports & Pastimes of the People of England,
Late 18th century

"CORNELIA IS MINE, YOU KNOW," SAID ASTERION, lounging against the closed door to Skelton's bedroom as the Major slid home the knot on his tie.

Jack Skelton ignored the Minotaur as he turned slightly, checking his reflection in the wardrobe mirror to make sure his uniform sat straight.

"I've had her ever since that moment she begged me to sleep with her," Asterion continued. "Genvissa was right. Cornelia was always a tramp."

Skelton turned about so he could look the Minotaur in the face. His eyes were weary, ringed with dark circles, the expression in them resigned, almost hopeless.

"Then why hasn't she given you the final two bands?" Skelton said.

The Minotaur laughed. "Oh, she will, soon enough."

Skelton smiled. "Yes? Then why traipse about over London after me? Why torment me, if there is no need?"

Asterion straightened, snarling. "Because I enjoy it!"

Then he was gone, and Skelton was left staring at the back of the bedroom door.

"Major?" Violet called from the other side. "Frank's waiting for you. He has the motor outside." She paused. "Waiting."

"Aye," whispered Skelton. "Waiting, as are we all." He raised his voice. "I'll be but a moment, Mrs Bentley!"

But Skelton did not immediately move. Instead he continued to stand, staring at the closed door, one hand raised to his shirt where he scratched softly at that spot where Matilda had touched him earlier.

He could hear a rumble outside, and Skelton knew that it was not, as might be expected, the sound of Bentley starting up his motor.

Instead he recognized it for what it was: the sound of the white stag with the blood-red antlers running wild through the forest.

"I'm ready," he said, and the only one who heard was the running stag.

Chapter One

Mid-September 1066

HE NORTHERLY WIND BLEW STRONG, WHIPPING the waves in Somme Estuary into man-high, cream-foamed crests that slapped against the hulls of the scores of galleys at anchor.

On shore, standing atop a tower, which overlooked the harbor and the small town of Saint-Valery, William glanced yet once more at the weather vane on top of the church spire.

The northerly wind showed no sign of abating.

Matilda, standing with her husband, saw the direction of his glance. "Hardrada is moving."

"With this wind? Aye. His ships will be close to northern England by now."

The spring and summer had been a curious mix of frantic activity and a soul-deadening wait for intelligence. As William had built his military expedition and garnered support from the European heads-of-state and Church (all of which had, thank Christ, been forthcoming), so Harold had consolidated his hold on England, and built his own forces up to meet the expected challenge from Normandy.

But Harold Hardrada of Norway was also moving. He'd built up a huge flotilla of three hundred ships with which to invade the north of England and, like William, now awaited propitious weather conditions in which to launch his ambition.

This northerly wind provided Hardrada his chance. William had received intelligence a week ago that Hardrada had embarked. If he wasn't within sight of England now, then he would be within the day. And while the northerlies sped Hardrada toward England it kept William pent up in the mouth of the Somme . . . waiting.

"And Harold?" Matilda asked softly.

"Preparing to meet him." William let out a pent-up breath. "At last. At *last* we are moving."

"But we are *not* moving," Matilda observed, and William turned to her and grinned.

He leaned down and planted a kiss on her forehead, and rested a hand briefly on her belly. Matilda was five months gone with child, and William was grateful for no other reason than the child would keep Matilda at home when otherwise she might have insisted on embarking with him.

"We shall be soon," he said. "This northerly will not last a lifetime, and the instant it changes, we sail."

"Yet in the meantime Hardrada threatens to seize England from us."

William shook his head, his eyes now scanning the fleet as it bobbed at anchor. "Harold is good. Very good. Hardrada may test him, but I doubt very much that he will best him. He *will* tire him. With luck, my love, Harold's force will be exhausted by the time it meets mine."

"I wish my agent was still in place," Matilda said, her voice sad. She'd heard some time ago of her agent's death, and Matilda worried that it was her orders that had placed Damson in danger.

"We will manage without her," William said, kissing the top of Matilda's head.

"I wish I knew who killed her," she said.

"When I have England, then we shall hunt down her murderer. I promise you that."

Matilda relaxed, trusting in her husband. She, too, looked over the fleet, reviewing in her mind all that had happened in the past months. The Norman magnates' enthusiastic acceptance of William's plan; the pope's blessing; the aid—both monetary and in the form of troops—sent by the nobles of Flanders, Maine, Brittany, Poitou, Burgundy, five of the Italian states, and a score of others.

All lusting for the spoils William promised would be theirs at his victory.

"I will keep Normandy safe for you," she said, and William again smiled and kissed her. He was leaving Matilda as coregent of Normandy with their eldest son, Robert. At fourteen, Robert was coming into the age where he needed to shoulder the responsibilities of the duchy, which would eventually be his. William had needed to fight for decades to establish his right to rule Normandy; he intended to make the process of succession much easier for his son. He loved his son, as he loved Matilda, but not with the deep-hearted passion he was capable of. *That* he reserved for . . .

His eyes slipped over the estuary and out to sea. Wondering what was really happening in England . . . in London.

Swanne had been quiet. Too quiet for his liking, and for the events that were gathering. He'd heard that she'd kept her place in Aldred's bed, and he found that increasingly disturbing.

Why?

Harold, he had understood (if not yet Swanne's neglect in telling him that Harold was Coel-reborn). William's chance to take his rightful place on England's throne (as England's Kingman) had been delayed by so many years because of the (Asterion-driven) revolts within Normandy itself. In the meantime, Swanne had needed to establish a place within the English court, and Harold had been the perfect vehicle with which to do that.

William could forgive her Harold. Could *understand* Harold.

But not Aldred. The man was not unknown to William, for the corpulent archbishop of York had acted as one of Edward's emissaries to Rome on numerous occasions, and when traveling through Europe, Aldred had often stayed with William. Aldred's sympathies were clearly with William—he'd acted as the go-between for the letters between Swanne and William for years.

William repressed a sigh. Perhaps that's why Swanne was with him. Payment owed?

No, that wasn't Swanne at all.

"Your thoughts?" Matilda said beside him, and William jumped a little guiltily.

"I was thinking of Swanne," he said. "I was wondering why, out of all the intelligence I've received from England, so little of it has been from her. I had expected more."

Far more, dammit. There is not just a throne riding on this!

"You're worried," Matilda said.

"Yes." *What was Asterion doing? Where was his hand in all of this?*

"You can do nothing save what you have already done," Matilda said, leaning in against him and placing her arm about his waist.

"Aye. You are right. As usual." William lightened his face and tone. "Tell me, how do you think I can possibly crown you queen of England when in all probability you shall be too round and cumbersome to fit onto the throne?"

She laughed. "You shall be a great king."

William's face sobered. "I hope so."

CHAPTER TWO

$\mathcal{J}$T WAS ALL FALLING APART—HAD BEEN FOR months—and Saeweald had no idea how to stop it.

It had all seemed so simple: pass control of the Game into the hands of Mag and a resurrected Og and all would be well, for ever and aye.

The land would flourish, and no one and nothing, ever, would be able to stain its brightness again. Asterion and all malevolence would be contained, Swanne and William and all their ambitions would be broken, Mag and Og would again reign supreme, and the waters and the forests would rejoice.

Yet nothing had quite happened that way, had it?

Saeweald had known that Caela had always felt that she lacked something, an emptiness within her where there should have been fullness, and that she somehow had failed to truly connect to the land. Since the failure of her "marriage" to the land, that night she'd lain with Silvius, that sense had become even greater, undermining Caela's confidence within herself. Now, since that terrible day when Swanne and Asterion had slaughtered Damson, Caela had rejected the Mag within her completely.

It wasn't so much that Mag, or her potential, was dead (as Silvius had so melodramatically cried), it was that Caela had been so ill—physically and emotionally—for so many months after Damson's death that she had completely suppressed the Mag within her. She refused to acknowledge its existence, she would hear nothing of the Game, would not speak to Silvius and barely to Saeweald and Judith . . . she *wallowed* in her guilt at Damson's death.

Even the Sidlesaghes, undoubtedly knowing she would not want to see them, had stayed away.

Ah, Caela had allowed her guilt to overwhelm her. In the months since Swanne and Asterion had killed Damson, Caela had seemed to go into a fugue. She didn't know what to do, or where to go, and to all suggestions that there must be some means of redressing the emptiness within her, or fulfilling her potential as Mag, she had refused to act. She had merely smiled sadly, and shaken her head, and then turned aside. Caela continued to live quietly within St. Margaret the Martyr's, and Ecub and Judith stayed close. Silvius came occasionally, but Caela did not respond to him any better than she did others, and so his visits became less frequent. Caela spent her days sewing, talking quietly with one or the other of the sisters of St. Margaret's, or, more and more, she took solace in wandering the hills and meadows beyond the priory's walls.

She did not enter London.

So far as Saeweald was concerned, the Mag within Caela might not be dead, but it might as well be, for Caela refused to acknowledge it.

And without Caela, without the *Mag* within her, everything was doomed.

Saeweald tried to talk with Caela, tried to reason with her, tried, on one disastrous day, to seduce her (if Silvius had not aided her, then Saeweald could have, surely!). But to all efforts, words, hands or mouth, she had only smiled, shaken her head, and laid a gentle hand to his cheek. For months, Saeweald had felt sure that he was to be Og-reborn, but in his failure to touch Caela, to be able to communicate with her, he now began to doubt even that. He wasn't strong enough.

And Caela wasn't strong enough.

Meantime, Swanne and Asterion went from strength to strength.

Or so Saeweald supposed. He'd had very little to do with Swanne in recent months—he had no reason to see her and would only arouse her suspicions if he insisted. Besides, knowing of her alliance with Asterion, Saeweald frankly didn't feel like going within a hundred paces of the woman. Instead, Saeweald heard of Swanne only through gossip and the occasional glimpse of her moving through the streets of London. He assumed that she and Asterion were biding their time, waiting for William to arrive so they could . . .

Saeweald shuddered. So they could seize him. William would arrive, fall straight into Swanne's arms . . . and find himself trapped by Asterion.

Saeweald didn't know what to do. These months of inactivity, of *nothingness*, had drained him. Caela turned aside her head, Silvius had slunk off somewhere unknowable, Swanne and Asterion planned and shared nights of passion, and Saeweald paced and fretted and wondered what in creation's name he could do!

Warn William?

That would be the sensible course of action, but *how*? Saeweald had no avenues of communication open to him by which he could reliably reach William. Anything he sent, whether spoken word or written, might well be intercepted by one of Asterion's minions—and thus expose both Saeweald and, through him, Caela. If by chance a communication did reach William, then Saeweald doubted seriously that William would believe it. If he understood that it came from Loth-reborn then he most certainly would *not* believe it.

Frankly, Saeweald wasn't sure if anyone could convince William that Swanne had allied with Asterion. He'd never believe it. Never.

Just as Saeweald and Silvius and Caela had not thought it possible . . . had never considered it a possibility.

Meanwhile the land slid toward chaos and despair.

Almost two weeks ago, Hardrada and Tostig had invaded the north, sailing up the Humber and defeating the earls Edwin and Morcar in a desperate battle before seizing the northern city of York. Harold had been caught surprised, even though he'd known of Hardrada's intentions, and had marched north to meet the Norwegian king and his own brother.

That had been ten days ago. The only word that had reached the south was that a great battle had been fought, but as yet no word of the victors and of the defeated.

In one hateful part of his being, Saeweald almost hoped that Hardrada had been successful, that Harold had been killed, and that England would suffer under a Norwegian king rather than, briefly, a Norman one, before that king succumbed to a great darkness.

But why pretend that darkness belonged to the future? Wasn't it here already?

chapter three

CAELA SPEAKS

I KNOW THAT THOSE ABOUT ME REGARDED ME WITH disappointment, perhaps even with shame. I know they wanted me to rage, and do, and act.

But I could do none of these things.

They thought I had suppressed the Mag within me, had suppressed all that Mag had given me.

But I had not. Not truly.

I was simply waiting.

Damson's death shocked and appalled me. I had been responsible for it, not so much for deciding to approach Swanne, for I truly believe I had little other choice, but because I had not been able to protect Damson. If I'd been at full power, at full strength, in command of all of me and without that damned lack within that tormented me, I should have been able to protect her.

That I was not in full command of my potential, that I had not reached the full height of that potential, was my responsibility. Not fault so much, I did not think of it in terms of fault (although I know Saeweald thought I spent much of my time wallowing in guilt), but in terms of responsibility.

It was my responsibility to reach that potential, to protect others, where before I could not protect Damson.

I knew how to do it—I needed to mate with the land, *marry* the land, meld with it completely. Silvius had told me that. The Sidlesaghes had told me that.

But how? I had thought that laying with Silvius would have accomplished it perfectly. After all, he was the warm, breathing representative of the Game, and as the Game and the land had merged . . .

Yet that had been a failure, even if a reasonably enjoyable one.

The consequence of that failure had been Damson's death, and I could not afford to fail again. The next time, far more people would die.

I did not wallow in guilt or grief, although I had to deal with both of those damaging emotions. Instead, I waited.

I waited, and I approached the problem from a different direction. In order to aid the land, I needed to ritually mate with it, to meld completely with it. That was not only my problem and responsibility, but that of the land as well.

It had to act. *It* had to do, as much as me.

I waited, and what I waited for was the land to show me what to do and where to go.

CHAPTER FOUR

AROLD HUNCHED ATOP HIS WEARY, PLODDING horse; he was exhausted, bruised, despondent. His cloak clung to him in great sodden patches, his hands—his gloves lost days ago—were gripped cold and tense about the horse's reins as if they would never let go. About him rode the men of his immediate command: the rest of the army was following as and when it could.

Harold's command sat as hunched and bruised over their reins as did their king, their eyes fixed on some point between their horses' ears, unblinking, unseeing.

The horses, under little instruction from their riders, simply moved forward in the direction their riders had set when they'd still retained some purpose. South, south, ever south away from the battle that had been fought and toward the one that still needed to be fought.

Stamford Bridge had been a nightmare of rain and mud and blood. Harold had arrived in the north the day after Alditha's brothers, the earls Edwin and Morcar, had met Hardrada and Tostig in battle at Gate Fulford, two miles north of York.

The earls had been routed. Indeed, so many Englishmen had died that it was rumored that Hardrada reached the earls to take their surrender by walking across a fen of dead bodies.

Harold then did what few men could have done: he turned a disaster into a means of eventual victory. While Hardrada and Tostig were celebrating, and conducting lengthy negotiations with Edwin and Morcar over the fate of hostages, Harold and his army had arrived unannounced from the south and attacked without even halting for sustenance to fuel their effort.

The battle at Stamford Bridge was long and desperate, and, apart from the surprise of his attack, the only thing that tipped the balance in Harold's favor was that Hardrada's men were either bone-weary, or drunk with their previous victory, or both.

Hardrada had died on the field. So had Tostig. Harold had faced him, in the end, battling his way through the fighting bodies of the living and the slumped bodies of the dead, and had taken the head from his brother's body with such an immense swing of his great sword that Harold had all but stumbled to the ground with the weight he'd put behind it.

He'd not needed his balance, for by then the invaders were themselves routed, their leaders dead, the greater of their numbers dead or crippled enough to wish they *had* been killed.

Olaf, Hardrada's son, had survived the carnage. Morcar, who had acquitted himself better in this battle than in the one of the previous day, brought the young man before Harold.

England's king was standing before a sputtering fire, still in his chain mail and stained tunic, his bloodied sword hanging at his side.

Olaf stood before him, his head high, his eyes glittering proudly, expecting nothing less than death.

"Take what remains to you," Harold said, his voice harsh and exhausted, "and take whatever ships you need, and go back whence you have come. I want you no more in my land."

Olaf had stared, then nodded tersely, bowed his head, and turned on his heel and left. In the end, he'd needed less than twenty ships of the original fleet of three hundred to take what remained home. The rest of the ships remained at anchor in the Ouse River where they'd arrived a week or so earlier: their timbers kept Yorkshiremen warm through the five following winters.

When Olaf had gone, his pitiful twenty ships vanishing into the northern sea mists, Harold had sighed, cleaned his sword, and turned south once more.

He'd won against Hardrada, but at a frightful cost. Edwin and Morcar's original defeat had cost him almost half of the men he could have summoned to battle William. Moreover, many of the elite among Harold's personal troops had been killed or wounded at Stamford Bridge.

Fate—and Hardrada's ambition—had dealt William a kind hand.

HAROLD HAD EXISTED IN A STATE OF HALF-WAKING for hours. He'd been riding for days, barely taking the time to stop and rest, or take sustenance, or allow his horse to do likewise. Now, when he was, at last in conscious thought, and about a half day's ride from London, Harold was so exhausted he could barely think, let alone take note of what was taking place about him.

The weather had closed in. Misty rain had surrounded the horses and riders for hours; now it had thickened into a dense fog that obscured most of the surrounding countryside. Harold occasionally blinked and wiped the fog from his eyes; whenever he did so, he saw that his companions drifted in and out of the mist, almost as if they were ghosts. Even the hoof-falls of the horses were curiously muffled, and the constant jingling of bit and spur and bridle faded until it was little more than a distant memory.

Harold had ceased even to think. He sat, huddled within his soaked cloak, swaying to and fro with the motion of his horse, and descended into a trance that was not quite a sleep.

Thus he was not truly surprised when he finally blinked himself into a state of semi-awareness and saw that one of his men had dismounted and was now walking at the head of his horse, a hand to its bridle, ensuring that his king's mount did not stray off the road.

And then he saw that the figure walking by his horse's head was not one of his men at all, and that it had led his horse so far off the road that now it plodded silently through sodden meadowlands.

"Who are you?" said Harold, shaking himself and sitting more upright. "What is—"

He stopped, for the figure had halted the horse and then turned about, and Harold saw that it was not a man at all. Oh, it wore the shape of a man, but there was something in its long, bleak face, and in the knowledge in its gray-flecked eyes that told Harold this was a creature of great enchantment, and no man at all.

Strangely, Harold did not feel the least sense of fear. "Who are you?" he said, leaning forward a little in the saddle. "Where do you take me? Are we in the realm of faeries?"

That would not have surprised Harold in the least. His sense of unreality had been growing stronger and stronger over the past few days. Now he wondered if that had been the precursor for this other-worldly journey.

The creature smiled, but sadly, and Harold saw that his teeth were rimmed with light.

"I am Long Tom," he said, "and I am taking you to your bride."

"Alditha?"

"No," Long Tom said, drawing the word out until it was almost a moan. "To the woman you will never leave."

Harold frowned, but then the creature gestured to him to dismount.

"We need to take a journey, you and I," he said.

"Where?" said Harold, swinging his right leg over his horse's back and jumping lightly to the ground. His weariness was falling away from him as if it had never been; even the horse snorted and pranced a little as it felt the weight of its rider vanish.

"Do you remember?" said Long Tom.

"Remember what?" said Harold. He was standing directly in front of the creature, and, for all his own height, he had to crick his neck slightly in order to look the creature in the eye.

"This," the Sidlesaghe said, and nodded to his right.

Harold looked, and the mist parted.

HE SAT NAKED IN A STEAMING ROCK POOL, AND IN HIS *arms, very close, he held a young woman, as naked as he. He was kissing her deeply, his hands tight against her back so that he pushed her breasts against his chest.*

"Coel," she said, pulling her face away. "No."

"You want to," he said.

"I . . ." she said.

"Your mind has barely strayed from the pleasures of the bed since we set out," he said.

"I was thinking of Brutus." she said.

"Really? And now?"

HAROLD GROANED, AND THE SIDLESAGHE RESTED A hand on his forearm, as if in support.

"Who was she?" Long Tom asked.

"A woman I loved," said Harold. His eyes brimmed with tears, and he held forth his hand and cried out incoherently as the vision faded.

"What was her name?" Long Tom said.

"I don't . . . I don't know . . . *how could I have forgotten her?*"

"Watch," said Long Tom.

HE BURST IN THROUGH THE DOOR, AND SAW HER *kneeling, keening, in the center of the house.*

"Cornelia?" he cried, and he could feel his heart breaking. "Ah, Cornelia, I am sorry. I had thought to be here before you."

The woman rose, but slipped over in the doing, sprawling inelegantly on the floor. He ran to her, and wrapped her in his arms, and whispered to her soothing words.

"You knew that Brutus had gone to Genvissa, and taken Achates, and everything I hold dear?" she said.

"I saw Hicetaon come for Aethylla and the babies," he said. "I knew then. I wanted to be here for you when you returned. I am so sorry. I came as quickly as I could."

She clung to him, her weeping increasing, and the man rocked her back and forth.

"Cornelia," he whispered, "don't cry, please don't cry."

"ENOUGH," SAID THE SIDLESAGHE. "YOU NEED SEE NO more."

"I remember," Harold said, his voice thick with tears. "Oh gods, *I remember!*"

"Good," said the Sidlesaghe, "for there is much more I need to tell you."

He leaned close to Harold, and he began to whisper at the speed of wind in Harold's ear.

CHAPTER FIVE

CAELA SPEAKS

I HAD TAKEN TO WALKING THE HILLS NORTH AND west of St. Margaret the Martyr's during these late summer days. Here I could escape the bewilderment in Saeweald's eyes and the vain hope in Judith's. Here I could wipe my mind free (or as free as possible) of my responsibilities.

Here I could just walk, and here, if ever it was going to, the land could speak to me, and tell me what it wanted.

On this day I had walked until I had exhausted my barely recovered body, and had sat down in the center of the weathered circle of stones atop Pen Hill.

The view from here was beautiful. Before me spread fields and meadows that ran down to the silvered banks of the Thames, their purity marred only by the huddle of buildings and roadways that consisted of London.

I tried not to look at the city. I tried not to think on what it contained: not only Swanne and Asterion, somewhere within its huddled walls, but the Game . . . waiting, as I waited.

Well, they could wait.

I tried also not to look too closely at the stones that encircled me atop Pen Hill. Today I did not want to see the Sidlesaghes. I did not want to see their long, mournful faces. So today they were just stones.

To my relief, after I had been atop Pen Hill for an hour or more, a low-lying thick mist closed in, shutting out the view, but leaving the summit of the hill and myself in sunlight. I was happy, for this meant I might sit amid the waving grasses and flowers of Pen Hill, my arms wrapped about my raised knees, in solitude, and not have to fear any disturbance.

Thus it was some shock, eventually, to hear the faint thud of footfalls approaching up the mist-shrouded lower reaches of the hill.

I was irritated, more than anything. It would be Saeweald, come to ask me questions. Or Ecub or Judith, come to sit with me and think to offer me some comfort. Or it would be some peasant woman who, finding the space atop Pen Hill occupied by a former queen (and one with her hair all loose and blowing in the wind at that) would blush and mutter in confusion, and depart, taking my peace with her.

So I turned my face very slightly in the direction of the footfalls (*thud, thud, thud* up the hill; whoever this was, they sounded as if they had the gods at their heels), my chin still on my arms folded across my knees, and I arranged my features in a scowl.

Not very welcoming, I know, but I truly did not want company. As if in response to my irritation, even the sky had clouded over.

Then, in the space of a breath, Harold appeared out of the mist as if he were a spirit, striding resolutely up the final few yards of the grassed slope to reach the summit of Pen Hill.

He walked forward, pausing between two of the upright stones, a hand resting on one of them. He was clad as if for war, a tunic of chain mail, a light linen tunic of war-stained scarlet embroidered with the dragon over the mail, a sword at his hip.

He looked terrible. He'd lost much weight and, while he'd always seemed lean, now appeared gaunt under his mail.

His chest was heaving, as if he'd found the climb tiresome.

His face . . .

But I did not see his face, not immediately, for as my eyes traveled up his body, a ray of sunlight burst through the thin clouds that had formed across the sky and caught Harold in its grip.

I cried out, falling a little sideways in my surprise, for that shaft of sunlight had crowned Harold in gold as surely as Aldred (*Asterion!*) had crowned him in Westminster Abbey; only here he had been crowned, not by a monster in the guise of a man, but by the sun itself.

By the land.

And I understood. *Harold was the land!*

I scrambled to my feet, painfully aware that my robe was loose and grass-stained, and my hair all-tumbled about my shoulders and blowing about my face.

He didn't say a word, not at first. He stood, his hand still on the stone, staring at me.

Then he just walked forward, *strode* forward, grabbed me to him, and kissed me, deep and passionate.

"Harold," I said finally, when I managed to snatch some breath.

"Don't," he replied, his voice harsh with desire, and something else . . . I

am not sure what. "Don't say anything to me. Not yet." He buried his hands
in my hair, and groaned, and I think I did, too, and we kissed again, our bodies almost writhing, each against the other.

He had remembered. Someone had told him, or he'd simply just *remembered.*

"I cannot!" I cried, suddenly, frightfully fearful. "To lie with you will be to
kill you!"

"I am your king," he said, his mouth trailing over my jaw, my neck. "Do as
I ask."

"Coel . . ." I whispered.

He grabbed at my shoulders, and shook me, only a little, just enough to
tumble the hair over my face.

"I am this land incarnate," he said. "Are you *really* going to refuse me?"

I was crying, I think. Gently, but crying with all the strength of the emotions that were surging through me, and with relief and fear and desire all
combined.

Then he gentled. "We are safe here, in this circle." He smiled, and my
heart could have broken at that moment for love of him. "Will you accept me,
my lady?"

And it was not just Harold asking, but Coel, and the land besides. Harold
would die, and he would die through William's actions, as Coel had died, but
this time, in this place, we could bless each other . . . and the land.

Give me yourself, Caela, and you grant me joy and life.

I do not know if he spoke those words verbally, or in my mind, but I did
not care. I smiled at him, overcome with emotion, and I did not have to
answer. Not verbally.

Take what you want of me, for it is all yours.

And he gathered me back into his arms.

When, finally, we lay naked and entwined on the grass, and he entered
me, I cried out with joy, my arms extended into the skies, and wept at the feel
of the land embracing me completely, utterly, filling all my empty, desolate
spaces.

WE MADE LOVE ALL THROUGH THAT AFTERNOON, THE
gentle warmth of the sun bathing our naked bodies, the mist still shrouding
the lower portions of the hill and the flatlands beyond. This was loving such as
I had never experienced, not even with Brutus, for this passion encompassed
both earth and sky and water as well, and they were blessed as well as I.

This is what both I and the land had wanted.

This is what I had needed to open up those strange, dark spaces inside me, and fill them.

I wept, and he kissed away my tears.

"HOW DID YOU KNOW?" I ASKED EVENTUALLY.

"I was riding the northern road, when a strange mist enclosed me. A creature came, tall, and pale, and with—"

"The most mournful face!" I said, and laughed, cupping Harold's own face in mine.

He smiled, too. Slow, loving. "You know of what I speak?"

I told him of the Sidlesaghes and of Long Tom, and Harold nodded.

"He is of the ancient folk."

"Yes."

Harold grinned. "He showed me that day, in the rock pool."

I colored. Even now, after all these years, and all that had happened (and even now, lying naked, with this man), I still colored as easily as a girl at that memory.

"Now *that* is a memory to treasure," Harold said, kissing my neck, my shoulder, his voice light and teasing. "Inside you, Brutus not twenty paces away."

I did not smile, for my mind had jumped then to that moment later, when Coel was inside me, and Brutus, a great deal closer than twenty paces, and with a sword, gleaming sharp and deadly in the lamplight.

Harold was looking at me, his smile gone, but his face still relaxed. "He is not here now."

"But he will—"

"Shush," he said. "That does not matter. Not here, not now."

"Oh, Harold," I said, my voice cracking, and he gathered me tight, and held me, and I knew then that whatever else happened, whoever else I loved, this man would always be . . . would, quite simply, always *be*.

Later, after we had made love again, I looked over Harold's shoulder, and laughed.

"What?" he said, rolling off me.

Then he jumped, using his hands to cover his nakedness, and I laughed the harder, not bothering to hide mine.

We were encircled by Sidlesaghes, all standing with great smiles on their faces, all clapping, slowly, soundlessly with their strong, brown hands.

"They are happy," I said. Then I added, and where these words came from I have no idea, "They are our children."

"Then they should be in bed," said Harold tartly, and I rolled over, my sides aching now with my laughter, and the Sidlesaghes clapped the harder.

AND THEN, YET MORE TIME LATER.

Harold had decided to ignore the Sidlesaghes, and began a long, slow, sensual stroking of my body. I loved it. I sighed, and arched my back, and begged him never to stop.

"Will you do something for me?" he said.

"Anything," I groaned, "so long as you complete here what you have begun."

He lowered his head, and ran his tongue about one of my nipples, and I clutched at his hair, and thought I would die with the strength of my wanting.

"When I am gone," he whispered, lifting his mouth momentarily, agonizingly, "will you be my future for me? Will you watch over this land for me, and all those I should have been able to protect?"

"Harold . . ."

"Promise this to me."

"Yes. You did not have to ask."

He grinned, moving his head just enough that his tongue could now draw the other nipple deep into his mouth. For a long moment there was no talk, only the soft sound of my moan, and his heavy breathing.

"Then my future is assured," he whispered. Then he moved, pivoting across my body, burying his hands tight in my hair, his face only inches from mine.

"The Sidlesaghe showed me many things." His body was moving over mine now, and my legs, of their own accord, parted under his weight.

"Yes?" I whispered.

"Of how the Game and the land are married."

"As you and I."

He smiled, but only briefly, his body moving very slowly, very teasingly atop mine. I wriggled, trying to tempt him inside, but for the moment he stayed a breath away from entering me.

"The Sidlesaghe showed me how you are Mag-reborn."

"Yes." That was more moan than word.

"And how Og one day, too, will be reborn."

"Yes." Then I had a sudden, horrible thought that I could hardly bear, and my body fell still beneath his. "Harold—"

He kissed the tip of my nose. "I know," he said. "I know that will not be me. And I know who it will be, and I am content enough with that. This is a long path you travel, my love. A long way to go."

"I know. There is so far . . ."

"All every path needs is but one step at a time."

I was silent.

He smiled, and the warmth in it was stunning. "And all every path needs is a companion with which to share it."

I was shocked at what he suggested, particularly because of the understanding he'd shown just before it. "But you know that at the end . . ."

"All I want is to share the path with you. I know I cannot be your destination. I've always known that."

I began to weep. What had I ever done to deserve this man's love . . . to deserve what he now offered me?

"Oh, sweet gods, now I've made you cry again!"

I started to laugh through my tears, and, determining that I'd had enough of his teasing, I pulled him down and into me. "At least you will never hear me say 'No!' again!"

"Oh, my lady . . . how I love you."

MUCH LATER, AS EVENING DREW NEAR, ONE OF THE Sidlesaghes wandered over, waited until we both became aware of his presence, and gestured us to follow him.

ChAPTER SIX

THEY ROSE, REACHED FOR THEIR CLOTHES, THEN dropped them as another of the Sidlesaghes—some forty or fifty were still gathered about—shook its head.

A Sidlesaghe led them down the northwest face of Pen Hill, the side farthest from London and closest to the Llandin, toward a small grove of trees at the base of the hill.

Harold looked about as they neared the trees. It was now almost twilight, the fading of the light intensified by the close gathering of the Sidlesaghes. Gods, there must be several hundred of them waiting just before the trees!

He looked to Caela. She was close enough to him that he could feel the warmth of her skin, smell the womanly scent of her rising in the coolness of the evening. He slipped an arm about her waist, half-expecting her to pull away, then smiled as she relaxed against him.

Harold kissed the top of her head, then nodded at the Sidlesaghes. "What is happening?"

She gave a slight shake of her head. "Something . . . momentous. Something good."

She shivered, and he knew it was in anticipation. "Should I be here?"

She raised her face to him, and smiled. "*I* would not be here, if not for you. *This*," she indicated the encircling crowds of Sidlesaghes, "would not be happening if not for you. I think, Harold of England, you are to be very welcomed in whatever is about to happen."

"You are not afraid." It was a statement, not a question.

"No. I am content." She touched his bare chest, briefly. "I am whole."

Harold's eyes swept over the Sidlesaghes. "Where have they all come from, Caela?"

"From the stones of England," she said. "From the past. From the future. We have to follow them. Look, they are moving into the grove of trees."

He looked, and saw that she was right.

Caela took his hand, and they followed.

The stand of trees numbered only some twenty or thirty. They encircled a small rock pool, its waters emerald green and as still as the sky above them.

"I had not known this was here," Harold muttered.

"Nor I," said Caela. She had stopped, looking strangely at the pool, then again she turned to Harold. Under the trees it was almost full night, save for a gentle glow that came from the water, and it lit up Caela's eyes and teeth as she smiled. "It is for us," she said. "Just for us. A doorway."

"Into what?"

Caela remembered a conversation she'd had with Saeweald a long time ago, when she had been Cornelia and he Loth.

"Into a light cave," she said. "Pen Hill is a sacred mound, and I think that this evening its sacredness is about to be revealed to us."

"Are you sure I should—"

Before Caela had time to even interrupt his protest, one of the Sidlesaghes had stepped to Harold's other side, taken his hand, and led him forward toward the pool.

"I think that might be a 'Yes,'" Caela said, and followed.

AT THE POOL'S EDGE CAELA TOOK HAROLD'S OTHER hand—he was now visibly tense—and together all three, the king of England, a Sidlesaghe, and a woman who was about to become something that not even she had yet fully realized, stepped into the water.

It was not wet. Rather, it felt to Harold like the soft caress of a warm breeze. Led by the Sidlesaghe and Caela, he walked forward until the water reached his chest, then at the insistence tugging on both his hands, and with a quick, silent prayer in his heart, he ducked beneath the level of the water.

It was a different world beneath, and yet strangely similar. It was a reflection of the world above, only smaller, more compact, and far, far more magical.

They stood in a green meadow, the grasses weaving about their knees. Above them shone a clear sky—a soft gray—and before them rose a low hill.

On its summit stood something that Harold could not quite make out. It appeared to be a building constructed of something so indistinct—almost so out of focus—that he could not make out its lines.

He felt a slight squeeze on his right hand—the Sidlesaghe had now let go of his left—and found Caela smiling at him.

"Is this not beautiful?" she said.

"Aye," he said slowly, again looking about. *Thousands* of Sidlesaghes were now wandering about this soft, gentle landscape. They hummed—a sweet, reassuring melody.

"Aye," Harold said again, then paused. "What is it?"

"The Otherworld."

Harold jumped. It was not Caela who had replied, but a Sidlesaghe, standing a pace or so away.

"Am I dead?" Harold said.

"No," said Caela. "We are, I think, merely being granted an audience. Look." She pointed to the hill.

A figure had emerged from the indistinct structure atop the hill.

A small, dark, fey woman.

Caela gasped and, her hand still linked with Harold's, pulled him toward the hill.

By the time they reached its summit Harold was out of breath, but Caela didn't seem affected by the climb at all. She let go Harold's hand and wrapped the shorter woman in a tight embrace. *"Mag!"*

Harold felt himself freeze in awe. *Mag?* But was not Caela Mag-reborn?

The woman, Mag, returned Caela's embrace, then smiled at Harold. "Caela is my heir, she is not me," she said. She reached out a hand for Harold and, hesitatingly, he took it.

Immediately a sense of peace flowed through him.

"Will you come into England's water cathedral?" said Mag, and she drew Caela and Harold forward.

She led them into wonder, and the moment they stepped inside, Harold realized why it was he found it difficult to put this building in focus.

It was, unbelievably, constructed entirely of water.

They had entered a massive hall—columned and vaulted entirely in flowing water. It was the most magical sight that Harold had ever seen, or could ever have imagined seeing. The vast interior of the hall was colonnaded on either side by twin rows of water columns rising to some fifteen or twenty paces above their heads, where they merged into a gigantic circular domed vault that rose at least a further twenty paces above their heads.

They walked to the center of the hall, directly under the dome, and Harold looked down to the floor.

It, too, was made of water, although it felt solid under his feet. The water (*floor*) was of a deep, rich emerald color, but running through it, apparently at random, were lines of blue that trailed haphazardly, crisscrossing each other at random intervals.

Harold raised his head to find Mag smiling at him.

"The island's waterways," Mag said. Then she stepped forward and embraced Harold with almost as much emotion as she'd hugged Caela. "Thank you for bringing her to us," she said.

"It *was* my pleasure," Harold said, and Mag laughed, and kissed him on the cheek.

"We wished she could have found you sooner, but that she found you at all is a blessing indeed."

Harold was going to say something more, but then stopped as he saw that a score of shadowy womanly figures had emerged from behind the columns to walk to within several paces of where Mag, Caela, and Harold stood. Most appeared in their late middle age, but apart from their shared femininity and the gentle smiles on their faces, that was their only similarity. Some were fair, some dark, some tall, some slim, some plump, some beautiful, some homely.

Harold gave a small start . . . there was one other thing all these woman shared in common. They all had knowledge and power shining from their bright eyes.

For once, Caela seemed as puzzled as he.

Mag took Caela's hand, ignoring for the moment the other women. "Caela, you have had trouble accepting the heritage I bequeathed you."

"Yes. It has been . . . difficult. I felt myself empty. Lacking."

"Aye. For that you have blamed yourself. Ah, my dear, that was my fault, not yours. Here, let me explain."

Mag gestured to the encircling women with her free hand. "These women are all my predecessors, as I am yours."

Caela so forgot herself that she gaped. "There were others *before* you?"

"Indeed. I will explain, but first, if they may, my sisters will introduce themselves to you."

"I am Jool," said one of the women. "I came three before Mag."

"And I am Raia," said another. "I came ten before Mag."

The women all introduced themselves in turn. There were thirty-one.

Mag turned to Caela and took both her hands in hers, giving the woman her undivided attention. "I was the thirty-second in line from the dawn of time," she said. "You will be the thirty-third. Each of us has lived long lives, millennia-long, and at our given time we have passed into this world, handing the responsibilities we shouldered to our successor. Part of that succession was, first, ensuring that the woman we picked was mated with the land. That normally happened *before* we left our successor to her work. In your case," Mag smiled sadly, "well, in your case, events, and Genvissa's darkcraft, intervened. I was not able to ensure that you had mated with the land. No wonder you found it so difficult in this life."

"But," said Caela, looking between Mag and Harold. "Coel and I . . ." She stopped, remembering.

"Brutus murdered Coel before the act was completed, before that moment when both of you sighed in repletion. And besides, that act took place before I had told you of my decision. That was not in any sense of the word a true mating of my chosen successor with the land, although the souls were right.

You both needed to be reborn into the places you are now to have accomplished the act you have."

Caela nodded. Mag had told Cornelia, as she had been then, of her plans many months after Coel's death; the night Genvissa had forced her daughter from her womb.

"Normally," Mag said, "the old Mother goddess of the land and the waters passes over at the moment her successor and her mate have sighed in repletion. I went too early. I could not aid you to the place that both of you found today."

"With the Sidlesaghes' aid," said Harold.

"For my lack of being there," Mag said, "I apologize from the bottom of my heart."

"We all do," said the woman who had called herself Raia, "for we all should have aided you."

"And welcomed you," said a woman called Golenta.

"But late is better than never," said Mag, smiling. "You are here now. And Harold," she nodded at him, "is here because he is a beloved man both to you and to us, and because all of us need a witness when . . ." she stopped, and arched a questioning eyebrow at Caela, to see if she understood.

"Ah," said Caela, after a moment. "You said that only part of the responsibility in handing on succession was ensuring that your chosen successor was mated and married with the land. There is something else which needs to be accomplished, and that needs a witness."

Mag nodded, pleased. "None of us share the same name, my dear. And in the past few months, you have felt awkward using the name 'Mag', have you not?"

"Yes, indeed."

"You have avoided using it," Mag continued. "It has not felt comfortable to you. That is as it should be. My dear, when each of us came into our own, when we came into that power, that *embrace* which you know as the essence of this land, the soul of this land, we each chose for ourselves our own name.

"Now," she said, "you must choose for yourself a name, as I chose Mag when I shouldered the burden, and as all the other women present chose a name when their turn came. Your name, your goddess-name, is not only most sacred, but most powerful. One day you will wear it openly, but for the time being, until this land is free of the burden that currently consumes it, it will be your secret name, and the more powerful because of that."

"I can choose any name I wish?"

"Indeed, my sweet. But listen, for this is important. Your name will become your nature. It will dictate who you are. You will never be able to act beyond the confines of your name, for be certain that your chosen name *will* confine you. Do you understand me?"

"I'm not sure," Caela said.

"I chose the name Mag when I ascended," Mag said. "In the language of the people who inhabited this land, when I lived only as a mortal woman, it means welcoming . . . intaking . . . nurturing. I thought it the essence of motherhood, and for me, that is what I wanted to be for this land."

"Of course, thus Mother Mag."

"Yes. And as I had chosen that name, so it confined me—and eventually it damaged the land. Can you know of what I speak?"

Harold saw Caela's brow furrowing, then it cleared and understanding replaced the puzzlement on her face.

"Ariadne. When she came begging a home, you welcomed her. You took her in, because that was your nature, that was your name."

"Yes. Mag was who I *was,* and it meant that once I took Ariadne in I could not reject her. What mother can reject any of her children? The Darkwitches attacked me, and drew away my power, but that was not the only reason I weakened. My time was coming when I needed to pass into this world and pass on my responsibilities. 'Mag' was no longer what the land needed."

"You all passed on when the 'who' of you became irrelevant?"

"Aye. And now you must choose your own name, Caela. Your secret name, your power name, your goddess name. Choose well and choose wisely, for it must be a name that will provide this land with what it needs to repel the malevolence that assails it."

Caela drew in a deep breath, pulling her hands from those of Mag. Harold thought he saw a fleeting expression of panic cross her face, and he didn't blame her. *Choose well and choose wisely . . .*

For if you don't . . .

Caela turned away, her head down, thinking. She paced very slowly about the room, her arms wrapped across her breasts as if in protection, then, after a few minutes of total silence, with all eyes in the hall upon her, Caela came to a stop before Harold.

She lifted her eyes, staring at him, and Harold felt tears come into his own eyes at the depth of expression and of love in hers.

"I have chosen," she said softly, looking at no one but Harold.

There was silence, and Harold felt the breath stop in his throat.

"Eaving," Caela said. "My name will be Eaving."

Harold's breath let out a sob, and the tears that had welled now flowed down his cheeks.

Eaving! It was a rustic word, used generally only by shepherds, herdsmen, and sailors. Yet even by these men, eaving was a word used only once or twice in their lives.

Superficially, "eaving" meant shelter, but its meaning went a great deal deeper than that. Eaving was used by shepherds and sailors, men who were exposed to the worst of the elements, to mean "an unexpected haven from the tempest." They used it when they and their flocks or ships were caught in a storm that had blown down from nowhere, which threatened their very lives, and from which there appeared to be no shelter. Then, suddenly, as if god-given, there appeared as if out of nowhere the unexpected haven—an over-hanging cliff that protected the shepherd and his flock from the worst of the weather, or a small bay or estuary in which a ship could ride out a storm.

Eaving, the unexpected haven in which to ride out the storm and from where one could reemerge into the sunlight.

"You wish to use the name Eaving?" asked Mag. "Once you accept this name you will be tied to it and by it."

Eaving turned to Mag, then looked at each of the other women in turn. "It is who I have always been," she said, "and what I want only to be. Eaving. I accept this name."

"Then welcome, Eaving," said Mag. "Welcome to yourself." She held out her arms, as if she would embrace Caela—*Eaving!*—but then the hall appeared to disintegrate into its elements, and water crashed about them, and the next thing Harold knew, he was standing atop Pen Hill again, shivering in the cold night air, alone save for Caela who lay at his feet.

FOR ONE TERRIBLE MOMENT HE THOUGHT SHE WAS dead, but then Caela rolled on to her back and smiled at him.

"I feel whole," she said. Then she held out her arms to him. "Let me make you warm."

His shelter from the impending storm . . . and suddenly all of Harold's fears and anger and frustrations at his impending, unavoidable death vanished. He knelt down beside her, then lay down, and felt her take him in her arms.

"Eaving," he whispered, and then she kissed him.

CHAPTER SEVEN

HEN SHE RETURNED TO HER CHAMBER within St. Margaret the Martyr's, it was to find Judith, Saeweald, Ecub, and Silvius waiting for her.

"What has happened?" said Silvius, taking a step forward as Caela entered.

She looked at him as if slightly puzzled, then smiled agreeably. "I have spent the afternoon with Harold."

"Harold?" Judith, Saeweald, and Silvius said together.

To one side, Ecub looked carefully at Caela, and nodded very slightly to herself.

"He is tired," said Caela. "Dispirited." She paused, her brow furrowed as if trying to remember something, then said, "Our brother Tostig is dead. Harold killed him at Stamford Bridge."

Judith and Saeweald looked at each other, not sure what to say.

"Caela," Saeweald said.

She came to him, and kissed his cheek gently. "Forgive me for being so dispirited myself these past months, Saeweald. I have come to my senses now. I will do what I must."

"What *has* happened?" Silvius said. He walked forward, and took Caela's chin in his hand. "Caela?"

"I am well and I am at peace, Silvius," she said. "There are no more empty spaces. No more lack. I am this land, I am the soul of its rivers and waters, the wellspring for its fertility. I accept it. I have embraced it."

"How is this so?" Silvius said. His black eye was narrowed, searching Caela's face. "Why so confident, so . . .?"

"Unexpectedly confident, Silvius?" Caela smiled, very gently, and moved her face so that her chin slid from his grip. "I am tired," she said. "I would rest. Do you mind . . . ?"

As they filed from her chamber, Caela added, quietly, "Ecub, I beg you to stay a moment."

"Harold?" said Ecub once the door had closed behind the others.

Caela's face broke into a huge grin. "*Yes!* Oh, Ecub, you cannot know—"

"I can guess," said Ecub, laughing. She stepped forward, taking both of Caela's hands in hers. "He was your mate, yes? He was your means to mating the land. We all should have seen that sooner. Even in the past life, we should have seen it."

If anything, Caela's grin broadened, and Ecub laughed again, and enfolded the younger woman into a tight embrace.

"There is much I need to tell you," Caela said as finally Ecub pulled back.

"Indeed," said Ecub. Her face was sober now, her eyes searching. "But what *I* want to know, first, is why you tell me, and not the others."

"I am not sure." Caela turned and walked to the window, gazing out to the looming shape of Pen Hill in the darkness. "There was a caution within me that lifted only when you were the last left in the room." She turned back to face Ecub. "And perhaps it is because you were the one with me at Mag's Dance. You were the one to watch me dance Mag's Nuptial Dance."

"And Blangan."

Caela smiled, sadly. "But she is not here now."

"But *you* are." Ecub breathed deeply, then bowed low at the waist. "Mother Mag."

"No," Caela said, and Ecub looked up, surprised. "Eaving," Caela said. "My name is Eaving. Mag has passed, and only I remain." Caela sat down on her bed, and patted the space before her. "Sit, and I will tell you what transpired this afternoon. Oh, Ecub, it was so beautiful!"

An hour later they still sat on Caela's bed, their hands gripped, save that now Ecub was weeping, shaken by what she had heard, and by the power of her own joy. *Oh, how fortunate she was that she should have lived to hear this!*

EVENTUALLY ECUB SNIFFED, QUIETED HER EMOTIONS, and said to Caela, "You are Eaving, the shelterer, but you also shall need a shelter, and a protector."

Caela's mouth curved in a small smile. She had been right to trust this woman as the first—apart from Harold, of course—among those who would know her for who she truly was.

"I," said Ecub, "and my sisters, will always be yours. We shall exist for only one purpose, and that shall be to provide you with a haven, in whatever manner you might need it."

It was a powerful promise, and Caela's own eyes now brimmed with tears. She leaned forward, kissing Ecub softly on the mouth. "I accept," she said, "although you may one day regret—"

"Never!" said Ecub. Then, more softly. "Never. I watched over Mag's

Dance, and saw you come to your own within it. I will watch over you now, and ever so long as you need me."

Caela nodded. "Thank you."

MUCH LATER, WHEN EVERYONE ELSE HAD GONE, ECUB bedded Caela down in her chamber. Judith had gone off with Saeweald, and Ecub was glad of it.

"What is it that you 'must' do?" asked Ecub, tucking the bed linens about Caela's shoulders as if she were a child. "Warn William? Move against Asterion?"

"I must wait," said Caela. "I can do no more. I shelter. I cannot avenge. I cannot warn."

"Do you not fear for William?"

"Oh, aye, I do not think I can sleep for the fear I hold for him. Swanne . . . oh, dear gods, Swanne is his walking death. But I must be true to myself, Ecub. I cannot go to him. I cannot seek him out. He must come to me. He must need the haven."

"Swanne and Asterion will . . ."

"I know. I *know*. But I have to trust in myself and in what will be, Ecub. I can do no more."

Ecub sighed, patted Caela on the shoulder, then retreated to a stool under the window, blowing out the candle as she did so. The stool was uncomfortable, but there was no point in her sleeping; Matins service would begin within an hour or two, and she might as well spend the time between now and then in contemplation . . . and thanks, for the unexpected joy this life had brought her.

chapter eight

ILLIAM HAD BEEN IN ENGLAND ALMOST TWO weeks, and during this time he'd had barely the time to even *think* about the underlying "why" of his presence here. Certainly he was here to win himself a kingdom and all the spoils it could provide him, but there was far more at stake that he had not allowed himself to consider.

There had been no time.

He'd sailed from the Somme Estuary on the night of the 28th of September, arriving at Pevensey Bay early the next morning. Here William had constructed some initial defenses, but then had decided that the small port town of Hastings, which lay a little farther up the coast, would serve his purposes better. Hastings stood on a small peninsula and could be more easily defended, and William wanted to protect his ships, his men and, he admitted in his darker moments, his escape route.

He was a more cautious man now than he had been as Brutus. If Brutus had been forced to linger in Normandy, or Poiteran as it had been then, for over thirty years he would have marched on London the instant he'd landed. William was far more circumspect. He knew the English would be hostile, he was not sure where Harold and his army were . . . and he knew Asterion was here, somewhere, waiting for William to make that one, grossly stupid move which would see him fail.

So William proceeded with care, determined not to move so precipitously that it left him no escape route. Just outside Hastings, William set his men to work, constructing earthen defenses and a bailey castle. Neither defenses nor castle would withstand a siege, nor even a sustained bombardment, but it would buy William the time he would need during a forced retreat.

Now William was standing atop the bailey castle, one booted foot tapping impatiently on the floorboards, gazing northwest over the countryside. There were a few pillars of smoke in the distance: his men had been out pillaging. William had not wanted them to do it, but they had to be fed somehow, and William did not want to deplete what few stores he'd brought with him. A few paces away stood two or three of his commanders, watching William more than the landscape.

William had called his commanders for a war council, but that could wait for a few minutes.

A few moments more of quiet, where he could think on the underlying reason for his invasion. The real reason, the true reason why so many men were about to die.

To retrieve the bands, and to then complete the Game with Swanne by dancing that final, concluding dance of the Game, the Dance of the Flowers.

Ah, stated in so few and such bold words, it sounded all so easy, didn't it? Just retrieve the bands, grab Swanne by the hand, and execute the Dance of the Flowers. No need even for the accompanying dancers that they'd had two thousand years ago. All that was really needed was the Mistress and the King-man. Two people, six golden bands, a relatively uncomplicated dance, a dab of magic, and all was done.

All so simple, so easy, all so terrifyingly unachievable, should even one or two things go awry.

Like . . . Swanne. William drew in a deep breath. Where was she? He could *feel* her, somewhere close (and yet somehow closed to him; she was near, but he could not read her), but he knew there was no way she could approach him openly at this stage.

Yet that did not explain why he had not heard from her in months. Oh, Aldred wrote occasionally, or sent word via trusted messengers, but Swanne had not contacted William since that moment she'd appeared before him on the cliffs of Normandy, and that was before last Christmastide. *Ten months!* What was she doing? Why this silence? Was Asterion too close for her to risk contact?

It was the only reason William could think of for her silence, and it concerned him that Swanne might be so close to danger.

It terrified him to consider that there might be an even more terrible reason for Swanne's lack of communication.

He tore his thoughts away from Swanne. Yes, she was close, but he could feel others, too. Somehow, the mere fact of setting foot on this land once more connected him to others. Loth was here, much the same as he had been; William knew he would never like Loth as he had learned to like and respect Harold. Erith was here, too, as another Mother—he could not remember her name, but that woman was the one who had been intimately connected with Mag's Dance.

And Caela. He could feel her, far stronger than he would have thought possible. William closed his eyes, scrying out the sense of her: contentment, peace, even a little happiness, and something else that he could not identify . . . a depth that he could not understand. He suddenly realized that he could well meet her soon; odd, that he'd never thought of that until now. If matters went well, then he would soon meet Caela face to face.

His heart began to race, and William opened his eyes, apparently staring ahead although he saw nothing. Caela was lovelier now than she had been as Cornelia. What was she doing? Did she still yearn for him?

What would *he* do if she came to him, and offered herself to him?

What would he do if she did *not*? William found the idea that she might not yearn for him anymore as unsettling as the thought that Swanne might somehow be in danger. No, *more* unsettling. What if Cornelia-now-Caela no longer yearned for him?

He recalled the vision in which he'd seen her as Caela lie beneath his father, and he recalled also his vision of two thousand years earlier when he'd seen her as Cornelia lie down beneath another man, offering him her body.

Asterion, who had then slaughtered her.

What did those two visions mean? Were they truth? Or delusion?

Was Silvius the reason for Caela's contentment now? William tried to scry out his father . . . and found nothing. He frowned. Strange, for if Silvius was flesh, and ambitious enough to seduce Caela, as well as shift the Trojan kingship bands, then he would be flesh enough for William to feel. But there was nothing, almost as if his father did not exist, or was a phantom of delusion only.

William realized that his commanders were watching him impatiently, but he allowed his thoughts to roam just a little further.

Harold. There had been a great battle at Stamford Bridge, and it was long ago enough now that details of it had reached William. Hardrada and Tostig had both been killed in the struggle. Harold had come back to London, rested there some few days, and was now . . . close. William could sense him. Very close indeed—and as strangely at peace with himself, as content, as Caela seemed.

Was Harold so at peace because he had come to terms with his own imminent death? At that thought William felt a gut-wrenching sense of loss, the strongest emotion he'd felt since he'd been standing here in the open air staring out into nothingness. He didn't want to kill Harold. He didn't want to be a party to his death.

Not again.

Why hadn't he taken the trouble to know Coel better?

Or Cornelia, as Caela had once been? Why hadn't he taken the trouble to treat her better? To *understand* her?

William gave an almost indiscernible shake of his head. He might as well wish the sun to rise in the west. Brutus had not taken the trouble to know anyone well, not even himself.

"I have a command," William said suddenly, making his commanders jump. "I would that in the coming battle, if we prove victorious, that King Harold be taken alive. I do not want him killed."

"My lord duke," said Hugh of Montfort-sur-Risle, one of William's most trusted men, "is that wise? If we prove successful, then to have Harold still alive would be to invite—"

William, keeping his eyes on the landscape, had not looked at Montfort-sur-Risle as he spoke. "I do not want him killed. Not by my hand, nor by any of my men." William finally turned to looked at his commanders. "Is that understood?"

As one, they bowed their heads.

CHAPTER NINE

AROLD SAT ON HIS HORSE ON A RIDGE SOME NINE miles from Hastings. Behind him came his army, weary, footsore, straggling in disjointed groups rather than in the units into which they'd originally been organized. Harold turned so he could see over his shoulder. He knew the true depth of his command's exhaustion, and he wished he had the ability to bring the full complement of men he'd commanded at Stamford Bridge against William.

But that could not be. Many men were wounded, many more scattered along the long road between here and the north. William had both Fate and Luck on his side.

Harold looked back to Hastings. He could *feel* William. Somehow, in the few days since he'd been with Caela, Harold had grown far more attuned to the land, to its spaces and intimacies, and to those who trod upon it. William was out there staring toward Harold as Harold now stared toward him.

There was no animosity, only an infinite sadness, and that gave Harold great comfort. William had changed in this life, and that meant there was hope for the land. He may not have changed enough, but he had begun that road.

Harold closed his eyes and thought on Caela . . . Eaving. He remembered the feel of her body, he remembered her scent.

He remembered how she had smiled into his eyes, and blessed him.

Whatever happened, all would be well.

Eventually.

The sound of horses' hooves behind Harold disturbed him, and he looked to see who it was.

One of the English earls, come to receive orders about deploying what was left of their ragged army.

"We will make our stand here," Harold said, pointing along the long ridge. "The escarpments to either side mean that William can only attack us from the front. He cannot outflank us. We can make a good defensive stand here, my friend."

"We will win the day," the earl said, but Harold could hear the bravado in his voice.

"Of course we will," said Harold.

SWANNE ALSO STOOD, SECRETED WITHIN THE EDGES of a dark grove, staring across at Hastings. Like Harold she could sense William's presence and feel his vitality, but unlike Harold it was not her connection with the land which enabled her to do this, but her ability with the darkcraft.

Asterion moved up behind her, running his hands from her shoulders down her arms.

She nestled back against him. "Bless you," she murmured.

He smiled. "The darkcraft suits you. Imagine how much better you shall feel once William is dead."

"Soon."

"Oh, yes, soon."

Asterion's fingers kneaded slightly at her arms. She was really quite thin now, the imp within her continuing to sap away at her vitality. But she remained beautiful, and Asterion had no doubt that William, the fool, would not last for more than a few moments against her writhings and pleadings.

"He will be yours within a day," he murmured, his muzzle buried within Swanne's dark, curling hair. "This time tomorrow you will be in his bed, trapping him with your dark power."

With my imp, he thought. *Finally working its vile talents to their full potential.* Poor, dead William.

Swanne shuddered. "I cannot bear the thought of lying with him."

Asterion's fingers tightened where they rested on her upper arms. "You must. It is the only means by which to kill him and utterly negate his power."

"Asterion, my love, I don't really know if I can bear to—"

"You will lie with him!"

She cried out, stunned, and one of her hands fluttered to her belly. *Why was the imp nibbling now, when Aldred was not here?*

"Yes," she said, her voice dulled. "I will lie with him. If that is what you wish."

"Blessed woman," Asterion said, kissing her neck. "You will scream with pleasure. You *will*."

She moaned, her entire body relaxing back against his. "Aye, I will do that for you."

"But," Asterion whispered, his hands now running all over her body, "that pleasure will be as nothing compared to that we will feel together, as one, when we finally take the Game."

She moaned again, and turned about in the circle of his arms, and offered him her mouth. There was nothing left now but her need for Asterion, and the thought of the power she would enjoy with him when they led the Game.

EAVING.

The word came as a low moan, a breath on the wind, and it made Caela shiver. She was standing atop Pen Hill, staring south, feeling the swirling emotions that came from the land about Hastings. Harold was there, and William, but so also were Asterion and Swanne.

"*Eaving.*"

She turned her head, very slightly. A Sidlesaghe stood a pace or two to one side. No, several of them, gathering about her on the breeze.

"*Eaving!*"

"What may I do for you?" she murmured.

"We beg your aid," said Long Tom, stepping forth.

"You have it, you know that."

"Now that you have achieved your union with the land," Long Tom said, "have you felt it?"

Caela did not have to ask him what he meant. "The dark stain in its soul," she said. "The tilt in the Game. Yes, I have felt it. Asterion's hold over Swanne, over the Mistress of the Labyrinth. The shadow that hangs over us all.

"What can I do?"

"There are two more bands left."

"Aye."

"Eaving," said another Sidlesaghe. "Shelter them."

"Move them?" said Caela.

"No," said Long Tom. "Shelter them."

"Moving the bands may not be enough," said one other Sidlesaghe. "They can still be found. William can always find them. And if William . . . if William . . ."

"If William is trapped by Swanne and Asterion?"

"Aye," said Long Tom. "Eaving, there are two final bands. Will you shelter them?"

"From William as much as from Asterion," said Caela.

"Aye. In case. Just in case."

She thought a long time, staring sightlessly south, feeling all that the land told her.

"There is a way," she said, finally.

* * *

IN ROUEN, MATILDA LAY ABED. SHE SLEPT RESTLESSLY,
the bed covers twisting about her body, her dark hair working its way free of
its braids and tangling on the pillow, her face covered in light perspiration,
one of her hands fluttering over her rounded belly.

In her dreams, Matilda walked a strange and unknown landscape. About
her tumbled the ruins of a once great city. Columns and walls lay in piles of
great masonry, flames flickering from fires that still burned within them, dismembered bodies sprawled in sickening heaps, a great pall of thick, noxious
smoke hung over the entire terrible landscape.

She did not recognize the city. The architecture (what she could see of it
amid the ruins) was of an unknown and exotic form, and the bodies, which lay
about, were clothed in armor and held weapons of a type she had not seen
before. This was somewhere she had never visited, and, even within her
dream, Matilda wondered at the power of her imagination that it could con-
jure this vision to disrupt her dreams.

Matilda walked carefully, avoiding as best she could the tumbled masonry
and the bodies. She turned a corner and came upon a cleared space.

She halted, transfixed by the sight before her.

A stag lay in the center of a clear space. He was magnificent, larger than
any stag she had ever seen before, with a pure white pelt and a full spread of
bloodred antlers.

"You are a king," she said, and the stag blinked at her as if it were suddenly aware of her presence.

Matilda looked away, studying the rest of the space. Initially she had
thought the space was entirely clear. Now she could see that it wasn't. A
labyrinth had been carved into the entire circular space—

*Matilda's mind instantly leapt to that strange gift her husband had sent
Edward—the ball of golden string that unwound into a labyrinth—the labyrinth
he'd said was carved into the golden bands he thought might be in the possession
of either Caela or Swanne.*

—and the stag lay within its heart. Before the stag, also within the heart of
the labyrinth, were carved letters. They had been dug deep into the stone of
the labyrinth floor, and had been filled with red paint, or perhaps blood.

Matilda stepped forward, unfearful, curious to see what the word was.

Resurgam

Matilda frowned, for she knew her Latin well enough. *I will rise again?*

The stag began to move, struggling to rise, and it distracted Matilda. She raised her eyes to the stag, pitying the creature, for no matter how greatly it struggled, it did not seem to be able to rise to its feet.

Then the stag paused, its ears flickering as if it heard something, and its stunning head twisting so it could look over its shoulder. It trembled, and its struggling doubled, and a sense of great dread came over Matilda.

"What . . . ?" she said, and the stag turned its head back to her, and looked at her with black eyes that Matilda instantly recognized, and it said: *Begone from here, Matilda. Begone!*

"William," she whispered, and stretched out her hands to aid it.

Begone! the stag screamed in her mind, and Matilda wailed, and then she also screamed, for out of the tumbled ruins that bordered the open space behind the stag crawled an abomination such as Matilda had never dreamed before.

It was a gigantic snake, or a lizard, she could not tell, but it had a sinuous, writhing body covered in black scales, and a head with a mouth so vast and filled with fangs that Matilda understood how it could eat entire cities (and had indeed eaten this one, which is why it lay in ruins about her).

In the instant before the snake-creature struck, Matilda also understood one other thing. That this terrible demonic creature was a woman's revenge incarnate, and Matilda knew the woman who had created this revenge must surely be the greatest Darkwitch that had even walked the face of this earth.

The stag was screaming continuously now, its struggles maddened as it sought to escape the snake-creature writhing ever closer.

Matilda shrieked, backing away several paces, her hands to her face.

The snake-creature struck, lunging down with its vast mouth, and before Matilda could manage to wrench herself from her dream, she saw the demon's fangs sink so deeply into the stag's body that it tore asunder, and blood spattered all about.

SHE WOKE, DRENCHED IN SWEAT, STILL CAUGHT IN the terrible imagery of the stag's murder.

"William," she whispered.

CHAPTER TEN

ON THE FOLLOWING MORNING, WHEN THE NOR-
mans faced the English on the battlefield of Hastings, there were
not two forces ranged against each other, but many. Harold and
William were, and always would be, the face and tragedy of Hastings, but
behind them and at their side ranged other forces that influenced both the
battle of that day and that which would come over the following centuries:
Asterion, the Minotaur; the Troy Game itself, determined to ensure the
future it wanted; the land, and Eaving, who spoke on its behalf, as on the
behalf of Og, her all-but-dead future; and finally, Swanne, the Mistress of
the Labyrinth. All of them, in their own way, participated in the battle at
Hastings.

Harold had massed his army on the ridge that lay nine miles from Hastings.
Fate could not have picked for him a better site. The ridge was a natural fortress.
Before it the land sloped gently away before rising again toward another hill. To
either side of the ridge were steep escarpments that were in turn flanked by
marshy streams. If William wanted to attack Harold—and there was no way he
could ignore the English king and allow him time to build up his forces—then
he would need to attack from directly forward. There was no real hope of trying
to outflank the English, because that would mean lengthy delays and the splitting of the already small Norman force into two or even three tiny and weak
secondary forces.

Harold was as ready as he could ever be by the time the sun rose. He'd
deployed his men so that William would face a mighty shield wall. William
had armored cavalry—but even they would be of little use against a phalanx
of armored and shielded men who could range pikes, lances, axes, swords,
stones, and arrows—as well as the supporting landscape—against the attacking force.

Weary his men might be, but Harold knew that in theory they had a very
good chance.

Save that he knew they would not win. Not in terms of a battle victory.

Where would the treachery come from? he wondered.

* * *

WILLIAM ATTACKED SOON AFTER DAYBREAK. HE'D
marched his army from Hastings, massed on the hill opposite Harold's ridge,
then sent in both cavalry and infantry in three divisions.

If William thought to break Harold's shield wall, then he was grossly disappointed. Harold's men held, and wave after wave of Norman attackers were
driven back.

By midmorning it appeared that the battle was turning into a rout. The
Normans were milling, often ignoring the shouted commands of William, who
fought within their midst, and falling one after another to the axes and swords
of the English.

William changed tactics. He screamed at his archers to direct their missiles into three or four concentrated areas of the English line, and then to his
horsemen and knights to follow up the arrow barrage with a concentrated
attack on those areas. While the English were still in disarray from the arrows,
the knights stood a better chance of breaking through the shield wall.

Crude, but effective. Very gradually, as the day wore on, the English were
worn down. Where they held in the earlier part of the day, their weariness
caused them to stumble during the latter.

Very gradually, the Normans began to break through the shield wall and
engage the English in terrible hand-to-hand combat.

"I want Harold alive!" William screamed to his men as he saw them break
through in a half a dozen different places. "I want him alive!"

"AND I DO NOT!" MUTTERED SWANNE, STILL STANDING
within the embrace of her dark grove. She could not see the battle with her
eyes, but she could with her power. "Ah, what a fool you have become,
William! The Game has no use for such as you."

Then she relaxed. She must not think this way. She must practice the
pretty, smiling face she needed to present to William. In the meantime,
she needed to ensure that he actually won this battle. The bands could be irre-
trievably lost (for this life at least) if the damn fool was killed by some stray
English sword.

"Harold!" she whispered, and she spoke with the voice of passion.

HAROLD!
It stunned him, for it automatically drew him back through the years to
that time when he and Swanne had been young lovers, and he'd entertained

no doubt that she loved him, nor that she was anything else but that which she appeared.

Harold!

He was fighting desperately in the very thick of the battle where the Normans had broken through. Covered in sweat and grime and blood, hearing the shouts and grunts and cries of those crowded about him, feeling their thrusts and hopelessness and dying, *still* he heard Swanne's voice as clear as a clarion call.

Harold!

He looked up, and never saw the arrow that plunged directly into his eye, killing him instantly.

CAELA MOANED, ALMOST DOUBLING OVER IN THE intensity of her sorrow. How pitiful a death, to be so duped by Swanne.

Then she managed to collect herself, and wipe the grief from her eyes, and straighten, and compose her features and smile.

She stood in the stone hall—save that only the western end of the hall was stone. The eastern half, which stood at Caela's back, was built entirely of flowing, emerald water.

Caela stood at the border of this life, and the next.

A figure appeared at the far western end of the hall. He was not dressed in battle garb, nor did he bear the stains of sweat and grime and death.

Instead he walked straight and tall, as beautiful and as content as ever she had seen him. England's king, as William would never be.

She drew in a deep breath, and could hardly see for the tears of joy that now filled her eyes.

"Harold!" she said as he drew near.

"Eaving." He smiled, and it was composed of such pure love and acceptance that the tears spilled from her eyes. He lowered his head and kissed her, then gathered her into a tight embrace, lifting her from the floor and spinning her about. "I had not thought to meet you here!"

"How could I let you pass without . . ." she stopped.

"Saying goodbye?"

"It will never be goodbye," she said, very softly. "You should know that."

"Aye, I know it."

She had pulled back slightly from him now, and her face was grave and angry all in one. "Swanne murdered you with her darkcraft."

"Again." His voice was virtually inaudible.

"Do you know," Eaving said, "that for this you are owed vengeance?"

Harold laughed shortly. "When shall I collect it?"

Whenever you will. Harold, the Sidlesaghes showed you, as well as me, the paths between this world and the next. You can travel them as well as I.

"Whenever you will, Harold," she said, her eyes locked into his.

"Ah, Eaving," he said, resting the palm of his hand against her soft cheek, and she knew that he'd put Swanne from his mind for the moment.

"Harold, I need you to grant me a favor."

"Anything."

"Take these with you."

He looked at what she had in her hands, then his eyes flew back to hers, shocked. "I cannot touch those!"

"Please. For me."

He laughed, the sound bitter. "These will eventually take you from me."

"You already knew that."

"Oh, gods, Eaving . . ."

"Please, Harold. Please."

He sighed, and reached out, taking the two golden bands from her. "Where shall I put them?"

She shrugged, and suddenly he grinned, and then laughed. "You are so beautiful to me," he said.

Then, kissing her one last time, Harold walked past Eaving, through the water cathedral and into the Otherworld.

CҺAPϹƐR ƐLƐVƐN

ILLIAM HAD SPENT ALL OF HIS LIFE, SINCE the age of seven, fighting battle after battle. He'd lost a few, he'd proved victorious in more, and he'd walked the field of death in the aftermath of combat more often than he cared to remember.

But never before had he been as sickened as he was this evening as he picked his way slowly over the ridge where Harold's army had made its stand.

It wasn't the dismembered corpses—Norman as well as English—that lay about in their thickened, coagulated blood.

It wasn't the moans and the screams and the pleas for mercy or quick death that came from those maimed men who lay twisted in indescribable agony amid their silent, dead companions.

It wasn't the shrieks of the crippled horses, or the stench of spilt blood, and split bowels.

It was sadness that sickened William, and the fact that he could not quite understand the reason for this sadness, nor even comprehend its depths, only made it worse.

He picked his way slowly through the battlefield, stepping over the piled corpses, ignoring the cries of the wounded, save for a jerk of his head to those companions who trailed after him to see to their needs.

William was looking for Harold. He'd not been among the captured, and William knew the man well enough to know that neither would he have been among the few score of English who'd managed to escape the field. Harold was lying here somewhere amid this stinking, reeking, shrieking carpet of humanity, either dead or wounded, and William feared very much that he was dead. He found himself praying over and over that Harold would still be alive, but William *knew* that he was dead.

He could no longer scry out his presence, although, oddly, he could still feel Harold's sense of peace and contentment.

It was, finally, one of Count Boulogne's captains who raised the shout, standing thirty or forty paces away toward the northern end of the ridge, waving his arms slowly to and fro above his head.

William's stomach lurched, and he froze momentarily, staring at the man's waving arms as if he signaled the end of the world, before he managed to collect himself and stride over.

He stopped as he reached the captain, then looked at the ground that lay between them.

Harold's body lay bloodied and twisted, his legs half covered by the headless corpse of an Englishman. The dead king's arms lay outstretched, as if Harold had willingly relinquished his spirit; his body, so far as William could see, was unscathed.

Save for the arrow that protruded from his left eye.

William could not tear his eyes away from it. He stared, unblinking, then his stomach suddenly roiled, and he turned away and retched.

The arrow! There as solidly as if William had thrust it in himself.

As he had thrust the arrow into Silvius' eye in order to seize his heritage.

Was he cursed to repeat this foulness over and over, through this life and all others? Was everything he set his heart on to be destroyed with the cruel thrust of an arrow deep into a brain?

William straightened, and wiped his mouth. He did not look back at Harold.

"Take him from here," he said to the men who had gathered about, "and treat him with all respect. We will bury him tomorrow."

Then William turned, and walked away.

BY MIDNIGHT, WILLIAM WAS BACK WITHIN HASTINGS, conferring with his captains about the likelihood of the remaining English regrouping and attacking, when a soldier entered the chamber, saluted, then stood expectantly as if he had news of vast import to share.

"Yes?" said William.

"My lord," said the soldier. "Harold's wife is here and craves an audience."

William froze, staring at the man.

"The Queen Alditha?" said Hugh of Montfort-sur-Risle, frowning.

"No," said the soldier. "The other one. The lady Swanne."

As one, everyone looked to William.

He was sitting in his chair, his face now expressionless, his eyes still glued to the soldier. "Bid her enter," he said, finally, his voice very soft. "The rest of you may leave. I think we have done this night."

Count Eustace of Boulogne shared a glance with Hugh of Montfort-sur-Risle. "My lord," he said, shifting his gaze back to William. "She might be dangerous."

William gave a soft, harsh laugh. "Oh, I know that all too well. But I will be safe enough, my friends. Pray, leave me alone with the lady for the moment."

Again his men shared concerned glances, but they did as he bid them, and as they filed slowly out, the soldier reappeared with a darkly cloaked woman.

William nodded to the soldier, and he turned and left, closing the door of the chamber behind him.

William rose slowly from the chair. "Swanne."

"Aye!" She threw back the hood of her cloak, then undid the laces about her throat and discarded the heavy garment entirely

Beneath, Swanne wore a simple white linen robe, a low scooped neckline revealing the first swell of her breasts, her narrow waist spanned by a belt of plain leather, the heavy skirt left to drape in folds to her feet.

The simplicity of the robe, its starkness, set off her beauty as nothing else could have done. William felt the breath catch in his throat. Even though she was a little too thin, as if she had been ill recently, Swanne was still as desirable as she had ever been.

And yet there was something about her, something apart from her thinness. Something . . . harsh.

"William!" she said, shaking her head so that her heavy, black curls shook free from their bindings. "William!"

She held out her arms, her eyes shining, her red mouth slightly parted, the tip of her tongue glistening between the white tips of her teeth. "William!"

"Swanne," he said, feeling ridiculous, as if he'd been caught in a child's play. *Gods! Could he do nothing but stand here and mutter her name? Is this not what he had waited for, lusted for, so many years?*

Then, in a moment of a stunning—almost horrifying—revelation, William knew that she was not. Swanne was not what he sought at all. She was merely his unavoidable companion.

Was this what Theseus felt when he abandoned Ariadne on Naxos? Did he feel as I do now when I look on a woman I once thought to love, and think, "Murderess?"

As cold as ice, William stepped forward, took one of Swanne's outstretched hands, and laid his lips to it in a courtly fashion.

His eyes never left her face.

Something shadowy crossed Swanne's countenance, but vanished within an instant.

"William!" she cried yet one more time as she threw herself against him, pressing her body against the length of his, her arms tight about his waist, her face uplifted to his. "Finally . . . finally . . ."

He gave a small, tight smile, then lowered his face to hers, and, reluctantly, kissed her.

Her mouth grabbed at his, her hands tangling within his hair, her body writhing against his flesh.

William felt as though he were being devoured.

Worse, her mouth tasted foul, as if it were full of the coppery aftertaste of old blood . . .

He pulled back, pushing her away with his hands on her shoulders.

"William? I have waited for this moment for so long. I have been through so much for this moment! Shared Harold's bed—"

"Harold is dead."

"Yes! Praise all gods!" Swanne clasped her hands before her, her face alight with delight. "And you must ensure his children die as well. You cannot have any of his blood lurking in the hills, ready to make a play for your throne."

William's face froze. "They are *your* children as well!"

"Ah," she said, making a deprecatory gesture. "Mere necessities to keep Harold happy. They are of no importance to me. A discomfort, only. I could not wait to rid my body of their weight."

Swanne leaned froward again, lifting her face to again be kissed, but William turned away. He walked a short distance to a table where lay a scattering of parchments: intelligences and reports.

He did not touch them.

"William?" Swanne stepped up behind him, and laid a hand on his back. "What is wrong?"

"Harold is dead."

"Yes . . .?"

"God damn you, woman!" William swung about to face her. "You shared his bed for over sixteen years! You bore his children! Have you not a care for the fact that this man is *dead?*"

"Harold discarded me!" she snarled. "*No one* discards *me!*" Then she relaxed, and smiled again. "Have you seen his body, my love?"

William gave a terse nod.

"Did you like the arrow? I thought it a nice touch. I thought . . ."

Swanne stopped, appalled at the expression on William's face. "He was nothing to us, William! Why look at me as if I were the most loathsome witch on earth?"

"He was a good man, Swanne. He did not deserve to die. *And not in that manner!*" William paused, his face working. "And to now beg me to murder his children? *Your* children. I cannot credit it! Is there *nothing* within that breast of yours but hatred and ambition? Nothing?"

"What is wrong with you, William? *You* and *I* are the only things that matter. And the Troy Game. Nothing else counts. We are here, we are together, and we can complete the Game. *Nothing else matters!* Why look at *me* as if I were a vile thing?"

He turned away again. "I also used to think that nothing mattered but the Game," he said quietly. "I used to think that nothing counted but that you and I would live together, forever, caught in the immortality of the Game."

Swanne stared at his back, her face a mixture of confusion and frustration. *What was the matter with him?*

"Forgive me," William said, his voice now drained of all emotion. "I am tired. I know I am not what you want me to be right now . . . but . . . I am tired."

"Of course." Again she approached him and put a hand on his back, rubbing it gently up and down before she reached for one of his hands, turning him about as she lifted it and put it on one of her breasts. "I understand. Of course I do. Perhaps in the morning . . . ?" She smiled seductively. "All we need do is lie side by side tonight if you are too tired to . . ." Again she grinned, and rubbed his hand back and forth over her breast.

He pulled it away, watching her face cloud in anger. "I am *tired*, Swanne. I am sick in the stomach from the slaughter that has ensued this day. I want to be alone. I want solitude. I want to grieve for Harold, even if you do not. I am sorry if you thought that I would leap instantly into your arms, but . . ."

He stopped, too tired and heartsore to even continue arguing the point. The thought of lying with Swanne—*the thought of that blood-sour mouth running over his body, taking him into her flesh*—made his very stomach lurch over in nausea. He grimaced, and that told Swanne more than words ever could.

"*What?*" she said, her body stiff, her brows arched. "You think to lust after your damned Cornelia again? She's a pale, hopeless wretch who has retreated into a convent, William. I can't see her offering her body for your use!"

"I am married to a woman whom I respect and honor," William said, holding Swanne's furious stare. "I have no thought to demean Matilda by taking another to my bed."

"I cannot believe you said that!" Swanne said. "What is a *wife* when compared to *me*? First Cornelia, and now this Matilda?"

"A wife is an honorable thing, Swanne."

"That is not what you believed when you had Cornelia mewling at your side!"

"Perhaps I *should* have thought of it then," he said quietly.

"I am your—"

"Matilda will be my queen, Swanne."

To that, Swanne could make no immediate verbal response. She merely stared at him, her mouth closed grim and tight. Finally, she said, "*I* am your queen, William. *I* am your mate, your partner. How have you forgotten that?"

"We will dance the final enchantment together, Swanne. We will make the Game together. We will—"

"How can you possibly want another woman before me?"

Although Swanne was still angry, her voice sounded genuinely bewildered, and William gave up trying to argue with her. He took her in his arms, and pulled her close, and hugged her. "I am tired, Swanne. Forgive me. My mind and mouth are too muddled to make sense."

"Ah, my sweet . . ." She lifted a hand to his cheek. "You must pardon me as well. I know you must be exhausted, and we have eternity before us to consummate our love. Our power. Kiss me one more time, and I will leave you in peace for this night, at least."

She grinned lasciviously, and William's mouth gave a tired twitch in response. Swanne looked up at him, her body relaxing against his, and William gave a capitulative sigh and leaned down to kiss her.

After all, what was a kiss?

He pulled away almost instantly, again appalled at the foulness he'd tasted in her mouth.

But Swanne did not seem to notice his revulsion. She gave him a smile. "Soon," she said, and left the room, picking up her cloak as she left.

William stared after her, the fetid taste of death still filling his mouth.

chapter twelve

WANNE GAVE WILLIAM A FULL DAY AND NIGHT before she came to him again. He'd kept himself busy with the aftermath of the battle, with orders and worries, and the sheer and unexpected weight of Harold's death, which he had yet to deal with effectively.

Harold's death had been a far more bitter blow than William had imagined. He hadn't known Harold well, but what he had known . . .

And he had fought to save him. *Damn it!* He had fought so *hard!* The fact that it hadn't been a Norman arrow that had felled Harold gave William no comfort. Instead he felt even more responsible; that it was Swanne's hand (again . . . no matter who wielded the weapon, it was always Swanne who struck with it) made William feel even more guilty than he would have otherwise.

So when Swanne had herself admitted into his presence on the third day after the battle, William raised his head wearily from the maps he'd been studying and gazed at her with such clear aversion that any other woman would have turned on her heel and walked straight from his presence.

"I am weary, Swanne," William said. "What is it you want from me?"

"How can you ask that, my love? You must be fatigued if you cannot even remember what we have fought toward for so long." She smiled at him. "Come now, give me a kiss, and then we can, perhaps, share our noonday meal and discuss what we should do. Whatever your weariness, William, we must consolidate what we have gained. Asterion can no longer keep us apart, and we must work toward the Game with all the strength we may."

"You are right." William called to his valet and asked him to bring some small ale and whatever food he could barter from the kitchens, then he waved Swanne toward his own chair, which sat before a brazier, while he took a bench.

As the valet set a platter of food before them—fresh bread and the remains of the pigeon pie that William had partaken of the previous night—William gestured to Swanne to eat as he poured some small ale from a jug into beakers.

"You're looking thin, Swanne. You should eat."

"I have been mildly unwell, but nothing of any true concern." She smiled, and once more William found himself thinking that it looked more like a grimace than a genuine expression of warmth. "And I have been aching for you. To be with you."

Her smiled stretched, becoming almost predatory. "I remember how we were interrupted that day in your stables, when Matilda made her ungracious entrance. I think, William, that it is time we consummated our union." She pushed aside the stool on which sat the platter of food and, rising from the chair, unlaced the bodice of her gown so that her breasts swung full and naked before William. "William, do not deny me. We have already begun the partnership of the Game. You cannot now turn your back on me, or on the Game. Once started, it *can't* not be finished. We have obligations we both need to fulfill, and the sexual union of both Mistress and Kingman is the mightiest of them."

He sat very still on his bench, only his eyes moving as first they ran over her breasts then moved back to her face. "Swanne . . ."

She knelt before him, and lifted his hands to her breasts. "This does not arouse you?" she said.

Now William shifted, uncomfortable. In truth, it did arouse him, the memory of her foul-tasting mouth notwithstanding. It had been many weeks since he had slept with Matilda, and now, to have these warm, soft breasts filling his hands . . .

"William," Swanne whispered, running her hands up his thighs, kneading and rubbing, until they reached his groin. "William . . ."

He slid down from the bench, thinking, *Just this once . . . just this once . . . then she will be satisfied and she will leave me alone . . . just this once . . . it will surely do no harm . . .*

"William!" Swanne said, more powerfully this time, and she also slid so that she lay on the floor, and she pulled William down atop her. His mouth ran along her shoulder, her neck, her jaw, not touching her mouth, and his hands kneaded at her breasts.

Smiling in triumph, Swanne hauled her skirts over her hips, then began to fumble with the fastenings at William's crotch. "Thank God," she said, "that your petty wife is not about to interrupt us *this* time!"

"And I say, 'Thank God she is!'" came a voice, and William rolled off Swanne so fast that he knocked over the stool carrying the platter. Food scattered everywhere as he fumbled with his clothing while trying to rise at the same time.

Matilda walked into the room, very calm, very dignified, very in control of herself.

"Husband," she said, nodding to him in greeting as if she'd disturbed him at nothing more than his morning shave. Matilda continued into the chamber until she was close to Swanne and then, very tightly, also nodded at her.

Swanne had made no attempt to cover herself. She had propped herself up on her elbows so that she could see the better, but her breasts still hung bare from the front of her under tunic, and her naked body was exposed, from her hips downward.

"And thus you expected to be *queen* beside my husband?" Matilda said, letting both incredulity and disgust fill her voice.

The barb struck home, for Swanne flushed, while with one hand she jerked her skirts down and with the other pulled her bodice over her breasts. She looked to William to aid her rise, but he had stepped several paces away and now stood slightly to Matilda's left.

Unwittingly—or not, as the case may have been—William had placed himself so that he and Matilda stood together, confronting Swanne.

Swanne managed to rise to her feet with as much dignity as she was capable. Her flush had deepened, clearly now through anger rather than through humiliation, and her eyes flashed. She opened her mouth, but Matilda forestalled her before she could speak.

"You are the lady Swanne, I think. Yes? Ah, William, look at that red mouth, and those sharp teeth." Matilda's voice hardened. "Lady Snake, more like. Swanne is too gracious a name for *you*, my dear."

"Matilda," said William. "What are you doing here? Are you well?" He kissed her quickly on her mouth, recovering far more quickly from his initial fluster than Swanne liked.

"I had a bad dream," Matilda said, her voice now rich with love. She laid a hand on his cheek. "A terrible dream, and so I acted on it." Her eyes slid back to Swanne, and her tone and features became glacial. "Just in time, I see."

Swanne's mouth opened and then closed as she fought to find something to say. As William and Matilda continued to watch her with impassive faces, Swanne finally managed to summon enough dignity to give Matilda a sharp nod, and William an even sharper look, before she stalked for the door.

As it closed behind her, William's shoulders visibly relaxed. He took his wife's face in his gentle hands. "Thank you," he said. "Thank you."

She smiled, her eyes full of love and relief.

"WHY NOT?" CRIED ASTERION, STALKING BACK AND forth before Swanne as they stood in an unnoted corner of William's camp. "Why not?"

"I had him," she ground out, still so angry that her flesh almost vibrated.

"He was mine . . . and then that damned *wife* intervened! Gods help me, I will have her torn apart limb by limb!"

"You failed me," Asterion said, and there was enough coldness in his voice to make Swanne look at him in panic.

"I will have him, I *will!* He cannot resist me for long. Besides, she is pregnant, and so soon will be too unwieldy to take any man atop her."

"I need William dead, Swanne."

"I know! I know! I promise you, my love. He will be!"

"*Before we get to London!* I do not need William breathing over my shoulder when I retrieve those bands!"

She leaned against him, placing her hands against his chest. "I will let nothing come between us, Asterion. Believe me. William will be mine before we arrive in London."

He nodded. "Make sure of it." *Damn her! William should be dead by now!* For a moment Asterion contemplated the possibility that Swanne might not be able to seduce William. If that were the case, could he use . . . ?

No, they were imps of different natures. Swanne carried the deadly imp within her. The destroyer.

She was the only one who could murder William safely.

"Make sure of it," Asterion said again to Swanne, and there was enough threat in his voice to make her blanch.

Chapter Thirteen

Caela Speaks

I SAT WITHIN ST. MARGARET THE MARTYR'S FOR THE six weeks it took William to reach London, and felt every pace he and his army took as England disintegrated before its conqueror. From Hastings, William marched on Canterbury, then farther east on the road to London, fighting skirmishes here and there, but facing no real opposition.

The might of England's earls and nobles had died on the field at Hastings. Not merely Harold, although for my heart he was the most of it, but his brothers, his uncles, Alditha's brothers, everyone who might have had a faint hope of uniting the remnants of England's pride against William—all had died on the bloodied field at Hastings.

London, as most of England, was terrified. What would William do? Would he burn and rape and pillage? Would he set England afire? Would he destroy lives?

If I had been able, I would have answered them "Nay." William would want nothing but those bands. He might strike down any who stood in his way, but if his way to London remained open, then England would remain safe.

If I did not fear for England, then I remained taut with worry about William himself. I knew Swanne had gone to Hastings—and where Swanne walked then so must Asterion walk close by—and I knew that Swanne and Asterion meant to trap William.

But had she—*had they*—managed it?

I didn't know. I didn't think so. I was sure I would feel it if she had, feel her triumph if nothing else, but I would also feel it through the land. I could still feel that dark stain on the land, and that made me realize that Swanne was still alive, but the darkness had not spread, and that gave me hope— William had probably not yet been infected with Swanne's foulness. What gave me more hope was the news of Matilda's unexpected arrival in England. If William had Matilda by his side, would he then still succumb to Swanne? I did not think so, but there had been some days between Hastings and Matilda's arrival, and what could have happened in those days was almost too frightful to contemplate. Yet for all my concern I could do nothing until I laid eyes on William, and spoke to him, and felt his warmth close to me. Until then I would not know for certain.

The Sidlesaghes worried also. I often saw them, slowly circling atop Pen Hill, and sometimes on the more distant Llandin. Long Tom, or one of the others, would also come to see me from time to time, and sit with me for a while, silent, holding my hand in his.

I tried to hope that William would have enough sense to recognize the dark change in Swanne . . . but then, he'd not let her darkness scare him away when she had been Genvissa, had he? *Then* he'd willingly allowed himself to be enveloped by it.

So why not this time? William was not to know that in this life her darkness had a more frightening edge to it, a fatal entrapment, so why would he view her any differently? Why shouldn't William already be seduced into Asterion's trap?

Because Harold had trusted him. Because Harold had thought him a changed man—and changed for the better.

I had to trust Harold. I had to . . .

I had to *believe* in what he had felt from William.

I had to trust William.

I had to believe that he had grown.

ONE GRAY, COLD MORNING IN EARLY NOVEMBER, Mother Ecub came to me and said that four members of Harold's witan waited within the convent's chapel to speak with me.

"They say," said Ecub, "that since Alditha has fled to the north—" Alditha was heavy now with her unborn twin sons, and I cannot blame her for trying to put as much space between her husband's nemesis and her husband's unborn children "—that you are the voice of the nation. You are Edward's beloved widow," her own mouth quirked at that, mirroring the action of my own, "and they wish to hear your advice."

I rose, smoothing down the folds of my robe and reaching for the cloak Ecub held out for me. "How satisfying," I said. "Gods' Concubine has finally achieved some purpose."

Ecub grinned. "If only they knew the true extent of that purpose."

"Who is among them?" I said.

"Regenbald," Ecub said, and I nodded. The Chancellor had been at the forefront of both Edward's and Harold's witans. Of course he would be here.

"And Robert Fitzwimarch," Ecub continued, ushering me toward the door, "Ralph Aelfstan, and the archbishop of York."

I froze.

"Aldred," Ecub finished, watching me carefully, knowing the fear that name would cause me.

"Aldred?" I whispered.

"He was a member of the witan as well, Eaving. He is doubtlessly here in *that* capacity, not as . . . as . . ."

"Asterion," I whispered. I closed my eyes, and collected myself. I should not fear. Aldred would not recognize me for what I truly was. I had not shown myself to him as Eaving as yet—nor to any, save Harold, Ecub, and the Sidlesaghes—and whatever tiny "difference," if any, he picked up, he would undoubtedly put down to Caela's much-lauded acceptance of God and religion since her time in St. Margaret the Martyr's.

I was more powerful now. I could hide myself and my true nature from him. I could. Besides, he thought he'd murdered Mag in Damson. He would not be looking for her replacement within me.

I merely had to be Caela.

Ecub squeezed my hand in comfort. "I will be waiting outside the chapel," she said. "With an axe."

I burst out laughing. "And I had thought to escape attention!"

And thus, smiling, we proceeded to the chapel.

"MY LORDS?" I SAID SOFTLY, ENTERING THE CHAPEL with my shoulders bowed in Caela's habitual thralldom.

"My lady Queen!" said Regenbald, stepping forward to greet me with great courtliness and respect.

Oh, that I had received this respect when I'd truly needed it as Edward's down-trodden wife!

"Disaster brings you to me," I said, nodding to Fitzwimarch, Aelfstan, and Aldred, upon whom I was careful not to allow my eyes to linger.

"Aye," said Aelfstan bitterly. He was an aged man who had once been a renowned warrior, and I could not imagine but that the events of the past weeks had caused him great pain. No doubt Aelfstan wished he had died honorably in battle, rather than being left among those few who would oversee England's complete humiliation.

"William marches on London," Aldred said, stepping out of the shadow where he'd been standing. "He is but a half day's march away. Good lady . . ."

Aldred was wringing his fat hands over and over themselves, and I could not help but admire the depth of the creature's disguise. Who could have thought *this* the dreaded Minotaur? "Good lady, we fear greatly!"

"And . . . ?" I said, looking between the four men, but wondering within me if Aldred's presence here (*Asterion's presence*) indicated that he and Swanne had not been as successful with William as they'd hoped. Or was this but another part of his greater plan?

"Lady Queen," Regenbald said, "we face a stark choice. Lock London against William, and watch it starve into submission over a half year, or capitulate it to him without a fight, and watch him burn it to the ground."

"Oh, I doubt that William would—" I began, but Fitzwimarch broke in.

"Lady Queen, we would beg you that you surrender London to William, and in the doing, plead for its life, and the life of its citizens. He would the easier listen to your pleas, we think, than those of men he has good cause to loathe and distrust."

I thought furiously. This is undoubtedly what three of these emissaries thought, but what of Aldred? Would he truly believe that William would listen to anything that Cornelia-reborn pleaded? Did he hope that William would just push me to one side and burn the city to the ground anyway?

Was he just here, adding his silent support to this plan, merely because he needed to keep up his disguise as wobbling fool for a while longer?

The hope that William had thus far resisted Swanne grew stronger, and, I must admit to myself, the thought of finally facing William was something I could not resist.

Finally. To see him again, to be in his presence, if only briefly.

"I will do it," I said, and did my best not to allow my anticipation to flood across my face.

"What a good girl you are," said Aldred, and the anticipation froze within me.

CHAPTER FOURTEEN

ILLIAM PACED BACK AND FORTH, BACK AND
forth, knowing that Matilda was standing and watching him
and wondering why he was so nervous.

But he couldn't stop himself from pacing. Back and forth, back and forth.

One of his men came into the chamber with some trivial question and William snarled at him.

The man fled. Matilda raised her eyebrows.

William made a gesture composed of equal parts frustration and impatience, and forced himself to sink into a chair. He gripped the armrests, for otherwise William thought he might have sprung up almost as soon as he had sat down.

It had been six weeks since Matilda had arrived, and in those six weeks little seemed to have been accomplished. William had consolidated his hold on the southeastern county of Kent, secured the port of Dover, and had moved on London, but had not managed much else. London was William's prize, he wanted it desperately, but almost as desperately he did not want to destroy it in the taking. London was a fortified city, it could be defended, and it had by all accounts a good militia. The very last thing William wanted was to become enmeshed in a siege that kept him from his kingship bands for months, if not years.

So William had hedged and threatened and negotiated, moving his army eastward, swinging south below London, then marching west and crossing the Thames at Wallingford. From there William moved his army to the small town of Berkhamsted. Here he had moved himself, Matilda, and his immediate command into a large and comfortable abbey house while his army made do with sleeping more roughly in the frosty meadow fields or, if they were lucky, the outbuildings and barns of local farmers.

And so at Berkhamsted William waited, until, two days ago, had come news that a delegation was moving west from London to meet him.

And, perhaps, to surrender.

Heading the delegation was the dowager queen, Caela.

They were due this afternoon; they had, in fact, arrived, and William and Matilda only waited for the delegation to be escorted into their presence.

William, Matilda thought, was far more nervous than he should be, and she wondered why.

Personally, Matilda was more than looking forward to meeting Caela. She'd heard so many intriguing things about the woman over the past years (although intimate, personal information about the queen had largely ceased to come her way after Damson's terrible loss) that now Matilda could barely restrain herself from hopping from foot to foot.

Was Caela the reason William was so nervous? Matilda suddenly wondered. *And if so, why?*

At least Caela could not possibly be the threat that Matilda knew Swanne posed. Since her arrival, Swanne had kept her distance; from Matilda, at least, although Matilda had seen Swanne talking to William on two or three occasions when she managed to catch him at some distance from his wife.

There was a knock at the door, and William of Warenne, one of William's senior commanders, entered.

"They are here, waiting outside," he said.

Matilda saw William draw in a deep breath and slowly rise from the chair. She also saw him briefly clench and then relax his hands.

"How many, and who?" William said.

"The dowager queen," said Warenne. "Harold's Chancellor, Regenbald. Aldred, the archbishop of York. Robert Fitzwimarch. And a small retinue, unarmed."

William was silent, a little too long, for Warenne glanced at Matilda in concern.

"Pray send in only the queen," William said eventually. "Entertain the rest with good wine and food and warmth, and tell them that I shall receive them later."

Warenne nodded, bowed, and left.

Matilda watched as William drew in yet another deep breath, and again clenched and relaxed his hands.

Sweet Christ Lord, she thought, *what has he to be so nervous about?*

And then the door opened, and Edward's queen and Harold's sister entered, and Matilda took her first step on a journey of mystery that she could never have imagined.

THE FIRST THING THAT MATILDA NOTICED AS CAELA hesitated just inside the door was that the woman, if not stunningly beautiful according to court tastes, was nonetheless one of the most arresting figures

Matilda had ever laid eyes on. It was not her features so much, although Caela's face and form, and most particularly her stunning deep blue eyes, were most pleasing, but that Caela had a presence about her that was extraordinary. She was lovely in the manner of a still summer's day, and she carried about her a sense of peace and strength that Matilda would have given her right arm to acquire. She wore very simply-cut clothing, and had left her dark hair unveiled and unworked, save for a loosely bound plait that twisted over her left shoulder, but, even so, with her presence Caela could be recognizable as nothing else but a queen.

The second thing Matilda realized was that Caela was as nervous and as tense as William.

The third thing that Matilda noticed was that William and Caela could not take their eyes off each other.

Matilda was put out by this, only in the sense that it was so unexpected. She did not feel any presentiment of jealousy or of disquiet. She was consumed only by a sense of great curiosity and by a desire to understand what lay behind this extraordinary tension between her husband and Caela.

"My lady queen," Matilda said softly, but with enough strength to make Caela's eyes flicker, then move away from William to his duchess. "I do welcome you to Berkhamsted, although"—Matilda smiled, quite genuinely, and reached out both her hands as she walked over to Caela—"I confess I feel most awkward in welcoming this land's queen into the presence of its invader."

Caela returned Matilda's smile. "I am but its forgotten queen," she said. "The wife of two kings past. Alditha should truly be here."

"No," William said, and Matilda was more than a little relieved to hear that his voice was strong. "*You* are this land's queen, whatever brief claim Alditha might have had to the title. Thus you are here now, not Alditha."

He had also walked over, and Caela took her hands from Matilda's and held them out for William.

As William took them, Matilda had the sense that both William and Caela had quite forgotten she was there.

And again, Matilda's only reaction was one of deep curiosity.

What went on here?

"I am sorry about Harold," William said.

Matilda noticed he had not let go of Caela's hands.

Caela nodded, and tears sprang to her eyes.

"It was none of my doing," William said.

"It was Swanne's doing," said Caela and Matilda as one, and both women looked at each other, smiled, laughed softly, and, in that single moment, became friends and allies.

"Harold told me so much of you," the two women said together, and their laughter deepened, and whatever awkwardness had been in the chamber dissipated, and Caela let William's hands go to lean forward and embrace Matilda.

"Thank you," Caela murmured for Matilda's ears only, "for coming so quickly to William's side. He is whole, thank all the gods."

"I would not allow the snake to take him," Matilda muttered, and Caela leaned back, her face sober now, and nodded at Matilda.

"We should speak later," she said. "You and I.

"But now," she turned back to William, "my lord of Normandy, I have come before you for two reasons."

He inclined his head, his black eyes very steady on her face.

"The first," Caela said, "is to beg for the lives of Harold's children, and that of his wife, Alditha. She is currently with child, and greatly fearful that you intend her harm."

"I did not wish him dead, Caela. I would have done anything to prevent that."

"I know," she said softly.

"I vowed to Harold that Alditha and his children would remain safe, Caela. And so they shall. As shall you. He asked for your life as well. Did you know that?"

"I do not fear you, William."

Matilda felt that she should say something, if only to reassert her presence in the chamber. "William has already hammered his orders into the heads of every one of the Normans with us," she said. "They are not to be harmed, and given every assistance possible."

"Then thank you both," said Caela. "The safety of Harold's family means a great deal to me. The second reason I stand before you is to hand you London." She paused. "It is, after all, yours."

Matilda frowned at that. What did Caela mean?

William's mouth twitched in a tiny smile. "Then I will gladly accept London's surrender, madam."

"Other members of the witan wait outside. Shall you—"

"No, leave them for now. Perhaps . . ."

"Perhaps William and I can remember the more courtly among our manners," Matilda put in smoothly, "and offer you a chance to sit and perhaps have a cup of fine wine. Will you accept?"

Caela smiled. "Gladly, my lady."

THEY SAT FOR SOME TIME, SIPPING WINE, CHATTING agreeably; every look, every spoken word reinforcing Matilda's growing belief that her husband and this queen were only reacquainting themselves rather than establishing an acquaintance.

William and Caela also focused too much of their discussion on Matilda. What Matilda had expected (before Caela had actually entered their chamber) was that there would be tense verbal parrying as the queen tried to ensure the safety of her people and country, and William tried to ensure every concession possible. Instead, Matilda found herself in the slightly surreal situation of fielding constant questions from both Caela and William as they both tried very desperately not to engage the other one in anything other than banalities about the weather or the state of the rushes on the floor. Caela asked a score of questions about Matilda's children, and about her current pregnancy. William asked Matilda to relate amusing incidents from their life together, and from that time in their youth when they'd had to fight so hard to marry against what felt like all of Europe combined against them.

It was only during this last topic that there came a very deep and personal interaction between William and Caela.

As Matilda finished relating the three years of struggling with princely and papal objections, Caela actually looked at William directly.

"How strange for you," she said, "that you had to spend so much energy and time fighting for the right to occupy your wife's bed. From what I know of you, I should have thought you would only have taken her as you willed, and damned all consequences. I had no idea objections had come to mean so much to you."

There was a stillness between them as Matilda tried to frantically work out the hidden meaning in what Caela had just said.

"My sensibilities have changed," William finally said.

"How fortunate for Matilda," said Caela, and now there was a decided edge to her voice.

"There have been deeds in my past that I have come to regret," William said. "I wish I had not forced . . ."

He stopped suddenly, his eyes sliding his wife's way.

You! Matilda thought, her face very calm. *You! That's what you were about to say.*

"I have learned from my mistakes," he said, and now his voice was as hard as Caela's.

Caela inclined her head toward Matilda. "Patently, my lord of Normandy."

"Matilda," William said very slowly, his eyes first on his goblet of wine and then lifting to Caela, "has taught me how greatly I should have treasured . . ."

You! Matilda felt like standing and screaming that single word that William was so loathe to utter. Yet for all the implications of this conversation, Matilda still did not feel a single pang of jealousy or of possessiveness. All she wanted was to somehow discover what these two were talking about, and how it was—Matilda took a deep breath as she finally allowed the thought to form in her mind—how it was that William and Caela had come to love each other so deeply.

Then, as Matilda struggled within herself, Caela turned her lovely eyes to the duchess and said, simply, "I am sorry . . ."

A pause, as Matilda wondered what that apology referred to.

"I am tired," Caela continued, "and I admit that my reception had worried me so excessively on the journey to Berkhamsted that now I feel over-weary. I speak nonsense, my lady. Forgive me."

You weren't speaking nonsense to William, Matilda thought, *for you have not begged forgiveness of him.*

"We can find a quiet space for you within this abbey house," Matilda said, "where you might rest. Tonight, perhaps, you and your delegation may sup with the duke and myself."

Caela inclined her head, but Matilda had not yet done.

She turned to William. "My lord," she said formally, and she saw the wariness surface in his eyes; "my lord" was only a title Matilda bothered to use when she wanted something of him. "My lord, may I request a boon from you?"

William, still wary, raised an eyebrow.

"I wonder if I might request the presence of Queen Caela within my ladies. Not," she added hurriedly, shooting Caela her own look of apology, "as a member of my retinue, but as my honored companion and, indeed, my better. It would ensure your safety," she said to Caela, "if you remained within the duke's company, and would provide me with a companion for whom I would be most grateful. I would like to know you better, Caela. I . . . you intrigue me."

There, best to be honest.

Caela looked at William.

"You would not object?" he said.

She shook her head, and smiled back at Matilda. "I, too, would like to deepen my acquaintance with you, Matilda. I will stay awhile, gladly."

"Good," said Matilda.

THAT NIGHT, WHEN MATILDA AND WILLIAM ENTERED their bed, Matilda turned to her husband, and offered him her mouth.

He made love to her, sweetly and gently, and for that sacrifice, Matilda loved him more than ever.

Chapter Fifteen

Caela Speaks

H, BY ALL THE GODS OF HEAVEN AND HELL, I could not believe he was so handsome. Brutus had been good-looking enough, but his features had been too blunt for true handsomeness. But William, William . . . I lay in my bed that night, grateful for its privacy, and thought of him in bed with his wife, and I envied her so desperately that it became a physical pain within my breast.

I had not expected this: not his handsomeness, his vitality, nor my instinctive gut-longing for him. I do not know if this was simple sexual desire (I cannot imagine any woman coming into the presence of William the duke of Normandy and not feel her belly turn to water as he looked at her), some greater depth of love, or that much greater need I had of him for the future of both this land and the Game.

I was so grateful for Matilda. I had mooned over William like some virgin girl, and she did not berate me for it. He and I spoke in what were riddles to her, and she did not ask for an explanation. Beyond that, I was most beholden to Matilda, for it was stunningly obvious to me that William's transformation away from that hard-hearted, ambitious brute he had once been into something more reasonable was all her doing. But what I blessed Matilda for most of all was her gut instinct about Swanne's danger, and her actions according to that instinct. I'd heard that she'd come most unexpectedly to Hastings a day or so after the battle, and I had no doubt that it was her arrival that had kept William whole.

Safe.

I had felt that from him the moment I took his hands in mine. *He was still safe from Swanne!* I swear I almost threw myself at his feet and wept in relief at that moment of realization. Instead, I did the better thing and embraced Matilda, for she was the one responsible for his current wholeness.

Matilda had managed to find for me a small, but, most gratefully, private space within the abbey house. I had no women with me, not even Judith, and so I was almost like a child in my sense of freedom as I did for myself that night (Matilda had offered me one of her women, but I had declined). So I lay there, sleepless as my thoughts tumbled about, thinking almost entirely of William (my thoughts oscillating between relief at his wholeness to a slight feminine numbness at his attractiveness), and occasionally of Matilda.

Eventually, my thoughts were rudely drawn to Swanne.

She came to visit me in the small hours of the night.

I had not been asleep, but the soft footfalls approaching my tiny chamber nevertheless disturbed me. At first I had thought they might be William, and I was terrified, for I did not know what to say to him, but then I realized that whoever it might be was far too light for his tall frame.

In the end, I wished it had been William, for Swanne was far more terrifying than anything he could have been.

I had not seen Swanne since that terrible night when I had gone to her as Damson. There had been no reason for us to meet, and I, most certainly, had not tried to instigate a meeting. I had wanted to leave her well enough alone.

So, as I raised myself to my elbow and studied the dark figure that slipped in my door, I had a sudden, terrifying moment of sheer panic as I realized who my visitor was.

Could she harm me?

Could she see whom and what I had become?

And then I felt a moment of self-loathing for my cowardice. I would need to deal with Swanne eventually and, moreover, I *needed* Swanne. Nothing in my future could be achieved without her aid.

Somehow.

But still, knowing her alliance with Asterion, I simply could not help a tremor of fright as she came to my bed, saw me looking up at her, and then sat down on the edge of the mattress.

"Well, well, Caela. Come to your man, have you?"

"He is not 'mine,'" I said, grateful my voice remained steady. "Nor shall he ever be."

"Good girl," Swanne said patronizingly, and reached out and patted my cheek. "What do you here then?"

"I come to surrender London into William's hands."

"And then run back to your convent, I hope."

I said nothing. It was difficult to see any details of Swanne's features or her expression in the dark, but, silhouetted against the faint light coming through the doorway, I could make out an ever-changing landscape of lines and angles about the outline of her face. "Snake," Matilda had called her, and I thought that an apt name for her.

"I am amazed that you lie here so quietly," Swanne said after a moment's silence, "when William undoubtedly heaves and grunts over Matilda in their chamber."

"I am unsurprised to find you here so unquietly," I responded, "when William undoubtedly makes love to Matilda in their chamber."

I saw her stiffen.

"She is nothing," Swanne said.

"I do not think so," I said.

"She is not the Mistress of the Labyrinth!" Swanne hissed.

"She is far more to him."

"You simpleton! You have no idea—"

"To everything a purpose," I said, edging myself up in the bed so that I sat upright. "Is that not what the Bible says?"

"The Bible is nothing but worthless—"

"Matilda is your penance," I said, very softly, "for what you did to me in our former life."

I think I struck her dumb. I know she sat there, rigid with emotion, staring at me for a long time. Finally, she broke the silence.

"And where have you found your backbone, my lady?" she asked.

"From life, and experience, and tragedy. Through loss of innocence, Swanne. For that loss, I think, I have you to thank."

Again, a silence. I considered her, and I remembered how powerful she had been as Genvissa, both as MagaLlan and as Mistress of the Labyrinth. I remembered also her years as Harold's wife, when she had been so influential within the court. Yet, as Swanne, Asterion's creature, she had lost all power, whatever she may have thought. Oh, she was still dangerous, and could command magic, but she had lost completely that aura of extraordinariness that had once so set her apart from everyone else.

I realized that Swanne now, even as menacing as she remained, had become little more than a shadow flitting like a forgotten ghost through the unlit hallways of whatever court she thought to seek power within. Few people paid any attention to her, most people had likely forgotten her existence, or ceased to care about it.

For the first time since I had even known her, either as Swanne or as Genvissa, I felt sorry for her.

At that thought, my mouth opened and words tumbled forth from some dark, intuitive place.

"Swanne, if ever you need shelter, I will give it to you."

"What?"

"If ever you need harbor, I am it." *This is what I should have said and done when I went to her as Damson!* Suddenly I knew what I was doing. It had become clear to me, as I had trusted it would. In offering Swanne shelter, in offering to be her friend, I was opening the way to the day when Swanne would hand to me the powers of the Mistress of the Labyrinth. Willingly. As Damson, I had tried to bargain with Swanne, tried to exact the powers of the Mistress of the Labyrinth from her as payment for services rendered. That had been a foul thing to do. Instead, I should have offered her friendship.

Freely. No conditions.

Swanne started to draw back, but I reached out a hand and grabbed her wrist. "Swanne, *if ever you need harbor, then I am it!*"

"Let me go!" She wrenched her wrist from my grip and rose, almost stumbling in her haste. "Your wits are gone, Caela!"

"If ever you need a friend, Swanne, then I am it." Suddenly, as I said that, I no longer hated her, nor even feared her very much. *Poor Swanne . . .*

She took a step backward, again almost stumbling as her heel caught in her skirts.

"If ever you need a friend, Swanne . . ." *then I am it.*

Then she was gone, and I found that, as I lay back down to my pillow, sleep came easily to me, and I slept dreamlessly until the following morning, when the sound of Normans clattering down to their breakfast awakened me.

MATILDA AND I SAT, CHATTING, PASSING THE DAY IN idleness while about us men and horses bustled about the courtyard outside as William prepared to march on London.

London had been given; he wasted no time taking.

It seemed to me that I had wasted a lifetime in idle chatter over needlework. I had certainly wasted most of my marriage to Edward bent submissively over wools and silks. And here I was yet again, a former queen with the queen yet to be crowned, talking of children and babies and childbirth and, of course, wools and silks.

Thus it was that when Matilda sighed, placed her needlework to one side, and said, "I am curious as to how it can be that William loves you so deeply," I was somewhat dumbfounded.

Then, as I stared at her with, I am afraid, my mouth hanging slightly open,

wondering how on earth to respond, she smiled with what seemed like genuine amusement.

"I have misphrased that question," Matilda said, "for I did not mean to
suggest that it could not be possible for William, or any other man, to love
you, for you are a greatly desirable woman, but that how it is that William can
have come to love you. Has he fallen in love only with rumor? Or did he somehow hold you as an infant, he but a small boy, and conceive then his great passion for you?"

There was absolutely nothing in her voice but intense curiosity, and I think
that surprised me as much as . . . as the idea that William loved me.

He hated me. He'd always hated me.

"I . . . he can't love me," I said.

In response, Matilda simply nodded to my lap. "You're bleeding," she
said.

I looked down. At some point in the last few moments I'd stuck my needle
almost completely through my left index finger. I pulled it out hastily, wincing, and sucked at the pinprick of a wound, feeling like a child.

"On our marriage night," Matilda said, "William paid me the courtesy of
being honest. He said that I would never be the great love of his life. Ah, do
not fret, Caela. I accepted that then, and I accept it now. But for these past
sixteen or so years I have thought my great rival to be Swanne. Now I realize
that it is you that William loves beyond all others—and you him. Caela, I ask
again, and in simple curiosity and not in judgement, how can this be so?"

My left hand was back in my lap, and now I looked down at it, and wondered what to say.

"And all my marriage," Matilda continued in a soft voice, "I have known
that William was somehow very, very much more than 'just' the duke of Normandy. That there is another level, another purpose to his life that he has kept
entirely from me. Is it you, or are you just a part of it?"

"A mere part of it," I said.

She was silent, waiting.

"Matilda, to tell you would be to involve you in such dark witchery that—"

"Swanne is dark witchery," Matilda said. "You are not. Swanne had the
power to ruin my life. You have the power to enrich it. I am not afraid nor
threatened by you, Caela. Please—".

"Matilda."

We both jumped slightly, and looked to the door.

William stood there, leaning against the door frame, his arms folded, his
eyes unreadable.

I had no idea how long he had been standing there.

"Matilda, my love," he said, unfolding his arms and walking into the room. "I would speak privately with Caela for a time. Do you mind?"

"Of course not," Matilda said. She rose, kissed first me and then William on the cheek, almost as if she were blessing us, and left.

Finally, my heart pounding, I raised my eyes and looked into William's face.

CHAPTER SIXTEEN

OU ARE WELL SERVED IN YOUR WIFE," CAELA SAID
after a long, uncomfortable pause.

"She is a better wife to me than you were," William said, taking Matilda's chair.

"She has made you into a better husband than I managed," Caela said.

The skin about William's eyes crinkled in humor. "So Cornelia is still buried in there somewhere."

"We are all who once we were, only . . ."

"Changed," he said. "You are far lovelier than you were as Cornelia, and that loveliness is not just reflected in your features. You are calmer, more at peace with yourself. Stronger. Wiser." *And more still,* he thought, but could not put words to that difference.

"And you?"

"As you said, I am a better husband."

Silence, as both looked away from each other.

"Why did you lie with my father?" William said eventually.

"You saw?"

"Yes. My *father,* Caela?"

"What care is it of yours?" she said.

"Why?" His voice was very soft now.

She lowered her gaze, her wounded hand making a helpless gesture. "He reminded me of you. He had your look, save gentler, and kinder. More weary. I was lonely and in need, William. I was in no mood to reject what he offered. He was a mistake. I lay with him only that once."

"Did he please you?" His black eyes were steady on her face.

"No." She paused. "Not as once you did. He was your father, but he was not you."

"You should not have lain with him, Caela."

"What concern is it of yours? *What?*"

Now it was William who spread his hands in a helpless gesture. "None. I know that. I just . . . I just wish you had not. Not with my father . . ."

"I'd wished it was you," she said, "but I could not have you. I thought Silvius could fill the void. I was wrong."

"I heard what Matilda said to you, Caela. But I do not love you. There is too much shared hatred for us to—"

"I know. You do not have to explain."

"Dammit," he muttered, looking away.

"William—"

"I did not come here to talk to you of love," William said. "There are more urgent matters, as I am sure you realize."

"Yes."

"Caela, do you remember those bands I wore about my limbs?"

Her shoulders tensed at this change in subject, and he did not miss it. "Yes."

"Someone has been moving them."

"Yes."

There was a long, heavy pause. "Do you know who?"

"Yes." Another pause, and Caela kept her eyes directly on him. "I have."

William's mouth dropped open, and he stared at her for so long and so incredulously that Caela eventually had to look away.

"*You* shifted the bands?"

"Yes."

"How? *How?* Only I or the Mistress of the Labyrinth could have touched those bands! And *possibly* Silvius, as he was once their Kingman also." William's voice was rising, and Caela flinched as he slid forward on the chair then stood up. "*How* could *you* have moved them, Caela?"

She studied her hands clenched in her lap a long moment, then looked up. "The Troy Game has changed, William."

"What do *you* know of the Game?"

Caela visibly steeled herself. "The Game was left alone a long time, William. Uncompleted. It changed." She gave a small, helpless shrug. "It became attuned to the land, and the land to it. William, the Troy Game is no longer the passive thing I think that maybe you believe it to be. Something that waits for your touch. Yes, it wants completion. Yes, it wants the strength that will come with that. But it also wants that completion and strength on *its* terms." She paused. "And this *land* wants the Game completed on its terms as well. The land and the Game are agreed on how this should be done."

William stared at her for a long moment in silence. *How was it that she spoke on behalf of the Game and the land?* He spoke one single, expressionless word: "Yes?"

"The Game wants the male and female elements of this land to complete it, William. It means it will become one with the land. Completely melded with it."

"Explain that to me," William said, his voice now dangerously quiet.

"In simple terms—"

"How *good* of you."

Caela winced. "The Game wants the female and male elements of this land, the ancient gods Mag and Og, to complete the Game as the Mistress of the Labyrinth and the Kingman. It does not want you or Swanne to—"

"What have you done?"

"I have done nothing! William, the Game has—"

"Are you still Asterion's pawn?"

"No! William, I beg you, listen to—"

"This Game is *mine*, and *Swanne's!"*

She took a moment to respond, steadying her nerves and her voice. "The Game is its own, in partnership with the Mistress of the Labyrinth and the Kingman."

"Who you say are to be Mag and Og."

She nodded.

William abruptly stood and walked over to a window. He stood for long minutes, staring outside. "I have not come all this way to be told that," he said finally, turning about. "I have no reason to believe you."

Caela stood, and approached William. He tensed slightly as she neared, but made no move to stop her when she lifted his hand and placed it flat against her breastbone. "See who I am," she whispered, holding his eyes with her own.

He found himself standing within the circle of stones he had once known as Mag's Dance.

Save that the stones were no longer solid, nor even stationary, but instead appeared to have become creatures of wraith and movement and song.

He spun about, both scared and disorientated, and saw that a woman approached him through the spinning circle of dancers.

It was Caela, clothed only in mist and her loose, blowing hair and with such power in her eyes as William could never have imagined her—or any woman— possessing.

"See," she said, and looked to one side of the circle.

A white stag lay there, its head crowned by bloodred antlers.

"He is my lover," she whispered.

William snatched his hand back from Caela. "By all the gods," he whispered. "You are Mag?"

She hesitated, then nodded. "I am what she once was, yes."

"Ah," he said. "Now I understand you. And to think that once all I thought you wanted was my attention and my babies. No. You wanted power. You wanted revenge, against both me and Swanne. And this is it. You have now taken Swanne's place in the Game, or at least fooled the Game into thinking you were what it wanted, which is why it allowed you to touch the bands, and—"

"I am to this land what Mag once was. And yes, I am what the Troy Game now wants—one half of it, at least. I did not 'fool' it, William. I only accepted the decision of both the Troy Game and the land."

"I cannot believe that you would do this to me! And yet . . . how could I not expect it? You always were ready with the dagger to plunge into my back. You were always ready to—"

"Stop! No, William! No! None of this is *my* plan, but that of the Game itself, and of the land!"

"And who do you—oh, I offer my apologies—the *Game* and the *land* think to replace *me* with, then? Loth-reborn, whoever he is?"

"His name is now Saeweald, William. He is a physician tending the wounded as he tends this land."

"Saeweald? Well, Saeweald then. Oh, how it would please him to have me crawl to him and offer him my powers! Or Harold? Is Harold the one who you mean to take as your mate and partner? Yes, I can see that. Harold. I imagine you have a plan to raise him from the dead."

"Don't do this, William," Caela whispered. "Don't become that man of hate again."

"Did you think that you could walk in here and seduce me with face and body and tender voice into betraying everything I have fought for . . . through *two* lives?"

He topped, swore, and stalked away.

"William—"

"You are not the Mistress of the Labyrinth," William said, turning back to face her. "I don't care what *else* you are, but you are *not* the Mistress of the Labyrinth. You do not have the power, and you do not know the steps to complete the Game. *It* cannot teach you. *Silvius* cannot teach you."

"One day, eventually, Swanne will hand to me her powers as Mistress of the Labyrinth."

"What? You have lost your mind! *She* will *never* willingly hand over her powers! *I will never willingly hand over* . . . oh, I cannot *believe* I am having this conversation with you!"

"Will Swanne willingly hand her responsibilities as Mistress of the Labyrinth to me one day? Yes, she will." Caela's voice was very certain.

"You are a fool, and out of your mind."

"Swanne has betrayed you to Asterion."

She could not have said anything else to more stun William into silence.

He gaped at her, his face paling from its fury-induced red, Caela's words bouncing over and over within his head. *Swanne has betrayed you to Asterion.* No. Those words could not mean what they seemed to. Swanne could never have betrayed him to . . .

The taste of blood and decay suddenly overwhelmed William again, and he grunted, as if someone had punched him in the belly, and he sat suddenly on a chair.

Caela walked very slowly, very carefully, over to the chair, kneeling before it and taking one of William's hands in hers. "This was none of my doing, William."

William was not looking at her, slowly shaking his head to and fro.

"I do not know what powers or persuasions Asterion used to so capture Swanne's heart and loyalty, but that he has is undoubted. William, Asterion does not want to destroy the Game. He wants to control it. *He* wants to become its Kingman, using Swanne as his Mistress. She has agreed to this, thinking that in Asterion she has a more powerful Kingman than in you. If you ask why I have moved the bands, then that is why. To protect the Game, and through it, the land, from Asterion and Swanne combined."

William was still shaking his head back and forth, back and forth, but Caela's calm, soft words were beginning to make terrible sense. *Asterion wanted to control the Game, become its Kingman, dance his ambitions out with Swanne. Yes, that made sense. Why hadn't he ever considered this before?*

"Who is Asterion?" he asked finally, softly.

"Aldred."

William winced. *Aldred had been playing both him and Swanne all this time . . .*

"Asterion and Swanne want to trap you, to use you to find the bands. Then, once they have them . . ."

"Stop!"

"William, *listen* to me! Swanne is Asterion's creature now! Everything she says and does is said and done on *his* behalf! Do not trust her. Do not—"

"And everything you say and do is done on *your* behalf, yours and Silvius', no doubt!"

"Everything I say and do is for you, William."

"That is not what you have just been saying. In one breath you tell me that you want me to relinquish all control I have of the Game into Saeweald's or Harold's hands."

"I never said that. What I said was—"

"Get out, Caela! *Get out!*"

"William, don't push me away!" The words tumbled out of Caela's mouth, so desperate was she to have him hear them. "Beware of Swanne and Aldred, and trust me. *Trust* me!"

"Don't you dare say that to me!" He grabbed at her hands and pushed her away roughly so that she sprawled on the floor.

"William!" Caela cried. "Don't push me away when I can—"

"Get out!"

She rose to her feet. "William, when you need me—"

"*Get out!*"

"When you need me, whether in this life, or in any to follow, seek me out."

And then she was gone.

CHAPTER SEVENTEEN

HE ONLY SPACE SWANNE COULD FIND FOR HER-
self in the abbey house was a small, dusty attic space within the
roof of the building. It was filthy, there were rats and lice in the
thatch, and she was forced to sleep on a pallet that was padded only with her
cloak.

It was an existence far different from the one she'd enjoyed as Genvissa,
or even as Harold's wife.

But Swanne did not allow herself to think of such things. These discom-
forts became as nothing when she thought of what would be hers, once she'd
trapped and killed William, Asterion had the bands, and both of them controlled the Game.

But for now she could neither dream of future powers and glories, nor
even sneer at the terrible state of the thatch, for Asterion was with her, and he
was angrier than she'd ever seen him before.

"I cannot understand," he said in a low hiss, "why it is that you have not
yet taken William! How many weeks? How many opportunities?"

"I have tried!" she said, her words stumbling in her haste to placate
Asterion. "But . . . oh! He has some nauseous commitment to his wife. He is
afraid of her. The simpering fool. He says he cannot abide to annoy Matilda.
And she, the *bitch,* she won't allow me near him."

Asterion's hands were on Swanne's shoulders now, soft and caressing, yet
somehow managing to convey an infinite threat in that caress. "Are you sure
it is not *you* he cannot abide?"

"Ha! I almost had him, even though he is terrified of his wife. I had him on
the floor, and then that . . . that *dwarf* interrupted us!"

"What manner of woman are you," Asterion continued, "that you cannot
even seduce a man to your bed? What manner of Mistress of the Labyrinth is
scared of a mere 'wife'?"

Swanne wrenched herself away from his tight hands, furious at him, terrified at his anger. "I have done all I can! Rubbed my nakedness against him!
Taken his member in my hands and roused him! Do not accuse me of—"

Asterion grabbed her shoulders again and gave her a hard shake. "I need William dead, you fool! Neither of us can dare to have him wandering about—"

"You are afraid of him," Swanne said, wonderingly. "Perhaps I was wrong to think you would make a good Kingman, after all. Perhaps William *is* the preferable—"

Swanne stopped as if struck, then her eyes widened and a whine of sheer agony escaped her mouth. She tried to say something, but couldn't. Instead, as Asterion let her go, she sank to the floor and curled up about her belly, whimpering in agony.

"You *will* do what I need," whispered Asterion. "You *will* kill William, and you . . . will . . . do . . . it . . . soon. Before he has a chance to ruin all our plans. Do you understand me?"

She gave a tiny nod, and then visibly relaxed as the imp within her ceased its vicious nibbling.

"There's a good girl," said Asterion in a sickenly soothing voice. He leaned down and patted Swanne on the head. "There is no escaping me, my dear, and it is far better to work with me than against me."

SWANNE LAY ON THE FILTHY FLOOR OF THE ATTIC space clutching at her belly for hours after he had gone. She felt as if her world had disintegrated about her.

Never before had Asterion treated her so cruelly. Why? Did he hate her so much? Had she failed him so badly?

Swanne succumbed to a fit of weeping. She felt hate sweep over her, but not for Asterion. For Matilda, who stood in her way, and for Caela, who had once thought to stand in her way and who now had somehow managed to retreat into a smug complacency.

Why, Swanne had no idea.

She remembered what Caela had said to her last night.

Swanne, if ever you need shelter, I will give it to you. If ever you need harbor, I am it.

"Silly bitch," Swanne muttered, and managed to struggle into a sitting position. *Shelter from what, for the gods' sakes?* All Swanne had to do was murder William, and then Asterion would be grateful, and pleased, and would love her again, and would give her all the dark power she craved.

"I'll kill Matilda first," she said. "Yes. I'll kill Matilda, and then I'll take William. Easy. Simple. I should have thought of it sooner."

They would be in London soon, and there Swanne knew she would get what she needed.

chapter eighteen

HINKING ONLY OF FLEEING WILLIAM'S NOT unexpected anger, Caela did not immediately register the fact that the door to the chamber had not been closed when she fled. All she could think about was returning to her own small chamber, gathering her cloak, and then making her way to the courtyard where she might prevail upon someone to escort her back to London.

But the moment she entered her own chamber, leaving the door open, as she only needed to snatch at her cloak, Caela heard a footfall behind her, and then the sound of the door closing.

She spun about.

Matilda stood there, staring at her. Caela began to speak, but Matilda waved her to silence. She closed the distance between them, lifted her hand, and placed it firmly on Caela's breastbone.

"Show me what you showed William," she said.

"Matilda—"

"*Show me!*"

And so Caela did.

Eventually, as William had, Matilda stood back, her hand falling away from Caela, her face pale. "Who are you?" she whispered. "What are you?"

"Matilda, I did not want to involve you in this."

"I have been involved ever since I married William! *Tell me!*"

Caela closed her eyes, and tried one last time. "If I tell you, I will involve you in witchcraft so malevolent that it will destroy . . ."

"What? My entire life?"

"This life, and all future lives," Caela said softly.

Matilda stared at Caela, and suddenly everything fell into place. "That is why William and you know each other so well . . . this is not your first life together, is it?"

Caela shook her head.

"But how can this be so? Nothing that the Church teaches can explain—"

"We come from a time long before the Church existed. It cannot know of us, and of what we do."

"A time of dark witchcraft!"

"And a time of great beauty," Caela said gently.

"Tell me," Matilda said.

"Matilda, are you sure that—"

"Tell me."

And so Caela drew Matilda back to the bed where they sat, and Caela told her.

FOR HOURS AFTER CAELA HAD LEFT HIM, WILLIAM SAT in the chair, head in hands, his entire world a turmoil.

Aldred . . . Asterion.

Swanne . . . perhaps even now lying with Asterion, plotting William's downfall.

Caela . . . a part of this land as William had never imagined.

For the moment, Asterion and Swanne, and what they planned, *what they could accomplish,* were too frightful to consider, so William concentrated entirely on Caela.

Oh, God, how beautiful and desirable she had been. Perhaps, strangely, he had no trouble believing what she had told him about her nature as it was now, and not simply because of what Caela had shown him of herself. He remembered how only relatively recently Swanne had told him Caela (and Cornelia) had harbored Mag within her womb. As Cornelia, she had loved this land the instant she'd seen it. He remembered how she'd stood on the deck of the ship, their son Achates in her arms, staring at the line of green cliffs in the distance. He remembered how she had once told him that arriving in this new and strange land was not "strange" at all, but felt rather as if she was finally coming home.

He remembered how she had instinctively known what the Stone Dances were for, their purpose, their magic.

He remembered how effortlessly Cornelia had learned the Llangarlian language, as if she'd merely been remembering it, not learning it at all.

He remembered how immediately close she had been to the people of the land—to Erith and her family.

To Blangan.

To Coel.

Cornelia had walked onto this land and instantly become one with it.

He, as Brutus, had walked onto this land and instantly become its enemy.

Why? Because he'd only seen Genvissa? Only seen the power and lust she'd represented?

William's mind began to worry at him as he tried to piece things together. Genvissa had been Cornelia's instant enemy. Genvissa had done nothing but plot Cornelia's murder from the instant she'd known about her. Genvissa had used the excuse that Cornelia was Asterion's tool—but that wasn't only it, was it? Genvissa had seen within Cornelia a terrible threat, and it had nothing to do with Asterion but everything to do with this land.

William groaned, wondering how he could have been so blind. How could he have so blithely ignored everything Genvissa *was*? Everything she *did*?

Ariadne had wrapped the Aegean world in catastrophe. Genvissa—and in her rebirth as Swanne—was doing the same.

No wonder the Llangarlians had been so antagonistic. No wonder they had fought so hard against Genvissa and all she stood for.

William rose and paced slowly about the room, thinking now on the Game. Caela said it had changed, become attuned to the land.

Could it? William tried to remember everything he had been taught about the Game, but nothing he had been taught catered to the current situation. No Game had ever been left so long uncompleted between the opening and closing dances.

Had the Game become attuned to the land to the extent that it had all but merged with the land?

There was no reason that it should not have. Two thousand years left uncompleted. *Gods!* It could have done anything in that time.

Slowly William's mind began to unwind from its turmoil into a peculiar kind of peace, even though he felt disjointed and a little disorientated. He found himself standing in the center of his chamber, seeing not the cold stone walls, but the labyrinth as it had stood atop Og's Hill, the maidens and youths with their flowers, dancing about him and his Mistress.

He saw the Mistress of the Labyrinth standing before him, dressed only in a hip-hugging white linen skirt. He saw her lithe body, her breasts glowing in the torchlight.

He saw her deep blue eyes and her smile, as they rested on him.

He saw Caela, and William was suddenly hit with such a longing that he again groaned, and doubled over, as if in pain.

Could Caela be the Mistress of the Labyrinth? Yes, of course she could, if she were taught, but she *had* to be taught, and it could be none of his teaching. The mysteries of the Mistress were alien to William. He could dance with a Mistress as her partner, but he could never truly understand her power.

Was he angry that Caela sought to become the Mistress of the Labyrinth?

No. Not truly.

What angered and embittered him—even as he could not understand it—was that she did not want him to dance with her as her Kingman.

What frightened him was what he had seen when she had lain with Silvius.

When all was said and done, she had possibly betrayed him as deeply as had Swanne.

"THERE," SAID CAELA EVENTUALLY. "YOU HAVE IT ALL."

Matilda felt numbed by what she'd heard, and yet she disbelieved none of it. Everything fit her own experience and observation.

"You do not seem overly surprised," said Caela, watching Matilda carefully.

"The details have shocked me," Matilda replied, "but I do not find them difficult to believe."

Caela took the other woman's hands. "Matilda, listen to me carefully. Do not become involved in this, no more than you are now. I could not bear that you should be injured in a battle that has nothing to do with you. I have hurt and murdered too many innocent people, sometimes willfully, sometimes unintentionally. I could not bear to have your hurt or death on my conscience as well."

"'Murdered' is a strong word, Caela."

"What else can I call the death of my father, Pandrasus? And my nurse, Tavia? All the people of Mesopotama? Damson! Oh, Damson . . ."

"Damson? How can you blame yourself for Damson's death? Caela—"

"I used her unwittingly, and sent her into danger. She was a sweet and simple woman who—"

"*A sweet and simple woman?* Ah, Caela! Enough! I cannot have you carry this burden. Listen to me . . . Damson knew precisely what she was doing. And her greatest 'talent' in her life was that she fooled most people into thinking she was 'sweet and simple.'"

"That is good of you to try and make me feel better, Matilda, but—"

"For sixteen years, Caela, Damson was my agent within Edward's court."

Caela's mouth dropped open.

"Damson was a cunning and knowing woman," Matilda continued, "Not 'sweet and simple' at all. I met her several times in the days before I sent her to Edward's court, and I am very well aware of precisely who and what she was. Do not berate yourself on Damson's account. She had long previously accepted the risks of the life she led, and if you want someone to blame for putting her in Swanne's way, then blame *me*. I was the one who sent her to Swanne when she moved to Aldred's palace."

"You sent her to spy on Swanne?"

"When I discovered that William and Swanne were lovers in the first month or so of my marriage, I sent Damson to be my own personal agent at Edward's court. She was to report on Swanne to me . . . if Swanne moved to destroy my marriage and my life, then I wanted to be warned of it. Later, my dear, I set Damson to watch you. After Harold came to visit, I became increasingly curious about you."

"But . . ." Caela still could not believe what she was hearing.

"Do not fret." Matilda smiled. "Damson discovered nothing about you that she could report to me, save a sense that you were far more than you appeared to be." Matilda shrugged. "You thought you were using her. She was spying on you. You thought you had sent Damson to her death. I already had. Caela, Damson is not your guilt to bear. Nor mine neither. Damson had responsibility for her own life."

Caela was silent.

"And your father Pandrasus, and Tavia? Your fault? No. They were victims not of any single ill will, but of circumstance. Mesopotama was destroyed by the miasma of hate, Caela, not by any single person or action. Everyone hated: you, Brutus, Membricus, Pandrasus, the Mesopotamans, the Trojans. A small boy walking down the streets of Mesopotama could have sparked the disaster that ate it as much as anything you did, or anything Brutus did. Forgive yourself, Caela. Don't carry around a burden of useless and unearned guilt."

Caela gave a small smile. "I wish you had been with me in my previous life, Matilda. I think somehow it would have been a happier time for me."

"I can make it a happier time for you in the future," Matilda said, and squeezed Caela's hand where it lay in her lap.

CHAPTER NINETEEN

C AELA AND MOTHER ECUB STOOD ON PEN HILL, THE stones humming gently about them, and watched as William the Conqueror took London.

His army had been split into four, and it approached the city from four directions, entering from the south via London Bridge, from the northeast via Aldgate, from the west via Ludgate, and the largest column from the north via Cripplegate.

This last column approached Cripplegate from the northern road, which took them past Pen Hill, and it was with this column that William and Matilda rode.

Caela and Ecub could just make him out: William was unmistakable in his brilliant jeweled armor.

"Did you tell him?" Ecub asked.

Caela shook her head, her eyes not leaving the distant figure. "He did not want to hear. He is not ready."

Ecub sighed.

"His wife, however," Caela continued, "did."

Ecub turned to Caela, an eyebrow raised.

"Matilda will be coming to visit you," Caela said. "Eventually."

Ecub laughed delightedly. "Asterion has his own Gathering," she said. "And I shall have mine."

William saw Matilda glancing at the crest of the hill, and his mouth tightened.

"They are watching," Matilda said. "Caela, and a woman I think must be Mother Ecub."

WILLIAM SAID NOTHING, HIS EYES NOW BACK ON THE road before him. He was still furious that Caela had told Matilda.

Unbelieving that Caela had told Matilda.

It was not so much anger that Matilda now knew—in a sense William was relieved that he no longer had to deceive her, or hold anything back from her—but anger because William was terrified Caela had now trapped Matilda within the same maelstrom of rebirth and disaster that caught so many others. Matilda did not deserve that; she deserved only to live out this life with as much blessing and peace as he could manage to give her, and then to die without lying on her deathbed wondering how and when she would be drawn back.

William was also angry because, of all things, Matilda's sympathies seemed to be leaning more toward Caela in this mess than to him. *Women!*

Is it so bad that Caela might be the Mistress of the Labyrinth? Matilda had asked him the previous night.

He had not answered her, and, after a silence, Matilda had said softly. *You do not mind that at all, do you? You are truly only angry because you think she has not chosen to dance the final enchantment with you. You are riven with jealousy. You love her, you want her, you cannot bear her choosing another over you.*

At that, William had been so infuriated that he had not picked up on Matilda's carefully chosen words. *I do not love her!* he'd shouted.

Matilda had only smiled at him.

"Keep away from them," William now said as, gratefully, the hill slid past. Matilda only smiled.

"I command it!"

She tipped her head in a gesture that might have been acquiescence.

Not wanting to fight with her any longer, William nodded. "Good."

Tonight, he thought, *the bands. Tonight I shall retrieve the bands.*

CHAPTER TWENTY

*L*ONDON! IT LAY SPREAD OUT BEFORE HIM, windows and torches glittering in the cold midnight. *His!* Finally.

Few Londoners had taken to the streets to witness the conqueror take his city. Most had stayed indoors, windows shuttered, anticipating, perhaps, riot and pillage.

But William had his Normans under tight command. He established control of the city within hours, securing it both within and without, then sent the majority of his army to establish encampments a good distance without the walls, so that the Londoners might not feel too severely the humiliation of Norman victory.

William took for himself and Matilda the bishop of London's great house, preferring for the moment not to remove himself to Westminster. To his captains he said that he wanted to ensure that the Londoners felt the full power of his domination, but privately William could not have borne to remove himself from that for which he had lusted for so long.

He had entered London.

He was not going to willingly remove himself from it until he had what he wanted.

The Trojan kingship bands. His limbs burned for their touch.

At dusk William had come to St. Paul's atop Lud Hill. There he had brushed aside the murmured concerns of the deacons and monks and strode down the nave toward the small door that gave access to the eastern tower. Waving away his soldiers, saying only that he wanted some solitude with which to gaze upon his new conquest, William climbed the tower's rickety wooden stairs three at a time, emerging on the flat-topped tower just as full night set in.

Here he'd stood for hours, *feeling*, sensing out the bands. Oh, William remembered where he'd buried them two thousand years before, but over two thousand years the landscape had changed remarkably. The city had grown, buildings stood where once had spread only orchards, streams had been enclosed . . . and yet nothing had changed. The Troy Game was still here.

William could feel it beneath his feet. By sheer luck (or design, perhaps?), this tower stood over the very heart of the labyrinth, by now buried many feet below the crypt of the cathedral. Now the power of the Troy Game throbbed up through soil, wood, stone, and the leather soles of his boots, surging through William's body as strongly as it had done when he stood with naked feet on the labyrinth itself.

More strongly.

Caela had said the Game had changed, and William could feel it. It had grown . . . independent.

It was going to be very hard to control.

It would be impossible to control without his kingship bands.

William shivered, and gazed over the nighttime city. Caela had moved all six of the bands; or, at least, all six had been moved. William could feel four of them very clearly, calling out to him, longing to be touched and slid over his flesh once more. They were now scattered to the west, north, and south of the city, miles away, but he could feel them, and could feel how the Game had grown to meet them.

The remaining two bands . . .

They were not where he'd left them two thousand years earlier. Caela had taken them, but he could not sense them at all.

What had she done with them? Where had she hid them?

"My, what a fine man you have grown into. Taller than I imagined. I wonder if those bands will still fit you . . . if you ever discover them."

William whipped about. Silvius stood two paces away, his arms folded, dressed in the manner of Troy, with nothing but a white waistcloth and boots.

His flesh was very dark in the low light, but his good eye flashed, while of his left there was nothing but a seething pit of darkness.

"What do you here?" William said, trying to keep his voice level. *Gods, how much power had both Silvius and the Game accumulated if his father could appear this solid, this real, this . . . here?*

"Come to see my son. What else?" Silvius let his arms fall to his side, and he took a half pace forward. "Come to wonder."

"At what?"

"At you, of course." Silvius paused. "Come to see what my son has made of himself."

"Do you like what you see?"

"Does it matter anymore what I think or like?" Silvius paused, his eyes running up and down William's body. "You have seen Caela. Did she tell you that she and I—"

"Yes," William said curtly. "You have become most intimate with Caela, it seems."

Silvius' face took on a lecherous cast. "Very intimate. She has changed, and vastly for the better. It seems you have not. Vile corruption has forever been your creed, has it not? You founded this Game on it, and you seek it out still."

There was a strange note to Silvius' voice, and William did not know what to make of it. "Did it make you happy to lay with her? Did that give you satisfaction? She is not *yours*, Silvius."

Silvius laughed. "Oh, yes, she is. She gave herself to me freely. *Gave* herself to me, William! Freely!" He paused, and when Silvius resumed, his voice was roped with viciousness and contempt. "You lost her two thousand years ago. She can never be yours now."

William regarded his father with as much steadiness as he could summon. "Why do you interfere, father? What has any of this to do with you?"

"*You* made me a part of it! *You* founded the Game on my murder. I warned you not to found the Game on corruption, that fratricide was no way to—"

"This is none of your business, Silvius. Crawl away back to your death. Leave Caela alone. Leave me alone. Leave the Game to play out as it will."

"The Game will play out according to *my* will, William. *Mine*."

William's eyes narrowed, and for a moment it appeared as if he did not breath. Then he said, very softly, "No wonder my mother Claudia died in my birth. It was her only means of escaping you."

Silvius' lip curled. "You killed Claudia. Not me. *You* tore her apart."

William stared at Silvius, his own eyes almost as clouded and dark as his father's empty eye socket.

"You shall never succeed," he said. "The Game is mine."

And with that he pushed past Silvius, and disappeared down the stairwell.

WILLIAM RACED DOWN THE STEPS AS IF HIS LIFE depended on it, his breathing harsh and ragged as it tore through his throat. Four times he stumbled, almost falling, sliding inelegantly down five or six steps before his scrabbling hands managed to find purchase on the stone walls.

When he finally reached the bottom, he took a moment to steady his breathing, glancing back up the stairwell as if he expected Silvius to come bearing down upon him at any moment, before he stepped out to meet the concerned faces of his men.

"Robert," William said to one of his most trusted men-at-arms, "there is a priory about two miles out of the city on the northern road. Ride there, and deliver a message to the dowager queen Caela. Let her pick the place, but demand that she meet with me *tonight*! Impress upon her the need for urgency. You have that?"

Robert nodded, then left at a trot.

William closed his eyes, and took a deep breath. *Gods, let her agree! Let her agree!*

The situation had been bad before this night. Now it was almost irreparable.

When he had been Brutus, and Silvius had been his living father, his mother's name had been Lavinia.

Not Claudia.

Never Claudia. When William had left her earlier that evening, Matilda waited until she'd heard the clatter of his horse's hooves as it left the courtyard, and then she'd snapped her fingers at one of his sergeants.

"Find me a quiet mare to ride," she said, "and an escort. I need to visit a priory just beyond the walls."

The sergeant thought about arguing with his duchess for all of two heartbeats.

Then he nodded, and within a half hour was riding with the escort surrounding Matilda through Cripplegate.

A half hour after that, Matilda stood before the gates of the priory, watching as the door slowly swung open.

"You are Mother Ecub," she said to the woman who stood there, and Ecub nodded.

"Sister," she said, and stepped forward and embraced Matilda.

SWANNE SAT IN HER CHAMBER, ONCE AGAIN WITHIN Aldred's palace. She didn't know where the good archbishop had got to, and she didn't care. Asterion was the only one who came to her now, and for that she was heartily glad.

All Swanne could think about was Matilda's, and then William's, murder.

Aldred's palace held many comforts. One of those had been a blessed bath—Swanne had soaked for what seemed like hours within a tub set before a fire—and the other had been having access again to Hawise. Hawise had not accompanied Swanne south (Swanne had told her to stay within London, thinking then that she'd be able to take William and return to London herself within a day or so of the battle), and Swanne had missed her sorely. Not for her company, for Swanne had grown to detest Hawise's prattling, but because Hawise was one of the best people she had ever met for procuring things.

Now Swanne sat in a comfortable chair, holding in her hands a vial of one of the deadliest poisons she had been able to concoct. Hawise, of course, had no idea she was procuring a poison for Swanne, nor did she have any idea what Swanne was going to do with the collection of herbs her mistress had sent her out for.

But when Hawise had brought those herbs back, Swanne had spent a delightful hour or two mixing and fermenting them, distilling from them the purest, blackest poison she could manage.

Matilda's death.

It would look like a miscarriage gone terribly wrong. She would lose the child, and then bleed to death. What could be simpler? All Swanne would have to do was slip the poison into Matilda's wine cup herself or, more like, pay someone a handsome sum to do it for her.

For gods' sakes, London was full of resentful Saxons who would jump at the chance to hurt the Norman cause in any manner they could.

And then poor William. Distraught. In need of comfort.

Swanne smiled, setting the vial to one side. Soon, within the day.

She closed her eyes and imagined how it would be, when William finally rolled atop her, and entered her, and the imp snatched . . .

She looked forward very greatly to his scream of terror and agony, a scream that would, within the moment, disintegrate into a whimper of submission. Then she could roll him away, and leap from their bed, fall to her knees before Asterion, and say, *I have done it! I have worked your will! Love me!*

Meantime, she would comb out her hair, and pinch some color into her cheeks, and perhaps Asterion would come to her and would love her again.

Soon. Swanne closed her eyes, dreaming.

"Will he love you enough to take your imp, do you think?"

Swanne's eyes flew open, her heart pounding, then she stumbled terrified to her feet. The far end of the chamber seemed to have opened into a huge hall made entirely of emerald water, and Swanne remembered enough of her previous life to have some idea of what she was seeing.

"No!" she whispered. "Go back! Go back!"

Harold was walking toward her out of that watery emerald cathedral. He looked fit and well, better than she could remember having seen him in many, many years.

He looked as he had before he had touched her, except, *more.*

And however much she screamed, and shrieked for aid, he kept walking toward her, closer and closer, until she could see the terrible gleam in his eyes, and she understood it for what it was.

Vengeance.

"I will not let you do to William," he whispered, "what you did to me."

And he reached out his hands, *stretched* them out over the three or four paces that still separated them, and seized her by the neck.

* * *

ASTERION FOUND HER ON THE FLOOR SOME TWO
hours later. Her neck had been twisted until it had snapped.

Her black eyes, dulled by death, were staring at something that Asterion
could not even imagine.

*Who had done this? William? Those strange and as yet undetermined compan-
ions who had aided Caela to move the bands?*

"Useless bitch!" he snarled, and dealt Swanne's corpse such a massive
blow with his booted foot that it skidded away some three or four feet.

Asterion stepped forward and kicked the corpse again. *Curse the idiot
bitch! Curse her!* Not only had she failed to kill William, but she'd managed to
get herself killed instead.

And now Asterion was left without a Mistress of the Labyrinth.

Damn her to all hells! Now they'd have to come back again!

Another life, another set of years spent scheming, planning, maneuvering.
Waiting!

Asterion's lips curled, and he began to batter Swanne's body with slow,
deliberate, hate-filled fists.

After a long time, time enough to almost cover himself in Swanne's blood,
Asterion paused and raised his head.

She was moving. She!

She was going to meet with William.

Suddenly, in all his anger and frustration, Asterion forgot his caution
about meeting William face to face.

"I think it might be time to ruin a life or two," he muttered.

And grinned.

CHAPTER TWENTY-ONE

CAELA SPEAKS

I RECEIVED WILLIAM'S MESSAGE AFTER SUPPER when Ecub and Matilda sat with me.

I had no choice but to go. He had asked for me, and the last thing I'd said to him that night was that should he need me, then he should seek me out. I could not refuse to go. It was my nature not to refuse him, should he need shelter.

Besides, I wanted to see him again. I hungered for it.

So I told Ecub and Matilda not to worry (a useless piece of wordage), and I sent William's man off carrying a message containing place and time.

The time was unimportant, save that William's need seemed so urgent that it needed to be as soon as possible, but the place . . . the place . . .

I sent word to William that he should meet me over his dead body.

I thought, if nothing else, that would make his mouth curl in dry amusement.

So here now I stood, early, wanting to have time before William arrived to contemplate what we had been, what we were, and what we might be one day, all gods permitting.

This was the first time I had been here (the first time while still breathing, of course). It was unbearably sad.

The chamber, rounded out of living rock, was bare, save for the two plinths of stone, each of which bore a shrouded corpse. One, that which was Cornelia's corpse, had its wrappings disturbed, and my fingers briefly touched the bracelet that still I wore about my left wrist.

But my eyes were drawn irresistibly to Brutus' wrapped figure. I stood a long time, staring at it, before I walked over and, hesitatingly, rested a hand on its chest.

Brutus. Oh, gods, how I had loved him. Why? I wondered. What was there about Brutus to love? He had mistreated me and abused me, humiliated me and abandoned me, and still I could not resist him. Still I loved him, when there were others who would have suited me better, and who offered me more than Brutus ever had.

But perhaps even then I had known.

My hand drifted slowly up the wrappings covering his chest to his throat. Here had swarmed the growth that had, finally, killed him. I remembered the long months of his dying, his fading from strength into weakness, the rough rasp of his voice as he ordered some servant or the other to remove me from his presence.

How he had hated me.

My eyes filled with tears and I tore my mind away from the memory. I slid my hand further up, over his cheek, and then his forehead, imagining the features that lay swathed below my touch, to the crown of his head.

Did that wondrous, thick, long curled hair still live beneath these tight shroudings? If I unwrapped his beloved head would I be able to run my hand through its blue-black crispness again?

Would there ever be any way of recapturing that single moment we had, that moment in the hills behind the Altars of the Philistines, when he had lowered his mouth to mine, and for a heartbeat almost loved me?

A tight hand closed about my throat, jerking me back, and, terrified, I let out a strangled cry.

"Caela," he said, his mouth close to my ear, and pulled me back against his body.

His other hand was now about my waist, as hard and as cruel as that about my throat. I was caught, I could not move . . . I could barely breathe.

And then he let me go, stood back from me and looked about the chamber. "This is where they buried us? In this chamber?"

I nodded. I could not take my eyes from him.

He walked slowly over to the plinth on which lay poor Cornelia's corpse, and he touched the wrappings. "They have been disturbed. Why?"

I raised my wrist, and showed him the bracelet. "Silvius took this from the corpse, and put it on my wrist."

William's eyes darkened. "And why did he do that?"

"He thought to make me remember. At that time I lagged in forgetfulness, remembering nothing. It was a device to make Asterion think me no threat. To make him believe that Mag was dead."

"And that artifice worked, of course."

He was looking at me strangely, and I found myself shivering. "Yes."

In truth, of course, Asterion had then found out about Damson, and had "murdered" poor Mag all over again, but I sensed that now was not the time to leap forth into such explanations.

What was wrong with William? Why did he regard me with such wild-eyed strangeness?

"William? What is wrong? Why summon me here?" *Sweet gods, was this the time for us?* I felt a mad rush of hope and joy within me, and even though I tried to suppress it, I knew I could not keep it entirely from my face.

He lifted those unsettling eyes from me and began to walk slowly about the chamber, sometimes running a hand about its walls, sometimes touching briefly one of the plinths. "I have seen Silvius," he said.

"That cannot have been pleasant."

He shot me a look, but continued speaking in a normal tone. "From what you said to me, and from what I have gleaned, he has been of great aid to you."

"And to this land. I owe him a great deal."

"Be careful you do not owe him too much," he said. "Caela, how much does he know?"

I frowned. "Know about what?"

"About the Game, about the bands—and their locations—about *you*."

My frown deepened. "He knows many things. He has been at my side for almost a year, now. And at Saeweald's. He has become our closest ally."

At that, William closed his eyes briefly, as if I had said something so painful he could hardly bear it. And I suppose I had. Brutus had ever hated his father.

"You lay with him," William said. "You *lay* with him."

"I wanted to," I said steadily, wishing William would leave this be. "I had no wish to stay God's eternal virgin concubine."

"You gave him your virginity," he said, his voice bitter. "That gives any man a powerful hold over a woman."

"It certainly gave you a powerful hold over me."

"But with Silvius, even more power, Caela, considering what you are now."

I shrugged. "He is my friend. He will not think to use it to—"

"The gods curse you, Caela! Have you no wits?"

I flinched, taking a step back. William's face was suffused with fury, and something else, which frightened me far more than did his fury: fear.

"It is not the time now to discover yourself jealous, William. I—"

"*Damn* you for your unthinking naïve stupidity!" He strode forward and, before I could stop him, before I could even think, or utter a protest, he seized me in cruel hands, and forced his mouth down to mine.

For an instant I resisted, and then all my want and need, all my desire for him flooded through me, and I opened my mouth under his.

How many years had I wanted him to kiss me?

Oh gods . . . I melted against him.

"You bitch!" he exclaimed, almost throwing me from him, and, horribly, wiping the back of his mouth with his hand. "You corrupted piece of *filth!*"

I could not believe it. How could he possibly say that to me?

"Don't you understand, Caela?" he spat. "The apparition of Silvius which walks this land is not my father, nor Brutus' father." He paused, and in that instant, seeing the terror in his eyes, I suddenly knew what he was going to say.

I went cold, frozen with horror.

"*Silvius* is Asterion! Asterion may have used Aldred's body from time to time, *but Asterion took Silvius' form as well!* I tasted it, the corruption in your mouth. You are as much his as is Swanne."

"No." I gasped the word, taking yet another step back. My stomach coiled and then clenched, and I thought I might vomit. "No!"

"Yes! Curse you again, Caela! *How much does he know?*"

I could not think. My entire world had torn apart around me.

William had walked up to me, and now he grabbed my shoulders, giving me a little shake. "How much does he know?" he said again.

"Silvius cannot be . . . he cannot be . . ."

"How much does he know?"

"Many things," I managed to whisper, my mind churning. "Saeweald and I . . . we trusted him. We trusted him. He knew so much that . . . things only Silvius could have known . . ."

"And what did *you* know of what Silvius knew? Answer me that?"

"He knew the Game . . . as he would, being your father . . ."

"No one knows the Game better than Asterion. And no one knows it less than you, or Saeweald. You were his willing fools. You knew nothing of Silvius, and nothing of Asterion, save for their existence." His mouth twisted, and I could see contempt burning in his eyes. "All he had to do was come to you, wearing my face, and say, 'I hated Brutus, too. I was his victim, too. I want to help.' And you fell into his arms. Literally. You were so grateful, you lay with him."

He grunted, disgusted, and pushed me away. "You *lay* with Asterion. You stupid, sorry bitch, Caela. What have you done?"

I could say nothing immediately. All I could do was stare at him, appalled more at myself than what he'd said about Silvius. One thing stuck in my mind—how Silvius had known all about glamours.

Of course he knew, because he used them continually himself.

Eventually, running my tongue over my lips to soften them away from their dryness, I managed to speak. "How did you know?"

"When I was Brutus, and you Cornelia, I had a vision. I saw you lying with a man in the stone hall, a man you loved. I could not then see his face, but as your loving continued, he changed, changed into Asterion, and before my eyes, he murdered you. You accepted him into your body, thinking he was a man who loved you, and he took that and murdered you with it."

He paused. "The night you lay with Silvius I again saw a vision, save that this time I did see the man's face. My father's—or at least a glamour of him."

I was shaking my head, desperate to deny what he was saying, but William continued on. "And last night I saw him, he who pretends to be my father. I spoke to him of my mother and his wife, Claudia. He talked of her as well."

"I do not understand."

"My mother's name was Lavinia. My *father* would have known that. Asterion would not."

I raised trembling hands to my face, finally facing the fact that William might be speaking the truth.

"He does not know where the bands are," I said. "Silvius never knew."

He almost spat in my face. "He doesn't *need* to know where they are. He has *you*, Caela. He is going to reel you in at any moment. You are his creature. *You* will take him to them!"

He stopped, his face roiling in contempt, and suddenly the full enormity of what he'd told me hit me.

Everything I'd done had been a jest. All those times I'd laughed with Silvius about fooling Asterion. All the times I'd confided in him.

I remembered, in a bolt of stunning clarity, how Silvius had made such a point of making me agree that I lay with him freely, that it was my own choice. How he insisted that I had to come to him as myself, and not as Damson.

I remembered how he'd never appeared with me, or Saeweald, or Judith, or anyone else close to me, when he was within Aldred's body.

And I'd given myself to him. Freely. I'd given Asterion not only me, but Eaving . . . this *land!*

When I'd become Eaving, I'd felt the shadow which hung over the land, the blight that tainted it. I'd thought that shadow and blight was Swanne. I was wrong.

It was me.

"He has you, thus he has the bands," William said softly, driving home each word with cruel intent. "He has Swanne, the Mistress of the Labyrinth. He has the Game, Caela, in his hands, and you and Swanne have given it to him!"

I gagged, nausea suddenly overwhelming me. I could hear screaming, and I realized it was the Sidlesaghes, atop a hill somewhere, tearing themselves apart in their agony.

And I, I, *I*, had done this to them, and to this land.

I had given it to Asterion.

There was a step behind me, and strong hands seized my body and held it back hard against foul, muscular flesh.

And then a voice spoke, its breath caressing my cheek, its sound filling the chamber.

"Not Gods' Concubine at all," said Asterion. "But mine."

CHAPTER TWENTY-TWO

"NOT GODS' CONCUBINE AT ALL," SAID ASTERION. "But mine."

William sagged, grabbing at one of the plinths for support, only at this moment finally allowing himself to believe what he had shouted at Caela: that she'd given herself to Asterion, that she was his creature as much as Swanne.

He'd wanted her to somehow deny it, perhaps explain it, account for the stench of foulness he'd tasted in her mouth as he'd tasted it in Swanne's.

But she *was* Asterion's creature. Both of them. Asterion's.

The Minotaur had his eyes fixed on William, kept them on him, even as he lowered his head and nuzzled at Caela's neck as a lover might.

Caela did not move, but she stared at William, and in those eyes, William saw terror, and guilt, and hopelessness, and desperation.

And something else.

An entreaty.

No!

Please! She begged him with her eyes as Asterion's mouth moved to the back of her neck, then into her hair, a faint trail of saliva clinging to her skin where his mouth had been. *Please! Please!*

No!

Gods, do this if you never do anything else for me, my love.

And it was that "my love" that persuaded him. That, and the fact that Caela resisted, where Swanne had succumbed.

"Caela," William said and, stepping forward, snatched Caela from Asterion's surprised hold.

"Caela."

Then, before the Minotaur could move, William lowered his head, kissed Caela as fiercely as he could and, as she grabbed at him, sank his sword deep into her belly.

Caela!

* * *

ASTERION WATCHED CAELA, STILL SOMEHOW ALIVE, sink to the floor, the blood pumping from her belly, saw the expression of torment on William's face—and laughed.

Caela lifted a bloody hand and grabbed at William's wrist, her eyes locked into his, her lips moving soundlessly.

"What?" said Asterion, still chortling. "You think that will save you, and your Game? She'll only be reborn, fool, at my behest, and then I *shall* have her. She *shall* be mine, all mine—mind, body, and spirit."

He paused, and the laughter in his face and voice died as he saw that William watched only Caela in her dying, and paid him no attention. "Never yours. Never."

Caela's hand slipped away from William's wrist, and, as he tried to seize her, and lift her up, she closed her eyes and breathed one last final sigh, blood bubbling from her mouth.

There was a moment's silence, a vast stillness, and then William let Caela's body slump to the floor.

He took his sword, lifted it, then tossed it across the chamber toward Asterion, now watching him warily.

"Kill me, as well," William said. "I see no reason to continue this charade."

But he said it to empty air.

Asterion had vanished.

CHAPTER TWENTY-THREE

E DIDN'T KNOW WHAT TO DO WITH THE BODY.
Should he leave it here, in this mausoleum? Carry it to the surface
and lay it before the stunned, angry eyes of those who had cared
for her?

He sank to his knees before the body, gently straightening out its limbs,
his eyes avoiding the congealing blood across its abdomen, his heart racing,
his mind screaming that this wasn't happening, that this hadn't happened,
that he could not have . . . he could not have . . .

He had killed her?

"Caela," William whispered.

He had killed her? No, how could that be . . . Brutus had constantly held
his hand, and yet Brutus had hated her.

Hadn't he?

William moaned, and bent forward until his forehead rested on Caela's
still breast.

He had killed her.

That Caela herself had begged him to do so was of no matter. He had
killed her.

"Gods . . . gods . . . gods . . ." he murmured, over and over, everything
within him turning to ice.

"William," said a voice, and William jerked to his feet, wild-eyed, his hands
spread defensively to either side of his body.

Harold stood a little distant away, dressed in the scarlet tunic with the
great golden dragon emblazoned across its breast that he'd been wearing
when he'd been struck down with Swanne's foul arrow, but without his
warrior's chain mail beneath it, merely simple cream linen trousers. His hair
was pulled back and tied with a thong in the nape of his neck, his beard
close-trimmed to his cheeks, his face calm as he regarded Caela laying dead
at William's feet.

"You promised you would not harm her," said Harold. "You *vowed* it
to me!"

"I—"

"This is a bad day," Harold said, then raised his eyes from Caela to William. They were steady, impassive.

"I had no choice—" William began.

"This is a bad day that, after all the days and years and aeons you refused her that simple grace of a kiss, the moment you do kiss her, you choose only to taste foulness."

"I—"

"Did you taste foulness because that is what you *wanted* to taste, William?"

"She had lain with Asterion, willingly. She was his creature."

"You are a fool, William." Suddenly Harold had closed the distance between them, although William did not actually see him move, and, his hand tight in William's hair, had wrenched William's head back until he screamed in agony.

"You are a *fool!* You tasted only what you wanted! I lay with her, did you know that?"

"I—"

"I lay with her, and kissed her mouth, and because I loved her, I tasted only sweetness and goodness. *You* bring corruption to everything you touch, William. No one else. *You.*" He wrenched William's head again, and the man cried out, but made no move to pull himself free. "Who corrupted her, William? Asterion . . . or *you*, that first night you lay with her in her father's palace in Mesopotama? That night you raped her."

Harold let William's head go and the man staggered a little as he regained his balance.

"No," Harold said, his voice thick with contempt. "No one has corrupted Cornelia-Caela, not even you. She is incorruptible, did you not know that?"

"But she, too, thought that—"

"She thought so because she looked into *your* eyes, and *your* face as you told her how depraved she was. She looked at the man she has always loved, and what she saw in his eyes and his face made her believe in her own corruption. She had waited aeons for that kiss, William, *lived* only for it, and you used it to *destroy* her!"

Harold paused, his chest heaving, then laughed hollowly. "Have neither you nor Asterion thought, pitiful fools, that if Caela said to Asterion-as-Silvius, thinking he *was* Silvius, 'Yes, I lay with you willingly,' then that promise was given to your father, even if he was not there, *and* not to Asterion?"

William stared at Harold, his eyes unblinking, trying to make sense of what Harold said.

"You sent her into death believing she is Asterion's creature," Harold said, his voice now expressionless. "What a magnificent parting gift for the one woman who has always loved you, eh? How you must always have hated her."

"I do not hate her!"

Harold raised an eyebrow.

"I do not hate her!"

Harold turned his back.

"I have always loved her," William whispered, sinking to his knees and holding out his hands in supplication. "Always."

Harold turned his head slightly, enough to see William over his shoulder. "Then may mercy save her from a man who loves as you do," he said, and vanished.

ChAPTER TWENTY-FOUR

OTHER ECUB HAD SAT IN HER PRIORY WITH Matilda at her side and had *known* the moment Caela died. Concomitant with that knowledge came such a terrible wave of despair and fear that Ecub knew that Caela had died in the worst possible circumstances.

And then the Sidlesaghes atop Pen Hill had wailed, and then lifted such a cacophony of mourning to the night skies that Ecub understood that even "worst possible circumstances" was possibly being a little too optimistic.

The women of the priory, known among themselves now as Eaving's Sisters, came to sit with Mother Ecub and with Matilda. They formed a circle, and held hands, and spoke quietly, wondered, and wept.

Two hours after the knowledge of Caela's death had overwhelmed Ecub, there came a ringing at the priory gate.

"I will go," said Ecub.

And she set her face into harsh lines, rose, lifted a lamp, and walked to the gates. Matilda at her heels.

When she swung them open, she was not overly surprised to find William of Normandy—*Brutus*—standing there, Caela's bloody body in his arms.

Matilda gasped, her hands flying to her face. She started forward, but Ecub held her back.

"Help me," William said. He did not seem surprised to see his wife standing with Ecub.

"Why?" Ecub said.

"I loved her," he said. "I want . . ."

"It is too late to 'want' now," she said. But Ecub stood back once she had spoken, and beckoned William inside. Having closed and bolted the gate, she led him to the priory's chapel where she directed him to lay Caela's body on the altar.

Matilda followed behind, crying silently.

The chapel's altar was clothed in snowy linen, its hemline embroidered with depictions of the running stag and the twists of the labyrinth. The altar's surface was bare, derelict of any Christian paraphernalia; waiting, perhaps, for a duty such as this.

As Matilda straightened Caela's limbs and smoothed her hair away from her brow, Ecub stood behind the altar, arms folded, staring at William. "What happened?" she said.

William's face was haggard, that of an old man, and when he lifted a hand to rub at his close-shaven beard, Ecub saw that it trembled.

He began to speak, in a broken, stumbling voice, and he told Ecub everything that had happened in the crypt. Everything that had been said, and everyone who had been present.

"And so you killed her," Ecub said as he faltered to a close.

"It was what she wanted."

Ecub did not reply, not verbally, but her face set into hard, judgmental angles, and Matilda hissed in disbelief.

"Mother Ecub . . ." he began, then whipped about, shocked, as a new voice spoke.

"Well, well, Brutus of Troy, William of Normandy," said the Sidlesaghe, walking slowly forward from where he stood within the chapel doorway. "Grimly met, I fear."

"Who are you?" William said, one hand at his sword.

"William—" Ecub began, fearful, but the Sidlesaghe waved her to silence.

"I am Long Tom," he said. "I am a Sidlesaghe. I keep company, I sing, I watch over her." He nodded at Caela's corpse.

William addressed the Sidlesaghe again. *"What are you?"*

"What I am does not concern you at this moment. Tell me William of Normandy, Kingman of the Troy Game, are you going to retrieve the bands of Trojan kingship now that you are here?"

"What is the point?" William said. "Asterion will only haunt me if I try to find them, and as for Swanne, well she is so corrupted that—"

"Swanne is dead," said Long Tom.

William just stared at the Sidlesaghe, shocked.

"Harold came to her before he came to you," Long Tom finished.

"Well, the night has some joy in it, at least," said Matilda, speaking for the first time.

William shook his head, as if trying to shake some understanding into it. "Gods," he said. "What am I going to do?"

Ecub and the Sidlesaghe shrugged simultaneously. What William did, so long as he let the bands be, was of no concern to them.

"Go now," Ecub said finally. "There is nothing more you can do here."

William looked at her, then walked forward until he stood by the altar. He laid a hand on Caela's face and then, as Matilda had done, smoothed the hair back from her brow. "Next time," he whispered.

And then, without word or look to either Ecub or the Sidlesaghe, he turned and strode from the chapel.

Matilda hesitated a moment, looked at Ecub, then hurried after William.

As the door slammed behind them, the Sidlesaghe smiled at Ecub. "Do not fear, Mother. All is not lost. Asterion does not know about Eaving. He does not know about me. And he does not know . . ." he raised his eyebrows at the Mother.

She nodded, understanding. "He does not know about Harold."

"Yes." The Sidlesaghe's smile broadened. Then he sobered, and looked again on Caela's corpse. "Will you care for her?"

"Aye. We will wash her, and stitch her wound, and clothe her in fine array, and then we will bring her to you atop Pen Hill."

"And there," the Sidlesaghe whispered, "we will watch over her."

EPILOGUE

CHRISTMAS DAY, 1066

LDRED, ARCHBISHOP OF YORK, CROWNED
William of Normandy and his wife Matilda as king and queen of
England on Christmas Day in a lavish ceremony held in Westminster Abbey.

It was a celebration day in London also, although there was little in the
way of feasting or joy, or even mild cheer. Most craftsmen stayed home, their
workshops closed, while the markets were empty of all save children playing
hopscotch on the pavements.

Don't jump on the cracks, or the monster will snatch!

The ceremony in the abbey went well enough, save for a peculiar episode
when Aldred lowered the crown onto William's head.

"I find this most amusing," Aldred whispered. "Crowning you, most witless
of fools, as king of England. Enjoy it while you can, William, for when I
return—Caela and Swanne chained to my hand—I will take the Game and
bury you. The bands shall be mine, the Mistress *is* mine, and you shall be irrelevant. *Are* irrelevant."

The eyes of the entire abbey were on the king, sitting on his throne, and
Aldred, standing with his hands on the crown as it rested on William's head.
Aldred had murmured something, but most believed it to be a blessing.

They were stunned, therefore, when William reached up his hands and
seized Aldred's wrists.

"She promised to Silvius, fool, not to you."

Aldred gave a small laugh. "Her verbal promise meant nothing. It was a
ruse to upset you only. Don't you know how I shall control her? It is what I
planted in her womb, as what I planted in Swanne's womb, that binds her to
me. She may not be a willing tool, but she *will* be a tool."

Aldred stepped back, wrenching his wrists from William's grasp.

"All hail the king of England," Aldred intoned. "Mighty among men."

And then he turned his back and walked slowly away down the center of the nave between the ranks of Normans who cheered both their new king and their new realm.

Only their king, sitting on his throne, knew how empty his kingdom truly was.

THE STONE HALL STOOD EMPTY.

Empty, that is, save for the black imp that sat in the shadowy recesses of one aisle, playing with a red woollen ball to while away the time.

Waiting.

It grinned suddenly, and its teeth were white and sharp.

Waiting.

Its jaws snapped closed, then chewed as if they had bitten off something delectable.

The black imp sat.

Waiting.